# VILNIUS
# POKER

# VILNIUS
# POKER

## RIČARDAS
## GAVELIS

TRANSLATED FROM THE LITHUANIAN
BY ELIZABETH NOVICKAS

OPEN LETTER
LITERARY TRANSLATIONS FROM THE UNIVERSITY OF ROCHESTER

This work was published with support from Books from Lithuania,
using funding from the Cultural Support Foundation of the Republic of Lithuania.

Gracious acknowledgments to Professor Violeta Kelertas for her assistance.

An excerpt of *Vilnius Poker* originally appeared in *Two Lines* #15.

Library of Congress Control Number: 2008926605
ISBN-13: 978-1-934824-05-4 / ISBN-10: 1-934824-05-4

Printed on acid-free paper in the United States of America.

*Design by N. J. Furl*

Open Letter is the University of Rochester's nonprofit, literary translation press:
Lattimore Hall 411, Box 270082, Rochester, NY 14627

www.openletterbooks.org

# PART ONE
## THEY

Vytautas Vargalys. October 8, 197 . . .

A narrow crack between two high-rises, a break in a wall encrusted with blind windows: a strange opening to another world; on the other side children and dogs scamper about, while on this side—only an empty street and tufts of dust chased by the wind. An elongated face, turned towards me: narrow lips, slightly hollowed cheeks, and quiet eyes (probably brown)—a woman's face, milk and blood, questioning and torment, divinity and depravity, music and muteness. An old house entangled in wild grape vines in the depths of a garden; a bit to the left, dried-up apple trees, and on the right—yellow unraked leaves; they flutter in the air, even though the tiniest branches of the bushes don't so much as quiver . . .

That was how I awoke this morning (*some* morning). Every day of mine begins with an excruciatingly clear pictorial frontispiece; you cannot invent it or select it yourself. It's selected by someone else; it resonates in the silence, pierces the still sleeping brain, and disappears again. But you won't erase it from your memory: this silent prelude colors the entire day. You can't escape it—unless perhaps you never opened your eyes or raised your head from the pillow. However, you always obey: you open your eyes, and once more you see your room, the books on the shelves, the clothes thrown on the armchair. Involuntarily you ask, who's chosen the key, why can you play your day in just this way, and not another? Who is that secret demiurge of doom? Do you at least select the melody yourself, or have They already shackled your thoughts?

It's of enormous significance whether the morning's images are just a tangle of memories, merely faded pictures of locations, faces, or incidents you've seen before, or if they appear within you for the first time. Memories color life in more or less familiar colors, while a day that begins with nonexistent sights is dangerous. On days like that abysses open up and beasts escape from their cages. On days like that the lightest things weigh more than the heaviest, and compasses show directions for which there are no names. Days like that are always unexpected— like today (if that was today) . . . An old house in the depths of a garden, an elongated woman's face, a break in a solid wall of blind windows . . . I immediately recognized Karoliniškės's cramped buildings and the empty street; I recognized the yard where even children walk alone, play alone. I wasn't surprised by the face, either, *her* face—the frightened, elongated face of a madonna, the eyes that did not look at me, but solely into her own inner being. Only the old wooden house with walls blackened by rain and the yellow leaves scattered by a yellow wind made me uneasy. A house like a warning, a caution whispered by hidden lips. The dream made me uneasy too: it was absolutely full of birds. They beat the snowy white drifts with their wings, raising a frosty, brilliant dust, the dust of moonlight.

How many birds can fit into one dream?

They were everywhere: the world was overflowing with the soundless fluttering of delicate wings, sentences whispered by faces without lips, and a sultry yellow wind. The dream hovered inside and out, it didn't retreat even when I went outside, although the yard was trampled and empty, and parched dirt covered the ground in a hard crust.

4

It seemed some large, slovenly animal had rolled around there during the night. A scaly, stinking dragon scorching the earth and the asphalt with its breath of flames. Only it could have devoured the birds: they had vanished completely. There wasn't a single bird in the courtyards between the buildings. The dirty pigeons of Vilnius didn't jostle at their feeding spots outside the windows of doddering old women. Ruffled sparrows didn't hop around the balconies. There wasn't a single bird left anywhere. It seemed someone had erased them all from the world with a large, gray eraser.

People went on their way: no one was looking around with a stunned face, the way I was. They *didn't see anything*. I was the only one to miss the birds. Perhaps they shouldn't even exist, perhaps there aren't any in the world at all, and never were? Perhaps I merely dreamed a sick dream, saw something menacing in it, and named it "birds"? And everything I remember or know about birds is no more than a pathological fantasy, a bird paranoia?

These thoughts apparently blunted my attention. Otherwise, I would have immediately spotted that woman with the wrinkled face; I would have sensed her oppressive stare. I consider myself sufficiently experienced. Unfortunately . . . I walked down the path that had been trampled in the grass, glanced at the green stoplight, and boldly stepped forward.

Instinct and a quick reaction saved me. The side of the black limousine cleaved the air a hair's breadth away from my body. Only then did I realize my feet weren't touching the ground, that I was hanging in the air, my arms outstretched. *Like a bird's wings.*

My body saved me. I jumped back instinctively; I won against the car fender by a fraction of a second. My heart gave a sharp pang; I quickly looked around and spotted that woman. Her wrinkled face yawned like a hole against the background of the trampled field. Her stare was caustic and crushing. She gave herself away: none of the people at the trolleybus stop were standing still; they looked around, or glanced at their watches. She stood upright, as motionless as a statue, and only her cheeks and lips moved—you couldn't mistake that motion, like sucking, for anything else. I also had time to notice that her gray overcoat was frayed (*severely* frayed). Without a doubt, an ordinary peon of Theirs, a nameless disa. She suddenly shook herself as if she were breaking out

5

of shackles and nimbly leapt into a departing trolleybus. There wasn't any point in following her (there's never any point).

I glanced at her for a second perhaps—the black limousine was still quite close. As if nothing had happened, quietly humming, the limousine sailed over the ground. The back window was covered with a small, pale green curtain. They really had no need to cover themselves. I knew perfectly well what I would see if the little curtain weren't there: two or three pudgy faces looking at me with completely expressionless, bulging eyes.

The birds came back to life only when I got to the library. Two dazed pigeons perched by the announcement post. They practically ignored the passersby, merely rolling their deranged eyes from time to time, without moving their heads. They could neither fly nor walk. Perched on three-toed feet, they listlessly bulged from the grayish cement, as if they were in a trance. The ancient Sovereign of Birds had forsaken them.

O ancient sovereign of winged things, shepherdess of a thousand flocks, give all those hiding in the thickets to me, throw a skein of wool before the man who is searching, tracking the footprints; lead us forward in the eye of day and in the light of the moon, show the way no human knows!

She waited for me in the library corridor. I say "me," because sometimes it seems that everything in the world happens *for me*. The grimy rains fall for me, in the evening the yellowish window lights glimmer for me, the leaden clouds contort above my head. It's as if I'm walking on a soft membrane that sinks under my feet and turns into a funnel with steep sides; I stand at the bottom, and all incidents, images, and words tumble down towards *me*. They keep sticking to me, each one urging its particular significance. Perhaps only a presumed significance. Although, on second thought, *everything* could be immeasurably significant. I have found her leaning on the window many times before. She's probably not waiting for me; maybe she's waiting for her own Godot, a tiny, graceful Nothing. I know how to distinguish *those who wait*. She always stands by the window *waiting* and smokes, the cigarette squeezed between her slender, nervous fingers. Perhaps her Godot is the grayish-blue sun— the color of cigarette smoke—shining outside the window. Or maybe

I am her Godot after all, stuck at the bottom of the slick-sided funnel, beset by dreamed-up birds vanishing and appearing again and beating the dusty twilight of the library's corridors with their wings.

She rocks back and forth almost imperceptibly, a slightly bent leg set in front. It seems she intentionally intoxicates with the hidden curve of her long thighs. They're not particularly hidden: no clothing can cover her body. I don't understand her, or perhaps I want her to remain mysterious as long as possible. I don't turn my eyes away from her; even if I wanted to hide myself, she would force herself on me anyway, through hearing, touch, through the sixth or seventh sense. What is she—fate, or a treacherous snare? She doesn't force herself on anyone, she *simply exists*, but incidents, images, and words constantly slide down the funnel's slopes, *closer* to me each time. I avoid her a bit, maybe I'm even afraid. I can't stand it when some person turns up *excessively close*.

We worked together for two or three years and it meant nothing to me. I scarcely noticed her. And suddenly, one miraculous moment, my eyes were opened. Since that moment she's all I see.

She's unattainable; she doesn't pay the least attention to me. Why should she? I'm old, she's young. I'm hideous, she's beautiful. She could at least stop irritating me and distracting me by her mere existence. I know my destiny; I'm not reaching for the stars in heaven.

When was this; when did I think this—surely not today?

She sensed me, turned and showed her eyes (probably brown), wandering in from that morning's vision. She doesn't look at me; that brown gaze is always turned towards her own inner being, there, where the drab sun's rays do not reach. Inside, she is teeming with hidden eyes, while the two eyes that are visible to everyone are merely two lights, two openings breached by the world squeezing its way into her unapproachable soul. Soul, spirit, *ego, id* . . .

But when, when was this, when did I think this way?

I slipped into my room and quickly closed the door. I closed the door, pulled the curtains shut, and unplugged the telephone. I know perfectly well what I'm hiding from. Particularly today . . . Although what does "today" mean? What does "yesterday," "a week ago," "a month from now" mean? What does "was," "will be," or "could be" mean? I grasp the world far more essentially, without the deceptive entanglement of time. I was first taught the secret art of understanding in dreams and visions, and then here, in the world we feel with our fingers. I pay less and less attention to humanity's banal time; it's too deceptive, it leads you astray from the essence that hides in one great ALL. I can't allow myself to be deceived by thinking that something has "already passed by," or that something else is still "to come." Thinking that way destroys the great ALL's unity. *Now* I sit at my desk in the library's office and painstakingly lay out stiff paper cards. *Now* I stand entirely naked in front of the mirror. *Now* I plunge into the dizzying black-eyed Circe's body. Now I fearfully step into the old house in the depths of a garden . . . I stepped into, I will step into, I could step into . . . All of that happens at the same time in the great ALL, those purported differences have no meaning, they aren't essential. What is essential? That always, every second, slowly and quietly, I molder in one great ALL.

*"How old are you, snot-face?" asks the sniffler.*

*"A hundred!"*

*"See—the little bastard is still yapping."*

*Swinging his arm, he strikes, the brains disintegrate, from the wall the shit-god of all dogs, the mustachioed dog-god sniffs around Georgianly and smiles.*

*"Now, how old are you?"*

*"Six hundred twenty-three!"*

The morning's events weren't, of course, accidental. I'd *like* to not pay attention to anything, to say to myself that it was accidental, that there was nothing to it at all. I'd like to forget the wrinkled woman's oppressive stare, the pigeons by the announcement post, and the murderous black limousine's fender. But I don't believe in accidents. They don't exist. Everything that happens in life is determined by you yourself. All "accidental" failures, all misfortunes, all joys and catastrophes are born of ourselves. Every fiasco is an unconscious fulfillment of our desires, a secret victory. Every death is a suicide. As long as you cling to the world, as long as you don't surrender, no force can overcome you. Everything, absolutely everything depends on you yourself; even *Their* tentacles don't reach as deep as *They* would want.

I've summoned *Them* again; once more I've given myself away, I've attracted attention. There can be no doubt: the shabby disa's stare, the unmistakable movements of her lips and cheeks were excessively clear . . . The horror is to know that it's as inevitable as the grass greening

8

up in the spring, as the dragon's fiery breath. For a little while *They* stopped hiding and took aim at me again. My life is the life of a man in a telescopic sight. There would be nothing to it if the shotgun that is aimed at me would merely kill me. Alas . . . Who can understand this horrible condition, a condition I'm already accustomed to? Who can measure the depth of the drab abyss? The worst of it is that the trigger of that unseen shotgun is directly connected to you. Only you can pull it, so you have to be on your guard every moment, even when you are alone. Perhaps the most on guard when you're alone. Mere thoughts and desires, mere dreams, can give you away. *They* watch you, they watch you all the time and wait for you to make a mistake. With the second, true sight, I see the crooked smirk on *Their* plump faces, a smirk of faith in *Their* own unlimited power. But I barely try to inspect the mechanism of *Their* actions when I run into a blank wall. It's easy to get into Buddha's world; hard to get into Satan's.

God's world, Satan's world, the worlds of spirit, pain, fear . . . But there is an ordinary world too, the *real* world; you always return to it, you'll never escape it—just as you'll never escape from Them. It counts its absurd time, never missing so much as a second. Now its clock says it's noon. Two hours have disappeared, devoured by silent jaws. *My* time frequently disappears that way. You'd think you've fallen into a deep pit of time; all that can be seen from there is a pathetic little sky-blue patch of time that's always the same. And the insane clocks of the empirical world don't stop going; death hides in their ticking. Thank God, I fall into the pit and calm down there. Sometimes I envy myself this ability. It's like sleep without dreams. In the forced labor camp I would walk and talk for entire days (*now* I walk and talk), but in fact I would be on the other side of the barbed wire fence, on the other side of *all fences*, on the other side of my own self. Later I wouldn't remember either my words or my actions; that may be the only reason why I survived all the horrors. Unfortunately, from any sleep there is an awakening. It falls to your lot to return *here*.

Strange—even here I'm appropriate, allowed, *possible.* That's practically a miracle. I should have long since flown out of this world to end up in God's, Satan's, or fear's universe. However, for the time being I'm still *here*. I even *almost* have friends.

It's probably all right now to pull back the curtains, to crack open the window—and immediately Stefa, without knocking, sticks her head in through the door. She invites everyone to take a coffee break: a charming little head with white-blond hair and sparkling eyes, hurrying to see everything she shouldn't.

*"Toast his pecker a bit," says sniffitysniffler.*

*The portrait on the wall twitches its mustache like mad.*

I follow behind her, down a low, straight corridor. Slowly I turn into the ordinary outward "I"; soon he will quietly sip coffee. Brezhnev's portrait hangs at the end of the corridor; Stefa's wide hips sway in front of me rapaciously. It's almost a scene from childhood: Robertėlis sits under a portrait of Vytautas the Great while Madam Giedraitienė, even in front of me, a teenager, sways her hips erotically.

Unfortunately, the portraits differ too much. Bloated Leodead Brezhnev, with grinning, artificial jaws. Even his brains are artificial. More and more like Mao's last pictures. In the end they all become as similar as twins—there's some secret hiding here. They're artificial, put together out of non-working parts; when they speak, barely grunting out the words, it seems they are going to disintegrate any minute. And yet they don't disintegrate. They're the live apotheosis of kanukism; *They* give themselves away, propping up stooges like that.

No, no, better Robertas under Vytautas's portrait. Later he sits down to play a minuet while I stare at Madam Giedraitienė's seductive hips, Stefa's hips, all the hips of all the world's women; they dive into the opening of a door, Virgilishly and slavishly lead to an apple cake and a circle of hell made up of plump, feminine faces.

*Because above the table, shit on the beans, hangs the portrait of the mustachioed man, the rightlower corner cracked, the mustachioed man's a bit battered. Stalin Sralin,[1] baby swallower. But we won't be afraid of him; we'll shove a rod up his ass.*

*Shit on peas, shit on beans,*

*Shit on Stalin's flunkeys . . .*

*One sits across from me, another paces along the wall; his neck is thin and he's severely adamappled. His nostrils are thin, they quiver frequently; he wants something. He peers at you sullenly, with fish eyes: maybe he doesn't*

---

[1] Note: *sral* in Russian means "to shit."

10

*like it that you are lying naked and spread-eagled like that. They themselves laid you down, they themselves tied you up. Plaits appear on the wall, they shiver and distort themselves. You sprawl at the bottom of a stone pit, all you see is a mustachioed Sralinish little piece of crackedsky. The plaits climb toward the sky, toward the mustache; they glimmer, twinkle, and blink, like little eyes. He gazes from the frame as serene as a god. This stone pit is his altar. But everything's backwards here—you're crucified, and he's praying to you. Backwards: first he says Amen. Amen to you. The holy spiritsralin smiles Georgianly; the tiny chewed bones of infants stick out from under his mustache. Why have they put you here? After all, you didn't have the time to do anything. They didn't even give you a pistonmachine; they were saving you for other work.*

"Beat him some more," *says quivernostrils.* "I'm soaked already."

*Steeling lamp gets up, waves a hose, there's lead poured into it, to gentlycaress.*

"Oh you, devil's spawn, yob tvoyu mat."

*By now you know what that means: to screw your mother. They can, they can do anything; the mustachioedgod Sralin screws all of your mothers. They hit you on the head, and your kidneys and groin and the soles of your feet hurt. Then they punch you in the void—the back of your head hurts. There are circles all about the stone pit and around the portrait, like cobwebs or bars. There are cobwebs like bars on the window too, or the reverse—you don't know anything anymore, you're hit on the head, you're tied up and there's nothing you can do. There's absolutely, absolutely, absolutely nothing you can do. You never could. You didn't have the time to do anything; they didn't even give you a pistonmachine.*

"My hand's tired. Lively bastard."

*The pain is white and blinding, like a lamp. Painlamp stands on the table and pokes the eyes with its flashing.*

"What a stink," *says the unseen one.* "The bottoms of his feet are all scorched."

"Burn his pecker," *say the quivering nostrils.* "Maybe that'll scare him. Just throw some water on him, he's not all there."

*The nostrilly face flies around you. There's smirking and sighing from the frame. Stadniukas is his name, shitty Russian NKVD.*

"Aw, go on, burn him yourself," *says the white blinding pain.* "The hell he'll get scared. If he'd say something at least, the little bastard."

11

*And Lithuania will be free again,*
*When we drive out the last Russkie,*
*Machine guns will soon howl bullets . . .*

*The door slams—it's over already? No, there's water yet, icecold, and trem-*
*blenostrils, he still wants something, he holds a flame and smiles. What is*
*he going to do?*
*"You need your eyes burned out," say the plaits and circles on the wall.*
*The water soaked into you; you soak up the water like parched earth.*
*It's spring now; grass will grow out of you. Narrowneck stands next to you,*
*smiles and twitches his nostrils; suddenly he unbuttons his fly and pulls out*
*a limp sausage of manhood. What is he going to do? He was supposed to*
*burn yours. His is slimy, like some strange slug; the hole in the end, like*
*an eye, looks at you. Like it's alive. And Stalin on the wall. Both of them*
*are alive and looking at you. What will he do now, what will he do? The*
*flame lowers into your crotch, the pain as even and shiny as a needle. Then*
*it curves, touches the heart, kidneys, liver; but you still see, you see every-*
*thing. The slimy slug slowly coils, raises its head, looks at you with its one*
*skewed eye. Looks at you and relishes it; the little flame between your legs*
*has turned into the flame of hell. You're an old castle, the Crusaders are*
*burning you. It hurts, oh Lord, how it hurts. The slug devours your pain;*
*it quivers with bliss, its stumpy head upreared. Can it hurt more, can it?*
*Where's the end, you ask of the slimy fetidstench slug's eye, and it suddenly*
*spits in your face, a sticky white spittle. The little flame slowly rises from*
*your crotch, you see nothing more: the slug's sticky spittle sealed your eyes.*
*You hear quivernostrils breathing heavily, everything in your crotch is prob-*
*ably scorched, quivernostrils buttons his fly, hides his slug; it feeds on others'*
*pain, and you're probably gone by now. Stadniukas is his name, remember,*
*Stadniukas.*

The elegant menagerie has assembled. Nearest, golden-toothed Gražina, the legendary heroine; even in a chair she writhes like a cat, crying,
pleading for a soft couch, white plush, and a gigantic fat dog—the flabby
philistine luxury of the period between the wars. Next, sunken-chested
Martynas with yellowed teeth. Stefa—a blond-haired little angel with a
spy's eyes. And further—a veritable lineup of thick-jawed women who
know everything in the world in exactly the same way. A postage stamp
series, imprinted with a single cliché. Clichés everywhere: ceiling and

wall clichés, the view from the window cliché, poster and slogan clichés. A book is the best of friends. Welcome to Vilnius. Regards to our most heroic women. A watery-eyed society of unusual harmony. Only Martynas and Stefa are worth even the most modest of inquiries. The others don't interest me; I've heard their talk yesterday, a year ago, five years ago—time has stopped here too.

"You know, yesterday I spent two hours looking for meat, I was already standing in line, and right in front of my nose . . ."

"They take everything away, you know. In Kaunas some men soldered freight cars, bound for Moscow with meat, to the rails . . ."

"Haven't you been to Russia? You've seen how thing are there? Completely . . ."

"Things have always been like that in Russia, that's why it's Russia. What do we have to do with it . . ."

"Don't worry, Moscow is choking on Lithuanian sausage . . ."

"As if stuffing your face is what matters most . . ."

"A Lithuanian always eats his fill . . ."

"Like there was anything else. There isn't anything else . . ."

"Ladies, just wait for eighty-four." That's Martynas now. "Orwell's ghost will appear, the system will disintegrate like a house of cards."

"Comrade Poška, think of what you're saying!" There's Elena's hippopotamus alto.

My eyes start hurting from this talk. Of bread and circuses, only bread is left today. I sneak a look at her. She doesn't sit with the others, she stands leaning against the shelves and is the only one who is quiet. Her dress lies softly on her thighs, just hinting, just letting you know how perfect they are. Her calves are covered with high boots, but I've observed them carefully; in front of my eyes I see the long thin calves of summer, the skin as soft as willow buds. Strange currents, menacing fluids of beauty, flow through her legs. They rise upward, to her waist, caress her flat belly and curvaceous hips, fall downward, turn a circle around the knees, slide down the calves and pour through slender heels into the delicate feet, all the way to the toes. Her legs are a work of art. It seems to me that at night they should glow, enveloped by the fluid's tender halo. It's dangerous for me to look at them; I ought to lower my eyes, to cover my face with my hands, to hide from myself—but I greedily eyeballed them, nearly losing consciousness.

She felt my look; she feels everything. At intervals she would slowly raise the cup to her lips and freeze. She didn't glance at me even once; she didn't glare angrily. She didn't hide from me; I was allowed to admire the barely visible wrinkles of thin material in that place where the legs secretly join the flat, even belly. Her beauty is *full*, it breathes with real life. It's dangerous. She is like a live rose in this garbage-pit of deformed bodies. That's why an ominous doubt slowly creeps into my heart. *Can it possibly be, I think involuntarily, is it at all possible? Beauty should be limited; otherwise it inevitably turns into evil.* This was etched into my brain by an incident from long ago, the first bell that invited me to the great spectacle. A wretched spectacle, where all of the roles are tragic and bloody; an intricate and brutal performance, whose rules will sooner or later drive me out of my mind.

Gediminas was still alive then, and I was only forty years old. Was, is, could be . . . I don't know if Gediminas *could* be alive. I don't know if I would want him to be more alive than he is *now*. A person's non-being isn't absolute: the thread of fate breaks, but after all it doesn't burn up, it doesn't melt in the air; it remains among us, the living. Every one of us could seat our own dead in front of the hearth: our own Gediminas, our own grandfather, constantly griping sullenly about God and all of his creation. There shouldn't be such a feeling on earth as "lost to the ages." Only *you yourself* can be lost to the ages. Loss merely freezes a person's existence, as if in a piece of clear ice. Now Gediminas will never turn gray or be sickly; he can't be that way anymore. Now he'll never climb the Tibetan peak he dreamed of; he'll always just *want* to climb it. Perhaps it's for the best, that now he can't do what he didn't do, say what he didn't say, turn into that which he wasn't (*now* isn't). I don't need to be afraid he drinks too much—he will *always* drink and always enjoy it, now he really won't turn into a doddering wreck who can't hold a glass. He won't betray me or neglect me in misfortune. He is *the way he is*, now he will never change. Maybe it's better that way: it would be better, it could be better, it will be better . . . Gediminas hasn't vanished anywhere; even now he's standing on the corner of the sidewalk (*that evening* he stood). The impassive Vilnius autumn lingers about; the air smells of damp dust—like a giant whale pulled out of a sea of dust. The evening wraps itself in a barely noticeable mist and the wet glitter of lights. No one drives by, everyone has forgotten us, Vilnius has abandoned us. A gust of wind carries off the mist, the ripples in the puddles slowly settle down, the pale reflections of the lights float again. This quietly steaming broth of autumn quietly intoxicates. On evenings like this, Vilnius, with its toothless whale-mouth, whispers hoarse, mysterious words, entices and lures you, swallows you up and spits you out—appreciably the worse for wear and soaked in the smells of the whale's guts: vapors of wine, vodka, and rum.

When you've been spat out, you see the damp, dusk-enveloped buildings of Vilnius lurking in the dark corners of the streets in an entirely different way (*that evening* I saw it that way). It seemed they were lying in ambush. It seemed Vilnius no longer breathed at all; it crouched and settled down, grimly waiting. The drab monuments and the dirty, smoke-ridden lindens of Vilnius waited too. Something had to happen; this the two of us, deluded into the depths of Old Town and saturated with the city's fine rain, realized particularly well. We stood (*now* we stand), waiting for something to happen. For a mangy, wet dog to cling to us (all stray dogs love Gediminas; they all consider him their only leader and master). For the wind to suddenly whistle *like a bird*, and a vengeful moon, marked with mysterious crooked symbols, to show up in a rift in the clouds. But nothing happened; the toothless whale spat the two of us out, and forgot us.

Gedis saw that woman first. She emerged as if from the earth, or perhaps she was born of the fall dampness—she hadn't even managed to wipe the dew off her cheeks yet. It seemed an eddy of wind had brought her here from a gloomy side street. She swiveled to the sides, as if finding herself in this world for the first time. This can only happen in dreams or at night in Vilnius: just now, as far as you could see, the street was empty, but here a black-haired woman in an expensive elegant overcoat is standing next to you, and you aren't in the least surprised. She's one of yours now; she *had* to show up here, according to the imponderable laws of the dream of Vilnius. A gust of wind whisked the thick black hair from her face, but a shadow hid her eyes. It was the clothes I saw most clearly—the kind sewn by only the most expensive of tailors. I had no doubt she was the *something* we were waiting for. Vilnius's Greek gift, immediately attracting the eye (and not just the eye). You would instantly spot a woman like that in the thickest forest

15

or crush of people; you would see her dressed in any fashion, hidden under a dark veil, or disfigured.

There didn't seem to be anything special either about her oval face, or in the predatory thighs, visible even through the cloth of the coat, or in her indolent breasts. There wasn't that mysterious harmony in her that sometimes links coarse details into a wondrous whole. However, she attracted me (*attracts* me) like a large, warm magnet. She wanted touching. She wanted us to think only of her. Gedis and I had just been getting ready to go somewhere, to do something, and now we stood there, forgetting all of our plans, completely stunned. The woman smiled and waited for us to come to our senses. A beautiful, long-legged, perhaps twenty-five-year-old, with dreamy breasts and hair tousled by the wind. A strange, damp warmth, like that from a heap of rotting leaves, emanated from her.

She really did want touching. She craved this herself, she entwined us both with long, invisible arms; you wanted to obey her, but within that sweet obedience a melancholy fear flared—it seemed as if this Circe of Vilnius's side streets could at any moment turn you into a soft, brainless being.

An automobile, apparently lured by her, stopped next to us. Naturally and inescapably, she turned up inside it with us, naturally and inescapably, she got out at Gediminas's building and went up to the fifth floor. She smiled the entire time. I leaned on an armchair, secretly watching her, and still she smiled; she never uttered a single word. *She wasn't made for small talk.*

In the room I finally saw her eyes. I had never seen eyes like that before: huge, enormous, velvety, inviting you closer. I had never seen hair like that before: soft black curls slid down her grayish dress all the way to her waist. Later, when I felt them, I discovered that you couldn't squeeze them in your hand—they writhed and slipped out like a nimble black snake. *Hair like that doesn't exist in the world.* Probably there was never a body like that, either: the regal clothes, supposedly designed to cover it, denied their purpose; her nakedness strained and forced its way to the surface. She couldn't hide (maybe she didn't want to, either) her long legs or her oval breasts that shouted for caresses. She couldn't hide even the smallest details of her hypnotizing body. She was more naked than naked.

16

I completely forgot Gediminas, and he forgot me; both of us saw only her. He sat closer, but he didn't dare touch her; he didn't even dare to open his mouth. I didn't, either: it seemed words would instantly break the spell. I would never have dared, but Gedis nevertheless carefully caressed her with trembling fingers, then again and again, more and more—sensing she desired that herself, desired only that. I slouched on the other side of the table, but I knew, I felt, that she was with *me*—it didn't matter who caressed her or how. She was *my* woman that evening—from beginning to end. Gedis, completely forgetting himself, caressed her with *my* hands. *My* hands slowly stroked her neck and breasts, which swayed to the sides, felt them growing heavy and full, beseeching me not to pull away. Her gigantic velvet eyes asked the same thing. I couldn't hold their gaze, I lowered my eyes; she thought I no longer saw her. *Unfortunately*, I always see everything. I see in the dark, when others go helplessly blind. Looking straight ahead, I see everything around me, even what's going on behind my back. I saw everything then too: Gedis's groping hands—by now they had pried their way to the naked body—a trembling twofold shadow in the corner of the room, cigarette ashes herded along the table top by heavy breathing. I saw her face too. She secretly fixed her gaze on me, the *second* gaze, the eyes of the ashen desert, which I know so well now. At the time it occurred to me that it was a hallucination, a brief nightmare that hadn't appeared from without, but had emerged from within me. That gaze destroyed space; it seized everything for itself (it seemed that with her gigantic eye sockets she would suck in me, and the armchair, and the entire room). It seemed as if narrow cones of pale light, two steely barbs, emerged from her eyes. I flinched as if I had awoken during the night and felt *cockroaches* crawling on my face. I lifted my eyes, and Lord, I believed I was imagining things. I was caressed by the glossy black velvet eyes of a beauty begging me to approach. And breasts. Gedis peeled the pale blue lace from her shoulders and, stunned, looked at two dreamy hemispheres with dark, erect, brown nipples. "Oh Lord, Vytas, do you see?" I saw; I stared *there* as if entranced. Breasts strikingly inclined to the sides; each one swayed entirely separately, you could put a palm between them. *I had already seen these breasts*, as white as the ivory figurines in my father's study.

*Only the nipples are dark brown. And you are red, blood rushes to your entire face. It's red as well, it protrudes from below, and you are even more*

17

ashamed because she's looking there too.

"Come on, come on, don't be afraid," say her voluptuous swollen lips, "It'll be nice, really nice in a minute."

Janė sits on the cot, leaning against the wall, bent legs spread a bit, and smiles gently. There are boxes and pieces of lumber thrown about the shed and colorful rags hung from the hooks under the ceiling. The cot by the window is hard; your knees even hurt, but you kneel, anyway. Janė smiles encouragingly; her teeth are white, white. She's white all over, only her nipples are dark brown, and the hair below her belly. You look there and you feel faint. You've tried so many times to penetrate there, through the clothes, with your stare, and you would die, die, die. Now you see, and your head spins, and it's awful. With her clothes off, she looks thinner; her legs have grown even longer. And she keeps looking at it.

"That's an unusual little beast you're growing. How old are you, anyway, fourteen? My, what an early little gent you are . . ."

You tremble when she touches it; it seems she'll burn her hand—it's so hot there. Her breasts are acutely inclined to the sides; you could put a palm between them. Janė lies on her side, pulls you down with her, not letting it out of her hands. She smells of bitter herbs and the steam of the kitchen. You throw back your head to catch your breath, and suddenly your heart stops. Outside the shed's window floats a man's head. He's looking at you. Looking straight into your eyes and chewing a yellowish blade of grass. You want to run away, to escape, but she holds you firmly in her embrace and doesn't let go. Don't be afraid, little gent, she whispers, don't be afraid. Her eyes are closed, she doesn't see anything. And the man is still looking; he's spat out the grass. You want to tell her, but you can't catch your breath. You want to vanish into the earth, but you're tied down: it's tied down, it's disappeared inside her. You want to die, you want it to break off, so you could run away. The man looks, his eyes huge. She gently lies on top on you, she's going at it from above, breathing heavily. And it's doing something inside of her, chomping and shuddering, extended like never before. Now it has become part of her. Janė has completely turned into it; she writhes and wriggles without your consent. The man's head licks its lips, swallows its saliva. He's looking straight into your eyes, as if he wants to suck in all of your insides, all your blood, all your brains, leaving only an empty skin . . .

Completely stupefied, Gediminas carried her out in his arms. Without a sound she invited me, begged me, to come along. But I remained in the room, remained alone with breasts inclined to the sides, these and the others. And with her *second* gaze. No, the gaze didn't re-materialize; rather I seemed to imagine those dreamy breasts, black hair, long legs, and slightly wry smile. Perhaps everything about her was invented; however, the barbed gaze was *real.* I remembered it—no, not that; something nameless, perhaps even senseless: the gray emptiness of the abyss, an obscure picture, an invisible light. People are accustomed to ignoring indistinct accumulations of memory like that. They are horrendously mistaken.

The most important episodes in life aren't lit up by the rays of the sun; fate does its dreary work in twilight, in a murderous clarity, in a sooty dusk—out of it, bats come flying; the eyes of meaningless nonexistence lurk within it. Our fate is measured out there, where owls hoot gloomily. Only the gray, dirty pigeons of Vilnius escape it into the light of day.

I felt the black-haired woman's *second* gaze spreading through the room like an invisible will-o'-the-wisp. In vain, I tried to hide from it. I drank the cognac left on the table and looked around with growing suspicion. I had been led into an invisible labyrinth where roving eyes followed me from its identical corridors. Her second gaze reminded me of my mother's gaze as she stroked my head, of the grim stare of the camp barracks's broken windows, of the stare of the colorless river pool—numerous spines piercing straight through, but most significantly—it *reminded* me of eyes I had never seen before. It reminded me of the narrow little snouts of rats and dilated pupils. Reminded me of reddish foam on painfully compressed lips, of the eyes of the yellowish, vine-entangled old house. I didn't try to understand anything, otherwise I would have run out of Gedis's room, to wherever my feet took me. *A person who starts remembering the future shouldn't expect anything good of it.* But I still didn't know my "future," I hadn't realized that only the one huge ALL exists. I was blind, I was a headless stuffed dummy, a doll drowsing on a bed of dreamy breasts; no signals could arouse me. I swigged cognac and stared moronically at the window. No, not out the window—there were neither buildings nor lights outside it, Gedis's windows looked out straight into the void. Perhaps that was why frightening memories slowly encompassed me. A strange presentiment would flow over me in gusts and then retreat, the way a headache sometimes momentarily comes and goes again. I looked around at Gedis's pedantically arranged living room; I even counted the leaves of a spreading, flowerless plant. *It seems to me that this counting determined everything.* The memory stood in front of my eyes like a large, old painting. Only the dust needed to be brushed off. It was hidden in between the real things, inside them themselves, in the ghostly forms of Gedis's living room, quietly playing a melody heard once upon a time: the melody of some other room, some other space.

On the right a mahogany dresser, submerged in an indistinct shadow, some other gloomy low furniture. On the left, a mirror and a wall with torn wallpaper. A pale-colored runner on the floor and a window—most significant of all—a window, outside which yawns a gray void. It's dim in the room, but it's brighter there than it is on the other side of the grimy glass; through it, the interior is lit up by the darkness, by the drab rays of the pallid sun. Just exactly that: the darkness *lights up* the dimness; the blackish rays suck the last remains of the day out of the room. This picture didn't so much as breathe; it cowered in a boundless silence, grimly waiting for me to guess its secret. On the right an old dresser and some other low furniture . . . on the left a mirror, a full-sized mirror with a carved frame; an empty glass left by father . . . And all of it is *looking at you. All of it is looking at you.* Looking without eyes. There are no eyes in the picture; there is nothing that would remind you of eyes, nothing that would even let you think of eyes. There's *nothing* there; however, the picture stubbornly, annoyingly, *is looking at you* with the biting stare of the spiritless void. The stare of a maw entangled in yellowish vines. I do not remember who saved me from it at other times.

That evening Gediminas did the saving. He crept into the room like a thief, or perhaps like the victim of a theft—he kept glancing backwards, as if an apparition were following him. I didn't recognize him. I couldn't believe that indistinctly babbling figure with sunken eyes was The Great Gedis. It was some other person, frightened and enfeebled. No stray dog would rub up against a person like that. I *didn't recognize* Gediminas. Someone else looked at me with a stare full of horror: "Go on, go on in yourself, you'll see." Lost between the dreamy breasts and the barbed eyes, everything seemed clear and inevitable. I had to get up and go into the bedroom. There I had to slowly undress and feel a strange, damp warmth rising from the bed. As if from a heap of rotting leaves. Only the smell, sugary and voluptuous, was different, entirely different. Everything was ordinary and inevitable, like the grass turning green in the spring, like the dragon's fiery breath. The scene was satanically real, but entirely unreal—a dusky shot from a Buñuel film. In the swath of bleak light sprawled the intoxicating body of a woman, inviting me, waiting for me. She lay naked and not naked (doubly, triply naked), wrapped in strands of black hair, in a frame of shiny black snakes. The legs were outlined in long taupe stockings (those stockings hid treachery, I know that *now*). The breasts fell completely to the sides and looked at me with the large, dark brown eyes of the nipples. But *her* eyes were even bigger, brimming with intoxicating voluptuousness and a mute invitation. Her look seductively and despairingly whispered that she is waiting for me alone, that she lives for *me alone*, that she surrenders all of her essence, to the very end and beyond. *Just for me alone.* Slightly bent knees spread open like a flower bud, enticing and brooking no delay: she had waited for me for so long. I kneeled between her legs, put my hands on her breasts (they were somewhat limp, like those *others*). My fingers, it seemed, would instantly melt, disappear within her, meld with her breasts, her shoulders, her thick black hair. Her intoxicatingly scented body even rose up in the air to meet me; it clung to me, the silk of the stockings gently stroked my sides and back. In astonishment I dived into her, *it* instantly dived into a damp, sugary heaven; it was at once caressed, fondled, embraced by myriad tiny little hands and mouths. Her breasts thrashed and nibbled at me, the hair snakes wound about my elbows, and it *constantly* reveled in sweet heaven, continually climbing, climbing to a boundless height. In her body the bodies of all women intertwined, the bodies of women who could or could not possibly be, everything that could be the best in them. *She was created for this alone.*

I came to completely sucked dry. I wanted to flee as quickly as possible, but she didn't let go of me; even the limp breasts rose, following my receding body, and the black hair snakes shackled my elbows and pulled me back. A single thought throbbed in my head: *it can't be this good, in this world it isn't this good.* I got up, even though a thousand gentle little hands held me back. I didn't look at her; I knew that if I looked back I would instantly end up next to her again, inside of her, inside the damp, sugary heaven. I returned to the living room naked and sat down across from Gedis, probably repeating out loud: *it can't be that good, it's a lie, in this world it isn't that good*. Gediminas looked at me with sad, stray dog eyes; it seemed at any moment he would lick my hand. I knew he had experienced the same thing. "Vytas, what will we do?" he mumbled quietly. "If she stays here, *the two of us won't be able to do anything else*. It's all we'll be able to do." "Yes," I answered, "it can't be that good in this world." "She's like a cosmic black hole, she'll swallow us both, Vytas." "Yes, there's no point in useless discussion. I'm going to her." "Who sent her, who sent her, Vytas?" "Just one more time, one little time, the last . . ." "Get hold of yourself, Vytas, get hold of yourself. It'll be the end of us!" "Yes. I'm going now . . . We're not dreaming?" I was blind, I was on the verge of falling into a trap, but Gedis saved us both. I believe he *knew* even then. He shoved me into a corner and blocked my way. It's a rare person who can block my way by force. Gedis could. I was left to squat stark naked in the corner and I cried genuine tears. I cried that it could be that good, and that it *could no longer* be that good. Her entirely real breasts, legs, belly, damp, warm vagina (particularly that, particularly that) probably came from the Other Side, from the threefold cosmos of Nirvana, where thoughts aren't necessary to understand the world. That had not been just a perfect act of lovemaking, that had been . . .

Had been, is, could be . . . If Gedis were alive, I could ask where it was he put that woman—one way or another, she wasn't a spirit; blood coursed through her veins. Maybe he would tell me now. Then he was quiet. He expelled her by force. She left dismayed and sad—sorrowful in a pure, pure way. Cinderella in a princess's gown, driven out from the king's palace. Gediminas, that black-winged angel, cruelly separated us. After all, she was *mine*. I sat, shoved into a corner, completely crushed. And she obediently went out the door, throwing a longing glance at me. *Throughout it all she never uttered a word*. She just looked at me: not just with her eyes—but with her shoulders, her breasts, her knees, and with her incomparable vagina, the black hole, which shone through all her clothes, sucked me inside, and perhaps wanted to destroy me. I wanted nothing more than to be destroyed within it. I craved that sugary, damp annihilation. But Gedis was stronger; he locked me in, and when he returned he was alone.

I searched for that black-haired woman—fitfully, depending on vague instincts. It seemed to me that she would, without fail, show up at twilight, on just such a damp, murky evening, in just such a labyrinth of Old Town's streets. I stubbornly scoured the crumbling gateways and the narrow courtyards that reeked of urine. Sometimes I would go around to the nastiest of drunken dens, where unshaven lumpens guzzle cheap wine, and then, remembering her expensive clothing, I'd tumble into one or another of the expensive dives and, to the maître d's horror, scour the private niches. At first I probably wanted only to experience the miracle's sugary blessing once more, and later . . . Later my life was lit up in an entirely different light; I began to search for Old Town's Circe, wanting something else. Unfortunately, she vanished like a flame. She no longer inhabited the wet streets of Vilnius, Old Town's filthy bars, or the automobiles flying by. All that was left was Gediminas, scowling angrily, like a killer. He probably buried her underground, submerged her under water, dissolved her into the air. Or perhaps, having appeared out of nowhere, she vanished into nowhere; born of the wind, she disappeared in the wind—but here another appears, she stands in front of me, and *again I want to touch her.*

Of course, Lolita is completely different: different eyes, a different body—not open, but as secretive and quiet as an abandoned lagoon. She is still standing there when the others finish jawing, start to disperse, and Martynas is saying something to me.

My head's in a fog—that's forgivable in a person who was caught in the vortex the moment he woke up, who once more parted the curtains of the secret spectacle, once more remembered the script of the inevitable role. Sometimes I think the best thing for me to do would be to go out of my mind. It's too difficult to grasp everything with a clear mind. There are things that no human can do. *Almost* cannot bear, no matter how strong he is or how powerful his intellect may be. It is this "almost" that is my foolish hope, my wise hope. It is this "almost" that is all of me. For the time being I still am. In this world the easiest thing is to lose yourself. Most of the time you don't even realize *you* no longer are, that only a stuffed dummy crammed with blood vessels and nerves, truly not your "I," remains. You aren't aware that *They've* already devoured you. You aren't aware of anything. You don't even remember that you once *were.*

23

It wasn't easy to understand this, to open the door to the vague world of drab nothingness. For such exploits *Their* secretive system takes a cruel vengeance. I'm already *almost* a corpse. I've paid dearly for every crumb of understanding. What is the world worth, if it imposes so many tribulations and such pain without promising anything—neither paradise nor felicity on this earth? I didn't expect requital, but I fought nevertheless. And I continue to fight. For what?

What the hell—for you, and you, for all of you!

I know that no one will put up monuments to me: I am a nameless soldier. But I fight every minute, even now, sitting in my office at work, repeating like a prayer: a clear head, cold logic, and caution. Those are the three whales on which my world depends. Outside the window the dirty pigeons of Vilnius are once more lazily soaring about, and once more time is throbbing in my temples. On the other side of the glass—bushes whitened by cement dust and construction scaffolding. Two figures drag themselves along slowly; one steps inside the shrubbery and unbuttons his fly. Between his spread legs I see a little stream watering the ground.

*You don't see anything, it's dark, there's nothing, although you strain to see, even your belly hurts. On the right an old dresser, on the left a mirror, they help you to see. It's there! Really, really, it's there, pale little faces coming up to the window.*

"Mama, they're looking! Little chubby faces! Who are they? What do they want?"

"Bugbears," says mama. "They live in the forest beyond the Giedraitis house, and in the evening they look for naughty children. They search and hunt high and low."

"Where do they hide in the daytime? Why doesn't anyone find them?"

"During the day they turn into rats. Gray rats. When they catch some naughty child, they suck out his blood, so he walks around all white."

"Like little Giedraitis?"

"Even more so, without even a drop of blood. The child doesn't want anything, he doesn't remember anything . . . but you're a good boy, they won't touch you."

*You raise your head quickly, quickly—really, they've disappeared; it wasn't you they were looking for.*

"I already know. They're kanukai."

24

"What, what?" Mama's red lips smile.

"They're not bugbears," you say proudly, because you've thought up a new word. "They're kanukai. When I grow up, I'll catch them."

Let's reason this out logically. The black limousine intimidated me far less than it would have once. I've experienced too much to be terrified by the chilly whiff of Death's shroud. I've consorted with that eyeless one for a long time; on meeting, we smile at one another like old acquaintances. Death is a woman whom I once *had*, but cast aside. Always expect revenge and treachery from a woman who's been cast aside; don't allow yourself to be caught by surprise. *They* know this perfectly.

Let's reason this out logically. *They* couldn't have intentions on my body. *They* need more, far more. True, *Their* plan could have been this: a broken spine, paralyzed limbs, battered brains. That's hard to believe: *They* know I couldn't be dealt with like that. And I know, but all the same I'd rather think about realistic, common sense punishments. However, every last thing—even my liver, kidneys, and lungs—is screaming and shouting that the great game has begun again, and the price is my "I."

Besides—where had all the birds disappeared to, anyway?

Some other, more fundamental logic must be sought in this case. Images and moods speak more effectively and astutely than words, you just need to listen carefully. You need to listen in a particular way; after all, I've studied this art in my nightmares and while awake, in dreams and behind the barbed wire of the prison camp. It's imperative to hear what the united ALL whispers to me. *Now* I enter the old house in the depths of a garden. *Now* I pass slowly between the bookshelves, shadowing the small head of a woman with closely cropped hair. *Now* I slowly pull back the little curtain that hides two grim paintings. *Now* I shake Suslov's flaccid hand. Incidents arrange themselves into a complex tangle, announcing the great secret in a drab script.

A clear head, cold logic, and caution! The clock shows two o'clock in the afternoon; more than anything, I want to slowly die. If only someone were to know how *solitary* I am!

The black bricks of the boulevard's paving reflect a woman bent under the weight of a shopping bag, the emptiness of windows crammed with junk, the roof cornices' ornamentations. Vilnius pants convulsively, like a dying beast. It's close to three, prime work time, so no one is working: faceless figures keep trudging by—I don't want to grace them with the word "faces," those skulls with skin stretched over them. They walk along without even suspecting they *no longer are*. But after all, at some point they were, and could still be. Although no, they couldn't, it's too late. They're all doomed already. All that's left is to socialize with Vilnius itself—it understands me, and I have compassion for it. Vilnius suffers, oppressed by inactivity and somnolence, remembering the Iron Wolf like a dream. It should have howled through the ages, but grew decrepit long ago, sickened with throat cancer; its metastases eat away at the city's brain too. Perhaps only we two, Vilnius and I, are still *alive*. The stream of the unalive constantly flows down the boulevard like a murky river. The messengers of gray nonexistence crawl over the city's body like an invincible army of cockroaches. The history of the world is a chronicle of humanity's futile war with cockroaches. Alas, the cockroaches always win. Vilnius sprawls helplessly, almost paralyzed, its hands shackled and its mouth gagged. However, it can still *think*. The two of us are still alive; for the time being still alive.

The best place to hide yourself from passersby is next to Vilnius's real river. The Neris is the river of Vilnius's time, the river of memory. It remembers nothing itself; it just carries other's memories. It's not true that you can't wade into the same river's stream twice. Heraclitus was mistaken, or more accurately, he had some other river in mind, certainly not this river. The water of the Neris turns and turns in a circle, you can wade into the same stream many times. You can scoop up a handful of water that saw the founding of Vilnius, drink a gulp the Iron Wolf once drank. You fling a pebble into the murky current, it plops into the water, and its echo summons some ancient sound, words pronounced once upon a time—maybe even your own. The Neris remembers everything; it's a miraculous river, you just need to hear it talking. Sometimes I hear it.

There now, I pick up a small stone and throw it into the current. You'll find the river said something, but I didn't make it out: the cars got in the way. You need to listen to the Neris talking in the quiet of the night, or at least not here, where automobiles roar by.

I walk away from the river; I'm drawn to wander aimlessly, even though I've long since memorized all the byways of Vilnius. Saint

Jacob's church nestles beyond the square where Lenin rules. The church doors are securely locked, and the stairs to the bell tower are fenced off with the thickest possible grade of sheet metal, so the nonexistent Lithuanian terrorists won't climb up during some parade and aim a shotgun above Lenin's bronze pate—straight at the government podium. It really would be handy to shoot from here, but who aims at puppets? Except perhaps the spirit of our platoon leader Bitinas.

Lenin has turned his back to me; his arm points at the KGB building. I obey; I go straight up to it and stop for a minute, although others automatically quicken their step here: the building repels them, acts like some sort of anti-magnet. No one wants to be guarded, to be *even more secure* than they are. Only I don't hurry away; this building hasn't intimidated me for a long time, I've already been where this earth's tortures seem like silly games. Only someone who has borne *real* torture can stand here calmly and think about the newest legend of our times: people say the KGB has outfitted bunkers under Lenin's square, connected to the buildings by a tunnel. Times change, and so do the legends—earlier in Vilnius they would tell tales about ghosts and the accursed gold buried in churches' naves. *And about the Vilnius Basilisk.*

Most likely there's neither tunnels nor bunkers here, but there are other, invisible tunnels and cells, I know quite a bit about them. The things that matter most in this world aren't those you can see with ordinary sight. Only *the second sight* perceives the essence. Looking casually, you see only one interesting thing there: a deep hole dug up in the middle of the sidewalk—for absolutely no apparent reason. Bending over, I peer down: there are no bunkers to be seen.

I've been gawking too long: a figure with puffy eyes dressed in canvas clothes blows his nose right by my ear and declares angrily in Polish:

"What's the gentleman standing around for? There's people at work here, we don't need any gawkers!"

A Pole. One head of the multilingual dragon of Vilnius. A dragon that speaks ten languages, but doesn't know how to speak a single one correctly. Someone from Warszawa or Kraków wouldn't understand his accent. He spoke Polish on purpose, even though he sees that I'm Lithuanian. Many Poles still haven't backed off; they naïvely remember the period between the wars, when they had seized Vilnius. Jokers—

they seized it without even knowing why, the city always suffered economically. Vilnius, the city of Polish poets: the city of both Mickiewicz and Miłosz. Apparently, it's the city of this bard of canvas clothes and cheap wine too. The poets wrote poems and the simpler Poles raged over Vilnius. It's not just them; all of the dragon's heads bite each other—the Lithuanian one, the Polish one, the Russian one, and . . . No, the Jews live here quietly. Folk wisdom gives birth to myths, but there is no mythology that would reflect Vilnius. Where else would you find a dragon like this, whose heads fight among themselves, swearing in different languages?

"I'm talking to you—can't you hear?"

The puffy little eyes stare, enraged and insolent. The righteous fury of a lumpen who's forced to work hung over, aimed at a well-dressed idler. It's horribly depressing and dull; around us it's even thick with the stinking pigeons of Vilnius, and here that still-not-sober Pole too.

*There's your grandfather, he's a hundred years old. His jaws tremble frequently, but his eyes flash lightning. A disheveled bag of bones in a corner of the hospital room, he moans and rocks his bandaged hand like a baby.*

*"Grandfather, can I help?"*

*"I can still walk," say his angry, narrow lips, "look out for yourself."*

*Staggering, he crosses the room; he is followed by perhaps ten pairs of old, feeble eyes. Along the ground hovers an oppressive smell of sweat and carbolic acid. Grandfather is making his way down the narrow corridor by now, bracing himself constantly against the wall.*

*"When I was fifty years old, you were born," says his hunched back, "Now you're fifty yourself, and who has been born to your son? Where is your son? Where are your grandchildren?"*

*The nauseating smell of corpses emanates from the beds lined up in the hall. The eyes of the live corpses next to the wall follow us. The hall is jammed full of patients, they moan and writhe like little worms.*

*"Give me a cig," says grandfather's trembling chin.*

*He blinks frequently from the smoke, but he doesn't cough. He carefully looks to the sides, leans down over the stair railings, and finally he raises his withered head next to your ear:*

*"There are eleven carcasses in my room. At least seven are Poles."*

*He stares at you without blinking, testing if it's possible to trust you with the great secret.*

28

"Three of them are pretending to be Lithuanians," he explains further. "They've invented Lithuanian last names for themselves. They don't speak Polish. But I saw through them: they're secret Poles. The secret Poles are the worst."

He scratches his leg with a scrawny hand, pulls up one leg of his pajamas. Grandfather's calf is mined with deep scars, something like a rotten tree trunk.

"You know," he says with his head hanging, "It'll turn out they've slipped in among the doctors too. They're giving me the wrong medicine on purpose! ... They're not ready to murder me ... They want me to rot alive ... They're taking revenge: I've ruined a lot of blood for those Polacks . . . They saw Vilnius like they saw the back of their heads . . ."

Grandfather giggles foolishly, winks at you, and nods his head, inviting you to come downstairs. He doesn't manage to wink with one eye; he flaps both eyelids at the same time. You go through the landing below and descend to a door under the stairs. By the time you adjust to the dark, a sickening lump comes up at the back of your throat. It's an unbelievable hospital latrine, walloping you with soured excrement. The tiles on the wall have been broken out, the floor is fouled, there are puddles stagnating everywhere. Grandfather, giggling, squats by a hideous heap of waste, an entire tower of it. It looms there like a symbol of humanity; it's the Absolute, the Shit of All Shits, with a puffy, pulpy body. Tongues of fresh waste cover it like a mantle—all colors, from yellowish to black. You feel sick, you want to scream, but the old man just giggles insanely.

"You know a person by his shit, Vytie!" His hands grub around in the heap of waste, separating them by color. "I'll get even with those Poles! Let them all devour their own shit . . . See, these pale ones—they're Vacelis's. You hear, Vyt, they all gorge themselves without blinking an eye, they're just surprised: why does that gravy have such a strange scent? A scent, you hear, it's a scent to them! And they devour it—the more they shit, the more they devour, eh?"

The black tiles of the boulevard, laid, incidentally, during the Polish period, remain behind my back. I climb the steps to Pamėklių Hill. The Polish years, the German years, before them and after them—the Russian rule. You won't even remember Vilnius's Lithuanian years; it flows only in the Neris, with its waters it keeps turning and turning in a circle. I'm almost the only one climbing the stairs, everyone else is headed down. Why are they so *ugly*? Surely there aren't people like that walking around in other beautiful cities? Do faceless figures tread the streets of Bologna too? Or Lisbon's? Do people's innards spill out so vividly everywhere, does consciousness shape existence so clearly everywhere? I keep asking myself this, even though I know very well that *They* paint the landscape of both Portuguese and Italian faces. *Their* system didn't show up yesterday, nor a century ago. And certainly not in Lithuania. When and where? No one knows. The sphere of the earth, speedily spinning to destruction, doesn't bother with such metaphysical problems; it's too busy spinning to destruction.

I had already raised a leg to take a step, but suddenly I froze. I had expected it, waited for it, but the sight still caught me by surprise: around the corner a black limousine quietly hums; two (or three?) pudgy faces, with large vacuous eyes, stare from inside. The faces of priests who were never ordained.

"Don't pay attenshion," a wheezing voice suddenly says.

I jerk back, but the speaker has already shuffled off. An old, old Jew—Lord knows, there aren't any like that left these days. You'd think he'd climbed out of a Chagall painting or a Sholom Aleichem book. Just now he was walking on the roofs, or perhaps even flying; barely a second ago he put away his flea-ridden, dirty wings. His face is nothing but wrinkles and the round glasses with fractured lenses on his nose; his clothes are practically from the last century. A genuine eternal Jew. Maybe he really is Ahasuerus. I've seen him somewhere before. He approached and mumbling horribly, said:

"Don't pay attenshion!"

The automobile suddenly roars and screeches, tearing off down the street. Only now do I realize this is the same place, maybe even the same time, the same fear, the same despair. The Russian Orthodox Church sullenly waits for something; on the left darts a girl with a cocoa-colored raincoat. The morning image of the old house I'd never seen before has unlocked the fateful day's fettered box. Today the birds, grandfather pressing his soiled hands to his cheeks, Lolita's divine legs, eternal Ahasuerus in the middle of moribund Vilnius, and the pudgy faces of unordained priests were hidden inside it. *Now* the box is left empty, because I myself am as empty as a dry well. I have arrived at the critical juncture; beyond it is the final stretch. I begin the inevitable race to doom. A race with myself; in it, the faster you run, the more you try to stop. Lord, give me secret powers, give me strength and reason. Strength and cold reason.

I began on The Way against my will. I had already settled down and forgotten all the quests for meaning. Even chest pains no longer upset me—it was just the first ones that were frightening. I no longer tormented myself if I didn't feel the slightest desire when I saw an ideally sexy woman. I was forty-three years old.

I remember the day and the place very well. *The same place*: across from the Russian Orthodox Church on Basanavičiaus Street. The day was sunny and clear—not just externally, but also *on the inside*. A brilliant clarity ruled in my soul. On days like that your intellect works smoothly and gracefully; you suddenly understand a number of things you hadn't even tried to grasp for months. Perhaps it's only on days like those that you sense you have a *soul* at all, not just a computer of brains crammed with neurons.

I made careful note of the date: it was the eighth of October, the height of Indian summer. I sensed that something particularly important was about to happen. My internal clarity allowed me a brief glimpse of the future, to see that which was yet to be. It was probably the first time it occurred to me that there is no past and no future, there is only one great ALL. To the left, a girl in a cocoa-colored raincoat kept darting by. Lazy cobwebs—witch's hair—floated in the calm sea of the sky. Every single thing was *infinitely significant*. Every single thing brought the climax closer; it was inevitable. Everything had already been determined before I was born.

Suddenly I felt a strange stab; it hurt the most tender, delicate places of my being. A keen danger signal flew from the deepest nooks of my soul. I quickly looked around, but all I saw was a grimy cat, furtively crouched by the Orthodox Church's stairs. The piercing danger signal resounded louder still. I felt brazen proboscises shoving their way into the very core of my being, there, where there is no armor. I automatically looked about for the limp-breasted woman of the dusk, the Circe of Old Town: at that time, I still naïvely believed that only she could have such proboscises.

Instead I saw that man. The sight changed my entire existence;

31

however, I can't relate anything particular about him. The man's hair was the color of straw and the pupils of his bloodshot eyes were colorless. He stood unsteadily on his feet; he kept pulling up his falling pants with his left hand. With his right he pressed a puppy, a few weeks old and blinking in fright, to his chest. A drunk like thousands of other drunks, selling stolen pedigree pups or flowers from someone's garden. But I immediately realized it was a disguise. I abruptly turned around and hastened to catch the glance of his pallid eyes. My past and my future lurked inside them. Inside them hid the last drop, the critical link that joined *all* the connections. *I finally saw through it all.* The long, narrow cones of pale light protruding from the man's colorless eyes instantly vanished, but it was too late. I understood him. I looked at him for an endlessly long moment, the kind of moment that escapes the real world's time. Somewhere else, in some other time, it lasts for centuries on centuries. During those centuries of divine clarity, my intellect surpassed its own self; for a short time it turned into *not just intellect.* Even the most perfect logic doesn't reveal the kind of connections that opened themselves up to me. Suddenly I understood what Saul heard on the road to Damascus. What Mahomet saw during the short moment before the water poured out of the overturned jug. *I experienced that myself.*

In the meantime, the straw-haired man looked about, frightened; from him, as important evidence, emanated the smell of rot, like from a damp pile of old leaves. Suddenly he flung the puppy aside and galloped off into the gateway, *not staggering in the least.*

It seems to me I saw Ahasuerus that time too. I could swear that at that moment he was shambling over the nearest roofs. I really do remember; he had taken his shoes off, and he carried them in his hand. He was walking around the roofs barefoot, but proudly and at the same time respectfully, as if he were walking through a palace hall. I believe he looked me over from above.

At that moment he wasn't what was on my mind. I realized I had to find Gedis right away, and not waste a second. The fateful spectacle's curtains opened wide; I saw everything with *the second sight,* with pupils narrowing from an invisible light. Facts, incidents, dreams arranged themselves into a harmonious system (an *excessively* harmonious system); every thought, every detail strengthened my conviction. I hurried; I was in a huge hurry to see Gediminas. I didn't know yet that it was already too late.

When discovered, *They* immediately change tactics. There are numerous means of damage, a host of methods of crushing a person, within *Their* power. It's impossible to surround *Them*, to trap *Them* in a corner, to push *Them* up against a wall—it's *They* who surround you, who hold you in a siege like a live castle, whose walls, alas, are pathetically weak. A human being can't withstand a siege. He can hold out for a month, a year, a decade; but sooner or later he breaks, at least temporarily. He doesn't even feel when and how *They* break into his inner being, crawling inside like omnipotent cockroaches.

I had found *Their* ghostly organization. I am surely not the only such investigator. There are no *unique* things in the world, just as there are no *unique* people. Certain books prove that I am not *completely* alone. That is all that upholds me in moments of absolute despair.

When defending yourself from *Them*, even thinking about *Them*, you cannot give in to feelings—fear in particular. The most important thing is to not allow yourself to be lulled or intimidated, to keep your hold on cold reason. The only way to save yourself from *Them* is with the constant vigilance of reason. In a certain sense, *They* behave logically—true, according to their own peculiar logic, which is nearly impenetrable to man, but they behave *logically* regardless. It's probably *Their* only weak spot (if they have a weak spot at all). Only facts deserve attention; it's worthless to trust in feelings or speculations. A clear head, cold logic, and caution. A clear head, cold logic, and threefold caution. That's what keeps me alive.

At least now I'm alive; until my great insight I merely vegetated, passed the days like everyone else, knew what everyone else knew, was doomed like everyone else was. Although no, I wasn't doomed in any case, my Lithuanian luck was different. Nothing in this world happens *accidentally*. Only a complete idiot, a completely blind person, could suppose that I saw that straw-haired man by accident, that I discovered the link between his and the black-haired Circe's gaze by accident; after all, it's possible it would never have happened if I hadn't paused by the Russian Orthodox church on Basanavičiaus Street that day and stayed to watch that furtive cat. No! All of that *had* to happen, a crack had opened in *Their* harmonious system, and it was exactly *my* fate to break in. Years upon years, entire decades went by, unconsciously preparing themselves for that moment. Only great insights give meaning to a person's existence. I've already justified my existence: I discovered *Their* system. My life at last took on meaning when I took up my clandestine investigations. Let me die, even if today—all the same in the book of fate it will be written: *he was able to understand, he fought until the end. He tried.*

For the sake of my clandestine investigations, I got employment at the library. It's convenient to have the necessary books at hand. I say "necessary" even though I don't myself know (*no one* knows), which ones they are. There are not, and cannot be, specialized studies about *Them*. This sort of knowledge has to be gathered by the grain. Not only that, but egoism and vanity keep whispering that I am *the first* to uncover the configuration of the world. The structure of Good and Evil. This is the most dangerous blunder a person walking The Way can make. It isn't possible that The Way has gone undiscovered for thousands of years. There are hints of it in many books—hints that are perhaps excessively vague, sometimes *almost* incomprehensible, however, those quiet warnings and lessons are essential to someone who has begun clandestine investigations. Numerous names have been lost to the ages, but one or another survived. Saint Paul, Bosch, and Blake tried to warn humanity about *Them*—each one differently; de Sade, Nietzsche, and Socrates all paid for their daring in different ways. I am convinced that *there have been direct studies of Their organization as well.* Fires in the most magnificent libraries, the *auto-da-fé* of well-known books, manuscripts, and papyruses, weren't accidental. We can only speculate about the *real* role of Herostratus in the history of the world. *They* know perfectly well *what* they're burning every time, *which* of a thousand burning treatises had revealed *Their* secret. *Their* logic is truly ghastly: *They* don't destroy one or several books; *They* understand perfectly well that this would give them away, attract attention. Sensing the danger, *They* destroy everything at once; *They* can destroy a city of millions on account of a single person who has grasped the Essence. The demise of Atlantis and the tragedy of Sodom and Gomorrah carry the traces of *Their* work to this day.

And how is someone supposed to bear it *all alone*, seeing the wisdom of millennia going up in flames, hearing the moaning of millions of innocent people?

When I found myself back at the library, Martynas instantly cornered me. He announces himself, without fail, the moment I want to be left alone. A short Vilnius thinker: hair shaved in a crew cut, sharp eyes, and the pale tongue of an invalid. He blocked my way, apparently emerging from the dusky corridor wall. A shabby pale blue couch and a crooked little table protruded from the wall; an ashtray made of bent tin, full of cigarette butts, billowed dust from the table. Tufts of hair and dust dirtied the linoleum floor; distorted, cheerless rays fell inside through the grimy windows. Scattered pieces of boards and little piles of brick dominated the world outside the window. The only thing that drew attention was a lonesome, miserable dog: a horrible mutt with a big, square head, a long rat-like body, and a thick tail dragging on the ground. He was snuffling at the earth; this he did so diligently, so devotedly, that the thought came to me automatically: he's shamming. He's *sensed* that I'm watching him, so he's acting as if he has nothing to do with anything, that he's idling about without any purpose. He vaguely reminded me of something—not some other dog, but an object, or an incident, or even a person.

Martynas was the only male in my absurd group of programmers who didn't have a computer. And the only one to study the humanities. According to someone's sometime plans, we were supposed to eventually computerize the library catalog. Martynas would have been the one to prepare the index, bibliography, and classifications of literature. Under that pretext, he scurried about writers' homes, ostensibly for consultations, but really just wanting to meet them and chew the fat. Like all of us, he essentially did nothing. In my eyes, he had no firm answers, but he craved an explanation for absolutely everything. His very life was an attempt to explain something. His apartment, in a cramped room, was stuffed to the gills with the oddest things. He called it his collection. You could sit in that room for hours on end, just staring at those things: vases, clothes, ashtrays, scrubbing brushes, canes, little boxes. It seemed that even they questioned you, that they wanted something explained. But that wasn't enough for Martynas—he would keep questioning you himself too.

"Listen, Vytautas, hasn't it ever occurred to you that we have no past?"

I had calmed down by then and caught my breath, so I could answer:

"It depends on what we call the past. On who those 'we' are."

"Me, you, that bowlegged babe outside the window. And that laborer on the scaffolding . . . We have no past, we never were. We just ARE, you know? We've lost our past and now we'll never find it. We're like carrots in a vegetable bed. After all, you wouldn't say a carrot has a past?"

Martynas's chin quivered, ever so slightly, with emotion. His own worldly discoveries always shocked him. I was more interested in the dog: he suddenly started wheeling about the yard, sketching a crooked circle in the dust with his tail. As if he were trying to write a giant letter.

"So, what of it?" I growled. "If we don't have it, we don't have it."

Martynas's little eyes popped out; he gasped for air with his mouth open. I didn't understand why he was getting so worked up.

"Whoever doesn't have a past, doesn't have a future, either. We never were and we never will be, you know? We can't change anything, because we don't have a past, you know? . . . We're a faceless porridge, we're a nothing, a void . . . We don't exist, you know? We don't exist at all. Absolutely! Someone has stolen our past. But who?"

Martynas even broke out in a sweat. He had fingered the secret's cloak, crumpled it fearfully in his hands. Had he sniffed out *Their* scent?

"I keep thinking—who was it?" he murmured breathlessly. "And it's not just people . . . I had this white ashtray . . . A featureless mass production. It had no past—like us, you know? And one day it suddenly disintegrated, crumbled into white dust—and that was it . . . It didn't have a past, either. It affects even things, you know?"

I glanced at a tuft of dust and hair that had wound itself up in a corner. It suddenly fluttered, even though there wasn't the slightest draft in the corridor. It slowly rose up from the floor, as if picked up by a live human, hung in the air, and descended again into the corner. Some invisible being turned that tuft around in its hands and put it back in its place. I quickly glanced out the window: the dog glared at me and shambled off. Carp walked down the path next to the slowly growing brick wall. He tiptoes past our windows several times a day, but every time I see him I get agitated. He is my talisman. I don't remember his real name; in the camp everyone called him Carp. It's a terrible thing: when we meet in the street, we don't greet each other. Many of the camp's unfortunates don't let on they know one another when they meet. Maybe we really don't have a past?

*The shagfelted Siberian dogs didn't chew through the backbone of his spirit. There he is, walleyed Stepanas, nicknamed Carp. He's pestering the Russkie commies again:*

*"You're like those carp! Carp! They're frying you in a skittle, and you're writhing and singing a hymn to the chef! It's Stalin that's cooking you, Stalin—don't you understand? Are you as stupid as a carp?"*

*He raises his arms to heaven and thunders as if he were on stage:*

*"I'm ashamed that I'm a Russian! Ashamed! I'll never be a carp!"*

*You look at him, and it's easier for you to breathe, easier to bear it, easier to wait for your doom. No incisorfanged Siberian huskies will bite through the backbone of his spirit. To you Carp is beautiful, even his crossed eyes don't spoil his face. If you have a spirit, you're beautiful.*

Martynas is probably right: I don't have a past. It's like a boundless country, one I'm destined to never find myself in. On long winter evenings I fruitlessly attempt to remember *my own past*. Memory willingly recreates sights and sounds, but those talking pictures *aren't my past*. What of it, if those episodes once happened? That jumble of people and things doesn't change anything in my life, doesn't explain anything. It *cannot become* my past. All of that probably happened to someone else, not to me at all. That's not the way my Vilnius night was, not the way *my* camp's fence was barbed, not the way *my* sweat smelled. The real past couldn't stay so impassive, it has to be *your own*: recognizable and tamed. It's like the nails with which your present is constructed. There are no nails holding mine together. I do not have a past, although there *were* many things in my life. It seems all I have is a *non-past*. In the great ALL there are no episodes that once were, and are now past; inside it everything is *still happening*.

That's why I took note of Martynas's unexpected unveiling and his ideas, though they've been heard elsewhere many times before. That's why the image, yet another vision of my non-past, engraved itself: Martynas, the thin little deity of all those with crew cuts, stands leaning sadly against the wall; cigarette ashes billow indifferently at his feet, and walleyed Carp tiptoes outside the window, stinging my tired non-heart.

It was all too much for me already: the morning's half-witted pigeons, the Russian Orthodox churches, the girls in cocoa-colored coats, Vilnius's stray dogs, the flat kanukish faces. That day (if that was *one* day) had tired me to death. A crushing, stunningly lucid despair came over me. All I wanted was to die on the spot. Nothing in heaven or on earth had the power to drown out that desire.

All there is left to do at moments like that is to wait. To wait for who knows what, because there is no hope whatsoever. It's as if you were sprawled all alone in a broken-down dinghy with your legs and arms paralyzed, and a mountain stream was quickly carrying you closer to a waterfall; not a soul about—only steep rocky shores and the thunder of water plunging into the nearby abyss. The spray from the waterfall hangs above the foaming rapids, the end is near, and you can't even roll out of the boat and sink to the bottom with a rock, to finish everything in an instant. You have to suffer until the chasm snatches your body for itself: the stream of the waterfall will smash it against the splinters of sharp rocks, and then cast you, still alive, into the boiling cauldron of the gray vortices. You're already dead, but you can think; that's the worst of it: you grasp everything.

Danger hid everywhere, just about anything could determine the outcome: the grim, hunched-over laborer on the scaffolding, the books on the shelves, the smell of linoleum. *They* watched me all the time, themselves invisible, inaudible, indiscernible. I was absolutely alone, but I couldn't for a moment be *by myself*; I couldn't avoid *Their* hellish guardianship.

It seemed to me that the office was slowly widening, that the walls were receding from me—or perhaps I was the one cowering and shrinking and growing ever smaller. I knew I was sitting in my office, that the wide dirty window yawned behind me, but the inner vision was stronger: the room slowly turned into a desert, a scorched, sallow expanse where no plants grow and no animals wander. This landscape of gloom was *more real* than the view of the real office. It was empty inside of me, so the surroundings became empty too. I was suffocating; I was so alone and unhappy that all that remained was to die immediately. I was already on the verge of dying. Some life, even the most miserable desert creature, could have saved me—anything. But the desert was absolutely empty—only a distant thunder reminded me that the thunderlord is also always alone.

It took me a moment to realize that it wasn't thunder, but just a knock at the door. Somebody's knuckles ordered me to come to my senses, tapped to a swinging rhythm, one of many of Gediminas's swinging rhythms. Creaking, the door opened; Lolita stood on the threshold.

"May I come in?"

She carefully closed the door, awkwardly fixed her hair, and smiled guiltily:

"If you only knew how sick I am of those women . . . Is it okay if I sit with you for a bit?"

Somewhat flustered, she settled on the sofa, stretched out her long legs and leaned back, lowering her eyes. She probably expected that her pose, her slender waist, and her loose hair would explain everything on their own. She had never been to see me like this before; we rarely exchanged so much as a word. But there she sat on the sofa with her eyes lowered; with her forefinger she gently caressed her other hand. That defenseless caress completely did me in. Lolita, it seemed, begged me to sit down next to her, to help her, so she wouldn't have to caress herself. She showed up just in time; she came true, the way an intoxicating dream comes true. A moment ago I *really* could have died. She saved my life. My dream came calling on me, even though I had never dared to summon it.

And I stood there like a blockhead and got even more breathless. The silliest of all possible thoughts ran through my head: it's not proper for a boss to turn red like a teenager in front of his employee. That was how much was left of my intellect. I was probably hallucinating. Her appearance was much too unexpected, entirely impossible. It was a miracle, although she sat there in an exceptionally earthy and ordinary way: a somewhat irregular oval face, not particularly symmetrical features, legs that had blundered their way out of my dreams, rather large, upright breasts. But the brown eyes, always turned in towards herself, towards her own inner being, suddenly looked *at me*. They spoke to me of plain and simple things, so plain and simple that I couldn't believe it. I ought to have rushed to kiss those nearly unfamiliar (so familiar, so

wished for and dreamed of!) woman's hands, to tell her everything—
not silly words of love, no—to scream that she is *everything* to me,
that she had saved me from death . . . that I had *conceived* her during
sleepless nights . . . That without her the world wouldn't exist, the stars
would stop moving . . . I ought to lick her feet, to crawl in front of her
. . . I needed to at least temporarily go out of my mind and risk it, but
I stood there like a statue and felt I would ruin that miracle myself. *I
didn't believe* the signs in her eyes. *I believe in nothing.*

I probably gave her a terrible look—she bit her lip and again smiled
guiltily. Unfortunately, my eyes don't give away any feelings, they simply
look. At the very best they frighten or insult. She fidgeted as if she were
sitting on hot iron, then suddenly leaned forward with her entire body,
closed her eyes, and murmured despairingly:

"Vytautas! Vytautas, t . . . t . . . touch me . . ."

Some sort of gigantic bubble instantly burst, splattering me with its
hot spray. My gigantic bubble of fear and absurd doubts. In that instant,
I understood everything I should I have understood some time ago. A
difficult, hysterical happiness took my breath away. Why, she had been
searching for me for some time already, searching for me *herself*! She
would wait in the corridor for me to pass by, aim to stand as near as
possible, to catch my glance with all of her body. Why, she had been
searching for me herself: suddenly I saw her breast heaving in fear and
her hands desiring caresses with entirely different eyes. That divine
woman was desperately searching for *me*! Crazy circles swam before
my eyes, and when they cleared, I saw her smile, Lolita's familiar, dear
smile. Everything was so plain and simple that I was mortified, and
felt some other, nameless sensation—perhaps shame. After all, she had
walked next to me for a year, for two, for three; *I saw* her a long time
ago, but I was blind and an idiot, and a coward, and . . .

"Lord of mine," I squeezed out by force, "Lord of mine . . . A hundred times, a thousand times . . . What nonsense . . ."

"Jesus. At last . . ." She kept smiling; that smile cut me like a scourge,
punished me for the lost time, for my blindness and my wretched fear.

I still didn't believe that her hands, her lips, her breasts finally
belonged to *me*, that she was perhaps even happier than I . . . that here
she is . . . that here is Lolita . . . that I, wretched fool, could have ruined
everything today as well . . .

I didn't hear what she said afterwards. She glanced archly with her brown eyes and spoke as if we were old lovers who had no end of common memories, as if no wall had been left between the two of us for quite some time. And still I feared that I was only imagining it all, that I had concocted that miracle while sitting in the sallow, empty office, trying to save myself from death, that I had put my faith in a hallucination and would soon pay for it dearly . . .

But Lolita was as real as my pain, as my despair; she laughed soundlessly, throwing back her long chestnut hair.

"Jesus, Jesus," she kept repeating, "all this time! . . . And if I hadn't happened for no reason whatsoever to . . ."

Again she laughed soundlessly, as if the heaviest of rocks had rolled off her chest, while I, in horror, sensed the sallow desert, the dirty city pigeons, the flat faces of the kanukai, Ahasuerus, and the Orthodox Church receding and disappearing—the whole lot slowly receding and disappearing. I sensed an empty hope reviving within me, a hope I'd lost many times before; the desire to do nothing but caress and kiss Lolita was strangling me—but my heart was knocking a warning to Gediminas's beloved swinging rhythm.

*Now* I stand completely naked in front of the mirror—my body's chilled, but I stubbornly look at myself—for an hour now, or a day, or a week. My dusky, tanned skin stands out from the red wallpaper in the background; the portrait in the mirror, painted in excessive detail, stands motionless, hinting of a slick kitschy spirit: the overly pretentious red color of the background and affectedly smooth lines. Something here's not real, not believable, as if the painter had merely sought a cheap effect. Or perhaps he was seeking a *genuine* effect, but inadvertently overdid it: the portrait's particularly fatalistic stare . . . the convulsively clenched fists . . . the coarsely emphasized sex . . . the theatrical pose . . .

I myself am in the frame of the mirror, but at the same time it's not me, it's some he, looking at *me* with angry eyes. Sometimes he rubs his temple with a finger or brushes his palm across his chest. You would think he was ashamed of his nakedness. What could Lolita have found seductive about this person in the mirror? What attracted her to this mistrustful person with edgy nerves and an enigmatic martyr's smile?

41

I still cannot convince myself that she was really searching for *me*. I looked through her file at work: she is *exactly* half my age. If I were rich, or at least a minister, I could understand. If she were some awful old maid I could understand. But her body, her eyes, her mystery would seduce any man. And she picked an old geezer. I see all of him; he won't hide anything from me. That man really is large and powerful, tall, and broad-shouldered: a person accustomed to pushing others aside by force. He really doesn't look even slightly aged, or *exactly twice* as old as somebody. His smooth skin is nicely tanned, his muscles aren't flabby, there isn't an ounce of fat on his waist. His body's still very firm (*outwardly* firm); a truly rare firmness in these days of flabby bellies. So far, *he's* not even graying: only the hair on his temples and chest is scattered with silver dust. A peculiarly attractive, mostly older youngish Apollo, who apparently knows his own worth very well. A male by no means beset with infirmity, a voracious predator grinning with healthy little white teeth. The Vargalyses' teeth don't rot. That brazen man in the mirror *almost* believed he could catch the eye of a beauty half his age. But why doesn't he calm down, why doesn't he leave the mirror?

Merely because he's afraid. He's afraid of losing, afraid of being left disappointed. Afraid of falling into a trap, but most of all he fears that all his faith in himself is no more than a pathetic deception.

I do not love this person. He isn't repulsive or unpleasant, but I don't see the light in his eyes, the light that indicates a healthy spirit. I don't sense the strength in him to give anything *to others*, even to Lolita. His gaze, brimming with rage, is the gaze of a prisoner who has been sentenced to death. Don't tell me Lolita doesn't see his eyes, doesn't understand the despair in the blackened irises?

True, Lolita is, in any case, a woman. Women hate abstractions; they place more value on tangible things. I'm sufficiently cynical; I can spit the disgusting truth in his face, explain *what* most attracts and astounds Lolita. It senses this as well: that thing hanging threateningly under his belly, that *abnormally* large organ of love, full of seductive, beastly power. *His* masculinity isn't like others'— convulsively crooked with the foreskin always pulled completely back and deep scars marring (or decorating?) the head—signs of a brutal duel in a soft, one-eyed face. A man by the name of Stadniukas burned those scars in for eternity. He wanted to cripple it, but instead he strangely improved it: that scarred beast, instead of frightening women, awakens a tripled desire. So that's how I would cynically explain to him *what* most attracts and astounds Lolita.

But that would be a terrible deception too. For some reason, I don't just crave demeaning him, but her as well. After all, she has never seen or experienced that thing. She hadn't seen it when she started *searching* for me; she hasn't seen it even *now*, as I stand in front of the mirror and pointlessly torment myself.

But what, what, did she see in me?

*Grandfather sits hunched over in a deep armchair in the middle of the room, as always scowling angrily, soundlessly muttering curses on the entire world. Through the open window yellow and red leaves have fallen inside; they move as if they were alive, striving to get back to freedom. They are afraid of grandfather.*

*"So, you're fourteen," says grandfather. "Seven times two."*

*He beckons with his finger; you must come closer. The dry leaves angrily rustle below your feet; for some reason it's uncomfortable, almost frightening. Everyone avoids grandfather. When he shuffles down the little street of Užubaliai village, people quickly close their windows. Even the leaves of the trees fear him.*

*"So, you're fourteen . . ."*

*Again you hear the rustle of dry leaves: grandfather's big dog, as black as coal, is sitting next to the armchair and staring at you with an impenetrable stare. Grandfather stretches out a withered hand and starts feeling you over. With his fingers he kneads your shoulders and your elbows, squeezes harder on your upper arm, and despite yourself you stiffen your muscles.*

*"All right," grandfather mutters. "Rock and earth . . . Copper and flint . . . Everything is all right . . ."*

*His words are strange, while his hand probingly explores your body. At last he has poked around all over you, you think you'll be able to go now, but suddenly you break out in a sweat. Grandfather thoroughly prods everything there too, and angrily blurts out:*

*"Unbutton it . . . Give it here!"*

*You feel sick; you don't want to obey, but the dog growls threateningly and you give in immediately. Frightened, you take out that thing, throbbing and flinching from every touch. Maybe grandfather has gone completely insane; but no, he's as serious and intense as if he were praying. You look at*

43

*the leaves on the floor, at the fire in the fireplace, and suddenly it starts to seem as if all of this has already been; at some other time you stood in front of a gray old man with long hair down to his shoulders and a wild beast as black as night. You've already waited for them to inspect you all over and give their blessing.*

*Grandfather carefully turns your masculinity over in his hand, weighs it in his palm, squeezes its head.*

*"A good pecker!" he says at last. "A genuine Vargalys pecker. With a copper end."*

*He hides it and buttons you up; probably he realizes you'll keep standing there, completely dumbfounded. The dog gets up and rustles the red and yellow leaves, while tears gather in your eyes: grandfather is grandfather, but why did he have to show everything to that angry black beast?*

*"You know, my child, you can have a woman already, any woman," says grandfather. "Every Vargalys can have any woman. Even your shitty father."*

*You're dumbfounded again, because grandfather is smiling. That's impossible, grandfather doesn't know how to smile, he doesn't have the section of the brain that creates a smile. Even now, hardly born, the smile dies.*

*"Go on!" says grandfather in his usual brusque voice. "And remember— you're a Vargalys now. Persevere, my child, being a Vargalys is no kind of luck. And don't try to understand yourself. No Vargalys has ever understood himself."*

*You walk out as if you're dreaming, turn back once more, and see grandfather in the midst of the red and yellow leaves scattered about the floor, already muttering curses under his breath. He curses everything by turns: first Żeligowski and the Poles of Vilnius, then all the Poles in the world, the Russians and the Germans, life, God, the sun and the moon, father and mother, the Milky Way and every last galaxy.*

Unfortunately, she has never seen or experienced *me* at all; all she knows is the Vytautas Vargalys who walks the corridors of the library or the streets of Vilnius. Then *what* did she choose, *who is* that person who is twice as old as she is? Is it me, or not me? This person in the mirror, or maybe the phantom of her dreams, whom not even the *real I* could equal?

If she really chose that person in the mirror, the one who has lost all hope, I must warn her, restrain her, before it's too late. I don't even

44

know what's more important to me—to help her, or to harm her, to take revenge (revenge for what?) on that mean-eyed man, attentively inspecting my nakedness. Surely she sees, surely she understands that beneath that solid-looking exterior hides a body that disobeys its master, a body living an independent life? That's a *dangerous* body, the husk of an unnamable creature, into which my innards have been forcibly stuffed. You can look at that husk for hours upon hours, but you'll see nothing *real*. *I'm* not there; there's only that sad person of the mirror. Even I'm not able to penetrate his depths. And thank God for that!

I have an inkling of what would happen if you were to worm your way even a bit deeper, if the exterior armor were to open itself up and uncover the weedy undergrowth and cobweb-caked corners inside. What would go on, if, somewhere in the world, there were a torch you could use to light up all of the little nooks of the spirit, or better yet—to scorch the bestiaries of the interior, so that all of the inner creatures, all of those abominations, would start clambering out in fright. It would be appropriate to classify people based just on the monstrosities crawling about inside them, on the basis of their profusion, types, and variety. All you would need to do is invent that torch, and nuns with modestly lowered eyes would instantly be stuck all over with warty toads, and holy martyrs would be covered in swarms of poisonous mosquitoes. So then what would it tell us about all the others?

I know that naked person of the mirror well; I know what a procession of hellish monsters would swarm out of him. Creatures with the bodies of toads and the eyes of birds, lurching along on short little legs, twisted long-nosed heads with deranged stares, old women with swollen bellies splattered with warts, greenish slimy faces, fish-human servants of Satan with the snouts of mice, birds with hairy beaks and transparent guts in which pieces of human flesh were being digested, round glassy eyes without pupils, rotting bodies overgrown with tree bark, gigantic breasts with pimply, bloody nipples, spreading a hideous stench with every movement, clumsy dwarves belching waste, innocent girls run through a meat grinder and put together again into a single thing, smiling little figures pierced with needles, and then women, women, women, embracing the rot of tree trunks, with pockmarked frogs greedily mouthing at their crotches and blood-sucking bats stuck to their bellies, women distorting their faces in pleasure, giving themselves to

45

long-bristled boars in lacy beds . . . And that's just the edges of the gray hell, the good-natured periphery; the most essential thing is to see how *he himself*, that motley crew's leader, appears, to see what *he himself* is up to . . .

I stand completely naked in front of the mirror and almost admire *him*. His body has gone completely numb, but he patiently (and probably insolently) continues to stand against the bloody background, defying me. Suddenly I realize he sees straight through me too. I confess: I like those kind of people.

Only those who have lost their spirit fear the monsters of the interior. Only those who have lost their balance pretend their insides are pure and refined. You can only become truly great by joining your heaven with your hell. All of the good in people is the same, but the kingdom of evil is different in everyone. I truly *think this way*, but could I confess this to Lolita? Does she have even the slightest idea of what's going on inside of me, of what a quagmire she's stepping in to? Wouldn't she be frightened, seeing even one of my billions of Bosch-like inner landscapes? And how could I show them to her?

Maybe I have to stand completely naked against a bloody background in front of her too, stand for hours upon hours, so that she could scrutinize my graying temples, my nearly pupil-less eyes with their darkened irises, my scarred masculinity—so she could look until she saw the headless monsters inside of me (or see me myself as a headless monster), until she could hear my inner music, until she could sense my *true* scent . . .

No, all the same *I do not understand* why she chose me. There's no explanation for it, or more accurately, there is only one explanation (so far only one) that I don't even want to think about.

*Now* I stand on the street by the bus stop across from the Russian Orthodox Church and absentmindedly look around (who knows when I stood and looked around). Not far off a girl in a cocoa-colored raincoat flashes by, on the church's steps a furtive cat curls itself up; but that's not what matters most. What plagues me the most is the memory of the limp-breasted Old Town Circe, her spirit hovering about. Even the trees are as quiet as she was then.

*Now* I see the man with straw-colored hair, unsteady on his feet, now I sense the glare of his pallid eyes fixed upon me, smell the odor of rotting leaves. And it's in that glare, in that odor, that the answer hides, an answer that unifies the scattered details into an *excessively* harmonious whole.

All of *Their* subspecies watch you, secretly shadow you—even if they're eyeless; eyes are not at all what matters most in this case. I could call *Them* "the observers," "the watchers," "the stalkers;" however, these names would imperceptibly lead away from The Way. Our language is merely a collection of *labels*, stuck alike to entirely different things, because those labels always run short, there's never enough of them. (It's *They* who always strive for words to come up so short, to be so inaccurate and deceptive.) But after all, it isn't *Their* oppressive meddling that determines everything. The crushing groping about in the dark and the unceasing shadowing are probably the most obvious, but by no means the most dangerous things.

I had been warned about *Them* when I was still a child, but I didn't pay attention to it. I suppose that *everyone* (or almost everyone) *is warned*. Unfortunately, our civilization has taken such a turn that no one pays attention to the warnings. They drown in the stream of other impressions, images, and words. They're decided, almost by agreement, not to notice, not to explain the odd things. Sooner or later that custom will push humanity to its doom.

It's imperative to save ourselves before it's too late, to take at least the first small step towards The Way. Everyone must ask themselves if they have ever seen the stare of *the void*. I can't think of a better description. I've devotedly investigated *Their* stares (a stare that's one and the same), overcoming fear and disgust. And I always saw one thing in it: a hopeless void. *Their* boundless subspecies, *Their* infinite hierarchy, in which, it seems, even they ought to get confused, doesn't help matters . . . Brazen youngsters, sullenly staring at you in a cafe. Pale-faced, pustular women spying on you through the glass of unwashed windows. Straw-haired, broad-shouldered men, secretly piercing you with the glare of colorless eyes. Filthy city pigeons, hypnotizing with their soulless bird pupils. Cockroaches twitching their antennae, staring at you from all corners *without any eyes*. Swamp sinkholes smelling of rot, they're looking at you too, they're destroying you too . . . Let's start from the beginning, with humanoid creatures (*Their* subspecies, having the form of human beings). You will, without fail, see signs of an inner life in even the most miserable little human's eyes. Even a lunatic's eyes flash with a live spark from time to time. Lord of mine, even a dog's eyes are alive! But not *Theirs*. Look around, I beg you . . . spot those who are secretly watching you . . . they don't even particularly hide . . . examine their eyes . . . study them . . . study them well . . . You'll surely see: all of those brazen youngsters, pustular women, broad-shouldered men with obnoxious faces, look with the stare *of the void* . . . No, their eyes aren't empty; they simply look with the stare *of the void*. I can't say it better . . . Imagine a beast that devours light—and not just light: words too, and love, and music, and dreams, and . . . Imagine its stare . . . No, I don't know how to express it. All I can do is hope every thinking person understands what an absolute, oppressive *void* is.

Study them, first of all study those deranged gawkers, those kanukai in human form, maybe at last you'll feel uneasy. Follow them *yourself* and perhaps you'll begin to see things clearly. Perhaps you'll grasp the danger that's impossible to overestimate; perhaps you'll even have the strength to resist. Perhaps you'll at least have the strength to shout for help. Perhaps it won't be too late yet.

*They* start with the children first of all. For the love of God—guard the children!

I wanted to run, to flee, from that accursed Russian Orthodox Church, but in spite of it all I held on to cold reason. I walked slowly, placing my feet carefully. Around me an unfamiliar world was in its death throes: angry women with puffy faces, crumbling gateways where staggering apparitions and withered trees with dried-up leaves took refuge. It even seemed to me that all the passersby spoke some unintelligible, hissing language.

A murky brew bubbled in my brain. My head puffed like a steam boiler without a release value, ready to explode at any moment. My swelling skull did nothing but hum and clatter: inside a multitude of tiny little doors opened and slammed shut, and my thoughts ran along new, unfamiliar routes.

At the instant of insight you fall into a new, absolutely *different* world. A universe of strange episodes and images that your mind isn't adapted to, that *no part* of you is adapted to. Your eyes and ears, your arms and legs aren't suited to this novel world. You could trip in a level place or crash into an invisible wall that everyone else sees and goes around. I passed through Vilnius and sensed that the streets were no longer streets, the trees no longer trees, even I was no longer myself. I couldn't even stop, close my eyes and calm down—I didn't know if that might not be the most dangerous thing of all. A strange equilibrium only slowly (very slowly) appeared. The streets once more turned into streets (*different* streets), the trees—into trees (*different* trees); however, the new status quo only deepened the inner upheaval. I couldn't orient myself in this new world. The ground eluded my feet. It seemed I understood everything, but I experienced no joy. I kept thinking: it's much better not to know anything at all. It's really not worth envying Saul, fallen to his knees on the road to Damascus, or Mahomet, transfixed in front of the falling jug. The grand insight brings only torment.

I had to find Gediminas right away. Things that had been long since forgotten and had been thrust to the very bottom of my consciousness became enormously significant in the new world. Vague images flashed in front of my eyes, stories without beginning or end, which brought on a strange presentiment. In that muddle, like a leitmotif, Gedis kept appearing. I saw his sarcastic smile, heard his hoarse voice whispering, "Who sent her, *who* sent her, Vytas?" I could swear he once said, "I always feel like someone is *watching* me when I'm with a woman." Yes, yes, he'd say something like that to me all the time.

I hurried. I still didn't know how to express my great revelation in words; I didn't know what I would have said to him. However, I didn't in the least doubt that he would understand me. I spun the telephone dial and considered how I should begin. Gedis, I have finally grasped the secret: *They* are watching us. Did you know? Aren't you horrified? Or perhaps like this: Gedis, surely you remember the black-haired Circe who wanted to destroy us both. Did you notice *the look* she would secretly steal at us? . . . Or maybe start straight off, like this: Gedis, surely you don't think that those observers, those pathological stalkers, are merely snooping, merely registering facts? Surely you don't think they're gathering the consummate card index just for the sake of the index itself? Do you have any idea of what their intentions are, or could be? . . . Finally his work telephone answered: "Riauba just ran out to the repair shop to get his car, and then probably he'll get it into his head to take a spin around the highways."

Of course he'll get it into his head: besides logic and music, Gedis also worshipped speed. In the middle of the night he'd get up from his work table and go tearing around, who knows where, with his Opel. He always drove like a god.

I waited for him for an hour, then another and another. Calling over and over, I slowly aligned the most important observations. *They* spy on you with pathological attentiveness, even when they really can't see anything hidden or meaningful. *They* hysterically avoid publicity and openness; *They* are always obscure, sodden, and colorless. (Then what about the Old Town Circe?) I carefully prepared for my visit with Gediminas: in discourse he recognized only logic; he left emotions to music, and ecstasy—to speed. I gathered theses for a simple introductory lecture. First: we have all experienced that oppressive evening mood, when we're compelled to pull curtains over the windows. We say "it's more comfortable that way," but actually we're unconsciously hiding ourselves from *Them,* from the empty expanse of the evening's stare. Second, how many times have we heard Vilnius's impotent intelligentsia complaining: "Oh, I can tell when the KGB is following me." How many times have I had the urge to irritably reply: stop posturing, you just want to convince everyone that you're aren't a nothing, that you're secretly fighting for justice—after all, The KGB is supposedly interested in you. Now those complaints were illuminated in an entirely new color. That evening *everything* colored itself in different colors, *the true* colors.

Gedis didn't come home; neither at ten, nor at eleven. I got dressed and went out to wander the streets. Something inside of me forced me to take just exactly that route, pushed me along like a doll. Vilnius turned into an empty, meaningless labyrinth in which you could wander until you died without ever understanding there is no exit, that this is an *absolute* labyrinth. The kind where you'd never come across a dead end—that's how gigantic it is. But you will never get to freedom. I walked aimlessly; I didn't even go by Gedis's apartment—even though his phone could simply have been out of order. The streets grew narrower all the time, they kept pressing in on me more and more from both sides. At first I didn't pay any attention to this (I didn't pay attention to anything); then I was astounded. A ceiling had appeared above my head; the labyrinth's burrow did lead to a dead end after all. Something incomprehensible was going on: the narrow little streets turned into corridors and bloody, beaten figures sat along the walls. It seemed some of them had no eyes or noses. I tried not to look at them. Someone tried to restrain me, demanding something. Horror slowly came over me. I didn't understand where I was; I started suspecting that something evil was going on. I doubted whether I was still in the real world—there was nothing recognizable left around me. I kept hearing a strange noise— something like the shoving of paper cartons, like the whispering of giant lips. Someone spoke to me (or I spoke to someone); then a young woman led me somewhere (or I led her somewhere).

I came to my senses in a small, uncomfortable room. The intent stare of a man in a white coat brought me back to reality.

"You've found out already?" he asked, somewhat surprised.

The man was impossibly lean. A bearded head, overgrown with curly hair, was stuck on his thin neck as if on a pole. An ascetic, truly Semitic face, the face of a man who had gone through the desert and fed on the manna of heaven. And in it—an ideally straight Grecian nose and bright, bright eyes.

"Kovarskis is what I go by," the man blurted out, "Remember my name, we may meet again sometime. I'm Kovarskis."

His gaze studied me for a long time, at last he decided (I saw it in his bright eyes), that he could tell me the truth.

"Don't get your hopes up. He's ground into a mush. I don't understand how there could be that much vitality in him. His heart and lungs are still working. His Opel was smashed by a run-down old MAZ truck without a license plate. It drove off. The strangest thing is that no one saw a driver—you'd think the MAZ was driving itself. Without any plates."

It was only then I understood he was talking about Gedis.

"How long?" I believe I asked. "A week, a day?"

"Until the first infection. Then there'll be pneumonia—and the end."

"Lord willing that happens as soon as possible," I answered.

It was imperative I see Gedis. I don't remember how I convinced the doctor. Probably he thought I was in a hurry to give Gedis that redeeming infection as quickly as possible. Once more I was led down narrow corridors between bloody, bandaged figures. A young nurse shot glances at me curiously from below. I'd like to know what I looked like then.

Gedis was lying in a room by himself. He resembled a giant spider: wires were strung from him on all sides; he was joined to the shining machines. It seemed he was feeding those metallic contraptions with his own blood, his own fluids. At first sight, I wanted to rush and tear out all the wires. Gedis *couldn't be* trusted to machines. Gedis was never a machine; even his *body* wasn't a machine. I procrastinated for a few seconds, weighing how to push the people in white coats out. Gediminas himself stopped me. He suddenly raised his right hand and waved convulsively.

"The remains of his motor reactions," Kovarskis muttered.

He understood nothing. Gediminas moved his hands, writhed like a bug pinned to a board. A well-known bug. With his finger he *perfectly repeated* the movements of a smashed cockroach.

I didn't ask anything; I didn't jump up to pull out the wires. I didn't stay in the room for a second. I calmly walked out and went home. The facts stubbornly pounded in my head, but still I resisted. The facts can be arranged in various ways, particularly when they are incomplete. I *avoided* grasping everything in the only possible way.

While I was still wandering the labyrinth of Vilnius that had led me to the hospital, I remembered with amazement and horror an interesting item that could have become yet another introductory (and not just introductory!) thesis of my lecture on *Them*.

From Marshall Zhukov's memoirs about Stalin.

He was never likable, not even for a second. Everyone who saw him up close noticed his stare: rude, biting, pricking the visitor's softest spots. You would go into his office as if you were going into a torture chamber. Anyone who had been there could testify: you left there sucked dry, debilitated—as if you had left part of your strength behind with him.

I rode home completely on edge. I was prepared to at last see through everything, all I needed was a sign, a crucial stimulus. I began to understand what a terrifying game I had become embroiled in. The first naïve conclusions scattered like fog. It seemed to me I awoke from an oppressive dream (it seemed to me like an oppressive dream) in order to clearly see that it was merely a respite before the real nightmare. I began to understand a thing or two. *They* don't exist just so, of their own accord. *They* are the product of our dismal existence and at the same time its cause. During the twenty-minute trip many things became clear to me, although I just couldn't fathom *Their* purpose, the great worldwide purpose. Now I know it. Many things that people value or fear appear equally insignificant to me.

The night trolleybus was practically empty; I had a good view of all the riders. The stage was set, the only thing lacking was the lead actor. It didn't take long for him to show up: a young, perhaps twenty-year-old imbecile. I craved an answer, anything could turn into *an answer*, so I attentively examined his round head, stuck right onto his shoulders, and his fleshy nose, which was reminiscent of a beak. Overall he looked like a large, swollen bird. His fleshy, markedly bloated face shone with a friendly smile. I was just waiting for a sign; I stared at him with a pathological hope. Perhaps he was the one who was to send that sign. Perhaps he himself was that sign. He behaved sweetly and excessively politely, almost perversely so. He loitered between the seats and spoke to the riders. With impeccable pronunciation he asked what time it was; he asked nearly everyone where they were going. His urgent craving to socialize, his desire to please everyone, was revolting. He spoke to the riders by a strange logic which apparently only he understood—not in turn, but not in random order, either. He *knew* what he was doing. By no means did he appear wronged by nature or God; more as if he was just exactly the way he should be. The irritated riders, scowling as soon as he gently reminded one of them it was time to get off, were less convincing. The imbecile's inner satisfaction grew right before your eyes, it shone in the pudgy, full-cheeked face. There was no room for sadness or pain in that face, it could only show a cretinish impassivity or bliss. Its owner was satisfied with himself and others, he *loved* himself and others . . . and the trolleybus, and the rain outside the window, and the trashed bus stops—he loved the entire world without discrimination. He wanted for nothing, everything was clear to him. His pronunciation annoyed me most of all; it nearly drove me out of my mind. He spoke exceedingly properly—like the linguists on a television show. His lumbering body at times even twitched from the effort, he fawned so violently. But I saw a strange fear hiding in him too. That he could even have those kinds of feelings surprised me, but I quickly figured it out. He was afraid to be left forgotten and alone, to fail to attract others' attention for even a second. Every person who still has a thing or two left inside is able to be alone with himself. There was nothing inside this lumbering figure that could be relied on. He no longer had *himself*, so a secret fear constantly gnawed at him.

A chill suddenly pierced me; then in horror I felt a nearly inexplicable stitch, a strange stab that wounded the most tender, delicate places of my being. The stench of rotting leaves emanated from the imbecile; it seemed the danger signal that had sounded inside me before was recurring. Involuntarily I thought: so it's *They* who sucked out this person's soul; the kanukai kanuked him. Once he was human. The spectacle was probably over, the sign given, even though the actor was still standing on the miserable stage. Gediminas's final convulsions, the black Circe's gaze, all of the horrifying pictures were numbered and *almost* explained. Everything was much too clear—I actually felt faint on account of that purity and clarity. But what of it—I didn't know what should be done. *No one knows what should be done.*

But still the spectacle continued. The imbecile, with his piggish little eyes, stared at a girl who was sitting not far away. Apparently she had emerged from underground, or appeared out of nowhere. She sat quite close to me, daydreaming and completely forgetting herself, and looked at the rainy window glass. Both her coat and skirt buttoned up the front and had spread out somehow obscenely—they uncovered her long thin legs and the lace of her underwear; under them the dark, warm triangle of hair was apparent. Her dreamy face and that voluptuous, dangerous tunnel extending between her thighs straight to the tempting, damp mystery was horrifyingly incongruous, but all the more enticing. The imbecile felt it too; he carefully sat down on the neighboring seat, quickly stuffed his hands into his pockets and froze as if he'd had been paralyzed. I was completely done in by that girl's involuntary voluptuousness, the imbecile's fingers moving hysterically in his pants pockets, and his face, which he suddenly turned towards me. He looked at me *as if I was one of his own*, smiled knowingly, and turned back again to the sugary damp tunnel. Strings of slimy saliva dripped from the corners of his lips. He pulled his hands out of his pockets and intently stretched them towards the girl's legs. Slowly, carefully, he thrust them into the tunnel between her thighs. I swear, at that moment there wasn't a drop of fear left in his face.

I jumped out of the trolleybus; I thought I heard the horrified yell of the girl as she was awoken from her daydreams. There was just one thing on my mind—that my apartment was right near by, and I had to get to it. I doubted I would succeed in returning home alive. Afterwards, an interval of several days disappeared from my consciousness.

Thank God, Stefa took care of me. Thank God, the Academy of Science took care of Gediminas's funeral. Thank God—after all, like me, he lived all alone. And he died all alone (as I am destined to do). It's just that the Academy of Science, which suddenly honored the eternally chastised Gediminas Riauba after his death, won't bury me.

In Lithuania, truly great people are valued, if at all, only after their death. In the very best case.

*That live skeleton crawls on all fours through the pen and nibbles at the grass. That skeleton of a tall man with a toothless mouth and bloody gums rips out a dried-up clump and slowly chews it. There is nothing left in his eyes; Plato and Einstein are dead, Nietzsche and Shakespeare are dead. In his eyes a void remains, a boundless, bare expanse. You know this man. You know his name. You've spent hundreds of nights talking together. Vasia Jebachik sprawls next to you and giggles. If they should catch us, we could end up in the pen ourselves. The man suddenly stops and spreads his legs. It seems some kind of thought flickers on his face. He strains to think, tries to remember something, while between his legs hangs a thick sausage of waste. It dangles for a long time and finally falls down. Your heart wants to jump out of your throat, but you can't pull your eyes away from him.*

*"Bolius!" you say in despair.*

*He doesn't hear. That human animal no longer knows his own name; he turns around and sniffs at his waste. He calmly leans over and chomps the steaming, reeking sausage with his toothless mouth. He chews it blissfully, with his head thrown back no less. You know this person.*

*"They've done your prof in, Ironsides," Vasia Jebachik grins, "And there's another one."*

*The second shaved head is much younger; he doesn't crawl, he reclines with a pained expression on his face. He still has a human face. The older* one suddenly yowls. You're wracked by spasms, because you know this person's name. All of Lithuania knows his name. You want to kill someone, because it's impossible to go on living. Whom should you kill? Perhaps Bolius? Or maybe yourself? It's the fundamental question of philosophy: do you kill someone else, or yourself? God was killed a long time ago.

"The other one's supposedly a Swede," Vasia whispers. "Balenberg, or something . . . Ha! Do you see a Swede? He's the King of the Jews! I'd recognize a Jew a mile away!"

Your hands shake, your heart no longer beats, you've died already. You no longer are, there is only an all-encompassing NOTHING, which has no meaning nor objective, no purpose, which looks with a multitude of invisible eyes, gorges with a multitude of invisible mouths, and blankets the entire earth—it has no cracks, no weak spots; it's invincible, eternal, unchanging. Under it cities disappear, people disappear, the whole lot disappears, Bolius disappeared, you'll disappear in a minute, sooner or later nothing will be left—just that nothing, existing for itself and because of itself, but it's almost all the same to you, since you no longer are. You're dead already.

"Let's get lost, Ironsides," Vasia Jebachik blurts out. "If they catch us here, it's all over for us. They're hiding that Swede like you wouldn't believe!"

For two or three days I lay in a fever, then suddenly I came to my senses—with a dull head and an empty heart. I felt somewhat like the only life left among the dead. Everything in the world appeared to be as usual, left standing *in the same place and the same way*. But everything was illuminated in a new light, arousing the second, the true sight. It's not difficult to get used to obvious, tangible changes. It's much more difficult when things seemingly haven't changed, but *mean* something else entirely. If you were to try to reconcile the old and the new perspectives, you could go out of your mind. I saved myself simply by not even attempting to remember the old world; I accepted the new without any stipulations. I saw it clearly, like a finished painting, like the dragon's fiery breath.

All of *Their* subspecies—from the commissars of gray powers down to the last peon, all of the beasts marked by *Their* sign, seek the same thing. They suck, devour, and ingest your essential powers, the inner strength, thanks to which you are *human*. *They* devour people, but leave them looking perfectly healthy on the outside. They suck out just the insides, leaving an ashen emptiness inside. They suck out fantasy, inspirations and intellect, as if it were everyday food or a refreshing drink. *They* are able to adjust to circumstances better than any other living creature. It's impossible to avoid *Them*; *They* are everywhere. It's *They* who fixed things so that in the eternal war between the darkness and the light a soulless gloom always wins. *They* discovered the *near* truth, which is worse than the blackest lie. If the human race really is doomed to extinction, it will be solely thanks to *Them*.

A hundred times I tried to logically refute *Their* existence. But I reached the opposite goal—I unarguably proved that *They* really exist. The simplest proof—an argument *ad absurdum*. Let's say *They* don't exist. There is no such subspecies of live creatures whose sole purpose is to kanuk people, to take away their intellectual and spiritual powers; that kingdom of sullen, flat faces doesn't exist. Let's say none of that exists.

Then how can you explain humanity's structure, all the world's societies, all human communities, their aspirations and modes of existence? How can you explain that always and everywhere, as far as you can see, one idiot rules a thousand intelligent people, and they quietly obey? Whence comes the silent gray *majority* in every society? Would a person who wasn't kanuked think of vegetating in a soulless condition and say that's the way everything should be? Why is it always enough to arrest a thousand for the just cause of a million to be doomed? Who raises and sets all governments on the throne, who hands the scepter to Satan's servants—to all sorts of Stalins, Hitlers or Pol Pots? How do thousands, even millions of people disappear in the presence of all, and the others supposedly don't even *notice*? How does humanity manage to forget its history and repeat that which has already caused catastrophe more than once? Where does everyone's intelligence and memory disappear to at such moments? What instills the tendency in a human to betray the seekers of justice, knowing perfectly well that they are seekers of *justice*? Where does that secret desire come from, when a person is up to their neck in shit, to use all his strength to drown another who's still trying to scramble out? How could censorship, whose *sole* purpose is to hide the truth, exist in a human society that hasn't been kanuked?

Why doesn't a single theory answer these simple questions? Why do all the great philosophical systems, all the Hegels and Kants together, fail to explain these basic things? Why?

Maybe that's the way, and just that way, that man unavoidably is? Maybe all of these horrifying things aren't the province of theory, but rather axioms that you'll neither prove nor disprove? Maybe a soulless doom is programmed into all of us from the start? Every nation has the kind of government it deserves, and so on?

I cannot bear assumptions like that, assumptions that acrimoniously belittle people. I can't bear them! But an investigator must be calm and objective, he must rely only on facts.

Children deny those revolting assumptions. The very existence of *children*. A foolish boy who tries to boss the neighborhood kids around will be ridiculed immediately. There is no silent gray majority in the world of children. You could arrest a thousand, a million children, but as long as *at least one* remains alive and free, there will be a child's view of justice in the world, there will be someone to shout that the king is naked. An unspoiled child tries to be more like the stronger or smarter ones, not to pull them down. No, no, *a human isn't born a kanukas!*

The ruination takes over later, when children *are taught* to rat on others, when they learn it's not worth ridiculing the kid with pretensions to be a little king, since he's the boss's son. When someone convinces them (convinces without presenting any arguments) that it's imperative to participate in the idiotic play of life, even knowing it's idiotic. Convinces them there is no choice—either float in the ship of fools, or drown.

How can you explain all of this, supposing *They* don't exist?

ERGO: THEY EXIST.

Thank God, even *Their* system isn't omnipotent. Not everyone gives in to being kanuked. Some people have an incomprehensible metaphysical power (frequently not even suspecting it themselves) to elude the thickest of *Their* nets. Alas, there's very few of them, terribly, tragically, few.

*At that time* I hadn't comprehended *Their* abnormal logic (*Their* patho-logic). I didn't know even a hundredth part of their methods, but I had already started to grasp what sort of threat hung over all of us. Gedis was the first victim to die in my presence. To this day I'm not sure he knew about *Them*. Without a doubt, Gediminas was better, smarter, more energetic than I am. Unfortunately, it's by no means a given that every good and intelligent person will come across *Their* system. You must experience a great deal of evil in your life, *real* evil; you must thoroughly scrutinize its pupil-less eyes. Besides, you must have a seed of real evil in yourself. It's awful, but that's the way it is: if you don't have evil within yourself, you won't be able to recognize and comprehend the evil in the world. So I cannot be sure that Gedis *knew*. He was only the first victim I *recognized*—who can count how many of them I had seen just in the Stalinist camps, without even suspecting they were *Their* victims. I have no doubts about the reasons for Gedis's death. I hastened to find regularities of a more general nature. I searched gropingly: I tried to remember all mathematicians, all musicians, all car crashes. At last, I turned up a significant car crash in my memory. I remembered how Albert Camus died. That was how my research moved into a completely new sphere.

The entire story of Camus's life always seemed somewhat strange to me. Hidden in the sands of Algeria, he could, of course, come across more *essential* things than the inhabitants of large metropolitan centers can. In a center of culture and science, in the hum of people, *They* feel safe; *They* blend into the throng, into the profusion of words and opinions. *They* always dictate intellectual fashions, by this method concealing things that are troublesome to *Them*. Inhabitants of obscure places have far more time to delve into the essence of the world, but also far fewer chances for their ideas to reach humanity. Camus successfully reconciled the qualities of a hermit and Europe's darling.

His spiritual activity was twofold. Some of his writings, let's say, *The Myth of Sisyphus*, seem to indicate that Camus was practically an apologist for *Their* activities. This is confirmed in part by his Nobel Prize (*almost* always it's *Their* emissaries who determine the awarding of official prizes: I emphasize—neither Joyce, nor Kafka, nor Genet received any prizes).

On the other hand, *The Plague* or *The Stranger* brazenly intrude into *Their* inviolable domain. The portrayal of the plague is strongly reminiscent of an allegory of *Their* system, while Meursault is one of the most influential portraits of a kanuked being. There's no sense delving into Camus's actual activities—the most significant things won't be found in the tangle of his biography. But his death is worth pondering. Perhaps at first Camus was an obedient (let's say an inadvertent) servant of *Theirs*, and later he saw through things. Maybe he was cleverly feigning all the time, secretly damaging *Them*. We can only speculate. One way or another, he slowly began behaving in an unacceptable manner; maybe he even did things to *Them* that we are forbidden to talk about (even *to think* about them is dangerous). Retribution was quick. The fatalistic death, the lost manuscripts—all of that's in an all-too-familiar style. Gediminas's letters also disappeared without a trace.

Camus's precedent was the first I wrote into the great list of *Their* victims.

*The fact that you won't find straightforward information about* Them *in books ultimately proves* They *exist.* It would be easy to fight with a concrete societal or political organization that everyone knows or has at least come across. An identified enemy is *almost* a conquered enemy. Everyone would have risen up against *Them* a long time ago; *They* would have been destroyed at some point. Unfortunately, *Their* race exists and works harmoniously. This proves that they're hidden, undiscovered, uninvestigated. But whether *They* want to or not, they leave traces behind. All of *Their* victims are indelible footprints. Let's take the story of Roman Polanski and Sharon Tate. Anyone who's seen Polanski's films will understand that he should have shut his trap (or more precisely—broken his film camera). Both his vampires and *Rosemary's Baby* slowly, but unavoidably, lead to *Their* lair. True, Satan Manson (his *leaders!*) miscalculated something, Polanski was left unharmed, his wife died (or maybe that was just exactly *Their* patho-logical plan). However, the time will come yet when some barb-eyed Circe of the Hollywood villas will do him in. It's silly to talk about a shortage of footprints. There are plenty of prints—it's even horrifying how many there are, those most often bloody footprints of *Theirs*.

Sometimes it's almost suspicious how far individual researchers manage to get. I'm not even talking about Kafka. There's another one who particularly astounded me. He's from Buenos Aires, by the name of Ernesto Sabato. I was simply horrified when I read his book. I couldn't believe my eyes: Sabato openly described some of *Their* methods—although it's true, he didn't mention anything at all about *Their* goals. In addition, he persistently associated them with the powers of hell.

That aroused my suspicions. Strangest of all, he wrote about *the blind*, and they, after all, don't have a gaze. At first I just couldn't understand this *inversion*. It sufficed to scrutinize two words—AKLAS and AKY-LAS: AK(Y)LAS, the words for blind and sharp-sighted. Perhaps the particularly archaic Lithuanian language has preserved even more secret connections, connections which *They* have managed to eliminate from other languages?

However, this discovery didn't solve the problem of Ernesto Sabato, and it didn't dispel my suspicions. It wasn't plausible that an Argentinean would know Lithuanian. Unfortunately, I'll never travel to Argentina, I'll never speak to him nor track him down. However, his picture fell into my hands in the nick of time.

A man with a pudgy *little face* and small eyes looked out of the photograph, a man who looked sufficiently satisfied with himself. Not at all like a man condemned to death, a man who knows the secrets of The Way. Besides, he's too well-known, at least in Argentina. Argentina—where a good number of Hitler's toadies hid! All of these facts opened my eyes. Sabato's book is merely a clever attempt to turn the search in an erroneous direction. *They* set quite a few traps like that. I was saved by my native language and vigilance. They didn't succeed in fooling me.

I don't know why it's the *Lithuanian* language in particular. I don't know why it's in Lithuania in particular that *They* so openly show themselves, or disguise themselves so poorly. I don't know why it's Vilnius in particular that's so important. All of that is still a mystery to me.

*They* overshot, if they think that I'll study only the books in my own library. I've spent quite a bit of time in the University's manuscript sections. There I came across a manuscript, a transcript of a pre-war dissertation, that shocked me.

During the time of Zygimantas Augustus (the second half of the 16th century), a Basilisk appeared in Vilnius that killed people with *its gaze*. It was the horrible metamorphosis of a *bird*; it killed people with the power of its eyes, or sometimes with a deep breath. It hid in the mysterious Didžiosios Street district and had been discovered, but later disappeared. It was possible to temporarily defend yourself from its powers with dry tree leaves—they absorbed the strength of its gaze.

In the dissertation, this unique information was described as if merely in passing, as one of many legends of Vilnius—with the author's (a woman's!) perfectly understandable caution. After I read this, I didn't sleep for several nights. I frantically looked for information about the Vilnius Basilisk—unfortunately, in vain.

Yet one more very important observation: students at Vilnius University used to organize ceremonies celebrating victory over the Basilisk, but later they were *forbidden and forgotten.*

How much more invaluable information from the past is still hidden in manuscripts!

She talks and talks; she's been quiet for too long. Even now she's silent the entire workday and doesn't even glance at me, while I fume, irritated by blond-fluffed Stefa buzzing around me. At one time I used her in some of my inquiries. Lolita avoids her; she avoids them all, but after work, left alone with me, she bursts out. We spend entire evenings walking around Vilnius; I haven't roamed through the city this much in a long time. Lola constantly scatters words, sentences, and difficult tirades about. In the narrow little streets, in the grim gateways, next to the old houses, the words she's spoken pile up in heaps. They are distinctive: smaller or larger, arranged tidily or thrown about any which way. They pretend to be rocks, tree leaves swept together, or even trash.

She talks incessantly.

"Vytas," is how it most often starts, "Vytas, do you want me to tell you about . . ."

A typical woman's question. How can I say what I want? But the worst of it is that I do enjoy it when she talks. I enjoy listening to her like music. She improvises as she speaks, returning to the same place (in the story and in the city) a hundred times, or turning in circles, or wandering aimlessly. She starts to talk about her village, about her grandparents, and I know we'll shortly turn up in Gediminas Square. Mentioning her husband, we're surely cutting across Vokiečių Street (now it's Muziejaus). Her jazz of words and routes has become *part of me*; we're not just walking through Vilnius, but through my internal streets too.

"I'm drawn to horrible people," she says with inner fear. This is a favorite theme of hers (down Gedimino Boulevard, then to Tortorių Street, deeper and deeper into the bowels of Vilnius). "I'm fascinated by doomed men, the ones that smell of misfortune from a distance . . ."

Now she's a bodiless, extinct, paralyzed fairy of Vilnius: a pale shadow on the dark background of a wall, a dark shadow on the background of a bright wall. The charms of Lola's body have vanished somewhere. I don't even notice her breasts or the mysterious roundness of her belly; I listen more than I look. I like Lolita's voice. In it I hear the quiet rustle of an inner fire; the fire there isn't extinguished yet. Her voice is *multifaceted*: you can hear her girlish dreams and her desires in it, her favorite music, even her breasts and her long legs wrapped in fluids of beauty.

*Now* I'm walking beside her; I see her lips, I even see the words themselves—it's a shame they fall on the sidewalk and roll into the dark portals; they should be collected and saved.

"I'm persecuted by people who are marked with the sign of misfortune," she repeats seriously. "It sounds silly: marked with the sign of misfortune, like in a Russian ballad . . . We no longer know how to say what we want to say, there are just strangers' phrases in our heads . . . Although, no, I know: if everyone were to speak their own language, we'd never understand one another. But it would be so beautiful! . . . The sign of misfortune . . . I look for that kind of person myself, that's the worst. The other kind don't interest me . . . What is a man, Vytas?"

"A face and sexual organs. To distinguish them from others and to multiply!"

"Jesus and Mary," she sighs, "You're a silly, foul-mouthed person. A man is his eyes. Eyes are everything, even if you're physically blind. And the invisible fiery brand on a person's forehead."

She suddenly stops. She frequently comes to a standstill this way, as if she had to hammer in a little stake here, to leave a sign. In just this spot. Here, where she spoke of eyes.

"And me?" I ask, because by now we have turned in the direction of the University and my turn to speak has come. "What's written on my forehead? Or written on some other spot? What's written there that's so significant, that you fell for a dying old man? It isn't by chance an Electra complex?"

"You're a pig. And terribly spiteful," she says, after a long, long silence (all the way to Stiklių Street). "You hate me. This always, always happens to me . . ."

Suddenly she stops on the very corner, and leans against the wall; her face looks up, straight at me. *Now* she has a body: and eyes, turned in towards herself, and breasts (they furiously press up against me), and the curves of the thighs hidden under her clothing, and her flat goddess's belly. She suddenly comes to life, her eyes blaze and her fingers angrily pick at the wall.

"And if I were to start needling at you too? We'd go on picking on one another? You'd get mad first. Men are very touchy."

I follow from behind, hanging back a bit, and wait patiently, because she speaks of intimate things only in Didžiosios Street. (Now she's in Gorky Street. What a sad, sad absurdity—what does some Gorky, a miserable kanukized servant, have in common with Vilnius?) It's only in this street, descending downwards, that she talks about what matters most to her. (Climbing up she always asks me about the camp.) It's probably still quite early, but Vilnius is empty. Vilnius gets emptier by the day—the emptier it gets, the worse the crush in the streets. A dead city, and above it hangs a fog of submissive, disgusting fear. Vilnius, which I love, Vilnius, which is I myself, buried under lava like Pompeii, under the seas like Atlantis. Lolita and I are shadows: the live Vilniutians, that throng of ants, that murky river, don't wander the evening streets, don't talk the way we do.

"I can't stand dead ideas," she suddenly says. "I can't stand symbols and metaphors . . . My mother was obsessed with the idea of innocence. The idea of consummate innocence. Do you know what innocence is?"

"This membrane in the vagina. Sometimes very difficult to tear."

"Vytas, stop it," she fumes. "You're making fun of me. I won't tell you anything . . . Although as it happens, it was exactly with a membrane that everything started . . ."

Agitated, she looks around as if she were searching for ears in the walls, then she cowers and whispers. Even her whisper plays its own music. She doesn't hiss like others do; you'd think she was uttering secret curses—only genuine fairies know them.

"Whoever walks between these walls can't be innocent. This damn city wouldn't put up with innocence . . . But no, I was talking about the past, about my mother . . . At first my maidenly innocence really was what mattered most to her. You can't imagine how much you can talk about that. How many days, evenings, nights. For years! Mother started

64

when I was about six. I'd run around the yards, mostly with the boys. For some reason I wasn't attracted to dolls; I liked hideaways, ruins and boys better . . . She immediately started in giving me lectures about innocence. She wanted to explain what innocence is. Abstract innocence—that's what mattered most to her. It was complete mysticism . . . Later she switched to concrete maidenly innocence, as a separate example. She explained in excruciating detail all the methods whereby, in her opinion, it was possible to lose your innocence. All night long— so I would know what I had to avoid. Her imagination was nightmarish. But enough of that . . . Of course, I didn't understand anything, but an image of mystical innocence formed within me. A live innocence . . . Practically a little beast . . . It was so . . . sticky, without any holes or openings, hairy, and really cold—so you wouldn't want to touch it. My six- or seven-year-old brain was full of that cold, hairy innocence, can you imagine? I'd dream of it. And how did everything turn out?"

She stops again, as if she needs to concentrate to answer, and takes a deep breath of air, Vilnius's gray air. It smells of decay. Every evening street of Vilnius looks like a narrow path through an invisible bog. If you were to go a couple of steps to the side you'd immediately feel the sweetish breath of the swamp, the smell of peaceful decay.

"Do you know how it all ended up? Quite naturally: I began to hate any kind of innocence. If I had only understood what my mother was explaining to me, I would have lost my maidenly innocence by all possible means. I'll tell you about my mother's fantastic invented methods later, all right?"

I can't be all right: we're approaching the Narutis, approaching the lonely portal that quietly chats with Saint John's church. There's no talking here; I have to go by calmly, without disturbing the old smells that have seeped into the walls. And Lolita understands me, understands without a word, by now she's standing in my room by the window and stroking the curtain. But no—she's lying on the couch with her legs curled up under her.

*Now* she's lying on the couch completely naked, her head leaning on her left hand, with her soft-skinned legs curled up under her. A secret fire burns within her—I still don't know if she won't set me on fire too. I only know what I see and feel *now*. I feel Lolita's warmth, and I see her herself: the large, firm breasts, the belly hidden in half-shadow, the folded, twisted legs. I understand why an artist took her for a wife: he wanted to have an ideal model at hand every day. You could draw her, exclusively, your entire life. Not just her portraits—you could paint a meadow or a room: on the canvas there really will be a meadow or a room, but actually you'd draw her *all the same*. You can delve into her, express her, even though at that moment your paintbrush will leave an image of the Last Judgment on the canvas, or a still life of space-rending green peaches, or symmetrical gray squares. That's just what the ordinary sight will see, but the second, *true* sight will invariably discern Lolita there.

"Why do I talk about it? I don't know . . . Sometimes it seems to me that she was a genuine Lithuanian, a Lithuanian of Lithuanians—with that idea of hers, of innocence. It's like a national illness, you know? She tried to be innocent in absolutely everything. It was practically a religious aspiration, an unrealistic yearning. Her slogan should have been: 'Never take a step!' And: 'If someone comes close to you, don't wait, don't stand in place—run as fast as you can!' She wanted to be innocent in absolutely everything . . . Not God's fiancée, no, no, not that at all . . . I'd say she didn't want to surrender to the world, or something. If it were at all possible not to do something new, something unknown, something she hadn't experienced yet—she wouldn't do it. Understand? . . . If she had never been somewhere, she avoided going there. She tried her best to never go beyond the borders of the smells, events, and ceremonies she had already experienced; anything new could injure her mystical innocence . . . Don't touch that flower, she would say, don't show it to me! . . . Don't tell me about the sea, never, ever, tell me about the sea! We got into a horrible row the first time I secretly ran off to the sea! . . . Never mind the sea, she had never tasted lemons! A lemon could injure her innocence, you know?"

"So, it's always about your mother. And you?"

Lolita moves her legs uneasily, rubs her cheek with a finger; bars of light slink over her chest, briefly light up her navel and the lower part of her belly, the thick, curled-up hair. Her mother intimidates me. I don't want to hear another word about her mother. She was my age. Someone my age, obsessed with a pathological idea of innocence.

Lolita suddenly sits up, bends her somewhat spread legs and leans on her knees with her elbows, her hands hanging down, her fingers almost reaching her ankles. The halo of thick hair glows with an angry fire around her head. Her body, unusually coarse, almost vulgar, looks at me rapaciously; the plainly visible dark sexual opening irritates me. It's only like that for a few moments. The lamp is ashamed and hides behind her back; now her face, her entire front, is in shadow, and her voice is much calmer.

"Don't make fun of my mother. Her world was bigger than ours. Just think how much she *invented* about those things she never experienced, the things she denied herself . . . I envy that ideal world of hers . . . Imagine it—you invent a lemon yourself. With all the details, with a bunch of non-existent characteristics . . . Come on now, a real lemon compared to an ideal like that—nothing more than a fog, a banal yellow fruit, while yours . . . She was a theoretician, an aesthete; I went for practice and experimentation. She pounded that abstract idea of innocence into me so thoroughly that to this day I'm dying to lose my innocence in every possible sense, to try out everything immediately, to run looking who knows where, and to constantly look, to look for something never seen, never experienced, never known . . . And I like just exactly the kind of men I can't understand, the kind I don't know what to expect from . . . Understand?"

"And I'm that kind?"

"You understand . . ." she blurts out, and continues down the street. "You understand everything perfectly well. You're intelligent. Besides, you have your secret, and I don't know what it is . . . And I don't want to know . . . If I were to know, then at least I could predict what you'll do, how you'll behave . . . And I don't want that . . . I want to experience everything myself, understand?"

She gets more and more furious; her voice angrily cuts the air of Pilies Street into pieces, and then flings them in my face. It is slowly getting lighter, or it hasn't gotten dark yet. By now we have almost *gone the entire street* to the end. By now she has almost gotten all of it out— earlier, now, later.

"What did you ask me to begin with?" she says sadly. "Why am I telling you this drivel?"

"You were explaining why you're attracted to horrible people."

"Oh . . . Because I can see only two signs in a person's face—either unhappiness, or peace. The kind of peace that means stupidity, clean business, bacon, money, *very* soft furniture, fear of authority, endlessly just and moral behavior, shiny shoes that are never dirty, perfectly even dentures, a precise daily schedule, peaceful sleep . . ."

In an instant the mood changes; suddenly Lolita is quiet, and without her voice something inexplicable is going on in the dimness. I'm walking down a street of Old Town, a woman walks beside me, but I have absolutely no idea who she is—I know her name, a few of her real or invented stories, but does that really mean I *know* her? A completely strange, dangerous woman is walking next to me and probably wants something from me—at this moment or in general. She probably wants to use me, like all women do, or perhaps even to deceive me cruelly. An extremely graceful woman—I can't get enough of her walk, her legs gliding as smoothly as in a dream. She's very young; it's not clear what she wants from me, this fairy of Vilnius. At any moment she could look at me with a magic glance and turn me into a stone, or a submissive slave. I feel I am in her power. She controls me with magical powers, or at least she could control me: if she were to look at me with her entrancing eyes I would obey, I would carry out any order. But she doesn't look—maybe she thinks it's still early, maybe she's saving her authority for the critical moment. You have to guard against her; you shouldn't admire her.

There's practically no fog left; I see the streets, the square and the most important thing—the hill and Gediminas Castle. Here the Iron Wolf howled in Grand Duke Gediminas's dream and promised the castle a great future. Now Vilnius itself is a dream city, a ghost city. Among the faceless figures walking the streets, the good dead of Vilnius (the old ones and the entirely new ones from the post-war period, the last Lithuanian aurochs) look much livelier. It's not clear which is a dream—the ancient city or the Vilnius of today. Only the ancient castle in the new city is unavoidably real: a lonely tower, emerging from the overgrown slopes of the hill—the phallic symbol of Vilnius. It betrays all secrets. The symbolic *phallus* of Vilnius: short, stumpy and powerless. An organ of pseudo-powers that hasn't been able to get aroused in a long time. A red three-story tower, a phallic NOTHING, shamelessly shown to everyone, Vilnius's image of powerlessness. The great symbol of a castrated city, of castrated Lithuania, stuck onto every postcard, into every photo album, every tourist brochure. A perverted, shameless symbol: its impotence should be hidden, not acknowledged, or it should at least pretend it's still capable of a thing or two. But the city has long since lost everything—even its self-respect. Only lies, absurdity, and fear remain.

For some reason I'm sitting in the break room again, someone's tossed me into a room with peeling plaster and set women around me. Besides myself, there's only one man here—Martynas Poška, our library's sad little chatterbox, a weird variety of crew-cut deity, a pathetic searcher for justice, and a collector of absurdities. At one time I even thought he was walking at least in parallel on The Way; I was shocked by his thin, long face, his eyes brimming with horror, his spineless whispers: "They don't need it . . . it was done intentionally . . . a Satanic system . . ." But you scarcely start to think Martynas could be *one of your own*, when he brushes his hand across his face, suddenly changing it for another, and again I see the sneering crew-cut Martynas, the library's sad little chatterbox. Someone like that can't walk The Way, thank God, he can't be *Their* spy, either: in whatever company, he's the one that talks the most. And I always listen. I don't disdain any conversation, any company. He who knows The Way doesn't have the right to disdain people who have been kanuked; he knows all too well that his great discoveries and advantages are just a matter of fate, and only his mistakes are truly earned. You cannot condemn those around you; the desire to demean others is inspired by *Them*. Everyone should be viewed with secret hope, and their words examined for expression of a strong spirit. *Almost* no one is *completely* kanuked.

Take Martynas: some spiritual organ of his secretly manufactures anti-kanukas hormones; I've been convinced of this many times. Inside of him hides a deep protest against *Them*, although unfortunately, he hasn't an inkling of *Their* existence.

Martynas was always a person of faith. He had faith in the power of reason. He thought the majority of our misfortunes proliferate because there aren't enough virtuous, stubborn, and talented young men to sacrifice themselves and fix at least the biggest idiocies of our life. Martynas feels he himself is one of those young men. He dedicated his dissertation to the study of education, although its scope was much larger. He even flushed out a few substantial things. It wasn't just a standard dissertation, but two full-scale treatises. One was philosophical for the most part, written like Spinoza: axioms, theorems, and their proofs. The other was almost sociological: a lot of rich documentation confirming the already proven theorems. Martynas carried out a titanic labor: he began it in his sophomore year and labored over it twenty-five hours a day for an entire eleven years. He was even left without a wife or children. Martynas Poška was a scholarly fanatic.

He painstakingly studied the path of the Soviet citizen from preschool to a university degree, and with mathematical precision proved that everywhere and at all times the only thing taught is how to swallow ready-made propositions, lifeless tropes, and barren constructions. Nowhere is *thinking* taught. No one is taught to create images for himself, to find propositions, to arrange logical schemes. No one is taught to search for truth, no one is taught to *doubt*. And worst of all—no one is taught the fundamentals of morals and humanity. In a word, we raise imitators, talking parrots, soulless automatons—but not *Homo sapiens*. Martynas always had a boundless respect for the concept of *Homo sapiens*. In the second part of his opus he scattered a bouquet of the most dreadful examples—from moronic educational programs to young killers spouting off: they had murdered just for the hell of it—not even out of anger, nor out of any dark instinct, but merely because they hadn't grasped the simplest rudiments of human morality.

When his dissertation immediately stumbled on *every* rung of the bureaucratic ladder, Martynas understood nothing. He still believed in the power of the intellect. After all, an educational system like that ruined absolutely everything: the economy, politics, people's souls; in a word, his dissertation bolstered the entire country. But no one, *absolutely* no one, would even consider speaking of its shortfalls or merits. A multitude of identical faces and identical voices vaguely muttered, "Come on, now, how can you, you understand yourself, after all, you understand everything."

Force is neither *Their* only nor *Their* basic method. Treachery, deceptive persuasion, and a peculiar hypnotism are far more significant, far better suited to *Their* purposes. It's always *Their* bywords:

"Come on now, you understand, you surely understand everything yourself!"

"The time hasn't come yet for ideas like that!"

"Is it *worth* your while to be in such a hurry?"

*They* don't try to merely break your spirit, but to force you to break it *yourself*. Obviously, *They* must occupy key positions in the educational system. It's particularly important for *Them* to start with children as soon as possible.

For the love of God, guard the children!

Martynas refused to understand this. He still believed in the power of intellect. Besides, he was a sufficiently bold and brazen young man. He marched on Moscow itself, camped overnight in the reception rooms of the masters, took Olympus by a long-term siege. He climbed quite high; the only thing higher was the very apex, the banquet table of the gods.

One sad evening Martynas, well into his cups, leaned over to me and whispered enigmatically: "That muckety-muck talked to me for *two hours*! I understood it all . . . they don't need it . . . it was done on purpose . . . you can't imagine what a *Satanic* system it is!" He spoke in a whisper, casting furtive glances at the corners of the empty room. It was then I thought he probably was walking right next to me on The Way. Alas, alas.

On his return from Moscow, he quickly went through all the bureaucratic offices, collecting copies of his opus. That's when remarkable things started happening. He didn't find a single one. All of the offices claimed they never had a copy. The manuscript he had left at home vanished without a trace. Then they fired him from his post, quite officially, for not having defended his dissertation on time. He couldn't manage to find other work. Openings would mysteriously disappear as soon as he approached the personnel department's door. At last, late one evening, an unfamiliar voice telephoned him and suggested he apply at the library. That was how he ended up: without a wife, without children, without his great work. But he didn't fall into hysterics, didn't drink himself to death, and didn't start fearing his own shadow.

On the contrary, he started expressing dreadful heresies out loud—the way people sing as loud as they can when they're going through a haunted forest. I suspect Martynas sees apparitions too. Even now he almost never shuts his mouth. For some reason we're sitting at the coffee break table again and talking about something. And again it repeats itself: more and more often, my time turns in circles and returns to the same spot.

Leodead Brezhnev's portrait listens indifferently. An abundance of the usual conversational themes: Lithuanians and Russians, the food that isn't, rising prices, Russia as the kingdom of idiots, America as a paradise where dollars grow on trees, the decrepit government, youth has no ideals, the world's ecological system is disintegrating, we were born Lithuanians, will there be a war?

*Now* the theme approaches the eternal circle, which is nearly impossible to escape from: the absurdities of propaganda, what are they blathering, who do they think we are? The theme has been discussed and dissected to death, but Martynas is still pontificating:

"They actually know no one will listen to them. No one will hear what they say. So there's no need to put even a speck of logic into what they're spouting off about. It would be a useless waste of effort. Besides, they're concerned about people's health. Imagine what would happen if a political commentator suddenly said something *intelligent*. A catastrophe! Fifteen hundred people would get a heart attack. Three thousand would go into nervous shock from the unexpectedness of it. At least several dozen would start prophesying: they'll decide the end of the world is coming . . ."

"Comrade Martynas, Comrade Martynas . . ." Elena drawls lazily.

Pretty Beta, who separates me from Elena, is completely stunned: she showed up here recently and isn't used to Martynas yet. Whenever he opens his mouth, every newcomer or stranger thinks a platoon of soldiers will pile into the room at any moment and drag Martynas off to a penal colony. The old-timers are used to it, even Elena, even though she represents the Communist Party in our company. She interrupts Martynas's heresies with the monotony of a robot, but she doesn't even bother to scare him or lecture him.

Laima took advantage of the silence. She resembles a fish, a large cod. I always want to let her back into the ocean. She looks around quite serenely and announces:

"Last night I saw an evening with Marcinkevičius on the television. A very good poet."

My neighbor Beta's jaw even dropped: you need to get used to Laima too. She always speaks out of turn. That's her style. She's even weirdly secretive, like every fish.

Elena willingly takes up the theme of nationality. She likes to play the knowledgable Lithuanian. The wolf's satisfied, and the sheep's healthy too:

"He's the only true Lithuanian poet."

Martynas's eyes bug out horribly:

"Oh, yes, no one else knows how to exclaim with such sad, longing pathos: *O sancta Lituanica!* I suggest introducing a unit of yearning sadness, let's say . . . hmm . . . a marcinkena or a marcena. One marcena would be equal to . . ."

"His trilogy is a true Lithuanian epic." Elena's knowledge is wide, she reads the newspapers diligently. "The people create a national poet with their own hands."

"Yes, I see how that nation, its sleeves rolled up, under the careful eye of the KGB and censorship, dripping with sweat, swiftly creates a national poet," this from me, needlessly of course.

Elena gives me a murderous look, but lets it pass. She's afraid of me.

"And the national poet doesn't snooze, either," Martynas interrupts in a sweet little voice, "I can literally see him, taking heed of strict instructions from the authorities, practicing profound Lithuanian poses in front of the mirror. Do you know what's the most Lithuanian pose of all?"

"He's going to say something nasty!" Laima announces with cheerful horror.

But Martynas doesn't get the chance to say anything nasty. Elena cuts him off angrily:

"You despise your own nation, Comrade Poška. You don't like Lithuanian art."

The great Lithuanianist Martynas ought to explode in fury, but he just swallows his saliva three times and says rather calmly:

"Where is it? Where's the art? Where? Show it to me." Anxiously, he looks under the table, out the window; he even sticks his nose behind the cabinet. "You know, there is no art. I can't find it anywhere! Maybe someone took it and carried it off? Where, my dear, is your art?"

The newcomer Beta got truly intrigued, she even leaned forward. I've such an urge to stroke her little short-haired head, and then her firm, probably not very large breasts.

"You don't even know Lithuanian art, Comrade Poška!"

"That's a lie! I know eighty-five kilometers of Lithuanian writers, I'm an expert! Lithuanian writers are divided into the sad ones and the cheery ones. The latter I refuse to study. And the sad ones' sadness is of two types: a tearful sadness, measured in marcenas, more typical of poets, and a sighing sadness, more typical of prose writers. They sigh because the censor's framework is suffocating them. They sigh in an apartment with a custom kitchen, custom bath and custom toilet provided by those setting the censorship framework. It's particularly important that the Lithuanian writer have a custom toilet. He spends most of his time sitting on the custom toilet and writing nothing. Because his creative freedom is restricted. If he were given freedom, wouldn't he just write like mad! Now, it's true, he can't very well imagine what that 'like mad' would be, but that's secondary. You can't demand too much of a Lithuanian writer's imagination."

Martynas's high spirits were interrupted by a creak of the door. Fyodorov, a Communist from another section, is making some sort of Communist signs at Elena. Elena, with the proud grace of a hippopotamus cow, sways out to see him.

"Vytautas, what milksops we all are, huh?" Martynas sighs in my ear. "Why aren't we Irish? The same size country, the same number of inhabitants . . . Even Dublin's almost the same as Vilnius . . ."

"Only Russia's not next door."

"There's England!" Martynas continues buzzing in my ear like an evil spirit. "They fucked the Irish good too, but they held out."

"They lost their language."

"A language spoken by men with no balls is shit!" Now Martynas is hissing like a snake.

"Martis, maybe you really do hate Lithuanians?"

"I'm a hundred percent Lithuanian, and no one's going to force me to *love* myself," Martynas says in a deathly calm, and moans again: "Well, why aren't we Irish? Where's our IRA? Where's our Sinn Fein? Where are the bombs? I want to be a terrorist!"

"Martis, finish about the writers," Stefa offers lovingly, "the censor's gone, you can go on."

Stefanija is mistaken: the biggest censor is still hanging on the wall. A humanistic person, looking at that portrait, would have to feel pity and pain: a broken-down, barely creeping stiff, exhibited by his colleagues for threefold ridicule, like an old buffoon. But he's staring too, his grim eyeballs are even bulging from the portrait—just that it means nothing to Martynas.

"Yes . . . So, at night he prays to God that no one gives him that freedom, because if he got it, he wouldn't know what to do with it. Now Lithuanian writers have an ironclad alibi: there's no freedom. But what would happen then?"

A fog slowly comes over me again. Martynas mouths off soundlessly; all of the women and girls explode in laughter. Only Laima is completely serious. She'll laugh suddenly, ten minutes later, after she's returned to her room.

Why exactly did all of these people end up in the *library*? Why is Lolita hiding out here, why am I sitting here? There is plenty of other work for a good programmer. In our situation, who needs an experimental computerized card index? So someone can find out with blinding speed that he won't get this or that book, because it's hidden in a closed special collection? I myself suppose I ended up here of my own accord; I still naïvely believe in my own free will. But after all, only *They* could have let me in here. Maybe it's more convenient for *Them* this way to watch what I'm reading? Or maybe all books are nothing but *lies*, maybe reading makes *Them* happy, because it leads me further from *The Way*? Or maybe *They're* too lazy to rummage through books themselves, maybe I'm only supposed to come across the texts that are dangerous to *Them*? Maybe that's the only reason I'm kept alive?

Bookshelves, bookshelves, bookshelves. Books, books, books. Narrow passageways—a secret labyrinth where it's easy to get lost, to turn and turn in circles, never to return again. From all of the bookshelves there drifts an identical, barely noticeable warmth—as if from a raked-up pile of autumn leaves. Who knows what sorts of minotaurs wait in ambush for you in the dimness spreading from the concealed ceiling lights. (The library collection's lights always spread dimness, not light.)

The soundless picture continues to flicker before my eyes. Martynas has tickled everyone so much they'd laugh if you showed them a finger. Still going on about the writers?

". . . every seven years a creative fever overcomes him. The symptoms: muses and ghosts torment him. His entire body starts itching.

The pain is horrible. The time has come to beg the authorities for a new apartment. There aren't many apartments, but writers multiply like dogs. That's when the Shakespearean passions boil over. Sung in tones of the highest spirituality. What eloquence! What depth! You see at once that these are artists. What Greek tragedies! The Soviet writer could kill his brother or sister over a new apartment, or still worse—he could kill himself! I know at least six writers who publicly threatened suicide if the state wouldn't give them a new apartment."

"So what happened?" Stefa laughs.

"Two of them did it. One with tablets from America; the second used a really awful method. He categorically refused alcohol! His death was inevitable."

"Martis, tell us about creativity, something about creativity," Marija begs through her tears.

"My dear, it really is true creativity! The applications to get an apartment are great pearls of poetry! In it you'll find living pain, true torture. True passion. I'll devote the rest of my life to the publication of a collection of writers' applications for their apartments. Otherwise history won't forgive me."

"That's enough!" Laima declares, unexpectedly as usual. "It's time to go to work. The boss is already frowning."

The boss—that's me. I thought about Martynas and frowned despite myself. I listen to his mockery and sarcasm, more often I listen to his serious conversation, occasionally I visit his strange collection. All of it leads somewhere, unfortunately, not where The Way leads; Martynas has turned down a side path. Even people who aren't at all stupid frequently turn down them. Almost all do.

Most likely he thinks, as the majority do, that everything is determined by two elements; the battle between good and evil, black and white, light and dark. The great contradiction: we are light, while the others—darkness, underground vaults, bats, obscene birds of the night. Heaven and hell, God and Satan.

No one, *almost* no one draws the obvious conclusion: the battle between light and dark is always won by grayness and twilight. As long as the essential elements, black and white, God and Satan, exist—all is not yet lost. The end comes when everything mixes into a unbroken sugary fog, when nothing no longer differs from anything else.

It is this fog that is the eternal gaze that lurks even in our dreams. It is the Vilnius Basilisk's gaze, piercing me every morning, a morning that begins with the overcrowded trolleybus, the crush of figures, the journey from non-existence into non-existence: from the drabness of dreamless sleep to the unthinking work machine. It's only by *Their* will that the tired figures with puffy eyes cram into iron boxes with fly-covered windows and slowly creak towards their daily bondage. The day begins with smells: the stink of rancid sweat and cheap soap, the stench of last night's drinking, and a whiff of nightmares.

But most important of all—the birds have disappeared somewhere. (Which morning was it they disappeared—today, yesterday, always?) The birds have disappeared, and I'm slowly losing my soul, I'm starting to turn into something else. I'm even curious: who is this *other*? A beast or a demon? A madman? An envoy of the dark? My shape probably won't change—only my eyes will lose their fire, their secret signs; I'll quietly turn into a man blind to his soul, into a void, a fog. I'll feel the blessed nirvana of imbecility. I won't have to remember anything anymore.

For the time being I still remember. Like it or not, I remember my grandfather. Like it or not, I remember my father. Perhaps one of the secret gazes examining me is my family's history?

In front of me, pressing a glass of first-class liquor in his hand, father sits and pushes words out his twisted lips. He scans the shining table-top as if there, underneath his pointy chin, the words would quietly lie one atop another like dry tree leaves. My father, the one-time prodigy of Göttingen and Copenhagen; his intellect, probably equal to Dirac's or Einstein's, crumbled and turned into a sickening half-spirit gazing out of narrow, dull pupils. An invisible cudgel trounced him. But no, a cudgel wouldn't have vanquished him. Father is very large, like all of the Vargalyses, he would just shake a blow off—we're accustomed to blows. That intellect could only have been vanquished by a plague, a cancer slowly eating away at the brain.

"Except maybe a writer," father pontificates, "perhaps it's still possible to be a writer in this world. There was this colleague of mine in Göttingen . . . Sometimes he sends a line . . . His name's Robertas . . . He's writing the story of his life now. A book about non-possession. Do you know what non-possession is?"

The liquor glitters in the glass: Hennessy or Courvoisier. (Where does he get the money?) Father's hands are beautiful, their movements smooth. They reek of nobility and inborn elegance. Even on the worst mornings his hands tremble elegantly. I do not love my father (I never loved him), but his hands fascinate me. If I were to draw a real human, I would paint him with my father's noble hands. Hands are a man's beginning of beginnings. Hands and eyes.

My father, a downed bird floundering between Kaunas and Polish-occupied Vilnius, the doctor of Göttingen who sometimes raves about the new European physics and Dirac's delta function, now speaks of non-possession. He's always talking about non-possession and loss. He breathes non-possession and loss; he lives by them. Winning or possessing, he'd die, the way others die of hunger or thirst.

"Non-possession is our core," father lectures. "Even that which we possess—we don't really possess, understand? We only supposedly possess it . . . What do we have—this or that object: houses, cars, books. These or those ideas, or women . . . But is your woman really yours? Do your ideas really belong to you? Not true! When things are bad, you're invariably left all on your own . . . And all ideas instantly turn foreign . . . We're permeated with non-possession, Vytie . . . We ourselves are living non-possession. Even our daydreams are taken away from us . . . WHO takes everything away—there's the essential question of existence, Vytie. Everything that could really BE OURS is taken away and hidden somewhere . . . Or maybe there really isn't anything on earth that could be ours . . ."

Father's speech sometimes rises to holy revelation and sometimes falls to a drunk's blathering. His ruin is inexplicable and therefore even more frightening. We're born lost already, father likes to say; our birth itself is a loss. Sometimes I would secretly pray to all the gods for the slightest excuse for his ruin. He didn't have any and didn't even try to look for one, like other drunks do. (The greatest unwritten novels molder in the boundless inventions of drunks, blathering away about the tragic reasons for their downfall.)

It's unbelievably difficult for me to understand him even *now*—and at the time I was only twelve, and later sixteen. Father disappeared at the very beginning of the war; there was talk that he had, by unknown means, run away to Switzerland, and then to America. I don't know if that's true; no one knows if that's true. All I know is that father could do anything, overcome whatever obstacles. He could swim right across the Atlantic if he wanted to. The war meant nothing to him. I don't think there was anything in the world that would have meant anything to him. I don't think he vanished in the Americas; his mysterious disappearance and reappearance aroused completely different suspicions, the very worst of suspicions.

Sometimes I see my father writing articles (I see it *now*: maybe nineteen thirty-six, maybe forty). Suddenly he sits, leaning on an elbow, for three days, filling sheets with complex formulas, and then carelessly tosses the scrawled-over pile of sheets onto the armchair. There it lies for two, three, five months. Lies there until it's covered with a thick, fuzzy layer of dust, other papers, and forgotten time. Forgotten time hovers about our house constantly. At intervals someone finds those discarded articles and sends them off somewhere—probably grandfather, he visits us two or three times a year. The shabby sheets of paper disappear, do something in the secret cosmos of written sheets, and then they return multiplied; enormous bundles of paper descend upon the house. I don't know who publishes those articles—*Zeitschrift für Physik* or *Physical Review*—but the house is always full of author's copies, postcards from some physicist or another, and father's astonishment. Stunned, he turns those papers over in his hands, even forgetting his glass of cognac; it seems he keeps wanting to ask me something. Maybe he wants to ask me what's the point of it all. What's all this about, Vytie? Am I the one responsible for this? That's what happens when a person absentmindedly tries *to accomplish something.*

Sometimes I see my father drawing. He can draw anywhere and with anything, but above all else he values first-class Chinese ink. He has it sent from Paris. (Where does he get the money?) There is life and death in his drawings, there's soul in them. You can find God in them. Sometimes father draws without looking at the paper—his hand draws the lines itself, as if it had both eyes and memory.

All father needs from this world is paper and marks he can write or draw on the greedy surface of paper. And a glass too, into which this or that has been poured. Nothing more. The smell of paper and liquor lingers in his office. Here, the feeling experienced in a gloomy forsaken house, or in a dusty old attic filled with mysterious things, comes over you. Here, everything has died; inside you can only imagine ghosts. It's the excavated room of an inhabitant of Pompeii. Miraculously extant furniture. Ancient Pompeian books. The smell of thousand-year-old wine. You immediately feel like you're under thick layers of frozen lava, that the sun and light are far, far away. Here, only the stunning Pompeian drawings provide heat and light. It seems to me they weren't designed for this world, or for the light of day. My father (his hands?) drew them, so that, blazing up briefly in the real world, they would vanish again for eternity. And when the world tried to take them, father instinctively defended himself. Once some passerby visited his office and saw the drawings. I wasn't the only one to sense they were drawn by the hand of a genius. Several art buyers immediately flocked into our courtyard (they did resemble shabby birds); one of them moaned wordlessly, another conceived the idea of immediately taking the drawings to Paris. For several days the courtyard resembled a gypsy camp.

Father finally saw his drawings himself. Closed up in his office, he glumly looked through sheet after sheet, talking out loud to himself. He spoke a secret language that was unintelligible to me. Maybe he had thought up one that could *describe* his drawings.

He built the bonfire at night. The drawings went into the fire only at the very beginning. Then father started carrying his manuscripts, journals, and books into the yard: slowly, seemingly weighing things over calmly, he piled ever more bundles of paper into the fire. Soon clothes, grandfather's carved chairs and Turkish carpets began falling into the bonfire too. Mother stayed in her bedroom, never taking her eyes from that bonfire of the world, but she didn't even try to restrain father; she didn't say anything at all. She waited for father himself to stop—she waited all of her life for him to stop. But father continued burning his world according to a spectral scheme. He'd fling some item into the fire, and leave another identical item unharmed. He chose certain cups, plates, and glasses as sacrifices to the fire. There's no telling what gods he made offerings to, what demons he wanted to scare off. He finished that ceremony of fire just as calmly as he had started. It lasted for maybe an hour, maybe two, but that dance of fire didn't stay in the great ALL; it crumbled into bits. I see only individual burning things, my inhumanly calm father, and my mother's pale face in the window. There are no smells left, and neither the fire's crackling nor the hubbub of the agitated household can be heard. Everything goes on in complete silence, just from time to time a dry heat wafts onto your face.

I regretted father's sketched portraits most of all. He always drew the same person—a strange hermit of the swamps by the name of Vasilis. Vasilis would wander into our yard at regular intervals; father got along with him perfectly—you see, the two of them never said a word to each other. Vasilis would come silently and leave silently, piled up with healing herbs and bundles of roots. Grass snakes wound themselves around his arms and tiny, nimble little birds would perch on his shoulders. For posing father would pay him with salt. He would draw the portraits quickly, with enormous inspiration. The real Vasilis didn't appear in any of them; the people in those portraits would always be different, as if that hermit who lived on vipers and frogs changed his face every day. But actually he was always the same: ragged, tanned almost black, murmuring something to his snakes and birds, showing his eyes to no one. He came to the great *auto-da-fé* too, and helped father throw books and drawings into the fire. Then he slowly shuffled off into the darkness, accompanied by an owl flying in circles above his head. He didn't show up in our yard again; I would only see him out in the middle of the swamp, calmly walking through the most treacherous bogs, like Christ walking on water. When father burned his portraits, it was as if Vasilis lost touch with reality, with the ground beneath his feet. To me it seemed as if those portraits contained absolutely everything: the swamps, and the *auto-da-fé* that was to be, and Christ, and the night owls, and non-possession, and impotence. But it was all destroyed in the flames. I managed to hide only "Woman-spider," "Faithfulness," and "The Crane"—I stuck the names on myself. That crane is the most nightmarish bird ever drawn by a human. I've never seen another creature so obviously flying to destruction. That crane radiates pure despair; it knows itself that by now it's almost disintegrated, that it almost isn't there anymore. But it flies anyway—just above the ground, slowly and weakly. It's a flying stuffed bird of doom, a ghost appearing in broad daylight through some mistake. Perhaps a bewitched princess turned into a bird who will crumble into ashes at any moment. That crane is the sister of the woman who, in another drawing, is slowly turning into a giant hairy spider. Or maybe the spider is turning into a woman; one way or another, *change*, by some inexplicable means, is depicted in the drawing. The change is what's so horrifying; it's brimming in every line, in every little hair on the spider's legs. Horror reigns everywhere, except for the woman's face and eyes. She is completely indifferent; it's absolutely all the same to her that she will soon turn into a disgusting anthropod. Or the opposite— it's all the same to her that she's a spider almost turned into a woman. In "Faithfulness," an attractive young girl with gigantic breasts, on all fours, devours her dead husband. There's emptiness in her face and eyes, but her whole body, every seen or only imagined little muscle, is brimming with a rich, bloody ecstasy. She *loves* her husband—even dead. She wants to become one with him. Her gigantic breasts keep swinging lower, it seems as if the devoured flesh of the dead merges into them, embellishing them even more. The dead husband's body adorns her, beautifies her for another man.

My father could have been the best artist in the world. He truly could. However, he refused to budge from the spot. He didn't in general want *to move*.

Oftentimes I see him leaving the villa, slowly walking out to the car. Opening the door, he stops and starts groping for a cigarette. I follow his movements through a grimy window and I know very well (*now* I know) what it is he's waiting for, what he hopes for. Any incident whatsoever, the slightest excuse, so he could immediately return to his room, calmly settle himself in the armchair and pour himself a brimming glass. But no one will save him. I see so much suffering on his face that I want to scream at the top of my voice, to rush to mother, to grandfather, to everyone in a row, to every passerby in every city under the sun, today, yesterday, tomorrow, at all times, to shake them all at the same time and beg: leave him alone, don't torture him, let him, at last, *do nothing*! I want to lie down under the automobile's tires and shout: see, he can't drive, let him return to his drink!

But he has to sit at the wheel, he has to drive to the university, he has to go into the lecture hall and be a professor (act a professor?). To repeat words repeated many times before, to draw marks on the blackboard drawn many times before. To look at the faces of students seen a hundred times before. You can't shake all of that off. There is no bonfire that would burn up the Kaunas highway and his lecture hall . . .

and the alien ideas of long dead physicists . . . and the motley crowd of students . . . There is no such bonfire, so father futilely tried to set it on fire in his mind at least, throwing everything in one after another: our house . . . the surroundings' wretched meadows . . . the entire swamp together with Vasilis . . . the stream frozen in fear . . . mountains and seas . . . all of rotten humanity . . . the tiniest of creations, even bacteria . . . even ideas, all ideas of all time . . . And most importantly—man's immortal soul.

He begins speaking only on those mornings when, in spite of it all, he succeeds in escaping from the unbearable circle of events, in returning to his office and filling a brimming glass of champagne. (Where does he get the money?)

"Equilibrium is the lowest state of energy," his deep voice slowly explains. "The lower you get, the greater your equilibrium. That's a cardinal law of nature, Vytie . . . People do strive so for equilibrium, therefore they sink even lower . . . Into an even deeper pit, into an even greater equilibrium . . . There is no road up, Vytie, ALL roads lead only downward."

But father speaks less and less often. Speech is a type of interaction with the world, and father only wants to interact with himself. That's why he surrounded himself with mirrors. They're hung everywhere: in the hall, in the corridors, in the bedrooms, in the bath. Mirrored walls, mirrored ceilings, only mirrored floors are lacking. Mother couldn't bear those mirrors taking over the house, but father immediately found a Solomonic solution. Now it's as if they're not there—as long as father doesn't take possession of a room. Upon entering, he immediately takes it into his power. He opens every little cabinet's, buffet's, and secretary's doors (on the inner side of the doors are mirrors). He pulls back innumerable little curtains, drapes, *portières* (mirrors crouch, cowering behind them). He turns pictures hung on long strings around (mirrors are set into the other side of the canvas). When the ceremony's finished, father can see himself all the time. He can drink and painstakingly follow how he drinks.

Drunkenness is his separate world. Father drinks *all the time*. Grandfather, in one of his fits of cursing, said that if he couldn't find anything in the house to drink, he'd cut open one of father's veins and fill a glass with blood. A watery shit courses through most people's veins, grandfather sullenly explained, but this specimen differs from others in at least this respect: a cocktail of cognac, rum, champagne, port, and all types of vermouth flows in his veins.

Almost every day I secretly watch father. It's a shameless, dirty pursuit, the most disgusting of all possible thieveries—the theft of a person's solitude. Spying on father, I turn into the most revolting creation of the Universe, coming alive as eyes, as a kanukas sucking others' vital fluids. I curse myself afterwards, even slap myself in the face, but all the same I cannot stop. Our house itself tempts and entices you to secretly watch others. Corridor after corridor covered in carpets, doors always ajar, mirrors reflecting the view around the corner, around a bend, in a far-off room. Dusk always hangs over the house; it turns you into a nameless, faceless spy searching for a victim. Here, like it or not, you see what you shouldn't see. Here you are beset by the urge to inspect another person through the tiniest crack. In this house my acquaintance with the world goes on (*now* it goes on), it's only here that I can study a person from so close up, like a large worm pinned to a board with a cold silver pin. (The Russians burned our house down when they invaded again in forty-four.)

*Now* I kneel in front of a door that's been left ajar and in astonishment watch my father drink. My heart thumps in my chest and my head spins slightly. I can't believe my eyes. Father, stark naked, has rolled himself up into a thick carpet. At first it's even hard to notice him; it seems there's nothing more in the room than a roll of carpet and a glass set at one end of it. Father sticks his head out of the inside of the roll, takes the glass with his lips and teeth, turns it up, drinks a gulp, and carefully sets it down again. And then—strangest of all—he pulls his head back inside the carpet. For a minute father's not in the room, there's only a rolled-up carpet and the glass set at one end. Then father sticks his head out again, grasps the glass with his teeth again . . . The way a snail emerges and hides again in his rugged home. I'm not horrified at all. I don't think for a second that father's gone out of his head. I'm so stunned I don't think at all, I just look. I've turned everything into looking. Now I am an eye, an eye without a brain. Father sticks his head out of the carpet. Pulls it back again. Out again. He drinks in small gulps, barely sipping.

For a long, long time I don't understand *what* he's doing. My face gets hot, my thoughts scatter. At last I vaguely realize: he can't drink in the usual way; he's obliged to perform this absurd ceremony. He's obliged to pour alcohol into himself in an immeasurably serious, intricate, and aesthetic way. That's how he *lives*. And I steal his most intimate secrets: I look and don't close my eyes, not even at the most horrifying moments; that's how *I live*. I want to understand my father, because it's the only means by which to understand myself.

It's just unclear what the view outside the trolleybus window, of the gloomy wooden houses of Žvėrynas and dirty frightened dogs, has to do with this. And there *are still no* birds, although by now the metal box carrying me is turning to the left, shortly there'll be the bridge, and beyond it the library. But that doesn't concern me; I just want to understand my father. It isn't just a few isolated threads that join the two of us, but a wide current overflowing from one to the other. Once I seized father's limp hand: for some reason I wanted to feel his heartbeat, but I couldn't find his pulse. It seemed as if his heart had stopped. It was only after a few long seconds that I realized our heartbeats were *the same*, as if a common heart drove common blood through both our veins. Maybe that's why I always look at father as if I'm looking at myself. Maybe that's why I never understand *what he's doing*. It's only yourself you can't understand that way.

I don't understand now, either: he ordered Janė to undress, while he himself casually walks around, constantly sipping from a glass. Janė undresses without hurrying; I glue myself to the keyhole and nearly choke. I used to be dazed if she so much as leaned over to clean the table, generously revealing her loose breasts; I'd lose my breath as soon as I attempted to scrutinize the divine roundness of her belly through her flowered apron. Now she's undressing right here, without even glancing at father; she's undressing *for me*, she's looking straight at me, maybe she knows that I'm glued to the keyhole, whereas father's standing next to her and doing nothing. Why does he need it? Why does Janė need it? Why is she looking straight at me? She looked exactly the same way when four Russian soldiers raped her: two of them held her knees spread, one pressed her shoulders to the ground, while the fourth just couldn't hit the right spot. She didn't scream, she didn't struggle, there was no sign of suffering on her face, and her eyes gazed at me attentively. She didn't shout for help, not even with her eyes, she calmly gazed straight at me, although she *really* couldn't see me; I watched her unseen from a hiding spot.

Perhaps that look got confused with yet another—when she discovered me in a secluded spot, by the window to the inner courtyard. No one ever wandered by there, a thick layer of dust had settled on the floor. I sat on the window sill, horribly exposed, having pulled out that burning masculinity that wouldn't fit in my clothes, and looked at it with an imbecilic gaze. During those years there were moments when I felt I could rape a dirty wall or a window frame. Or all of the house's mirrors. Or the air above the hilly field. I just didn't know what to do with *it*.

I didn't hear her footsteps. I turned my head and realized she had been standing there for some time already.

"Poor thing! You don't know what to do with yourself anymore?"

She looked at me shamelessly, taking me apart bone by bone. I couldn't imagine how I was to go on living. In an instant she had realized my secret, learned of my great shame. She, of whose breasts, legs, and belly I would dream at night, whom I could not imagine dressed, who, in whatever clothes, would appear more naked than naked. My fantastical erotic plans collapsed in an instant; Janė became unattainable. I could no longer either buy her or catch her accidentally; now she would just laugh at me. I was eternally separated from her heavy breasts, from the secret blackness below her belly that quivered erotically underneath her clothes. Now she could only despise me. And she kept looking below, at *it*.

"Poor thing!" she repeated in a throaty voice. "Come to the shed after dinner. You know—where the boards are . . ."

And I went to the shed; it remained a sacred place to the very end. There Janė took away my virginity. There, four years later, the Russian soldiers raped her. There my mother hung herself. There, in the summer of nineteen-forty, my grandfather built his altar of horror. Misfortune after misfortune burdened our shed; it should have broken into flame sometime of its own accord.

I see grandfather ripping off the shed door so it will be brighter inside. I see a little silver pail falling out of his hands.

"Shit!" grandfather howls. "Shitty shit!"

I already know that the Russian tanks are in Kaunas, that Lithuania has met the doom grandfather predicted.

"Shit!" grandfather roars. "The little fools—they fought with the Poles over Vilnius, only to live to see the Russkies! A shitty nation!"

Grandfather rushes headlong with the little silver bucket from the outhouse in the bushes to the shed and back again.

"Over here!" he nearly roars, "Let's pray! I've built an altar!"

To me it's both kind of awful and funny; for the time being I don't understand anything, even though by now the stench has reached me. It floats along the ground, slowly climbs the walls, pushes through the windows, it's no longer possible to stand it in the house; it descends to the yard, but the stink lingers there too. It seems that nightmarish stench has permeated all of Lithuania's air; you can't escape it anywhere. Grandfather's already lining everyone up: Janė's brother, who's overslept (I cannot look at him, I'd strangle him); the frightened cook; mother looking about with horrified eyes, apparently waiting for grandfather *to stop*. We all turn our noses aside, but we crowd inside the narrow shed and stare, stunned, at grandfather's altar, blinking our eyes, teary from the keenness of the stink. The altar is a cracked pig's trough, decked with flowers, stuck with crosses made from old bunches of twigs and decorated with a yellow wax candle. The candle's flame quivers; it flutters from the stream of poisonous stench rising from the trough.

"Kneel! Everyone kneel! Kneel in front of God!"

But no one kneels, not even grandfather himself; everyone is staring at the teeming, swarming, reeking trough. The little silver pail lies tossed to the side, as if in mockery. It's as silent as a tomb, except that water irritatingly drips from the ceiling. I look too, gazing through fluttering spider webs, and I can't believe my eyes. The trough is full of reeking waste; grandfather carried it here with the little silver pail. That teeming, seemingly live waste, the waste of us all, in which satiated little white worms writhe. The sight is instantly nauseating, and the hideous stink is suffocating besides. Grandfather grins wickedly, fixes his hair with his befouled hand.

"Here's your god! A new kingdom's come, a new government, and here—the new god of the Lithuanians. The age of Perkūnas is over, the era of Christ is over. The Russkies brought you a new god, kneel in front of him and pray. Here he is, get to know him, The Shit of Shits, now he'll be the god of the Lithuanians! A shitty god for a shitty nation, and I'm his priest. Hosanna!"

Grandfather laughs raucously, while we stare at the trough as if in a trance. I no longer know what to think, the oppressive smell pushes the thoughts out of my brain, the air is nothing but a stench, the entire world is a stench, it's the only thing in my head, in place of thoughts, in place of words—just the stench.

"Today is the beginning of a new epoch! A new god has come to our land, by command of a prophet by the name of Stalin Sralin. Now he'll shit on your heads for the ages. Get used to it! Pray to him!"

A glass clinks; I see father, like a doll, drink a sip of champagne (he brought his glass with him even here). This infuriates grandfather. His eyes flood with blood like a bull's; he's no longer speaking, but rather hissing:

"It would have been better if a plague had overrun us, at least some survive. But we've been overrun with shit, and no one will stay clean! We ourselves poured shit on our own heads. Ourselves! Now we'll live in the kingdom of shit. The slogan of the Lithuanian people: it may be shit we're living in, but at least we're alive! Do you have any idea what the Soviets are? They won't leave a single person unshat upon, not a single thought unshat upon, do you understand? In the Soviet communion everyone will have to swallow a piece of fried shit. The Soviets discovered a great secret: the major part of any human being is shit, so you need to value him as shit, address him as shit, treat him like shit. This is Sralin's doctrine of faith: you are shit and don't even try to be anything else. Rejoice: we'll be slaughtered; we'll fertilize Siberia's fields! They'll grow bread for the Russians out of us!"

Grandfather has gotten hoarse; he jabs his finger at the trough, although he doesn't need to jab, everyone is looking at it as if they were entranced, the white of the little writhing worms is in everyone's eyes, the lush stench is burning everyone's nostrils. It seems to me that the teeming shit is looking at us from the trough—pleased and sated—it's mocking us; it knows that now will be its right and might. Horror overtakes me: suddenly I see a gigantic wave of shit relentlessly creeping towards Lithuania's meadows and forests, its cities and villages. It creeps along like a glacier, consuming everything in its path, flooding over the earth. Little figures wave their little arms, try to defend themselves, shriek and instantly suffocate—what can they do, if even hundred-year-old firs snap like matchsticks and drown in the teeming glacier. The wave of shit doesn't hear the moans, it has neither ears nor eyes, it's soulless and all it knows to do is to creep forward. Everything is done for; nothing remains alive, nothing *really* alive. I understand now what grandfather wanted to say. I'm the first to rush outside; I suck air in and look around, as if I really could see that novel glacier. Behind me father and Janė's brother come out, mother creeps out last of all; she looks around with eyes that see nothing, and, addressing no one, asks:

"How did you allow Lithuania to disappear? Why didn't you do anything? Were you poisoned in advance with something that took away your power?"

It was practically the first time I realized that mother also *thinks*. As if she had read my mind, she slowly turns towards the forest, smiles to someone unseen and clearly, intelligently, says:

"God is love. Is it possible that excrement can be love? Is it possible to love excrement? Is it possible that excrement can love someone?"

*A majestic vat of shit looms on the sleigh, filled with a hundred buckets, the entire camp's efforts. Two frost-covered men pull the sleigh, while other skeletons-to-be battle with dreams on three-tiered bunks. Not far away someone is furiously masturbating—it's always the ones who won't be around in a few days who suddenly start up. They want to reproduce themselves, but there's nothing here to impregnate, except for the air.*

*You and Bolius haven't slept for several nights, there's so much accumulated inside the two of you that there's no room left for sleep.*

"Then the Germans took a dislike to our university. They closed it and threw us into a camp. I remember the railroad meandered along a ravine, and on its slope Hilterjugend kids danced a devil's dance. There was nothing human left in them anymore, just the Nazi plague's bacillus. That's the worst of it—children! They unbuttoned their flys, shook their little peewees, and tried to pee on us. They were breathless with the sensation of power."

*The professor didn't see it, but you did: the fifteen-year-old stribai,[2] reeking of moonshine, with shotguns on their shoulders, were children too. And not some Hilterjungends, but the sons of Lithuanian ploughmen. Bolius didn't see them. Give a half-grown kid vodka and a gun—he'll do whatever you say. And those others, without pausing for a second, keep pulling and pulling at the sleigh with the vat of shit.*

---

[2] *Stribai,* "terminators, destroyers" from the Russian *istrebiteli.*

*"Before that they drove us in trucks, while we were still on Lithuanian soil. There were just a couple of guards; they were playing cards. And we rode—thirty healthy, unchained men—and did nothing, we didn't even try to run. We sat and waited for something . . . Why do we Lithuanians always just wait?"*

*Bolius looks sadly at the camp's night shit carriers and nods his head:*

*"There you have it: we obediently drag a pile of waste . . . There you have it . . . I'd lay a wager they're Lithuanians . . . that's so Lithuanian . . ."*

*But the professor is wrong: the wind carries their somnolent voices; you can easily hear that they're speaking Russian:*

*"Forgive me, colleague, but I cannot agree with that conception of yours. Besides, Berkley ultimately proved . . ."*

It's my mother I'm most sorry for. I never spied on her, but she was in view all the time—always with Janė's brother. I would accompany them to the bedroom and then retreat, I couldn't stand to see *more*, but sometimes I would hear *those* sounds. I saw how she paid Janė's brother money *for that*. The sullen, eternally unshaven boy would later shamelessly count the litai, and she would stumble down the house's corridors like a ghost. A slender, beautiful ghost with an upright posture. She was lost in the world; she never found *any* road. *They* poked out the eyes of my mother's soul, took away any feeling for life. All she saw around her was a labyrinth and steep walls, it was entirely the same to her whichever direction she turned, whatever she did. You could never guess what mother would do the next minute, what else she would think up. Sometimes she would chop the heads off the geese in the inner courtyard. Once a cat got underfoot—she did the cat in too. Perhaps she didn't distinguish cats from geese. Sometimes she would quietly swig from father's reserves, until she'd collapse, lifeless, on the floor in the middle of the corridor. Sometimes she would start breaking the mirrors. Sometimes . . .

It'd be better to be quiet about my mother. But I feel compelled to tell at least one person in the world some tiny speck of truth. Perhaps some time I'll tell Lolita about her. About her, about the labyrinth of the world, about the determination to do anything—whatever occurs to you.

Sometimes I get the urge to do almost anything, because I feel trapped, driven into a pointlessly spinning wheel it's impossible to escape from. It makes no difference that this wheel of life, or labyrinth, is alive. A strange vitality throbs below the cobblestones of the street, hums soundlessly in the walls of old houses. The gray houses quietly mutter curses and the churches whisper between themselves in Latin, so no one will understand. They exist *apart* from the city's morning clamor; there's nothing here that affects them. They seem ready to slowly, with difficulty, lift up into the air and float off somewhere, where it'll be better for them; it'd be better there for me too. Where? I don't know of a place like that, I only know the direction: as far as possible away from here, as far as possible from dead Vilnius. Vilnius has been dead for a long time: the rumbling of barrels rolled along the pavement, the motley little shops' signs, the secret tangle of narrow little streets are no more. The Lithuanian quarter, the Jewish quarter—the colorful towns within the city are gone. The face of Vilnius is gone; all the new neighborhoods are identical, they are *nothings*: soulless conglomerates of drunks, lines in the stores, and trolleybus wires. I look with my eyes wide open, but I can't perceive anything more. No secret signs, no deeper meaning; there is only a monotonous, endless dream I am forced to dream against my will. A soulless play staged by a half-witted director: against the mysterious backdrop of old facades, the pseudo-drama of the world's most dismal lifestyle goes on. The plot is known from the start, nothing unexpected can happen—unless the stage sets themselves were suddenly to start speaking in gloomy voices: they are the *most alive* things here. Vilnius's heart beats in the walls of the buildings; it alone here has a soul. The streets turn towards the lazily rising hill, and on it, like in the nightmare of an impotent, sullenly protrudes the short and stumpy phallus of the castle tower, the godsend of the inhabitants of Vilnius, a universal symbol of debility. Everything, absolutely everything here is a dream. The Italian Renaissance buildings that you'd think were transported directly from Bologna or Padua, the ornate church towers spiking the sky, and between them—the faceless crowd of the giddy spectacle's extras. It can't be this way; God or Satan got something wrong here. Either these people ended up in the wrong city by mistake, or they're in the right place, but the buildings, the churches, and the smell of ancient times have lost their way. Vilnius is a ghost city, a hallucination city. It's impossible to dream it up or to imagine it—it is itself a dream or the concoction of fantasy. The spirits of the Grand Dukes of Lithuania walk about Vilnius, greet acquaintances, accost the girls, and grimly shove at the trolleybus stops. Here the smell of the Polish years, the smell of fires and plagues, and the most banal stench of cheap gasoline hover and mingle. Here, at night, the Iron Wolf howls desolately, calling for help. Here you can unexpectedly meet the dead, tortured once upon a time by the Gestapo or the KGB, repeating over and over again the name of their betrayer, which no one wants to hear. In Prague or Lisbon the past lingers *next to* today's soullessness. In Vilnius, every building, every narrow little street crossing is simultaneously the scene of ancient life and today's catalepsy. Vilnius is innumerable cities laid one atop another. It isn't just the earth that lays down archeological layers here, but time, and air, and language do too. In the same spot, layers of Eastern and Western cultures lie hidden and turn into one another. Vilnius is the border where Russia's expansionism and Europe's spirit went to war. Here absolutely everything collided and mixed. Vilnius is a giant cocktail, stirred together by the insane gods of fog. If a city could exist *alone*, without people, Vilnius would be the City of all cities. But it's people who express the spirit of a city, and if you attempt to understand what the figures in Vilnius's streets *mean*, what that atrophying spectacle in which you yourself play means, you'd immediately realize you're dreaming.

I walk slowly through a dream called Vilnius, while the weird sensation that all of this has already been pierces my brain. Once I went down the street in exactly the same way, in exactly the same way I considered what the dream—the yellowish leaves, blown about by the wind, and the old house in the depths of a garden—could mean . . . The exact same pair of dazed pigeons have already perched by the announcement post. Lolita has already waited for me in the corridor, rocking her waist back and forth in exactly the same way . . . Everything has already been, everything, everything, has already been. I know it's just *déjà vu*, but all the same a sense of fear stabs right through me. In *exactly the same way* Stefa's hips sway before my eyes, the hips of all the women in the world, Virgilishly leading me ever closer to the secret . . . *The exact same* shabby dog with a huge head and still larger sexual organs and a long body like a rat's sniffs the ground outside the window . . . The coffee break table seems just as unreal as it has seemed many times before.

Why do I come here? Why do I waste the time—I should devote every instant left to me to a single purpose. I don't understand what my employees are doing here, why they gathered here (or maybe—*who* gathered them here?) Sometimes it seems they all have a secret purpose here—just as I do. The library is essential to my clandestine investigations. But what do the others find here? Don't tell me things are as ordinary as they seem at first glance? The majority found a place where it's possible to do nothing and get some kind of pay. The authorities needed to shove Martynas off into a corner, to dupe him with an abundance of books, to isolate him from the scholarly centers. The communist Elena was introduced to look after everyone. And so on. (It's not clear to me why Lolita ended up here.) Which of these women are nothing more than silent victims, and which are *Their* secret agents? Stefa is the only one I don't suspect—I have carried out certain experiments with her. Which one? Maybe Gražina, the plump petite with the greasy glance? Or Marija, the mustachioed green finch with the burned-out bass? Or Laima—the exhausted fish, constantly blurting out some sort of nonsense? Or maybe the newcomer Beta, blinking goggle-eyed? (Can *short hair* have some essential meaning here?) *They* could have picked any one of them, or all of them together. All of them in front of my eyes, all of them sitting at the table, only Lolita stands by the window and follows Carp with her eyes: he's hobbling by the construction site again. It's Saint Carp, my talisman, a person who even in the face of death wasn't afraid to call a tyrant a tyrant and a slave a slave. (Who knows which is more dangerous—probably calling a slave a slave to his face.) Lolita follows him with her eyes and smiles: I've told her about Carp. My Lolita. My, my Lolita. But can anything in the world really be *mine* anymore? Have I ever really had my own woman?

Like it or not, I think about my wife. After all, I had a wife—a loved one, the only one, the true one. *I had* . . . I should call her my savior and the one who opened my eyes (unfortunately, Irena opened my eyes not just to happiness, but to horror too). She showed up when my entire life was distorted into a hideous hallucination. That was the Narutis period; drunkenness, a premonition of insanity and a very real, boundless pain jumbled together in it. I had just been released from the camp. I have no idea where I lived; I have no idea how I scraped together money. I remember, as if though a haze, loading freight cars at night and hunkering down during the day in ground-floor rooms with broken-out windows and doors that wouldn't close, getting drunk with seedy companions. To me, the morning didn't differ from the night, and the sun never rose at all; in my Vilnius there was nothing but a lingering, dismal haze. I was drunk all the time. I don't know how long that lasted, but I do not regret those days, months, years. I was obliged to live through all of that; my path led through the Narutis, through syphilitic dumps, through the very bottom of Vilnius. Every true search is hellish; great discoveries are made on the edge of insanity. I don't at all regret ending up in the gutter, the same way I *don't regret* landing in camp. I had to go through all of the circles of hell, so that I would, in the end, grasp what matters most, so that I would discover *Their* footprints. My circles of hell were marked by barbed wire, and then by alcohol. Good Lord, the amount I drank! Only my father's iron genes saved me—according to all the laws of nature I should have gone insane or turned into a wreck. I searched for *truth*, delving into the very cheapest alcohol. I searched for an answer (already then *I searched* for an answer) by destroying myself. There's probably no other way. A person can escape his limits and exceed himself only by sacrificing a part of himself. But I sacrificed too much. Many times I thought I surely won't find any secret *here*, between the scattered, reeking clothes, puddles of vomit, and cockroaches crawling up the walls. I realized what direction I was heading in, but I didn't have the strength to stop. Returning to Vilnius after nine years, ostensibly released to freedom, I couldn't live just any old way: I *no longer knew how* to live. I had never been destined to experience *freedom*. I was the slave of a single, sole idea, and the worst of it was—for a long, long time I *didn't know* what idea. I understood just one thing: *everyone* lives in error, the world doesn't behave the way it should; once upon a time it erred, and it can't manage to fix its great mistake. Why did I, even though I had been exonerated, have to wander the garbage dumps like a stray dog, while the person (or dragon?) whom I was once supposed to hunt relished life in the radiance of absolute power? At that time I thought of nothing but him. *Now* I think about him too.

"Anyone can grab a pistonmachine and spray in every direction," Bitinas's long, bare head says softly. "Any fool. That's not your destiny, my dear Vargalys. You're destined for the great dragon hunt. Think about him, think only *about him. Dream of him, become one with him, my son. Devour him, like he devours Lithuania. Drag him out of his stinking tank . . ."*

Why, to what purpose was I assigned ordeals that made me doubt afterwards whether there is a *human* in the world at all? I doubted whether humanity is, on the whole, fit to exist. I couldn't understand who devised that horrible mechanism, or who controls it. The idea of a merciful God is absurd: if God exists, he is a madman and a sadist; he needs to be fought. The Buddhist theory of inescapable pain doesn't explain anything, it's merely an observation. The abyss of the Apocalypse is an effective metaphor—but who can get concerned about *all* the world's inevitable end? No, the explanation had to be *here*; I searched for it within myself and without. Nothing else concerned me. Not even myself. Nothing! I wasn't intimidated by the puffy faces of my drinking partners, the bloody knives that could stab me too, or the grotesque sluts indifferently smearing fetid unguent on hardened chancres in my full view. I was on *the other side* of everything. And still I drank, Lord of mine, how I drank!

Probably I approached the secret regardless, approached along the paths of death and insanity, gathering horrible experience grain by grain. It has been said that to kiss a leper all over is a holy sacrifice. It has been said that after long prayer and fasting, the Holy Virgin reveals herself. I sought that in my own way. Who can appreciate the sensation you experience when you watch your penis penetrate the rotten vagina of a syphilitic? Who tells the truth about the revelations that beset you after a week of drinking, when the vodka for sobering up runs short? I realized I was drowning, but I held it sacred that at the very bottom, before releasing the last gasp of air, I would find the answer. And I kept drinking. At the end of the inclined plane a church waited for me, Vilnius's Basilican Church. I very well remember the torn-down crosses in a corner of the courtyard and the walls sullenly bending in on me, ready to collapse at any moment. The old churches of Vilnius are desecrated in various ways—some as warehouses, some as museums of atheism. A little factory that made the crudest wine had been set up in that one. I came across a breach in the fence and slipped in with the entire gang; I could drink without restraint. Inside, contorted piping branched about, grim vats loomed, and dust reigned. The dust of dust. The drunken guards slept it off right there, on the stone floor, with their greasy faces turned to the vandalized altar. We would sit around a brimming vat like devils and drink to the point of insanity. The wine there was brewed from anything—from rotten fruit, from garbage, even, it seems to me, from the church's sticky dust. *They* must obscure everyone's intellect at whatever cost. I spent my nights right in the church; I wanted to meet my end there. The time and space of Vilnius were deranged. I would sit down on a broken chair in some dump, and I'd end up in the church next to a bucket of garbage wine. Occasionally I would be surrounded by talking animals or the chopped-off heads of people with little legs; sometimes Plato would climb out of the church walls—wearing a dingy cap with a peak and a leather jacket—the harsh commissar of the kanukai. There was only one way to determine what was a hallucination and what was reality—to drink still more, then the hallucinations would usually disappear.

I nevertheless prayed my holy virgin into existence. I don't know when she presented herself for the first time, there couldn't be a *first time* anyway—Vilnius's time was completely confused. Irena emerged from the fog, gazing at me pitifully. Sometimes she would come arm-in-arm with Plato, half-naked, vulgarly made up. I would seriously ponder why that pederast Plato gave up boys and broke his own famously declared principles. I would down a glass and still another glass, but only Plato would disappear, Irena wouldn't vanish, and one day I woke up not in a nook of the church, but on a folding bed in her apartment.

She lived in a decaying room, a former nun's cell; her window looked straight out at the breach in the wine factory's fence. To this day I still don't know why she stopped me on the very edge. I was a drunken scum with puffy eyes. More than once I again fought with headless figures or poisonous white rabbits. More than once I again climbed into the ruinous breach in the fence. But Irena didn't order me to do anything, didn't preach, and didn't scold. She simply opened my eyes. The road of my life was truly unique: I had already almost acquired the *second* sight, but I didn't have the first; I had never known the ordinary world that everyone sees. It was only thanks to Irena that I experienced for the first time what a friend is, what a woman is. She was my friend for a long time—that one and only, the true one, a part of your own self. Only Irena forced me to realize that in this world a man means nothing without a woman.

Up until then I didn't know what a woman was, I hadn't had the time to perceive it. Janė wasn't my woman, she wasn't anyone's woman; she was the live embodiment of a vagina, a mystical symbol, the goddess of a teenager's wet dreams. Madam Giedraitienė wasn't a *woman*— merely a voluptuous female, a voracious, sadistic slave driver. I didn't have the time to know a real woman, and the camp wrecked everything for good. Months upon months, years upon years, I didn't so much as see them. They slowly turned into mythological beings capable of anything—maybe even of bringing the dead to life. I wasn't even able to dream of women. I would dream of gigantic birds with breasts swaying to the sides and women's faces. Those women-birds would surround me, greedily stretching their long necks at me, wanting to peck at me, peck at me, peck out my masculinity . . . Released to freedom, every woman I met seemed miraculous but intimidating at the same time. They were all like unfathomable, unattainable beings from another world. I was afraid to go into the street because *they* walked there, I feared that fairy-tale world where *women* walked around as if it were nothing. I didn't know how to behave, what to do; I didn't believe it really was that way. It couldn't be that way. It wasn't just horrible to *touch* a woman, even accidentally; it was horrible to speak to her, or even look her in the eyes. Maybe I would have finally ended up in the madhouse that way, but three bitches of the ground floor snatched me in time. I don't remember why I gave myself up to them, why I didn't get scared they would feed on me (even they looked miraculous to me). They adroitly cured me: in place of the beings of my dreams, the goddesses of legends, I found a dirty, stinking female who wanted only money and an iron penis. I would find the money somewhere, and my thing suited them too— although it wasn't made of iron, but rather with a copper end.

And after all that, after a hundred months of drunkenness, Irena suddenly showed up: tall, slim, agile, with eyes as black as tar. I don't know if she was pretty. Probably not. Could that have been of consequence? Does it matter how my Irena's legs, breasts, or her face's oval looked? If someone had inquired about her figure at the beginning of our life together, I would have knocked him out cold. Who would dare to analyze whether a Madonna's body is sexy?

I would tell her everything. That's a huge thing—the opportunity to tell at least one person absolutely everything (now there's no such person near). Irena wasn't afraid of me, even though I threw out all the bile, the blackness, and the pain inside me. She got to see the disgusting wound—teeming with quivering, satiated little worms—inside me. But she didn't retreat. She was like a spring in which I could wash my soul without polluting it. It was impossible to pollute her. She bravely took on a part of my load, and her narrow little shoulders didn't so much as tremble. I could trust her completely. She *gave birth* to me.

Life was difficult, but we were the happiest people on earth. I remember the banged-up buckets in which I carried water, because the only tap was outside. A *Polish* tap; grandfather wouldn't have drunk a drop out of one like that, even if he were dying of thirst. I remember miserable, washed and re-washed duvets and sheets. But most often I remember Irena. Irena, Irena, Irena. Scores of her portraits, a secret photo album that's invisible to everyone but me. She smiles, having calmed my rage again. She sits with her chin on her hand. She speaks in a low, somewhat throaty voice, while I listen and understand that only she can give me *meaning*, that she herself is that meaning. She washes her feet in a large rusty basin, and I want to kiss her everywhere, all of her. I could think only of her; I experienced a miracle that was destined for no one else. The two of us really were the two halves of an apple that had miraculously found each other.

There was only one thing that divided us—she liked to stare at the television. I'm afraid of it. I hate it. Television is *Their* magic weapon; with its help *They* surround you with troops, throngs, legions of hideously kanuked beings. *They* strive to convince you those beings are the real, normal representatives of the human race, and if you're not like them—it's your own fault, it's *you* that's abnormal. At that time my *second* eyes were only beginning to emerge. I watched those television creatures almost morbidly. Understandably, I can't study American or Italian television, however, I firmly believe *Their* television traps encompass the entire world. *They* just subtly adapt to the country's traditions and political system. Doesn't an American or Frenchman experience the same fear and disgust—seeing some television beauty almost have an orgasm after taking a whiff of some toothpaste or tomato sauce—that I do? Doesn't it arouse the most hideous suspicions in him? After all, those television beings have nothing human about them in any country; they've traveled here from *Their* soulless kingdom. Of course, our television beats them all. The announcer tries to persuade you that these are some kind of workers . . . some kind of farmers . . . some kind of writers . . . or scholars . . . There's masses of them; they appear every hour, every second . . . planted on identical little chairs, by identical tables, frequently wearing medals or ribbons of honor, and most often with unhealthy, pudgy faces. There's something essentially unalive in them, something inhuman, particularly the eyes—or more accurately, the place where the eyes should be: those narrow cracks without any expression, without a spark of spirit. In those cracks you can perceive the grim wasteland's void, a pulsating swarm of innumerable cockroach legs. Those creatures repeat the same words over and over; they're very pleased with themselves, they know everything and believe in everything. They fruitlessly try to *act* like people, to give their face expression . . . Probably they haven't yet forgotten what a human should look like . . . And it's totally irrelevant that on American television the beauties' eyes are huge and the hosts' faces aren't fat—*They* know perfectly well how to disguise themselves . . . What matters most is the stare, the stare of the void. What matters most is that imbecilic ecstasy, no matter what provokes it in the television being—a slogan of the Russian plenary or a Japanese kitchen mixer . . . What matters is that they're all so *assured* . . . So *clever* . . . So *happy* . . . Such *idiots* . . .

I'm afraid of television; I've always been afraid of it. But Irena liked to stare at the screen—to her that spirit-crushing image was nothing more than chewing gum for the brain, as it is for most people. It doesn't seem there's anything so terrible about it. But for some reason everyone forgets that the brain is surely not the proper place to *plaster* with used chewing gum. Alas, alas . . . Every detail matters when you're up against *Them.*

Sometimes life's time rushes along too fast. One day it struck me that I'm already forty, that Irena and I live in a new, somewhat larger apartment, and that I am a programmer. (Gedis convinced me to finish in mathematics at the university.) Everything was getting on well, it seemed; I slid smoothly down the path of life, but somewhere years upon years had disappeared as if they had never been—I remember much less from those times than I do from the Narutis period. I was stuck in a calm, healthy, everyday bliss. It seems to me that I was *almost* happy—Irena

99

at my side, in the midst of intelligent books and my memories. But one morning I woke up and suddenly realized that something had happened. Something, something, had happened. I don't know who was to blame for that. Maybe Gediminas. It was just then that he started acting strange, stranger and stranger all the time. Perhaps it was Vilnius. Just at that time it was sprouting the new, *nothing* neighborhoods; for the first time it occurred to me that my city had died and would never rise from the dead again. Perhaps it was Irena. I suddenly noticed her gaze was worn and dazed, that more and more often she didn't hear what I was saying to her. Something, something, had happened; I had overlooked an incident of monumental importance and realized it only when everything began to *change*. I began to sense smells I'd never noticed up until then. I smelled the trees, the dust of the streets, my writing desk, and the sound of a distant airplane. I began to see things I hadn't noticed before: a grimy cat cowering under the balcony, or a hunchbacked dwarf quietly hobbling home along the wall. An abundance of details, details which had meant nothing to me earlier, mysteriously whispered something; they wanted to warn me that something fundamental and horrible had happened.

Then I had a terrifying dream. In this dream I sluggishly made love with a plump, overripe beauty. I didn't feel the least pleasure, but she kept pestering me, embracing me, virtually sucking me dry. At last I escaped by force, withdrew my penis in relief from the sodden damp space, and abruptly went into shock when I looked at it. It was studded all over with dark, moving spots; it was crawling, teeming, with disgusting brown cockroaches. There were hordes of them. They twitched their thin whiskers and rolled their unseeing eyes. My penis was covered with cockroaches, the way a rotten banana is covered with fruit flies. Hysterically I tried to shake them off, to clean them off, to pick them off one by one, but in vain. I had fallen into a trap; the cockroaches were in control. Meanwhile the plump, overripe beauty glanced at me sullenly; sharp, leaden barbs protruded from her eyes. When I awoke, I got really scared that something, something, had happened. I didn't feel like myself all day. Lord knows, I went to the toilet several times and determinedly searched for marks on my masculinity. Of course, I found only the old scars Stadniukas had burned on it, but that didn't reassure me. I went home early and waited for Irena, anxious to talk it over with her; finally I saw her through the window, but I didn't feel the slightest joy, much less relief. Something, something, had happened. Irena wasn't what she had been until then, even her walk was strangely altered. She didn't notice me; she didn't notice black Jake, either, the neighbors' dog, and our family's great friend. He ran up to Irena, sniffed her knees, and suddenly barked at her sharply. His entire pose showed horrified disgust and fear at the same time. I didn't get it: Jake? Irena? She stopped and fixed the dog with a serious gaze. She didn't pet him, but she didn't raise her arm, either; however, Jake instantly jumped back, curled up pathetically, and started to whine, as if he wanted to warn the entire building, his entire doggy world, about something horrible and sinister. He announced a great danger. I thought Jake had simply gone nuts. Irena continued to calm him with a serious look and smiled wanly. That was *not her* smile. She went on walking in that unfamiliar manner. Jake has gone nuts, I kept repeating to myself, but I didn't believe it. Irena was radically different. Her thighs rubbed together revoltingly under her dress. The joints of her fingers were unnaturally thickened and pale.

Suddenly I realized that the poor dog *didn't recognize Irena's scent.* She no longer smelled like herself. Jake barked at a strange, intimidating intruder, whose stench aroused a boundless doggy horror in him. But it was far worse that suddenly I didn't recognize Irena myself. I didn't say anything to her, I didn't complain. I merely began to secretly observe her.

All the gods in the world know how difficult it was for me: I was spying on the person who was closest to me—not just her behavior, but *she herself,* even her body. I didn't know which direction to turn, what to look for. I feared giving myself away inadvertently, I feared hurting Irena. I was still afraid of hurting her. I was afraid of many things, most often myself. It's always easier to be ignorant; the search for truth is fraught with mortal dangers. Something is invariably lost—either faith, or happiness, or the past. Or everything at once.

I started with what seemed like insignificant details. Visiting (I never did understand *why* we visited all those people), or at home when her so-called friends came over, I secretly listened to what she was talking about when she thought I didn't hear her. I was overcome with horror. Her melodious voice grew hoarse; it was left dull and hollow, like an echo in a mossy old cellar. It lost its colors and hues; it became a monotone, like tapping on a torn drum. But her speech was far more shocking. I had never heard such things from Irena's lips: she prattled on about clothing fashions and furniture, about wages and responsibilities. Explained that she had pulled me out of the quagmire. Complained about prices, about my lack of a career. With a strange malice she smeared friends who weren't there, and when they showed up, she would take apart those who had just left. Maybe it wasn't so terrible—she was exactly the same as others are. But Irena *couldn't* talk that way. I glanced at her through the crack in the door many times, risking discovery. She was the one talking, all right. I didn't understand where her real words had gone—her talk about heights and precipices, about man crushed and man defeated, her naïve attempts to understand all the wisdom of ancient and modern times—where everything I had loved her for had gone. True, even now she spoke to me in exactly the same way she had before. However, I immediately realized that she was lying to me, and speaking the truth *there*. The dull, monotone voice was ideally suited to those *other* words. It occurred to me that if I looked into her throat, there, deep, deep, inside that pink pipe, I would see a woven knot of little worms. Something was strangling and suffocating her, but at the same time she was becoming dangerous herself. She was intentionally playing a role for me. This dull-voiced woman probably had been playing my Irena for a long time; the latter was gone, vanished or degenerated. And until then I had felt nothing—I was deaf and blind. I was truly horrified. I grew three times as careful, three times as watchful, I feared inadvertently giving myself away. After all, *she* lived right here, next to me; I needed to hide my knowledge from *her*. Hide it from everyone. Who could I complain to? Except maybe Gedis.

I didn't discuss it with Gedis. I decided to act on my own, and I made one of my many irrevocable mistakes.

I began to follow *her* even more closely. *Her* skin turned gray and grew coarse; she wandered lazily through the rooms or the kitchen, doing pointless things: she ironed the same clothes several times, moved them from one shelf to another and then back again, and ceaselessly watered the flowers. Mostly she did nothing at all, just stared vacantly in one and the same pose, turning some object over in her hands. She didn't read books; she just stared at her television. True, as before, she would take my books and pretend she was reading them at work. Later, supposedly charmed, she would praise them, but I already knew they had been stuck in a kitchen cabinet all week, gathering dust. I just couldn't understand when I had missed what. After all, that transformation couldn't have happened overnight. I was deaf and blind: my Irena had been exchanged for another, and I hadn't even felt it. Everything *in her* was artificial: her ingratiating voice, and the words stolen from Irena, and her purported deep gaze. I didn't love *her*, I avoided *her*, sometimes I loathed her—and she didn't even feel it, didn't notice it! She'd drag me to bed even more often than Irena did. However, love play, that miraculous kingdom, suddenly turned into an oppressive, soulless exercise. It seemed to me that at any moment I would break into tears or start howling—*she* knew all of Irena's erotic games, you could *almost* confuse the two of them. *She* sucked my penis inside in exactly the same way, pressed it and caressed it with hidden little muscles, as if there, deep inside, were scores of tiny little hands. Against my will I would forget for a short time, I'd nearly feel a climax, but quickly, breaking into a cold sweat, I would get hold of myself. She destroyed my Irena and crawled into her skin, but couldn't play the part to the end. I was making love to a stuffed doll. Horror would come over me. To save myself I searched for *differences*. Thank God, the two were still different, even in bed. She always tried to end up *on top* (Irena didn't like positions like that). In addition, *she* pathologically avoided light, she made love only in semi-darkness—Irena would turn on all the lamps, even in the middle of the night. For a long time I wracked my brains over this, but the mystery was completely ordinary: *she* was afraid that I would *see* her. She was afraid that I would see *her* body.

*Now*, carefully, gropingly, I explore *her* body (I've already explored it a hundred times). The night spreads a somewhat bitter smell; not far off a dog barks gruffly. I practice seeing in the dark—not with my eyes, but rather with my fingers, my fingers turn into eyes, I see all of her in a halo of pale light. I see her for the hundredth time, but all the same I cannot control my disgust. That woman's breasts are swollen, three hideous rolls lie pressed together below. It seems that if you ran your finger over them, you'd clean a tangle of cobwebs and putrefaction out from those wrinkles. The waist has disappeared somewhere; square thighs stick out immediately below the bulging breasts. Between the legs, almost from the knees up, sprout fat globs of flesh—something like thick ropes. They rise right up to the hair below her belly; it seems that they twist themselves straight into that woman's innards and pierce her through. Under that woman's arms upright globules of fat converge. Coarse tufts of hair curl on her nipples and even between her breasts. I see only the threatening parody of a body; the separate parts don't suit one another—it seems she could crack apart at any moment, disassemble like a matrioshka doll. And from her entire body, from every pore in her skin, a sour smell spreads; the smell of night's blunt knife, the smell of mold. It intensifies my disgust; I realize that what I'm seeing is no laughing matter. It isn't *her* frivolous twaddle, or her husky voice; it's real and tangible. A mysterious deformation is ravaging that woman. It's not some kind of illness; the bristling mane of our neighbors' black Jake proves it's not an ordinary illness, one that medicine can cure. It's something else, entirely, completely, something else, something mysterious and somber, connected to mold . . . to cockroaches . . . to oppressive smells . . . connected to me, to my life . . . perhaps earmarked for me, aimed at me, destroying me first of all . . .

I sensed that the catastrophe couldn't hide *only* inside her. I knew I had to investigate what she did outside of the house, whom she met with and where she went. I had already caught on to a few things, but I still couldn't entirely grasp what path I was taking, my thrashing heart squeezed into a fist.

*She* didn't sense she was being followed (I had opportunities to convince myself of this), but she always escaped from me. This stunned me: even without sensing the real danger, she maintained an absolute conspiracy. She would disappear through courtyard passageways, or simply turn a corner and vanish, as if she had floated off into the air. I would search for at least a door, a window, a crack in the wall where she could have disappeared. Unfortunately, always unsuccessfully. She was attracted, drawn into the old part of Vilnius, closer to the narrow little streets and churches, the neglected buildings and gloomy, filthy courtyards. You'd think it was only in Old Town that she could disappear, in league with the spirit of Vilnius itself. That spirit of the city intimidated me. All of Vilnius grew faint and muffled, all there was left of it was crooked, fly-stained little streets and dirty courtyards with whitewashed toilet stalls. The city shrank into the narrow, decrepit buildings, into the realm of the ground-floor dives. In the courtyard passageways

I would be met by bandy-legged dogs and dirty chickens. The entire motley pack would furiously sniff me over. Dazed men staggered along the walls. Shrill women hung laundry on sooty clotheslines. In the squares, sullen groups guzzled the cheapest garbage wine out of bottles. Hoarse, drunken cries bounced between the thick walls; I practically didn't hear a word of Lithuanian anywhere. It seemed I was no longer in Lithuania, that at any minute I was going to have to speak a narrow gutter language I didn't know. My ancient, sacred city was beset by the lowest order of lumpen. I had to shove my way through them to follow the waddling woman's figure. She felt at home between the fly-stained walls, even her walk would improve. But I was an alien here, and not welcome. Bleary-eyed men looked at me with surprise and a strange malice. Surprised dogs would sniff at me, unable to understand what that smell was doing here. I was shocked: it had been many years since I had seen this Vilnius. But after all, my own old spirit had to linger here; I myself, as I was ten or fifteen years ago. Perhaps *she* was intentionally attempting to lure me back to the past.

There was no peace left at home, either. Increasingly weird characters began visiting, as if bugs had converged on my apartment from unknown cracks and corners. They beset my house like apparitions. They were seemingly different, even very different, but at the same time *exactly the same* as *her*. My practiced eye already distinguished the critical details: the unusual movements, the emptiness of the gaze. All of their hands were chubby, with swollen joints, and covered in small, tawny freckles. From every one emanated the familiar sour smell of decay. One sturdy fellow, by the name of Justinas, seemed especially typical to me. (He was some sort of party functionary, a representative of the *nomenklatura*, a person from a special world where everything is different than it is in our life: things, and food, and hospitals. Even bread is baked specially for them. Even the rules of the road are different for their cars.) I kept trying to talk to him, even though *I didn't know* what I needed to question him about. I simply tried to earn his confidence, to encourage him to chat freely. I would fix the coffee and make toast myself, leaving Justinas in the room with *her*. I would secretly listen to what the two of them talked about. But he didn't give himself away: not a word about Old Town, the Narutis neighborhood, or the courtyard passageways.

Justinas immediately made himself completely at home; it seemed entirely natural to hug my wife in a friendly (or not just friendly) way, or to pat her on the knee. Once, when I had stayed a bit longer in the kitchen and returned quietly, I caught him pressing her breasts in his hands. We were all a bit drunk. I pretended I hadn't noticed, but before going to bed I threw a jealous fit. I was stunned by her reaction. Suddenly she got really nasty and launched into an attack. I was the one who was to blame. I had invited Justinas over. I had created an unhealthy atmosphere. I alone. I listened to *her* croaking voice, looked at the pimply face, the deformed fingers, the bloated breasts, the globs of flesh between her thighs, which she hid under a thick nightgown but weren't difficult to infer; I looked and I couldn't help but be charmed. This time *she* played the part perfectly. She smeared her face all over with mascara, writhed like a snake, and heaved in the most disgusting convulsions of kanukism. She truly had not lost the talents with which she had deceived me our entire life together.

*She* didn't lose her ability to disappear, either. It seemed I should have given up my useless stalking long ago, but my determination never knew any limits. Determination sooner or later pays off. One time, as usual, I lost sight of her and aimlessly went in circles around the neighborhood of the Narutis; finally I went out into Didžiosios Street, stopped, and lit up a smoke. Apparently, the tension was already accumulating within me; the *second sight* was already emerging. I sensed that I *had* to look to the right; I sensed this command coming from *within*. First I saw *her*; then that creature too. *She* slowly crept towards him; without turning his head he muttered something to her and continued to stand there, as if he were rooted to the spot. *She* hunched over even more, and, obediently, as if she had received a blessing, hobbled off. *She* no longer concerned me; I fixed my eyes only on him. He was stocky and square. He stood by the wall next to the door of a store. Next to the scurrying, rushing figures he looked like *a hole* in a colorless carpet. He had no neck at all. His massive head was set directly onto his shoulders; if he wanted to look to the side, he had to turn his entire body. But he didn't turn; he merely *devoured* everything with his eyes. That neckless thing had grown into the paving stones, into the grim walls, into Old Town's close air. Passersby would slow when they passed him; it seemed they forgot for a moment where they were going. But this didn't interest him; he simply stood there and *devoured* everything with his eyes. He riveted my attention, riveted even my willpower. The eyes in his pudgy, flat face were like two holes—if it's possible to imagine *holes in a hole*. His face was completely expressionless, but it was just this lack of expression that broadcast his oppressive menace, his universal scorn, and his firm belief that this was *his* domain. Superficially, he looked like an imbecile, but I didn't doubt for a second that inside him an iron, dispassionate intellect was working like a machine. His head jutted out of his shoulders and was bent somewhat forward; he seemingly charged forward, but at the same time remained as unmovable as a rock. He was like a wolf poised just before a leap, but firm in the knowledge that it would be unnecessary to pounce—the victim would climb into his jaws *on its own*. A pathological threat, indescribable in words, was hidden inside him. It was only possible to *feel* it; it penetrated my innards like a plague bacilli, like a sense of impending doom. At intervals, faceless figures would approach him for a blessing; he would growl something, and they would slink off again. I saw he was the secret king here, whom everyone obeyed without knowing whom they were obeying, and naïvely thought that they were acting independently. He held all the strings in his hands (whose strings, what strings?); he loomed above Old Town like a gigantic octopus, connected by innumerable threads to the mass of drab figures who were crawling here and there. His proboscises reached everywhere; they reached my innards too—my chest was encompassed by a torpid weakness. I felt I had already *found* it, but I still couldn't understand what I had found. I was alone—frightened and helpless. I was and I remained alone.

Now I understand how lucky I was. I never again succeeded in seeing one of *Their* commissars, a high overlord, so close up—simply in the street, in the crush of passersby, for some reason breaking the codes of secrecy. I don't know what I would do now, but at that time I simply froze, gasping for air with my mouth open, feeling nothing but a boundless fear and a pain in my chest. That creature stirred and slunk off along the wall, but I couldn't budge: I was paralyzed. I had come across *Their* outpost, but I wasn't prepared; I didn't have sufficient strength to risk it. Apparently, *They* had undermined me too; the tree of my spirit was not exactly flourishing. However, there was still sap there, even though *They* believed they had already dealt with me. It wasn't true—I was still alive. It was just that the time hadn't come yet. Only a person who is focused and resolved to sacrifice himself can begin to do battle with *Them*. A person who has no other out.

*. . . and everyone's lounging about as if they were at a health resort. It's some kind of communist holiday today; for breakfast you each got a genuine roll with marmalade. You're sitting in your nook by the garbage cans again. A couple of Russkies rummage through the refuse—today no one will yell, no one will assign you to solitary, no one will knock your teeth out. Bolius is terribly emaciated; even here it's rare to see such a tortured face: a desiccated, sapped, disfigured face. But it's a human face regardless. No blind strength, no hatred can wipe off the marks of a great intellect, the marks of a great heart; nothing can extinguish his eyes. You're actually intimidated. The man who is probably the greatest intellect of Lithuania, the honorary doctor of a hundred universities, the intellect of Lithuania's honor, is sitting next to you, talking to you and teaching you, Vytautas Vargalys, as if you alone were all of poor strangled Lithuania, waiting for his word.*

"After the war the Russians took land, technology, and gold away from Germany, but they never managed to appropriate German Ordnung," Bolius lectures. "In a German camp, the sadism is precise and refined; here the sadism is primitive and brutish. Russia is still Russia—even in a camp . . ."

"You were in Russia before the war?"

"No, this is my first time here. They brought us here by train straight from Auschwitz—without switching trains, without any visas. Like in a relay race—straight from Hitler to Stalin. Not just me—all of us—millions . . ."

"Why?" You ask involuntarily. "In the name of what?"

"Why me?" Bolius rephrases the question, his eyes gleam with a strange sarcasm, "You? All of us? Because we're breathing. Because we're alive. Lithuania without Lithuanians! You know, after all, that's the Soviet leaders' slogan. You know that."

"Then why the Russians?"

"Oh, they're just along for the ride." Bolius grins, his crooked smile is awful. "It's nothing, they're used to it. It's worse for us, because we've already gotten a whiff of freedom and will never be able to forget it. Blessed are the ignorant . . . The Russians never experienced freedom, so they can't even dream about it. Blessed are the . . ." Bolius' voice unexpectedly trembles.

"In Auschwitz I used to secretly give lectures: about art ... about literature, philosophy ... Dozens of people risked their lives for those lectures ... They had to feel human, they couldn't do otherwise ... But these do without it quite nicely ... They don't need it, do you understand?"

You're sorry for the Russians, who have never tasted freedom, who need nothing. There now, a couple of them are rummaging through the refuse, they're happy to find a bite. Don't tell me man was created for this, to rummage through a camp's refuse, and then for weeks upon weeks, years upon years, to chisel out Stalin's portrait, as big as an entire village, on the rocky slope of a mountain? You no longer know what a human is. Perhaps Vasia Jebachik is a human? He's next to you, he's adjusting his still, but he won't make moonshine—it's a tea brewer. Vasia Jebachik is the ruler of this world. Bolius looks at you, and he sees right through you.

"You think I'm not sorry for them?" he says. "You think I'm not driven to despair that I can't do anything? ... Look around: this is what their world is. The sun shines, so they're all happy. They each got a roll, so they're all satisfied ... They have no doubt that things are the way they should be ... The doubting ones are long since under the ground ... Still others console themselves with the thought that it's an unfortunate mistake, but shortly a bright future will arrive ..."

Bolius closes his eyes; he doesn't want to show the suffering in them. He wants you to see only wisdom in his eyes, a clever Voltaire-like little smile, so that at least in your thoughts you'd forget your desecrated body and believe that the spirit can't be fenced in with barbed wire.

"They'll do the same thing to us," you say suddenly. "We'll be praying to the Shit of Shits too."

Bolius opens his eyes in a flash, you actually recoil—the anger that flows from his gentle eyes is so unexpected.

"Son!" he spits out fiercely between clenched teeth, "You don't know what a human is. Listen carefully: HUMAN! It's impossible to defeat a human. You can kill him, but defeat him—never. They've taken everything away from me: my wife, children, freedom, love, the world, God, learning, the sun, air, hope, my body, they've done everything so that I would no longer be myself, but they haven't overcome me. And they won't! Within me lies an immortal soul, whose existence they deny!"

Bolius roars, even Vasia Jebachik lifts his eyes from his still and glares sullenly at the two of you.

"Ironsides, shut your prof up," he says sarcastically, "He'd better be quiet. The Doc keeps staring at him, and if he takes him to the fifth block—none of his gods will help him. Neither Buddha, nor Shiva, nor that little Jew Einstein."

Justinas was like a splinter driven into my life: I stumbled over him wherever I turned. He acted friendly with me, but somewhat from above: after all, he belonged to the cream of the party, and I was nothing more than a computer specialist. I no longer listened to what he was saying; I sensed he wouldn't give himself away with words. I studied only his face and hands. I would look at the double roll that was forming under his chin, at his soft, indistinct features. His face was covered with a thin, barely noticeable layer of fat, but it wasn't just an ordinary layer of fat, the result of pointless gluttony. That layer—puttied over the sharp corners, protrusions, and hollows—was a natural part of his construction. Justinas's face couldn't express sudden or strong emotions, that's not what it was made for. It was designed for something *like* emotions, for half-feelings and a calm, stable existence. His eyes were the color of water. His hands, however, held the most meaning. A strange, unfathomable hieroglyph hid inside them. A hieroglyph of decay, stagnant water and twilight. They were pale and covered in brown freckles, with swollen joints. The fingers were stumpy, bloodless, and almost transparent. There were no veins to be seen on his hands. Those hands wouldn't leave me alone. An irresistible desire kept coming over me: to cut into Justinas's finger and see *what* would run out of the wound, what there was inside of him. Probably a continuous gray mass, a sticky bog of non-thoughts and non-feelings.

He got along famously with my wife—their thoughts and words, and even their movements, coincided. The two of them looked like brother and sister. I felt I was standing on the threshold of the secret. Sometimes I got the urge to track Justinas, and sometimes I unexpectedly felt sorry for *her*, or more accurately, for the pathetic remains of my Irena that would at intervals flare up in *her*. A human is weak: I would caress *her* secretly in the dark of the night, examine the body, lost in dreams, with the tips of my fingers. A human's sensations are deceptive: sometimes it seemed that I didn't feel the triple rolls under her breasts, I didn't find the disgusting globs of flesh between her thighs, I didn't feel the coarse hair tangled around her nipples. I was completely deranged: sometimes I talked to her, sometimes to my Irena. I had to resolve to do something, but I didn't know what. I kept trying to lure *her* out into the yard when I heard Jake barking. I wanted to bring the two of them eye to eye, and see either bristling hair on the nape, insane eyes, and bared fangs, or a tail wagging hysterically and a tongue trying to lick. But as soon as Jake's yelping sounded, *she* would find piles of work that couldn't be put off. The longer I failed to bring the two of them together, the more I believed the dog would decide everything. Sooner or later the two of them had to meet, and then . . . "Then" came one gloomy Saturday morning. *She* was bored and, of her own accord, suggested we go outside. I was about to argue against it; I wanted to read, but I glanced out the window and saw Jake romping around the yard. I went down the stairs with a numb heart; I almost wanted to grab *her* by the hand and drag her back home. I secretly hoped Jake would have run off somewhere.

But Jake was lying next to the bench, all tensed up, ready to jump up and bound towards us. *She* turned to him first, squatted carefully, stretched out her hand and, crying out, jumped back. A bitter smell of mold suddenly spread through the yard. My leaden feet wouldn't carry me closer, I didn't want to know anything, and for a few long moments I didn't know anything, but suddenly, almost against my will, I understood it all. It would have been better not to. *The dog was dead.* His infinitely lifelike pose, his open eyes gazing forward, completely did me in. An instant before he was energetically romping about, even now his doggy soul hadn't yet entirely left his body, but at the same time he was somehow especially, hopelessly dead. She wailed out loud, caressed the rigid, curly-haired body, and I dare say even forced out a tear. I didn't believe a single one of *her* wails, not a single one of *her* movements. That time she played her role badly, no one in the world would have believed her. The yard immediately got sickeningly colorless; the smell of mold or decay became unbearable. I was seriously frightened; I was afraid to even get close to *her.* The cowardly, nervous little person deep inside my soul just wanted to run, to escape as far as possible, to dig under the ground, to crawl into a cave and tremble there. The other—the brutal man who had gone through hell—wanted to strangle her with his bare hands. I wanted to howl, when suddenly *she* turned around and looked at me with Irena's pure, sad eyes.

I hardly moved all day. I was half paralyzed, and on top of it all, Justinas showed up that evening and tormented me with his talk about women and his sexual prowess. He had never spoken about it before. This time you'd think he'd opened a bag of obscenities and uncovered his filthy insides. He never said the most important word aloud, but it was heard *most*, without actually being said a single time; all the talk, all of Justinas's thoughts, revolved around it. It seemed he wasn't in the least concerned about the women themselves, just their vaginas. In Justinas's world, the streets were full of walking vaginas with completely unnecessary appendages: arms, legs, heads. The more I listened, the more I started becoming some kind of vagina maniac myself. To my own surprise, I praised my wife's erotic talents in a mysterious whisper, and wasn't in the least ashamed. He *infected* me with his mania; it was only a good deal later that I became disgusted. *They* really are capable of *infecting* people with all the forms of their plague; this must be strictly guarded against.

I needed to run off somewhere as soon as possible and think things over. I signed up for a business trip to Moscow and packed my bag in an instant. She didn't seem to want me to go, and she kissed me just like Irena when I left. I was stunned. She was intentionally driving me insane. I stood on the stairs for a long time, but I went to the station anyway. Too well I remembered the neckless ruler of the Narutis neighborhood. Too well I remembered the hopelessly, irretrievably dead Jake. Suddenly I felt there was no turning back. In the station bar, all my doubts began to bubble up again; once more, the simplest question arose: *what's going on here?* Suddenly I realized that people, entire nations, the greatest countries come to ruin in just exactly this way— they fail to ask out loud in time: what's going on here? (It's enough just to remember the birth of Nazi Germany.) Of course, man became man because he's able to adapt to anything; however, that adaptability will be his ruin in the end.

I hurried back home; I prepared to press *her* into a corner and force it out of her. I was brimming with resolution. I opened the door quietly (as it happened, I had greased all of the locks and hinges in the house a few days before), went down the corridor, stepped into the living room, and came to a dead stop. *Now* I'm standing in the doorway of my living room, still in my wet coat, water dripping from my hair (it's probably raining outside), heavy drops pressing on my eyelashes, but I see everything very clearly—it's impossible to see any more clearly. She has fallen back voluptuously on the couch, half undressed, her thick, knobby thighs spread out, repeating as if she's insane—don't, don't, we shouldn't, but she's ripping off the remains of her clothing herself, savagely grasping at Justinas, pulling him closer and continuing to senselessly repeat—don't, don't, we shouldn't. With horror I see how the globs of flesh between her thighs join perfectly with Justinas's hips, I see (or maybe I'm imagining it) how his fingers lie perfectly in the triple folds under *her* breasts, how they *assemble* themselves into a single thing like some mechanism: all of the parts sanded smooth and fitting perfectly. We shouldn't, we shouldn't, don't, but she herself paws at him, sucks him into herself, moans with her head thrown back, my heart will jump out of my chest any minute, but I can't move from the spot, my feet have grown to the floor, even my eyelids have turned to stone, without blinking I watch him screwing my Irena, my one and only Irena, I watch her body relishing him, endlessly, without respite, hypocritically and perversely, I watch Justinas fling himself on the rug completely worn out, and she kneels, her legs disgustingly spread, no longer repeating we shouldn't, we shouldn't, don't. My eyes hurt, my heart hurts, I no longer know myself who I am now, what I will do the next instant—trample them both under my boots or fall headlong into despair; I know nothing, my soul is gone, completely gone, but it hurts all the same, that supposedly non-existent soul of mine hurts piercingly—after all, *she* was once Irena, my one and only Irena. The two of them move again, come to life, and start doing something weird. Suddenly I realize that everything that has happened was no more than a prelude, a meaningless, primitive prelude, and the real things are only just beginning.

He crawls around *her*, and *she* continues to kneel, her legs spread disgustingly, her behind stuck up in the air; she keeps raising it higher, and curls up as if she wanted to turn herself inside out. Justinas sticks his nose right next to *her* grinning vagina and sniffs at it like a dog; they both sniff, it seems they're even wagging their tails and melting with bliss. I look and I don't believe my eyes, I look and I don't understand what they're doing *now*, even though by now I realize, without understanding anything I realize, that the two of them have slowly, with relish, begun *Their* act, *Their* dance of love. I feel my fury fading, *all* of me fading, but all the same I look at them, at their hanging tongues, their gray faces, the convulsive movements of their bodies (what's left of them—they're no longer human bodies), and I'm overcome with horror, I realize it's not me who will trample the two of them, but they who will kill me if they realize I'm watching them. *That* can't be seen by a human being; *that's* impossible and incomprehensible. You couldn't even imagine anything like it. Now they are like some kind of plant or jellyfish— I've never seen anything like it. Never. Nowhere. I don't know what to call *it*. You wouldn't find it in even the most horrifying dream. A human being couldn't even dream of such things. *It* has no name, I have no name myself, because I'm standing in the doorway of my living room and I see everything. It doesn't fit inside my head, there's a lot that no longer fits in my head, I need to save myself quickly, I quickly close the door, but all the same I hear *those* sounds, I go down the stairs, sensing an oppressive smell following after me, I'm as empty as a finished bottle (but maybe something's still there, at the very bottom?). And everything is greenish: a greenish sunset and a greenish Vilnius, my hands are greenish too—for some reason I examine them closely, I even feel over my joints with my greenish fingers, greenish figures pass by, and behind the corner a greenish death waits for me, craving to finally suck an infinite greenish emptiness out of me. I am no more; I am long since no more.

I wandered the wet streets all night. I turned circles through a greenish Vilnius, an accursed ghost city, a hallucination city, which has finished sucking out the last fluids of my soul. I do not know *what* I was that night. I was both a madman and a genius, a corpse and a newborn, a dead thing and the embodiment of a soul that had lost its way. I was horrified. I didn't recognize the streets; I didn't recognize my own city. If someone had spoken to me, I couldn't have said where I was. I banged on Gediminas's door several times, but behind it there was only silence and emptiness. In the near future the Russian Orthodox Church, the straw-haired man, and the crucial discovery awaited me.

I was left alone. *They* took away my support, the one I relied on most; they took away my Irena, sucked out the person nearest to me, sucked her out in full view, and there was nothing I could do. The worst of it was that I probably didn't want to do anything: a secret instinct ordered me to protect myself first. Once more I looked over my hands. They were slender-fingered and sinewy. I was still alive. *They* hadn't yet managed to turn me into not me. They try to turn all of us into something else: my former wife, the imbecile on the trolleybus, Bolius crawling through the bare meadow. *They* want to destroy all the hundreds (or more?) of our souls: the soul of the back of the skull and the soul of the forehead; the souls of the nose, elbows, lungs, and liver; the souls of laughter, sadness, thoughtfulness, and despair; the souls of unchanging habits and the soul of dreams—even the soul of all my souls. Every human's soul of souls. This thirst to destroy doesn't, it seems, make any sense. It cannot be their ultimate purpose; it can only be the means to attain *something else*. But what? For what pathological purpose? You smash into this question as if it were a rock the moment you start thinking about *Them*. If you could divine the purpose, you'd probably learn how to defend yourself. But you never succeed in solving the riddle. You think you've already given it a name, but again and again it turns out that it's just a *means* to attain some other, still more secret, still more mysterious purpose. When investigating *Their* pathologic, you have to pay attention to all the trifles, because there are *no trifles*. There are no trifles, there is no one to ask, there is no one to rely on, and there is no one to comfort you—except rickety, crazy Vilnius.

But even so, why did Vilnius become *Their* global lair? This is one of the most difficult questions.

In my search for an answer I have only one meager hint. Tadeusz Konwicki, a Polish writer, spent his childhood in Vilnius when it was torn away from Lithuania. When asked how he writes about Vilnius without being there, he answered: I don't need to visit there, you can find Vilnius everywhere—I see entire neighborhoods of Vilnius in Amsterdam and San Francisco: the streets, the houses, and the people of Vilnius.

There's something immensely significant hiding in that answer: *Vilnius is everywhere*. In every *real* city you can come across the houses, streets, and people of Vilnius. But neither that poor, naïve Konwicki, nor other poor, naïve people know the most important thing: those are all *Their* residences. Settling in some city, *They* quickly impart a Vilniutian form to entire blocks. In a neighborhood like that in San

Francisco or Amsterdam, you must immediately start looking about for *Them*.

But why Vilnius, anyway?

It's impossible to *understand* what Vilnius is. You can only believe in Vilnius or not believe in it. Believing is difficult, I know, it's very difficult. Even I sometimes cannot grasp that this geometry textbook of cement block barracks, this clanking concentration camp choking on fumes, is my Vilnius. That these ghosts, wandering aimlessly, without realizing that the remnants of their souls are surrounded by barbed wire, are Vilniutians too. Not everyone will see the real body beneath the drab clothing, not everyone will believe in Vilnius. I'm obliged to believe in it, because it gave me Lolita.

There she is—lying naked. I can admire her high breast and slender waist, feel the secret beauty fluids flowing through her long legs. Lolita entrances me, takes away my power to think logically. Her capricious spirit overwhelms me, forces me to forget what I should remember every minute. She is practically unreal; people like that can't exist. A body like that shouldn't have either a spirit or intelligence—its beauty should suffice. But she is full of both one and the other—even too much of everything. By her very existence Lolita mocks God and nature, and things like that are punishable. I'm terrified that I'm inadvertently bogging her down in matters that will sooner or later destroy me. I am a horrible swamp, but she too, only looks sturdy and dependable on the surface—she's like quicksand, in which you can sink for eternity, herself.

"You've got it good," I say, "you live in an old house. Old houses have a soul. The new ones don't even have a face."

"They can have one," she answers immediately. "In other places, even when they're building skyscrapers, they give them names. Whatever has a name can have a face too."

Lolita has a face, really she does (although sometimes I get a craving to cover it, to hide it). The spirit is inevitably reflected in the face; neither dark glasses nor a nightmarish grimace will hide spirituality. It's an unfortunate characteristic of a human: *They* immediately take notice of you.

"You've lived only in nameless houses?"

"The labor camps were named very astutely," I say. "Metaphorically! Above the gates there they write: work makes life sweet . . . Or: abandon hope, ye who enter here . . ."

We talk about the camp mostly when we're walking up Didžiosios Street. She starts the conversation herself, but I hardly get a word out when she gets scared, pushes me into a gateway and kisses and kisses me, shutting my mouth. And now she moves uneasily, curls up her legs, her body is ungracefully broken. I feel guilty that I've disfigured the ideal painterly lines of a nude: I'm a vandal, hacking at Goya's *Maya* with a knife.

"Before the war I lived in a haunted house. It surely wasn't nameless. That was a crazy house, no less so than the Lord God. And it created horrors no worse than God manages to."

I spoke of ghosts and horrors quite unnecessarily. The fear that Lolita is nothing more than my invention darts through me once more. Demented Vilnius willingly gives birth to fantasies: I simply thought her up, I just very much want her to be, that's why I see her, when in actuality she doesn't exist. I'm consorting with a phantom of fantasy. But who I am talking to? To myself? It seems not—I don't think the way Lolita does; her words frequently surprise me.

"There you go again," she says carefully, "your eyes are LIKE THAT again."

I've concocted a sad, melodious voice for her; it's a bit intoxicating. I've concocted amazing girlish breasts for her, breasts like I've never seen before. Is it possible to invent a form you've never seen? Then there are her eyes—real or concocted? Her legs, Lord, her legs—could they really be concocted? I carefully come closer; I try to walk slowly and smoothly, because a sudden movement could dissolve Lolita, woven out of thickened air. I'm afraid to touch her—my fingers could go right through her. I close my eyes—now I don't see, don't hear, don't touch her, but the scent is still there, the scent of the garden of Paradise, caressing my nostrils. I close my nose with my fingers, but there's the sixth, and seventh, and tenth sense; all the same I feel her, and I can't destroy that feeling. (Maybe that's what they call love?) Whatever I do, Lolita exists; I cannot hide myself from her. I could not see her, not smell her, not touch her, but she unavoidably remains both inside me and outside of me—if I still separate my inside from my outside at all.

I quickly open my eyes, draw in her scent, caress the long toes one by one, embrace the slender ankles—hesitantly, as if it could turn out that they're not the same as always. I stroke the velvet of the calves' skin, feel every little hair—everything is in place. With my palms I slowly fondle the thighs, the firm waist, the flat, smooth belly, where unseen little veins pulsate. All of her is waiting for me, the way the parched earth waits for rain. I sense her sweet warmth, caress the slender hands— their joints have actually softened from expectation. I know every one of her fingers. I love the elongated sharp nails of the hands. I adore the rounded porcelain of the toenails. I love the mole under the breast and the other one, large and light brown—on the nape of the neck, where the spine ends. I love the crooked scar on the right hip. I love the cracked skin of the lips. I love her forehead, the two wrinkles cutting deep; they grow distinct when she scrutinizes me. I love her breasts, formed of light and honey (they even thrash when I touch them). She is my song of songs, I've long since learnt her by heart, but she cannot bore me or seem, even for an instant, to be known, to not be hiding something unexpected. Her breasts that are always *the same* are *different* every time. I'm amazed that Solomon attempted to compare his loved one's body to something. Lolita isn't comparable to anything; she's not even comparable with herself, because she is different every time. She is like an entire world, like a universe—with stars, nebulae, and comets. Her flavor is heavenly: I lick her cheeks; with the tip of my tongue I brush the neck and shoulders. There are more flavors in Lolita than in the entire rest of the world. A tart grape sugar behind the ears, and the salty sweat of passion under the breasts. A choking September apple flavor on the mounds above the knees and a mixture of love herbs covering the entire length of the spine. There are a thousand varieties of flavor hiding in her skin, and I distinguish them all: the wrinkled skin of her nipples is one kind, a completely different kind between her thighs—an impossible, supernatural smoothness. Her dry lips attempt to moisten my tongue, while the belly's skin softly fondles it. It slides down the thin hair below the belly and unexpectedly gets entrapped in the hidden, damp space, where by now a slightly bitter flavor of desire is nascent, the flavor of Lolita's tumult. The secret space is like the gates to the unknown, with my tongue I feel all of the little wrinkles, the slightest mounds, I strive to plunge into Lolita as if into an abyss, she is my goddess and my ruler. She writhes like a ball of enchanted snakes, her trembling thighs caress my cheeks, convulsively clutch my head, the space of mystery nearly suffocates me, but I relish it, I relish it. I leave that bottomless unknown; I lick Lolita's nostrils, bringing her the flavor of her own desire, and then the wordless caress of the tongues begins. By now I hardly know where I am; I only feel her breasts pressing marks on my body. I hardly see anything, but I know that her face hinders me—it's *too much* of a face, *too much* eyes, *too much* spirit. I cover it with a corner of the gray curtain, as if in a dream I feel that faceless woman loving me like a panther, as if in a dream I see her body, now it is the body of all the women in the world. It no longer belongs to Lolita; it doesn't belong to anyone—only to me. I make love to all the women in the world at the same time. I can love that way—I have enough strength. This universal woman body is made up of that which I have never experienced; it isn't the body of my other women. I have never touched such overripe breasts, so fearfully pressed together. I have never felt such a flat, smooth goddess's belly with my belly. I have never penetrated into such a winding, multifold, branching sexual space. This is the body of all the women in the world. A changing, faceless, sightless body, my song of songs, my death and my resurrection. I die and I am resurrected, again I die and am resurrected, everything recedes from me, even now I am left completely alone. *Does Lolita really exist?*

Perhaps it's possible to dream up that giddiness, that apocalyptic melody of bodies . . . that beastly desire, those floods and ebbs . . . probably it's even possible to invent the sightless, universal woman body, her heavenly orgasm, when the entire skin becomes pure white and as thin as parchment . . . when every last vein shines through it—blue or dark red . . . to invent that supernatural, impossible vagina, in whose multifold space you go astray, which is different, unrecognizable, mysterious every time . . . you can invent even yourself, but it's impossible to fabricate that boundless *closeness*, it embraces all of me like a nirvana, more perfect than death . . . It gives me meaning; you can't invent that kind of closeness *by yourself*. Another person is essential here, in all of his wholeness . . . I am no longer alone . . . She doesn't let me be alone . . . It's a true closeness, a true connection . . . with her . . . with the trees . . . with all of oceans of the world . . . with hallucinating Vilnius . . . with me myself . . . A true connection, one that has nothing in common with the sexual dance of the body, little in common even with the erotic, it's a *true* connection. As long as such things exist in the world, they alone make life worth living. (Maybe that's what they call love?)

No, I haven't invented Lolita, she is: she walks around the room naked, and then puts on a robe . . . She sits across from me in the tub and splashes my chest with white foam . . . She is, she doesn't disappear anywhere, she won't vanish like smoke, here she is: kneeling at the end of the bed she helplessly nibbles at my thighs and belly, she wants to take a bite of her god's body, ritually taste of it, so that at least a particle of mine will remain within her, because if she were to lose connection with me, she would instantly crumble into a little pile of ashes. I lie on my back, and with all of my pores and veins I feel her take my scarred masculinity into her hands, stroke it with her palms, press it to one cheek and the other, brush it against her lips, look at it, no longer at me—only at it.

"My handsome one," she says in a hoarse voice, "It's like a flower . . . It's my prettiest flower . . . And it smells like a flower . . . A scarred warrior . . ."

Her head has fallen on my hips while she caresses and kisses her prettiest flower; I actually feel weak, and an emptiness spreads through my innards. She sucks me, sucks out my insides, it seems she is pulling everything out of me, only a sugary bliss remains inside; it should be very good, but for some reason it's dreary—for some reason I see a blue sky above me, it's not darkened by the least little cloud. The clearest of clear summers returns again, the summer of horror, the summer of the cattle cars. Grandfather's angry predictions are coming true; I don't understand anything anymore, I live as if in a dream, I rise and go to bed as if in a dream. Barely a year has gone by since the Russians came, and the world changed the way it doesn't change in centuries. Now I'm lying completely naked in a bed of luxuriant grass, the sun glares, right nearby a little creek swirls, and on my belly scrawled sheets of paper quietly rustle. Giedraitis Junior is naked too, still guzzling a half-empty bottle swiped from home. The wine we've drunk gently intoxicates, and I feel like I'm in a double dream, Lord knows, as if I'm dreaming in a dream, but there's no peace in it, either; the wheels of the cattle cars keep rumbling in my head. Everything is a dream—it's so easy to convince yourself of that. The trains to the East thunder by in the black darkness. The Russians are hidden, they do their black work in the blackness, but I know the secret. Every morning I run to the railroad tracks, where Giedraitis Junior is already waiting for me. After the night, the embankment looks like it's been covered in snow; it's white, white as far as the eye can see—as if the cattle cars were spreading a deadly frost. We quickly scoop up and gather that dirty snow, but oddly—it doesn't freeze, but rather scorches the fingers. It's probably not the paper that scorches (that snow is made of paper), but what's written on it. We gather up those damp little papers, but we don't manage to take even a hundredth part of them: the entire embankment is strewn with those moaning, wailing, screaming sheets that the trains of ghosts, rolling to the East, scattered during the night. This is the only place where everyone throws their little messages out—apparently, this is an enchanted spot. And I am the king of that enchantment.

I play a strange game, as if I were playing chess with strangers' fates. Every night people disappear without a trace, and then thunder off into a boundless void by the thousands. The Shit of All Shits is devouring Lithuanians; everyone is waiting for their turn to come. And when it comes—they throw out their ghostly letters, like sailors from a sinking ship. They believe someone will pick up their cries, tears, and groans from the ground and send them off as addressed. A naïve, naïve, hope: to once see the morning railroad embankment strewn with hundreds, thousands of little letters, is enough to be overwhelmed by a bottomless fear, a horror of the mute trains of apparitions dissecting the blackness. You couldn't manage to send out even the smallest part of those letters, so we play a strange game: we skim through them, and he who wins is the one that finds the most interesting one . . . or the most horrible . . . or the funniest . . . We haven't selected today's yet:

> *Elena,*
> *I know you won't get my letter, I'm writing into the void.*
> *I'm sitting in the corner of the car with my pants wet*
> *because the guards won't let us near the opening. So no*
> *one will see there's people in the cars. No one knows where*
> *they're taking us, maybe to shoot us. Maybe I'll be gone*
> *soon, but you won't be around for long, either. If that's the*
> *way it is—the Russians will shoot everyone. We'll die out*

*from them like from the plague. It actually makes me feel*
*better, that you'll die too. We'll meet in paradise, no one*
*will separate us there . . .*

I watch Robertas guzzle the wine; I try to guess what he's thinking. What does father think, drawing nothing but bloody trains that are
descending into horrible, gigantic, tunnel-like sexual openings? What
does grandfather think, he who doesn't eat, drink, or say anything? What
does mother think, she who shaved her head bare yesterday? What do I
think myself? Maybe that the end of the world is here? That I'm a human
and that I should love other people? In other words, those aliens too, the
ones who load the trains of apparitions at night? I cannot love them, for
the very reason that I am a human. Actually, I could add that they aren't
human. Yes, that's the only possibility: those aliens are not humans.

*Maryt, we're still alive. They stuffed us into black cars last*
*night, they're taking us to Rushia, we'll be like servants there*
*for the Balshevik masters. Don't you worry, I'll write you a*
*letter as soon as I can. You just learn Russkie, Russkie will*
*be all they'll let you speak and write, so learn it. Let Kazelis*
*run like hell from Kaunas, they'll take everybody from the*
*cities to Rusland, maybe out in the country they'll leave*
*some. The two of you just lie low, then maybe everything will*
*be okay. I had a slab of bacon so I'm fixed up a bit better*
*than the others. The Russkies aint never seen bacon, so it*
*was like manna from heaven to them. Only one guy didn't*
*eat it, he said at home they make it better, in factories, out of*
*speshal stuff. Teach Kazelis to say miravaja revoliucija and*
*tavarich stalin nash atec, and he ought to learn a Russkie*
*song too, they like it a lot when you sing their songs. When*
*some Russkie shows up in the yard, start singing out loud*
*right away, then they'll leave you alone. I'm throwing this*
*letter out next to some kind of bonfires, maybe some good*
*people will pass it on to you. Luv and kisses, Stanislovas*

And yet another one, some philosopher's; even in a cattle wagon he
wants to appear wise to himself:

*Lord God! Everyone is throwing letters out here, so I'm throwing one out too. I don't want to write to people anymore. I'm addressing this to Thee, Lord, surely Thou seest that Lithuania is on the brink—tell me that doesn't worry Thee at all? What have the honest, hard-working plowmen of Lithuania done to offend Thee, why are people who think, who have a heart and who believe in Thee no longer loved? Why take the side of the faceless mass pouring out of the East? Don't tell me Thou dost not hear what they say? They have no brains. Don't tell me Thou dost not see what they're doing? They have no heart. They're not made in Thy image. Why are they chasing us out of the land of our fathers? Maybe Thou hast proclaimed the end of the world by now, maybe the Revelation is already being fulfilled? Maybe . . .*

The letters rustle on my belly. There's no need to try to understand anything. There's the sun, there's the creek, over there's a rock overgrown with moss. It's just somehow unsettling; my heart is troubled. And Giedraitis Junior is looking at me so strangely too. I know he secretly hates me—because I'm so big and strong, because I have known a woman, because I'm already a man, while he, a year older, is still a puny little kid. And I envied him his dandy of a music teacher, the entire class envied him: he would meet junior Giedraitis by the school, put his arm around his shoulders and lead him off, whispering something in his ear. And I'm also envious of him because everything is always obvious to him. He doesn't reproach himself over the love of humans or unsent letters. Every human resembles some sort of animal: a bird, a long-legged hunting dog, a rat. Giedraitis Junior doesn't resemble anything, he's completely lifeless: he reminds you of drab ruins that absolutely no one visits. Sometimes it seems like there's bats flying around in his belly. Nature shorted him something; everything others take openly and honestly, he's forced to snatch secretly—like today's wine. He's missing something; something very, very important. No one likes him. All the more reason I should love him. They're packing up Lithuanians as fertilizer for the fields of Siberia; there's fewer of us all the time, we have to love one another. They'll take him among the first—he tried to buddy up to the Nationalist youth. I almost love him—as if he were a younger sister, neither pretty nor interesting, whom no one will marry no matter what dowry you'd offer. Robis smiles pitifully—he always instantly senses sympathy in another's eyes. He wants to be good to me, very, very good—like an affectionate puppy. He rubs against me, he's a puppy, and I'm a naked god knocked to the ground, great and unhappy in equal parts. Apparitions are writing letters to me about Lithuania. Robis blinks rapidly, he watches with a devoted gaze. I'm sorry for him, I want to do something nice for him. I stretch out my hand and tousle his hair—that dandy of a music teacher used to do that. He suddenly blushes, smiles pitifully, looks at me with an ever stranger stare. I don't get it right away when his hand starts feeling around below my belly, carefully strokes my hair, suddenly as lightly as a little mouse slides down even further and, quivering, embraces my penis. My face suddenly gets hot, my thoughts jumble, I should say or do something, but the wine is swirling in my head so pleasantly. I never imagined that Robis's hands are so soft—like velvet, like willow buds.

"It's so handsome!" says Robis in a thick voice. "It's so big and handsome!"

Yes, a strange inner voice whispers, yes, it's big and handsome, all of you is big and handsome, you are like a god. I don't understand what Robis is doing, my thoughts wilt, I don't think anything, I just wait to see what will happen. He sighs quietly, slides somewhere lower down, I wait, I keep waiting, and suddenly I feel a damp touch there, below, in the most tender of spots. I subside into a sticky, warm sweetness, and the strange voice keeps warbling: only for you, only for you can it be this sweet, because you are like a god. It's really hard to tear my stuck eyelids apart, I can barely see: Robis has lain down on my hips, his eyes are like a beaten dog's, it's some kind of a painting, in reality it's not like that, there's no such impossible sweetness, even my bones grow soft and mushy—any moment I'll close my eyes, helpless. Yes, the strange voice beckons, only gods dream such dreams, wait a bit, it'll be even better. I throw a last glance at the giddy dream, but my eyes stumble on the sheets of paper on my belly, suddenly I understand that this is no dream, that everything is for real!

Suddenly I realize *what's going on here.* Giedraitis Junior, sensing something bad (he always senses things), arduously tears himself away from me, panting heavily. I don't know what to do, I just assure myself that nothing happened, nothing, nothing, has happened and couldn't have happened. I want just one thing: that he too, would understand that nothing happened here; nothing, absolutely nothing, has taken place.

"Is it nice?" Giedraitis Junior asks quietly. "If you want, I'll kiss your feet . . . I collect things that you've touched . . . Let me finish . . . Soon, to the end . . ."

He looks at me again with big eyes, *like I'm one of his own*. It's green around me, everything is green, except for the white of the undelivered letters on my belly. What would those apparitions think of me, seeing their naked, spread-eagled god? I find myself thinking of what my grandfather would do to me and it takes my breath away. I'm completely calm; I'm just sorry that Giedraitis Junior spoke. I'm sorry for his voice, sorry for him himself, because now I will have to kill him. If he spoke up like that, it means everything really did happen. Now I will have to kill him, otherwise I'll never wash off the shame.

He's gone in an instant; I see only a helpless lump of a body, splatters of blood on the grass, and my beaten knuckles. He's choking on snot and blood, wheezing, slinging little whitish papers to the side. I need to calm down, otherwise I really will kill him. Giedraitis Junior is all bloody, even his glance is bloody; his words are bloody too.

"You screwed my mother!" he screams, "I know everything! You screwed my mother! I'll tell father! He'll kill you! Cut you into pieces! Tear out your eyes! Rip off your shitty peewee! . . ."

He eyes me so furiously that it seems he'll strangle me with his very eyes, his very look. Everything in my head is muddled: the night trains, the game with strangers' fates, the babbling of the creek, Madam Giedraitiene's limp breasts and commanding voice, starving grandfather's sluggish stare, Junior Giedraitis's doggish gaze, and a white ceiling which looms above me, presses down on me; I have to shake my head roughly so it will rise up a bit and grant me just a speck of freedom, just the slightest chance of remaining alive. For the time being still alive.

"What's the matter with you?' Lolita asks. "Have you been beset by ghosts?"

She is calm and good-natured, there's only a note of curiosity in her voice. By now she has put on a robe, only her legs are severely naked; they bother me. Her body should be different, perhaps old and tired— then neither her intelligent eyes nor her strange wisdom would surprise me. Sometimes it seems she should have been born a man. It's practically pathological: I want to turn the most beautiful of my women into a man—into an elderly giant who's seen everything, who could truly be relied on. She could substitute for both Gedis and Bolius—if not for those intoxicating legs, if not for those breasts rising up and forcing their way out of her clothes, like fish out of a net.

Lolita reads my mind: she carefully covers her legs, sinks into a shadow. Her profile is a bit predatory, it's one that could be a man's too. Maybe I should dress her in men's clothes for conversations? No, they would make it even more obvious that she is a woman, a woman of women.

"Talk about something. That's the only way to drive the ghosts away. Tell me about your mother. You promised."

It's true, I promised; I actually thought up a bargain. An eye for an eye, a death for a death. A story for a story.

"And you tell me about your husband. Even though you didn't promise."

"I didn't think you'd be interested," she says, and falls silent for a long, long time.

I see my mother standing in the intersection of the hallways, not knowing which way to turn. What can I say about her? Would she herself let me? I ask, even though I know it's all the same to her. Everything's all the same to her. She would listen to a story about herself as if it were the tale of some stranger. And immediately forget it all.

"She was rich. She married against her family's will. It's understandable—there a fattened burgher's family, and here—a crazed genius with flashing eyes. My mother was very pretty . . . or maybe not . . . I don't even know. It probably doesn't matter . . . She relied on father absolutely, that's what was the worst. No friends, no gatherings, no charity work. Her husband was the entire world to her; she existed only when he was next to her, afterwards she would seem to disappear, and all that was left was waiting until he would show up again . . . That's worse than death. To blindly rely on someone—that's worse than a slow, painful death . . . Without father she lived as if she were in a dream, she would drift up and down the corridors, she didn't even talk . . ."

Mother comes into the room; it seems she badly wants to say something—it always seems she wants to say something important. But she'll be quiet, she'll just stretch her slender arms out to me, and drops of blood will drip from her fingertips. She's killed something again, she's always killing something; you'd think she wanted to make the world smaller so it wouldn't be so complicated.

"You rely on someone . . ." I say quietly, quietly. "And then that someone spits in your face . . . I don't know why father turned away from her. They didn't interact at all; they lived in different ends of the house so they wouldn't, God forbid, meet . . . She was suddenly left alone, facing the world she had never tried to understand. Her world was her parents' family, then her husband and his affairs . . . She didn't know how to live, understand, she didn't have anything of her own: no goals, no aspirations, no worries. Can you imagine what it means for a forty-year-old woman to begin to get to know the world—like a child, like a naïve teenager? . . . And she was utterly determined to understand the world—by herself, independently . . . I don't know how to explain it . . . Well—we all know how our day will begin tomorrow, what we will need to do, what we want . . . She didn't know anything."

"She didn't adapt?" Lolita asks carefully.

"Not that, no, not that, Lola! She took on the world like . . . like a game . . . like a miracle . . . I don't know . . . She didn't try to adapt to it, she just as calmly as you please created her own universe with inexplicable, spontaneous laws. Whatever came into her head, that was a law of the universe. She was up to her ears in money; she had the complete freedom that all artists and thinkers in general can only dream about. It was just that she didn't know what to do with that freedom. She spat on society, family, children, making money, and all rules, and decided to try some kind of experiment. No one could predict what she would think up next. The worst of it was that she didn't know herself. She could sleep days and stay awake nights. Week after week, from morning till night, cook up fancy meals, and then dump everything out. I mean dump it out, understand—not parcel it out to some villager, or to us, or to some guest, but dump it out . . . You'd think she was trying to find the slightest minutiae that could concern her. But to her it was all absolutely the same. Her husband had turned away . . . I was of no concern . . . no activity concerned her . . . religion didn't attract her . . . nor any amusements, either . . . And yet she still tried to *live* . . ."

"You sound like you hated her guts," Lolita says carefully.

"Excuse me," I try to control my voice, "you're correct. It's not right to condemn a person who doesn't have the strength to pull himself together, to oppose *Them*. You'd have to condemn all of humanity. Everyone is given the opportunity . . . Oh, we're short of money, we're short of freedom! It's all lies! . . . If you think it's the surroundings or other people that are to blame—you're fooling yourself. Only you are to blame. Only you. You're amazed at other people's helplessness, weakness, stupidity? Don't fool yourself—you're that way yourself! You're oppressed by the injustice of the world? Look inside yourself more carefully! The only one you have a right to condemn is yourself!"

"I always dreamed of meeting you," says Lolita, "you're a terrible person. Perhaps the worst I've ever seen."

She looks at me with huge brown eyes (it seems I unintentionally said *They*: I'm losing my guard entirely), but Vilnius looks at me even more reproachfully. After all, by condemning others, I condemn Vilnius too. For what? Better remember one of my prayers. Lord, grant me patience and forgiveness, in order that I might understand everyone and forgive everyone. Do not let me forget they *suffer too*. Always remind me of my purpose, a thousand times bigger than myself, in order that I may disregard myself. Take anger and disdain away from me, give me the intelligence to always distinguish the victims from the executioners.

Have I calmed down yet?

"I'd like to feel that free," says Lolita, "to have my own hermetic world. And you . . ."

"Don't wish for it, oh no, don't . . . Maybe you don't even suspect how much you, me, all of us are protected by the cover of normal behavior, by automatic activities and banal rules. It's the most powerful of our defenses; it's our God, to whom we pray despite ourselves, even though we curse him all the time . . . You want to create a world? Right away you'll need both good and evil, and beauty . . . and a God, a strange, unique God, who would be God no matter what you call him . . ."

"Love," says Lolita, "You forgot love."

"And love. Of course, love . . . Do you know what love turns into if you throw caution to the wind, if you're left face to face with the world? Do you know what it turned into for my mother? She bought herself a stud, a gloomy giant, who screwed her . . . That illiterate, soulless animal ravaged my mother's slender, white body and took money for it too. There's the love of a unique world for you. Mother refused to accept the common world, but didn't manage to create her own, either. She was short of everything: God, goodness, beauty . . . It was horrible to listen to her when she tried, in spite of it all, to speak. She tried, Lord knows she tried . . . She wanted to do something, to change something, to exchange things, so nothing would be motionless, nothing would stay in place. And she kept killing all sorts of life: geese, cats, worms . . . This is bullshit, and not my mother's story, isn't it?"

"That's the only way you can say something genuine about a person," Lolita answers calmly, and for that understanding I really do love her.

I love, I love Lolita, she's the only living thing nearby; only my dead surround me. Grandfather, the great Lithuanian spy in Polish-occupied Vilnius. A hero, bravely fighting with the most windmill-like of windmills. Father, convinced by an unheard voice that the world isn't worth his efforts. My two forefathers, kanuked so differently. By what means do *They* inject a healthy brain with their pathologic; with what form of the drab spirochetes are they able to penetrate the joints, the blood, the sperm? How did all of my people fall into a trap they didn't see in time, which they didn't guard against? What did Gediminas fail to consider, the all-knowing Gediminas, gloomily leaning over the piano, his hands raised, but still not daring to press the keys? What did I overlook, squeezed for long years between the moldy walls of my wife's apartment? What unexpectedly wiped my brains clean and opened up the *second* sight? What do I have to guard my Lolita against? Lolita, my very own Lolita.

"I can imagine how your parents horrified their neighbors," she says. "In such a homogenous, commonplace group of people . . ."

"Oh, sister, how you've overshot! You really don't get it? The two of them were perfectly pleasant, acceptable people! For the yearly ball at the university mother would order a dress from Paris . . . Yes, yes . . . You don't really think that she went around town with her head shaved bare? You don't really think that father would roll around in a drunken stupor in the company of professors? No, he would talk politics, make witty remarks . . . It seemed they returned from a long, long journey, threw off their exotic clothes, and suddenly turned into the most proper bourgeoisie . . . Perhaps that amazed me the most. I kept thinking, where are they keeping all of that, what's really inside of them, what are they hiding from, what are they afraid of? That two- or three-facedness of theirs, that ability to undress themselves, their genuine selves, just like dirty clothes, drove me out of my mind . . ."

As I talk I feel a soft lump covering my brain and drowning it in thick silt. Everything recedes into a fog. A wall appears between me and Lolita; I can't step over it anymore, although I could just a minute ago. I'm slowly turning into *something else*. It's a whiff of *Them*, an attack of *Their* secret plague. My innards teem and swarm with gray spirochetes too; no one can predict how much longer my spirit will hold out.

"Why did she kill herself?" someone asks out of the fog. "Did she get lost in herself? Look into the abyss too deeply?"

"I loved her." I'm telling the holy truth, but that's not what I should be talking about, not at all. "She was the unhappiest of us all. She hung herself decently, while we're still living . . ."

"To me she resembles Lithuania," someone in the fog suddenly says, "The same senseless despair."

"Resembles? Maybe in the sense that Lithuania never was ITSELF either, foreigners were always glomming on to her—through force and deceit . . . Do you know why she hung herself? She persuaded herself she was going to give birth to a monster—large and hairy . . . yes, yes, it had to be hairy . . . She convinced all of us, it was all she talked about . . . She thought Satan had impregnated her. But not the black one . . . And not the one who says *non serviam* . . . The very worst of all—her own private Satan . . . How can I put this? . . . By the incarnation of the evil of the universe, understand? She found neither love nor beauty in her invented world, but she found evil in it . . . If she had given birth, she would have given birth to a monster that would destroy the world. And that monster would be her son, her beloved, even insanely beloved son . . ."

"Horrible," whispers the fog, slowly starting to resemble Lolita.

"No, not horrible. There's no name for it. We can't imagine even a thousandth part of her fear, her love, her responsibility to the future of the universe. She hung herself one calm, quiet morning, above grandfather's Shit of All Shits altar. She got up from the table and went out to hang herself."

"So she went crazy after all . . ."

"I don't know. Lord knows I don't. It's hard to say what 'crazy' means. What 'normal' or 'abnormal' mean. You could say that normal is pragmatism, the ability to adapt to circumstances. Are you abnormal if you understand the circumstances correctly, but still behave in such a way that death inevitably awaits you? If Mandelstam wrote and read his friends poems about Stalin, knowing full well that he would, one way or the other, be killed on account of them, was Mandelstam abnormal? I think it was Stalin who was abnormal. But anyway, this is all theory . . . And as for mother . . . she knew quite well how to exist in her surroundings. Perfectly well. Nothing threatened her. All of her nightmares were there next to her, understand? It was as if she would go in there, the way an artist goes into his creation, and then she could return. And live on, entirely properly . . . That's the thing . . . When she talked about the monster she was going to give birth to, you could understand it as a metaphor, the creation of a poem of horror. That's the way we all understood it . . . The time itself was insane. Russian tanks were rumbling in Kaunas, a handful of collaborators was already rushing to Moscow to sign the papers to join the Soviet Union . . . We thought mother was just reacting to everything in her own way. You think no one would have watched out for her if we had believed she could kill herself? We all thought she would keep talking and talking about it . . . But she went off somewhere THERE and, completely consciously, didn't want to return. She up and hanged herself. And what use was there in that? Unless maybe that sometimes I, I myself feel I'm that son of hers, that unborn monster."

"Stop!" says Lolita. "It's my fault, I provoked you. Out of curiosity. I really want to know everything about you. Absolutely everything. But it's just ordinary curiosity. You won't be angry if I admit it? You're as white as a sheet."

I look at her; now I see well. The drab fog has disappeared; once more sounds are no longer hollow. Lolita smells of milk and grass . . . and something else sugary . . . But I have to ask; I warned her I'd ask, even though I'm sorry for her. I have to ask. It won't leave me alone. I have to know everything. Practically every strange death is *Their* work.

"Tell me about your husband."

"I didn't think you'd be interested. I thought it might even be unpleasant. Why should I talk about some third person?"

"I'm interested," I say, as if I wanted to hurt her on purpose. "Five sentences. Who he was and why he's gone."

"He was an artist. A sculptor. Probably not a genius." She puts the words on the table in front of me carefully, one at a time. I clearly see how they tremble, how pained they are. "He died. An unfortunate accident. You haven't heard about it? It's a well-known story."

"Sort of: that he drowned or something."

"Let's not talk about him," Lolita asks. "I don't know what I could say . . . He was . . . he's gone . . . It's sad . . ."

I don't hear the siren of danger; I don't feel the pang there, deep inside, in the very softest spot. It's calm everywhere, even too calm. Every unexpected death piques me, but this one didn't bother me at all. Lolita didn't say anything stinging anyway, but I do see her eyes, I smell her scent, I even sense her bio-energy fields—I would notice danger at once. *I want* to sense it, but apparently it isn't there.

"It really is a sad story," is all I say.

Outside the window sprawls filthy, messy Vilnius: the new city collapsed on the old one. An inexplicable presentiment suffocates me, perhaps flowing from the future, since there is no stimulus for it from the present or the past. But it's not frightening, because Lolita is, and in her there is both a body and a spirit. A glass, and a noble drink within. Do I love her because of the way she is, or is she that way because I love her? Does she make me better, or have I already made her so? Is she that way because she knows I love her, or because she doesn't know how much I love her?

And again: do I really love her?

Vilnius, again and again: the old houses, cowering, trying to crawl underground, and the new multi-storied buildings insolently sticking out. The old ones are afraid; this is no place for them, they belong in Bologna, Padua, or Prague. The churches bend their spires down to the ground—they're afraid to be so different. I go down the street and don't even try to guess who's devouring me with their eyes today. No spy intimidates me anymore: neither the men with massive heads, nor the fine-featured women with short-cut hair, nor the straw-haired lumpens with puffy faces and colorless eyes, sullenly staring out of the gateways, out of the doorways, through fly-stained windows. They have all become a customary part of the landscape. The daily routine of the continually siphoned-off and *kanuked* human being. Getting on the trolleybus, I'm actually amazed if I *don't find* a hunched figure somewhere in a corner, glaring at me with the eyes of the meaningless void. I've known for a long time that the ones you see don't matter. The ones that matter hide in secret cracks, like cockroaches. Cockroaches ought to be *Their* organization's symbol, *Their* totem, *Their* heraldic sign—cockroaches on a greenish, moldy background, on the background of beloved, despised Vilnius—with all of its sounds and smells, which never abandon me. It's like a beloved woman whose body has been eaten away by syphilis and leprosy. But you love her anyway; that love is eternal, even though nothing is left of her body but ruins, rot, and reeking wounds. You stroke the reeking ulcers, your hand dives into the abscesses, but you see the divine body it once was. Love doesn't fade, it only grows stronger; you love even the wounds, because you know what that woman (that city) once was, what it could be. What it *should* be.

Vilnius, again and again: a narrow, little Old Town street, smelling of oblivion and wet leaves. With an uneven arc it turns to the right, no one knows where it ends or where it leads. Probably to nonbeing, to the void. An old wall overgrown with lichens should surround it, and above the paving stones a single light blowing in the wind should dangle. But the wall is evenly painted with bright paints and the lantern, merely pretending to be old, shines calmly and steadily. Everything here is unreal, like in a burned-down theater, and no one worries if you'll believe the acting. Everything is soaked in cheap pretense—no one knows why, or for whom. (Pretense is *Their* ploy too. They consider it extremely important that a person pretend to be something other than what he really is. They consider it extremely important that a person should sing about how full and happy he is, even though he's a half-starved slave. It's not enough for *Them* that a person is quiet; they need him to *sing* merrily. And the worst of it is that people really do sing.) In an ornamented gateway, a trio of teenagers loiter with their fists jammed into their windbreaker pockets. They spit constantly and swear every other word. They glare at me with wolfish glances and turn away: an easier target will show up.

You couldn't say Vilnius is suffocating in emptiness. It's full, that is, *full* of emptiness, the worst form of emptiness. Pure emptiness is an ideal, a type of divinity. *They* aren't worried about emptying; what *They* need most is simply to extract and embalm, and then to stuff the free space with surrogates. That's the only way to bring in the new order: an *ostensible* man, a kanukaman. That's the only way to create a new conglomerate: an *ostensible* city, a kanukacity. That's how an *ostensible* world shows up, a kanukaworld, where God has been exchanged with the Shit of All Shits, time has been turned into eternal stagnation, and space becomes despair. A kanukaman's virtue turns into the art of pretense, and honor becomes scorn. Even the blackest passions turn into oppressive drivel, while love becomes an erotic hymn of bodies . . . I saw *it*; that scene still stands in front of my eyes, but I do not want to name it or talk about it.

The kanukacity oppresses me; Vilnius annoyingly repeats itself: its sounds and smells, its people and animals. The faces are all the same; it's rare to come across a more interesting one. Although here's one that's really worth noticing: a thin, unshaven little face with cracked round eyeglasses. The face of an exhausted tramp, although the little guy is arrayed like he's on parade: there's even a bow-tie with red polka dots tied around his neck. I've seen him before; perhaps I've seen him many times. He's like the ghost of Vilnius—a short little Jew, so Jewish it's quite striking. A Vilnius Jew: not a banker, nor a sharp-eyed cheat, rather a small businessman or a craftsman, but brimming with archaic Jewish wisdom, able to cite from the Torah, the Kabbalah, or Hassidic teachings for hours on end. He slowly totters by, glances at me, and suddenly, quite clearly, says:

"It's a dangerous road. Oy, a dangerous road!"

Don't tell me we know one another? Surely he doesn't know where I'm going? Surprised, I stop, while he totters on unconcerned, easily climbs up the creaking metal stairs, and in an instant is already balancing on the edge of the roof, merrily waving at me from above.

I'm no longer surprised. Anything is possible in Vilnius. I emphasize: absolutely anything is possible here. Perhaps this is Ahasuerus himself, come from the depths of the Polish years or a painting of Chagall's. The main thing is, he's right. The Way truly is dangerous. Extremely dangerous—if even a unshaven descendant of Vilnius's old watchmakers warns me. At least someone spoke the truth. In the worn-down, played-out conversational record of Vilnius you won't, unfortunately, hear a word about *Them*, even though everyone, absolutely every person, feels *Them*. But all of the recitative street monologues and all the anecdotes whispered in smoking rooms repeat the same thing— it's enough to make your teeth hurt: the shortages, the stupidity of the authorities, the kingdom of universal lies. If those were the only things that mattered, we would be almost happy. How nice it would be, how simple and easy, if we could, even for an instant, identify *Them* with the authorities, the system, or the machine of compulsion. If *that were all* Their power would mean. If the threat were concrete and rational. No one even suspects that all the cursing of the government, even jokes told around the table, are dictated by *Them*, secretly regulated by *Them*. No one suspects that the most important part of their brain has been excised, the most important words taken out of their speech and the meanings of others deformed. At one time I myself thought *Their* goal was to suck out everyone with their pupil-less eyes, to wring out their secret powers, to feed on them the way blood-sucking insects feed on their victims' blood. But I quickly understood it was just the means to attain a totally, completely different goal. *They* strive to turn us into *something else*, something not ourselves; they strive to infect us with gray spirochetes. But why? At one time I thought *They* valued control most. It's entirely natural to think that way when you live in a world where idiots, having got hold of authority, hang on to it tooth and nail, determined to destroy millions just so they could freely rule the millions that remain. But by no means are *They* idiots. Power is also nothing more than a means. A mangy KGB agent is no more than a KGB agent; the government mafia is no more than a sullen mafia. It's just the upper layer disguising the true essence. You can dig in *Their* direction all your life, but *They'll* be hiding there anyway, in the depths. You get infected with *Them* like the plague and you feel (if you feel it) just the symptoms of the illness. To battle *Them* sometimes seems just as senseless as the hope of catching disease-causing microbes with your hands.

Even if we're all destroyed, *They* will remain. If we turn the earth into a desert poisoned with chemicals and radiation, nothing will be left alive in it. But not entirely! Cockroaches will survive even a nuclear war! Cockroaches are invincible. Let's think about that. Perhaps we'll sense how the flow of thoughts brings us closer to grasping *Their* essence.

Perhaps that's *Their* ultimate goal, to leave the world empty but for *Them*. Even if it's only in the form of cockroaches. In the end, do the great kanukai commissars—even Stalin—differ that much from cockroaches in their goals or essence? Even their whiskers are practically identical.

This sort of reasoning carries me, floats me through Vilnius; I don't want to think about anything anymore, I don't want to smell and hear my city, I don't want that which is long since dead to haunt me. I go where my feet lead me, and they can only lead me to a single spot. On its own my hand pushes open a familiar door; my feet stumble on the uneven stairs.

The Narutis is exactly the same as always. The same walls, the same faces. Little broken-down tables with crooked legs. Meager snacks, thrown any which way onto metal plates. Men indifferently swigging beer and cheap wine that turns the blood to sand and breeds worms in the liver. (It would be ridiculous to look down on them or condemn them—they don't destroy and ruin themselves any quicker than those who never touch wine, but voluntarily breed worms in their brains.) There's a smell lingering here that you can smell only in barracks and railroad stations. Nothing has changed at the Narutis, only I have changed considerably. My fashionably-cut suit and well-rested eyes are improper here. My appearance should irritate everyone. However, the regulars just look me over indifferently and turn away again. I know very well why that is. There is an indelible mark, whose meaning no one knows, pressed onto the face of a person who once haunted the Narutis. You won't find it looking in a mirror; you won't figure out what it is that gives you away as a member of the secret Narutis community. I can see that mark on other people's faces immediately. The oppressive mark of Mackus the Hunchback.

I even flinch: it seems like Mackus the Hunchback will come to the table at any moment and, as always, ask for vodka. Without doubt he will address me as "sir," he always addresses me that way. Only in the Narutis will you meet an alcoholic wreck who addresses everyone as "sir" or "mister"; he still remembers his associate professorship and his fiery speeches at scholarly councils. Mackus remembers a great deal, although there's one thing he tries very hard to forget: how, in fifty-three (I still hadn't been released), with several other *trustworthy* boys, he took secret KGB files outside the city and burned them, so that no one would even know the names of the people who are gone, and, even more, so that no one would find out that they had not, and could not, have committed any crimes. At that time the authorities were trembling and hiding their work; they desperately needed helpful hunchbacks. Mackus the Hunchback helpfully burned up those musty papers that dispassionately reported the suffering of Lithuanians and the genocide the government had commenced. They were the only documents, and he burned them up—later he vainly tried to forget it. But he unavoidably remembered those thousands of flaming files (probably mine too)—and with each burned file a person's fate burned as well. Mackus even started imagining that it wasn't paper he had burned, but rather thousands of live people. In his dreams, the charred pages turned into charred limbs and fried intestines. He desperately wanted to forget it, but after the third drink he would start telling all about it over and over again. I'd always pour him some vodka—and not just to hear about the dreadful bonfire of Vilnius again. I was sorry for Mackus the Hunchback: they didn't succeed in entirely turning him into a kanukas, a speck of conscience remained in him. Hundreds, or maybe thousands of much more serious criminals don't remember their crimes for an instant; they don't feel they've committed a crime at all. At least Mackus the Hunchback reproached himself.

"It was all of our memory I burned up," he would say glumly. "For that I'll burn in eternal fire myself. I'll be the first to get thrown into the pool of fire. I destroyed those files so that later anyone who remembered, who was seeking justice, could be cut off by saying: you made all of this up, how are you going to prove it?"

I took a gulp of warm beer and looked around again—after all, it's not Mackus the Hunchback I'm looking for at all. I came wanting to repeat the unrepeatable, the episode that had once occurred. Or maybe it hadn't happened at all?

At that time I stood on the edge. Gedis was already gone. The city drained me and ravaged me with its ghostly stares. I felt persecuted, pressed into a corner, but like a crazed beast I went straight for the hunters. I sat around in the Narutis; I frequented Old Town's dives. I was seeking destruction; I was provoking *Them*.

*Now* I sit in the Narutis, nearly gagging from the smell of scorched cabbage, and try to overcome it with vodka. The vodka is warm and disgusting, undoubtedly diluted with tap water; it turns your guts inside out. I sit all alone waiting for my Godot, like the others gathered here. Somewhere else perhaps there is a world, somewhere else rivers flow and winds blow. Somewhere else (Lord please, please!) maybe there are even *humans*. But here—only bitter, cheap cigarette smoke, the stench of scorched cabbage, and the monotony of time flowing backwards.

I came here looking for something: a thing, an animal, or a person. A thing, an animal, or a person? It's trivial, it's all nothing. A mysterious object that means something to me couldn't turn up here. The only life here is the cockroaches, dazed by the light, crawling out of the cracks. The gray ruler of Old Town's streets, the short, neckless spiderman, will surely not show up here. So why should I find an answer in this universe of boiled cabbage, vodka, and deformed faces? However, something tells me to wait *just precisely here*. The memory of the neckless spiderman won't give me peace. I sit and look at everyone in turn, not putting my hopes on anything, until my glance stumbles upon an unusual, unexpected figure of a man who doesn't fit in here. I could swear he wasn't here a second ago. He sprang from the earth; every wrinkle in his face, every fold in his clothes, screams and shouts that he didn't get here the way everyone else did. He has some sort of secret purpose. And his purpose can only be me. I feel a sharp pang in my chest; my hand pours the rest of the tumbler into my mouth of its own accord. The man looks straight at me. His eyes are brimming with quiet and . . . wait, wait . . . yes, a sweetish smell of rot. I have already seen his beautiful, elegant hands, so out of place next to the dirty shirt and frayed remains of a jacket. I already know he's come for me, but I have no idea what he could want from me (I don't want anything from him).

Don't tell me he'll simply take me out to the street and push me under a passing truck? I'm not Gedis, after all. Gedis knew something, and I'm just barely beginning to speculate. Perhaps he came to intimidate me, to break me, to take away my will? The man stands up, rises to his full, gigantic height, and approaches. I look only at him, at his glassy eyes with narrow pupils, and I know him, I know him well.

"Hello, Vytie."

It seems a hundred thunderclaps should roar; it seems the entire Narutis should sink straight into the ground. The man pats my hand. I don't pull it away because *across from me sits my father.*

"I thought you were in America ... or Australia ..." I say in a weird voice. "In Chicago, or Melbourne."

"As far as I know, this country is called Lithuania," father says calmly, as if we had separated only yesterday, "and this city is Vilnius."

I obediently followed him out, through the inner door of the Narutis, through the stench-spreading kitchen, through a small inner courtyard. We climbed up creaking stairs; several times my feet sank into rotten wood. Father's back swayed in front of my eyes, sometimes widening, sometimes narrowing. It pulsated like the naked heart of a giant animal.

"You think I'm dead?" father inquired without turning around. "In a certain sense that's true."

The two of us turned into a long arched hallway; on both sides there were doors, doors, doors. Some of them were open; slovenly women were working inside. Everything seemed natural, but there was something missing. I didn't immediately realize I wasn't hearing even the slightest sound, not even our own footsteps: their echo was apparently stifled by the rotten floorboards. They were rotten through—your feet stuck in them as if it were a swampy meadow; we should have left footprints as we passed by. I suddenly put it together that we were circling around in the places where my Irena would disappear; we were slowly penetrating into the kingdom of the neckless spiderman. My throat suddenly dried out; I fearfully asked myself what my father was doing here. Where was he taking me? Why does he feel at home here? His back no longer pulsated, it flashed regularly before my eyes, turned to the right, to the left, to the right again, to the left, to the right, to the right, to the left. In the empty rooms I discerned only rickety furniture piled in the corners. Those rooms were endless; we went and went, I could no longer understand *where* all of this labyrinth could fit: the Narutis quarter isn't all that large, we should have exited its borders long ago, maybe even Old Town's borders. Finally, father stepped into a large windowless room and stopped.

"Greetings, son," he said hoarsely. "Sit down, we'll talk."

For some reason it seemed everything had to be this way. I had to sit on the rotten floor, father had to stand off a bit—as if he feared I would suddenly touch him and convince myself he's woven out of fog. It seemed he had to say just precisely what he said. He talked a lot. I don't remember how the time passed, I don't remember where the bottle of Jamaican rum came from, or the tall candle in a bronze candleholder. The candle looked fake: its flame didn't flutter; it seemed the air in the room was solidified, not even our breathing could budge it. Father kept talking about mother, our house, and grandfather's altar; then he spoke about the war. I was seized by an unpleasant presentiment: he said no more about himself than what I already knew. You'd think thirty years had literally been erased from his life. He talked about the war like a person who hadn't experienced it, about foreign countries like a person who hadn't visited them. It seemed he had come from our last evening together, but for some unknown reason he was aged and hunched over, for some unknown reason his voice had lost its resonance. The conversation (or father's monologue) bobbed along over and over in the same spot; the good feeling that everything was the way it should be slowly disappeared. I no longer listened to his words, I just looked at father's face and tried to at least read something there. I started getting angry with this elderly person who had invaded my life without warning, confusing everything, even though everything was already confused without him. My face probably gave my thoughts away. Maybe I just imagined it, but my father's eyes suddenly flashed tenderness and fear, together with a desire to help me. Undoubtedly I only imagined it; however, it was enough—my anger instantly dissipated. I came to my senses and realized that *my father* was sitting in front of me. Father, whom I hadn't seen in thirty years. A man from whose seed I am created, whose weaknesses and strengths I inherited. My eyes involuntarily flooded with tears. I probably hadn't cried in a quarter of a century. But that time I cried. No, I wasn't sorry for myself; probably I was the most sorry for father, for the man with tousled gray hair sitting in front of me. I was sorry for the back nooks of Old Town, reeking of boiled cabbage and drowning in a drab silence, I was sorry for Vilnius, above which hung a fog of fear and despair, sorry for all of its inhabitants, the irretrievably dead, who don't even know they are no longer alive.

"Father," I interrupted his speech, "Father, what should be done?"

The two of us were like wanderers in the desert, only he was more experienced. He knew more. However, he was quiet; perhaps he was vacillating or deliberating. It was only then I felt how stuffy, how dead the room's air was. I was practically suffocating. But father was still quiet, intently looking me in the eyes, or even deeper, as if he wanted to look straight through into my brain.

"You don't know what to do now?" he asked in a thick voice. "You don't even want to think about what's waiting for you? You're tormented by obliterating stares?"

The questions were so unexpected and so well-aimed that I was at a loss for words. It seemed I should have anticipated something like this; now, however, my thoughts got confused, and I kept getting more feverish.

"You feel as if something malicious and evil is gathering about you, something you cannot explain or even decently name. You feel some kind of threat around you? A dreadful danger?"

"Yes."

"You've decided to find out for yourself what it is?"

"Yes. I'm trying."

"Strange characters keep getting underfoot more and more frequently? You want to investigate them, but you no longer know yourself if you're shadowing them, or if they're shadowing you?"

"Yes. I need help."

"Help? Help? There is no help. Don't go there, Vytie. Don't go there!"

"Do you know the way?" My voice trembled, I shook all over, I wanted to be quiet, but I spoke all the same. "Do you know where it leads?"

"Help?" Father gave a hoarse laugh; his voice no longer asked, but angrily asserted something. "As a child you weren't afraid of either the light or the dark; the worst thing for you was the dusk, the dimness."

"Yes."

"You liked to hide in the dark: in basements, in burrows, so no one would see you. You felt safe there."

"Yes. Vilnius's underground was my childhood paradise."

"People were disgusting and dangerous, they didn't at all act the way they should. This was truly horrible to you . . . You felt they were controlled by something evil."

"Yes. Probably yes."

"You fought off these thoughts, these sensations, but they persecuted you."

141

"Yes."

"You didn't want to curse every living soul, you didn't want to blame them. You understood that they were merely victims, that the cause was hidden somewhere else, on the outside."

"Yes. Yes!"

"Body deformations? The strangest degradations?"

"Yes! Yes!"

"Your friend transformed from the incarnation of wisdom into a dribbling idiot? A person close to you, sunk into an inconceivable swamp and trying to drag you along?"

"Yes! Yes! Yes!"

I screamed at the top of my voice, and father fell silent. Sweat poured down my face and chest; I felt as if I had been beaten, all my bones ached. Every one of father's questions multiplied the confusion. Earlier I could still doubt, I could blame my own excessive sensitivity, or chance, or coincidence. I could contrive a defensive wall of rational arguments. Now that wall crumbled and cracked—and I crumbled and cracked myself.

"It's not true, Vyt. You're imagining things," father suddenly spoke exceedingly softly. "It's not true. It's a lie, Vyt. Come to your senses, look around. People are people, faces are faces . . . Everything's all right . . . Everything's all right, it's okay . . . Look around—is anyone else raving the way you do? Come to your senses, Vyt . . ."

"You're lying," I hissed, "Why are you lying?"

He suddenly stood up and hung over me with his entire body, as if he wanted to crush me. He stuck his face, with its hot breath, right in front of my eyes. He looked at me with anger and despair. I still hoped for his help, and he looked at me *like at a condemned man*. I remember his eyes well. Inevitability has eyes like that.

"You don't even suspect what kind of hell you've opened the door to," he spoke quietly, swaying to the sides. "To a hell without flames, without the hot tar, the very worst hell of all: quiet, indifferent, senseless, where the victims are satisfied with their murderers . . ."

Suddenly darkness fell upon me. I heard a quiet rustle and felt a soft breeze on my cheek. By the time I collected myself, both the rustling and the draft were gone. I was left alone in complete darkness. Crazed, I sprang towards the now silent rustling, began groping about and banging on the wall with my fist. I was obliged to catch up with him right away, to recover my father. I had to hug him, to kiss him, to say everything I hadn't said. I didn't want to save myself, not myself at all—I wanted to save father. I didn't have the time to tell him I'm still strong. I could protect and defend him. The two of us could take on the entire world—me and my father. Why, we're Vargalyses! We must fight together—after all, we're branches of the same tree. I banged on the wall harder and harder, it seemed I even screamed aloud, "Give me back my father! Bring back my father!" I couldn't even imagine I would never see him again.

The walls didn't answer; I realized I still needed to get out of there. The way back was a live labyrinth. I slunk past repeating rooms, corridors, stairs, and covered balconies; I should have exited somewhere long before, but still there was no end. I kept returning to the same intersection of corridors, the same inner courtyards. Like it or not, I remembered the labyrinth of Babylon, whose center could be reached only by always turning to the left. But I didn't need the center of the labyrinth, I was afraid of it. I needed either an exit, or father. It seemed to me that *I felt* father somewhere close by; that sensation sometimes grew weaker—I would turn somewhere else, and the sensation would grow stronger again. I wandered around as if I were playing "warmer, colder": it was warm, then it was colder, warm again, warm, still warmer, and then it kept getting colder. It would seem father was right there, on the other side of the wall, but I wouldn't find a door in the wall. And if I did come across a door, beyond it I would see new stairs, new corridors, and new covered balconies. I wandered without sensing time or space; I came to only when my feet began to hurt. Who knows how many kilometers I had walked. I stood in a dead-end corridor; doors leaned on both sides. I opened the nearest one on the right, beyond it ranged rooms crammed full of broken furniture. A vague presentiment told me there was a constant twilight here both day and night—as if that broken furniture devoured the light during the day and vomited it back out during the night. Standing there, my legs slowly sank into the rotten floorboards. It seemed something alive was holding me by the ankles. That corridor didn't want to let go of me. For the first time it occurred to me that perhaps there was *no way out* of here. I rushed into a low gallery, ran out into yet another corridor, threw open all the doors in turn. It was the same everywhere: rooms stuffed full of broken furniture. That furniture looked like slaughtered people. An occasional door was locked, but I had neither the desire nor the strength to break them down. All I felt was the primitive fear of an animal trapped by pursuers. I tore up and down staircases and jumped over balcony rails onto the pavement of deep little courtyards. By now I heard the voices of the unseen pursuers surrounding me. I plunged through a creaking door and unexpectedly stumbled into someone's living quarters. There were beds along the walls and an idiotic little carpet with swans hung on the wall. I was particularly reassured by a night pot with a handle set alongside a child's bed. That was surely an object of this world. The awakened children's dirty little faces stared at me with big eyes. A naked woman with pendulous breasts stood upright in the middle of the room, not even thinking of covering herself. Right next to me, a tiny little girl with scrawny little braids turned over on her side in bed and in her sleep clearly said: "Please ring three times." Finally I saw a window; beyond it shone a completely normal, ordinary, dear, beloved street light. I leapt forward and half-dropped, half-fell down to the pavement. The window was rather high up, well above my head. I saw the woman, her breasts hung out in the street, close the window, unaccompanied by the slightest screaming or astonishment.

I was standing in a side street right next to the Narutis. Still not fully recovered, I was horrified to notice two figures leaning against the wall. They were loitering there in terribly evil, terribly dangerous poses. But at last the cool air revived me, and I realized that I was as safe as safe could be in the damp Vilnius night. The two men, concentrating intensely but staggering anyway, diligently relieved themselves against the wall.

"I'm a Lithuanian, and you're a Lithuanian," one of them slowly expounded. "We're both Lithuanian."

"Yeah!" the second nodded, actually smacking his head against the crumbling bricks of the wall.

"We won't give up Lithuania to any shitty Russkies!"

"Yeah! Give it to 'em in the nose, the rats!"

"Let's kiss, brother," the first one shook off the last drops and tried to hug his companion. His kisses were wet and slimy, like the damp-drenched pavement of the side street.

"You're a Lithuanian?"

"Yeah!"

"And I'm a Lithuanian. We're both Lithuanians."

"Lithuania is the land of heroes!" the second loudly declared. "Yeah!"

The two of them staggered towards the street, while I continued to think about father. Exhausted by the oppressive air of the corridors, the stale side street felt like a mountain resort. I almost felt good. From down the street an inharmonious duet drifted:

> Ride Lithu-uanians, up the castle hill,
> Ride Lithu-uanians, up the castle hill,
> Ri-i-ide on, ri-i-ide on, Lith-thu-uanians
> Car-r-ry on, car-r-ry on, wreaths of glory! . . .

The library bookcases are grim and monotonous (for some reason I'm walking through the library again), like the secret corridors of the Narutis quarter. And the dimness is exactly the same. I walk aimlessly; the bookcases slowly slink by. It seems it's a desert, a boundless desert of frozen thoughts and metaphors. Here, between the identical rows of books, I immediately remember the labyrinth of rooms cluttered with broken furniture. Earlier I had even hoped to come across father here, quietly dawdling around the corner, inhaling on a cigarette that's hidden between his fingers. Now I don't expect anything anymore, although the books charm me anyway. No, they didn't provide me with clear answers. But they helped me grasp a great deal. I came across many of *Their* attributes in books first, and only afterwards in the real world. Books protect me from aimless wandering, from hasty conclusions. There was a time when I thought *They* existed only here: in Vilnius, in Lithuania, in Russia. I didn't have the strength to think about everyone, about the entire world. A study of history dispelled this fallacy. In the twentieth century alone *Their* activities mark Italy and Germany, China and Cambodia (*They* have long been fond of China in general). And then there's Spain in the Middle Ages, where *They* ruled for entire centuries! It's enough to remember Charles the Bewitched, the impotent dwarf: when he was dissected they discovered that he had a heart the size of a child's fist, rotten intestines, and one black testicle. I came across incontrovertible evidence that Torquemada, the

Grand Inquisitor, a christened Jew who burned Jews at the stake with the greatest enthusiasm, was *Their* commissar.

Alas, *They* are everywhere, in every country, in every system. *They* are and were in every epoch—sometimes they were in control, more often they hid, but they always waited for their chance. My head spins from all the data about kanuked people, nations, and even civilizations. In the encyclopedia of the kanuked, the Roman Empire would nestle next to Plato, the first of *Their* world commissars. The kanukas of kanukai, Stalin, would end up in the encyclopedia next to the ruin of the Mayan civilization. Alas, even entire civilizations are kanuked, the same way people are. To this day scholars haven't managed to properly explain why all the old civilizations, without exception, came to ruin, or what laws of death govern them. After all, they don't die biologically, the way people do. Where did Greece and Egypt's power and wisdom disappear to, even though Greece and Egypt still exist? Where are the ancient Chinese, Mayans, or Aztecs? Researchers seize on any and all arguments, even co-opting space aliens, but *They* don't raise the slightest red flag. *They*, only *They*, are to blame! What other evidence do you need? Scholarly conjectures sometimes drive me into a rage. It's known that a civilization died over the lifespan of several generations, that it encountered no epidemics or cataclysms. And they vaguely babble on about some social reasons or who knows what else. How can they be so blind? It's always *Their* pupil-less eyes peering out of the ruins of a civilization. No, *They* don't control nature's powers or kingdoms, however, they manage to destroy what matters most—people's spirit. *They* penetrate into *every* person's brain, and then calmly retreat. Nothing more needs to be done. The kanuked destroy themselves.

But it isn't the study of individual nations that matters most to me, I'm most interested in the activities of individual people who have gone down The Way. It's not an idle curiosity or a desire to delve into strangers' fates. Oh, if only I could restrain my distant, secret friends, if only I could guard them from destruction! Alas, they are distant not just in space, but in time too. But their fatal mistakes are actually warnings of incalculable value. I can avoid those mistakes. It's not for me to die in a car crash like Camus (like Gedis). It's not for me to be stuffed into prison, like Jean Genet, or guillotined, like de Sade (the poor revolutionary Marquis—they made him into nothing more than a symbol of sexual deviation). Better to balance on the edge of the abyss, as Ortega y Gasset does, practically the only one in modern times who dares to survey *Their* methods. (Deception is possible here too: *They* could have purposely cracked the cover open a bit, calculating that reasoning about the revolt of the kanuked masses is useful to *Them*. On the other hand, Ortega duped them anyway: he showed how art has been stolen from the Western world—that's one of *Their* biggest achievements.) Alas, those who have protected themselves, like Ortega, are few, wretchedly few. Rummaging about in the lives of like-minded thinkers, I risk turning into a necrophiliac: there's so many corpses, madmen, and suicides there. Even Nietzsche, the divine, poetic Nietzsche! A man who dared to publicly declare that sooner or later we'll succeed in triumphing over *Them*, in healing kanuked man and in cultivating a true, inspired, *Übermensch* who doesn't submit to *Them*. It's awful to even remember Nietzsche's lot. In life he was destroyed, forced into insanity and suicide, deceived and misrepresented. But even that wasn't enough. *They don't leave even the dead in peace.* Their Satanic calculations are horrifying: Nietzsche's music of the heavenly spheres, his divine poetry, was handed over to one of the worst maniacs of the twentieth century. The dream of an unkanuked man, in the hands of the Great Kanukas, turned into butchery and labor camps. Is it possible to think up a worse method of discrediting someone? Millions of people, hearing Nietzsche's name, involuntarily remember Hitler and the Nazis. Yes, it isn't just that books give me support—at the same time they destroy me by degrees, and constantly deepen my despair. On some level it begins to seem we'll never succeed in penetrating *Their* secrets, much less in surmounting *Them*. I know only one thing for sure: whatever you do, you must always leave an escape route open. You can never burn all of your bridges. One of *Their* key pathological methods is to drive a person (or even an entire nation) into a real or imaginary situation with no escape route, so all that remains is a single, unguarded step straight into *Their* prepared trap. Convincing a person it's the *only* way is of utmost importance. It's the only way to reach the height of kanukism, to reach *Their* paramount sphere of prowess: a man accepting slavery as if it were a stroke of luck—a *self-satisfied* slave. (Once, well in his cups, our zone boss condescended to chat with us, the "incorrigibles"; he told us that in the mountains, twenty kilometers away, there was some sort of tunnel being dug, that people were digging it without a roof over their heads, practically without food, and without warm clothes.

"A tunnel's easy to guard," I observed. "Cover the opening with barbed wire, tie a couple of man-eating dogs to it—and that would do it."

"My boy," the zone boss edifyingly pronounced, "Wake up. There's no wire, no dogs, no guards. Why waste money if you can get by without spending anything? Those idiot Communist Youth are digging the tunnel. They are looked after and guarded by their own idiotic enthusiasm.")

Stalin's ultimatum to Lithuania is a classic example of *Their* pathologic: either Lithuania will let the Soviet Army divisions in to guard the Soviet Army divisions that are already in Lithuania, or the Soviet Army divisions will march into Lithuania without Lithuania's compliance. Total freedom to pick whatever your heart desires. The implied alternative—forceful resistance—circumspectly annihilated: the leader of Lithuania's army has long since been bought off. Lithuania was ruined when it let the first five Russian soldiers in, when Vilnius, thanks to the generous father of the people, Stalin, rode into Lithuania like a giant Trojan horse.

Vilnius, it's Vilnius again!

Bookcases; there are bookcases around me again. Breathing in the heavy dust of the books, I occasionally turn around and throw a word to Gedis over my shoulder. I feel a burning weakness when I realize once again that he is no more. The loss is irreparable. All losses are irreparable. I had a mother, but I no longer have her. I had a father—he showed up and disappeared again. I had a beloved wife—*They* snatched her for themselves. I had a friend—*They* killed him. What will *They* do to Lolita?

Gedis revealed the structure of the library to me (the structure of all libraries). Stumbling into a sea of millions of books, I nearly went mad with joy; I just tried to keep from drowning. I devoured as many as I could get my hands on. I didn't pay the least attention to the remote little rooms where dour figures with grown-together eyebrows sat. Gedis looked right at them. It was only at his urging that I realized for the first time what a *special collection* is. Of course I knew there are sections like that in libraries. But in my imagination a special collection was a small chamber hiding the couple hundred tomes that are taboo for a Soviet man. Oh, divine naïveté! . . . Our most extreme fantasies, our most horrifying theories, fade to insignificance when compared to *Their* reality; they turn out to be no more than the naïve babbling of babies. Gedis laughed out loud when he heard about my several-hundred-volume special collection. Actually, there isn't a single book in it, just a closed catalog, which is inaccessible to ordinary mortals. The size of the catalog shocked me. Hundred of thousands of books are buried there. God knows I shuddered in horror when I learned what portion of the world is hidden from us. Probably the best, the most important part. It's an extraordinary mockery that those books are floating in the common sea of books, but are nevertheless unattainable. Even without ever having been in a library collection it's not difficult to understand that among a million books you'd never find what you wanted without a catalog, without some coordinates. It's impossible. Those books are right there, but for us they don't exist. I discovered that there is also a special special collection with a separate catalog; those who aren't among the chosen aren't allowed to even come close to it. I was no longer surprised when I found out from the old-timers (I'll never forget their frightened whispers) that there is a special special special collection too: books piled in the basement, bricked in like a nuclear shelter, with hermetically sealed metal doors. Books that *almost* no one can access. I'd had enough already, but Gedis just smiled wryly. He calmly declared that there should also be a box made of a special titanium alloy, the special special special special collection. That box is impossible to open; it's impossible to even blow it up. Inside are hidden books that *no one at all* is allowed to read, or even to see.

Gedis always amazed me. I never understood (and I still don't understand), where a scrupulous kid from a Lithuanian village got his strange inclinations. I wasn't surprised that he defended his first dissertation in mathematics at twenty-five, and his second at thirty: a talent in mathematics doesn't depend on your place of birth. But how could he, still plowing fields at sixteen, manage to crack philosophical systems like nuts, recite page after page of Proust in French and Joyce in English? When did he have the time to learn and come to love all that? After all, he grew up where many see only patriarchal values, wells with sweeps, pure Lithuanian maidens with golden braids, folk wisdom, and other pseudo-folk concoctions. From what good fairy did Gedis get a soul of the highest order, a subtle taste, and a boundless predilection for novelty, what instilled in him a longing for the distant islands of the soul, a hunger to take in everything? What force, what gods ordered him to play jazz and just jazz? You'd naturally assume, provincial of provincials that he was, that he wouldn't even have known that somewhere in the wide world such a thing as jazz existed.

All of us Lithuanians, up against free Europeans or Americans, feel the way blacks do about whites: we envy them and we hate them, we have very well-founded accusations against them and we feel we're in the right, but at the same time we can never get rid of our inferiority complex. Gedis didn't have the slightest complex. Presenting a paper at some mathematical congress in Paris, he'd spend every free moment at the Louvre, in jazz clubs, or heaven knows where else. He drank coffee with Sartre, argued about painting with Picasso, and played a jam session with Coltrane. He didn't have an ounce of snobbery; even I would learn about his exploits accidentally, sometimes from him ("when I played with Trane, for some reason I got the urge to play this idiotic trill . . . like this . . ."), but most often from others—they would tell me about it with their eyes popping out in envy and amazement. I only learned how respected he was as a mathematician from the letters of condolence. It seemed every other topologist in the world, all the universities and academies, sadly brushed away a tear, knowing that without Gedis, topology would never be the same as it had been before him (that's what Professor Edwards wrote from Oxford). Even the mystic Grothendieck, for the first time in several years, awoke from his self-imposed exile in Tibet and wrote with a thin little brush in red ink: "By now I have forgotten what mathematics is, but I will always remember who Gediminas was. The Grand Duke of Lithuania." I was friends with Gediminas for ten years, and, from the way he talked, I thought he was merely one of a hundred thousand ordinary servants of mathematics. There is probably nothing more beautiful than a great person who doesn't value his greatness.

I remember many of his monologues, but best of all I remember how he played. Gedis's music wove itself into one great ALL, it even seems to me that it reinforces and supports the unity of that ALL most. When he was playing, I'd suddenly get the feeling Gedis had already lived in this world more than once, that there were Aristotles and Platos, Confuciuses and Lao-Dzes lying hidden inside him for ages already; he didn't need to study them—all he had to do was remember. He plays Shakespeare and Saint Augustine, resonates with Hume and Eliot's *The Wasteland*, Moore's sculptures, and Rauschenberg's broad compositions. And he doesn't play, Lord save us, what's already written, carved in stone or painted. Gedis plays *pure music*. He plays that which others leave *between* the words, the lines and the colors; what others aren't able to express. He plays scents, dreams, and illusions all the time. Once he organized a concert for me alone, a concert overflowing with horror, which, Lord knows, I'd think I'd dreamed up if there weren't live witnesses walking around. I know now that he already had some idea of *Them* at the time; a presentiment of *Their* intentions bid him answer quickly by way of his music. Up until then, Gediminas would only occasionally sit in with newly forming quartets in Vilnius. He would blend in instantly to any style, but it wasn't that he just joined in; rather he immediately raised the quality of the entire ensemble. He had an inborn talent for persuasion and teaching—without any imperiousness or force. The young jazz players of Vilnius unanimously confirmed that during the course of several hours, without saying a word, he would explain so much about jazz, improvisation, and music in general that, according to one violinist, "you start hearing the violin of God, even though you know very well that God surely never plays the violin." When Gedis announced he was organizing an ensemble, all of the invited came running headlong, throwing other work aside, even though he warned them that after all the trouble they would give only one concert. The jazzmen were determined to carry him on their shoulders, together with the grand piano, to wherever he wanted. Incidentally, that's just what happened. Gedis categorically demanded the concert be held in an abandoned church. At first it seemed to me the caprice of a madman: they needed to temporarily steal a concert grand and cart it off who knows where. Once more I witnessed how much influence Gediminas Riauba had over people; his colleagues accepted this whim without blinking an eye. The concert was entirely underground: no posters, no tickets, no invitations. They had to break into the church illegally, quietly breaking down the door. All of the participants felt like conspirators; it seemed to me that, despite themselves, they feared that uniformed officials would crudely interrupt the music at the crucial moment. Excited by these surreptitious preparations, I was hardly surprised to find out that Gediminas had selected *my* church. The little wine factory had long since closed down; the church was left completely forsaken—it seemed even the exterior was covered in cobwebs. I was calm; I got nervous only on the evening of the concert, walking up the stone-paved street and smelling the oppressive smell of garbage wine. It seemed I was stepping into my own past, full of secret dangers.

The inside of the church was virtually unchanged: the same dirty walls, painted-over frescoes, broken benches, and unimaginably grubby floor. Gedis didn't allow anything to be tidied. He invited only me, but apparently didn't forbid the others from inviting people. The church was practically crammed to the gills; everyone sat wherever they could: on dirty boxes, bags of fiberglass, rotten benches. Some thoughtfully brought folding chairs along. An eerie silence reigned; a couple of lively girls who tried to chatter and giggle instantly quieted down. You really had no inclination to raise a racket. A dusty dimness hung over the church; it was somber, harsh, and depressing. Every cough was echoed by gloomy rumbles in the vaults. The grand piano stood right below the altar; big drums and little drums, boxes, pots of all sizes, sticks and rods were stacked around it. Wooden bells had been assembled and gongs set up. All of it stood against a backdrop of crumbling walls, debris, broken parts of some sort, and ruined holy sculptures. Gedis had picked an ideal spot: sitting there, beholding that grimace of chaos, you automatically expected something even more morose. At last, Gedis sat down at the piano and announced in a tired, detached voice:

"This evening I play for my friend Vytautas. We'll play one thing. It's called 'Vilnius Poker'."

*Now* I sit cowering in the middle of the church of garbage and wine, *now* I hear the first chords, they aim straight at the heart, still quivering from the strange name. For the time being, Gedis plays alone, testing himself and me, his hands and my ears. I still don't know what he wants, I still don't hear the sharp rhythmic blows, even though a lame drummer, with the pained face of a jester, stands at the foot of the altar, by now he's selecting drumsticks, by now he's striking the tightened hide of the drum, he widens his eyes and turns his pupils to the sky, flashing the whites, waving the drumsticks right by Gedis's head, thundering a

152

dozen rhythms together, while Gedis flings me an inexplicable warning, his hands run up and down like crazy, the alto roars angrily, and Gedis distorts the melody, escapes through modal improvisation, through the *free*, he's flying into the realm of pure spirit, weaving a vision, and I suddenly feel *the first gaze*: only Gedis can create an illusion of such strength; the music itself is looking at me, it's staring sullenly, with the stare of my childhood years, with the enervating stare of Vilnius's streets; this music is truly meant for me, it looks, pries, stares, and leers at me, but not just at me—the others' faces also darken and contort, some of them look around in fright, but quickly stiffen and hang their heads: they have deadened and faded, the way their lives fade and die, but the music does not cease, the bassist is furiously driving nails straight into my temples, now three are playing, now four, now five, the alto saxophonist and a stout girl are shrieking, they scream over one another, the two of them are grappling in all seriousness, apparently they must fight, I look at them, I hear them: this isn't music anymore; they are fighting for real, a fight to the death that never ends, that no one wins and everyone loses: two or three whack the little drums, the big drums, the pots, it's a real rattling racket; I follow Gedis's hands, I don't hear the melody so much as I guess it, it's the nonbeing melody of our nonbeing lives: Gedis is dreaming now; a thunderous, raging dream, vague echoing towers (perhaps Čiurlionis?), confusing corridors, bookcases, plank beds, barracks, eyes of horror looking out from everywhere; cold spreads through my chest because it's the void, it's nonexistence looking at me, my fear looks at me, my past, the barbed wire of the camp, it's naked Bolius gobbling down grass, he keeps gobbling it down, again and again he gobbles—grass, grass, grass, Gedis stubbornly repeats the same phrase over and over, there's a mass of musicians beneath the altar by now, they all shriek, scream, wail, it's a wail over a human being (Bolius? My father? My grandfather?); they wail so loudly because they can no longer do anything else, the music grows, seizes the entire space, it wants to drown out the world, it won't let you think of anything, it imperiously stops time: everything takes only a second, an endless, timeless second, a second of penetration—I calm myself, I convince myself it's just music, it's just a concert, but the faces around me grow darker still, the debris under my feet trembles and rises from the floor, visions and dreams explode inside me, they glitter horribly with fragments of evil, I won't let them, I won't, I don't want to remember anything, it's a vision of death, it's a dream of death, I won't let them, I won't—but they don't listen, they, the musicians, they aren't listening to anything anymore, they've caught us all in a trap; the vaults send back horrible sounds in different echoes, they're playing a new phrase, but the vaults keep repeating the old—I concentrate, I concentrate even more, this is a nothing more than a concert, there they are: Gedis is practically poking the keyboard with his nose, the drummer tires and falls silent; at last, they let me catch my breath a bit, the saxophonists look at one another and converse gracefully in heavy, damp notes, I almost hear the melody again (some kind of blues?), the music shoves and thrusts itself inside of me, takes my breath away, it's sad, terribly, terribly sad, I've lost something and I'll never get it back, I'll never be the same as I was, the saxophonists still sling lazy, indulgent notes, slower, still slower—that's not allowed, that's impossible, the music chokes and suffocates, the notes stumble over one another, save, save the music! Now Gedis is playing solitude, a sodden, slow Vilnius solitude, he plays so sadly, softly, sadly, almost Chopin, but the others don't want to allow it; after an instant of rest, they join in again, the sounds push, squabble, shove their way in out of turn, the vaults send them back, the dirty walls, the ravaged stained-glass windows resonate, the fragments of chaos on the floor tremble and jump about, the church itself is playing—that's what's I find so horrible: if they rouse the church of garbage wine, it could play music that would drive us all insane, that's mortally dangerous, but they don't pay attention to anything, they play louder and louder still, all of them at the same time, the dusty dimness howls, all of my bones resonate—if you'd cover your ears, you'd hear with all of your body, every pore of your skin, your eyes and the tips of your fingers; they're determined to break down all the doors, knock down all the walls, to show the nightmare that solitude turns into: it's impossible to play any louder, but they keep getting louder, louder, and louder, in accord like a single instrument; Gedis truly has taught them miracles: the unified, constantly growing sound slowly pushes everything aside, it pushes me out of myself, it sucks out my blood, it extracts my brains (is this what Gedis was after?), I recognize Vilnius's oppressive, destructive power, it appears you can *play* it, but it's dangerous: the menace is strangling, a universal menace, around me I see frightened faces distorted by pain, apparently by now they're sorry they came here, while those others keep getting louder, even though there's no way they can, the lame jester bashes pots on the floor, splinters scatter to the sides (perhaps that's how our dreams shatter, our love, our spirit?), sweat pours down Gedis's face (they keep getting louder, still louder!), the thunder destroys me, I'm losing my mind because it's impossible to run from it, it's everywhere, like Vilnius itself, I start to turn into something else: an imbecile, a naked crawling Bolius, a bat, a cockroach, while insane Gediminas angrily rips away all the covers, tears the skin off me, there are maws everywhere about, devouring the light and happiness, devouring the world, devouring people alive, me first of all, and then all who have gathered here, before I come undone I grin with bloody fangs, I beat repulsive wings, I must stop them, shut them up, break their instruments, but I can't budge: the sounds have collapsed on me, overpowered me, pressed me to the floor, they can't go on anymore either, they ooze sweat and tears, they're wracked by spasms, they've lost sight of the world, the theme, harmony, everything—this cannot go on forever, they no longer have the strength, but Gedis suddenly grows a third hand, it plays that which no person with two hands could ever play: my pain and the despair of Vilnius, and Lithuania's ruin, and my endless waiting, and the barbs poking out of Their eyes, and the ruins of a soul, and that which I know has not yet been, but inevitably will be, and love, and even Lolita, whom I have not laid eyes on yet. Gedis has stretched himself out on the sacrificial altar, he's playing the real secret about the stares, about the stumpy phallus of Vilnius, about dangers, dangers, I'm probably weeping, because I've understood: I have to save everyone—from the stares, from doom, from the cockroaches (there they run between Gedis's fingers: a mass of hoarse, unharmonious notes): Gedis has played it, he has shown how the soul vanishes, how it is no more—only screeches, screams, insanity, soulless ecstasy, chaos remain—that's how Gedis imagines the eternal poker game of Vilnius. The two singers are no longer screeching—they're roaring, one can't stand it, she's unbuttoned her blouse to the waist, the alto has crammed two saxophones and a clarinet into his mouth, the veins in his temples will burst at any moment, the jester is no longer of this earth, he jerks about as if he has St. Vitus's dance, the bassist's hand has cramped, he's fallen out of the general fury, dazed, he looks around, while Gedis, that insane demiurge, rises from the keyboard, snatches at the piano strings and listens intently. *He still hears everything, every note; he's doing everything deliberately.* The others have probably gone deaf, because the sound has reached its culmination, neither the instruments nor the voices can bear more, neither the ears nor the church's walls can stand more. Wherever he swims to—there's nowhere to swim to, as far as the eyes can see there is no solid ground—save him, save him, he'll drown!

And suddenly Gedis straightens up, lowers his arms and freezes like a statue. That very instant everyone goes quiet, at that very moment, all at the same time—that's impossible, it's unnatural. It seems as if Gedis unplugged them. They wander off quietly, as if they had never stood there, as if that nightmare never happened, as if nothing at all ever happened. Not a single person remains below the altar, only scattered instruments, debris, and silence, in which the ears ring sharply. My hands are shaking, I'm short of breath, my heart splutters like a failing pump; it's not driving blood into my temples—it's driving lead. It's horrible, glum and depressing: I want to cry like a little child, because there is no hope and never will be. Gedis sensed that first and mercilessly convinced me of it. That wasn't music anymore, or at least not only music—that was a séance of black magic, an eye-opening ritual, a moment of truth, the Spanish *momento de verdad*.

I had already dreamed this music; I knew Gedis well. It was somewhat easier for me. That hideous, inhuman world crashed upon the others without any warning. I understood why Gedis didn't want to invite anyone. He was merciful; he knew what the consequences could be. Now there was a crowd of dead people sitting in the church. With his music Gedis turned them into what they already really were. The distorted, darkened faces didn't move; everyone's eyes were like glass. They all sat transfixed. They were sitting too long; I panicked momentarily, when I thought of what would happen if we had to *revive* them. After all, Gedis surely wasn't going to play lively wake-up music.

The seconds passed by mercilessly; they were all done for by now. A petite brown-haired girl saved them. She suddenly thrashed like a captured bird and cried out. That was a sign that it was still possible to live. As long as a person is able to cry, he still exists. All of them slowly came to, quietly stood up, and immediately started dispersing.

No one applauded, everyone was dying to get out of there as quickly as possible: not a one of the thoughtful ones took their folding chairs along. Many staggered as if they were stunned; some were led by the hand by their neighbors.

"What kind of poker is this!" a sad, bent-shouldered young man next to me muttered, "It's the nuclear explosion of Vilnius. We've all gotten a dose of radiation. Our hair and teeth will fall out."

"The insanity of Vilnius!" his girl answered fearfully.

Only then did I look at the musicians. They were alive, but incredibly worn out. They glanced at one another with stunned gazes; apparently they couldn't believe they had really played all that. Gedis was sitting in a side nave, naked to the waist, having thrown his sweat-drenched shirt aside. I wanted to tell him everything at once, I wanted to fall down on my knees in front of him; I was overflowing with despair and lament, but not a word would come out of my mouth. I could no longer return to the ordinary, normal world, but, like always, Gedis rescued me. He had understood long ago that music is just music, and people are just people. He shrugged his shoulders and muttered in an brusque voice:

"It's not my fault. They're just not used to it. Besides, I didn't invite them."

Alongside Gedis, leaning on the wall, sat the pale lame drummer, a bit further away the bassist Tonis was massaging his colleague's hand.

"I told them!" he grumbled angrily. "I warned them! Just be happy everyone's alive."

They looked as if they had just been rescued from a sinking ship. The saxophonist, filthy and covered with cobwebs, climbed down from the altar like a ghost and stared straight at me with the gaze of a madman. The singer, wrapped in the flaps of her blouse, staggered over from somewhere and looked everyone over with watery eyes:

"I can't find the buttons. Maybe someone has a needle and thread?"

"Just imagine, despite the entire forty-three minutes, one person, at the very least, didn't get it," complained Gedis in a dead voice. "This tousled guy came up to me and very politely asked what it was I wanted to *say* by it."

"What a Herod!" muttered Tonis, lighting a cigarette. "You practically finish off eight people, just to say a few unspeakable words to your friend. And for God's sake, explain why on earth you needed a title."

"There wasn't any title," Gedis answered. "It came into my head after I had already opened my mouth. I shouldn't have said anything at all. But no one is safe from stupidity."

"I broke my saxophone," the alto player complained, carefully picking the cobwebs off his jacket. "I was almost . . . almost climbing out of that hellhole already . . . but suddenly someone grabbed me by my coattails and pulled me back . . . and I couldn't play a single intelligent note anymore . . . nothing but holes around me, and no notes . . . horrors . . ."

"Let's get out of here," Gedis suddenly jumped up. "You can't hear this. If you've listened to the music, you can't hear how it was *done*. They'll recover in a minute and one after the other start sharing their impressions. Come on! We'll go out into the street, and then we'll walk and walk, right up to the river."

The old street had a difficult time penetrating the fog. Fall leaves rolled underfoot—fragments of Gedis's vision. No one was ever as close to me as Gedis was that night. I had no idea what I should do: console him or console myself, tell him about the camp, about the people with no brains, or ask him something. I couldn't remain silent, but I didn't know what to say. Any words seemed meager compared to the scream welling up inside me. I was no longer alone; I felt that Gedis would always be next to me. Our closeness was real: people aren't united by common victories or joys—only a common loss, a common despair, can unite them.

"You're really not sorry for them?" I asked.

"Which ones? Those who played, or those who listened?"

"All of them."

"I'm not sorry," Gedis answered without wavering. "To waken someone isn't a crime, it's a service."

That was all he said about his playing. The two of us went down the street (I will walk here with Lolita), smoking cigarette after cigarette (Lolita will tell me about her mother and innocence manias).

"An abandoned church!" Gedis finally spoke. "A true metaphor. The place where a dead God is laid to rest. Not Christ, of course, and not the bearded Sabaoth with the holy doves under his arm. The dead God of Lithuania. Every Lithuanian should go to an abandoned, desecrated church on a daily basis. After all, it's a reflection of our spirit:

the remains of former majesty, along with trash, debris, dust. We need to see every day that all of our gods are dead. So that even in complete despair we won't have anywhere to turn. After all, we stopped believing in anything a long time ago. Only idiots can believe in the Kremlin these days; fanatics—in Christ; paranoids who consider the current state of affairs desirable—in the spirit of the Lithuanian people. Only fools, unfortunately, believe in the power of intellect. We're not even destined to believe in the power of money, because our money is shit. You won't buy yourself anything with it—not even freedom . . . Maybe some Englishman or Frenchman doesn't believe in anything, either, but that's something totally different . . . Other enslaved peoples at least believe in their liberation, Lithuanians stopped believing in anything a long time ago. Not even in that absolute lack of belief of theirs. They don't even know how to be genuine cynics. Lithuania is a void, stuffed with rotting memories . . . there's nothing, nothing, nothing left—only the language. But a language can't be an object of faith. A thousand intelligent men all over the world analyze the Lithuanian language because it's incredibly interesting, practically unique. But who analyzes Lithuanians? It'd be better if one of those thousand analyzed Lithuanian's spiritual history, all that drivel, that nameless heartache and hopeless, grotesque attempts at *living*. I swear—they'd understand where humanity has been and where it's going! . . . Oh! I don't know what to do. Shoot at the political commentators on the TV screen? Listen, Vyt, let's start our own sect, huh? The soul searchers' sect. For sermons we'll read music or mathematical formulas. And you'll tell stories about the camp, about your father and grandfather . . . And when everyone asks what's our purpose, what our sect is after, where is it leading to, we'll answer: look, listen, smell—we've already told you everything; played it, wrote it, drew it. All that's left is for you to feel and understand it . . . and believe . . ."

And not a word about "Vilnius Poker." Gedis talked about this and that, gathered pebbles from the wet paths and slung them into invisible tree trunks, whistled unfamiliar melodies. It seemed he was secretly distancing himself from me, slamming shut the door that had just now been open, closing the shades, shutting the windows. I didn't know how to hold him back, which of his hands to grab, except for that third one, which was probably no longer there. The two of us finally reached the river, descended the steps, and stopped right next to the dark stream. It had been soaked in rain for some time; the water had risen up to the very bank. Gedis squatted and dipped his hand into the muddy current.

"The river! The Neris!" he muttered, shaking invisible drops from his hand, "Why not Joyce's riverrun? How is the Neris less than the Liffey? Why doesn't anyone immortalize it as the current of dreams and oblivion? When you think 'river,' you immediately remember the Lethe and the Liffey . . . Dublin and the Liffey have been forever impressed onto the world's brains, and old man Joyce sits in the heavens and jeers . . . What's the Liffey without him—a muddy stream, and nothing more. I saw it myself . . . But where's the Neris? Where's Vilnius? Why doesn't the world know anything about them?"

And not a word about his concert. Probably Gedis should have played quite a bit longer, so that there would be no words left in him at all. Suddenly I felt like I wanted to swim to the other, invisible bank of the river—as if the world would be different there, as if Vilnius would be altogether different.

"A smashed-up boat full of water should bob on the bank. Forgotten by everyone—no one wants to swim across the current to the other side." Gedis again nervously lit up a cigarette. "Have you noticed that Lithuanians have always feared and avoided water? Or more precisely, moving water: currents, rapids, ocean waves. The vital power of water horrifies them. They like *standing* water: Lithuanians like little lakes and swamps. Particularly swamps: the greatest victories in war were won thanks to swamps. Swamps are rotting, murky water. It's the mythological tragedy of the nation. They couldn't step past an unspeakable inner taboo, couldn't overcome themselves . . . Anything but a current, anything but ocean waves! What a weird horror: the Lithuanians lived on the seashore for ages upon ages and never got the urge to sail to foreign countries, to find something completely unknown, or even to dream of other shores. They only fished along the coast. Even Lithuania's head was cut off by the current of the Nemunas. Always that mythological power of moving water . . . the nation cut off its own head. Yes, yes, every country has a head, a trunk, arms and legs—like a Dogon house. The current of the Nemunas cut off Prussia and the Prussians from us. And that's exactly where Lithuania's head and brains were: its religion and shrines, the height of its culture and the rudiments of philosophy. It was all there. Even the ground itself is magical there: the Germans murdered or assimilated the Prussians, but they specifically drew the power for their state from Prussia . . . Lithuanian culture came from there even centuries later. Even when it's chopped off, a root sprouts . . . And it was all lost by free will. No one fought for Prussia; no one wanted to sail across the current to the other side . . . Explain to me why on earth we needed to rule over millions of Byelorussians and Russians, to lose and conquer some place like Vitebsk dozens of times, to drag ourselves to Moscow itself and exact tribute from it, to go chasing the Tartars across the steppes, to fatten an already fattened body, and at the same time lose the head . . . That's how it is: we're a headless people. By now it's been five hundred years. The evil powers deceived us and stole our brains. And it's very easy to enslave a brainless country . . . That's what the scholars studying the Lithuanian language should think about. Let every nation, every country, thoroughly explain where it's head is at, and then let them guard it."

Not a word about "Vilnius Poker." Gedis angrily spat into the water, raised his collar, and turned his back to the Neris.

"Let's get the hell out of here," he muttered brusquely. "Don't be afraid, the river won't follow us. I'm sure of that."

I felt the door which had, it seemed, slammed shut, was by no means closed, and that Gedis wasn't trying to hide; he was still leading me forward.

"The worst of all is what you could find here—the beasts of Vilnius," he looked down a little street creeping along a curve. "The dragon of Vilnius, which needs to have its head cut off. He's hiding here somewhere too."

"Not here," I said, my mouth suddenly dry.

"I believe you, I believe you: you know another spot, maybe even that abandoned church. But don't be mistaken: that beast is everywhere. A disgusting, scaly dragon, a Basilisk that kills with its gaze. There's no hiding from it. It must, it must be beheaded . . . Yeah, why 'Vilnius Poker?' 'The dragon of Vilnius' would be a hundred times better."

My head spun and I felt faint. Without warning, Gedis had touched my most sensitive spots. He turned around carelessly and broke my glass shield. I was left stark naked; every one of his words lashed me with tongues of fire. I had never seriously thought about the dragon, and yet it had splattered me with its poisonous spray too.

"It always seems you'll meet it any minute. It's completely for real: gigantic, overgrown with mold, with ghastly, greenish little eyes . . . Maybe it's hunkered down in Old Town's underground, or maybe it's hiding in the new neighborhoods, in between the matchbox geometry. When you wake up and look out the window, it's sprawling out there in the fog, across the new highway, spreading the smell of decay around. Content and confident in its power, in its invincibility . . . Satisfied . . . It's here, it's here somewhere. It has to be. It can't not be. But what is it? What does it look like? Where is it? Maybe around that corner?"

"No," I whispered to myself. "No, it won't be there. It's somewhere else."

*Bitinas sits with his head tilted sideways, looking at you intently. His skull, shaved bald, even shimmers. He's the only one who didn't take a nickname; he proudly calls himself by his real name. The only one to have the Vytis Cross, but he doesn't put on airs at all; he pins it on only on the sixteenth of February. The exploits he plans are precise and elegant. It's said that your group has lost the least men out of all the groups in Lithuania, and there's a lot of them.*

*"Of course you want to get a pistonmachine," Bitinas says in an icy voice. "Of course you want to fight and show your courage."*

*You swallow, but you can't manage to speak out, you just nod your head. Bitinas bewitched you long ago; you're afraid of him.*

*"You won't get a weapon. You are meant for other things."*

*Bitinas' shaved skull and small black whiskers intimidate and oppress you. He doesn't look like an inhabitant of this earth, maybe because you're conversing underground. Your bunker is an entire underground garrison: undetectable, unnoticeable. Bitinas even ordered the air vents run into the bark of trees; he even found a way to disguise it from the search dogs. You are moles, unaccustomed to the light of day.*

*"Our battle will be a long one, Vytautas. We'll punish the settlers; we'll punish the collaborators. The Russians must be left in a complete void, supported by no one."*

*"To me that's obvious," you say, surprisingly boldly.*

*"I don't doubt it. You're an intelligent person. Yes, we'll kill and be killed. A civil war is a terrible thing. It's not Christian. But there are special tasks."*

Bitinas opens an iron box, takes a photograph out of it, and carefully lays it in front of you. His hands are majestic; they spread a crushing calm. You won't escape from hands like those.

"Take a good look!"

In the photograph there's a bony-faced man, probably not a Lithuanian. You don't see anything special, maybe just that his hair is particularly unruly; it's standing on end. You take a good look at his eyes. There's no gaze in them; they're like buttons set in his eye sockets.

"Who is he?"

"The executioner of the Lithuanian nation. Remember his name: Suslov, from the word 'susas.' He really is rather mangy."

Bitinas smiles wryly, and scores of little veins in your temples start pounding; anger and mortification flood through your chest. They'll make a spy out of you, but you want to do battle. That's why you came here.

"He's the emissary from Moscow. Sent here to deal with the Lithuanian nation. He has introduced two slogans. The first—finish off Lithuanian-German fascism. Pay attention—it's the Lithuanians who are monsters, but he's not. The second basic slogan—Lithuania without Lithuanians! No colonizers have ever introduced anything like that before."

"I won't be able to do it," you answer, your voice trembles from that incalculable pounding.

"If we're in the position where we're forced to kill, we must first punish those who have truly earned punishment. Muravyov the Hangman, compared to Suslov, is no more than a babe in arms. He hung maybe a hundred, while Suslov's counter has ten thousand as its smallest unit. He is a dragon. A dragon that must be beheaded. His head has to end up on top of a flagpole in place of the Soviet flag."

Your head spins, you see the spike, and on it—a dried-up head. But not the man in the photograph, not the head of the dragon. Shudders shake you, but even with your eyes closed you see Bitinas's head on the spike. A flashing bare skull and black whiskers. The prophetic vision is so strong that despite yourself you step backwards, while the live Bitinas's ghastly head watches you attentively.

"We've selected ten men from various groups all over Lithuania, whose purpose is to track down the dragon. I picked you, Vytautas. I won't give you a weapon. You don't have the right to die in a ridiculous firefight. You're meant for other things."

You're wracked by shudders, because you have to talk to the transfixed head of a dead man. There are gloomy tunnels about; vague flames flicker in them; they commune with Bitinas's angrily flickering eyes.

"I believe if anyone can get to the dragon, it'll be you. The dragon must be destroyed. The widows and orphans cry for it. Hundreds of thousands of Lithuanians in the snows of Siberia pray for it."

"But why me?"

"You're an exceptional person, Vytautas," answers the head on the pike. "I can see it in your eyes: you'll manage. That creature has no right to live. He's driven us, the masters of our country, underground, and dares to breathe Lithuanian air himself."

You want to answer that underground is a place of sobriety and safety, that it's only here that you have nothing to fear, but you're quiet, since the dead man's bald head won't believe it.

"I'm inexperienced. Why not you . . . or some other old soldier?"

"Too many people know me and the others. A young man is what's needed, a man no one knows. You see—you're the son of working people. You've learned Russian at night, after backbreaking labor, studying Stalin's writings, for which you could have been shot. You will need to play your role well."

"It's that hard to find the dragon's lair?"

"Don't tell me you have no inkling of how afraid he is? He's afraid of us. He's afraid of his staff. He's afraid of the whole world. He doesn't show his face anywhere. He sleeps only sealed up in a tank: we got this from a reliable source."

The bald head lights a cigarette, and you breathe easier: the flame of the match lit up his waist and broad shoulders. There is no pike. Even Bitinas's sad grimace calms you. Creaking, the cover of the tank stopped by the forest opens, and out of the hatch the dragon's head emerges. It looks around and, just in case, releases a plume of fire into the nearest bushes.

"What do you think—who established the destroyer units in Lithuania? They didn't even look for a nicer name. Destroyer units, that's all. Sonderkommand. What do you think, whose idea was that?

"The dragon's?"

"You've guessed it." Bitinas smiles grimly, and you are stunned, because his eyes open wide and you see how much he's suffering: you sense the pain gripping him, him—the iron man with the icy voice. "As you know, after

164

*a battle our soldiers' bodies are gathered and laid out in the village and town squares. Just so that everyone who brushes away a tear while passing by can be seized immediately and sent to Siberia. Whose elegant idea was that, you think?"*

"The dragon's," I answer firmly now. "The dragon's."

*You know that you won't escape from Bitinas's sticky fingers. It will be your lot to face the dragon barehanded, and no one is promising you a princess or half a kingdom. No one is promising you anything.*

"How do you blow up a tank?" you suddenly ask.

The mothers stubbornly drag the children to the front, but the children aren't in any hurry; they look around. They want to see everything, feel everything, and understand everything—not just that bug-eyed drunk, but the shape of the trees' branches and the construction of the trolleybus. It'll be worse when they want to understand themselves. Or that young woman there with the sickly, dark bags under her eyes:

"I can't stand it anymore! I feel like a caveman. Yesterday they were selling decent pork—two Russian women in the line got into a fight. They drew blood!"

"That's the way it should be. As long as there's nothing in your head except a hunger for meat and winter boots, you're a proper Soviet citizen. What would happen if we had everything in spades? You'd start— God forbid!—to think. You'd become dangerous."

A thirty-year-old homegrown philosopher with a shock of hair. He glances around to see if anyone hears how brave he is. Every establishment, every café is full of people like that. If all of their words would turn into matter, it would fill the streets and cover the tallest houses: Vilnius would be destroyed by empty words. Besides, that speaker is terribly naïve. If having everything could save you from *Them*, the world would long since be a different place. A McCarthy suddenly shows up even in the wealthiest societies. Even Hitler can be chosen in a free election. You might think a thriving Englishman immediately rushes off to think about the Universe and the structure of human society. Not at all; one collects neckties, another—diamonds. Each according to his means. Not for God, but for Mammon. They let you have a lot of gold— if you renounce your soul.

At one time I had decided that *Their credo* is a dictate of pure reason: *They* merely calculated that a society of kanuked creatures provides the most stability. If an anthill is the most stable way of life, then you need to construct human anthills. There can be no talk of the individual, freedom, or the soul; all of that just gets in the way. *Their* great commissar Plato described a state of that sort. It's worth reading—it's the germ of *Their* pathologic. Stalin attempted to bring a society like that into being. *People* aren't necessary—every member of society is nothing more than a function. He lives by his function alone, thinks only of his function, dreams only of his function. Dzerzhinsky dearly loves children, but his function is to be an executioner, hence he becomes an executioner. Hess adores music, but his function is to kill the Auschwitz Jews, so he murders Jews. (Just thumb through Soviet books, look at the films—how many odes and thunderous apologias there are for people who sacrificed themselves and their inner beings to the functions thrust on them.) Every morning the only newspaper in the country announces what is to be done today, and everyone meekly obeys. Orwell described the life of such an anthill of the kanuked in detail.

But over time my delight with the theory of pure reason faded. It explained a portion of *Their* pathologic, but did absolutely nothing to reveal the *purpose*. Who needs all that? Plato proclaims the kingdom of kanukai until he's hoarse, drives the dreamers and poets out of his state, deceives the throngs without ever feeling a pang of conscience—but why? In whose name, to whose advantage? To the advantage of those who are called "philosophers," that is, the caste who assert that it's proper to live in just exactly this way? But what are the criteria for the caste? What binds and unites them? Maybe those "philosophers" are the smartest, or the most handsome, or the tallest, or must be brunettes, or have a mole on the right shoulder blade? There are no criteria; *They aren't united* by either government or reason. All I needed was to read Kafka carefully to understand there's no reason in *Their* system. Both Kafka's *The Trial* and *The Castle* are *a priori* senseless and pointless—actually, *Their* purpose hides beyond the boundaries of ordinary logic. I understood that the germ of *Their* system, the source of *Their* gray magic, must be looked for at an extreme depth—beyond logic and reason, beyond the understanding of ethics and beauty, perhaps in the depths of time and mythology. Only there can you find the crossroads where *Their* development turned in an entirely different direction than *human* development.

The biological aspect is extremely important here. *Their* biological origin obscures even racial differences: just look at how similar Brezhnev and Mao Tse-tung became in their kanukish faces. The depths of time must hide a hideous biological branching of species: *They* and humans. What's to blame for that? Radiation? Emanations from outer space? The finger of God?

The Arabian Gnostics mention a vague power, *Satar*, which turned people against the word of God; even though they heard it, they immediately forgot it. Ancient Japanese sources mention a handless god of the plague, a strange plague that killed only certain select people—most often poets and wise men. That's just where *Their* roots are hiding. Humanity wasn't entirely blind; they recorded *Their* traces on many occasions, and *They* are not so entirely omnipotent—they didn't manage to erase all of the traces. But where did *They* emerge from, when did they weave their cobwebs over Europe and Asia? There are simpler questions too, questions that are closer to me. For example, this one: from where and when did some kind of Lithuanians show up on the shores of the Baltic Sea, speaking a language extremely close to Sanskrit, but without any nomadic traits? Did they hatch out of a cosmic egg rotting in the Lithuanian swamps, or did they at one time, for just an instant, know how to overcome enormous distances, and then forget that knowledge? Did the Lithuanians escape *Them* this way, or conversely—were they a secret unit, a landing-party thrown into *Their* expanding sphere? A question from more recent times, connected with the first: by what means did Lithuania in the 13th century become *the only state in Europe* that wasn't christened, that didn't give in to the kanukish dictates of the popes of the Middle Ages? And why did an unappeasable desire arise in that state to penetrate into Russia and attempt to conquer it? Was this *Their* satanic influence, or did the Lithuanians simply have a sacred mission to get to *Their* center?

Kafka, understandably, couldn't write about *what* Joseph K. was accused of. In his will he ordered that all of his writings should be destroyed, fearing *Their* revenge even after death. (Could he have foreseen Nietzsche's tragedy?)

None of us know *what* we're accused of. *Their* purpose can't be described logically; only metaphors and presentiments, absurd associations, or poetic juxtapositions can be of assistance here. The majority of all definitions and terms are dictated by *Them*. (*They* really love creating terms and slogans.) Only poetic intuition can lead to The Way; it's the only thing that penetrates through their pathological armor like smell through solid rock. The thought that asserts that a river and a snake have a common soul because both of them *wind*, that all of the world's sounds hide in silence, accomplishes more than the most rational theories in the world.

Oh no, it's no accident that the champions of kanukism—starting with Plato, ending with Stalin—so hate and fear fantasies and poetics, that they tried so hard to make everything pragmatic, to explain it, to substantiate it.

Poetry kills *Them*, gives *Them* convulsions, wrings *Their* guts—like boric acid does to cockroaches!

But there is no poetry around; everything is familiar and deathly boring. The post covered with peeling announcements (next to it should perch two stupefied, lame pigeons), then the wide steps to the library (and there—a degenerate dog, sniffing at the ground that's been torn up by the construction workers, drawing strange hieroglyphics with its tail). All of this has already been or will be. And I must pay absolutely no attention to it all. I must not feel the world outside, not even my own body. Only by these means is it possible to guard against *Their* attack: to be a complete void, to be imbued with readiness to fend off an attack at any moment. Nothing concerns me and nothing can concern me. I am a tensed string; I am a compressed spring. I am nothing, so I am invincible.

But Martynas keeps waving his arms, flinging cigarette ashes to the sides. What does he want from me? I don't want to see this faded movie with third-rate actors. I have more important goals; I cannot waste time uselessly. I have to protect myself from *Them*; I need to hoard my black knowledge. I am no longer of this world; I am long since dead.

These thoughts are always inspired by *Them*. Thank God, once more a bright light flashes in my head, once more I feel I *love* this painfully blathering little man, I even love the women in our section, I love Stefa, constantly getting underfoot. I love this entire accursed city, because without it, without these women, without Martynas and

Stefa, I wouldn't be, either. If I were to forget the others, I would be destroyed in the blink of an eye. After all, I have set out on The Way; I torture myself and go out of my mind not for my own amusement, but in their name, in the name of all the kanuked and those who still resist, however pathetic that may sound. They're all that supports me. They and everyday life, in which you sometimes, at least briefly, succeed in forgetting the horrors and the secrets, in turning into an ordinary little person looking for a breather and amusement.

"Listen, Vytautas," says Martynas, "Let's go somewhere and get a drink, huh? Some place where no one will find us."

You must not just decline, not regret in advance the time you'll lose. You must obediently agree—when you're balancing on a razor edge above the abyss, every meager little pleasure could be your last. You must go everywhere, wherever you're asked: amuse yourself a bit, swim in a lake, or go mushroom hunting. You barely manage to nod, and Martynas has already reviewed the map of obscure bars in his head and unerringly picks Erfurtas: during the day it's absolutely empty in Lazdynai. If someone like us were to show up there, they would be looking for solitude too. All that's left is to find transportation.

With Martynas I feel more or less safe (like I do with Stefa): he's been carefully checked out. At one time I was convinced that Martynas was a dangerous spy of *Theirs*. I discovered that he had filled half of our computer's disk with some sort of text of his, which I couldn't read. The writing was encrypted, and if that wasn't enough, you couldn't get near it without going through a special procedure. It was like those books in special collections—it existed, but you couldn't get at it. If you tried to break into it directly, the writing would have been entirely erased— we'd rather die than give our information up.

An evil thought immediately began gnawing at me: *They* destroy every speck of our trust in other people. It's horrible to live without trust, but it's even more horrible when trusting no one most often turns out to be correct. That's the sad experience of the kanukaworld. I didn't count on Martynas a bit. I was *almost* convinced that he was hiding my kanukish dossier. It must exist; this is easy to prove. *They* keep me alive only because they aren't omniscient. They can't do away with me because they suspect I know too much. That's the paradox of The Way: as long as I'm alive, I'm forced to be silent; however, it's possible to find the means to proclaim your findings after your death. *They* can't destroy me as long as they haven't precisely ascertained *how much* I know and how I hid my information. My dossier in *Their* files is really worth a fortune. I decided Martynas was gathering data about me. I observed him and became all the more convinced he was *Their* agent: he touched upon dangerous themes without being punished; with Elena listening, he denigrated the most sacred topics of the Soviet religion. You must always be most on your guard around the quiet ones and their antipodes—the chatterboxes that speak boldly and insolently. These types fear nothing because *They* protect them. The poor guy thought he had guarded his writing by encryption, codes, and triple safeguards. He forgot the fundamental law: *that which can be written can also be read.* All it takes is time and intelligence.

Reading writings of that sort is even more disgusting than reading a stranger's diary. When a person writes something down in black on white, he is aware, at least unconsciously, that a stranger's eye might see it. Frequently he may even secretly desire this. Martynas's writings were *in essence* designed for him alone. I mucked straight into someone else's soul with dirty shoes, and by then it was impossible to erase the traces. Unfortunately, in the battle with *Them* it's impossible to keep to moral standards. *I had* to read those writings. I certainly would not use my knowledge for evil. With an enormous effort of will, I forced myself to forget everything, to literally erase it from my brain. I must go down my Way cleanly, without the theft of a stranger's soul. There was only one thing I didn't forget, one thing I took note of with joy: I could rely on Martynas.

Understandably, up to a certain point.

No one can be relied upon completely. I can walk this earth only as long as *They* merely *suspect* me. If I were to tell someone everything I know—I'd be dead the same instant.

Probably I'll perish one way or another. Perhaps *They* are restrained only by mysterious kanukish rituals or the commandments of some unknown religion. Or maybe it's quite simply because my turn has not come yet; maybe *They* are extremely scrupulous and pedantic.

We were set up royally in the bar: no one flitted in front of us. A single fellow next to us was drowning himself in drink: he'd order two drinks at a time, toast himself by banging the two glasses together, and in one gulp down the right-hand one. Then he'd sit there like a ghost for a long time, and suddenly coming alive, down the second one. Then he would order two more. He was a stocky, somewhat overweight man of uncertain age with coarse black hair. His hands were thick-fingered and clumsy and overgrown with thick fur. It hardly seemed he could have been sent to spy on us: he'd already been sitting there for quite some time. Besides, he didn't pay the least attention to us. The bartender was another story—a lively, elegant swell. His forehead, underneath his thickly curled hair, was unnaturally white. I acutely sensed him secretly squinting at us as he snuggled up behind a column. I wanted to go to a different bar, but a gulp of cognac settled me down somewhat. I looked around carefully, trying to sense what was hiding in the bar's twilight. The mood of a bar frequently testifies to what has gone on there once upon a time, and sometimes it even gives away what is only still *to be*. Places designed for human gatherings speak a strange language when they're deserted. This bar was just silent and waiting. A drunken couple made their way out of the restaurant, newcomers no doubt. From some Moscow or another: provocatively fashionable clothes, glaring make-up on the girl, and something essentially alien about them—the movements weren't right; the expressions weren't right; they had an unpleasant intrinsic vulgarity. People like that think they're *masters* everywhere and at all times. (Gedis explained that this is characteristic of Americans too.) The guy casually looked over the bar, shooting insolent looks at both of us. The bored girl leaned against his shoulder, embracing his hips. Unexpectedly nimbly, Thickfingers jumped off the barstool and, with a lynx-like step, stalked over to the newcomers. The guy looked at him as if he were an empty spot. I observed their strange pantomime attentively: Thickfingers authoritatively explained something to them, the guy tried to argue, but suddenly the newcomers quieted down as if they'd been shut off and obediently turned back to the restaurant. The victor, with a strange smile, returned to the bar and immediately grabbed a drink.

"You're Lithuanians!" he declared unexpectedly, turning to the two of us and pronouncing the word as if it were a curse—I had heard that tone a million times in the camp. "I can tell right off. This is my third time in Vilnius."

He spoke Russian carefully, enunciating his words—the way people talk who are accustomed, even after five drinks, to doing their work and demonstrating that alcohol doesn't affect them at all. He immediately turned away again.

"Thank God," the bartender accommodatingly hovered over us. "I was starting to think that you were from there too."

"From where?" Martynas inquired belligerently.

"That guy over there isn't letting anyone out of the building," the bartender announced furtively. "He's KGB. There's a pistol under his arm. He's stopping everyone going to work and checking them out. Maybe it's one of their conventions?"

"Stop it," Martynas boldly shot back. "They hold their conventions in ruins and garbage dumps."

"Well, thank God," the bartender smiled indulgently, "At least there's a couple of normal people."

He walked off to the battery of bottles and then hid himself behind the column again. I was disappointed. The bartender was an innocent bystander, and Thickfingers was just an ordinary KGB agent, the type that serves *Them* without even knowing who they're serving. Vilnius thrusts total solitude on you when you don't want it, but snatches away any hope of hiding when that's what you're after. It will invariably stick you with a girl who brazenly pokes you with her breasts, or a depressing citizen who insistently treats you to drinks you don't like. And sometimes it plants a KGB agent with a pistol under his arm next to you.

"The worst of it," Martynas spoke up sadly, "is that the Lord God is a humorist. At one time I considered God a madman, a sadist, and a criminal. Then I decided he suffers from an inferiority complex; that's why he tries to deride people as much as possible, so he can feel how great he is in comparison. But I've caught on at last. God is a global comedian. There's no need to search for meaning or depth in the world. The world is a black comedy, whose ONLY purpose is to make God laugh."

I wanted, for at least a little while, to believe that all the forced labor camps are nothing more than a giant comedy, that all of Vilnius is just a giant comedy, a silly joke in honor of God. But for some reason I kept seeing the children of the camps: it seemed at any moment sickly children with shaven heads would start climbing out from under the bar, from behind the brown curtains, from underneath the carpet, begging for help with their toothless mouths.

"Maybe that God of yours is a criminal, anyway, if he finds suffering and blood amusing?"

"No!" Martynas kept getting sadder. "You have to understand God! It's all just a comedy to him. A theater show! There are no victims, no blood, it's all fictitious. God laughs his head off when he hears little people making majestic pronouncements and then acting out pure stupidity. The way they honor morality before going out to butcher one another. He knows that the blood is squeezed from beets, that the torture sessions are intentionally laid on thick and senseless so that they'd be sillier, and that those who are supposedly burned at the stake shake off the ashes and are already preparing for the next scene . . . It's really sad to know that all of your painful work, all your aspirations have only one purpose—to make the Lord laugh . . . When you start INTENTIONALLY playing in the comedy of the absurd, it's easier . . . Let's drink!"

He poured the whole drink into his mouth and made a horrible face: Martynas never knew how to drink, which you wouldn't say about our neighbor with the pistol. He apparently was of the type that sobered up as they drank. He slowly moved over to us and fixed his gaze on me.

"Calm down!" he declared, smiling wryly, "I've come in peace."

He seemed to be ready to explode from self-assurance and self-satisfaction. I saw his eyes and I was amazed. They were not at all what I had expected. The beautiful light blue irises moved enigmatically; there was most definitely no emptiness behind those eyes.

"Lithuanians!" He rolled the word out again, practically spitting it. "And what is it you want, you Lithuanians? What do you expect? Who are you? I want to understand. To understand! I've always wanted to understand every variety of human, even the most pathetic."

He ostentatiously lit up a cigarette and carefully looked me over again, then Martynas. His jacket under his left arm really was bulging. From close up his fingers didn't look all that thick.

"You still believe the world's going to help you out? You're happy that the European Parliament, for the thousandth time, voted for a free

Lithuania? That the U.S. Congress commemorates Lithuania Day? What use is it to you? It's nothing more than a delusion . . . don't tell me you can't distinguish a delusion from reality? You rave about a referendum on the separation question? We could arrange that referendum for you, just for a laugh. And what of it? We'll apply a little bit of pressure, and you'll vote the way you should."

"And if we don't?" Martynas got his back up immediately.

"What do you mean, if you don't? You'd be afraid. Just try it—and there won't be anything left of you." His hand grabbed the glass the bartender shoved at him. "And by the way, let's say you don't. So, what of it? We'll make the ballots change color when they're already in the ballot box, so what should be marked on them will mark itself. But why the complications? My God, after all, we're the ones counting the ballots . . ."

"I'll flatten his ugly mug!" Martynas muttered in Lithuanian.

"Don't babble in that language of yours," blue eyes said good-naturedly. "You know I don't understand it. Besides, I can't understand you even when you're speaking Russian. Passive disagreement is the stupidest policy. It's a pipe dream policy! Forget that Europe for once. Did they help you out much when we took you over in the forties? . . . You need to think CORRECTLY, you need to get hold of reality. And you? . . . One burns himself alive in protest, others solder freight cars that are filled with meat and bound for Leningrad to the rails, and still others parade in the streets after a football game singing nationalistic songs . . . I don't get it. What's that all about? Come on, it's nothing but a pipe dream. Come on, it's all perfectly obvious. You won't run anywhere, you won't do anything! We won't let you do anything!"

"That's how Lithuanians differ from you," Martynas announced furiously. "When they're frying in the pan, at least they aren't rejoicing over it."

"What does a frying pan have to do with it?" Thickfingers was sincerely surprised. "What frying pan? You just need to be aware of how things are, and always will be. Always! For eternity! We won't let it be any different! Where does this superiority complex of yours come from, this thought that you are somebody? If we need to, we'll announce that you don't even exist, and never did. No one will miss you. The Europe and America you've dreamed of won't so much as peep when you disappear. We'll arrange it so they'll have other problems at the time."

"So we'll just disappear?" I couldn't hold out.

"Anything can happen, if that's the way we want it. The one who wins is the one who ACTS. There's more Czechs than you—and what of it? The West bitched about it for a year or two, but everything stayed the way we wanted!"

I looked at him carefully and couldn't get over my astonishment. He was sincerely sad, and there was neither stupidity in his eyes, nor anger—more like compassion. The way a good-hearted person is sad when he runs over a cat or dog with his car.

"All the same, you're hopeless specimens," he said thoughtfully. "You don't even have anything to say. It's impossible to understand you. It looks like the boss was right: you're doomed to extinction."

He deftly jumped off the chair, stretched himself almost imperceptibly, like a giant cat, and in a completely different, commanding tone ordered:

"You are not allowed to go outside! You'll have to sit here for a while yet."

Without staggering a bit, he marched off towards the toilet; halfway there he turned around and wagged his finger in warning. He had barely disappeared from the doorway when we both, without a word, got up and quickly went downstairs.

"Stinker!" Martynas spat out glumly.

"I wouldn't say so. But it'll end badly for him sooner or later."

"Why?"

"The rank and file are required to carry out secret policies in silence, without giving it any thought. This one thinks too much and goes on about things that should never be said out loud."

"He's a stinker all the same! WE! Who are those WE?"

"That's the most important question in the world."

Martynas looked me up and down closely and had already opened his mouth, but at that instant we both stepped outside and stumbled into a strange world that scattered all words in the blink of an eye.

The square around the fountain with a weathervane, which was always busy and full of people, was totally empty, as if it had been swept by a giant broom—only the autumn wind ruffled the dark water of the puddles. It was completely quiet. No people to be seen anywhere. No trash, no trace of people. They had never lived here at all. It seemed we'd stumbled into a dead zone. A lone puppy, whining, dashed by. He deftly worked his short little legs, scurrying like he'd been wound up: apparently, he was driven by the same force that had eradicated the people. Despite ourselves, we stopped and looked around in horror: we felt as if we had gone out some *other* door and ended up in some *other* Vilnius, perhaps the inverse side of Vilnius. The windows of the houses were dead, the leaves on the trees were dead, life had abandoned this inverted city. The two of us, stunned, stared at one another. The urge came upon me to immediately return to the bar, let there be a hundred KGB agents with a hundred pistols perched there. We were already turning back, but the stage set suddenly changed. Two broad-shouldered men with angry faces scurried towards us, furiously waving their arms. They did not look human. They were fake. There couldn't be real people in this inverted city.

"What the hell!" Martynas muttered.

I glanced in the direction where he was staring and saw indistinct figures looming in every other window of the building opposite. They surrounded the entire square, settled in as if it were an amphitheater. The glass of binoculars flashed in some of them. No, this wasn't a dead zone: I felt as if I had ended up in a giant theater set. Everything's possible in Vilnius. Everything *really is* possible in Vilnius. As if emerging from underground, four government ZILs with bulletproof glass lazily rolled up to the sidewalk (how could there be ZILs in Vilnius? Of course, this is an *inverted* city); elderly men in hats began to clamber out of them. As if responding to an unheard signal, several women with baskets came out of the neighboring houses and began mincing towards the store. A couple of young women with baby carriages followed them out. And they started to rotate around the fountain. One after the other, young men with optimistic expressions marched through the square in all directions. An instant ago it was completely empty, but now an unhealthy crush had formed—everyone moved stiffly, like mannequins. I still didn't get it. I knew this square and its fountain well. I knew this store well—just like all the others, for the sake of a vision of plenty it was filled with cans of inedible fish, cereal, and cheap candy, and instantly crammed with people if sausages unexpectedly showed up.

"Who the hell let you in here?" one of the broad-shouldered men, who had at last hurried up to us, snarled in Russian.

"Yankovsky has gotten plastered again and for a few cocktails let them go take a look," the other, a likable brunet, replied phlegmatically.

"I'm going to write up a report about this!" hissed the first one. "I'll trash him, the damn philosopher!"

To them, we didn't exist; they talked over Martynas's head.

"They see us," the brunet calmly observed. "They're coming this way already."

"Get into the store, now, and just you try something!" The angry one went so far as to shove me in the back.

The procession of hats really was close by. Stepping inside, I noticed a group of militia restraining a crowd around the corner of the building. I slowly started catching on to what was going on, while by now Martynas was poking me in the side:

"Look!" he hissed, stunned, "Just look! We're in Sinbad's cave!"

Again it occurred to me that we were, despite it all, in an inverse Vilnius. The store was the same, but completely different. The shelves were buckling with wildly colorful cans, packages, and jars. Saleswomen who looked like nymphs in bright blue smocks smiled at us; their eyes said they loved us. In the huge room a few buyers wandered about casually, occasionally stopping by the refrigerated shelves or cases.

"It's fantastic!" Martynas hissed in my ear. "There were narcotics in the cognac, we're hallucinating. Do you see the canned crab? Do you see three . . . no, four kinds of caviar?"

That wasn't all I saw; there were many more things an inhabitant of Vilnius wouldn't behold even in his pathetic dreams. The procession of hats advanced right up behind out backs; whether I wanted to or not, I heard the guests' questions and the guide's answers.

"It's a pleasant square," a hatted voice declared; a strange voice: hoarse, but biting at the same time.

"The inhabitants like it," the guide spoke Russian with a mild accent that merely emphasized the suggestiveness of his velvety voice. "It's particularly popular among young mothers. They like to bring their babies here, to meet and chit-chat. The air here is especially clean, and there are a lot of green spaces."

"It really is a pleasant square."

I recognized the hoarse voice; it froze my blood. An oppressive foreboding wickedly told me I hadn't been driven here merely to observe a strange spectacle, that something really evil was about to happen. My foreboding asserted that *They* had arranged this performance especially for me. Martynas wasn't choked by any foreboding; he grabbed several colorful cans from the shelves.

"Lobsters!" he whispered resignedly. "I thought I'd die without ever tasting lobster!"

"There aren't very many people here," the hoarse one observed.

"Most people are at work. In the evening there's more. We do avoid lines, however."

The hats were nearly stepping on our heels. The hoarse voice terrified me, even though I hadn't the slightest idea why I feared it so, feared it and probably hated it. The women with the baby carriages were still zooming around the square like they'd been wound up. The optimistic young men chatted, waving their hands about with excessive cheer. They depressed me; I so wanted to *stop* them all. Martynas poked me in the side again. With his glance he caressed cans of Lithuanian game destined only for export. The sides of the cans boasted in fancy type: "Taiga's Gift."

"As far as I know," he observed philosophically, "Lithuanian boar, moose, and deer have never so much as smelled the taiga. A little misunderstanding."

"It's a metaphor!" I made an effort to collect my senses and take up Martynas's tone. "Lithuanians have surely smelled it."

"Oh, I get it. In the sense that our boars are so tasty because Lithuanians were taken to pasture in Siberia? As clear as mud."

"We try to always have at least several varieties of meat for sale," explained the guide. "Some like game. Some—it's funny, really—have a high opinion of horse meat. It's probably a fad from the French."

"It's not good to chase after foreign fashions," muttered the hoarse one. "It's ideologically dangerous. Small things lead to bigger ones."

Martynas quietly cursed in Russian. If he starts to curse in Russian it means the end of the world is coming. Once more I looked around, once more I wanted to know if everything going on here was for real. I wouldn't have been the least surprised if that entire preposterous store were to sink into the ground and disappear without a trace. I almost wanted it to, because then the hoarse voice would have disappeared too. But whose was it? Whose?

"The sonofabitches!" Martynas seethed. "And if I were to turn around and explain to them how things really are?"

"We try particularly hard to provide ample fruit," the guide cooed. "Working people need vitamins."

I calmed down a bit, perhaps because the hoarse voice was quiet for the time being. I looked over the great performance's participants. The director's hand could be felt everywhere, but the actors played their parts badly. Their movements were nervous; they wanted *everything*, but apparently they had been warned not to take more than a few items. A few women, it seemed, went into shock. Their blank faces stared at some culinary miracle and their lips moved without a sound. Going by, the broad-shouldered men roughly jostled them, awakening them out of their trances.

"Our stores," the guide explained, "compare favorably with, say, American stores. In ours, people don't purchase groceries for an entire week. A working man knows he'll always find what he needs. He buys only enough merchandise for one time."

"You live well," the hoarse one declared. "And are there ever shortages?"

His voice was driving me out of my mind. I felt I was going to stop at any moment, turn around, and fix my eyes on the procession of hats.

"Unfortunately, it does happen," the guide reported sadly; you could feel unappeasable pain in his voice. "Unfortunately, sometimes a person comes into the store and can't buy what he wants."

"He's a bit confused," Martynas interjected between his quiet cursing, "He just now said that you can always find whatever your heart desires."

"Don't get excited, in a minute he'll add that not everything's been done yet."

"Of course, not everything's been done yet. We still have unused resources."

Martynas snorted and stopped cursing for a moment. It seemed to me that the pseudo-shoppers started going around faster and faster all the time, more and more nervously; the pseudo-mothers outside the window were practically running at a gallop; it seemed the entire mechanism was starting to turn more briskly all the time, that it was no longer possible to control it, that everyone would keep moving faster and faster, get carried away and start breaking the shelves, smashing the jars, and in the end sweep away and trample the procession of hats.

"Pineapple!" Martynas suddenly moaned, "I haven't seen live pineapple in fifteen years!"

"As it happens, we've been carrying out an experiment in this particular store," the guide lectured. "All of the saleswomen speak only Russian. The results are encouraging: an absolute majority of the inhabitants accept this innovation gladly."

"That's a positive sign," the hoarse voice agreed. "I'll report this to the Politburo. In other respects you have been dealing with the national question rather slowly."

At last we both got to the cashier. Martynas, smiling wryly, paid for the lobster and pineapple. I knew I was behaving in a suicidal manner, but I slowly turned around anyway. I could not believe what I saw; I wanted to scream, but a scream wouldn't have helped.

HE stood a few steps away from me. He had aged considerably: his chin shook a bit, and his unruly hair was quite thin. However, it really was HIM. I swear, for a few seconds my blood *stopped*. Bitinas's bald head, stuck on a pike by the cash register, moving its lips scornfully, spat out:

"That's the dragon. The dragon that's devouring a hundred innocent virgins a day."

I no longer grasped what was going on around me. I felt a hysterical movement, the barrels of pistols pointed at me from under jackets. HE stood with an indifferent expression and seemed to be chewing something with a slack jaw. Only now did I grasp what had brought me here, how *They* had decided to test me. I knew I had to do my duty, to fulfill my destiny. I wasn't at all afraid of the invisible but fully apparent pistols. I wasn't afraid of anything at all; it was perhaps the first time in my life I was so pure and empty, so impassive. HE stood right there and finally took notice of me. I felt that my life had to end in just exactly this way: I had to crawl and squirm through hideous swamps especially so I would at last end up in this deceptive store, and HE would be standing in front of me. The last instant had to be like this, a frozen instant: everyone staring at me in shock, with the baby carriages gliding past the windows. Unexpectedly, it cleared up, and the puddles shone in the sunlight. I thought about whether I had ever felt hate for HIM, or if I had thought about HIM at all. Probably not. With surprise, I sensed that in essence, I had never believed HE really existed at all. HE was just a metaphor, the embodiment of the indescribable smell of the camp, of the nameless letters scattered by the night trains, of mother's darkened, shaven head hanging above grandfather's altar, of the lame dog by the Narutis, and of Gedis moving his hands and legs like a bug. HE was nothing more than Bitinas's induced fantasy, an oppressive dream we were all dreaming. But here he stood right next to me and soundlessly moved his lips. The dream came alive. I had to take revenge on him for everything and for everyone, I had to bite through his throat like a wolf, but I just stood there and thought about how his arrival needed an entirely different stage set: that square with the fountain full of laid-out corpses, one next to the other, some of them castrated. The puddles lit up by the sun and surrounded by optimistic high-rises—and the square completely full of corpses, with a procession of every, every, every last one sent to Siberia, and rotting live bodies, and the sweetish stench of the camp. At any moment I'll jump forward, the faceless broad-shouldered men will press the pistol triggers in unison, and everything will be over. At last HE will no longer be, since I will no longer be. But he insanely wanted to live; I sensed this when he looked at me attentively, and—I could swear!—*recognized* me. He had never seen me, never heard of me, but he recognized me. I felt it in every nerve, smelled it like a scent, read it like an open book: how weak he was, how afraid. Unexpectedly, he stepped up to me, smiled ingratiatingly, and *stretched out his hand.* That's what the fiery dragon's breath was like.

"Hello," his raspy voice croaked, "How's it going? Is there anything you need?"

In the square the pseudo-mothers with baby carriages came to a standstill. Everyone stared at me. My heart paused. That was HIS futile attempt to avoid the inevitable, to stop me from doing my duty, to beg a miracle. The attempt was senseless; the dragon couldn't stop everything forever, all the same someone had to move. Martynas's lips moved first:

"It's a wonderful life!" he said clearly. "The only thing missing is bird's milk."

"Ha, ha!" the guide laughed gently. "We manufacture this candy that everyone likes, called 'Bird's Milk.' Apparently, we ran out of it today."

HE continued to stand right there, I could stretch out my hand and strangle him, but I stood there unmoving and *did nothing*. I could have said something, I could have spat on him at least, but I did nothing. It was all pointless. He stood right there, and I did nothing. Next to us it reeked of the camp's vomit, next to us crawled Bolius with his shaved head, next to us glared the straw-haired men's kanukish eyes. My hands were free, I definitely knew what I should do, but at the same time I knew that no actual retribution would encompass even a millionth part of his guilt. Or perhaps—like a genuine Lithuanian—I literally stood there and waited for everything to slowly resolve itself on its own. And everything did resolve itself: he felt he was free, tipped his hat and slowly swayed off past the cash register. Martynas poked me with the pineapple and snorted. The broad-shouldered men bustled around us, the handles of their pistols finally released. The mechanism moved again; I was its only motionless detail. Fate had given me a single chance, and I did nothing. The procession crawled along the square, dissolved among the sun's reflections in the puddles, climbed back into the black ZILs, and sailed off. Martynas and I already stood outside. The optimistic young men quickly parted, the young women abandoned the baby carriages, the broad-shouldered men collected them and slung them into a covered truck. Others, after locking the doors to the store, set about unloading the colorful boxes and cans from the shelves. The militia at the cordon lit cigarettes and released the real Vilnius crowd into the square. People rushed headlong to the door of the store and pressed up against the window, trying to discern, from a distance at least, the miraculous cans disappearing in front of their eyes, and stood there, disappointed.

The two broad-shouldered men, panting, caught up with us.

"Hand over that pineapple," growled the dark one.

Yes, yes, despite it all we still had the pineapple. I watched indifferently as they looked around anxiously and wrenched it and the can of lobster away from Martynas.

"Give me back MY pineapple!" Martynas quietly babbled. "I paid money for it! Give me back my pineapple!"

The light-haired one marched off with the plunder, while the dark-haired one, intrigued, raised his eyebrows.

"Are you a complete fool? What money? The merchandise doesn't belong to this store. They don't even have a price. You really gave them money?"

"Give me back my pineapple," Martynas repeated, louder this time.

The dark-haired one's expression suddenly changed and he hissed like a snake:

"You're still talking? Get lost, you rat, or I'll write you up for provocative activities. Understand? Get lost while you still can."

I believe I was the one who dragged Martynas off to the side. I believe I mumbled something to him; maybe to calm him and keep him quiet, but he kept going on like a broken record:

"Why did he take my pineapple away? He ought to give my pineapple back. Why did they take my pineapple?"

"Listen," I finally said. "Was that really Suslov, or was I just imagining it?"

Martynas looked at me as if he had just now awoken.

"You didn't recognize him?"

"That REALLY was Suslov? REALLY?"

"Of course. I completely forgot . . . You know, everyone was talking about it . . . His first visit after who knows how many years."

Martynas suddenly started shaking all over. Shocked, I stared at him, while he kept trembling harder and harder, slowly swayed forward and grabbed at the air with his arms, until he finally fell to his knees on a wet, dirty bench and started jerking as if he was being wracked by spasms. The shocked face of an elderly woman looked at us through the window of a nearby house. She blinked frequently, as if she were trying to chase a hallucination away. It seemed to me that anything could happen now. I expected that woman to fly straight out through the glass and flutter above my head. I expected a monstrous patrol of *Theirs* to jump out of the stairway and devour me. Or a tank, caterpillars smiling, to crawl out from around the corner and crush us. *Anything* could happen, but nothing happened, absolutely nothing. The sun shone like it was summer; a gust of wind drove a few yellowish leaves towards us. It was quiet, except that somewhere someone panted and moaned as if they were being strangled. I didn't realize at first that it was Martynas.

"Jesus, Jesus!" He finally stuttered out through his tears. "What artistic powers! I practically believed it! . . . Some Peter Brook mounts a production of *Orghast* at an Iraqi shrine in some invented language and thinks he's creating great theatre art! He's an ignoramus! A mangy dilettante. Could he have managed to mount a spectacle like this? No! I'm completely certain—no! He couldn't get the stench! Poor Brook. Poor, naïve Brook!"

He gasped for breath again, it seemed his laugh was a hard, choky thing that just couldn't get through his throat—neither in nor out.

"There's true theater for you! There's the art of arts! Did you see all of it? Did you feel the rhythm? Did you see those babes pushing the baby carriages? What was in them—walkie-talkies or machine guns? Have you ever dreamed of anything like that, eh, boss?"

He fell silent, sobered up in an instant, and jumped up from the bench. He came up to me, he even stood up on his tiptoes, and, looking me straight in the eyes, spoke quietly. It seemed he was turning over every word, literally pleading with me to understand him, wanting to convey something or other to me.

"Listen, what's Kafka . . . What's Orwell . . . The number of participants, the way everything was arranged . . . What a show: a member of the Politburo inspects a run-of-the-mill store . . . Where did they get all those cans from? A government hoard? . . . Go on, tell me—isn't God a comedian of the absurd? What was that? A tragedy? A folk lament? *Prometheus Bound?* . . . The folk, as you saw yourself, just ran headlong to pick over the leavings, but they didn't even get that . . . Go on, answer me, what was that?"

"A nightmare." I surprised myself that I could speak in a completely normal voice. "An offering to *Their* god, to the Shit of All Shits."

"What, what?"

"It's just a single line from the poem of universal drivel. How does it differ from the interminable speeches no one believes? How does it differ from the list of slogans for a demonstration, printed in the newspapers in advance? How does it differ from the election farce? It's the same genre."

"Maybe," Martynas suddenly backed off and gave in. "Probably. It's just that it was a new one to me."

"Me too."

It was new to me that *Their* net could encompass me *like this*. *They* stuck Suslov on me, thinking I wouldn't control myself and I'd do myself in. *They* decided to exchange me for a mangy, worthless kanukas magistrate. There are no coincidences in *Their* system. If the dragon, for no reason whatsoever, came to Vilnius, then apparently that suits the laws of pathologic. If I ran into him, then apparently that suits the laws of pathologic.

I was overtaken by horror at these thoughts. I no longer heard what Martynas was saying; I didn't even see the sun. I was wracked by spasms of fear. I wanted to burrow into the ground, to turn into a blind worm that no one would find, that no one cares about. It seems you can *wait out* danger. Lord knows, getting as far away as possible from any light whatsoever, burrowing into the earth, relentlessly attracted me. But the sun, as if on purpose, glared like crazy. *They* could start anything. If the slope of the mountain moved, the avalanche must surely follow; the only unknown: would it bury me, or roar on by. Identical buildings, stamped out of a duplicating machine, loomed all around, surrounding me, preventing me from breaking out into freedom. I hate the new neighborhoods. When you find yourself inside one of them, you have no idea where you've ended up—it could be Vilnius, or it could be any other city. In neighborhoods like that you feel like you're in a trap. They don't have a face, they don't have a soul, and anything can happen in them. There are good-natured neighborhoods and angry neighborhoods, dangerous neighborhoods and dour neighborhoods. You recognize them, you have some idea of what to expect from them. But faceless neighborhoods are no different than people in whose eyes you can't read anything. It's no big deal to be on your guard when you see an angry spark in a person's eyes; it's easier to escape in time when you see a sullen threat in them. The worst is when there's no expression at all, when the shape you simply took for a pole, a rock, or a withered tree suddenly comes to life and bares its bloody fangs. It's worse because you're not expecting it. After all, you can't go around being afraid of every pole, every rock, and every withered tree.

Now *They* could start in on me at any minute. I felt I was a target in a gigantic bombing range, where every shot is precisely on target. Martynas's fussing distracted me somewhat, but I kept thinking about *Their* notorious schemes. When necessity compels, *They* aren't choosy about the means. *They* can assassinate the Kennedys, even while they're sitting in the White House. (I always felt a pang reading the news about the investigations of those infamous murders. Not just because I was sorry for John and Robert, but mostly because I knew very well that no one will ever come across the *real* killers. No one. Never.) They can pretend to be anything—terrorists, madmen, maniacs. They can blow up a subway train so that a single person *They* found inconvenient would die. Manson, who declared himself the servant of Satan, was selected for Polanski. He intentionally disguised himself as the Prince of Darkness, to turn everyone's attention away from his true color—a complete colorlessness. *They* won't even bother arranging a grand attempt for me. I'm not a Kennedy, nor even a Polanski. I'm called Vytautas Vargalys, I'm already fifty-three years old, but I am completely, utterly unknown. Although that may just be what saves me. At least for the time being.

It's still possible to save me from myself by remembering Lolita—but not in moments of love, not when she's surrounded in beauty, but rather in the most banal, everyday situation.

Lolita is standing next to me, so I'm fine. She really does perform miracles. A moment ago, there was a terribly irritating desolation here, and now everything's changing. We're standing in a line for sausages. I cannot bear the sight—chains of sullen, exhausted figures. They stand in silence, their eyes fixed on the ground. But today I'm at peace, because Lolita is next to me. She *changes* the world. If she touches wilted flowers, their petals straighten out, fill with the fluids of life and start to give off a soft scent. If she pets a dog, a human expression shows up in its eyes. And now something is starting to happen to the entire store, to all the figures; they've raised their hanging heads—someone even cracked a joke. Decrepit, irritable old women slowly turned into lively, red-cheeked grannies. The faded, dirty curtains glistened in brighter colors and the saleswomen smiled at everyone. Everyone felt a miraculous change, but only I know the reason: Lolita changed everything.

In front of me, a skinny old lady with a strange Russian accent wails: these Lithuanians, these damned Lithuanians! The government did the right thing when it sent them North, oh, they did the right thing! She clams up for a bit and then starts in again: those Lithuanians wrong us, oh, they wrong us! The long, gray hairs on her upper lip quiver like petals tossed by the wind. I'm sorry for the old lady; I'd like to help her somehow. She's a poor thing, it's not her fault: she ended up here, this isn't the place for her—maybe her children dragged her along with them. She can't get used to different people and a different lifestyle, and her poisoned brains don't help her any—unless by whispering to her that a good government would send all the Lithuanians to hell, so they wouldn't get in her way. But she's not to blame; it's the fault of the kanukai magistrates, the dragon Suslov most of all. Poor old lady, I think, and I smile, because I think of how I would perceive her if Lolita wasn't next to me: that disgusting Stalinist witch with gaping lips, seething with murderous ideas, quivering with lust the moment she can destroy someone. But, thank God, Lolita is standing next to me, so the old lady slowly calms down, stops whining, turns to me and gently asks: tell me, my son, what kind of sausage did they bring today—is it for two-twenty or two-eighty, I can't make it out.

Shortly we'll separate, but after an hour or two we'll meet again—maybe at my place, or maybe in the streets of Vilnius. The two of us have allocated the streets and squares according to mood: Cathedral Square when we're a bit tired, but not irritable; the square by City Hall—nervous but promising fulfillment; University Square—thoughtful and in the mood to reveal secrets. We don't even discuss where and when to meet, we'll both sense the time and the place, neither one of us will have to wait. It's a shame that a person has to eat, to sleep, to carry out incomprehensible duties; just walking through Vilnius with Lolita, going from one street to another, from one mood to another, would be perfect. That would really be living—the two of us and the streets: from one street to another, from one mood to another, from one dream to another, from one old hurt to another, from one renewal to another . . . That would really be living . . .

But the only certain thing in my life now is fear. I stepped over the last boundary a long time ago. Up until that evening I had still hoped for something. I remember I was over at Martynas's; he was driving me nuts with his television. An important basketball game was on, but I was in constant fear that a talking kanukas head was going to leap out onto the screen. Half of Lithuania was waiting for a crucial move on the part of the Zalgiris team; Martynas jumped up and down in his chair with every shot, while completely unexceptional things were happening on screen. It could have been predicted in advance. Zalgiris needed only one last step, but the basketball players, unfortunately, were Lithuanians too; at the very last second they were losing—hopelessly and completely idiotically. Martynas chewed his nails and cursed in Russian, while I thought about the Darius and Girenas complex, our age-old complex, originated by Vytautas the Great when he lost the Lithuanian crown at the very last moment, when everything, it seemed, had already *almost* happened. It really is our authentic complex; it's not borrowed from anyone. It was exactly the same with Darius and Girenas flying across the Atlantic first—they did everything, heroically overcame all the difficulties, and smashed into the ground three steps away from home. The basketball players acted exactly the same way now—they had flown over their own Atlantic, overcome all the difficulties, and suddenly lacked the spirit one step away from the goal. We all lose our crown at the last minute; we always smash into the ground three steps from home. That's the misfortune of our fate.

They announced a timeout, and a talking head really did show up on the screen. In my surprise I didn't even turn off the television. I recognized the long face with the bristling eyebrows and the uneven, piercing gaze of the eyes: it was Stepanas Walleye, nicknamed Carp, my talisman, my great hope, the symbol of human resistance. I was at a loss for words; I thought—maybe they mixed up the programs, maybe by mistake some other program's sound track was connected. I watched Carp's lips hopefully, but their movements matched the text. It couldn't be; all my guts, filled with that long face, told me it couldn't be. It could be anyone else—just not Carp, not walleyed Stepanas! But it was him. It seemed I had turned up in a world where rabbits devour snakes, flowers fly from bee to bee, and stars shine brightly in the middle of the day.

"The new Party Plenum's resolutions," Carp's low voice monotonously intoned, "express the deep hopes and wishes of the working people. We, the working people, indubitably know that the Party always was, and always will be, the conscience and wisdom of our epoch. We will greet the new resolutions with even greater triumphs of work and creative achievements."

I knew he couldn't be saying words like that. I knew that any minute he would turn around, wink at me, and say: that's how carp talk, now listen to how real people talk. But he didn't stop talking; he just changed the subject for some reason:

"Yes, I have had to go through this hell. Not a single criminal should elude the retribution he deserves. Reactionary regimes hiding those who had a hand in the horrors of the Fascist concentration camps commit crimes against humanity. As a former prisoner at Auschwitz, I agree with our government's appeal with particular zeal."

"What is he talking about?" I asked, totally at a loss.

"They've found another escaped Auschwitz participant in Paraguay," Martynas answered. "We, as the most humanitarian country in the world, hasten to lodge a protest."

The eyelid of Carp's walleye twitched—that hadn't changed in over thirty years. The last time I saw him in the camp, he was in a pit where we used to dig gravel. He stood there, huge and run-down, with his head bloodied, staggering heavily, and, coughing blood, spit out through his teeth:

"Never! Never! Remember, guys: never!"

And now Carp, my sacred hope, my talisman, sat inside the television set and babbled something in the language that brings on despair, the language that has nothing in common either with the Russian language or in general with whatever *human* language: the drab jargon of the kanukai, which speaks *itself*, without a human being, in incomprehensible words of satanic absurdity. It seemed to me that I had seen Carp just this morning, passing under the library's windows; just this morning I had prayed to his soul like it was some kind of holy relic.

In the camp he was a symbol of the resistance of the spirit to me; I feasted upon it, it kept me alive! These were always his words: *they can eat me alive, but they'll never break me! Never! I'm invincible! I'll never say out loud that they're right! Never!*

He held out against what no human could—even Bolius didn't have the strength to hold out. And now Carp had perished. He betrayed not just my faith in him, but even his own church.

*They* had destroyed even Carp! Neither Auschwitz nor our zone boss had overcome him, but the calm, soulless stare of Vilnius finished him off.

That was yet another direct warning to me: no one, but no one, holds out against *Them!*

It's a rule of *Theirs* that's cast in stone. *They* always finish their work to the very end; *They* don't lose their crown at the last minute. It's a matter of *Their* honor that Stepanas Walleye be the one to sit himself down in front of the television cameras. Just about anybody could have been planted there; someone who hadn't languished in any forced labor camp, or someone who had sat in Auschwitz but hadn't afterwards stumbled into the Soviet meat grinder (if there are such people at all). Someone who had languished in both places, but had always been and always would remain blind, would have sufficed too. But this couldn't have satisfied *Them.* It was precisely Carp who was needed. It had to be him, Stepanas Walleye. He was precisely the one who had to publicly honor the cancer that had eaten him up. I clearly understood that only this could be enough. Only a complete, universal grayness, voiceless birds, exterminated bees, and blind swallows with their wings ripped off could satisfy *Them.*

In the camp, he despised those of his partners in misfortune who just didn't want to see through it. They were an indescribable, absurd, gut-wrenching clan. They founded underground communist cells and tried to persuade others, and themselves, that Papa Stalin didn't know a thing about the horrible mistreatment that had befallen them. The Father of the People had to show up one day in a shining cloud like the Messiah, announce eternal Justice, and extol the members of the underground communist cells. Stepanas Walleye called those paranoids carps.

"You're like those carp," he'd scream in their faces, "You're being fried in the pan, and you writhe and sing hosannas to the cannibal chef. You don't belong to the human race and never will. You're carp!"

He called them carp with such fury that the nickname Carp stuck to him.

He'd sidle up to me and Bolius and to the other Lithuanians, and repeat glumly:

"I'm ashamed to be a Russian. I'm ashamed! Guys, accept me into your nation."

He even learned some Lithuanian and proudly twisted his tongue, muddling the words with a dreadful accent. He'd assert to Bolius and me:

"I'll get out of here. I know that I really will get out. And even if I live a thousand years, I'll never be a carp. I have a brain, whoever it was that gave it to me—God or nature. I'm invincible!"

He really did leave the camp and settle in Vilnius.

And now there he is, hanging around on the television screen and singing hosannas to the old and new cannibal chefs.

Even Carp was vanquished in the end! *They* took away the brains he was so proud of!

I could just see all of our zone guards, and the zone boss himself, sitting comfortably in front of their screens and lazily applauding with gloved hands. I can just see a hundred thousand guards sitting in a gigantic open field, so they can see one another, enjoy one another, and feel their combined power. They lazily applaud Stepanas Walleye for his accurate and timely words. Now he was their *colleague*.

It was no different than if Giordano Bruno were to take up preparing firewood for the bonfires of the Inquisition. If Thomas Jefferson were to demand that the Bill of Rights be recalled forthwith. If Saint Paul were to start persecuting Christians and profaning Christ by all available means.

Once upon a time he sat in front of me—his lip split, sucking on the hole left by his knocked-out teeth—and told me about his dream:

"We're worse than the Germans . . . Yes, yes, only we're to blame . . . One mustachioed Georgian couldn't accomplish anything . . . But the world has already punished the Germans and will continue to punish them, while these will remain righteous for eternity, my child . . . Russia never knew how to admit its own guilt. We love tyrants: Ivan the Terrible, Peter the Great, Stalin . . . We're afraid of them, but we respect them, we LOVE them, my child! That's what needs to be burned out of the Russian soul first of all! . . . The love of the whip, as Pushkin, Alexander Sergeyevich said . . . And by the way, I wouldn't take Pushkin into the new nation. I'd take Dostoevsky, Fyodor Mikhailovich . . . And Bulgakov I'd take, with his *Heart of a Dog* . . . Too many Russians have a dog's heart, my child . . . Way too many . . . I'll establish a new church, a genuine Russian church. I must establish it, my child! And I won't accept a single person who believes in the sacred Russian destiny to rule other nations, to create an eternal empire. Not a single one raving that Moscow is the third Rome . . . I'll only take those who will understand their guilt, who will understand what they really are, who will want to become real . . . Real humans, my child. Who will fear nothing, bow to no one, but won't oppress anyone, either . . . That's how a new Russian nation will be born. A great nation! Perhaps I won't be in it myself, maybe I'm too lowly for it too ordinary . . ."

Stepanas was quickly taken on by the zone boss himself, and this meant the end. Our boss was the paranoid demiurge of the camp. You could sense a satanic system in all of his pathological activity; he had some purpose that was comprehensible only to himself. For example, he wouldn't prevent the carps from gathering, but later he would suddenly add ten years to the sentences of all the members of the communist cells for starting up an illegal organization. There is no communist party of the zeks, he'd like to reason, ergo, they're illegal. He thought it amusing that the carp, whom the Communist Party had shoved in there, secretly made sacrifices to it, and because of that got extra punishment. He wanted to perceive some kind of paranoiac essence in this, to "understand a person's liver," as he himself would say. (The gypsy baron from the neighboring barracks swore that during the annual celebration of the Revolution, the boss ordered him to serve up a human liver.) The majority of people are brainless manure, he liked to repeat, they'll not only eat others up, that's too ordinary—no, they'll eat *themselves* up.

"I need to understand your liver," he said one day to Stepanas Walleye. "I'll take you on."

This meant the end. When the boss would take someone on, nothing would be left of a person, not even that liver of his. The boss had taken on Bolius just before Stepanas.

The last time I saw Walleye in the camp, he was in the pit where we used to dig gravel. There was only the shadow of a shadow left of him. He staggered and repeated:

"Never! Remember, guys, never! I'm invincible!"

That hideous summer at the camp I made an eternal vow to myself to never have children. It's inadmissible to bring little creatures with souls into the world, souls that *They* will instantly devour. At least I can't do that. Millions of people don't even consider that they're merely giving birth to sustenance for *Their* spiritual cannibalism. Millions of mothers don't even ponder the hideous doom they're sacrificing their infants to. Not a single child asks his parents to bring him into this world. Not a single father has tried to ask his child this.

That's a hideous crime—to give birth to a little thinking creature, whose soul will be left untouched for five years at the most.

In Lithuania *They* start the kanukizing procedures through day-care nannies. In other places perhaps they do it differently.

*They* need the mass of humanity. *They* encourage procreation by all means. *They* aren't in the least interested in the extinction of humanity. The more brainless beings, the more carriers of the gray spirochetes!

Even if, through some miracle, you hold out against *Them* during your teens and young adulthood, even if you reach such heights of resistance as Carp did, sooner or later *They* will grind you up.

For the love of God, don't make children for *Them*!

Carp sat on the television screen, praised the Divine Party and condemned the Auschwitz guards as if there had never been any guards in the Gulag. It seemed someone had torn out a piece of my heart, took away my one and only sacred talisman. It seemed I had suddenly found out that my beloved sister was a horrible slut, and that in her free time she manufactured pliers which were designed to rip nails off of fingers. I realized that even Stepanas Walleye needed to be *saved*. I had to save that tall girl over there on the other side of the street, those children there, who are running like mad to who knows where. I must save the old, abused city outside the window. I must save the calm Swede sitting next to a fireplace in Stockholm and smoking a good pipe. Perhaps I *especially* needed to save him, because he doesn't so much as suspect *Their* existence; he thinks that everything evil will pass by and leave him untouched. Like an aristocrat, he believes that all misfortunes are destined for others. He doesn't notice the secret sucking stares; he has a sacred trust in his centuries of stability and doesn't even suspect that his thinking alone shows *the kanukai's proboscises have already* touched him, that the pupil-less eyes are already stalking him around every corner, that the drabness already covers both him and his neighbors.

I felt an irrepressible urge to talk things over. I had to try to save Martynas too.

I talked to him about Stepanas Walleye, told him about his nation, made up of five Russian writers, about the zone boss's boots, which always shone—in whatever weather, at whatever time of year, as if he hadn't touched the ground, and about the pen where Bolius grazed.

"The worst of it," I got naïvely hot-headed, "is that what he says seems like the truth: they, the brownshirts, committed hideous crimes against humanity; they have to suffer retribution. But he condemns those hundred scumbags in hiding, and doesn't say a thing about the quarter of a million of the same kind of scumbags who continue to live quite peacefully next door to him, and don't even think of going into hiding. What may be may be, but he knows it! Because of his sufferings in the German camps he can feel like he's a part of mankind demanding retribution. For his sufferings in the Gulag no one will let him feel a part of humanity, they won't even let him mention it, and he obediently agrees to that. He's betrayed us all! He, Stepanas Walleye! The invincible! He himself agreed that he's a nothing. He did it himself, that's what matters most."

That, or something similar, was how I reasoned, attempting to understand something, but I only felt that absolutely everything was covered by a sticky layer, a cosmic jellyfish. I felt that I had to help all the *people*, before it was too late, while the trees still turn green and you can hope to find something alive beyond the lazy hills, as long as somewhere there still are all kinds of Swiss or Swedes, who at least already know that it's inadmissible to admit, even for a second, that you are NOTHING. And to save them too is essential, because they have too much faith in themselves, they think there's no way the fate of Spain in the Middle Ages or Atlantis could happen to them. Those naïve people! . . . They don't sense the pulsating of the cosmic jellyfish, or, feeling it, they run to a psychoanalyst, thinking it's just something broken inside of them and everything around them is all right. They must be saved quickly! Gedis's beloved dogs scampering around Vilnius must be saved, and the warbling birds, and the smell of flowers, and little girls' smiles, and that part of all humans that's called . . . that's called . . . it

194

doesn't matter what it's called, but it must be saved!

It was only then I realized I had been quiet for some time. The brakes engaged without my will; I didn't say what I had no right to say out loud. Martynas was quiet too; he even turned off the television set despite the basketball game. The two of us were quiet, because that was perhaps the only means to communicate to some extent. Through long centuries humanity lost the habit of speaking *straightforwardly*, sensing that *They* could overhear everything. It's only the voiceless conversation of two minds and four eyes that they cannot invade. The most difficult thing in the world is to communicate somehow. (I feel, I believe, I want to believe, that Lolita and I communicate this way.)

At last Martynas sighed and insensibly stared at the city outside the window. Then he turned to me and in all seriousness asked:

"Vytautas, has it ever occurred to you that Vilnius is God's outhouse? That this is merely where he urinates and empties his bowels? Have you ever thought that we, even you and I, are nothing more than God's excrement?"

You'd think Vilnius itself, its gray eyebrows dourly compressed, had asked me that, had asked me what I take it for—a beast or a cosmic jellyfish. Outside the window Vilnius was cloaked in dusk. Buried in a ravine, it seemed to be sinking deeper every minute. Only solitary church towers attempted to escape from under the earth, from out of the drabness. The towers of the churches and the short, stumpy phallus of Vilnius. Vilnius looked at me. Its stumpy, powerless phallus looked at me (looked, because a male sexual organ is an eye, while a vagina is a mirror). Your soul abandons you when Vilnius looks at you that way. You can feel you're already a dead man if Vilnius starts *talking* to you.

I felt tiny, utterly tiny, and horrible—a monstrous dwarf, a midget of the soul, hiding all the horrors of the world within. I felt terrible because I *know*; I know everything (but at the same time I know nothing). I was physically ill; I was nauseated. Outside the window, Vilnius sank below ground for the night, the toothless children of the camp crowded around me, and there I was in the middle of them—a disgusting midget with no right to live. It's impossible to live knowing *everything*; at least the tiniest bit of deceit, a sugary dream of drabness, is imperative. What should I have done? What should I do now? I should have grabbed everything (like those Jewish children) and carried it all away to a safe place. But I, the midget, was pierced through with a numbing premonition that *there are no safe places.*

I rushed to the toilet. I threw up green spit and a few gulps of dry wine. My life was like that reeking, vomited wine. I already knew a great deal and sensed a great deal, but I hadn't saved anyone in my life. I didn't save mother, or Janė, or Irena. I didn't save Bolius, Walleye, or Gedis. I didn't slay the Dragon. I only saved three large-eyed little Jews.

*You're sitting in ruins that smell of death next to St. John's Church; the dark, as always, protects you from evil. Everything is evil now: the crooked streets of Vilnius, the murky air, even the bland hum of silence. Even silence itself is evil. Your city has been injured again—who can count all of its injuries, all of the notches left on the old pavement by the boots of foreigners.*

*You're not allowed to sit here; at dusk you can no longer sit anywhere—only at home. But as soon as the clock strikes the commandant's curfew, you sneak out into the city's labyrinth. No one misses you. Father is gone. Mother is gone. Grandfather falls asleep right in his armchair.*

*The emptied city is particularly beautiful; it's not marred by people's bodies. That beauty is geometrical and oppressive—as befits a labyrinth. You know you'll be able to hide in it. This is your city; you sense all of its nooks and crannies the way you sense your arms and legs; you rule this labyrinth. (All rulers are unhappy.) You could be its Minotaur, but you have no need for innocent maidens. To you it's important to feel the breath of the mute void and the quivering of the pained air; it's important to feel that this labyrinth, unknown to others, belongs to you. German patrols crawl through its corridors constantly, like worms. They're aliens here; they wander aimlessly. They'll never find the center of the labyrinth, where you sit in safety. You hate them, and the city hates them. Who can come to terms with foreign conquerors? Rats, toads, and cockroaches. But you are a human.*

*You don't know what it is you're seeking of the Vilnius night. Perhaps you simply can't leave it alone with the Germans, you must suffer along with it. With the two of you together, it's more comforting and encouraging.*

*You sit in the ruins and look at the illuminated street. Light is bad, it's the kingdom of the German worms, while the ruins and the crooked, pale blue moon protect you. Just now the quiet was ripped like a finger piercing an engraving of ancient Vilnius; you heard shots and shouts of "Halt!" You wait for the runaways to show up in the illuminated corridor of the street; you still don't know what you'll do then.*

By now the tromping of heavy boots is close by; you plainly sense the inhabitants of the nearest houses secretly peeking through the windows. You'd think you would have gotten used to people being hunted long ago. By now the runaways are close, any minute they'll emerge into the dimly-lit street. They must emerge—there's no other way. You know all of the burrow holes of the labyrinth.

There they are, they've already dashed into the pale lake of light.

First some kind of hunchback staggers in, barely dragging himself along; at once his retinue shows up too. Hunchback can't hurry. He's followed by three Lilliputians; sweating, they work their disgusting, short little legs. He can't hurry—he looks back, it seems he keeps dragging them along by invisible strings. The traveling circus of Vilnius: the leader and three trained Lilliputians. No Lilliputian tricks will save them now: the street is illuminated; the German worms will detect them. Now you are their lord: you can let them die against your will, but you can save them too.

However, that's just the way it looks in your foolish lordly head. You can't choose anymore, because you're already standing on the edge of the street, right under the lantern, you're already waving to them, never mind that the patrol worms could show up any minute, spitting little leaden pieces of death. You're risking your life, but in these times life doesn't matter. You're used to that by now. Meaning that your own life doesn't matter, either. You wave to them, beckon them into the ruins; they instantly obey you—the ruler of the Vilnius night. You quickly dive through disintegrated corridors, descend invisible crumbling stairs, step over chunks of stone: anyone would get lost here, but you know where to go. You know all there is to know about night in Vilnius.

At last you stop; the breathless hunchback stops too, and the three hideous Lilliputians huddle against the damp walls and melt into the darkness. The man's face is old and wrinkled; glasses hang on his nose and flash eerily in the moonlight. That man is some three times your age and maybe half your size. He catches his breath with difficulty; an unpleasant smell of sweat emanates from him.

"You're a Lithuanian!" he says with conviction in a heavy, heavy, Jewish accent. "What are you doing here, my boy? Don't stand there, lead us on! Let's run!"

"These are my ruins, my underground," you answer firmly. "The Germans will get lost in my labyrinth. They couldn't explore all of my underground in time for the Day of Judgment."

"You've read the Revelations, my boy?" the hunchback asks in surprise and his accent gets still thicker, "And you know how to hide from the beast whose number is six hundred sixty and six?"

That's the way the Vilnius night is: there you can meet even a hunchback-ed, bespectacled Jew and three degenerate Lilliputians, runaways from death, declaiming about the Revelations of St. John next to St. John's Church.

"It's safe in my underground. In the dark it's always safe. Light is more dangerous."

You don't know what else to say. They won't listen to you, anyway. Jews only listen to their rabbi. As a child you once snuck into the old synagogue. They sat with their heads covered and read something from the Torah. You didn't understand any of it, while they all sat motionless and stared at their Jewish infinity.

"Why were they chasing you?" you ask, but immediately understand it's a foolish question. You are a naïve fool, like all gods.

"Because we're Jews," the hunchback answers and gets nervous: "What if they bring dogs?"

You could answer him that you are the Minotaur, that the dogs won't smell you, but he doesn't need an answer. His thoughts grow confused; he speaks again from another angle:

"We're from the ghetto. Do you know where the ghetto is?"

"Where are you running to?"

"Nowhere. Through the ages we Jews run to the void, because the Prom-ised Land is only in our heads."

"Why the Lilliputians?"

He looks at you in surprise, and then he snaps his fingers as if he were summoning an obedient dog. The Lilliputians separate from the wall—it's three children, large-eyed little Jews, dirty and disheveled. They are as sickly as the Lithuanian pensive Christ; their eyes gaze defenselessly in the moon-light. There's no telling whether they're boys or girls.

"Save them," the hunchback says proudly, without begging. "Save them, if nothing else. I won't go anywhere now, my end was written a long time ago in the books of fate. Remember—every human is an entire universe, and a child is a universe of universes. Save them, my boy, and you'll save a countless number of worlds."

"What do I have to do?"

"You're the Lithuanian. In the villages they secretly take in our children. Lead them out of Vilnius. I have faith in you, my boy."

You feel that now you are their God. You can read to them from your own Torah; they will listen to you, gazing at your infinity. But what can you do? How are you going to take three little Jews, the most Jewish in the world, through the entire city? It's no good to have children, you shouldn't have children.

"You say that the dark loves you? Hide them in the dark, take them out to a village."

"Not today, it'll be light soon."

He no longer has the strength to stand; he suddenly collapses on the stones' sharp edges. He doesn't feel the pain, though the sharp edges pierce him in the thigh, into live flesh. Now he looks like Moses in grandfather's picture. All the old Jews of Vilnius look like Moses on the verge of delivering a great sermon. The three large-eyed children suddenly fall on their knees in front of you. They don't stretch their arms out to you, they don't cry, they don't beg—they kneel as motionless as statues, their eyes have turned to silts of silver in the moonlight.

"Do this, my boy," Moses begins his sermon.

"Let them hide themselves," you order, "And let them stay here, no matter what happens. Until I return."

The Jew says something in his language; the large-eyed children suddenly vanish. You know that they're here, you even feel their breathing—but they've disappeared. They've crept into the cracks of the disintegrating walls, blended into the piles of bricks, turned themselves into muddy drops dripping from the ceiling. Hunchback Moses has bewitched them, has turned them into a part of the ruins.

"I won't thank you, my boy," says Moses in a dying voice. "I'll say just one thing. However many years should go by, wherever you should be, when you meet a Jew, look him straight in the eye. Don't say anything, don't ask for anything—just look at him intently, straight in the eye. He'll understand everything—if he's a real Jew. He'll understand and he'll help you . . . And now lead me out of here. If they find me, they'll start looking for the children too. Lead me out of here."

Without saying anything you lead him through the ruined, wrecked labyrinth. Exiting into the air right by the Dominican Church, you push Moses down a side street where the patrol worms aren't crawling, and you yourself climb the stairs, proud and happy, until you see that your door is open. Open doors in the Vilnius night can only mean something bad.

"Listen, Herr Vargalys," you hear a voice with a horrible German accent, "we're all Europeans. You Lithuanians are almost Aryans. What are these Slavs to you? You should help us."

"But I don't know anything about the Polish secret service," grandfather says calmly.

"Herr Vargalys, we've inspected your old dossier . . . We're grown adults, we're professionals. Don't tell me I'll have to threaten you? By the way, the Armia Krajowa is opposed to the Lithuanians too."

Through the crack you see a German neck and a protruding Adam's apple. The German smokes a cigarette with a gold-plated cigarette holder and looks at grandfather with inhuman eyes. He doesn't need to threaten; he's scary just as he is. He's like a mummy who's lain in a pyramid for three thousand years; now it's arisen and in vengeance wants to put everyone six feet under.

"We're both professionals. Who'd believe the Lithuanian secret service's resident spy in Vilnius doesn't know anything . . ."

Yes, grandfather knows everything: about the Polish secret service, the counterintelligence, Mikołajczyk, Sviderski—whatever you want. He's even told you about some things that aren't terribly secret. Grandfather knows everything, and in this world, it's bad to know a lot.

"How unfortunate that I don't know anything worthwhile," grandfather repeats pleasantly.

"You love the Poles?"

"God forbid. I've fought them all my life."

"Then help us!"

"Unfortunately, it's not within my power to do so."

"I intentionally came at night, so that no one would see us or know anything. We know how to disguise the sources of our information. No documents, no commitments. Just information. Perhaps you're afraid of those measly Poles?"

"I'm not afraid of anything," grandfather says firmly, and you know he's not bragging.

"Then help us!"

"It's out of the question!" grandfather smiles gently and pleasantly, like he's sitting at a diplomatic reception. "I'm so sorry . . ."

"I thought we would converse like colleagues," the SS officer says indifferently. "Sorry? It really is too bad. You're as stupid as a genuine Lithuanian. What do you want, you Lithuanians? What do you expect? You think you'll recover your independence? . . . That's just a hallucination. Your destiny is planned out for a thousand years in advance. Don't tell me you can't tell the difference between a hallucination and reality? You should act rationally; you need to come to terms with reality. To finally understand that you don't exist and never will. And what does the lot of you do? . . . Some give lectures that doom the university, and end up at Stutthof themselves. Another sits with his mouth shut and won't tell us what we need to know. What's all that for? After all, it's all so obvious. Where does this superiority complex come from, this thought that you're somebody? You won't accomplish anything. We won't let you accomplish anything! Everything will be the way it is, and only that way, through the ages, through the entire thousand-year Reich . . . No, it's impossible to understand you. It looks like the boss was right: you're doomed to extinction."

"It's such a pity, Herr Standartenführer, that we, Europeans, can't help each other out this time."

"It's a pity," says the uninvited guest, standing up, "I really wanted to help you . . . Well, others will speak to you. They'll torture you. And for what—for some Poles. For Slavs!"

Two cross-eyed SS officers drag grandfather right by you, nearly bumping into you. You flatten yourself against the wall and think about how much grandfather must hate the Germans if he can sacrifice himself like that on account of the detested Poles.

Their footsteps echo down the stairs, then it's quiet. Now you are left entirely alone. (All rulers are lonely.) You don't need Vilnius anymore. And Vilnius doesn't need you anymore. However, you still have a house on what was the border between Lithuania and Poland. The Russians haven't taken it yet; Janė and Julius are still sheltering there. A long journey awaits you tomorrow night. You'll have to take a lot of food, since you'll be bringing three pairs of giant Jewish eyes.

After Carp's horrifying downfall I couldn't recover for a long time. They couldn't buy him, they couldn't convince him—nicely or not. There was only one explanation: the pupil-less kanukai's stares had slowly drained him: They had cleaned out his brains. It wasn't Stepanas Walleye sitting inside the television set, but a nameless kanuked creature. That meant a great deal. That meant that the stare of the void is worse than the barbed wire of the camp, worse than the bonfires of the Inquisition—worse than anything. Unfortunately, like it or not, we have to live in the glare of that stare—there's nowhere to hide from it. The drab spell of that stare ravages a person more thoroughly than the strongest radiation—you won't protect yourself from it with a suit of lead; no dosimeter measures its effects. No one knows how many doses of kanukism they've gotten by now, or if a fatal dose is still a long way off.

I needed an assistant, a person I could depend on. Martynas wasn't suitable, he was too intelligent and too curious. I was completely sick of Stefa 'accidentally' getting under foot all the time, but she had already served her purpose. I needed a person who would help without asking too many questions, whom I could satisfy with vague stories about a dissertation or some scholarly work. Vilnius didn't want to give me that kind of person. An impossibly damp time had settled in; the city's red and yellow trolleys crawled through the streets half-blind with their windows fogged over. Even their drawn-out, irritating clattering was muffled. Vilniutians wrapped themselves in their raincoats and huddled, but the city's damp hands nevertheless penetrated wherever they wanted. I saw clearly how every passerby dragged himself along, pressed by damp, slimy fingers. All of Vilnius coughed and sneezed. The women of the department looked like plucked hens (Lolita wasn't working with us yet). And suddenly the heavens sent me a rookie by the name of Vaiva. She stung my menagerie to the core. For an entire three days they all came to work in new clothes, carefully made up. On the fourth day Vilnius won out: the collars of the new clothes frayed and their hair-dos came undone. Vilnius always wins.

The rookie seemed different; she wasn't entirely ruined yet. Maybe she wasn't particularly pretty, but she was gushing youth, still looking for something, still hopeful. A short-cut little head of hair, a slender energetic body, and large gray eyes. I carefully examined her intellect. I didn't need a fool, nor someone who was too intelligent. Vaiva was exactly that, and besides—she wasn't as irksome as Stefa. She willingly accepted the boss's attentions, stayed to work evenings, visited me at home a couple of times. She behaved properly: she didn't act cheap, but she didn't hide her legs, either. I was truly happy that I had found an assistant; I trusted her with secondary work. I was already thoroughly resolved to include her in an important experiment. I tried to make her like me, if need be I would even have married her—details couldn't block my essential aims.

But for the time being, I continued to wander through the library's collections alone. At night, there between the bookcases, I read Plato's *Republic* for the hundredth time. I attempted, to no avail, to comprehend the species of *commissars* he had originated. A species in which Robespierre and Mussolini shone. A species whose development says a great deal to a sharp-eyed investigator. I kept asking myself: why do you always end up alone in the presence of the commissars? Where do friends and like-minded fellows, in general any agreements with others, disappear to?

How do *They* manage, at the fateful moment, to separate everyone, so they're left alone? That was the question of that fateful evening.

Otherwise the evening was no different than any other, just that the strangest visions kept raging in my head—fragments of angry sentences, oppressive premonitions—anything you want, just not thoughts. And those that I managed to knit together anyway were *alien*, not mine. It seemed like someone else was thinking with my brains. It was an indescribable sensation. A ferocious being settled inside of my skull, perturbing my brain, sullying it with disgusting proboscises. I saw it, taken out of my head and set on the floor, stinking and blackened. At intervals it occurred to me that it was stuck all over with fat, pink leeches that quivered with relish. Plato was probably one of them—the very fattest one, full of *me*, twitching with idle overindulgence.

I knew quite well that Plato had nothing to do with it, that I was being devoured by a very genuine being; it had made its way inside me and was delighting in my helplessness. I imagined I was beginning to slowly *turn* into something else. I was fully conscious, not even overly tired, but suddenly I felt as if I had landed inside an oppressive dream. In this dream I was supposed to turn into something at any second. I was still myself, but I had already begun to inexorably change. I didn't turn into a different person, nor into some other thinking being. *They* had a different purpose: I was supposed to turn into something sticky, nasty, and soulless. I was threatened by a mortal danger, but there was no way I could defend myself.

Kafka's *Metamorphosis* doesn't describe *change* itself. Samsa wakes up already transformed into a gigantic bug. That's awful, but the metamorphosis itself, even the premonition of changing, is still worse. Kafka knew about it, surely he knew; apparently, in spite of everything, *They* had destroyed a part of his manuscripts.

However, I was no Samsa, I wasn't anyone's fictional character. I was a real person, I was sitting in a real library, and this waking dream was suffocating and choking me. Horrified, I looked around at the identical rows of bookshelves. Something was stalking me in the labyrinth of dusty book spines. Alas, alas, it was not I who was the Minotaur; the real beast was patiently waiting for me, or maybe it had even begun to quietly masticate me, its eternal victim. I didn't know which direction to turn, where to go look for it. It was identical on every side: defenseless book spines in the drab, spiritless light; turns, nooks and traps. Going one or a dozen steps to the side wouldn't change the view: once more—an aimless chaos of book spines, a distorted, dusty silence. I asked myself why do I sit here evenings and read tattered books? Why do I look for answers to questions, why do I wrestle with something if no one, absolutely no one, needs it? The soaked, fog-drenched inhabitants of Vilnius need only bread and meat, cushy furniture, and easy work; then there are some who need to whine about a dying Lithuania too—just whining, don't you dare lift a finger. And what could *I* give them? Vague premonitions, a quadrille of toothless camp children, a pile of portraits of people who once *were*? Who needs me? Vilnius, perfectly justifiably, wants to strangle me, the disturber of the peace. I had an urge to set the library on fire, to set all of Vilnius, the entire world, on fire. Even though there was (there always is) a simpler way—set yourself on fire, one way or another. Kalanta burned himself alive in a square in Kaunas for just that reason—whatever purposes and motives others would pin on him. And still simpler and more human—simply calm down. Why the torture? It's much better to bow your head and to feel a flawless, drab benevolence overtaking you. Let the dead bury their dead. Lord knows, why do I want to open my eyes, what in this godforsaken city is *worth* fighting for? (*Now* I'd answer—for Lolita. It's worth sacrificing a hundred like me for her.)

I don't know where these thoughts would have led me, but suddenly I heard a completely extraordinary noise. I didn't even hear it; I couldn't hear anything—it was completely quiet around me. I smelled that sound, I felt it with the seventh sense. Through the long evenings and nights I had grown so much a part of the library that I would have sensed even a stranger's dream there.

This time no such sensitivity was needed; I felt the hapless intruder's breathing, his clumsy movements. He carefully floated in the library's labyrinth, thinking he was undetectable and inviolable, absolutely trusting in himself, like all of *Them*. He had no suspicion that I could feel him. Heated blood throbbed at the top of my throat, raising a barely detectable salty taste. In the dusk the bookcases resembled ancient ruins. The variously colored book spines faded, the corners of the bookshelves crossed and changed places, and I was surrounded by all shades of drabness. It seemed I had ended up between the camp's barracks on an early, murky morning. All of the guards and the zone boss himself tried to turn me into a bug, a slug, a rock. They sat about inside their well-heated little houses and greedily sucked my soul. Everything was over; all that was left for me to do was to surrender. But suddenly I saw a dusky light squeezing under the book shelves; like a madman I rushed towards it, turned a corner, still another, and finally exited into a dead-end corridor at the end of the bookcases. He was covered in a dim light, permeated in a strange, bitter smell. A live creature sat there, my mortal enemy, a sullen octopus that had sucked out my fluids. *At last I discovered him.*

The octopus was named Vaiva; it had a short-cropped little head of hair and nervously smoked a cigarette. She stood at the end of the dead-end corridor, turning the pages of a book. Her movements were jerky; her fingers crawled over the pages, devouring the letters. I immediately recognized the place, the corridor, the row of books. She was looking over the books I had selected and put in a safe place the week before. She greedily turned the pages, photographing them with her eyes. I wanted it to not be true, I wanted it to be just a dream. But Vaiva was only too real. She stood leaning her shoulders against a shelf, her sweater kept rising and falling against her chest. A gray miniskirt barely covered her crossed legs. She turned the pages of a French book; I immediately remembered that she hadn't put down on her job application that she knew French. I quietly slunk closer; some ten steps still separated us. I still hoped that everything would end up as a joke, a small fright and explanations. But I couldn't deceive myself; the sensation that had brought me here was much too strong and real. She was just exactly the beast who had been stalking me. An impostor, worming her way into my immediate surroundings, knowing what books I read, even writing up summaries for me.

I expected a start or a smile, I expected what she would say, knowing full well that I would sense deceit immediately. There was a great deal I expected, but not what happened. She suddenly bared her teeth like a trapped wild beast and pressed herself into the corner. She didn't even try to *feign* anything; she had been caught too suddenly. She furiously shot her eyes to the sides, but I had blocked her path. Unexpectedly, her lips distorted into a pale smile. The short-cropped little head of hair turned coquettishly to the side, but the veins in her neck immediately tensed up again. She hunched her back and fixed her stare on my face. It seemed someone had whipped me in the eyes with a switch. The shadow of a smile on her lips vanished; she firmly planted her feet on the floor and leaned forward. That young, pleasant girl turned into the twin sister of the neckless spiderman, the ruler of the Narutis quarter. The pupils of her large grey eyes widened, and I couldn't pull my gaze away from them; I felt a lazy warmth flowing over my chest; my legs and arms began to melt. The corners of her lips turned upwards, instantly changing her face into a doughy mask. She took control of me; I stood there as if I had been turned to stone, I couldn't even budge. I suddenly forgot everything I had wanted to do. Her face slowly paled, her cheeks sank in, her firmly pressed lips lost their color. It seemed she was insistently sucking something in, siphoning something into herself with all her might. Barely visible barbs emerged from her eyes and pierced my numb arms and legs. A lazy, sticky warmth flooded over my entire body; I wanted to sit down and rest. I was a traveler who had walked a thousand steps, I needed to sit down and rest. Agile little fingers intruded into my guts, into my kidneys, gently caressed the most secret, most sensitive places. I saw a dull, bloodless smile on her face; I wanted to smile too. After all, the two of us were good friends. All of my fury was silly and unnecessary. She was my friend, and at the same time my ruler. The gentle but tenacious little fingers penetrated deeper and deeper, I felt good, better and better all the time. It always feels good to obey—to obey and to humble oneself, to dissolve in another's will.

A book plopped to the floor unexpectedly and released me. It seemed someone had pulled it off the shelf and hurled it down. Vaiva gave a start and scowled to the side, momentarily releasing me from the grip of her stare. A cold wave of sobriety washed over my head. I was still alive. I had met a disgusting octopus in the shape of a girl. Straining, she stood opposite me and attempted to injure me with a sharp, biting glance. I saw her unevenly lit pale face quite well. An unnatural face—there wasn't even the tiniest wrinkle on it. The gray skin was smooth, dull, and lifeless. She moved her completely narrowed, bloodless lips convulsively, as if she wanted to suck in all of the air in the library and thereby suffocate me. She rolled her eyes hopelessly, trying to stab me with her glance's barbs. She was powerless and revolting; she had finally and irrevocably given herself away. I had sidestepped her kanukish tricks; I was saved by the book falling to the floor with a crash.

*Now* I stand, trapping her in the dead-end corridor, and attentively follow her barbed eyes. *Now* the lamp with the colorless shade slowly sways, the lines of the shadows intertwine, crossing over and shoving one another aside. I feel horror rising inside me; I feel how my legs and arms slowly come back to life. By now I know what I will shortly do; by now I know why I slowly snuck over here and what must be uncovered. Now I am her ruler; I have triumphed. She stabs me with her barbed pupils, futilely seeks extra support for her feet, but her spectral efforts are in vain. I feel the strength in every tiny muscle, and most importantly—I feel how my brain has freed and focused itself. I see every wrinkle in her short skirt, her knees pressed together: she curls up her left leg, as if trying to hold up some thing falling from her crotch. I could crush her with a single look, reckon with her for this evening's nightmare, for the hideous *change*. It was she who oppressed me from afar, who wanted to turn me into a bat, a jellyfish, a cockroach. Now she turns her eyes away, now *she's* afraid; she knows there's no help coming.

I have the urge to tear her into pieces, to pull off her arms and legs, to fling the bloody pieces in all directions. She intruded on my world, broke into it by deceit, at a time when I particularly hungered for help. But she fell into her own trap. No punishment would be enough for her. My hands reach for her throat of their own accord, sweat beads up on my forehead, and below my belly a hard lump writhes. I have pressed her shoulders; I didn't press them hard, I was just trying it out. She finally raises her eyes, which are brimming with horror, but immediately cowers again—now she's the one who is cowering! Her body goes limp and surrenders. She doesn't dare to oppose me; she doesn't defend herself with either words or movements. I can no longer stop my hands; they let go of the stiffened shoulder blades and slide heavily down the sloping shoulders. I see the sweater's buttons fly to the floor, I see the smooth skin uncovered to the breasts. Only then do I understand what I must do.

Calmly, I pull off the camisole and bra straps; she tries to get away, but my hands are firm, she is in my power. With gusto I clean her body of its layer of deceitful clothes, she struggles and writhes, red indentations remain on her back from the shelves, and there are blue circles from my fingers on her shoulders, but the more pleadingly she looks at me, the more my fury boils. I know what I'll shortly see: withered breasts with multiple layers of disgusting folds and lumps on a deformed belly, those familiar abominations with which *Their* bodies are marked. I've already seen the body of a woman like that, I came to know it very well; soon I'll be disgusted again by one just like it. I've torn the last scraps off her torso, she's still curling her left foot up, the skirt writhes as if it's alive, but at the moment I'm more concerned by what's above it.

I pull back to see better, because she covers herself with her chin and shoulders, now I see it—I don't believe my eyes, but I see—she stands in front of me naked to the waist, breathing hard through her mouth with her arms lowered helplessly. But I search in vain with my eyes for what I expected, in vain I widen my pupils, blink and want to wipe my tearing eyes. I don't see the slightest sign of abominations; her skin is smooth and soft, the firm young breasts tremble in agitation, the small dark nipples stick out to the sides, and the smooth, slender stomach heaves heavily. Unable to restrain myself, I touch it: I don't believe my other senses. It can't be: I stroke and squeeze the soft breasts, still naïvely hoping they're artificial, buttoned on, stuffed. She winces terribly at every touch; I finger the skin under the breasts, I search for scars, the marks of an operation or something similar. It's hopeless, it's all hopeless; I audibly release a breath, it's gone musty in my lungs during that long moment. Everything was so clear, so absolutely clear—but suddenly everything fell apart. What have I done?

*Now* I stand in front of her like I've been struck by lightning. I don't believe it, I don't believe it, it can't be! I look at her, my eyes widened; I look at what she's hiding with her curled-up left leg. I remember the globs of flesh between Irena's thighs, I remember the wrinkles and the stinking abscesses, that image crashes mercilessly into my brain—I no longer control my hands; they grab her again, tear the short skirt aside, pull and rip off the stockings, losing all reason, all patience. I must hurry, because a horrible doubt keeps escalating, and I don't want to go there. She writhes and struggles like a fury, squeezing my hand with her knees, it seems I hear breaking bones. I must hurry, because the doubt keeps growing, by now it's bigger than I am, the stronger it is, the more furiously I tear at her clothes and skin, she defends herself like mad, I brutally twist her arms and push her knees apart. And the hideous doubt keeps getting closer, it's no longer doubt, but reality: of all her clothes, only pale blue lacy underpants remain, and I see, I feel with my hand, nothing but turned, polished thighs with a soft nap, they're long and graceful, I have nowhere to hide anymore, I see, ever more plainly, that *I have done something insane.* Her nearly naked body thrashes, squirms out of my hands, my eyes are covered in a red veil, because I have done something insane, I don't even dare to think of what will happen next. I cannot stop, because I cannot admit I've done something insane, the triangle of blue lacy underpants still remains, under it I'll find the answer, surely I will find the answer of all answers. It's there! I lift her from the ground, bend her in half, but she still presses her knees together, I can't tear off the blue barrier guarding the bottom of her belly, but I must do it, I want to do it, I want to find, to take her vagina, she's entirely in my power, all that's left is to enter her, I want that, *I want it,* no one will get in my way. Totally insane, I rip off the underpants, sling the remnants aside and wait, totally at a loss: something has gone wrong here, something has fallen apart. *There is no vagina; there is nothing there!* The body in my hands suddenly goes limp, turns slack, I pull out my convulsively curled fingers, then, not believing it, stick them into her crotch again. That is where the answer is. I let go of that doll-like body, set it on the floor; it stands there like a statue, even though just now it struggled and raged.

She stands and looks at me with complete indifference. I still don't want to believe it; I wait for something to change, even though I clearly see everything in front of my eyes, even though I just now felt of it with damp, trembling fingers. The lamp with its colorless shade has stopped swaying; it illuminates everything with a lifeless light. She stands in front of me, disgustingly bent over; I don't want to see it, but all the same my glance slides down her smooth belly until it reaches the long, slender thighs. Trembling, my hand stretches out, the fingers slide sluggishly between her legs, and Vaiva (or *how* would you call her?) nonchalantly crooks her thighs, letting my hand in. Once more I see, once more I feel it with my palm, once more I realize: she has no vagina, no labia, no mound of Venus, no pubic hair. Everywhere there is smooth, shining skin—like a plastic doll's. My head feels slightly dizzy and I desperately want a drink. All of my phobias, fury, and rage have disappeared. Casually, sickeningly, she squirms out of my hands and squeezes by me. I quickly recoil: now I'm afraid to touch her, I don't even want to look at her, because she's not human, she is *something else*. I want a drink something awful. The book that saved me lies under my feet, I pick it up and vainly search for a title—there isn't one anywhere. The binding is leather with an impressed ornament, and then the text starts up immediately—in Italian, it seems. A nameless Italian book.

Of course, Vaiva (or *how* would you call her?) didn't show up again. I knew it was hopeless to search for her traces, but I checked, anyway. Her documentation had vanished; no one knew where it had disappeared to. The number of the building on Minties Street she had given for her address had never existed. I quietly rejoiced at avoiding the danger, until I realized a simple thing: she hadn't been sent accidentally. *They* had come across my traces; only God knows what information the pseudo-Vaiva had managed to collect. At the very least, *They* now knew for sure that I was secretly looking for information about *Their* activities. It was just that *They* hadn't grasped what I had already found.

I was stunned by that body, by that unearthly doll made of flesh and bone—*almost* like that of a human's. In my mind I arranged and adjusted all of the details of her behavior, but I found nothing peculiar in them, nothing provocative. That ideal mimicry was intimidating; it nearly drove me out of my mind—it's terrible to trust no one, to suspect every last person. I couldn't get used to it, probably I eventually would have had a nervous breakdown, but this time Stefa came to my aid. She had anxiously followed my Donjuaniad with Vaiva; it seemed to me that she breathed a sigh of relief when she disappeared. And immediately, without a pause, she shoved me into the very midst of the kanukai. One gloomy morning she brought an elderly gray-haired man into my office. An expensive suit and a markedly correct pronunciation immediately gave him away as a stranger; he reminded me of a foreign diplomat. I chatted with him about the weather for some ten minutes before I realized it was Vasilis sitting opposite me. The eccentric Vasilis from the hut in the swamp, the sorcerer Vasilis, who understood the language of birds. I still hadn't managed to collect my wits when he finished me off completely: he cold-bloodedly explained he had come to Vilnius to attend Stadniukas's funeral.

Thank God, I was too exhausted and too dim-witted to feel all of that news' absurd menace to the hilt.

Stadniukas the scab, Stadniukas the pervert, Stadniukas the executioner, who had lived like a gentleman for all those years practically next door to me in the Executive Committee Building, had just now died. He wasn't struck by lightning, he didn't burn in the fires of hell; he expired peacefully in his bed! Both of us walked the same sidewalks, probably passed each other a hundred times, and I didn't see, didn't hear, didn't smell him! This can only happen in Vilnius, only Vilnius can hide a person that way for years upon years!

*"You should have your eyes burned out . . ."*

*"Burn his pecker . . ."*

*"Shit on peas, shit on beans . . ."*

*Sralin twitches his mustaches in the frame, and the nostrilly face flies around you. He minces and giggles, shitty Russkie NKVD.*

I got so wrapped up in disconnected memories of Stadniukas that I almost wasn't surprised at the miracle worker Vasilis. The nearly seventy-year-old looked my age at the very most. The dumb wizard spoke a foreign language fluently. The hermit of the swamps paraded his aristocratic manners.

He was terribly suspect. What did he show up here for? Why just now? I looked at his infernal eyes and had no idea of how I should act.

"You don't resemble either your father or grandfather," Vasilis observed calmly. "All the Vargalyses are very different. I know the Vargalyses well, better than they know themselves. After all, I'm writing a history of the Vargalys family."

"Where is it?" I went pale.

"In my head. In this world, there's no sense in trusting everything to a piece of paper."

Those words miraculously calmed me. I felt that Vasilis was *one of my own*. We prepared to go to Stadniukas's funeral together. Vasilis ponderously explained why it was not to be missed on any account.

"In attempting to understand certain people," he lectured me, "I decided that the drab spirit of the swamp reigns in their heads. The name means nothing; all that matters is that it's an evil spirit. Without question Stadniukas was beset by that spirit to an unusual degree. I believe when a person like that dies, the swamp ought to give an important sign."

I wasn't mistaken—Vasilis was *one of my own*. As if I had lost my mind, I threw all sorts of hints at him, and nearly spoke up about *Them*. Thank God, he was more sensible than I. He said what he could say, and clammed up like he'd been sewn shut. He really was *one of my own*.

At the funeral I stared more at those who had gathered than at the coffin, uncovered according to the Russian custom. Even now I hate the expression of Stadniukas's face, his thin, predatory nostrils. I was afraid that if I stared enough at his mug, I could attack it and tear it into pieces, or even worse—get even with him, an eye for an eye—unbutton his fly and rip out all of that stinking seed of evil. In those days I could have done anything.

Groups of NKVD agents had gathered at the graveyard—all of them outfitted in civilian clothes, but they couldn't, after all, change their eyes and faces. We stood a bit farther off; Vasilis watched the coffin with infinite concentration. The oppressive burial speeches came to an end; in them, the murder of innocent children was called a battle for the Communist cause, and denunciations—the embodiment of the highest morals. The refined sadist Stadniukas flew out of them as half angel, half holy martyr. It seemed to me that after every speech he got more and more bloated, the kanukai's hypocritical words penetrated into the rotten body through the ears and nostrils; they exploded Stadniukas's remains from within. By now the gravediggers had raised the coffin lid and grabbed for their hammers. The disappointment on Vasilis's face grew ever more obvious. Even I fixed my eyes on the corpse. The body was swollen to nearly triple its size; a black steam seemed to rise from it. The gravediggers attempted to close the coffin, but the swollen body resisted.

And at last, what Vasilis and I had come for *happened*. Stadniukas's long head suddenly *broke off like an overripe pear*; a black, sticky gruel flowed out of the crack over the entire face. I gave a hoarse cry, while Vasilis only grew more engrossed, straining in his effort to avoid missing the slightest detail.

I got a good look at the attendees' reaction. The gravediggers, acting as though nothing was the matter, closed the lid and pressed it down, even throwing themselves on top of it. There was no trace of Stadniukas left, only black steam continued to rise from the cracks in the coffin. The disguised NKVD agents pretended that absolutely nothing had happened. However, they gave themselves away; they had all, to a man, *seen everything*: for a brief instant their flat faces distorted, and terror flashed in their pupil-less eyes. But just for a brief moment: a second later they again stood there as if nothing was going on—full and satisfied, overflowing with self-satisfaction. Only one undersized gray-haired figure looked completely done in, but not because of Stadniukas: he kept cowering and glancing at me.

I had seen him somewhere before, but I didn't have the time to think about him. Vasilis was all that interested me. He cleared his throat in satisfaction and immediately turned to leave the graveyard. I barely managed to keep up with him. I didn't say anything, but my face and my eyes screamed and yelled: he couldn't have misunderstood my question.

"You saw it all yourself," Vasilis maintained his remarkable restraint to the end. "What more is there to say?"

In the meantime, that gray-haired figure kept staring at me, pressed up against the graveyard fence.

He meant something to me sometime in my life, but I couldn't place him.

I'll trap Vasilis in his cabin in the swamps yet; I'll get myself there straight through the mire. He'll answer all my questions yet.

At the time I practically didn't notice how or when he disappeared. I didn't see what was going on outside myself; I was only wandering around inside. The period of guessing and suspicions ended that day. The fateful performance, which will drive me out of my mind sooner or later, had begun. Up until then I could still hope everything that was going on was not *really* for real; I could convince myself that it was my excessive sensitivity, my predilection for fantasizing and making strange comparisons, that was to blame. Now everything was finally clear. Before it was too late, I had to do what I had not thought of doing until then. I had to thoroughly inspect Gedis's apartment. The six-month period after his death was coming to an end; in a few weeks some mathematician, rejoicing that he would at last have his own home, would take it over. The apartment would go to a stranger—Gedis didn't have any relatives and didn't leave a will.

Suddenly I asked myself: did he really not leave one?

*They* cannot bear a spiritual legacy. *They* tried in every possible way to destroy Lenin's political legacy.

*They* fear any kind of spiritual inheritance. *They* strive to have a person disappear without leaving a trace upon this earth. *They* honor and support a material inheritance by all means possible.

I broke into Gedis's sealed apartment without the least apprehension; I felt no danger. The rooms met me with an oppressive smell of dust; they were ill-disposed and foreign. Nothing there was the same as what it once was. Gedis's spirit didn't hover there; *They* hadn't just taken him away from me—they had taken him away from the entire world. I couldn't even come across any memories there. All that met me was the oppressive smell of dust and a dead silence. My hope—that I would be visiting Gedis—was in vain. He was gone, only a portrait, not at all similar to the original, gazed from the blue wallpaper. My hope—that I would find his secret testament here—was in vain. Neither Gedis's spirit, nor his scent, nor his memory were there anymore. There was only a labyrinth of things, which memory told me to call his things. But it seemed even the things were different. I found no sign of Gedis, neither in the office between the books nor in the drawers between the pages of formulas. Despite myself, I remembered *how* he died. Only *They* could erase a person from the world like that. Gedis vanished without a trace. With trembling fingers I stroked his piano, but even in its depths no memory of the music that had been remained. It was gloomily, irreparably dead. The dark polished surface was covered with a wanton layer of dust; I suddenly decided the dust was to blame for everything. I started angrily brushing it off—with my hands, my handkerchief, my sleeves. Hysterically, I cleaned the piano, the books, the windowsills. I crawled around the room on my knees, trying to bring it back to life. The dust I had raised came down again like gray sand. It stuck to my clothes and skin; after a minute or two I was just as drab as the dead things in the room. I realized that *They* had lured me here, probably wanting to warn me of what happens to those who are not submissive to *Them*: a dusty heap of dead things. I was no more than one of those things myself. Something snapped in my chest, under my heart; I cried like a small child, sorry for what, I didn't know, not for Gediminas, not even for myself—for something for which there is no name. Every tear would instantly soak into the carpet of dust without leaving so much as a darker spot—only a tiny indentation. Those indentations in the dust were all that was left of Gediminas. Still not understanding what had driven me here, I looked around the bedroom and the office for the last time, then turned into the living room to say goodbye to Gedis's piano, silenced for the ages. I sadly opened the door and froze on the threshold.

In the very middle of the living room, sprawled in the leather armchair, sat a tall, gray old woman in dirty clothes, the queen of dust. The thick fabric of her skirt didn't even cover her knees; her scruffy sweater was tied together with strings. She sat there comfortably, as if she were sitting at home, and pulled at the stuck-together ends of her hair with chewed-up fingernails. She looked at me without blinking and said nothing. She waited for me to recognize her and say something first. I looked attentively at the repulsive, wrinkled face; I sensed the stench of a long unwashed body growing stronger all the time. I wasn't surprised that she had suddenly shown up here, where no one should have been. I vaguely sensed that, not finding Gedis, I was obliged to find *at least* her. I went right up to her; she smiled wryly, suddenly let go of the ends of her hair, stretched out her hand and insolently, shamelessly, grabbed me *by the very crotch.*

"Come closer, Vytuk," she croaked in a low voice, "Don't be afraid, it's me. Come closer!"

*Even by the creek it's hellishly hot, although it's still only the end of spring. Grandfather is right: the summer of the apocalypse is coming—and what will be left standing? The sun hungers to burn everything up; dust* hangs over the fields, threatening to swallow everything; but your mouth is parched for other reasons too. You stand on the scorched grass next to the black ravine and look at Madam Giedraitienė lying on a sky-blue blanket. Everyone else from the two villas is gone, the two of you are alone today. She came down to the water, although the heat probably doesn't bother her—it's enough for her to wave her hand and even the weather would obey her. She's as majestic as a queen, or maybe even a goddess. You've always hungered to touch her, but you don't dare—that would be sacrilege, your arms would wither away. She slowly opens her eyes—she felt your presence. She'll drive you away immediately, put you to shame for secretly admiring her. But no, she looks at you kindly, her head gracefully turned.

"Come closer," she says in a deep queen's voice. "We'll chat about something. It's so hot and boring."

Her deep, dewy eyes pull you like a magnet, they scorch more fiercely than the apocalyptic sun. You approach carefully, looking only at her legs. You've never seen such long and slender legs. When you and your friends crawled under the stairs at school and stared greedily with your heads upturned, you saw thousands upon thousands of them. But none of them were so long and slender, none of them could be: Madam Giedraitienė is special; she's a queen, or maybe even a goddess.

"We've been left by ourselves, Vytuk . . . Giedraitis is in Kaunas; he's in meetings all the time. Robertas ran out to the Nationalist Youth gathering . . . The two of us are all alone, like on a deserted island . . . Well, come on, why did you stop?"

An intoxicating scent, the scent of enchantment, emanates from her; you dive into its lush waves. Can a human being smell that way? You should close your eyes and stop looking at her long, slender legs. You're sinful and disgusting, you're not fit to even stand next to her, next to a goddess.

"Sit down!"

"I'm wet, I'll dirty the blanket."

She laughs unexpectedly, stretches out her hand and touches your knee, then even higher up. It's so unexpected that you go numb all over, and then shudder like all the electricity in the world is shaking you.

"You little wet thing! You're even shivering. It isn't healthy to have wet pants on."

The irises of her eyes are crooked; she looks at you: not at your face—at your belly, your legs and somewhere else too. Her gaze burns, the places where she glances even hurt. Your thin white shorts are soaked through; you're completely transparent, you're more naked than naked. You stand right next to her face, she sees all of you. It's torture: her glance and her white-toothed smile will kill you.

"Just the two of us . . ." she says pensively.

Her voice intoxicates even more so than her scent. You shouldn't look at her legs; you close your eyes and try to hide in the reddish-brown fog of your eyelids. Once more you see yesterday's scene: the window of their villa, Giedraitis with your grandfather; in place of her intoxicating voice you hear their angry argument; thank God you can save yourself from her for at least a little while. "We've gotten in touch with Estonia and Latvia—it's the same thing there," Giedraitis thunders. "Their market is flooded with counterfeit money too. There's millions of counterfeit litai circulating here." "The Russians?" Grandfather asks impatiently. "Yes, it's Moscow's work. It's an absolute state secret, Mr. Vargalys . . ." "Is it still worth talking about a state?" Grandfather says bitingly. "Europe will spit in our beards and mind their own business." "You're a pessimist, Mr. Vargalys. It's an old trick, they want to provoke our financial ruin, but they won't succeed. Lithuania's currency is one of the most stable in the world." "If the Russian dragon has opened its maw, everything will go to hell!" Grandfather angrily cuts him off. "The English will suffer a bit without Lithuanian hogs, but they won't tangle with the Russkies. Remember Czechoslovakia . . . That Georgian will swallow us whole. He feeds on infants and snacks on states . . . Pack your bags, Mr. Giedraitis. Or drink champagne." "There's no point in declaring the apocalypse, Mr. Vargalys. The government is taking very serious measures . . ." "Shit!" Grandfather throws back, "It's all shit! When the end of the world is nigh, it isn't the time to sit in meetings." "Mr. Vargalys, the Cabinet has decided to ask you . . ." "My thanks to the Cabinet!" Grandfather bellows, "Thank you for the warning. At least I'll buy up some champagne while it's still to be had. Pretty soon Russian vodka will be all that's left." "But Mr. Vargalys . . ." "And there won't be any misters, everyone will be comrades! Where's the Russian army, I ask you? Who let it in? You let it in yourselves, you blithering idiots!" "Mr. Vargalys, all civilized countries . . ." "Those countries of yours have hidden themselves under the bed! The Führer and the Georgian have sliced up Europe like a cake. That's it! Bring on the champagne! We'll hold a wake for Lithuania!"

"You'll shiver to death," you come to your senses and instantly feel how the muscle in your thigh is trembling, as if it wanted to jump away from her fiery fingers. "What shall we think up? . . . Listen, you take off that wet stuff, those shorts. What's the big deal? We're like family, after all. Don't be afraid, no one will see us here . . ."

You don't believe your ears, maybe you're imagining her voice speaking of impossible things—you quickly open your eyes and again you see her legs, then the contour of her belly under the smooth fabric, then her bosom. Then the neck of a swan, then the eyes; they scorch your masculinity with the thin, wet cloth stretched over it. She really said that. Doesn't she realize you're already grown, that there's nothing that could make you do that?

"Listen, Vytuk," she coos, and keeps pressing you with her fiery fingers. "You'll get sick like this . . . Don't be afraid, no one will come by. It's just the two of us. Don't tell me you're afraid of me?"

Doesn't she understand? You look sadly into her eyes, but you can't see anything through the tears. How much you've dreamt of her! How you'll dress up in a new French suit, and she'll say in surprise: how handsome you are, Vytuk! How you'll save her from drowning, she'll press her wet hair to your shoulder and say: you're my hero, Vytuk! Is she teasing? You stand opposite her face more naked than naked and as hot as if scalded by fire.

"Now, what's to be done with you?" she bites her lip and lowers her voice. "All right, if that's the way it is, I'll get undressed too. We'll be like two Robinson Crusoes on a deserted isle . . . After all, we're like family, aren't we?"

You don't have the time to either be surprised or to cry out, and she's already undressing. Her swimming suit catches on her breasts, it doesn't want to come down, but finally they squeeze out; thrashing, they roll down her chest as if they were alive. You can go crazy from such beauty, you try not to see them, while she looks at you and says commandingly:

"Well, help then, what are you waiting for?"

You can't disobey the queen; she kneels, her hands pressed on her naked hips, and transfixes you with her eyes. You kneel next to her and pull the suit all the way down to the ground—roughly, with your face turned away, but your face turns on its own, on their own your eyes look at her belly button, then farther down, at the hair, from which spreads an even more intoxicating scent of enchantment. She laughs hoarsely, gracefully wriggles out of the collapsed material.

"And you? Can I help?"

*You jump up like you've been scalded and quickly take off your dripping shorts. She keeps smiling, and you stand there like a blockhead.*

*"Well, see now . . . nothing to it . . . We're simply Robinson Crusoes, floating to hell with all of Lithuania, and what is there to do, if not . . ."*

*You feel weak in the knees and ashamed, hopelessly ashamed. Your masculinity hangs frightened and shriveled. Even now it's bigger and more handsome than her husband's, even if he is a minister—but you know what it can be like! Suddenly you realize that you have long since wanted to stand in front of her as naked as can be—big and strong, a real, wild Crusoe, so she would see all of you, so she would be charmed and say: I didn't think you were such a man, Vytuk!*

*"Well, lie down, you'll warm up."*

*You stretch out carefully, not touching her. You insanely want to caress her breast or her slender leg. You want it to the point of pain—and what would she do? But after all, she won't kill you. You slowly move your hand closer, infinitely slowly, it'll move that way for weeks and months. But afterwards, after those weeks and months, you'll touch her at last—and what will happen then? She'll draw back and cry out, and you'll crush, squeeze, squeeze her breasts, squeeze . . . She sighs aloud, moves strangely, you get scared and close your eyes again. She probably sensed your horrible desires.*

*"Vytuk, I'm so hot and lazy . . . My blood's not moving at all. Be good, massage me, will you? . . . Press hard, you hear?"*

*You may touch her, she said so herself! You kneel with your knees secretly nuzzling her hip, slowly stroke her stomach, knead with your fingers, and stroke in circles again. You know what a massage is; if she'd let you, you'd massage her a hundred times a day. Her eyes are closed; you can look at her as much as you want. Your masculinity swells, raises its head—what will happen if she opens her eyes and sees it? Let her just say so—you'd lick the bottoms of her feet and between her toes . . . One by one, you'd lick every one of the barely visible little hairs on her calves . . . With your fingers, no, with your lips, you'd clean out the most horrible places—if she'll just lie with her eyes closed and smile.*

*"Lower, lower," she whispers, "Still lower . . ."*

*You rub your fingers in circles, twist and turn them around as best you can, and she moves her belly strangely, raising it, maybe you're not doing something right.*

*"Lower!" she orders hoarsely.*

*But there's nowhere lower to go! Your fingers tangle in the hair; you don't know what to do. Her long slender legs slowly spread out, the thighs separate from one another, and there, in the hair, something is showing by now, something you don't dare look at. She opens her eyes, her glance is angry, almost furious—in a minute she'll slap you and drive you away.*

*But she doesn't drive you away, instead, angrily, horribly, she grasps your swollen masculinity and rapaciously pulls it to herself, scarcely getting her fingers around it. It seems your insides will tear in half any minute, but she yanks at you without easing up, pulls at it and smiles wryly, horribly.*

*"Enough! Come on now!" she orders in a croaking, drinker's voice. "Just don't pretend you haven't tried it!"*

The old woman reeked, overwhelmingly and irredeemably. Was it possible Giedraitienė was somewhere close by all the time? Maybe I'd even run into her, looked at her without recognizing her?

"I knew you'd come . . . I waited . . ." It seemed an old, rusty mechanism creaked out the words. "I knew . . ."

"You . . . you live here?"

"What do you need here?" She didn't listen to me; she just continued to croak her strange sing-song. "Haven't you noticed the smell? Haven't you seen those hands with the swollen joints?"

I recoiled involuntarily: that live pit of offal was impossible to bear.

"Don't run off, this is just the beginning," the old woman croaked patiently. "No, I don't live here, I came just because of you. I live in the house of cheer, the cheeriest house in Vilnius . . ."

She laughed; her laughter had survived intact: hoarse and seductive, and at the same time unconstrainedly free—like music. It sounded in the middle of Gedis's living room in place of the dead piano. That was all I found here. When was the last time I had heard that laugh? The summer of the night trains of cattle cars, or the same one, but different already—the summer of the insolent swastikas and bored SS men? I stood in Gedis's dusty, dead living room, while across from me in a leather armchair sat Giedraitienė, as alive as could be, mockingly staring at me with her crooked irises. A hideous, oppressively reeking old woman with sagging cheeks and matted, greasy hair was looking at me.

"Do you know where you're heading, my child?" she spoke again. "Have you ever seen leeches suck out a mouse that's been thrown into the water? Have you seen it? . . . At first they latch on by the neck and under the belly . . . The mouse struggles, it fights like mad. It tries to throw off the leeches . . . It rushes around in the water, raising a terrible spray . . . But for some reason it doesn't go towards shore, that's what's odd: it thrashes, splashing terribly, but it stays in the water . . . The leeches don't get alarmed; they're never alarmed . . . The mouse's struggles change nothing; the water just slowly turns reddish. And the mouse keeps getting calmer and calmer. That's particularly beautiful— how it keeps getting calmer. It slowly realizes that's the way it should be, that it's the essential truth of the world . . . It's unbearably beautiful . . . It's like absolute knowledge . . . Or coming closer to God . . . Have you ever seen that, Vytuk?"

"No."

"Too bad. Too bad you've never sensed that beauty, that your blood is still calm and cold . . . But I feel it, I'm a mouse like that myself . . . What are you after, my God, what are you after? What are you looking for here: don't you understand yet that everything in these rooms has been changed? Even the books on the shelves aren't the same anymore, and the papers in the drawers aren't the same . . ."

It was all unreal. Outside the window a heavy, black rain was falling, but swirls of dust still spun in the corners of the courtyard. Reflections flashed on the wall, as if the old woman, disgusting old Giedraitienė, was glowing. Even the dust-covered room was impossible, its shapes twisted and corner-less. The paintings had disappeared from their frames; empty, barely painted canvases stared at me. The old woman was like a crumpled, rotten rag, on which someone had fixed a crumpled, rotten, inhuman face. Drool gathered in the corners of her lips; she continually brushed it away with the back of a hand that was covered in age spots.

I had to squeeze everything, as much possible, out of her. Across from me sat a creature of *Their* species—for the first time this close. I sensed that without a doubt, the way you sense a familiar smell, or grasp cold or warmth with your fingers. *They* had erred greatly in sending me Giedraitienė. *They* make mistakes too. The answer, the live answer, was in front of me; there was only one thing I couldn't understand: *why did the secret smell so bad?*

I don't very well recall how I grabbed her and shoved her into the armchair, how I squeezed her crackling neck and stared at her protruding eyes with malice; I don't very well recall what it was I was preparing to get out of her. I looked at her like an executioner waiting for his victim to release his last breath, and I just couldn't understand what was obstructing me more and more. Only after a few long seconds did I realize she was *laughing*, choking and suffocating in my grip, laughing soundlessly, and in the protruding eyes there was only a strange fascination and the smirk of a condescending, superior being. I let go, involuntarily wiped my palms on my pants, while she coughed, choked, and laughed, wiping away the tears that gathered in the drooping face's wrinkles.

"So you're still a madman," she finally choked out. "Why, you'll strangle me, Vytuk. And where will you put the corpse? You're still the same; grab someone by the throat and don't ask a thing . . . Ask first! I'll answer!"

"Where did you come from?" I was amazed that my voice was so weak and tired. "What hole did you crawl out of?"

"From the cheeriest house in Vilnius!" she announced with a strange joy. "Don't you know it?"

"No."

"Strange, everybody knows it—but not you." She once more settled herself comfortably in the chair. "It's the most important and most interesting house in Vilnius . . . It's the symbol of the city, its core. An infinitely BEAUTIFUL house, you just need to grasp its beauty. In every REAL city there is a house like that—sometimes open, sometimes hidden, sometimes it's full of people, sometimes it's empty and forsaken. But it's definitely always there . . . Come on, think about it, Vytuk, don't tell me you don't know? Once the Tsar's Okhranka was in that house . . . Then the Polish security . . . Then the NKVD office— do you remember it was precisely there we separated? . . . A house of miracles, a house of ghosts: have you noticed how easily entirely new inhabitants keep settling in there? . . . Then the Gestapo was in it, and later still the NKVD again. And now the KGB . . . Some come, some go, but the house still stands . . . How many sounds there are in it—they're in every brick of the walls. And how many smells! Someone should write a poem about it, a divine poem. But that would require a new Dante . . . Vilnius will fall, but that house will still be standing!"

"What were you doing there?"

"What I'm still doing," she said sharply and again stared at me wryly. "What do you think, what can I do? Always the same thing, Vytuk . . . What works out best for me . . . The very first interrogator talked me into it. He was almost refined; he even undressed me with his eyes politely . . . I thought, two or three times should be enough . . . but even two thousand wasn't enough . . . There were more and more interrogators all the time . . . They put me into a separate, luxurious room . . . Then they came in twos and threes, at whatever time of the day . . . I didn't keep track of the hours . . . or even days . . . or the faces . . . or the uniforms . . . I do the same thing over and over again, over and over . . . I didn't notice when the Germans showed up. Only the uniforms changed . . . You say, the language? It seems to me they all spoke THE SAME language. Not Russian and not German, some language of THEIR OWN. The uniforms kept changing, and I tried; I did this and that, I sensed that in this way I'd accomplish something. They kept wanting more out of me, but I became absolutely necessary to them too . . . More and more necessary . . . By then it wasn't they who were doing something with me, but I MYSELF started DOING something with them!"

Her voice softened, her face shone with a bright smile. She was changing in front of my eyes; it seemed something was driving a life force, an inner warmth, into her. She was becoming *almost* pretty, but she stank unappeasably.

"They need me, they can't bear it without me! They can go without food or drink—but they won't get by without me! . . . I became important, oh, how very important! I've spread myself throughout the entire house; I'm everywhere, Vytuk. Year after year I spread roots in all directions . . . They changed, but I stayed the same . . . Together with the house . . . We're both unchanging; we two are eternal. It's a pity you won't understand WHAT I do in the most cheerful house in Vilnius . . . You're too weak, too primitive . . . Or maybe? Maybe you have a hunch of WHAT your Irena used to do?"

I'd long since been short of air. I didn't want to hear anything, to know anything. I was being pulled deep into a horrifying cave; its walls could collapse at any instant and bury me for eternity. I needed to run, but my legs had been taken away.

"I'm a queen, Vytuk, or maybe even a goddess." I was no longer surprised to find that her voice had become melodious. "My roots reach everywhere. Our house is no more than a minor detail—they themselves are nothing more than little puny cogs, who don't know what they do or why . . . After all, the Gestapo or the KGB, Iran's Savak or Haiti's Tonton-Macoûte, they don't concern us, or you. We both understand they're nothing more than trained monkeys, who aren't worth wasting time over . . . We both know that only those who invented all of them, who contrived them, can be of concern . . . You can't even imagine how much I learned during those years upon years, learned without words . . . even without thoughts . . . I suck out their knowledge and secrets; come here, I'll share it with you, I'll teach you. Come here, Vytuk!"

She grabbed me again, the same way she always did, drew me closer; I couldn't resist the inner strength that emanated from her—together with the hideous stench. She looked at me with her crooked irises and smiled indulgently.

"You little fool . . . You're afraid? You're afraid of wrinkles, afraid of rags, afraid of the stench . . . You see just the surface and you don't comprehend the essence . . . I told you, after all, that I'm a queen . . ."

She began leisurely unbuttoning herself. I didn't even want to imagine what I would see, but I didn't close my eyes. I had seen the deformed joints and bones of insignificant little kanukai—so what sort of body could this one be! Many layers of clothes hid her body. She'd tear off one, another would turn up under it; she was something like an onion, and the smell wasn't any less biting. At last she wriggled out of her clothes; I looked at the white body that was revealed and couldn't pull my eyes away.

"Do you recognize me, do you recognize me?" she asked in a soft, trembling voice. "Come here, hurry!"

I couldn't not recognize that body. It was my Irena's body. Not similar, not just alike, but really her body, the body of the woman of the best years of my life. She knew I wouldn't have the strength to resist. There was nothing I wanted—only to drown in it, to touch the rather small breasts and the mole on the belly that was as white as milk, to hear her voice once more. It was as if I were under a spell.

"You do recognize me," the voice spoke gently. "Take me, come into me . . . You'll recognize me right away . . . come inside me, I'm waiting . . ."

I really did seem to be under a spell. By now I was standing next to her; I was already touching the smooth, cool skin with my fingers, fearing that Irena would suddenly disintegrate. At that moment I needed nothing more, I didn't want to know anything more. It felt good. For moments like that anyone would give half their life. I missed only Irena's face; it was in the shadows. I carefully grasped her fluffy hair, with the tips of my fingers caressed the earlobes I had not touched for so long. I gently pulled her head towards me; I tore it from the shadows. Into the vile dusk of the room appeared a wrinkled old woman's face, greasy gray hair, and a craggy chin. Giedraitienė looked at me greedily and commandingly. I tore away from her hands as if she were hot iron, once again I sensed the boundless stench; it filled the entire room, the entire world. I felt my heart would jump out of my chest at any moment. She really knew what I needed. It's nothing to defend yourself from exterior enemies. However, it's *almost* impossible to resist when you're attacked *from within*. It was hideous. It was unjust. *They* don't pay attention to any rules; they stick needles into the softest, most defenseless spots. My feet carried me out by themselves. At that instant my running feet were all that was left of me. Behind my back Giedraitienė, the hellish monster with sacred Irena's body and the disgusting, trembling head of an old woman, laughed hoarsely.

"Coward! Coward!" she screamed. "You'll never find out anything that way!"

At that point I thought it was, one way or another, the end for me. However, for a long time *They* left me alone—I don't know why. You'll never understand what *They* do or why. This uncertainty is one of *Their* worst weapons. I could only guess that maybe Giedraitienė snuck over to Gedis's apartment alone, on her own initiative; that she had confused and deceived even *Them*—this gave me a slight hope that it was nevertheless possible to deceive *Them*.

I had fingered and felt the slimy octopus of Vilnius, the murderous flashing of the eyes of the Basilisk of Vilnius, but I wasn't able to grasp its meaning. I saw what *They* did, I saw the dreadful effects of *Their* work, but I still couldn't grasp *what* all of this was for.

Do I really have to say that an absolute meaninglessness is the great meaning of it all?

Only one answer could save me: *my* meaning is to follow *Their* footsteps to the very end, wherever that should lead. Even if the world *itself* hungered for destruction, I was obliged to prevent it. I had barely thought of this when, at once, oppressive fetters fell from my brain. It wasn't worth torturing myself over *Their* meaninglessness; *my own* meaning was enough for me. Even if the world itself sought destruction, I was obliged to prevent it.

I know this for sure: as long as at least one person thinks this way, everything is not yet lost.

I dragged an old sofa into my hiding place between the library's bookshelves. *I lived* between books in the literal sense of the word. Unconsciously, books became everything to me. They smelled like flowers and thundered like storm clouds, caressed me like a woman and hurt me deeply like the vilest of enemies. Every last thing was an open book. A full-breasted beauty, glaring at me in a cafe, was no more than the leather cover of an old book; you could open it, inspect it, and then rudely toss it aside.

If it were possible for me to write books myself, I would know what to do. Unfortunately, genuine secrets cannot be trusted to either paper or to magnetic disks—as naïve Martynas thinks. The only way is to hold everything in your head, in the worst and most insecure place. It's the easiest to destroy, but nothing can be stolen from it. What matters is that I *know*, and if I know, ergo it's *possible* to know, ergo, sooner or later someone else will realize it, the one who will come after me. (I left him signs in the river!) That hope is all I live by—that I'm not really alone, that there are others who have studied this even more deeply, who have sensed everything more acutely. There must be. You won't overcome *all of us* that easily, even though we're forced to hide ourselves and to go it alone; we keep accumulating information, the murmurs of the heart, dreams—anything that will save mankind from the cosmic jellyfish, from the colorless pincers of the Vilnius Basilisk, which secretly entangle you, me, that green-eyed beauty there, the lame cat in the dirty courtyard, all of us.

Once I *searched* for traces of *Their* work in books. Now I couldn't escape them. I found them everywhere. *Everything* was marked with *Their* signs. We live in a world where *They* alone rule. I yearned to find at least one meager historical period, some more significant event, in which *people* would have arranged everything themselves. I searched for a book in which, having read it, I *wouldn't find* any hints about *Them*. In vain! The whole lot screamed of *Them*—from the history of the Inquisition to Hitler and Stalin's duet. *Their* commissars manifested themselves everywhere, attired in the masks of philosophers or politicians. I searched in vain for a country, a place where *They* hadn't encroached. *They* quietly crept into music, art, and philosophy. I read books and I saw how playfulness, fantasy, and metaphysics disappeared from European literature—the kanukized throngs demanded block-headed descriptions of everyday life. Painful and tragic dreams disappeared; their place was taken up by idiotic realia, a hundred Zolas and Dickenses. The throng was concerned about bread, so literature had to write about bread. The soul slowly disappeared from it, the body came to rule over everything: how some character is dressed, what house he lives in, how much money he has. After Vivaldi, improvisation disappeared from music; music slowly lost its depth of meaning. Hegel, drowning in alcohol, blathered about his trinomial dialectic, and Europe immediately fell behind a thousand years, since even the dialectic of the ancient Chinese *I Ching* is many times more complex and real. With horror, I followed how *They* strangled God, and in his place proposed fictions in *Their* favor: the Progress of Science and Historical Materialism. I saw how the iron Moloch's hold on man grew ever stronger; the automobile became a hundred times more important than a line of poetry. The idle rich had yachts and heaps of free time, but they didn't advance either souls or art, like the wealthy of ancient times; they merely competed to see who could internalize the most *dolce far niente*. *They* didn't hurry, but functioned effectually. The soul was irrevocably driven out of people. *They* intruded everywhere.

But my most nightmarish discovery was this: *They* exceed humans in their knowledge. I understood this when I researched my darling Stalin. One way or another, he was the closest to me; his hairy hands had once caressed me too. The strangest thing in the mustachioed Georgian's work was his implacable appetite to destroy millions, entire nations. Over and over again I researched all sorts of revolutions, the reigns of the cruelest tyrants. A dozen times I looked over the theories of *Their* great commissar Machiavelli. I sniffed out the logic of Robespierre's terror. And I kept getting more confused. All tyrants murder thousands; they all destroy real and imagined enemies. I understood *almost* all of

227

it—thanks to maestro Machiavelli and his impeccable reasoning. But not a single autocrat murdered millions the way my darling did. What was he after? I'd stare at Stalin's portrait, as if by such mystical contemplation I could revive him and make him speak up. I myself was revived; I suddenly remembered a trusty old rule: if you want to discover the hidden motivation of someone's work, find out what he is most afraid of.

The macabre Georgian vigorously devastated the study of genetics. Therefore, he was afraid that it could reveal something. The conclusion was so obvious and simple that at first I didn't believe it myself. Stalin *understood genetics perfectly*. He murdered millions *particularly consciously and scientifically*; he genetically changed the entire human race! Wholesale, he snuffed out anyone who was the least bit bolder, smarter, or more determined—anyone who could get in *Their* way. The Father of Peoples thoroughly changed the genetic code of his empire and *lost no time* in accomplishing a great deal. The slightest suspicion that a person has a gene for intelligence, courage, or stubbornness dictated a death sentence. If an entire nation was known through the ages for its resiliency and originality—the entire nation needed to be destroyed. (I probably could take pride that the Lithuanians belonged among the nations to be destroyed.) The tyrants of earlier times simply didn't understand—it wasn't enough to destroy your true enemies, you needed to burn out *the entire genetic field* with fire. The worst of it is that Stalin profoundly understood genetics at a time when humanity knew almost nothing about it. *They* always surpass our science and manage to appropriate the newest ideas first. *They* make deft use of our caution and laziness. Individual geniuses don't save humanity; the gray throng snuffs them out. While the throng greedily chews on *Their* discarded charity, *They* leisurely smother anyone trudging The Way. *Their* most popular methods are insanity and incurable illnesses. Earlier *They* selected tuberculosis or syphilis. *They* never work crudely; they strive to make their work look as unavoidable as fate, as eternal and unchangeable as the movement of the constellations. Although sometimes they enjoy more macabre methods too. Roman Polanski barely attempted to hint of *Their* work's superficial characteristics; he merely created a few films in which *Their* scent was discernible, but that was enough. No, *They* won't drown you, or crush you with an automobile. They'll send you, say, some sort of Manson, to slice open your pregnant wife's belly.

Everyone, everyone who tried to stand up against *Them* was destroyed, crushed, sacrificed their life, and *didn't change anything*. At least you know about the famous ones, but how many thousands of nameless ones have perished on The Way? I am one of them.

But one great thing really is *mine*; I won't let anyone take it away from me. Everything else aside, I am still a *human*. I am alive. For the time being I am still alive. I still have hope.

This meager hope of mine was aroused by the great kanukai duet—Hitler and Stalin. The two of them were very different. Hitler was somewhat superficial and too open. He would frequently give away his *true* intentions, and therefore *Their* operating mechanism as well. Stalin disguised everything masterfully; he was a true kanukish sneak, a global Basilisk. Without a doubt, Stalin felt himself the superior in this duet.

They fell out over something. The war between Germany and Russia wasn't *Their* conflict—after all, it certainly wasn't kanukai who died in the battles. The war was planned and coordinated between Hitler and Stalin as one of *Their* spheres of action. (Don't forget it's the courageous who are the first to die in battle.) Who would formally beat whom was entirely beside the point. The two of them fell out over something more essential.

How thoroughly Stalin hid Hitler's death! He even invented a legend about him running away to Argentina. Why, to what purpose? There can only be one answer: he made a fatal misstep and tried to hide it from *Their* highest authorities! He could kill off tens and hundreds of millions, but he had no right to touch another kanukai leader. That was Stalin's fateful mistake, the creature of his ambition.

War, squabbles, even slaughter, go on in *Their* midst too. *They* cheat, plan intrigues, and make mistakes too. That's what's most important: *They're* neither extraterrestrials, nor machines, nor gods. *They* are also *live* beings. Ergo, it's possible to overcome *Them*.

I still have hope.


I blew off the library and went out into the city streets. Vilnius is the most interesting book there is. By the Lenin monument the girls, their skirts pulled up, were tanning their legs in the sun and smoking cigarettes with hashish. Fat aunties in hideous clothes pulled up slightly wilted flowers and planted new ones—the square must always be full of

fresh flowers. "I'm not going to have children for the benefit of this hell,"
a deep, hoarse woman's voice spoke. "Better to strangle them to start
with. Why should I wait for someone else to do it?" Curious women
crowded around a van in a store's yard: what have they brought? Deep
sighs floated about, one huge Vilnius sigh, wind and rain, I couldn't
tell anymore if I was still myself, perhaps it really was me who said in
a unfamiliar man's voice: "You know, it feels like they've trampled on
my brains. They're forcing me to obey: calmly, with restraint, without
a fuss. And they just keep squashing and squashing that brain of mine
with their feet."

At night the confusion of sounds would quiet down; then they'd be
heard one by one. At three in the morning a taxi suddenly would start
roaring; for maybe a couple of minutes it would approach along the
empty street, its tires squealing, before screeching harshly under my
windows and finally quieting down. The driver would turn "Radio Liberty" on, full blast, and hang out there—why didn't anyone complain
about him? Then the entire street would growl and rumble, the window
panes would rattle, I'd jump out of bed and see a powerful procession
of armor-plated army trucks. The procession of death, the spikes of the
weapons covered in tarps, would fly howling through the Vilnius night.
The silence would not return. It seems Vilnius trusts in me; it presents
me with all of its night—right up until the morning bustle of the street
sweepers. The workers repairing the trolleybus wires rudely banged
their hammers on the iron poles and laughed over dirty jokes at the
top of their voices. Tired drunkards would drag themselves home. On a
bench between scrawny bushes, a couple who couldn't find themselves
a private spot tortured the silence for a long time with their mysterious
whispering. At last, a dress rustled, expressive details stung the ears:
the snap of underwear elastic, the damp, sticky sound of the beginning
of an act. The young lady quietly moaned in Russian, the young man
quieted her in Lithuanian, hurriedly squeaking the bench. On the other
side of the street a car bristling with radio antennas stopped, a drunken
militiaman quickly jumped out onto the sidewalk and started vomiting
into a garbage can. Vilnius thrust and shoved its nightlife at me. And the
day would begin with our neighborhood cat, a long-haired, brown bandit with metaphysical leanings. He would wait in the little dug-up plot
across from the building, scrutinize me probingly, and then scornfully

turn away. He always expected something meaningful from me, and he would always be disappointed. There was nothing I could do to make him happy. Shamed, for a long time I'd look at the cat's back, turned away in indifference, and his nervously twitching tail. The next morning he would be waiting for me again. He still hoped for something, with a true fanatic's stubbornness. I was ashamed. Or maybe it wasn't me—I really didn't know anymore if I was still myself. It seemed to me that I was *everyone*. I was those morning drunkards sitting together by the fountain, waiting for eleven o'clock (only at eleven!), when the liquor section would open. That was *my* red, wrinkled face with bags under the eyes. *My* hands shook, and my throat convulsively swallowed saliva. I saw frail little old ladies returning from church, live relics of Lithuanian villages. They dressed in dark clothes and tied spotless white scarves on their heads. Their calves were naked; the blue veins and shrunken gray muscles shone through the transparent parchment of their skin. Their faces were no longer of this world. They would walk in twos, arm in arm, supporting one another with their shoulders. (I myself was a little old lady like that, yanked out of the village by my children, quietly moldering away in a windowless little closet.) At intervals, so you wouldn't forget whom Lithuania belonged to, Russian officers' wives, with gigantic knots of white, peroxide-bleached hair, would proudly pass by. They never walked alone. They would pass by in twos, in threes, boldly casting glances in all directions, just waiting for someone to harass them. I saw it all. I saw the three lunatics on the loose in our neighborhood; one I took particular note of: he was fat and always wore a military uniform without epaulettes and an empty pistol holster. He hung around the workers who were endlessly digging around in the street and casually followed their progress, at intervals solemnly unbuttoning the pistol holster. Apparently the ancient gene of the camp guard dynasty lay buried within him.

In Vilnius nothing has progressed, in Vilnius everything has merely crumbled and shattered. Perverted old exhibitionist Vilnius doesn't in the least try to hide its blunt, powerless phallus. My eyes hurt. Vilnius jangled my nerves. My brains were exhausted from impressions.

"Let's transform Vilnius into a city of outstanding order!"

"The Party's June Plenum resolution—to life!"

"Everything the Party has planned—we'll accomplish!"

I needed someone. I needed someone who could see and hear with me. I couldn't take it alone anymore. I desperately needed someone, but no one could help in this search. No art, no philosophy advises you how to *find someone*. Great minds take up great subjects, but no one explains this—the most ordinary, but most important of things.

How was I supposed to look for someone? Where? By what: scent, shape, words?

Unfortunately, I don't have any advice, either. I don't know how I found Lolita. I found her in parts: first her body, and then—slowly, with enormous difficulty—her soul too. She doesn't even know that she has to take the place of all of my dead and even of disgusting, beloved Vilnius. She doesn't know that sometimes she has to take my own place for me. And thank God she doesn't know. If she knew, she'd probably be frightened at such a horrifying responsibility.

Now I no longer stand naked in front of the mirror; I don't keep asking myself what she sees in me. But I still doubt it's me she *really* needs. We've never become completely intimate; an invisible wall looms between us. Sometimes I want to break it down, to smash it to pieces, but I hardly clench my fist before I suddenly take fright. In this world *fulfilled* happiness isn't possible. With all the walls broken down, becoming one with Lolita, I would either have to die, or to kill her. Maybe it's a good thing that her spirit keeps escaping and hiding itself in a cave, like a frightened little animal. From behind that wall she surprises me with the weirdest stories and with her unpredictable behavior.

"I'd like to be your sister," she says unexpectedly, looking out the window at the slanting rain. "I'd like to feel we're part of the same seed . . . Although I'm more to you than a sister . . . We're doing something forbidden; we're enjoying spiritual incest. It'd be better if I really were your sister. At least I'd know what it was I'd decided on . . . Now I don't know anything anymore . . . It's bad enough that we both are, each of us on our own. But it's a hundred times worse that we're together . . . When I touch you, I melt completely. To me it seems like you're my death . . . We're doing something God has forbidden. We're closer than a brother and a sister . . . We shouldn't be together . . . I know I'll pay dearly for it, but I want you anyway—more than anything in the world. And at the same time I want to run away from you, run, run, run, as far away as possible . . ."

She wants to leave me, because I am her love and her death. These enigmatic horrors aren't even necessary—she could simply leave me for another. That *possibility* alone drives me out of my mind. Our love itself is insane. Suddenly I want something terrible to happen to Lolita. I long for her to break her legs and spine, for her face to be mutilated, so that no one, absolutely no one, would need her. So that everyone who saw her would feel pity for her, or better yet—revulsion. No one, no one would need her anymore—but I would need her no matter what shape she was in. Only then, when the entire world has turned away from her, will she understand how much I love her. I literally relish the insanity of this desire, before my eyes I see a Lolita who belongs *to me alone*— inseparable, for ages upon ages. And somewhere, at the very bottom, writhes a disgusting, stinking worm: my insanity calmly confirms that I could do this *myself*, mutilate her *myself*. All it would take . . .

She finally turns from the window and looks at me with her deep brown eyes. My supposed insanity bursts like a soap bubble. A stinking soap, boiled from the corpses of the camp. What right do I have to seize her for myself? What right?

Can a person want God to belong to him alone?

"We talk too much," she says. "We try to be too intelligent . . . Why can't we do whatever we want and not worry about it? Why do people want to justify their existence so badly, why can't they simply be, and that's it?"

I could tell her what happens when a person longs to *simply be*. In the labor camp we all wanted to *simply be*, to simply survive. *They* are preparing an existence like that for us all. I could tell her why I can't stand Beckett, the most *moral* writer of our times. (I can't stand Beckett, even though picking up a book of his I feel a quiver of respect. He is perhaps the only one who was able to look at man with God's indifferent eyes. He quite honestly showed the sorry state of the kanuked man *the way it really is*. He showed that which is, but refused to even hint at *why* it's that way, *who* is to blame for it. He categorically refused to make even vague mentions of *Them*. He left man on his own, because he looked at him with God's eyes. You need to look at a human with a *human's* eyes!)

Lolita stands in front of me like a dream come true. I don't know if I want to pray to her, but I really do want to kiss her feet. How pathetic

I am compared to her! She needs someone much more pure, more worthy, more powerful. I'll find her someone else myself, someone who would be worthy of her. I've practically no will of my own anymore. I merely catch at the slightest hint of her desires; I literally no longer am, I want only to please her, to do whatever she may want. I really no longer am—there's nothing I want for *myself* anymore; I am nothing but her reflection. I don't see anything anymore—just her. She takes up the entire world for me, she herself has become the entire world, and Lord knows, that is my good fortune. A dangerous fortune—one person isn't allowed to take the place of the entire world.

But we're already going down the street, so nothing matters—neither the wet sidewalks, nor the rain, nor the long-bodied bow-legged dog, my old acquaintance, sticking to the two of us. Her wet hair shines like blocks of coal; under her raincoat the sturdy hips move furiously. I do not know this woman in her entirety. She doesn't talk about her former husband. She refuses to move in with me, much less—to marry me. She categorically does not want to have children—best not to even mention it to her. But she won't explain why. She hides from me.

Don't tell me she doesn't sense what I could do on her account? If she were a miserable leper with rotten fingers, I would kiss those stumps all over one by one, infecting myself with leprosy, knowing full well what I was doing. If she were to turn into a chrysanthemum (she resembles a chrysanthemum), I would be the grave on which she would grow. Whatever she would be, I would recognize her immediately and turn into her shadow. Even if she were to turn into an intangible fabrication of the mind, a mysterious dream, I would be her dreamer.

We're going down a neglected path in the park to the foot of the hill, and for the hundredth time I think of how we don't fit in here. An over-aged Romeo and Juliet in the heart of black Vilnius. We don't fit in with the quietly weeping city, with the spiritless kanukish life. Vilnius doesn't accept such passions, such thoughts, or such behavior. Soon it will start to hate us (it already hates us). It will laugh at us with a drab, barking laugh. Love is impossible in Vilnius. We are partially digested pieces of flesh—can things like that be allowed to love? Can you imagine Romeo and Juliet suffering their tragedy in a sewer pipe, up to their waists in a stream of excrement, unable to move, armless and legless?

We approach the river; I feel the sad breath of the water. The secret wall continues to loom between us, a wall of treacherous rain. A cold mist rises from the water; the other shore is barely visible. The mist enshrouds Lolita's legs, slowly rises to her waist, and caresses her with damp fingers. I *envy* even that mist. Lolita is mine; no one is permitted to caress her. I can destroy even that mist, even the wind raging between her breasts. I get the urge to burn the books she likes, that she thinks and talks about. I get the urge to destroy the music she listens to alone. I envy everything. Our love is truly insane. I keep remembering how two wolves fought over a bitch with a white neck next to the camp fence. They forgot everything, even their fear of humans. They thrashed and bit each other as if they were alone in the entire world. The old one won, the pretender shamefully limped off, but heaven didn't take pity on the winner, either. Half the camp witnessed his end. The old gray was angry at the entire world. He scurried after the white-throated bitch and defended her from everything. He showed his fangs and growled at us. He attacked dry twigs and the gigantic Siberian mosquitoes. Sometimes, snapping his teeth, he grabbed at the emptiness, at phantoms no one could see; he'd battle with drops of rain. Perhaps I am that wolf.

"I'm like that dog," says Lolita, slowly descending the slope, "I follow you and wag my tail. You see how good you have it: you'll never need to buy a dog."

The river flows slowly and indifferently, like a gigantic vein; the blood of us all flows with it. The river of our forgotten blood. Vilnele, run to the Vilija, and Vilija to the Nemunas. So, say we love freedom more than life. Where is it, that freedom? Where is it, that life? The city swallows the river and poisons it with its sewage. The fish that are still alive stink of tar. And what do we, unable to smell ourselves, stink of? The Shit of All Shits?

Lolita's irregular face smiles sadly; wet strands of hair cling to her cheeks. Her body is gone; it's disappeared under the drenched coat. A dream must be intangible.

The river emerges straight out of the fog, flows in from who knows where—maybe from hell. Even the dog got depressed, stopped sniffing at the wet grass and stiffened, his long snout turned in the direction of the dumbfounded willows on the shore. What can I say to Lolita? We've long since exhausted the permissible subjects, and I don't have the right to invite her on The Way—for her own good.

I need an assistant who could tell her what I cannot say myself, things I probably don't even know myself. A mysterious go-between, maybe some Vasilis, a ruler of the swamps who knows the language of birds. Unfortunately, all of the people who are close to me are far away; all of them are in the other world. I can only hope to summon spirits, but they are, after all, bodiless and speechless.

But what spirits could I summon? Save perhaps that lonely figure: you'd think he'd emerged right out of the river, a damp being in a crookedly buttoned coat coughing damply. The edges of his hat collapsed from the dampness, streams of water cover his face like cobwebs, there's no eyes peering out of it—just the shattered lenses of round glasses. Where did he pop up from? Maybe he climbed down from the old roofs of Vilnius?

"Goot day!" that old Jew sniffles, smiles wryly, tries to pull off his limp hat, throws up his hands, and finally fixes his gaze on me.

He has eyes all the same; they're wise and *kind*.

"Your face tells an old Jew a great deal. Vhere have I seen you? . . . Maybe in da time of Grand Duke Vytautas or Grand Duke Gedhiminas? Or maybe in Spain in da time of Torkvemada? You invited me?"

Maybe I really can summon spirits? It's been a long time since anything surprised me: all things are possible in Vilnius. It'll turn out I called him here myself. What will he say?

"I'm an old, old Jew of Vilnius . . . my great-great-grandparents served Gedhiminas and Vytautas. My great-grandparents lent Zygimantas money . . . Ja, ja . . . My grandparents suffered under da Russian pogroms, and my parents fooled da Poles . . . Oi, how dey used to fool da Poles! . . . I myself lived and died in da ghetto! Ja, ja! I know everyting about Vilnius! Ja, ja . . . Listen to me, an old Jew knows everyting. An old Jew knows more dan all da Lituanians . . . but I can say to a Lituanian, Lituanians didn't hit da Jew, didn't make pogroms, didn't drive him into da ghetto . . ."

He walks unsteadily; the brim of his hat has collapsed entirely and covers his ears, from which long gray hairs stick out. Dressed in worn-out clothes, his shoes squelch water and mud. But none of this engenders scorn—it seems this is the only way this ghost of the rain could look. He turns to the dog and politely nods a greeting to him. Did I really summon him? Are his stories interesting to me at the moment?

"Vhy is it vortvhile to listen to an old Jew? Because Jews are a special people! Every civilizashion only sees vhat it IS, it never plans vat it should turn into. Ja, ja . . . Dey can only long for der past, but Jews long for der future . . . Only Jews invented demselves a future . . . Dey alvays had two great ideas: Messiah and da Promised Land. Look over da history of da vorld and you'll see dat only Jews long for da FUTURE . . . Only da Jew Marx could tink up communism . . . Listen to an old Jew . . . He sees da vorld differently!"

He talks and all the while entwines himself further into his many-folded clothes, as if he wanted to disappear into them completely. The mist slowly disperses. Only the river is always the same black; it flows past us apathetically, and probably listens secretly. A river of words—how many words has it swallowed by now? If you stuck your ear into the current, you'd hear them, floating up from forgotten ages.

"How strange," says Lolita. "A gloomy river, the fog's covering everything. We don't know where we're going or why . . . And an old Jew rattling on about the Messiah and the Promised Land. It's all like a dream . . ."

"But I am a dream!" he confirms willingly. "Don't be afraid, I vill not interrupt your love."

"It's nice that at least you didn't call her my daughter."

"Am I blind? Am I insane?" His eyes suddenly widen, it seems even his wrinkles smooth out. "Maybe you tink you can tell an old Jew about love? It's da old Jew can tell you about love."

He even got angry; Lolita calms him with a gentle voice:
"Tell us . . ."

"About love? You don't need to talk about love, you need to love it," he smacks his lips, picking the words. "Everyone asks—vat is da meaning of life. Da meaning of life is to live. And to live is to love. Love drives everyting. Da world moves because tings love one anoter. Fire burns, because da coal falls in love vit da fire. Da river flows, because it loves da sea . . . If der vere no love, da vorld vould stiffen and stop. It's awful to tink vat vould happen if der was no love left . . . People don't have a name until dey find der love. If you vant to ask a person's name, ask him whom he loves. People don't have oder names, only der love name. Love is everyting . . . Grain vouldn't sprout, if it didn't love da sun. Da sun vouldn't rise, if it didn't love da eart . . . Everyting is love . . ."

He falls silent, moving only his lips; tasting the words he's uttered, it seems. The fog is lifting, crawling back into the water of the river. Something has cleansed my brain—like a school blackboard with a damp sponge. Jews, love, and Marx—everything in its place.

But Lolita for some reason turned pale; this Ahasuerus of Vilnius drove all the blood from her face.

"And if you love a person," she suddenly asks in a weak, barely audible voice, "do you have to tell him everything? Absolutely everything?"

"Everyting!" he answers and screws up his dark eyeballs again. "If dere's someting you don't say—you have to trow it out of yourself too. If you can live vitout dat and be yourself—you don't have to say it. But if you hide someting deep vitin yourself, if you dream of it at night, if it doesn't leave you—you have to tell your lover . . . or else love dries up like a poisoned flower . . . Ja, ja . . . like it's been poisoned . . ."

He unexpectedly escapes from our midst, turns towards Žvėrynas and in the old-fashioned manner puts his fingers to the sagging brim of his hat:

"Ja, ja . . . only love!"

He shuffles off, but I no longer see him. Lolita's face is in a state I've never seen before. Her eyes are bloodshot; her lips compressed, even white. He did something to her! And I didn't defend her! What will happen now?

"Let's go to Teodoras's studio! We have to! Right now!"

I automatically swallow my saliva and think I haven't heard her right. Only after a few seconds do I understand why the old Jew, the soggy Ahasuerus of Vilnius, showed up here. He shoved me into a world that had been closed to me until now and then he disappeared, vanished in the fog again; he was probably wandering the rooftops of Žvėrynas, remembering the fires and the plagues, and the floods, and foreign armies, and the din of church bells . . . Who sent him?

Whoever or whatever had sent him, I wasn't prepared to avoid my fate.

The studio, with its high ceiling, was as surreal as a memory. A tiny fireplace and battered antique chairs, all of them different. Lolita sat in one with her feet outstretched; she was guarded by a mass of beasts, people, plants, clay, and metal Bosch-like phantasmagoria. This room had a soul; these sculptures hadn't turned into soulless things like Ged-iminas's piano. The dead owner could walk inside at any moment—and what would I have done then? And how would Lolita, suddenly forced to choose, behave—maybe she would grab *us both*? I shouldn't have come here. I tried to quiet my beating heart; I attentively inspected Kazys Teodoras's world. On the shelves, on the fireplace, around me, under my feet, above me stood, lay, hung his works—from matchbox to man-size. There was a mass of them—as if Teodoras had wanted to construct an entire world. A five-meter monster rammed against the ceiling crowned everything; it spread invisible proboscises, it wanted to snatch up everything in sight. Me first of all, me and Lolita.

"That's the Deformer," explained Lolita, following my stare. "When I asked Tedis what that meant, he said, after thinking about it: a reformer reforms, and a deformer deforms."

Teodoras really did want to build an entire world around himself. He formed it from clay, cut it from stone, poured and polished metal, soldered the most fanciful metal sheets, carved wood, poured glass, and wove all of it into a stunning tangle. By way of this studio I hoped I would find a road to Lolita's inner world, but *some third being* lurked here, the secret *third one* of Vilnius. What was it holding in its posses-sion, what part of Lolita? I was disconcerted by its insolence, by its evil intentions. It seemed to be lying in ambush and looking at me disdain-fully. A large red cylinder with green lumps, carelessly thrown into the corner, irritated me the most.

"That's the irritator," Lolita said hollowly. "Tedis explained that every studio has to have something whose sole purpose is to irritate visitors."

I tried to imagine this Tedis, a shaggy athlete with sleepy eyes, in the long autumn evenings carefully, lovingly, decorating the red irrita-tor with green lumps.

"It's strange that you don't remember him. Half of Vilnius knew him . . . I don't know why: he was a quiet guy . . . nothing bohemian about him . . . He raved only in his studio, all alone . . . Others would rather rave in public, and turn impotent in the studio . . . and cast busts of Lenin."

I slowly recovered from the studio's gloomy spell. One way or an-other, this was still a sculptor's studio, and not a mausoleum. Appar-ently Teodoras's spirit wasn't getting ready to bother us. But Lolita was afraid all the same. Her uneven face twisted up entirely; her cheekbones protruded. She was still too young; she wasn't accustomed to keeping company with her dead ones. She glanced around as if she were afraid one of the figures hanging from the ceiling would speak in her former husband's voice. She turned ugly, horribly ugly; she tormented herself, but I *wanted* her to tell me about it. I wanted to hear as much as possible. Perhaps I envied even her ghosts, even the dead. I turned into a tiny kanukas, quivering with greed; I wanted to suck everything out of her.

"I was an eighth or ninth grader, I spent the summer at my grandparents'," she spoke in a sad voice. "Four of them showed up; they were making some kind of relief or mural for the Cultural Center. Four young artists with patched jeans . . . I was probably fourteen or fifteen: a tall, skinny girl with unexpectedly swollen breasts. To others I already looked almost like a woman, I probably aroused desire, but actually I was as naïve as nature . . . There was too much of something in me too little of something else . . . I was missing a human, or an animal . . . or a thought . . . I was ready for anything. If someone had fixed me up with a child, I probably would have grown up a mother of mothers. If someone had given me a dog, I would have become the biggest dog specialist in the world. Anything suited me . . . But there was nothing in the village, absolutely nothing. Some other summer I wouldn't even have noticed Tedis. He was about thirty; to me he looked like a retiree. All four of them looked that way—like gray old guys, idiotically trying to act young . . . But all the same I preferred talking to them, rather than to the kids my age from the neighboring farms . . ."

As she talked, she recovered somewhat; sometimes she would smile at a completely unfunny part and her eyes would turn transparent. It seemed she was enjoying something, only I didn't understand what.

"So, what more? Milk. Warm, fresh milk. With foam . . . I kneeled on the wet grass and sucked it straight from the pail with a straw . . . Grandmother went off to the left, behind the bushes, to milk the second cow. It was impossible to tie them next to one another, they'd start fighting immediately . . . I drank warm milk, and Ted kneeled down next to me, with a straw too . . . I saw how he looked at me . . . He looked at me like God evaluating his creation. I felt as if he had created me. As if I were his sculpture . . . Probably that summer I really was like a rock waiting to see what would be hewn out of it . . . I don't know . . .

I probably stuck to him myself, with all of a silly girl's annoyance. And the milk had nothing to do with it. Probably he tried to shake me off . . . But from that moment I became his—and that was it. It wasn't love at first sight; I came to love him much later. But at that time he literally enchanted me—and that's it. It seemed all of my quests met within him, it seemed he was just exactly what I was looking for . . . Even when I hated him the most, I never forgot I was His and there was nowhere to escape from him. That's how it was . . . He became my God. I suddenly felt that's the only way God could be: a thirty-year-old, shaggy, silent type . . . I am his idea . . . His dream . . . His fantasy . . . At that time my body changed a lot, I frequently stood in front of the mirror and God knows, I BELIEVED it was he who was changing me, making me the way he wanted . . . Not to mention the soul . . . He sculpted me anew, patiently peeled off husk after husk, tore off veil after veil; he entirely remade my childish mind. He cleaned out all of school's phantasmagorias. It was only thanks to him that I grew up as a HOMO SAPIENS, and not a HOMO SOVIETICUS. I am a SAPIENS, aren't I?"

"You didn't feel any force?"

"No, no force." She slowly examined her hands. "See, he even sculpted my hands . . . Just imagine, a Cinderella of the soul, suddenly settled into the Prince's palace! What force could there be? . . . In place of all the Michurins, Makarenkos, and Brezhnevs I was flooded by an inner stream of Rasselases, Shakespeares, and Coltranes. I'd dream of Camus, Kierkegaard, and even Archbishop Berkeley . . . In my dreams I slept with an entire galaxy of geniuses . . . Ha, I'm probably the only woman in the world Kant raped! . . . My God had no mercy; he gave a woman intelligence. I'm not bragging too much? . . . You have no idea what it means to change from the top student in school to the accessory of a thirty-year-old shaggy-haired intellectual. Imagine you are being BORN and you see yourself being born. Tedis was a guru to me first of all, and not a man. A guru, and not a loved one. A guru, but not a lover . . . A year or two went by, I had time to get used to men looking at me, at night I would sigh, dream about lips swollen from kisses, on the trolleybus I would lean my entire body up next to him 'accidentally,' but he stubbornly remained JUST my guru . . . HEAVEN ONLY KNOWS what he wanted to make out of me—just not a lover, and not a wife. A spiritual disciple? Disciples are always men! I never understood him.

I'll never forgive him. He threw me to the wolves. It wasn't enough that I was entirely his creation, I didn't even know what it was he had made of me," she suddenly gazed with a stare that saw nothing, and said angrily: "If I had understood him, I wouldn't visit here, I wouldn't sit here nights and talk to the walls. I'd sell this entire morass. They pay well for the dead ones."

Her lips were firmly pressed together, she seemed to be speaking without opening her mouth. Suddenly I was afraid of the evil little flickers in her unseeing eyes. She wasn't talking to me, probably to her God, but I had no desire to be God. I was a man; I had an intense feeling that in a moment I would say something I shouldn't say. I was afraid of this angry woman with the insane flickers in her pupils, chopping the air with her words. I wanted my Lolita back, but she had disappeared without a trace. All that was left were the tin mobiles hanging from the ceiling, three fat Buddhas with animal heads set on the fireplace, and a bitter foreboding that something horrible was yet to happen.

"I'd purposely wear dresses with nothing on underneath, I flounced about and showed my charms however I could. He drove me out of my mind; he was impossible to understand, as suits a God. An absolute ruler, who needs to be cruelly punished . . . One of his buddies snatched me up, and in the course of a month he taught me absolutely everything, never even noticing he had taken my virginity. And it was all fine with me, just because he was a close friend of Tedis's. I took my vengeance; I slept with his friend. While with Teo we would discuss Beckett . . . In the end I did what I had to do: I broke in here and destroyed everything I could. The works prepared for his one and only show. Intimate masterpieces, put away and not shown to anyone. I spoiled his entire world, and when he himself showed up, I nearly killed him with some bas-relief . . . He tore off my dress, tore it into tiny shreds, placed me naked in front of himself, examined me with a professional eye and said he would put me in his show: naked, covered with shit, stuck all over with scraps of newspaper used to wipe yourself in the toilet. And he would name it "Lithuania" . . . And afterwards everything was as strange as a dream and as short as a single day. We got married as soon as I turned eighteen. My mother was hysterical—she was probably hoping to raise a vestal virgin . . . There was just one thing I wanted: to understand Tedis, but I didn't even manage to see him clearly. I even secretly wrote down his peculiarities. He never brushed his teeth. He wore a beard, but he had bought himself piles of razors and electric shavers. He didn't eat tomatoes or chocolate. It seemed to me that even those ridiculous details had some secret meaning . . . He was horribly afraid of fire and anything sharp . . . He had a strange way of categorizing every philosopher's and artist's work. For him there was a BEFORE and an AFTER. He divided everything that way: Kant BEFORE and Kant AFTER. As if all of them at some moment had caught some dreadful disease . . . He could be unconditionally charmed with some person BEFORE, and abhor the same person AFTER. But it was never the other way around . . . I kept asking, before WHAT and after WHAT? Teo didn't explain. He didn't explain anything about himself . . . He would look at me and repeat: you are my best sculpture. Yes, I'm his creation. Made for who knows what purpose. He didn't create me for himself, for his own good; I just knew that he broke and tortured me for my own good . . . He was saving me from something. But from what? From myself? From hexed Vilnius? Or from those annoying people who kept crowding into his studio? . . . He couldn't stand to have someone look at him intently. He imagined that it was possible to steal the thoughts right out of your head that way."

"What, what?" I asked, feeling my tongue slowly growing numb.

"I know, it's funny . . . And then when he was drunk he would sometimes say that people aren't really people, that on the road of evolution some horrible mistake happened, that the real people are somewhere ELSE . . . and then he was killed . . . And nothing was left . . . Until you showed up."

"He was killed? You didn't tell me."

"I thought you knew. Everyone knows. It's a famous story. He was burned alive."

The room tilted. I tried to pull myself together; I clenched my teeth together firmly, chasing away the circles that flashed before my eyes. He was burned alive. He talked about not-human humans, an evolutionary mistake. He couldn't stand kanukish stares. Shuddering, I looked around: the Deformer? Deformed bodies?

"It's a hideous story," Lolita said hollowly. "He was sitting in a camping trailer. Smoking, drinking, talking . . . with that same buddy, my sexual tutor . . . His friend left to lie down in his own trailer. Tedis was drunk, he fell sound asleep . . . and the trailer started burning like a box of matches."

I had to say something. It was imperative that I open my mouth, but my lips stuck together and my tongue wouldn't obey me. Suddenly I felt I didn't want to know anything, I felt I was on dangerous territory. Dangerous to my mental health. The premonition turned into conviction; the sculptor's studio was a trap. Does clay burn?

"Well, none of that matters anymore. I have to show you what I brought you here for. The thing Tedis told me not to show to anyone. Maybe you'll make something of it." Lolita got up and went into a dark corner of the studio. "Teodoras's testament."

I followed behind her like a robot. Stupefied, I watched her carefully take the head off of some animal sculpture. Only after a few seconds did I realize it was the Iron Wolf. It really was iron; on the sides in crooked letters was written the entire legend of Grand Duke Gediminas's dream. Like an automaton, I fixated on the wavy lines: "and he dreamed an iron wolf howled on the hill . . . establish a city here, Duke, and news of it will spread throughout the world, like the howling of the wolf . . ." Was Teodoras also of the opinion that the secret lay hidden within Vilnius itself?

"Look," Lolita nervously lit a cigarette and spread two rolls of canvas in front of me. "These are Tedis's only paintings. Ordinarily he never painted. He guarded these canvases like the apple of his eye. The Iron Wolf was his safe."

Fumbling, I unwound the rolls and weighed down the corners with some clay animals. The field of the paintings slowly stopped rippling before my eyes. *Now I saw.*

From the left, not directly at me, but somewhat to the side, gazed the pale green face of a woman, taking up the entire painting, squeezed within the borders of the canvas. The woman's eyes were large and lifeless; no soul, no personality hid behind them. And from the pupils, like the thorns of some poisonous plant, vague gray cones protruded—calm and indifferent, but not hunting for a victim, because every last thing was to be their victim.

Out of the right painting—this time straight at me, at all of us—stared a legion of little faces—each one out of its own cage or frame. A legion of little faces, all arranged in much too orderly a fashion, all piercing me with identically insolent eyes. They were seemingly different—with beards and mustaches and without; with hats, caps, and bareheaded; bald, disheveled, and plastered down. But I immediately realized that the face was always the same—a weak-willed, but at the same time insolent face, repeated over and over. Changing its makeup, disguising itself—but always identical: the horrifying, flat as a pancake face of a kanukas.

I didn't sling the paintings aside. I didn't get dizzy, and I didn't lose my breath. I didn't fly home like mad, and I didn't lock myself in with seven locks. I simply turned to Lolita—and only then was I really petrified.

She sat leaning forward somewhat, her legs spread apart awkwardly, as if she were just about to stand up or was already beginning to stand up, and had suddenly stiffened. Her lips were opened unevenly; in their right corner hung a thread of spit. Her face was crooked, her fingers twisted unnaturally. It looked as if she'd been paralyzed. And it wasn't just her: the cigarette smoke was frozen too, and the flame in the fireplace had turned to stone. I first thought it was a vision, a momentary illusion, but everything stayed that way. *Only I alone could move.* I worked my fingers and looked around. I don't know how long this took. The raindrops outside the window hung suspended next to the glass. A filthy Vilnius pigeon, maneuvering between the church towers, hung leaning to one side, right by the cross.

I wasn't afraid of anything anymore. It was all the same to me. I sensed how *They* had pervaded everything, penetrated all of our brains like a virus, shackled even Vilnius itself. Vilnius loomed outside the window, surrounded me from all sides, its power lost, deprived of the slightest will to resist, renouncing everything—even motion, even time itself. Its own soul, that which drove and moved everything. That frozen moment reminded me of something—maybe a wicked fairy tale, maybe a dream, a vision, or a nightmare. It didn't take long; suddenly everything moved again. Even then I didn't believe my senses. I tried to convince myself that nothing had happened; I looked at Lolita slowly rising from the chair, at the filthy Vilnius pigeon disappearing from sight, sensing a acrid bitterness in my mouth. *They* had encompassed everything. It was impossible to hide.

"So, what did you find out?" Lolita asked hoarsely.

The sun shines, that's the worst of it. Darkness would save you. But a streak of light falls through the barracks window and caresses your beaten knees. Your entire body aches. If you could manage to close your eyes, if you closed your eyes and forgot everything, you'd think you were sitting on a bench at home. The sun is the same everywhere. The sun heals wounds. The sun invites you to live.

"Well," says the one who sits on the bunk like a king, "shall we try again?"

His Russian bandit's eyes look at you gently, gently. Again a darkened, dented bucket appears before your eyes. The bitter stench of urine spreads from it; it worms its way into your nostrils, into your throat. It would turn your guts inside out, but you don't have any guts. They have beaten the guts out of you.

"Drink, my child," a gravelly, lame little voice says to you. "You drink it—it's over. Don't tell me you don't want to live?"

This one, as tall as a pole, sticks the bucket under your nose, pours the tepid, reeking liquid over your chin.

"He won't drink it, Vaska," says a voice that sounds like it's coming out of a barrel.

"He'll drink it with pleasure," the king on the bunk lifts his eyebrows. "Is he made of iron? He'll drink piss, and suck all of our little pricks too. He just doesn't know it yet."

And immediately it starts up again. For the second day they no longer beat you. Now they've found themselves a cross-eyed Korean. He presses a bit somewhere under the heart with his fingers and smiles. That's the face of pain: a smiling Korean with cross-eyed slits. It's not just you that hurts—it's the entire world. If you had a voice, you'd scream, but they've torn out your voice. The Korean suddenly releases his fingers; that's the worst moment. You don't hurt anymore, you're all right. You only need to drink—and the torture would be over. If you don't drink—this will go on forever. Should you drink?

"I'm tired of this," says the voice out of a barrel. "He's iron. What do you need this for, Vaska? If you don't like his mug—let's slice him up and be done with it."

The king on the bunk scowls, picks his words without hurrying.

"He walks around with his head up. And he looks proud. Whether he's beaten or not. And what does he have to look proud about? Because he's a political? Because he's a shitty Lithuanian? He has to understand. He has to bow. Bow to us."

"So, he walks around with his head up. Goga has it right—chop off that head—he won't walk around that way anymore. Do you want to see your own chopped-off head?"

You can't understand. After all, you're sitting in the same camp. You walk behind the same barbed wire. Why are they torturing you? True, they're criminals, they're Russians—but why? And furthermore you don't understand: why don't you give in? All that's needed is one little instant. Why are you holding out for the third day? Or the fourth? Or the fifth?

Their king, the famous Vaska Jebachik, climbs down from his throne and comes closer. He looks at you with his large, beautiful eyes and chews on his lips. The Korean will soon press other spots in his particular way, then still others. There is an entire galaxy of painful spots in you. Should you drink?

"I need to understand this shitbag," says the king quietly, as if to himself. "I want to climb into his kidneys and liver. And see what sort of little things are lying there. What's assembled there. But what could be assembled there? There's nothing there out of the ordinary. After all, he'll drink the pee, he'll lick us in front and in back too. I like it when Lithuanians lick. Their tongues are softer."

He knows his place in this world order. In every camp there is another camp, and in that camp another little camp. And in that little camp there is another tiny camp. And so on forever. Everyone has to choose which little camp of camps he will command. Otherwise you'll just be a prisoner everywhere. If you don't choose anything, you'll be the prisoner of all of those little camps of camps simultaneously.

Is it at all possible to escape from the very largest camp's fences, or is the entire world a camp, and you'll never escape it?

"Let's try once more," says the king, sitting on his throne again.

"Drink, you puppy, lap it up," the beanpole roars.

"He's iron," says Goga.

"You see how much I love you," says the Korean with the tips of his fingers.

"Let's try once more," says the king.

"It's like some endless piece of gum," says Goga.

The beanpole, angered, splashes the bucket in your face. The salty liquid burns your eyes, drips off your nose. You stink all over.

"Ass!" says the king. "He has to drink it himself. Himself, get it? He has to drink it like the finest wine. And thank us too."

"This is some kind of idiocy," says the beanpole. "It'd be better if we showed him his chopped-off head."

The king chews his lips again, chews them for a long time and unexpectedly smiles. His smile is handsome; he could be a movie star.

"He can't see his own chopped-off head. But he can see something else. Come on, take his pants off! Beanpole, you tossed it out, now piss some more yourself."

"But I can't anymore."

"For this cause," says Goga, lighting up unexpectedly, "for this cause I can make an effort."

He takes the dented bucket, unbuttons himself, and assiduously lets a thin stream inside. The beanpole fumbles around inside your fly and pulls out the musty, sweaty thing.

"Not an ordinary one," he says, "But it kind of looks like it's been chewed."

"The girls chewed on it," Goga smiles sweetly and pulls out his famous razor. "Now you'll drink anything for me, bro. Now I'll be able to piss straight into your mouth."

"Understand?" the king asks. "Do you understand, finally, that we can do anything? Do you understand who has the upper hand?"

The razor approaches like a little glinting beast. Below, you feel cold and the prick of the blade.

"You'll be left with nothing. Your beard won't grow. You'll be as fat as a pig and you'll speak with a woman's voice. You'll be a big, fat, disgusting old woman. Okay, let's cut. Drink!"

Taking aim, you kick the bucket with your foot. They won't piss anymore today. They won't have anything to make it from.

The king leaps from his throne like a beast, shoves Goga aside. The razor catches anyway; you feel warm blood below. King Vaska Jebachik looks at you insistently.

"Don't you understand? You're not sorry?"

"It's just flesh," says your voice, appearing out of nowhere.

"Just listen to him! Listen! His prick is just flesh! Do you understand what you're saying? Are you in your right mind?"

"Let's chop off his head and throw it in the politicals' barracks. Now, *that would be a laugh!"* says the beanpole.

*"Flesh? Flesh, you say? And what else might you be?"* says the king. *"All right, I'll cut off your prick. I'll poke out your eyes. I'll chop off your arms and legs. Tear out your tongue. And what will be left, what more will be left of you?"*

*"Me. I, myself. Who hasn't drunk piss."*

*"He's a psycho,"* says the beanpole in his lame little voice. *"Let's cement him into the foundation and be done with it."*

Goga's unhappy; he's getting unhappier all the time. He snaps the razor: now folding it, now unfolding it. The sun is shining, that's the worst. Through the barracks window you see a little tree. A puny, little green tree. If they cement you into the foundation, maybe you'll be a little tree.

I found out quite a bit:

1. Teodoras went down The Way and was burnt to death;
2. Gediminas went down The Way and was crushed to death;
3. The Basilisk of Vilnius is still hiding in its lair;
4. I am going down The True Way and I am the closest target for its murderous gaze.

The only thing I didn't know was how *They* would take me on. I look at Stefanija with pity—she kept trying to help me, but mostly she just got in the way and was underfoot. I look at Lolita with horror—she doesn't even realize that she's become a hostage.

I didn't have children on purpose, so *They* couldn't take them hostage. But now I have Lolita.

I looked at Gediminas in hope—he was the only one who could have helped me. Gediminas saw a great deal and knew a great deal. Innumerable cities, hordes of people, were tucked away inside him. He cruised the streets of Greenwich Village and drank beer with farmers in Montana. Caught shrimp with Japanese fishermen. Clambered around the Mayan pyramids. Gediminas was my eyes; he saw things I will never lay eyes on. I have only Vilnius, while he wanted to take in all the continents. The borders of his camp were much wider than those of mine. Paris and Amsterdam fit inside them, the world's tallest towers jutted up in them—not just the stumpy, powerless phallus of Vilnius. People swarmed and teemed inside of him, people whom he had met far away and spoken to—in hope of finding an El Dorado of the human spirit, a place where *Their* proboscises don't reach. It's terrible, but he never did find those people or that miraculous place. People are the same everywhere, he would say after every trip; they aren't *safe* anywhere. At the time I didn't understand what he had in mind. People are the same everywhere. There are no chosen nations that are safe from *Them*. It's actually even worse for people who live in free countries than it is for us. Our very life, our very surroundings force us to search for answers, because it's so obviously bad here—nauseatingly bad. It's very easy, Gedis kept saying, for the others to blissfully snooze off.

I will never fully understand who he was—that jazzman mathematician plowman. Who was this Gediminas? A lone warrior, or the leader of a legion? A fearless investigator, or a novice barely taking his first steps on The Way? Sometimes he'd be so much like his father, the patriarch of a Lithuanian village who had become one with his farm and his land. Gedis wandered a great deal through the world, but he kept returning to the shabby, ulcerated Iron Wolf. Apparently, it's only in Vilnius that you can uncover the great secrets. In a city turned into a province of provinces by force, in a city on the edge between Russia and Western Europe and infused with both one and the other spirit. Only in Vilnius, in the farthest bastion of the Catholic church, the city of the many-headed, multilingual dragon, of the oppressive Basilisk, of the fog of oblivion.

And yet there's more—in the city of the river of mystery.

Gediminas loved to sit on the bank of the Neris and wordlessly speak with the murky flow. The river names its city, he liked to say; it floats secret knowledge to the city and washes away the dirt of the soul. Now I, too, frequently sit on the bank and stare aimlessly at the wet bushes. The hung-over fishermen of Vilnius offer me fish that stink of tar. Gediminas is right: this river really does absorb words that are spoken in secret. It floats them away, and later, unexpectedly, brings them back from obscurity.

"Look at the Neris," Gedis would say, "There are rivers of the dead and rivers of oblivion in the world. There are rivers of history and the river of all rivers . . . But the Neris is the river of memory. Our spilled blood flows with it, our lost memory . . ."

On the banks of the Neris, if you listen carefully, you can hear the names of all of the lost Lithuanians. Those who fell at the hands of the

Teutonic Knights six hundred years ago, and those the Russians took to Siberia thirty years ago. It's the only place the chronicle of Vilnius survives . . . The gods only know what it told Gediminas. Only the gods know what Gedis wanted to say with his "Neris Blues," which was by no means blues. Gedis played only avant-garde jazz—if that really can be called avant-garde jazz. But it was *music*. I carefully researched how *They* went about destroying contemporary music; nowadays jazz is perhaps the closest to *real music*. Real music was always improvised one way or the other; both the East and the West recognized this. You cannot write the human spirit into a musical staff and play it the same way every time. Earlier everyone knew this. Johann Sebastian Bach played swing like a born jazz musician; he felt the pulsation of the spirit. However, *They* cleverly locked spirit into staffs, measures, and beats. It was no accident *They* so persecuted the jazz musicians who longed to escape those restrictions. It was no accident so many jazzmen were butchered by persons unknown or went out of their minds. Jazz is enormously dangerous to *Them*, the ones who thrust the idea on the world that music is the careful repetition of rules and worn-out melodies heard a hundred times, and that to play is to get *identical* sounds out of *identical* instruments via *identical* means. Gedis wanted to play everything, whatever is possible. And even more so whatever is not possible.

But besides jazz he delighted in the strictness of mathematics. More and more often I think he was digging closer to *Their* pathologic through mathematics. In his mathematical work he was just as unruly and insane as he was playing music. I am *almost* sure it was in this fashion he attempted to break through the wall of logic and enter the domain of the *pathologic*. He wanted to grasp the entire mechanism of *Their* activities. And who knows if he hadn't succeeded—otherwise why would they *have needed* to make all of his papers disappear? Some KGB could confiscate the manuscript of a novel, but why steal mathematical work?

I miss Gediminas very much. Vilnius itself misses him, that eternal *third one*, about whom Gediminas used to say:

"In Vilnius there can never be just the two of you. If you sit with a friend or a woman, Vilnius will, without fail, sneak up on you like some odd *third one*. You can't get away from Vilnius. There isn't another city like it in the world . . . America's blacks know this sensation well. Their

Vilnius, that *third one*, is called the blues. Not a song, not the music . . . I don't know . . . a mood, or God fluttering in the air . . . In a word—the blues. One old man in Harlem explained it to me this way: when some other old negro talks, and I listen, it ain't just the two of us, there's always a third, and his name is the blues . . . And our blues is called Vilnius. Horrible, beloved Vilnius."

Filthy, dazed Vilnius, where you get up every day and think you didn't go to bed there last night. Where you go to bed, thinking that tomorrow you won't be getting up there. A soulless blues, of which only a rhythm and a melody are left, even the *blue notes* don't sound anymore, because music has irremediably lost its spirit. Blues without a soul is always horrifying—it's like a dead man walking. Gediminas is the dead soul of Vilnius's blues.

I cannot go it alone anymore. I never could look at others from on high, I never could turn into a demiurge indifferent to God. I always felt that those others are part of me; their weakness is my weakness, their kanuked brains a reflection of my own dissolving brain. I never tried to stand above others and talk to God about my own private matters. Who knows if it's worth talking to God at all. It seems to me *God has also been kanuked.*

Every seeker needs direction. *Their* secret lingers everywhere—in the constellations of the stars and in the morning fog of a dream that hasn't dispersed, in the pavement of every Vilnius side street and inside the most disgusting slut's vagina. *Their* secret cannot be coded into any one sign, any one scent, or any one dream. It hides *everywhere*—like the name of God—you just need to know how to read it. The blond-haired girl slowly going down the evening street carries *Their* mark within her. If you could understand her completely, you would solve *Their* secret too. The fissured wall of an old house most certainly conceals *Their* hieroglyph; perhaps if you overlaid a drawing of those cracks on a map of Vilnius you would see *Their* secret pathways. But it's the river that matters most.

The river is paramount. I cannot write anything down on paper (*They* destroy papers). I cannot encrypt anything (*Their* pathologic deciphers everything). I cannot carry everything in my head (*They* will rip my head off). The river is the only place my information can survive. I whisper my secret prayer, every day, only to the river: do not try to name *Their* purpose, because there are no words for that; do not identify *Them* with any government, any system, any organization—that's just what *They* are waiting for, for you to attack particulars instead of universals.

I have offered the Neris hundreds of my prayers, most often at night. Night and the dark always guard me. In the dark you are invisible; the oppressive stares of the kanukai don't reach you. The river's current saved me from the unbearable weight of knowing. The Neris is Vilnius's ear; it heard me.

*Now* I walk along the bank and for the hundredth time arrange the secret signs, checking to see that none have gotten lost. The Neris flows in from the unknown, from the depths of the ages—just as *They* did. No one has yet determined the epoch when *Their* development turned aside from humanity's development, no one has researched *Their* evolution or *Their* history, although all of that should be tucked away somewhere deep within every person's memory. In their genetic memory—no wonder *They* try so hard to change humanity through genetics. Lithuania without Lithuanians! The Crimea without Tatars! Europe without Jews! Vilnius without a memory! The genes of memory hide in the Neris's current too; there's extinct nations flowing there, and death factories, and witch hunts. Across from Žirmūnai's first bend there is a small patch of land dotted with multi-colored stones. Every little stone there has its own hidden meaning. The two giant boulders—they're the two great geneticists, Hitler and Stalin. I can sit on either one of them. The boulders stand opposite each other. The one on the left, without doubt, is Hitler; I seem to see that famous shock of hair, fallen on his forehead, or maybe the little kanukish eyes, or maybe I hear the hysterical voice. That rock *is* Hitler. The second sits there more quietly, sunk into the ground; he weaves his plans in secret. When I'm standing here, I'm afraid to turn my back on him. It seems he'll start moving any moment, deftly crawl over and sink his poisonous teeth into my ankles. I'm *still* afraid of that rock, of his Georgian mustache, of his sticky fingers. But he is just a rock, both of them are just rocks. Never get distracted by politics and government leaders, they don't matter as much as the ordinary backyard kanukas who's devouring everyone with his stare. All politicians are just robots; police intelligence organizations—second-rate robots; government officials—third-rate robots. Don't look for answers in the system of government. I know *Them*, believe me. I look over the huge number of little stones rolling under my feet. There must be millions of them lying here. The six million Jews Hitler finished off; Stalin tried to better this number, but he didn't make it, he didn't make it. Why Jews (dark gray smooth little stones) in particular? Perhaps they really did transmit secrets no one else knows through the ages? But it's impossible to look for the logic in *Their* doings—take that pile of white stones looming over there. Several million Ukrainians, starved to death by Stalin. So it turns out Ukrainians also know something they shouldn't? And what do the Crimean Tatars have to do with it? Questions without answers. And a continually growing suspicion that it's all done for no reason whatsoever. Why does a river flow? Because it flows. Sometimes *They* act with the particular inevitability and senselessness characteristic of inanimate nature. If Hitler's death factories had reached their planned capacity, they would have destroyed *more* people in a year than were born in all of Europe. Thanks to *Their* secret doings the world's countries have stored up *more* weapons than are needed to destroy all of humanity.

A withered bush juts out beyond the garden of stones. There I hid yet another thought of mine, one born in a difficult, nightmarish dream: *Their* dialectic isn't the world's dialectic. *Their* doings unravel the world's harmony. The bush's branches are dead; the rotten leaves hang on crooked stalks. *They* can only kanuk a human; neither rivers nor trees submit to *Them*. When sucking out people's souls, *They*, willingly or not, contradict nature. The community of soulless humans destroys nature by its very breathing, even *with its thoughts*. Particularly thoughts. That's how ecological disasters happen. That's how the one that still awaits us all will happen. The ancient Chinese knew very well that a person's spirit, his thoughts, and his morals affect nature directly. A human spirit changes air, fire, water, the origins of the cosmos, and cosmic harmony. When the spirit fails, so does the great harmony. Futurologists delving into ecological balance with computers are ridiculous. They count external symptoms, but they don't know the deeper reason. They have no idea what I've encrypted into this poor, puny bush. They can't see a bush like that right in front of their eyes. They don't live in Vilnius. They are blind—I was like that too, not so very long ago. If we want to save ourselves, we don't need to count the smoke coming out of factories, but rather the remains of the human spirit.

Why, what's it all for? Why do *They* need it? Why did the kanukai metropole settle into Vilnius in particular? Why not in Bangkok, Port-au-Prince, or a nameless valley of snakes in Burma? Don't tell me *They* are attracted by the Neris's broad banks and the high-rise building boxes that are slowly wading into the stream? Vilnius really could drown; the houses could, in a sad row, crawl into the water. Unfortunately, the Neris is too shallow.

I can sit on the bank across from the double whirlpools by the Žirmūnai bridge for hours on end. It is one of the Neris's most dreadful spots. Every bit of straw that floats by, swallowed by the throat of the vortex, turns into a ruined human spirit. See there now, a scrap of paper floats in, thrashes, and disappears into the black funnel. Perhaps that's Freud, who got a craving to pull *Their* image out of oblivion, out of the subconscious, and was instantly dealt with. What's left of him after diving through the whirlpool? Naked biology, the libido, and sexual impulses. And perhaps that little stalk over there is Tolstoy, searching for the human in humanity, but ending in complete drivel. Or Picasso (a Spaniard!), striving to breathe spirit into art, but turned into a joker by *Them*. Or perhaps the little stalk will never again rise from the whirl-pool; it'll be swallowed up and left on the bottom for the ages. Then it will be one of those who never gave in, let's say, Lorca (a Spaniard again!), snuffed out like a smoldering candle the moment he tried to hint of *Them* less indirectly. (Do you remember "El publico"? Do you remember the fake Juliet and the scream, "That's not the real Juliet, *They've* tied the real one up and pushed her under the chairs"?)

I'd really like to announce my knowledge to everyone, but it's impos-sible. The Neris is the *only* place that can safeguard my thoughts. If I name all the nameless stalks, if I give them meaning, even *They* won't be able to destroy those meanings. *They* can't drink up a river. The one who comes after me will understand everything. The Neris will float my memory to him. I hid everything I know in the current of the Neris. I hid it well—even *They* won't decipher those signs. Only the one who will come after me can read them. The Neris is my encyclopedia, the *magnum opus* of my life. Heraclitus couldn't wade into the same stream twice. He didn't have his Neris. He didn't have a river whose current is eternal and cyclical, where not just water flows, but thoughts and words flow too, where my cry flows. The entire river current is full of my cry; it pours into the sea. Its particles splash with the spray of ocean crests into the shores of Australia, America, or Africa. And no one, no one hears it. No one. Except maybe *Them.*

Only *They* always hear everything, that metaphysical tribe that broke off from the human family in times past, the carrier of bulging little eyes, the parasite of the spirit, the apologist of deformed bodies, Vilnius's secret ruler. I cannot bear it anymore. It would be better if *They* shoved me into the Neris, so I would float downstream like someone's recollection myself. It would be better if *They* strangled me in my sleep. Why do *They* let me live? What task of *Theirs* do I fulfill without being aware of it myself?

I have only one answer: *They forgot their own purpose long ago.* They do everything as if they were automatons, as if they were creatures driven by a pathological instinct. They themselves no longer understand the reason why they have to bear crippled bodies and kanuk everyone in sight. *They* themselves want to know what it all means, or if they have a purpose. And they hope *it will be I* who will discover it, who will read it in an old folio, or dream it, or sweat it out during some night of kanukish nightmares. If there is such a purpose at all. What is the purpose of the movement of the stars? For what purpose do we dream of white horses or stares without eyes? What is the purpose of Vilnius's existence, the purpose of this river, the purpose of us all?

*"We're not going to finish this Judas off just any old way, but in a true Lithuanian way," says Bitinas calmly.*

*He speaks ringingly, like a preacher; his voice flutters in pale yellow stripes among the thick tree trunks.*

*"We won't finish him off because he's a stribas. Not because he's a spy for the Russkies. The NKVD tramped over our heads six times and brought dogs, but even they couldn't sniff us out. A bit longer, and one Judas would have betrayed everyone. But that's not why we'll finish him off. It'll be just because we are human beings."*

*The men are standing in a small group, disheveled and shabby. Of course, they're humans. They are human because they suffer and have hope.*

*"We're neither beasts nor gods," says Bitinas. "We're in the middle. Animals don't betray anyone and fight only for a mate or food. But we betray*

*first, and then we kill. Or first kill, and then betray. It's all because of our hunger for love, for sympathy, and for the welfare of our loved ones. Do you know how our forefathers punished a traitor? They would slit his stomach, pull out the end of his guts, and nail them to a pole. And then they would force him to walk in a circle around the pole, so that he could see his own traitorous intestines wrapping around it."*

Bitinas stands hunched over and aged, looking like a pagan priest who's condemned a victim to the ritual of fire and knife. You still don't believe it. You look again at the men who have assumed the names of trees; they stand there leaning as if they really were trees. They have nothing—neither sun, nor air, nor real names—only a bunker and pistonmachines.

"I wonder how our forefathers dealt with the traitors of traitors?" Bitinas asks himself. "Who turned him in?"

"Giedraitis," answers Ash. "With all the evidence."

"Mr. Giedraitis's son?" Bitinas turns to you. "Your friend, Vargalys?"

"We were only neighbors," you say, and remember the junior Giedraitis's puppyish eyes.

"A nice neighbor! He shows up wherever someone dies—one of ours or a stribas . . . It seems he's attracted to carrion."

Bitinas looks at you without blinking, his eyes really are like a pagan priest's: cold, penetrating, sucking out of you what you need yourself. You sadly think of where you are and what you're doing. Fighting for Lithuania? Seeking the dragon? You glance at Birch. He's a human too, after all, sitting with his hands and legs tied, propped up against the trunk of a tree, his long eyelashes blinking frequently.

"We'll pull out your intestines, you hear?" Bitinas has already decided.

"I knew where I was going," Birch tries to keep his courage up, but his voice gives him away: it trembles and squeaks.

"You don't know anything. There's nothing in the head of a Russkie agent. What kind of birch are you. What kind of Lithuanian. Are you a human being, damn it? You didn't know anything and won't know anything. But maybe seeing your intestines you'll find out . . . You start, Vargalys!"

"No," says your voice. "No, I can't. I won't stay here. I won't even watch. I'm going back to the bunker."

"You can," Bitinas says calmly. "You can do anything. After all, you're a human. After all, you're great. You must be able to do everything. Imagine that you finally catch the dragon; you trap him in a corner of his stinking cave. And suddenly he starts crying human tears and speaks in a human voice. Don't tell me your hand is going to start shaking? Don't tell me you won't slit the dragon's stomach?"

Could you cut up a living person? If your brain were empty and your heart completely empty—perhaps you'd manage to. But then you wouldn't be there yourself. What's going on here? Soon it'll be YOU whose stomach they slit and it'll be YOUR intestines they wrap around a tree. YOU are sitting with your hands and legs tied, propped up against a tree trunk. YOU blink your long eyelashes frequently.

"Enough," says Ash. "Leave the kid alone. I'll do it myself."

Petrified, you watch him lumber over to Birch, bend down on one knee, and tear the clothes from his belly. You should have been the one doing this. You'd calmly unfold a short, crooked knife and, without hurrying, cut through the ropes around his legs. Pausing a bit, you'd deftly slit Birch's belly; you'd pull out an intestine, hooking it with a bent finger (inside of it, under the slimy membrane, something would move). You would push Birch over on his knees and nail the end of the gut to the old tree trunk, nailing it in simply with your fist, with several angry blows.

"So how did our forefathers force them to walk?" Ash asks. "Maybe we should finish him off and be done with it?"

You see everything clearly; the evening glow is at its height now. It seems a long, whitish worm crawled out of Birch's stomach and bit into the tree trunk.

"You didn't understand a thing," Bitinas nods his head. "Death threatens us, the warriors for a sacred cause, every day. While this slime bag . . ."

You don't want to; you fight it, but unavoidably you turn into Bitinas. Your knuckles slowly become gnarled and your head bald. You start scowling just like he does; you become more and more gaunt. But most important— your thoughts turn into Bitinas's thoughts (or his thoughts turn into yours).

You hate yourself and love Birch. And that which we love we must kill. To feel the sacrificial knife plunging into the body of love, its handle transmitting the pulse of another's life to you, the blade easily slitting the live flesh. You turn him on his back, no, you can't . . . you turn Birch on his back, no, you just can't . . . you turn him on his back, Bitinas forces him on his back and slashes his entire belly with the knife. The woods smell of sap, the men and the trees have stiffened, while Birch's belly grins a wide, bloody smile. Inside are the intestines; there are lots of them, they teem like worms, you never thought there were so many. *You don't run, something inside you attracts you to the dreadful smile of the slashed belly, now you almost want to be in Bitinas's place, to plunge your hands into Birch's warm guts and squeeze them with your fingers. Can there be any greater way of being so close to someone? Bitinas cuts the guts into pieces, at first he hurries like he's being driven, but later he can barely move. Birch's legs slip out from under Bitinas's knees, he convulses as if he's dancing, then he moans and quiets down. He looks at you with surprise and regret. Only with surprise and regret.*

*Suddenly you ask yourself what Bitinas is doing here, what has he already done. Blood rushes to your face; you recoil, but by now it's too late to run. You also TOOK PART. What happened here? How will God punish you all? What will you all turn into now? You should poke out your eyes, because you watched everything. Bitinas slowly stands up, wipes his hands on a clump of grass. He slowly raises his head. He no longer has a gaze, the eyes have disappeared from his face, there are no eyes.*

*"Stick those guts into a bag," says Bitinas grimly, "and take them to that junior Giedraitis."*

Where did the birds go?

The same smell of rotting leaves hovers over the city again. On the way to work I'm again accompanied by the exact same stares. The day is exactly the same again (or maybe *it is* the same?). Two stupefied pigeons should perch next to the announcement post across from the library. Today is marked by their three-toed feet, a heap of yellowish leaves, and the dusty intestine of the library's corridor. And Lolita's exhausted face—a memory or reality? When was this already? When was it exactly the same (or maybe *the same*) day? The bright bluish-gray sun outside the window and Lolita divining with cigarette smoke? Her legs are truly a work of art. Her breasts are every man's dream. Beauty must be limited; otherwise it inevitably turns evil.

Evil? I don't know what evil is. *They* are not evil; perhaps *They* are an inevitable part of the world, without which it couldn't exist at all.

I look at Lolita and for the hundredth time it occurs to me that I never have guessed her secret. Lolita, Lilita, the ruler of demons. "Lilith" means a devourer. What is my Lolita Lilita devouring?

An evil premonition presses at my heart, presses convincingly— shouldn't I take some drops? But instead of drops, coffee awaits me.

Stefa has already stuck her head in the door; she smiles charmingly and bumps me with her plump hip as she goes by. Powerful hips and three rolls of fat on the stomach. Giedraitienė's hips and flat belly, the hips of all the world's women, the common body of all the world's women sprawling in front of me—it's faceless; I hid its face myself, because I wanted to have all the women in the world at the same time. Stefa flies forward: today everything is speeded up, time itself hurries, as if it wanted to reach a secret boundary and suddenly come to an end. Even the current of the Neris is probably speeded up, the murky water, with its last strength, attempts to wash away, to destroy my encyclopedia. Lolita smiles at me, her teeth are even and as white as can be. Teeth hungering to bite. I fruitlessly try to remember what I dreamed of today before I woke up, what image the day began with, what inaudible morning chord should be ringing in my head.

No, today the city doesn't ring—by now I'm going down the street, by now I'm smoking a bitter cigarette and counting the slovenly pigeons of Vilnius.

At what moment did the birds show up again?

Are the pigeons of Vilnius the dirty spirits of the dead, or simply *Their* disgusting envoys? No other bird would dare perch on your windowsill and pierce you with the hideous stare of their glassy eyes. There really is something kanukish about pigeons.

The streets of Vilnius are kanukish today too. The sun shines, it's bluish-gray, like cigarette smoke, like the star Metallah, which will smash into the earth any moment and shatter into a thousand fragments, poisoning all of weary Vilnius's streets. Or maybe it's already poisoned them, since it's so empty everywhere—only a miserable dog apathetically trots over the pavement. In all likelihood he was once the Iron Wolf. Or maybe I was once the Iron Wolf myself, but now I'm walking all alone and the wind angrily glues muddy tree leaves onto my face. Although no, I'm not alone, Gedis is walking next to me and whistling one of his rondos of Vilnius.

I have no itinerary. Gedis and I have no itinerary today. Perhaps that wet day has returned again, maybe in an instant the black-haired Circe will appear from around the corner, grab us both, and force us to forget everything: grandfather, father and mother, the camp and Bolius, my church and the Narutis, everything and everybody—even Lolita.

But how would she suck the Neris dry—could her vagina really manage to devour my entire flowing, whirling, stinking encyclopedia?

The wind blew passersby from out of a gateway; no, Vilnius hasn't died yet, it still shows its convulsively distorted face. Why is there such a plethora of old people in Lukiškių Square? Why did they choose today to crawl out of their slovenly, cobweb-ridden holes? Probably something really does have to happen today. I walk down the boulevard, but it seems I've stumbled into a museum of wax figures. The old people's faces are unmoving, *almost* dead; even the wind doesn't stir their sparse gray hair. Wouldn't you think they've gathered for a secret convention, where no speeches are made and no one socializes, they just sit for a while and stand for a while, without even looking at one another?

"Young man, come wit me!" a ringing, remarkably familiar voice suddenly says.

Once again I see the Ahasuerus of Vilnius, wrapped up in a moth-eaten scarf, rhythmically tapping the worn-down ends of his shoes. His shrewd eyes blink frequently; his gap-toothed smile sends me a secret message.

"Here, vere da bronze Lenin now stands, der vas a market square once," this guide of mine explains, "And even earlier, or maybe later, I don't remember anymore, gallows stood here . . . Dis square is magical. Dose who tink dat ghosts appear in Vilnius's underground are wrong. Dey're not dere!"

"I know. I'm familiar with Vilnius's underground."

"Ja, ja, dey're not dere! People are wrong to search for secrets at da extremes. Black und white! Underground und up in heaven! Black und white aren't vat's most important, it's gray! Neither da roots nor da top are da most important, it's da trunk! Don't search underground, don't search in da heavens, search on earth . . ."

I begin to remember him; his name is Šapira. He's already been part of my life, before he turned into an Ahasuerus—but what? I might remember, except that he keeps hurrying more and more, dragging me along; we're a really fine pair. A broad-shouldered, nearly six-foot-five man with a haggard gaze and a shabby Jew, two heads shorter, with bright little eyes. Yes, it's Šapira; once upon a time we drank wine at the railroad station. But where are we going now?

"Far! Very far!" he shoots back. "To hell!"

Ahasuerus flies with the wind (or against the wind?), holding on to his slumping hat. But I still can't get those old waxen men in the square, with their somnolent eyes and the gray stubble on their unshaven cheeks, out of my head. Maybe I've turned into an old man with trembling hands myself; maybe that's why I'm panting, why I can't keep up with that flyer? I want to grab him by his flapping scarf, but he's already turning to the right, brushing the sidewalk with his coattails, then suddenly turning to the left, maneuvering between leafless bushes. I know these little paths well; we've come to the clinics. What will he show me here? Dying people, deformed bodies? Yet another grandfather of mine, come down from the heavens? But by now Ahasuerus has dragged me inside, he's weaving through the corridors, descending all the stairs, climbing only downwards, heading towards hell; finally he leans against an iron-clad door with all his weight, bursts into a cramped little room, and, not even winded, fires out:

"I've brought someone, you'll find you have tings to talk about."

Šapira and I really did know each other. I'll have to ask Stefa.

The man sitting at the table slowly turns to me; instead of a greeting he says in a low, distinct voice:

"Just don't ask me if I'm Jewish. I don't even know myself. My name sounds Polish—Kovarskis. But I learned Polish when I was already grown. I don't know Yiddish, not to mention Hebrew. You can consider me a Lithuanian or a citizen of the universe, if that improves things. Do you believe in God?"

"No."

"It's a hopeless business. I don't believe, either. Without a doubt God exists, but I see no reason to pollute the brain with the idea of God. Do you smoke?"

I take the proffered cigarette and finally get a good look at the room's owner. He's impossibly thin: nearly my height and probably weighs half as much. On a long neck perches a proud face overgrown with a beard and hair—an ascetic, truly Semitic face. The face of a man who's crossed the desert and fed on the manna of heaven, who's been persecuted and suffered for thousands of years. And on that face—an ideally straight Roman nose and pale, pale, barely visible gray pupils. I look around uneasily, but my guide has disappeared.

"Šapira's always like that," the light-haired Semitic face says calmly. "He emerges from underground at the most unexpected moment and always vanishes without saying goodbye."

He speaks as if we've already known each other forever. I have seen him, I have heard his name. And I've seen this room, but not in this world—in a vision or a dream. I've been lured into a trap, a trap of my own visions. On the walls (it seems to me even on the ceiling) hang glass cabinets; inside them, neatly arranged, are countless nameless torturer's instruments. Glistening lancets with mirrored blades are lined up by size; the smallest is the size of a match and the largest is designed to disembowel giants. But all those knives are merely a small part of the horror show; there is still an infinity of saws upon saws, sharp pincers, and needles upon needles. You could hide the tiniest little saw in a coin, like a prisoner; with the big one it would be possible, with two quick thrusts, to cut a *live* person in half. A bit further on glitter pliers upon pliers, hooks, and little hatchets. Whether I want to or not, I see them covered in blood, sticking into a live body. That's what they're made for: they scream for blood and live flesh. Those instruments are arranged carefully, with *love*. A strange love lurks within them. There are scores of them, there's no end to them; I look around and suddenly realize this many *cannot fit into such a small room.* I've been lured into a trap. Unconsciously, I retreat backwards and quickly turn around, but behind my back is the iron-clad door. Knives upon little knives, sharp pincers to rip intestines apart, everything shines and glitters, everything streams blood. I quickly turn to the door and see that it *has no handle.* How simple it all is! I've ended up where I had to end up sooner or later; they'll carry me out of here ripped to pieces and feed me to the pigeons of Vilnius.

"Yes, you could call me an anatomic pathologist," the low distinct voice suddenly says. "I dissect the stiffs and announce the final diagnosis. I earn buckets of cognac if my enlightened colleagues were mistaken. Five mistaken diagnoses, that I will refute, and someone's career is over. Do you like cognac?"

The light-haired Semite finally moves, casually opens a cabinet door. I take the proffered glass and take a sip without sensing the taste.

"I see you don't care for instruments of destruction," the owner says calmly and pushes open another door. Beyond it, I see a tangle of glass tubes and hoses, instruments with a number of little handles and numeric indicators. "Maybe it'll be more comfortable in here?"

"An entire laboratory," I say—feeling better that I've recovered my voice, that the cognac has a taste again, that I'm still alive. For the time being still alive.

"It's a hopeless business. The number of times I've demanded an basic spectroscope! But what of it . . . And I need a spectrometer. I need a laser . . . For cryogenics . . . I knock around all of Vilnius with a piece of someone's ass. They fear me in every laboratory, in every institute. I'm a beggar . . . But let's not whine. You're not afraid of corpses?"

I could tell him about how I hid out in Vilnius's underground. My quarters were piled up with a gigantic stack of corpses. It was summer and they stank hideously. It was even more unpleasant when they started heaving from the gas. Maybe they were Lithuanians shot by the retreating Russians, maybe Jews murdered by the SS—I didn't have the time to investigate. And for the most part we didn't bother one another. We were each engaged in our own business: I in hiding, they—in decomposition.

And he asks me if I'm afraid of corpses.

"I see," the light-haired Semitic face states, looking at me carefully. "Just put on a gown. And gloves. Stick your fingers somewhere you shouldn't and your fingers will have to be cut off. A classic thing it is, dissecting fingers. Reducing them to little pieces. When you disassemble a single lone finger, when you arrange all of the veins, muscles, cartilage on the table, your eyes can't take it all in at once. You just can't believe that so many parts of all sorts fit into such a small mechanism . . . And actually, it's not just fingers I've dismantled, I've done an entire man. Every little piece of him. I've reduced a man to a million bits, strings, lumps . . . it's an unbelievable sight, I'd never even suspected it myself . . . The laboratory absolutely full of ONE MAN: thousands of glass jars with little pieces of flesh or splinters of bones, a dozen or more flasks of various liquids . . . And you just keep reducing it and reducing it, reducing it again and again . . . If I was a hero of Dostoevsky's, I'd probably announce that's how I'm looking for where a man's soul hides . . . That shitty soul . . . But I've always just cut up the dead; maybe that's why I still haven't found a soul. It's already flown off to heaven. I need to cut up LIVE people. Good Lord, how I'd love to see how the entire mechanism works . . ."

We pause at one more iron-clad door and go inside. Just the sight I expected: anatomy tables. On one there's a young girl who is only half dissected. Her head hangs to the side; the glassy eyes gaze at us intently. She's waiting for me. The girl's right side is slit from her armpit to her hip, her legs are disgustingly spread; it appears she's lewdly, all aquiver, awaiting a man. It's just that a man wouldn't find anything to do here: her crotch has been dissected up to the very uterus. There are no lips, no vulva, no vagina—just a straight-edged hole with even sides. One breast has slid to the side, the other stands upright; apparently it hasn't relaxed yet. From the side I look at her spread legs, at the line of her thighs, and suddenly I feel attracted to her.

"You've probably heard yourself many times that it's only alcoholics who've been exiled to the basement and hardened necrophiliacs who work here. That's partly true," Kovarskis announces nonchalantly. "Only the necrophilia is imaginary. Our poor, worn-out little doctors have nothing to do with it. It's the babes who are to blame. Just the babes . . . You wouldn't believe the sorts who show up wanting to get screwed here. You just wouldn't believe it! Babes—the most disgusting and obscene creatures on earth. Working here, you get to know women a bit. You wouldn't get to examine them this closely even if you drilled a hole in the women's toilet. You perhaps respect women?"

"One."

"It's a hopeless business. Look at this one. Even dead she lies there with her legs spread. The symbol of women. You just need to put a brain into that hole between the legs. They THINK with that place."

"Usually it's impotent men who talk that way," I say, a bit angered.

"True," Kovarskis agrees. "Or queers. Anyway, it's all rubbish. Yes, there are a few alcoholics and semi-necrophiliacs here; there are a few boys who hope, after working here, to then operate like gods. But the most important thing here is me."

His tone is enough to make you shudder. The Lord God could use a tone like that to announce: this world was made by ME! Once more I look over the bearded relic and meet a calm, searching gaze.

"So, what brought you here?"

I understand it's my turn to talk. But I don't know why I came here.

Ahasuerus dragged me here; he promised I would find something important here. Maybe that girl? She reminds me of something. Maybe Janė, raped by the Russian soldiers? She lay there the same way, completely unable to press her knees together.

Kovarskis sits down on the corner of the table, chews a cigarette, and looks at me. He looks at my eyes, searching for something in them.

"Once I asked Šapira to bring me someone. Maybe a year ago. He brought you. You're the first . . . No, brother, I'm not looking for a soul. More like a disease. A disease with my name . . . Even in my earliest childhood, I was determined to find a disease with my name. Kovarskis's disease, which no one had discovered yet. That's my mania, my *idée fixe*. You're not a medical man, maybe you don't quite understand what it means in our times to find a REAL, BIG disease no one has discovered yet. That's exactly why I cut little bones up into pieces and pull nerves out one at a time. I've looked for it everywhere. I am a walking encyclopedia of pathology . . . I've discovered dozens of specific anomalies, minor deviations, but I needed a DISEASE. A hundred times I completely lost hope . . . But God finally enlightened me. If you want to find an essentially HUMAN disease, he said to me once while I was perched on the shitter, research the brain. Because a person is a brain and only a brain. Everything else is a mechanism . . . Come here!"

He nimbly jumps off the table and goes over to a refrigerated cabinet. The girl, her head tilted, attentively watches him from behind.

"Do you know why she stares like that?" Kovarskis throws over his shoulder. "Because her brain hasn't been taken out. You wouldn't believe how a stiff's face immediately loses its expression and its gaze as soon as you take out the brain."

He finally manages to work the locks and opens the heavy door; I see hundreds of brains arranged on shelves: some larger, some smaller, a few with spots, still others with horrible growths.

"There you are," Kovarskis announces grimly. "Although you don't see much here."

"And you? What do you see?"

He suddenly turns to me, burning me with a terrible look, and then unexpectedly stares at his own hands. Without looking, he pulls out a brain and weighs it in his palm. Now he resembles a pagan priest, or more likely a sorcerer.

"Everything. When I look at a brain, I see a human. It grows around that brain; it's born out of emptiness. At first I see a face and eyes . . . Then the neck, shoulders, and arms show up . . . The torso and the legs . . . The sex shows up last of all. The women slowly grow breasts; a man's penis shoots up like some kind of sprout . . . I see everything. But that's not what matters most. What matters most is that expression . . . That expression . . ."

Sunk into thought, he throws the brain back into the cabinet and slams the door. The girl's left breast suddenly thrashes and slides down.

"Everything goes by the expression," says Kovarskis as if to himself. "It won't give me any peace. I dream of it at night . . . I hear it in music. I read it between the lines of books . . . And I keep meeting people with that expression in the street . . . you see, it's the expression of a stiff with its brains taken out. An indescribable expression! As if all the features had become rounded and distorted. As if the hieroglyph of the face had become hazy, indistinct . . . I don't know how to describe it . . . And just imagine—I see that expression on the faces of live people. I saw it first in the hospital, then right in the middle of the city . . . I found it, dammit, I FOUND IT!"

He's nearly screaming, the veins on his neck strain, no sign is left of his Semitic seriousness. Astounded, I watch him stack frozen brains on the table, pile them every which way, hurriedly put them on the girl's stomach, on her breasts; he's even panting.

"I have hundreds of examples to prove it! Hundreds!" Kovarskis hisses, "Here, look! You see? See? See?"

He pokes the frozen brains with a finger, but I don't see anything special—just a gray mass, convoluted wrinkles and the girl's body. The nipples of her breasts have reddened and distended.

"I don't see anything."

This works like a magic charm. He suddenly calms down; taking off his gloves, he rubs his forehead with a finger and smiles for the first time. No, he's no madman. Let him, when he's looked at a brain, see an entire person, but I can spot the smile of a madman instantly. No, he's no madman. Matters are much worse than that.

"Well, now . . . well, now . . . Look here. Here, here, by the hypothalamus. No, right here. You see that little lump? That barely visible growth that resembles a bug? A bug devouring the brain? Huh? . . . And on these brains, do you see? And on these? There you have it—there SHOULDN'T BE a lump like that." By the triumph and horror in his voice I understand we're getting to the heart of the matter. "And here's a good brain. See, no lump. And this one's good. And this one . . . I named this the Vilnius Syndrome."

"Vilnius? Not Kovarskis?"

"I couldn't refuse to share the discovery with Vilnius."

"A syndrome? A syndrome is a particular complex of symptoms."

"Clever man! Well-educated! And you think a lump like that right by the hypothalamus doesn't raise, as you say, 'a particular complex of symptoms'? I found it. It's Kovarskis's disease, which gives rise to Vilnius Syndrome."

He turns away from me and starts quickly piling the brains back into the refrigerator. I clearly see the pained wrinkles by his eyes; I feel the trembling of his hands. He is afraid; he is afraid of what he has found, and even more he fears sharing his suspicions with me.

"I know the human expression of a face," my voice speaks *by itself*, it's not me in control, it's not me choosing the words. "I know an inhuman expression too. Kovarskis, have you ever sensed stares that suck you out? Have you seen fingers with lumpy joints reaching for you?"

Finally I silence my voice. It's said too much. Kovarskis sits on the table again and fixes his gaze on me, nervously swinging his legs.

"Old man," he says in a tired voice, "It's already been at least a year since not just those stares follow me, but the walls of the room too. You think I asked Šapira to find me somebody because I wanted to brag about my discovery? Why brag—it merely needs to be publicly announced. You see, that expression . . . I named it the Vilnius expression. I could show you hundreds, millions of faces like that. Look at the images in the newspaper and you'll see what I'm talking about . . . It's horrible how MANY people there are with that expression. In Vilnius—from seventy to ninety percent . . . There's too many of them . . . Ninety percent, can you imagine? And no one has noticed it until now? Something's not right here . . . No one noticed? . . . A person with that expression is most certainly ill with Kovarskis's disease, understand? That bug sits on his brain. If you look for it, there's no way to miss it. So why hasn't anyone noticed? . . . You ask, is it just in Vilnius? No, of course not. It's everywhere. By now I can spot that expression even in pictures of huge crowds. Kovarskis's disease thrives everywhere. It should have been discovered a long time ago. It has been discovered a long time ago, understand? But why isn't it described anywhere, not even hinted at? . . . The worst of it is that you can't tear that bug off the brain, you won't cut it off; it's joined to the brain's biochemical circulation. My disease is incurable . . . Vilnius Syndrome . . . I know all of its symptoms, I could describe even the most minor of them . . ."

If an abyss had opened up beneath my feet, if my own brain had been covered with cockroaches, if lightning had struck in that basement—maybe I would have withstood it. But now I want to scream, to howl like a wolf. I know all of it's true. I'm drowning. I'm somewhere else, running down the streets, shrieking like a madman. But no, I run quietly, spitting out the suffocating air. I'm not running, I'm standing. I'm drowning.

"What matters most is the dimming of the brain," Kovarskis lectures in a monotone, rocking back and forth as if he were hypnotizing me. "Constant, continually intensifying, almost blissful . . . As if the thoughts had softened and were becoming streamlined . . . One patient explained it to me this way: my thoughts became soft and warm, I understand, better and better all the time, that it's all right the way it is, and it doesn't need to be better. Helplessness isn't bothersome anymore, you're not in the least put out if you can't think of something or if you don't understand . . ."

The shadows draw closer to me. I listen to his speech like a curse; unfamiliar faces crowd around me, and my heart grows stiffer and stiffer. Cold penetrates through all the pores of my skin; I am in an icy desert where the sun never shines. *They've* even *physically* slithered into our brains; it's irreversible. Horror stuns all my thoughts, all of my feelings. My saliva is bitter, but I cannot for the life of me manage to swallow it.

"The feeling of love disappears . . . Self-respect . . . Pride . . ." he arranges the words on the butchery table, on the girl's stomach, on his own knees. "The language changes. Sometimes it seems to me I could instantly recognize someone afflicted by Vilnius syndrome with my eyes closed, just by the way they talk. Expressive words, color, and mood disappear. All that's left is a bunch of stiff constructions, always the same, meaningless and vacuous . . . At the end, deformation of the body begins. The joints get twisted, strange lumps grow in the most unlikely places, and the eyes are left empty."

I was waiting for this. I was waiting for this, but the blow is crushing all the same. An invisible blade pierces my heart, pliers squeeze at my throat. It's a strange thing, hope. After all, it was all obvious a long time ago, but I still hoped. I still hope. I look at the light-eyed Semite who's still talking, and I see that he is not kanuked. I remember Lolita—she can't be kanuked. Kovarskis himself showed me *healthy* brains. Returning home, I'll look in the mirror and see a *human* face.

"But I always only get up to a certain point," Kovarskis speaks without stopping, hurrying along, "The deformation of aspirations, the deformation of the body, the deformation of speech . . . But what happens next? I can't ever track down what happens next! Death? No, Kovarskis's disease isn't fatal. All of my stiffs with the syndrome had died of something else . . . Listen, old man, maybe those damned bugs can grow SMALLER after all?"

He looks at me with such hope, with such infinite pleading, that he could probably melt a rock with that look. But I'm not a rock. I'm a human. I ought to tell him the truth: No, Kovarskis, the bugs don't get smaller; your patients, overstepping the boundary, turn into kanukai. You're right, Kovarskis, no one dies from the Vilnius syndrome. It's much worse than that. You *live* with the Vilnius syndrome!

"I can't announce my discovery, my life's work." He's no longer talking, but hissing. "I cannot unveil the disease with my name, as long as I haven't found an antidote, or at least the cause. I need to work. Work, work, and work . . . I need to dissect the living, and first of all— THE GOOD ONES. I must find out why they have immunity. I need a genetic laboratory. I need to know if it's hereditary . . . Help me. Help me, if you can. If you still can."

He falls silent and fixes his horrified eyes on me. He stretches out his hand and cold fingers brush against my cheek.

"If you still can . . ." he whispers, as if it were the greatest secret of all, "because your facial muscles sometimes arrange themselves so oddly . . . Very oddly . . . Do you occasionally get the urge to follow others, to discover their secrets? Does it sometimes start to seem to you that someone's emptied your brains, that SOMEONE ELSE'S thoughts flutter around in your head? Do you look in the mirror often? And how do you like yourself?"

You'd think someone had smashed me up the side of my head. He said THAT. A purple mist floods my eyes, the strokes of my pulse hammer into an empty skull. He didn't *really* see something, did he? In an instant all my infirmities, all my old pains, flow over me; the most awful suspicions are reborn. I feel a strange ache in the joints of my fingers, then in my knees and the vertebrae of my neck. In horror I feel my neck shorten, my head grow to my shoulders. And my heart overflows with despair, a horrible despair and loneliness, unlike anything I've ever experienced. Even without a mirror I see my hair slowly turning the color of straw. I already know that behind my knees, between my thighs, on my sides, soft, quivering mounds of flesh have sprouted. *I am slowly turning into a kanukas.* I'm probably standing next to the Narutis by now, looking around and sensing how the entire secret world of Old Town obeys me; I sense my neckless, bug-eyed, deformed-finger power. But this merely strangles me with a still deeper despair and loneliness. I understand what I couldn't understand until now: *we, the kanukai, do not give birth to kanukai; we can only reproduce our kind by kanuking healthy people!* I'm lonely and sad, as lonely and sad as a single tree, Lord of mine, how I want to kanuk someone! Where am I, where am I? The trembling hand of the imbecile slides down the girl's long thighs, approaching the unseen but inferred secret opening, but the girl, drowned in her dreams, feels nothing. The black-haired woman's legs, in taut brown stockings, encompass me, I melt like wax, I no longer even hear the Old Town Circe's enchanting breathing, I sense only the sweetish scent of rotting leaves. Madam Giedraitienė, with a familiar motion, roughly pulls me closer, and blooming breasts reveal themselves underneath the old rags—Irena's breasts, I recognize the mole under the nipple, I recognize their color and smell; a short-cropped little head of hair watches me, hidden between the library's dusty bookshelves, the supple body thrashes, struggling out of my hands, but it's all predetermined, I tear the lacy underpants into shreds and recoil at the sight, because there is nothing between her thighs— just a smooth, empty spot, like a plastic doll's. Bolius slowly, thoroughly chews on the grass, Jebachik giggles quietly, even choking with it, while Bolius clumsily turns around, attentively inspects his own dung heap, and, bending over, sniffs at it. Even I notice the stench, the disgusting stench of formalin or something else besides, I am all alone in the basement with the girl's corpse, my head keeps reeling more and more, I have no strength left, I stagger and grab the corner of the table. My fingers are right next to the girl's now completely softened body, its breasts fallen over to the sides—a palm would easily fit between them. I get such an urge to put it there; I need to get out of here as fast as possible. I gather my strength and inadvertently lean against the girl's body, realizing too late that it is a magic touch, fingerless hands snatch me, carry me somewhere, stuff me into the dissected girl's crotch, the world is no more and neither is my body, because I have been completely stuffed into the square space with perfectly straight-edged sides; I'm choking on stinking blood, but I cannot escape, there is nowhere to escape to, there's no room, I'm returning to the womb, and my last thought, my last question is—what does it mean to return to a *corpse's* womb?

Once more, I go over my finger joints, my knees, and the muscles between my thighs. No, I am not a kanukas; I am a human. For the time being I'm still human. Kovarskis lied, intimidated me with his frozen corpses, but for the time being I am still alive.

I descend from Karoliniškės towards Žvėrynas—so many places and neighborhoods fit into a single day, a day that's always the same, or maybe *the very same* day. The air is indescribably clear—even the contours of the forest looming beyond the city aren't at all hazy. Everything tries to exceed itself, to brighten its features; it desperately wants to convince me it really exists. The filthy pigeons of Vilnius in particular are doing their best. They're everywhere. They peck at nonexistent crumbs on both sides of the road; an enormous flock of them rages above my head. They're following me. They pretend to eat (at that moment another flock rages above my head), and when I pass by and go off a bit, they quickly take off and fly ahead of me in a large arc, glaring at me with their empty little eyes. I turn in one direction, in another, intentionally stomp around in places where there really is nothing for them to feed on, but they don't desert me. That gang of atrocities really is following me. It seems as if the dragon of Vilnius himself is slithering from behind, choosing a spot to devour me. I hate pigeons. They're the most disgusting birds on earth. Any ornithologist will tell you that only a pigeon (like a human) can peck a member of its own species to death. Then what's there to be said about the pigeons *of Vilnius*!? They want me to turn into a kanukas regardless. I whip around Žvėrynas's crooked, unpaved little streets, trying to use the trees as cover, but I cannot get away. Crawl *underground* if you like. I no longer recognize the misshapen little streets, the passersby here are strange, I'm lonely and uneasy, for some reason I get the urge to knock on the door of one of the squat little houses and shout at the top of my voice: "I've gotten lost, save me!" I'm delighted to see the asphalt of a wider street; I rush into it at a trot and breathe a sigh of relief. It's Vytauto Street; a few dozen steps away looms the closed Russian Orthodox Church. The street is empty as far as you can see, not a single person about, but that's not what's most striking. I feel as if instead of meeting a live, active acquaintance, I've met a walking corpse. The life on my name-sake's street has vanished somewhere: the leaves on the trees don't stir, dirty cats don't slink along the walls, there's no fluttering of laundry hung out to dry in the courtyards. Even the church seems more inert, more forsaken than usual. I look at the shabby cupolas, the Orthodox cross; I'm already about to lower my head when suddenly I see a sight that could make you go blind. Two pigeons hang in the air next to the highest cross. They don't flap their wings, they don't move at all; they hang helplessly, as if they had stumbled into a giant, invisible cobweb. One, apparently, was getting ready to perch on the cross; the other, its wings folded, was probably gliding downwards. And both are trans-fixed, hanging in the air, neither moving nor falling down, as if time had suddenly stopped.

Time, rushing forward headlong since morning, *has really stopped.* I still don't want to believe it; gasping for breath, I go down towards the river and pause by the bridge . . . I want to close my eyes, but I can't. I want to cry, but there are no tears. I want to save Lola, but I don't know how.

The water of the river stands still, the eddies and whirlpools frozen in place. It resembles a grimy, knotted rug. On the other side of the bridge, I see motionless cars and the small figures of people. Only now do I believe it: All of Vilnius *has stopped.* I no longer hear my heart; I'm probably no longer breathing. Absentmindedly, I brush my hand against my forehead and rub my eyes. *I'm moving.*

It's horrible to move when the rest of the world *has stopped.*

I've ended up in the very center of a boundless torpor. The worst nightmare couldn't compare to my reality. It'd be better if everything exploded or went up in flames; it'd be better if Vilnius were washed over by a wave of some new deluge or crushed by a cosmic catastrophe. It'd be better if everything crumbled, cracked, and crashed down. But around me stretches a dead landscape; a ringing silence encases the city, and an uncontrollable horror grows within me. What is this, I ask myself. No signs of an apocalypse, no bloody glow. Vilnius had come to a stop in an off-hand and routine way.

The crystal-clear air clouded up like muddy water. Tiny dust motes hung suspended in the air; it seemed the sky was slowly mingling with the earth. And absolutely everything stands stock still. The reflections of the street in the glass of the windows aren't moving. The cars sit frozen in the middle of the avenue; you can clearly see that a gray Lada jumped into the intersection even though the light was already red. People are as rigid as statues, but don't resemble them in the least. There is nothing artistic or symbolic in them; they have turned to stone in a single instant, in the most unsuitable poses. At that moment a disheveled, pimply teenager spat; the flow of spit hardened, stuck to his lips. A balding fatso, with a sweaty forehead, twisted backwards, apparently he'd glanced to see if his trolleybus was coming and stumbled on a crack in the sidewalk. He should have fallen, but was frozen instead, still falling, his hands thrown out to the sides. Two women who had paused to chat came to a standstill that way, with their mouths wide open. It's the inanimate things that look the worst: the leaves of trees standing on end on the sidewalk; petrified streams of water, splashed from under the wheels of a car; a crumpled piece of paper hanging over the opening to a garbage can. It isn't at all like a photograph or even a stop-motion film—in those there is life; here nonexistence has pervaded everything.

They stopped, dammit, they stopped! The gallery of expressionless faces froze; an inner cold locked the joints of Vilnius's beast. Is this the end already? Maybe I'm to blame for this? Many times I've fought down the urge to shout out loud at them: stop it, quit running around pointlessly, just calm down and think for a second! Freeze! . . . Settle down! . . . And here they've done it.

"Vilnius has stopped," I say out loud to the transfixed statues, I say to the building cornices and the dried-up lindens, I say to myself—I must drive off the all-piercing silence. "This is how the true Necropolis looks. The Necropolis of the spirit."

I do not smell any scents—they're inert too. If I were to eat something, I wouldn't sense the flavor. Vilnius has become absolutely tasteless and soundless. I can only see. Shivers go down my spine when I realize what I would never have figured out by cold logic: my perceptions have no meaning if there *is nothing* to smell, touch, or taste. A person can be ideal and perfect, but if the world has no need for it, all perfection will go for naught. What should a person like this do? Without thinking, I lick the sweaty, trembling palm of my hand and feel salt on the tip of my tongue. I can *only* taste myself. I can smell only my own smell, hear only my own words and the hollow echo of my footsteps. Kneeling, I carefully touch splatters of splashed water. The water runs down, but when it separates from my fingers, the drops hang in the air again. I take one and slowly let it down. That's how it stays standing, barely touching the shiny street tiles, not even moistening the dust.

Could I perhaps touch people? Animate them?

I almost stretch my hand out to a raw-boned man leaning against a tree, but fear restrains me. I'm afraid the person I touch will crumble like a castle of damp sand dried by the sun. And even more I fear that in touching him I would turn into stone myself. Everything is lifeless, but fear remains—it's the hardiest. I do not know the rules of this changed world; I fear *everything* here.

I tear up the stairs to the library at a run. It's empty in the corridor; no one's in the common room, and Martynas isn't sitting at his spot, either. Maybe it's just the nameless strangers in the street who've frozen? Maybe my own are moving, or maybe they've disappeared entirely? But no, in Lola's room I see the women sitting at their work. Marija had leaned over Stefa's desk, piled her gigantic breasts on top of the papers, and froze with her mouth wide open. It's enough to make me nauseous; people who you know, stopped dead in their tracks, are particularly hideous. And if I should find Lolita here? I'd probably want to freeze stiff myself. I'm already on my way out, but through a gap I spot a slender figure at the corner of an open cabinet. Trembling, I poke my head inside—thank God, it's just Beta. She froze with her skirt hitched up high, her thin fingers straining to pull her stocking up.

I look at her, fidgeting next to her as if I had forgotten something. Yes, those stockings of hers are always perfectly smooth. And her legs are perfectly straight. And her little head is *short-cropped.*

A short-cropped little head! I fruitlessly try to remember the expression of Beta's eyes and the expression of *that other's* eyes, the face of that little parasite in the dimness between the bookshelves. It seems to me that Beta *sees* my hand; could it be her *brain* isn't frozen? I shake all over, but I can't manage to conquer myself. I carefully pull her skirt up even higher, push it entirely to the side. Nothing happens. I carefully stick my fingers behind her underpants and waistband. And nothing happens. I pull the elastic towards me, I wait for Beta to suddenly shriek, or fall over, or crumble into dust, or . . . But absolutely nothing happens. She stands there like she's planted to the spot. I quickly glance downwards—thick hair luxuriates under her panties. Apparently everything is in order, but the devil keeps pushing my hand; I let my fingers in deeper still, slide them between the lips, and grasp a rather large, slippery clitoris.

I pull my hand out like it's been burned and leap out into the corridor. Only now do I realize my forehead's covered in sweat, my heart is pounding, and my hands are shaking. And Beta, with her skirt turned to the side and her underpants pulled down, still stands before my eyes. What will she think when she wakes up? If she wakes up at all.

This is better than reading someone's diary. In a diary you can lie to yourself, but here everything is the way it is. I had to check Beta out, I stubbornly confirm to myself, but my thoughts go in an entirely different direction. I can do whatever I want. I can intrude anywhere. Perhaps I can even come across *Their* hiding place.

My arms go numb down to my very fingertips; I reel as I walk, as if I had forgotten how to. No objective invites me forward, nor backward, nor to the side. As if in a dream, I step into a darkened stairway. I stumble up the stairs; I rattle the doorknobs one after another. The third or fourth opens up; I end up in a large room that is jammed full of furniture. A sickly young man stands with his hands raised dramatically; the open mouth of his distorted face looks like a doorway to hell. A woman with a frightened face sits next to a round table. She's considerably older than he is, but she's too young to be his mother. Her hands are knitted together; the fingers of the right are nearly breaking the fingers of the left. But most expressive of all are her eyes: I plainly hear the horrible, inadmissible words of the sickly man reflected at the bottom of the woman's eyes, and I also see suffering and contempt. She was horribly frightened at his words, but suddenly her depths flushed with contempt and disgust, that he had dared to say what he had said. A neurotic lover with a mother complex? A disgusting jealous scene? Or maybe a brother who called his sister a slut, or who cursed her for his ruined life, having found the guilty party at last? The frozen instant of a stranger's time doesn't want to give anything away; I see only as much as I can wrest from it by force. I won't guess anything more, even if I were to dawdle here for hours. I quietly close the door and rattle more doorknobs. Yet another unlocked apartment, squalid and decorated with unmatched furniture whose colors clash. The trashed little hallway table is on its last legs; the corners of the shoe rack are battered and greasy papers are scattered on top of it. At the end of the corridor, a first grader with a shaven head is fixed to the keyhole, his thighs pressed together and one foot stepping on the other. A long string of saliva drips from the boy's protruding tongue, which he has bitten in suspense. I carefully push open the door to the room and nearly cry out, I even recoil. Looking straight at me is a girl's distorted face, covered in sweat and as pale as if strewn with chalk dust. It's a corpse's face—only by gathering all of my strength do I calm myself. She's alive and isn't about to die, but she looks like an embalmed corpse. Black circles under the eyes, lips crookedly pressed together, hollow cheeks. She stares at me shamelessly and angrily. The grubby, contemptuous corpse's face is horribly incongruous with the rest of the scene; for a long time I can't believe what I'm seeing. She smirks, her head thrown indifferently to the side, while a broad-shouldered, curly-haired, bandit-faced little bull has fallen upon her with his entire body, pressing her into the very corner of the sofa. There are no smells here, but nevertheless I sense how he reeks of vodka. The girl's bent legs stick out from both the man's sides—they are pale and bloodless, like some strange growths that don't belong to her. But it's her hands, dug into the lover's neck, that are the most shocking. Nails caked with dirt, black dirty half-moons and peeling pink polish. I move clumsily, catching the head of the young spectator; his skull rings like an empty clay pitcher. His eyes are narrowed in horror and satisfaction; the thread of saliva continues to hang as it was. The girl's eyes look at me without turning away; she looks like someone who has unexpectedly bit into a peppercorn.

Only out in the street do I remember that I left all the doors open. I cough as if I'm trying to retch. Something stirs in my chest, my ears ring; suddenly I feel drawn to Lolita's place. I've known what I want for a long time. I want to see Lolita rooted to the spot. I've always wanted that. I've always wanted to secretly observe her from the sidelines. I cannot reconcile myself to the thought that sometimes she is *by herself*, that she no longer belongs to me. That she can do things I'll never find out about. I crave, I desperately crave to take her by surprise, the way death takes us by surprise. I want to find Lolita frozen stiff, sprawled under someone's body. To find her inert, unable to either deceive me or hide herself. I wouldn't touch her, I wouldn't do anything to her. I just want to catch her, to see everything in secret, under cover. There's just one thing I want—to *know* everything.

If Vilnius isn't going to move, I'm not going to be able to take it much longer. Frozen Vilnius invites me, begs me, to a festival of insanity. A person never answers for his thoughts, but in this inert Vilnius he begins to no longer answer for his *actions*, either. I really am dying to visit her and clarify her betrayal. I want her to deceive me. I would be disappointed if she would simply be sitting in an armchair.

But what if she's moving too?

But no, probably not. I remember her husband's studio, her strange pose and the pigeon momentarily frozen in flight. She didn't move then, so she shouldn't move now, either; she's the same as the others. I would *feel it*, if she were moving.

No, nothing moves. On the other side of the avenue is the motionless Conservatory, next to it is Vilnius's cheeriest house—its doors are flung open; a fat little kanukas with a puffy face got stuck in the doorway. I won't go inside, really I won't, I'll just look at him from close up. The little kanukas looks like an animatronic doll. I squeeze by his protruding belly, but I stop, afraid again, just inside the door. It's been a long time since I last visited here. Would I still find my cell? The stairs invite me to climb them, but the offices don't interest me. The guard by the door, his petrified finger jammed up his nose, isn't of interest, either.

Why on earth did I come in here? Maybe *They* are intentionally trying to lure me here? I'll descend to the basement and a flat-faced kanukas, with a pale smile and swollen fingers that bend every which way, will be waiting for me. But the more fearful I get, the faster I move forward. Only a fool could fear that *They* would set such idiotic traps. Something much worse has long since been arranged for me, so for that very reason there are many things I don't have to be afraid of.

I came here the same way others go to a sacred place of their childhood or youth: to the lone hundred-year-old oak on their native homestead, or to their parents' graves. I could probably shed a tear, or simply remember who knows what—an undefined quivering fog, the haze of an existent or non-existent longing. But actually, this is a just business, an office like any other office, although it's true the basement windows are barred.

I angrily rattle the doorknobs, try to push the bolts, but even today it's not my destiny to go inside or to change anything here. I can only look through the little windows in the doors; I hope to see nothing but empty rooms and the indifferent walls of the cells. Only the very first one is empty. In the next one I see a raw-boned, gray-haired man standing in a yoga position on his head; it seems he's stood there like that for a hundred years and will stand there until the end of time. His face is completely expressionless. He's wearing a suit that doesn't stand out; every other Vilniutian could be wearing one like that. Who is he? A refractory suspect, or a lieutenant who had decided to relax in his own particular way? His inertness is particularly shocking. The people petrified in the streets look somewhat alive in spite of it all, but this one, it seems, never did move. All of the observation windows are the same, only the view inside them changes like a kaleidoscope; I don't even manage to check the faces out carefully. I'm in a hurry, all of Vilnius still awaits me. A man with a horsey face and a remarkably thin neck stares at the bars, an arm outstretched, as if he were preparing to rip the bars out with a single yank. A hollow-cheeked woman with neurotic features who looks like a drug addict stands in a corner, her blouse unbuttoned to the waist, both hands stuffed under her arms as if she were trying to pull her guts out. In a large cell, children concentrating on arranging toys have come to a complete standstill. How did they get here? What are they doing here? Their faces are unnaturally aged and much too serious. They can't really be prisoners too? Or maybe this is a secret school for born agents, agents from the cradle? In yet another cell sits a large, beautiful dog, a brown and white collie. He sits majestically on the bunk and looks at the ceiling. I don't even try to understand what that means; I keep hurrying on, something is driving me forward. One of the cells holds an aquarium: the seaweed is frozen, and huge lethargic fish hang motionless in the water; the bubbles are woven together like beads in a necklace. I hurry forward, only forward. The scenes grow confused, at intervals it seems as if all space is divided into myriad squares, out of which constantly changing images look at me. The ever more protuberant eyes of large-headed children. Pale women's lips ever more distorted in passion. Monsters without faces, only gigantic orbs—perhaps a special variety of kanukas. The corridor bends in the form of a horseshoe, although earlier it seemed straight. It leads back to the beginning, to the first, empty cell (although maybe it's some other empty cell), which waits for me. But it won't see me— once again I squeeze past the fat slob stuck in the doorway, once again I make my way down the avenue. I suddenly realize how sick I feel. Really sick.

*Vilnius has stopped.* Now I don't just see it, now I even smell that inertness; I sense its petrified taste. But it wouldn't suffice to close your eyes and pinch your nose shut. Immobile Vilnius has penetrated into every one of my cells, into every nerve. It will remain inside me forever, I will always know that it *stopped*—even if I'll see a bustling throng and smell the stench of gasoline and sweat . . . Even if I hear human speech . . . Everything has penetrated much too deeply inside me: the inert dusty leaves of the lindens . . . and the petrified statues in strange poses . . . Shout at them as much as you want. Shriek. Tear around . . . But they won't budge . . . The great power of movement has vanished . . . Vilnius Syndrome eats away at them . . . The bug of Kovarskis's disease eats away at them . . . They're helpless—and I'm helpless too, even though I'm still *moving.* I'm still alive. God knows how much I'd like to rouse them . . . God has to exist, if only to see this . . . How badly I want it! . . . How I crave it! . . . Move! Wake up! Burn the Vilnius syndrome out of yourselves . . .

God knows how much I want to stroke that long-nosed girl over there. To push those three children forward . . . To turn the branches of that linden to the sun . . . Let me be unseen and undetectable . . . Let me not exist at all . . . But you, move . . . Wake up! . . . There's just one thing I want to ask: is anyone else moving? Show him to me. I know that he must exist. I know that he is.

*What one person has experienced, someone else surely must have experienced too.* Somewhere there really is another Vytautas Vargalys (not necessarily named Vytautas Vargalys). Somewhere there is this person, living in his own Vilnius (it's not necessarily called Vilnius). Somewhere there is at least one person like that (many people like that), who, at this very moment, is walking the streets of Vilnius. Somewhere, perhaps in his mother's womb, hides the one who will come after me.

I know what everyone who is moving now is asking, because I'm asking the same thing: have *They* frozen in place too? Could I catch *Them* unawares—like those women, those men and children, and the trees, and the monsters, and the fish, and the streets, and the air, and the water, and . . . And everything else under the sun, because all of Vilnius (all the world) has come to a stop, only I move and every instant I grow ever older. I grow ever older . . . I remember something, I remember something, but it's maddeningly vague: if you want to awaken those sleeping for eternity, you need to kiss somebody . . . or stroke somebody (like that long-nosed girl there?) . . . Or make love to somebody . . . or . . .

But who could I kiss HERE—save perhaps the short, stumpy, and powerless phallus of Vilnius?

The frozen avenue looks downwards, towards Old Town, towards *Their* lair. I'm not walking on the street—I'm walking on the back of a corpse. Perhaps they'll never awaken—I chase this thought aside, but it won't retreat. The wind froze, the sky clouded over, the earth no longer breathed—I vaguely recall an old manuscript I read not so long ago. The wind froze, the sky clouded over, cows no longer brought forth calves, nor sheep lambs. Women no longer gave birth to children and water no longer flowed in the river, because all the gods had abandoned the world and nothing could change anymore. But what happened next? What solution did the manuscript offer? The frozen statues push me to the wall, to the avenue's bricks; even in their lifeless condition they try to block my way. A heavy woman with a red face. Three drunk guys with their chests bared. The same city, the same figures, but every single thing is sterile and dead, like inside Kovarskis's morgue. But a city should be shaken by convulsions before death.

Stinking currents should pour out from the sewers, the Neris should flood its banks, the drowned words should come up to the surface of its waters at last.

The statues and the trees, the belfry of the cathedral and the square, every single thing slides by my eyes; suddenly I grasp that I'm walking along calmly, *as always.* Vilnius stands still, as always. It's locked in paralysis, as always. The corpse of corpses, as always. Perhaps only the worms inside its guts are still moving.

By now I'm standing in front of the Narutis; a hunched-over old lady with a basket in her hands had set one foot on the sidewalk, carefully climbing down the stairs from the delicatessen. Two staggering red-nosed men had stiffened and were leaning in opposite directions, seemingly dancing an unearthly dance. A blond-haired child, dressed up as if for a parade, inquisitively stretched a hand towards a dirty rag. I turn into the courtyard and my heart throbs with a surprising fear. *The first ones wait here.* Even when they're frozen stiff I'm afraid of them. Two of them stand together, pressed together conspiratorially, as if they had been lying in wait for me for some time now. Their straw-colored hair looks like it's glued to their skulls; their eyes look right at me but see nothing. What should I do? Smash their heads open? Destroy them one at a time? The same way I could smash cockroaches one at a time, hoping to overcome them.

I go past the straw-haired kanukai; I even bump them with my elbow, and nothing happens. I slip over to the courtyard's stone well, and nothing happens. I look over the walled-over ancient stairwell; I even touch the bricks with my hand. And nothing, absolutely nothing, happens. My arms and legs are wracked with pains, with my entire body I sense I'll never escape from here, but I won't retreat either, not until I have come to the very end.

Isn't this where I've been going all my life? Isn't it my Way that led me here? I press my ear to the brick wall and listen carefully. I'd rather pretend, I'd rather not hear it, but all that remains is to be truthful: *I plainly hear the throbbing of a gigantic heart.*

That's not how Vilnius's heart beats; no *real* heart beats that way. Only the poisonous heart of Vilnius's Basilisk could thump like that. I've cornered it at last. I've come like a warrior to cut off its head, but I don't have a sword. But that's not what matters. I will overcome it. Man is invincible.

"And just exactly what are you looking for?" asks a loud, clear voice.

At first I thought I was hallucinating. Unfortunately, it's for real: a woman, her head wrapped in a heavy tawny scarf, glares at me intently. That's all. The Basilisk escaped, leaving me with a perfectly ordinary Old Town slut. Startled, I glance towards the street. The Indian summer sun is shining there; sparrows hop by on the sidewalk. A fleshy, mean-eyed old woman turns a bag of garbage right onto the heads of some scrawny cats. Vilnius is moving again. It's alive again. I step forward, inhaling a full chest of air, but the farther I go, the slower my steps become. *They* had lured me right up to the threshold of the secret, and cheated me at the last minute. I'm a genuine Lithuanian: I smashed into the ground a step away from the final goal.

Suddenly I turn around and manage to catch sight of a pudgy little face, with beady little eyes, jumping back from the window. I've been caught. *They* understood everything. I have stepped outside the safety zone; now I will have to pay dearly for it all. I still manage to creep into the street and turn a corner, where my strength gives way altogether. I lean against the wall and fumble for a cigarette. I'm a corpse already. It's weird to feel like a corpse. I see neither people nor the rumbling cars; I sense no smells. *They* certainly won't let me go now. I'm dead. There's only one thing I repeat to myself: you must not lose your cool. A calm, sound mind. That's what matters most. A sound mind and sober analysis always saved me.

What can they do to me?

1. Kill me one way or another. *They* could have done that a long time ago. Apparently, that isn't enough for *Them*.

2. Break me spiritually, turn me into an imbecile. It won't work. I'm invincible.

3. Take hostages and blackmail me with them. It won't work. That's exactly the reason why I didn't have children, ignoring even my family's curses.

4. Accuse me of an imaginary crime. Rubbish. I'm accustomed to prison. You can continue on The Way while sitting in a camp.

5. Lock me up in a secret psychiatric hospital. It's a popular alternative, but you can escape from it.

6. Inject me with drugs and get everything I know out of me. It won't work. I've been preparing for a long time. They will hear only incoherent ravings, but nothing important.

7. Do nothing concrete. Wait and intimidate. Torture me with the unknown. That's practically the worst. Only I can demoralize myself.

It's no use guessing. There's only one thing I want: to see Lolita as soon as possible. The world is no more, I am no more; only Lolita is left. Maybe *They* intend to take on Lolita?

For the time being, *They* haven't started on Lolita. She stands next to me and smiles entrancingly. I see an old house, entwined in wild grape vines and set in the depths of a garden, with a shriveled apple tree off to the right. A gust of wind comes tearing along from the left, the yellow unraked leaves rise from the grass and silently tumble in the air. The wind carries the leaves of the trees easily, but it doesn't stir even the smallest twigs of the bushes. This is my first time here, but I've seen this before—both the leaves flying in the air and the old wooden house— perhaps in a dream or a vision.

"My parents' garden plot. One of the first collective gardens in Vilnius. No one looks after it now."

I simply don't believe she's really here. Just now I was wandering the streets of Vilnius, bumping into the passersby, frightening children and dogs. All the streets smelled of autumn cobwebs. Yes, it's the height of Indian summer now. Lolita emerged from around a corner and walked straight up to me, as if we had agreed to meet at just that spot. For some reason it occurred to me that it was my own destiny coming towards me. She walked gracefully, her head raised proudly, and then suddenly threw her arms around my neck, as if she had thought she'd never see me alive again. She said she didn't know why she had acted that way.

Did she really not know? Why did she unexpectedly lead me here, to her parents' garden plot? The gust of wind has died down, but the leaves still flutter in the air. Other small houses are lined up nearby; a gray-haired man sits smoking a cigarette on the nearest porch steps.

"A neighbor?"

"Yes. The neighbors here are incredible. It's a magic spot. On the right, there's a lieutenant colonel of the KGB. On the left, that gray-haired man—a KGB colonel. Colonel Giedraitis."

The name pricks my heart like a needle. I try to remember what Giedraitis Junior looked like then, but only Bitinas stands before my eyes, his bald head and narrow lips spitting out the words: take him this offal.

"He's always sitting there like that and smoking," Lolita says hoarsely, "Just sitting and smoking, all the time . . . Probably remembering his victims . . . In a minute, you'll ask what his eyes are like. Colorless, expressionless. His gaze is like a beaten dog's."

A portrait of the junior Giedraitis. I should go over there and check it out, but there have been enough ghosts for today. The gray-haired man doesn't even turn his head in our direction, and Lolita keeps smiling; she's strange today. All of Vilnius, moving again, is new and strange, as if it had only just now been born.

Inside the little house everything is tidy, it's even been dusted, but the room is lifeless—a clean, nicely fixed-up corpse. The air is thick with the smell of the people who used to live here. Neglected houses always smell that way.

"You should marry me or something," says Lolita, completely out of the blue, "We'd get along nicely. During the day, we'd discuss what we'll think up for dinner. And in the evening, after eating, we'd stare at the television. And all our days would be exactly the same—right up until death. Is that such a bad way to go?"

"Better to die suddenly. I don't find a slow suicide appealing."

"You need to kill yourself somehow. Slowly isn't so bad. You don't even notice yourself fading."

The gray-haired man is visible through the window too; he really does smoke without stopping. It seems he's slowly smoldering himself. The yellow leaves have risen from the ground again; they want to soar through the closed windows. A wind, awakened by the thundering cattle cars, rages over the entire world. This time those trains aren't going to Siberia. But where? Where did grandfather go to, with the dish of excrement in his hand, where did mother, hanging with her shaven head, and father's drawings go?

"And I'd make you a pack of kids. A thousand little Lithuanian ants, who would continue to multiply and propagate. After all, the only way you can retaliate for your miserable life is by taking it out on the children—let them experience all this insanity too."

Today she is too physical. I haven't felt her body this intensely in a long time; it seemed to have disappeared, dissolved into something else: into her eyes, her speech, or her thoughts. Today I sense it with all of my essence. I even smell her sweat, which smells of old grass. I see the beauty fluids pulsating beneath the sleek skin of her legs. *My* Lolita sits in a sagging armchair; she cannot exist without *me*. Without me, those girlish breasts would wither and her face would be furrowed with wrinkles. She would age instantly. I am the source of her life and youth.

"It just seems to you that you're thinking of me," she says in a hoarse voice and closes her eyes. "I see your thoughts. I'm not there."

"What is there, then?"

"My ghost, a bloodless, transparent Lolita . . . My legs, but for some reason they're shining . . . And then there's a strange hallucination of a city. Not even Vilnius, just some city. Clouded over and frozen stiff. A city that has lost everything, even its name."

"And what else? What?"

"Twilight. An opaque dusk, where something is panting, giving off an unpleasant warmth and the oppressive smell of rotting leaves."

If I were a believer, I'd start crossing myself. How did she know that? Who is she, this inexplicable woman? All my perceptions insist she knows much more about me than I do about her. Perhaps she knows too much. How? After all, there's no one, no one, I can reveal myself to. All the underground movements of all time seem ridiculous to me. Only I know what a real, *absolute* underground is. I cannot talk about it, even to Lolita. But how did she read my thoughts? Who is she, this inexplicable woman? *Who sent her?*

I look over the interior of the house. A cramped little kitchen is visible beyond a rickety door. A gas burner, dented pots, and a huge knife on the table. Nothing of interest, except maybe for that blackened knife. Lolita sinks deeper into the armchair, only her legs keep sliding forward. Her dress keeps pulling up higher; her legs emerge from the darkness as if they were alive, darting hopeful glances at me. Lola knows full well where my eyes are looking; she enjoys my gaze.

"It's starting to get dark," she says mysteriously, as if she were telling a fairy tale. "The setting sun is looking at us. It's the time of charms, the time of miracles. Don't take your eyes off of me, just don't take your eyes off me, and you'll be mine forever. Ajingi! Nothing will worry you anymore, only me! Ajingi!"

Today she is an enchantress. All of the corners of the room are lit by the fading glow. By now the light is dying, but the darkness has not yet been born. Stunned, I watch as Lola stands up and slowly lifts her dress; she is wearing nothing underneath it. I look at her belly and the thick hair covering her sex, and desire rises in me like a threatening wave. I sit before her as if before a pagan goddess.

"Wouldn't it be better to forget everything?' she says quietly, quietly, but I hear her. "Is it worth it to think of other women . . . other things . . . a different life? . . . Come to me, come to me . . ."

She slowly, slowly, slips out of her dress; the last rays of the sun redden her body. She stands there blindingly beautiful, and as unapproachable as death.

"Do you know what the celebration of the body is?" she whispers, "The ancient, genuine celebration of the body?"

I can't make sense of anything anymore: she spreads her lower lips with her fingers, smears the open pink slit with a sugary smelling lotion. I don't even know how I end up naked next to her; I kneel motionless and look at that slit of scents pulling me closer, raising the desire to plunge into it fully. There's probably a city there too, and a library, and a labyrinth, and wind fluttering the yellow leaves of the trees. Probably everything I'll need to say goodbye to is there. I want her, insanely. Lolita falls on me, writhes, rumples my hair and moans, that enchanting smell fills my nostrils; I've never smelled anything like that before. My joints soften and melt. I want her insanely, but I can't do a thing—you'd think the short, stumpy, and powerless phallus of Vilnius had turned up between my legs.

I crave her like death, but my penis hangs helplessly. Blood doesn't gush to it; it doesn't want to look at anything. It doesn't belong to me anymore. The eternal mark of the Vargalyses has deserted me. I'm done for: I *can't anymore.*

I slowly slide off, stretch myself out on the old carpet, and long to cover the shameful phallus of Vilnius, but I can't. I long to close my eyes, but I can't. She looks at me, smiling. She understood everything; you'd think she'd been waiting just for this. Long fingers gently caress me, tangle in the hair below my stomach, and grab the shrunken mark of the Vargalyses. I'm done for.

"We're small and tired," Lolita murmurs, "The terrible spells frightened us. We want protection and love."

I'm helpless; I obey her completely. It isn't just this moment she rules me; she's long since ruled my every desire, every thought, every action. And now she acts like a ruler: she kneels firmly on her legs, her breasts pressing on her knees, greedily opens her mouth and bites me, voluptuously consuming all of the former mark of the Vargalyses, as if she wants to swallow it. I want nothing, except to die. I'm done for. While she devours me, choking, growling in satisfaction, I lie there as if I were shackled; I can only look at Lolita, Lolita, the ever-changing ruler of demons, who has taken away my last weapon. But most of all I'm driven out of my mind by the glance from her closed eyes: imperious and mocking, following my slightest movement, my slightest thought. Outside the window darkness is already falling, but I sense, inexorably sense, thousands of beady little eyes looking at me, sucking out my fluids; the multifaceted Lilita is merely leading that thousand-fold throng of kanukai, she's directing the choir, suddenly I clearly see *pudgy little faces pressed up against the window glass.*

"I want to bite it off," Lolita whispers harshly. "I'll bite it off. I want it."

She laughs a hoarse, cannibalistic laugh; her eyes already closed, her hair disheveled. The pudgy little faces quickly jump back from the window. I lie on my back and feel only cold: in my chest, in my belly, in the tips of my fingers. None of my muscles obey me anymore, even though I feel my hands, my legs, and my limp joints. Maybe it's paralysis, or maybe now I've *stopped*, the way Vilnius had stopped. Horror takes away my breath; I can't even scream. Although who would I call—save perhaps for Lolita. Lolita or Lilita? Can I still call her? I sprawl there, slowly suffocating, while she walks around the room naked, glancing at me occasionally. She's not surprised; she expected my paralysis, maybe she intentionally immobilized me. She despises me. A bitter scent emanates from her, one I've never smelled before. What were those kanukai doing outside the window? I saw at least three of them. The horror slowly recedes, I try to move my fingers again, but only my brain stirs. I feel it writhing about in my head. *I was intentionally brought to an out-of-the-way place. They* don't like a scene. But why just now? After all,

288

I've learned nothing new—except that *They* are forced to kanuk people. That's how *They* reproduce; to *Them* it's a biological necessity.

I don't want to, I don't want to believe it. I can't. Once more a vivid image rises before my eyes: an old house, entangled in wild grape vines in the depths of a garden, and yellow leaves fluttering in the wind. For an instant it seems as if I am watching myself from outside. That I approach the garden cottage where I am sprawling helplessly. Finally I remember where I saw this image. I saw it this morning, when I woke up: it began my day. Something inside of me knew I would end up here today. What can that dream, which foretold the future, mean? Sitting up, I quickly light a cigarette, and don't immediately realize I'm moving again. Even the smoke doesn't block out Lolita's enchanting scent. Her gaze pierces me. It seems that pale, narrow strips of light emanate from her pupils.

I grasp it all in a torturously slow manner, like swallowing barbed wire. *She lured me to my doom.* It's all very simple. That was *Their* plan. *They* feared liquidating me because I could leave secret notes. There was only one way left—to penetrate my inner being. Do I know what I've chattered about in my sleep, lying with Lolita? Perhaps while conversing with her I gave away my most secret thoughts. Perhaps I gave myself away precisely by trying not to give myself away. The ancient Chinese would interrogate a person for several days and nights. If the prisoner would stubbornly avoid some topic, or a place, or a word, or a hieroglyph, it would be obvious that the secret hid precisely there.

She's the one who's most to blame. I should rip a confession out of her: slit her throat, slice open her chest, pull the confession out of her guts. Cut it out with the blackened knife in the kitchen.

"I could cut you up into pieces and eat you up," she suddenly says in a covetous voice. "I totally understand women who used to keep their loved one's heart in a jar."

I have to talk as if there's nothing amiss. It's not time yet, it's not time. She could get suspicious.

"You'd probably keep something else."

"Your blazing brain. I want to turn into you. At night I dream I'm you. My grandmother told me that if you ate someone's brain, raw, you'd turn into him. If you ate a wolf's brain, you'd take on a wolf's power. A fox's would give you his cunning and cleverness. All the warriors used to eat the brains of aurochs."

"And you'd eat mine?"

"I'd eat all of you." She slinks closer; I see her eyes, which have absorbed the revengeful red of the sun. "Your fingers, your knees, your chest with all its little graying hairs. But first of all—that scarred beast of yours, that's a bit indisposed today."

She bites me, by no means playfully, but the pain is merely invigorating. All of the objects in the room quiver; dust motes scurry about in the air in leaps and bounds. She pulls away, but sits down next to me with her legs crossed, Indian-style. It seems like she's trying to bend herself into an arch, to push her swollen lower lips, emerging from the hair, ever closer.

"Or you eat me. Whatever you want. Even all of me."

The girl in Kovarskis's morgue had a gaping black hole with even sides in that spot. That's where I need to start, and then the long, blackened knife plunges into Lilita's belly, cleaves the traitor's soft skin and subcutaneous fat, uncovers the pink, pulsating flesh. There's practically no blood to be seen; it blends with the revengeful red of the sun. There should be nothing inside of her, or else some inexplicable mechanism. However, there are coiled intestines, and a striped liver, and something else, probably the spleen. Lilita is made the same way we are: this merely cheers me. The strangest thing is how easily the knife plunges, how easily it cleaves the still living flesh. Bitinas felt this sensation too. It's the symphony of a warm knife; bloody music, spreading the strong, enchanting smell of the sacrificial altar. I turn the handle of the knife to the left, to the right; the ribs crackle like dry twigs. But there's no need to hurry, there's no need to listen to the scream, this isn't a rush job, this is music. The liver can be divided into two, then divided again . . .

"They've beset you again?"

She's still sitting the same way; her eyes look out of the dusk gently and comfortingly. Not the slightest kanukish sign—only my Lolita. My own, my own Lolita. And I wanted to . . .

"Who are they? What are they?" I don't recognize my own voice.

"The ones I don't know. The ones who torture you at night. Whose traces show up deep inside your pupils. Who carve the expression of suffocation on your face. Do you know that sometimes you look like a drowning man letting out his last gasp of air? That's what you look like now. They've beset you again?"

She knew, she knew everything. She felt it with her entire essence. And she never asked about anything, never pried, never tried to worm anything out of me. She simply walked beside me and tried to help as best she could. And I suspected her. In my thoughts I picked up the blackened kitchen knife. Now I really am suffocating, really drowning. How far can fear take you? I'll never atone for my guilt, even if I were to lick her feet to the end of my days. No punishment would suffice.

The sun glimmers through the window in farewell; I glance at it and encounter an angry, narrow-eyed stare. The long face is familiar to me, but I simply cannot grasp whose it is.

"See?" I shout out loud, my hand outstretched, "See?"

Lolita flinches, turns around and freezes; she recognizes that face too. But I'm already running, bursting through the door, rushing through the dry leaves in bare feet, ripping the wild grape vines with my bare shoulder. The long-suppressed fury has erupted like a volcano; I'm not feeling as much as grasping intellectually that I'm stark naked and catching painfully on the branches. I want to finally catch *Them*, to beat them shitless. Not a trace of fear remains. It never was. I don't fear anything! I'm Vytautas Vargalys!

It seems that I see the narrow-eyed watcher's shadow; I battle with the branches and stumble in the flower beds, but he's probably more light-footed. The nooks of the garden are misleading; the hunched-over form flashes now here, now there, but too far away—I can't even say whether it's a man or a woman. An automobile rumbles somewhere close by; probably the figure has escaped, but I can't stop anymore. I run and run, until I'm entirely out of breath. At last I realize I'm naked and getting colder by the second. I ought to go back. But the cottages are so identical, and the orchards and gardens between them are identical. Identical currant and gooseberry bushes, and apple trees, and even the chrysanthemums in the flower beds are identical. I wander among the cottages, looking for the only sight that matters to me. An old house in the darkened depths of a garden, entangled in wild grape vines. Yellow unraked leaves that the wind carelessly scatters, even though the twigs of the bushes don't so much as stir. In that house Lolita waits. I have to hurry; this isn't the sort of place where you can leave her alone. Perhaps *They* lured me outside deliberately? I have to find her as soon as possible. It seems I hear the fading throbbing of her heart. It seems I hear gasping breath. But I don't know where to go. By now I want to shout, but suddenly I sense a faint, enchanting scent, Lolita's scent today. I go on like a beast, constantly stopping and sniffing carefully. Soon I no longer need to keep stopping, the scent itself draws me closer. The old house is engulfed in the darkness; the leaves are no longer yellow, but rather gray. And there's no wind anymore. It's calm around, and calm on my heart. By now a light is burning in the room. I'll tell Lolita everything about *Them*. I will no longer be alone; we'll be together.

I step into the room and see immediately. She is lying the same way *I was lying not so long ago*. It's just that she looks different. I've never seen such a sight before. Nowhere. Never. Not even in a dream. I feel absolutely *nothing*. Not horror, not pain, nothing. I'm not hot and I'm not cold, my brain is working soberly and calmly. Lola is lying on her back, her legs spread unnaturally, because the tendons in her thighs have been cut through. Their whitish ends are clearly visible amid the bloody flesh. The flat belly is unmercifully cleaved, the guts pulled out. As if that weren't enough, the intestines are sliced into pieces. My brain calmly registers only the strong smell of the sacrificial altar, not the stockyards. I didn't sacrifice her; I didn't tear her guts into pieces. I didn't rip the kidneys out of her belly and cut them into thin, round slices.

Who did this? And why?

Her liver, spleen, and lungs are cut to pieces and thrown about the entire room. Every single one of Lolita's little pieces is screaming, calling for me. Cursing me for leaving her alone. I go up closer and kneel next to her. Next to her corpse. She is gone, but this I simply cannot grasp. Her breasts are cut crosswise to the very ribs. I search for Lolita's face, but it's not there. Her eyes are poked out, her nose and ears cut off. Even the hair, Lolita's gorgeous hair, is ripped out by the strand and flung around her head—around that which once was her head. I look over her body scattered around the floor, the miserable remains of her body. A single place, for some reason, remains untouched. In the middle of the mad knife's work protrudes the mound of Venus, and beneath it—the vagina, not a finger laid on it. The knife with the darkened blade lies right there. I touch it with the tip of my finger. The blade is still warm and damp.

*They* chose the most horrible revenge possible. I look at Lolita's remains: I want to take them for myself, to carry them off somewhere and hide them. Why didn't I think of such an end the moment I first met her? A man condemned to death has no right to look for comrades. I bend down to her slashed lips—this kiss is truly the last. I take the knife into my hands. Its handle is still warm. I should probably slit my throat—even wider than Lolita's throat is cut. The smell of the altar doesn't fade; I probably look like a prophet lost in thought.

A car engine rumbles outside. It's a familiar sound—it was just that sound I heard not so long ago. Footsteps stomp outside the door, but I don't even budge. It's all the same to me now. One after another, five men sidle inside. I look at them indifferently. What do they want here?

In the light of an invisible flash, I suddenly grasp the entire plot. So it is *Their* revenge. The absolute worst you could possibly think of. *They* waited for an opportunity for a long time. I thought I had weighed all the possible scenarios, but no imagination could devise one like this. I literally see how they had waited for me to return to the cottage. Which one was the last to look in through the window? A familiar, a remarkably familiar face. No one, no one in the entire world will believe I'm innocent. No one will believe me, no matter what I say. Not even if I were to speak of *Them*. Particularly if I were to speak of *Them*. At last, *They've* swallowed me whole. They couldn't kanuk me, so they've mercilessly devoured me. I sit next to Lolita's defiled body while one of the arrivals starts snapping a camera. So far they haven't even touched me. I can look at them calmly. Three round little faces with even rounder eyeballs, set into collars with rounded corners. But the fifth one interests me the most—a gray-haired man with colonel's epaulets. I try to remember what Giedraitis Junior's face was like back then, but in vain. I remember nothing, absolutely nothing at all. There never was a Bolius or a prison camp; grandfather's altar never existed. There was no Gediminas stirring his appendages like a smashed cockroach. And I never was.

"Put on some clothes, will you!" the colonel says angrily.

I dress leisurely; God is watching over me. They are of no concern to me; they do not exist and never did. Father's drawings never were, nor Madam Giedraitienė in the morning dew. There were no cattle cars strewing little white papers. There was no Irena, no Martynas, no library's labyrinth. There never was a Camus or a Plato. There was no Lolita. There was no me.

The fat faces lead me to the car and shove me into the back seat. For the first time, I see a tiny little kanukas stronghold from the inside. The greenish curtains and darkened glass. There was no Circe of Old Town, there were no three big-eyed little Jews. There was no Mindaugas, Gediminas, or Vytautas the Great. Lithuania never was.

"Let's go," snarls the colonel, sitting down in the front seat.

The engine rumbles. I'm pressed in on both sides by the fleshy fat faces. And inside the car hovers a sweetish smell of rotting fall leaves. A strong, warm smell of rotting leaves.

Suddenly I think that despite it all, there has to be a God on high. *There must exist some being who knows I am innocent.*

The cottages run by, retreating backwards. And a bit further on, in a deep, deep pit, shine the first lights of exhausted, moribund Vilnius.

There you have it—the end of the Vargalys clan.

# PART TWO
## FROM THE MLOG

Martynas Poška. October 14–29, 197 . . .

veryone keeps asking me about Vytautas Vargalys. But what can I say? "The man has killed the thing he loved, and so the man must die."

It started raining just after the devastating events at the garden. Vilnius is steeped in mud that reeks of sulfur. It's as if the devils of hell had spat up everything. Picking linden blossoms in the city's environs has been forbidden for quite some time now, unless you have an urge to slowly poison yourself. When civilizations die, even nature opposes them. Like it or not, you feel like the chronicler of the dying Lithuanian civilization.

My height—five foot seven and a half inches. I cut my hair in a crew cut. At some point this hairstyle will return, victorious, to Vilnius's streets, so I'll instantly become fashionable.

I know, I know, no one is interested in me. No one asks how I'm doing. Everyone just keeps asking about Vytautas Vargalys.

News bulletin: I don't get myself involved in mysterious and dreadful affairs. I don't cut people to pieces. I can't even manage to write a genuine log. I call it the mlog—after my name.

And what should I write in it now?

What can I say about Vytautas Vargalys? Probably very little of the real truth: I don't know what he was like in his childhood. You can't really say much about a person if you don't know what he was like as a child. It's difficult for me to talk about him. I can only relate facts with certainty. Probably that's appropriate when writing a log. But writing an mlog?

When I'm asked if he could murder someone, and so brutally too, I answer honestly: no, he couldn't murder anyone.

But I'm quiet about something else: he could have murdered his mania, his past, his menacing ghost. That's just what he did. But I don't say this to anyone and I won't. They wouldn't understand. They just hunger for bread and circuses. They hunger for blood—someone else's, of course. To them, Vargalys is nothing more than a live sensation, a monster of Vilnius, stirring up our sleepy anthill for a moment.

I'm not interested in ants. I'm interested in humans. And I haven't known that many of them. They're so rare.

I state with conviction: Vytautas Vargalys was a human.

I first laid eyes on him some sixteen or seventeen years ago. I was a student at the university. I hadn't started my collection yet. I naïvely believed it was possible to search for truth, to honestly seek virtue in this decaying world.

I'm not at all ashamed to repeat the words "virtue," "truth," and "honesty," over and over.

I ran into Vytautas Vargalys on the main boulevard. He looked like a character out of some spectral carnival. An athlete of nearly six-foot-six, dressed in operatic tramp's rags, with the puffy face of a drunk. Greasy hair down to his shoulders. In those days, men didn't have long hair; the hippies only showed up some five years later.

In my mind's eye, Vytautas Vargalys appears in innumerable guises, but mostly I remember him the way he was the first time I saw him.

Looking like a bum soaked in cheap wine, with the eyes of a suffering philosopher. He felt my glance immediately, as if he had had eyes in the back of his head. He always did have more than two of them. He turned to me, sullenly looked me over as if he were measuring or weighing, and said in a voice that had been ruined by drink:

"Make a donation of twenty kopecks to the Villon of Vilnius!"

Yes, this was after the monetary reform. He didn't ask for a ruble in the old currency, but twenty kopecks in the new.

I didn't give him any kopecks. I don't support drunks on principle.

Later he told me that if I had given him that handout, the two of us would have never met again. But fate would have it otherwise.

And immediately after me, Lolita went up to him. I can't be mistaken: I would recognize her anywhere, at any time, in whatever form. I would recognize her even now, even though she's in the kingdom of the dead.

That long-legged ten-year-old girl walked gracefully by, turned around, and came back. She calmly looked over that monster—he was twice her size—and stretched out a coin that was pressed in her palm. In those days, ten-year-old girls didn't have elegant wallets and purses.

That really was Lolita. Her path crossed the convoluted route of Vytautas Vargalys's life over and over again. Wandering the streets of Vilnius separately, they considered themselves independent. But actually one drew nearer the other like hapless electrons in a computer circuit.

I hate computers. They're perfect idiots: obedient and brainless, but capable of performing their tasks flawlessly. They do not doubt, and they have no opinions. The Ruling Old Folks' Asylum, during their sleepless nights of drivel, dreams that people could be exactly the same.

The Ruling Old Folks' Asylum isn't a concrete government or anything like it—it's all the elderly mean-eyed guys who crave control over us, who want to dictate their will to us: it's the head of the apartment cooperative, it's reserve colonels, it's sauna directors. This vindictive and evil old folks' asylum is a unique contemporary phenomenon, something that never existed before, and never will again. It drags us backwards, restrains and impairs us in every way imaginable. Watch out for mean-eyed old folks!

From now on, I shall refer to the Ruling Old Folks' Asylum simply as ROF. For brevity's sake. And Vytautas Vargalys I shall call VV.

I already know how an mlog most differs from a log. A log is written for the future. But if there is no future—you don't have one, he doesn't have one, no one has a future—you're stuck writing an mlog. No one will read it. So there's no need to dissemble, to twist the facts in someone's favor, the way it's done in logs. There's no need to write, for that matter. Or even talk. It's enough just to think. That's what I do: I think all the time, but I'm as mute as a fish thrown out on shore.

I wouldn't be able to write a genuine log. My thoughts never want to fall in a logical order. They're terribly incoherent and tangled. They're like pebbles on the seashore: the ones broken from the same rock are lying a long way apart, while nearby lie completely different ones, of different colors, that seem to have nothing in common.

Those pebbles want to reflect or embody the entire boundless sea, but there's very few of them—too few to encompass those boundless waters.

I put these metaphors and similar beauties into words just for myself, for my mlog. No one would think I have it in me. Everyone considers me a biting ironist, perhaps even a bit of a clown. That doesn't hurt me and doesn't get in the way of my life.

But I have never been a clown. Irony isn't a mask; it's merely a means of self-defense. Like judo, like karate. Not a circus trick, but a means of defending one's health, and actually one's life, from attackers.

It follows that self-irony is a means of defending one's life from oneself.

It's all very well for people who can grasp the whole shebang at once, in whose heads everything relates harmoniously. They think as a matter of course; they don't have to exert themselves on that account.

But I have to collect myself every time. By the time I stammer out the sorriest little thought, I have to recall thoughts I've mulled over earlier, and get myself in the right frame of mind. But the time suitable for this, suitable places, and suitable moods are few and far between.

I would say that I write my so-called mlog in fits and starts. In this torn-to-shreds world of ours, even people's thoughts are tattered. It's hopeless to search for harmony, grace, or majesty in them.

I spew thoughts the way Vilnius's gypsy women spit sunflower seed husks. My thoughts are soaked in spittle and chewed up. Still, it's a good thing; at least there are those spittle-soaked husks.

I know scores of Vilniutians who don't in the least grasp what a thought is. What are their heads stuffed with? Heaven only knows. Little worries, calculations, banalities, and confusion.

Once a former classmate, well into his cups, opened his heart to me. I wouldn't know how to think, he explained to me, even if I wanted to. But I don't want to. I'm told to just repeat someone else's words and not ask any questions. So, that's what I do. It's not hard at all, but one question keeps bothering me: what am I? I'm not a human—obviously, humans are entirely different. But what am I then?

That was probably the first time I thought to myself about what distinguishes a *homo lithuanicus* from a normal person.

Half the world knows what a *homo sovieticus* is (excepting *homo sovieticus* himself). However, no one has studied *homo lithuanicus*, or even *homo Vilnensis*. These species matter as much to the future of mankind as to its history.

Mankind should be grateful to the Lithuanians that they exist. But it will never forgive them if they do not describe their experience of existence, if they don't introduce the entire world to it.

Only a Lithuanian is qualified to write the opus "What is the Ass of the Universe."

The history of the great nations has been explored backwards and forwards. It's impossible to learn anything more from them. It's paradoxical, but humanity knows much more about various archaic tribes than it does about the history of European minorities—that quintessence of injustice, absurdity, and errors. The world may be doomed for the simple reason that no one noticed our plight in time. An ethnologist who diligently researched some Albanians or another would be much more useful than one who had written up hundreds of obscure African tribes.

Never forget that we are all, in a certain sense, a bit Albanian. All of us are just a tad Lithuanian. And worst of all—every one of us, in the depths of our hearts, is a Vytautas Vargalys.

It seems to me that I actually know too much about VV. His and Lolita's stories aren't enough for me, I'm itching to tell about his father, and about his grandfather, and about her father and mother too.

The two of them were doomed before they ever met. If I were a writer, I would write a book about what the two of them could have been. In my opinion, that would be the only theme of a genuine book about Vilnius: what all of us could have been, if we hadn't been turned into what we are.

Lolita showed up in our office four years ago, in her last year at college. She immediately attracted everyone's attention with her quiet insolence and impossibly long legs. Because of these two things, the other women in the office hated her, up to the very end. And she hated all of us and would have been happiest living in a desert. They wouldn't have hired Lolita at the office at all, but her father made calls to the right places, so everything was instantly straightened out.

By the way, about Lolita's legs and other body parts. Call her a slut straight out, if you're more comfortable with that, if you think it's worth calling a person a slut just because he sells his body and not his soul, as is customary. But you will seem particularly old-fashioned— in these times of greater or lesser sexual freedom, a concept like that has no meaning whatsoever. Besides, she wasn't a slut at all. She didn't even look seductive. Maybe that's why she sought to sleep with every man worth the attention. Furthermore, I wouldn't say that she liked this change of partners all that much. It seemed to me she expressed her spite and contempt for men that way. She'd seduce them, and then kick them aside. They'd get a taste of what it's like to be no more than a defenseless puppy, a puppy that's petted at first, and then roughly driven away. I would say that Lolita squandered only her body, but her spirit remained innocent.

This is how I talk about a woman who led three great men to their deaths!

She latched onto VV like a leech; the first two weren't enough for her. I actually wanted to warn him off, to deter him, but, unfortunately,

VV was always beyond control. He was impelled to rush headlong towards doom. He was a madman.

On the other hand, only madmen can accomplish great things. They put their purpose on one side of the scale, themselves on the other, and the purpose always tips the scales.

By the way, I'm not taking it upon myself to decide. I'm Martynas Poška, a programmer by coercion, a collector of fortunes, the doleful clown of Vilnius. The mlog is not a collection of conclusions. It's only a collection of facts.

Maybe it's a good thing that I can only think seriously in fits and starts. You barely sense you're about to have some time and you start spouting off senselessly. It'd be better to always feel the lack of time—then you'd set down what you really know in a hurry.

Now, *post factum*, many rush to proclaim VV a monster and a madman. People remember the oddities of his behavior and his ungovernable character. I really hate to philosophize, but I'm forced to declare that every one of our lives could very easily be portrayed as lunacy. All that's needed is to tidy up a few things, be quiet about a thing or two, add a thing or two—not much; the very least will do.

For this reason, I state officially: VV was a man with an extremely healthy, extremely witty, and extremely well-educated mind.

I'm not by any means defending VV; I only defend the truth. The objective truth. That is the task of the mlog.

At one time, I was taken with intelligence tests. I had amassed a pile of them and bothered all of my acquaintances with them. I discovered that people are panic-stricken by things that could show their inadequacy. But VV took on the problems boldly and playfully. He cracked them like nuts. His IQ was one hundred sixty and still climbing; he made fun of the people who made up the tests and offered new ones of his own. No scale would be large enough to describe his intelligence.

So much is straight fact.

Now—about sexual perversions: if a person with that much intelligence sometimes acts in a way we don't understand, couldn't that mean he grasps principles of higher import, ones we cannot perceive?

At times he would be beset by ghosts. He would remember some participant in a long-ago incident and would want to explain something to him or ask him something. It would drive him totally crazy that he couldn't talk to people who were long since dead. VV liked to say: we should all carry our dead in our pockets like a deck of cards, so if the need arises we could play the decisive game of poker.

In essence, VV was a hardened poker player, even though he never played cards in his life.

He would summon ghosts, but he couldn't stand live witnesses to the past. When he came across someone he knew from his time in the prison camp, he would run away. Sometimes a neighbor from his childhood years would visit him, this woman named Giedraitienė, an alcoholic with a puffy face. VV would buy her off with a three-ruble note. He didn't go to his grandfather's funeral because he couldn't have avoided meeting his father at the burial.

I'll never understand his relationship with his father. At some point, VV's father re-emigrated from Argentina; he works as a doorman at the restaurant in Druskininkai. No big deal—Russian princes used to work as doormen in Paris too, and he's no prince. Sometimes I visit him and tell him about VV. I can't imagine what I'll tell him now.

VV behaved as if his father didn't exist at all. The strangest thing was that his father submissively went along with this.

VV had a strange view of his past: the dead were more real to him than the living. The latter he simply ignored.

Stealthily, I begin painting the first portraits; apparently I secretly hope to paint the entire gallery. Just that it's inadmissible to forget the most important of them all—the portrait of Vilnius.

The first draft:

Vilnius is a city of identical little cement boxes. A city of identical little clay figures. A city of identical tears and identical sperm. If some giant were to suddenly mix everything up completely, all the houses, the people, the tears, and the sperm, if he were to switch everything's place and muddle it all up, absolutely nothing would change.

And that's what's the very worst—Vilnius hasn't been capable of changing for a long time now.

It's unbelievably difficult to begin VV's story, so I look for excuses despite myself. Perhaps history can't exist at all? "Life is a tale, told by an idiot, signifying nothing." If that's true, I'd really make a good storyteller. I'm sufficiently idiotic. My entire life proves this. The smart ones build houses and zoom around in Mercedes-Benzes. Or defend dissertations and receive decorations. Or give speeches from podiums and ride in special automobiles to special stores.

But I was, and still remain, an idiot. I had a sacred idea. I was such an idiot that I believed in humanity's sacred future. After little Nikita censured Mister Joseph's actions, I thought things in this world could change for the better. I decided the new Soviet society would inevitably need a new kind of human. I resolved to dedicate my life to the education and raising of children. This was my *idée fixe*. This was my *magnum opus*. I even had myself a child, whom I swore to teach only by my system. This was to be the first modern human.

I sat down to write a dissertation about a new educational system. I must add that both of my parents were educators, and my father collected information about the educational systems of various countries as well. This also helped me—helped me to complete ruin. You see, I wrote a solid dissertation rather quickly.

I'm not at all ashamed to admit what an idiot I was back then. I proved logically that the lack of the free rein of thought is strangling the Soviet school. I demonstrated that the educational program is pedantic, practically medieval. I demanded an essential change in the teaching of history, that we present children with the hidden facts of history. I suggested teaching children how to think independently, to argue, and to draw conclusions. And so on. It's funny to even remember my stupidity. I suggested teaching Soviet children to think! I wanted to disclose the true facts of history! I was the Very Idiot of Idiots. I was VII.

Anyone with a solid education in this field could write a dissertation like that. But only VII could officially submit it to a scholarly council. And I kept perfecting the text's style! I was a cosmic cretin, an imbecile squared, a divine degenerate.

No one discussed my dissertation openly. However, unexpectedly, a departmental meeting took place to denounce the infiltration of bourgeois influences into Soviet pedagogy. Next, I was left unemployed when it was announced that I had not completed the requirements of the doctoral program. Then I couldn't find work anywhere else. The fate of the Soviet unemployed is no cause for envy. The majority of dissertators like myself get work as night security guards. But I took all of my savings and went to Moscow to search for justice. Even as the VII, I grasped that justice doesn't survive more than three days in Vilnius. However, I was a true VII: I imagined that justice had been cultivated in Moscow for the duration. At that time, little Nikita had already been kicked out; the ROF slowly but surely took over the government. The mean-eyed old men crawled out of the caves they had hidden themselves in and started to dictate their will, to control all of the minutiae of our lives. But I was blind, I didn't get it.

I rushed around the corridors of Moscow's bureaus searching for justice. I was treated like a harmless crank. Everyone kept asking me if I understood what I was suggesting. And I, as is appropriate for a divine degenerate, explained that I was suggesting a bright future of intelligent, thinking, and self-motivated people. At last I stumbled into the home of a former party mucky-muck; he explained to me what kind of people his system needed, what kind of children we should be raising. My eyes were finally opened. I understood everything. First I wanted to strangle my own son, before it was too late. Then I wanted to hang myself, but it was too late. On my return to Vilnius, I was invited to visit the KGB and offered a job at the library. Apparently, it had been decided I was a harmless crank after all.

Incidentally, every copy of my dissertation mysteriously disappeared. Even the manuscript from the drawer of my desk at home.

Unfortunately, I never did strangle my son. My wife left me, and she made sure my son saw me as little as possible. More often, he doesn't want to see me, either. I've long since stopped teaching him anything—by any system. He's already doomed; there's no saving him. I do not have a son. And that teenager or young man who's recorded in my documents, who uses my surname, has no soul. He is a true product of Vilnius. He scorns me because I've obtained neither wealth nor social status. He would respect me if I had a Mercedes or occupied a minister's post. That young man condemns me because I had intelligent and truthful ideas. He's by no means a fool; he agrees my ideas were good, but, in his opinion, that's exactly why they should be forgotten as quickly as possible. He intensely dislikes Komsomolites or party men himself, however, understandably, he's officially a Komsomol member—otherwise they wouldn't take him on trips abroad. He thinks what matters most is to have a lot of stuff. Not money—Soviet rubles mean nothing—but concrete, tangible stuff. The Ass of the Universe is slowly returning to a natural economy and the direct barter of goods. It's in this barter that my offspring sees the meaning of life. That young man sincerely doesn't understand that feelings of virtue, kindness, or justice can exist. He trains a bit as an athlete and speculates heavily, because sport takes him abroad to compete. He takes hard currency there as contraband, and he brings home the stuff he's dreamed of. He travels to places I'll never be, but he doesn't see anything there—only stores. I have nothing against sports. I once dreamed of becoming a basketball player myself. I loved and I still love basketball, but my offspring hates sports.

He makes fun of me. He lectures me on how to live. He's surrounded by the prettiest girls, even though he's as ugly as sin. The girls aren't at all interested in him, but the beauties of the Ass of the Universe can sacrifice anything for contraband rags. He knows with certainty that when he turns twenty-five he'll drop that despised sport and start up a rose farm. He hates flowers too.

I lost my son a long time ago. I should not have brought him into the world.

And now I've lost my only friend, or at least buddy. I discovered him as soon as I got to the library. VV greeted me, smiled wryly, and said:

"If you had given me twenty kopecks then, we would never have met again."

I hardly recognized him. He was clean-shaven, scented, and wore a tie. At first glance, you'd think even his insides were polished and scented. But the eyes were the same: the eyes of a fallen saint. He added:

"Our office is the strangest in the world. Or at least in Vilnius. I advise you to consider why they let the two of us into the book collections. What's their secret purpose?"

Our office really is the strangest in all of Vilnius. Computer experts, bibliographers and otherwise inexplicable types have congregated here. Sooner or later, we're supposedly going to computerize the library catalog. I think probably later: first, because we don't have our own computer yet, and second, no library has the right to convert to computers as long as the Lenin Library in Moscow hasn't done it. The metropole must be first, and if someone tries to outdo it—they must be reined in. So we're all in the dark as to what we're doing. I'm gathering my collection. Gražina knits. Elena is a Party member. Marija is growing a hussar's mustache. Laimutė tries a different diet every day, even though she only weighs a hundred pounds. Stefa takes care of VV. And so on.

And that's the way it will be until the central library in Moscow computerizes. Outdoing Moscow is forbidden. It's a verified fact: for example, the resources and technical capabilities in Vilnius would allow the telephone problem to be easily solved. However, that can't be done, because then the count of telephones per thousand inhabitants in Vilnius would exceed Moscow's.


I appreciated VV immediately. Egoistically, it bothered me that he had made friends with Gediminas. After all, I was the one who introduced them.

I remember Gediminas from my school years. Everyone in school knew Gediminas Riauba. His father was our principal, and Gediminas was the center on the basketball team. I always smile sadly when I remember how much I envied him. What Lithuanian boy doesn't dream of becoming a basketball star!? We're suspiciously similar to American blacks in that respect. I dreamt of it too, at that point not having reached five foot three. What didn't I do. I'd hang on a crossbar, hoping to stretch out that way, and cried at night. I practiced five hours a day—like a professional. I was the most energetic and tenacious player, I should have gotten onto the school team, but Gediminas Riauba drove me out. He could do that; the coach listened to him. He said, "Maybe let's not start a kingdom of dwarfs here." I'll remember those words until the day I die. Probably I secretly hated Gediminas Riauba. Not because he insulted and mortified me. Rather because, being generously endowed by nature, he never did finish anything to the end. I think he could have been the best basketball player in the world, but in the first year of college he completely stopped playing and devoted himself to mathematics. I think he could have been the best mathematician in the world, but suddenly he took up his cacophonous music. Later he started mountain climbing too. I probably hated him. I couldn't bear to see how that man wasted God's gifts and didn't finish a single thing to the end. He was a snob. He always went for whatever was trendy and flashy.

But VV was immediately charmed by him. The two of them would wander the streets of Vilnius at night and fall in love with the same women. Probably they were friends, although Lord knows I don't know what "friend" means. That's something no one knows.

I'm going to start talking about myself again, but there's no other way to write an mlog. I can only tell you what's reflected in me, like in a mirror—not a distorted one, I hope.

Now I'm reflecting the senior Riauba, Gediminas's father. He was a true Lithuanian intellectual. They tried to eliminate people like that. But he somehow survived and even became the principal of our school. I've never met a more radical man. All of his decisions were strict, categorical, and implemented immediately. He became the hero of my adolescence. Riauba was the only person who took up open battle in my presence. He independently changed the teaching curriculum. At that time, this could have cost him his life. He scoffed at the cult of Stalin and taught everything his own way. He wasn't at all naïve: when the inspectors came, we would go through a fictitious lesson we had rehearsed in advance. He taught history himself and began every school year with the legend of the Iron Wolf. We would hold our breath listening. I fell hopelessly in love with Vilnius without ever having seen it. To me, from our little town in Žemaitija, it seemed the Iron Wolf slowly cantered through the empty streets of Vilnius at night.

By the way, about the Iron Wolf. A stray dog used to hang around next to the Lithuanian Film Studio garages. He was sickly, mangy, and horribly bloated. His intestines wouldn't hold food; as soon as he ate, he'd rush into the bushes with the runs. An awful stench emanated from those bushes. He would trot about staggering, banging into the walls, but he just wouldn't die.

All of the Film Studio drivers called him the Iron Wolf—without irony or sarcasm, in all seriousness, and very sadly.

Riauba's Iron Wolf was entirely different. He really did announce us to the entire world. In art class, I drew nothing but iron wolves. If we were told to draw an autumn forest, an iron wolf would surely be hiding somewhere in mine. If we were told to draw a vase, an iron wolf would be impressed on the side of mine. Once they forced us to draw a

May Day demonstration. In mine, an iron wolf proudly marched at the front of people with placards and slogans. The art teacher sent me to the principal, threatening Siberia. Riauba patted my head and said:

"You might yet grow up into a human being."

I well remember the lessons Riauba prepared for the inspectors. We would rehearse those plays at the expense of classes on the history of the VKP(b), the Communist Party. Riauba would select the actors from all the classes; he watched Russian films especially for this purpose and used them to select faces that, in his opinion, best suited the stereotype of a Soviet pupil.

"Who wants to earn extra credit?" he would ask, imperceptibly giving Kaziukas Budrys a sign.

Kaziukas Budrys was a teenager with a pudgy face and fanatically burning eyes. He was very proud to get such an important role in the play.

"We must unfailingly emphasize Comrade Stalin's incomparable contribution to the theories of Marxism-Leninism!" he would shriek in a fanatical voice.

Then he would practically sing a text he'd learned by rote. Once an elderly inspector, listening to Kaziukas's oratory, automatically stood up at attention. I thought he was going to salute him.

During recess, Kaziukas Budrys liked to shape busts of Stalin out of the soft part of bread. He would make the mustache out of real hair.

Perhaps Kaziukas would have been a great sculptor. But he disappeared somewhere in the expanses of Siberia.

The other outstanding soloist was this Kvedaravičius. He spoke slowly; you'd think he was weighing and pondering every word. His speech sounded unbelievably convincing; the inspectors would unconsciously start nodding their heads, approving of Kvedaravičius in their thoughts.

"A Soviet man must, of course, draw from culture," Kvedaravičius would intone thoughtfully. I thought about it for a long time, but I never did understand what he could draw from Akhmatova's poetry or Balys Sruoga's scribbles.

Those performances would be rehearsed down to the smallest detail, but Riauba directed us with such inspiration that they weren't in the least boring. Those lessons got nothing but excellent ratings from all the inspectors. Riauba quickly understood that in this system, you don't need to be something, you just need to look like it. No one is concerned with who you really are; all that matters is what you pretend to be.

Every true *homo lithuanicus* thoroughly understands this open secret. A true *homo lithuanicus* pragmatically acts his role in the drama and carries out his duty—all the more since it's so easy to deceive the authorities. The one on the platform acts the part of a dignitary, knowing full well that he's just acting. A thousand in the hall applaud enthusiastically, knowing full well that he's acting, and they are as well. And the so-called dignitary nods, knowing full well that the entire thousand are only pretending.

On the surface, *homo sovieticus* behaves in a similar fashion. But nevertheless, in the depths of his heart, he believes in the system's principles; he's full of concepts like "the misrepresentation" or "the distortion of Leninist norms," and so on.

From the get-go, *homo lithuanicus* doesn't believe in anything, but he learns, while still in school, to feign it convincingly.

Incidentally, spontaneous emotions still erupt in school. At times proclamations show up on the benches and assorted graffiti on the walls.

Lately it's become popular to write on the walls in English. For some reason, no one paints over these graffiti. The inscription "RUSSIANS GO HOME!" has adorned the wall of my building for two months now.

VV and Gediminas Riauba complemented one another. Gediminas's boundless ambition and snobbism were balanced by VV's complete indifference to other people's opinions of him. I remember when Gediminas organized a concert in an abandoned church, which the militia raided. There were maybe twenty or thirty people at that concert, but the incident instantly became covered with legends the way an ocean rock gets covered with seaweed. I was there; I saw everything with my own eyes. The musicians played something hysterical (you couldn't even call it playing); it seemed to me that they were merely waiting to be raided so that they could become heroes, at least for a little while.

VV was absolutely delighted, and used the opportunity to break some militiaman's jaw. Then he barely managed to hide himself in time.

To the honor of Vilnius's snobs, I have to admit that all of the spectators, to a man, declared they didn't know who he was. As if they had agreed in advance, they maintained that VV was some outsider, since he didn't know a word of Lithuanian.

That was perhaps the only time in my life that I encountered Lithuanian solidarity.

For the most part, *homo lithuanicus* has learned one precept thoroughly: watch out for yourself, and let the other guy worry about himself. *Homo lithuanicus* has got it into his head that if the authorities have taken someone on, helping him is suicide. So why stick your nose out? It's better to please the authorities. I know what I'm saying. I've experienced this myself.

I should be telling Lolita's and VV's story, and instead only heaven knows what I'm going on about. But that's the only way an mlog can be written. I'm nothing more than a character in the mlog myself. Don't ask too much of me. I'm happy I manage to relate anything at all.

I've told Riauba senior's story because he came to be part of my great collection.

VV resembles the senior Riauba in that he too, perfectly understood the essence of our collective pretense. With him at the helm, our section does absolutely nothing, but always carries out the plans. Such paradoxes are possible only in the Ass of the Universe.

From my collection:

A friend of mine who's already in his fifth decade confessed that all of his life he had, with particular care and diligence, carried out all of the government's orders and directives—just think!—for reasons of sabotage. Even at home he acted by all the Soviet canons.

"Everyone should do it," he explained heatedly. "If everyone would act that way, the system would crumble immediately, because it's absurd. The only reason it's still in existence is that ninety-nine percent of people don't abide by its canons."

He spoke in all seriousness. Only *homo lithuanicus* could come up with a theory like that.

It was only a few years into our friendship that I found out VV is a veteran of the prison camps. He would talk about the camp with first-rate black humor. Only a person who has gone through all of the circles of hell can mock everything in the world the way he did. He never complained or whined; more than that, he feared nothing. Many a camp veteran acquires a peculiar paranoia. He imagines he's secretly being wronged, denied a better position, and so on. VV would only snort when I mentioned his secret dossier. It's extremely difficult to understand this man.

His drawings were incredible. Once he showed me drawings from his time in the camp. VV has an entire collection of them. There were some really horrifying things there, but I found one portrait particularly shocking. A youngish man with a philosophic gaze stared out from the paper. Deep within his eyes lay an understanding of the True Essence. I immediately asked VV who he was.

"This one I just had to draw," he answered. "He got twenty-five years—but only because at that time the death penalty had temporarily been abolished."

"What did he do? What?" I nearly screamed, looking at that supernaturally deep face.

I was certain this person's life had to reveal some impossibly important secret.

"Even in our camp he was the only one like that," answered VV. "He killed his mother, cut her into pieces, and ate her. By the way, he knew all of Yesenin by heart."

The worst of it is that VV landed in the camp when he was still quite young. His soul matured in the camp—in a horrifying, distorted world. It seemed to me that in our world he felt like a tourist who could be called home at any minute—behind the barbed wire again.

From the age of seventeen to the age of twenty-eight he saw women only once—during the naked revolt. They worked in one quarry, while the prisoners from the women's camp would be driven into the neighboring one. One swelteringly hot day the wind carried an entire cloud of the inexorable smell of men over to the women's quarry. And the women went wild. They swept the guards away together with all their dogs and submachine guns, and a eerie procession headed towards the men, undressing on the way. VV, with sincere horror, told of how they were suddenly flooded with naked women, stumbling, falling, and rolling from the quarry walls. The guards swore and shot their guns in the air, the dogs they had unleashed snarled and tore into whomever they came upon, but people paid no attention. Some coupled on the spot, others openly masturbated. VV got scared to death and hid between some rocks. He was lucky. A group of hurriedly summoned special guards, without a moment's pause, turned machine guns on the quarry. Some of the corpses were thrown in trucks as they were, stuck together in pairs. The next day the barracks buzzed and commented on the incident. The ones who survived unharmed didn't even remember the dead; they just bragged, one after the other, about how many women they had managed to use. VV, with a wry smile, explained that the masturbators, as always, claimed the largest number.

VV must have understood our grim world best. After all, our gigantic common prison camp is also surrounded by barbed wire and guarded by man-eating German Shepherds. For another thing, can a person who spent his best years in hell live a normal life? From an intellectual point of view, he actually lucked out—his had his learned abbot, like some Monte Cristo. He learned a great deal from his professor, but the teachings of a single person, even the wisest, will never reveal all of the world's subtleties. After all, his Bolius viewed the world from his own tower, so he inadvertently forced VV to see the world the same way.

And how was he supposed to regard women? In high school, he was probably taught that women are delicate and gentle creatures who must be taken care of and chivalrously defended. But what did he think when he saw the naked revolt?

Everyone saw that VV looked down on women. He had them in spades, but he didn't consider a single one human. Even Lolita frequently wept over him, ignoring her surroundings, her face buried on her desk at work. He would humiliate her in the most disgusting ways. I know. I saw this myself.

VV frequently acted like a child of perdition, but I understand him,

I almost condone him. On every form, in the box about your origin and parents, he ought to write: I am an only child of the prison camps.

When Lolita showed up in our ridiculous office, it immediately occurred to me that I had seen her somewhere before. I couldn't fall asleep at night; I kept trying to remember where I had met her. I even looked through my collection, which wasn't all that large at the time.

I began to suspect something wasn't quite right only later, when rumors about her husband followed her to the library. It's not every day a famous man burns alive in Vilnius. And Žilys really was well-known. In all Vilnius, he was the only one who organized underground exhibits in his studio, ones everyone dreamed of getting into. You could say to anyone, "Yesterday I saw Žilys at the Neringa. He announced the second coming of Christ," and no one needed explaining about who Žilys is and why he had suddenly converted to Christianity. He was a regular Vilnius preacher; he confessed all religions without confessing a single one—expect maybe for the religion of art.

And here we all find out that Lolita was his wife.

And then about a week later, I ran into Lolita at Gediminas's, wearing his robe, with the nipples of her tiny naked breasts showing through it.

That meeting eerily reflected the past; that was why it had seemed to me I had already seen her somewhere. This happens often in Vilnius.

VV starting making moves on her immediately. Once Lolita let it slip (we had already become friends): "I'm afraid of him—you can see right off that he's a monster. I asked my father to find his case in the archives. I'd like to know what all he's done."

VV got it on with her all the same. In the most disgusting manner imaginable.

I really don't want to remember it. However, an mlog requires the whole truth and nothing but the truth. It makes me sick to remember nasty things. But I've become convinced that in the long run it's no use to shut your eyes, even if you really don't like the view. Even if it nauseates you. Even if it sickens you. Incidentally, *homo lithuanicus* loves to shut his eyes the minute something displeases him. *Homo lithuanicus* has preserved an ancient belief in magic: if you don't see anything, no one sees you, either. With your eyes shut, it's as if you disappear from the world for a little while.

I'm not allowed to close them; the mlog obliges me to look at absolutely everything with wide-open eyes.

That Sunday I got ready to go visit Gediminas. We'd arranged this earlier. He had brought me books from Paris. In the Ass of the Universe that's a normal thing—even the tiniest crumb of truth has to be brought in from outside as contraband. It was a wonderful morning. The sun warmed gently, but it wasn't hot. The entire city was merry and playful. Vilnius likes to put a person into this kind of mood when it's setting him a horrifying trap. Vilnius brings to mind the hangman who treats his unsuspecting victim to bonbons before the execution.

No one opened the door, but it wasn't locked. In the front hall, your nostrils were struck by the smell of some strange herb or incense; I actually got a bit dizzy.

Lolita emerged from the bedroom wearing only black stockings and a narrow little garter belt. That was the only time in my life I saw her naked. That could have been a heavenly sight, but instead it was revolting, downright nauseating. Lolita was completely out of it; her tiny breasts were bitten all over and her pubic hair was disgustingly gummed up with sperm. She glanced at me with glassy eyes, got a cigarette, and returned to the bedroom, where an exhausted Gediminas was lolling about on the couch. It was only then that I saw VV sitting in the armchair, stark naked. He was totally tanked, or maybe he had snorted some drugs. Either way, he was talking to the angels.

"Circe, the black Circe," he said, sounding like a sleepwalker. "Who sent her?"

Then he swayed off to the bedroom, where Gediminas was already bonking Lolita. I don't know if they had planned that filth in advance, or just simply went on a rampage. The two of them defiled her by turns all night, or maybe at the same time too. They could do something like that! They broke her down, crushed her, turned her into trash. I know she loved Gediminas, and that was how he thanked her for her love.

I will never forget the look she gave me on Monday morning when she came into the office. There was despair and pleading in her eyes; she remembered it all. Unfortunately, she remembered it all.

Lolita started showing a strange kindness towards me after that wretched Sunday. Perhaps because the two of us were unexpectedly allied by the blackest black of blacks.

Perhaps it will seem to some that with a beginning of that sort VV could only have finished the way he did. No, things are by no means that simple. The two of them fell in love later, much later. It was always possible to fall in love with Lolita as if she were an innocent girl. No dirt could smear her. She was divine. VV understood this. So he was obliged to defile that divinity, as he was obliged to destroy every deity. But later he inevitably had to fall in love with Lolita. Did he consider that she would have to love him too? Love him, remembering all of his depravities?

VV really didn't worry about others' opinion of him. In this respect (as in many others), he was the complete antipode of the creature known by the name of *homo lithuanicus*. This type strives to not stand out in the least, so what others think of him matters a great deal to him. Similar objectives are typical of many nations, of all civilizations. An American will invariably install himself a swimming pool no worse than his neighbor's. His car must be a model no worse than his neighbors'. But while an American tries not to be left behind, *homo lithuanicus* just tries not to stick out. The percentage of Lithuanians who are maniacs or fanatics is the smallest in the world.

I've digressed from the subject matter again. Evidently, it's because I'm afraid to assert anything categorical about Lolita. It's difficult to comprehend any woman, but this one is particularly difficult. What did VV, the great monster of Vilnius, use to charm her? Why did she willingly suffer the torments of hell, surrendering to his will?

When she came to visit me, Lolita liked to sit right on the carpet, leaning up against the sofa with her divine legs folded up, blinking her innocent eyes. She used to talk a lot, but even more often she would be quiet.

"Martis," she would say sadly, "a person really is the author of his own misfortune. I sank into this mess myself. No one is forcing me into it, Martis. If I were being forced, everything would be much easier."

She was right. If you are forced into doing something, you are in all respects a victim of spiritual tyranny. It's much worse if they give you freedom and you continue to do what you've been doing. If *homo lithuanicus* were to suddenly get his freedom, he wouldn't know what to do with it. If you want to know what to do with it, you can't be a *homo lithuanicus*.

Lolita would come to visit me to cry and talk things out. Not that I was her confidant; to her, I was simply a blank spot. That was the only reason she told me so much—the way you talk to a dog, a mirror, or the empty walls of a room.

Why was it me she chose to visit? Maybe because the two of us were connected by yet another blackest black of blacks.

I never imagined I would carry deadly secrets around, ones I wouldn't be able to reveal to anyone—except perhaps my mlog.

I was born and raised in a small town in Žemaitija. My parents were ordinary civil servants and my fortune wasn't marked by any preordained events. My fate wasn't influenced by any planets, or metals, or signs of the Zodiac. When I was born, the stars had temporarily gone out.

Every proper *homo lithuanicus* could say the same about himself.

I doubt if I will ever finish my mlog. After all, if you want to study wolves, you can't be a wolf yourself. If you want to study fish, you can't be a fish. *Homo lithuanicus* can only be described by someone who isn't a *homo lithuanicus* himself.

And I really cannot say that about myself.

I am an idiot. What else can you call a person who threw away his family, his future, and even his career to write a dissertation that absolutely no one needs? And now writes an mlog dedicated to no one. To the void. Or to the decrepit Lithuanian God, who lives in a tree and lays rotten eggs. He stopped thinking about anything or doing anything a long time ago; he just bolts down those eggs of his and empties his bowels.

If you should go out looking for him, watch out so he doesn't fall over on you in his sleep.

But perhaps the will of a God like that could explain things, if nothing more than VV and Lolita's story. This Lithuanian God, gorged on moldering eggs, started to crap, whine, and flail his arms around in his tree, forgetting that every one of his movements, every sound coming out of his mouth, determines people's fates, their lives, and their deaths. It was exactly this meaningless flailing and whining that determined Lolita's and VV's story.

And my life was determined by that Lithuanian God's farting.

I saw this with my own eyes, so once again I have no right to be silent. I ended up next to them quite by accident. Accidents have followed me all of my life. Once, when I had set up my tent next to one of the Ignalina lakes, I saw Lolita with Gediminas in the distance. Any decent person would have moved to the next lake. But I'm not a decent person. I'm as curious as a child and I'm not ashamed of it. Anything left in us from childhood is a good thing. People are born decent, truthful, and natural. All of the awful stuff overruns them later.

*Homo lithuanicus* wasn't created by the Lord God, just by Lithuania's history and the ROF.

So I didn't move my tent an inch. What's more, I grabbed my binoculars, which I had just happened to bring along. I spied on their hermit-like existence; I even forgot to unpack my fishing rods. I was always interested in what it was that pushed Lolita into Gediminas's arms. Perhaps Lolita, in her shock, saw a reflection of her husband in his friend. Perhaps Gediminas provoked her; perhaps he deliberately took her to Teodoras's favorite places and used his sayings. Gediminas Riauba could do that. All his life that hardened bachelor and pervert went after women by means both fair and foul.

"Gedutis didn't love me," Lolita would say, sitting on my rug with her long legs stretched out.

She always called Riauba Gedutis.

"He was too immersed in mathematics, in music, but by way of all that—in only himself. To him, the whole world was just part of himself: I was too, and the clouds, and even his beloved dogs. I hated him, and that's why I lived with him."

At the time, I felt very sorry for her. Only much later did it occur to me that men only imagine or pretend to rule women. Actually, the women always lead us by the nose. Even if they really do submit to our will, they do it consciously—they have purposes we cannot grasp. Lolita was like that too. She just played with Gediminas as long as he was of use to her. And poor Gedutis rejoiced that he had supposedly enslaved her.

In our life, absolute victories always turn into absolute defeats.

It fell to me to witness the finale of such a defeat at that wretched lake in Ignalina. Towards evening, I suddenly heard a scream. I immediately knew it was Lolita shrieking. She was virtually howling. To this day, I don't know what he was doing to her, and now I'll never know. The screaming suddenly stopped. An instant later, a stark-naked Lolita staggered out of the tent, and behind her—a smiling Gediminas. As if nothing were wrong, the two of them kissed affectionately. Then, naked, they climbed into a rowboat and rowed out to the middle of the lake. The shores of Ignalina's lakes are hardly reminiscent of a deserted island. Some kids on the other shore happily waved their arms and made obscene remarks, but the two of them didn't pay any attention. The forest ranger in his yard stared at them through binoculars (I saw the sun glint off of its lenses). Finally, he couldn't stand it anymore, and he got on his bike and pedaled around to our side, apparently prepared to fine them for disturbing the public order. I just threw him a quick glance, and when I turned to the rowboat again, Gediminas was already floundering in the water.

I spoke with the investigator looking into Gediminas's sudden death. Lolita had told him she absolutely couldn't swim, and she hadn't stretched out the oar because she was in shock. The investigator believed her. I would have believed her too, if I hadn't seen her face at that moment. She watched Gediminas choking and still floundering in the water, and smiled wryly. Her expression was furious and scornful. It seemed death rays were emanating from her eyes. It wasn't a human expression; it wasn't a human smile. I don't know whose—God's or the devil's—but not a human's. Lolita drowned Gediminas without even touching him. Such are the paradoxes of Vilnius—the great snob Gediminas, with his grand intentions of understanding all sorts of essential things about the world, swam like a rock.

I remembered that moment's horror a few years later. Our office is very fond of arranging outings by the Žaliųjų Lakes, with little rowboats, water bicycles, and a modest picnic. Unconsciously, I would keep an eye on Lolita. It seemed she really was afraid of water. She'd wade in up to her thighs, wash herself off and leap back on shore again.

But once I needed to relieve myself in a hurry. I found myself some out-of-the-way bushes by the shore; what I saw there knocked me off my feet. In a remote backwater, hidden from everybody, I saw Lolita swimming. She swam with firm strokes, without raising any spray. She swam like a fish.

I've thought up a thousand premises, a million fantasies on this subject, but I can't set them out here. The mlog accepts only indubitable facts. Unfortunately, only facts. Thank God, only facts.

I've come up with a theory explaining why horrible things must always happen in Vilnius. It could be called the balance of passions theory. It occupies a significant place in my general theory called "What is the Ass of the Universe." I think the universal dullness of Vilnius is terribly lacking in deep human passions. The majority of Vilniutians' passions boil and bubble in a glass of water. Writers overdose themselves with sleeping pills when they don't get a new upgraded apartment. Engineers take to drink if they aren't promoted at work. When there aren't any truly important objectives, passions flare up over comical trifles that a normal person wouldn't pay the slightest attention to.

My theory asserts that the world (even Vilnius) cannot exist without genuine human passions. To keep the world in balance, it must fall upon at least one real human to be an example to a thousand *homo lithuanicus*. Unfortunately, in order to supplement the passions raging in the glass of water, his own passions have to be inhuman. He rages, laments, and raves enough for us all. He lives enough for us all! That's why every one in Vilnius who even remotely resembles a real human being burns up alive, is drowned by his own great love, or cuts her into pieces himself.

I think that Vilnius has reached such a level of general soullessness that a single human can no longer compensate for it by normal, civilized methods. Those who try to climb out of the general manure pile inevitably step over the permissible boundaries.

From my collection:

"Oh, Lithuanians . . . what will tear you out of your lethargy? Oh unhappy country, worthy of compassion in these days . . . What do you need? A dangerous revolution, total rearrangement, a terrible shock . . . stagnation can no longer be overcome by civilized methods, fire is necessary in order to burn out the gangrene eating you."

That's a bit of mystification. The text actually starts with "Oh, Italians" and its author is Casanova.

I intend this quote for the skeptics who think that the theory of the Ass of the Universe and the balance of passions is suited to only one puny object—our poor little Lithuania. This quote proves that theories like this have universal validity too.

From my collection:

"Neither the crushing force of the civilized state, nor the teachings of mutual hatred and merciless struggle that come adorned with the attributes of science from obliging philosophers and sociologists, can root out the feeling of human solidarity deeply lodged in man's consciousness and heart, because this feeling has been nurtured by all of our preceding evolution."

The author of this text is Prince Kropotkin, the famous anarchist.

I'd like to believe, at least in my dreams, that someone will show solidarity with *homo lithuanicus* and attempt to save him from destruction.

My citomania has begun to express itself. I swear: no more quotes.

I wonder if I'll hold out for long.

In my thoughts, I always envision Lolita in one of two guises. Sometimes she's sitting in my room, right on the rug, leaning against the sofa, silent. But much more often, she's swimming towards me through black waters, propelling herself with impeccable strokes, rudely pushing aside other thoughts of mine afloat in those boundless waters. Swimming and swimming straight at me, with a strange smile on her lips, maybe wanting to drown me too, because I know too much.

She and VV fell in love like a pair of nineteenth-century teenagers, even though both of them had gone through several circles of hell—each his own—before then.

I cannot bear religions that intimidate people with a single, common hell. There's already a hell common to everyone here on earth—that's the Ass of the Universe.

Apparently, Satan forced VV to fall in love with just that sort of father's daughter. Povilas Banys is a particularly famous person. "The Voice of America" or "Radio Liberty" is always reading excerpts from memoirs in which he appears in all his glory. He was an apologist for the total annihilation of the human soul, a spiritual executioner with imagination and fancy. The authors of memoirs remember him with reverent horror. He was so horrible, so consistently satanic, that he even inspired reverence. Povilas Banys was the poet of night interrogations, spiritual sadism, draconian judgments, and the ravaging of innocents. This Lithuanian writer, who died in the United States, recalled with sacred trepidation how Povilas Banys beat him with a wooden hammer on the head in his torture chamber. After thirteen blows (exactly thirteen!), he would order him to write one more sentence of his ostensible confession. "I'm perfecting your style," he explained tenderly, "You'll learn the fastest way of expressing the essence."

Colonel Povilas Banys, the bearer of government decorations, was Lolita Banytė-Žilienė's father. That's the kind of person's daughter VV fell in love with. Their story couldn't have ended any other way; their love was doomed from the start.

Incidentally, Povilas Banys was an enormously educated person, a true scholar. But why do I say "was"? He's still living today, as pretty as you please. He loves avant-garde jazz, Joyce, and Buñuel. He simply adores the latter.

An American or European would never understand how a person like that could be a poet of spiritual sadism. It's never fallen to the lot of either Americans or Brits to live in the Ass of the Universe. The corresponding neurological connections don't exist in their brains. Once I nearly choked with laughter listening to a Harvard professor on the radio defending this Muscovite psychiatrist. The world accused this psychiatrist of stuffing dissidents into secret nuthouses. That's not true, it can't be, the Harvard professor railed, that Muscovite is a true scholar; he's published serious work. I even fell out of my chair laughing. No Harvard professor would be able to understand that a perfectly serious scholar could, of his own free will, be a complete butcher. No American or Frenchman would understand that the manager of a gas chamber in Hitler's Germany could have played the piano like a virtuoso and worshipped Chopin. No, they won't understand it. Those American and French brains aren't constructed right.

I feel sorry for those Americans and Frenchmen. When the all-powerful Ass of the Universe overtakes them, they'll die in the prison camps without ever catching on.

Lord knows, sometimes I'm glad I was born in the Ass of the Universe. There's a lot I could teach to the English, and the French, and the Italians, and . . . It's just the Lithuanians I couldn't teach anything to.

The inhabitants of the Ass of the Universe figured out paradoxes like that much too well. So well, that they've completely reconciled themselves to them. Even I, the great writer of the mlog who's seen everything, am sometimes astounded by this reconciliation.

From my collection:

VV socialized with this Stadniukas, who I believe was one of his former camp guards. Only in the Ass of the Universe can a victim nonchalantly sip cognac with his executioner. They socialized as equals. VV didn't condemn this Stadniukas openly, and in turn the latter didn't lick his boots or humiliate himself to atone for his past sins. Lord knows, they acted as if they'd been students together.

But VV wouldn't be VV if he hadn't, sooner or later, blown his top. My theory of the balance of passions was once again indisputably confirmed.

This Vasilijus Ivanovičius, who showed up from who knows where and then disappeared again, had his finger in it too. VV, in all seriousness, maintained that this Vasilijus lived in the mud of the bog and only emerged to breathe air once every seven years. He looked that way too—as if he had crawled out of the muck. I never got who he was—a former prisoner, or a guard. He downed vodka by the tumbler and spoke in nothing but swear words, and when he got really drunk, in inarticulate sounds. VV explained that this was the language of birds.

This Vasilijus flew in like a vulture as soon as Stadniukas kicked the bucket. He and VV got it into their heads to bury Stadniukas and beat off the gang of veterans. Who knows how they got hold of a coffin made of rough pine boards. Inside they stuck a half-finished bottle of vodka. They spat on the coffin lid and put their cigarettes out on it. The veterans, sniffing out the funeral anyway, ran off to call the militia; the gravediggers, afraid of trouble, hid themselves. VV and this Vasilijus, as cool as could be, filled up the hole; the militia, hurrying to the scene, found a fresh hillock and an Orthodox priest. It turned out that Stadniukas had managed to convert just before he died, taking communion and the last rites.

It was all like some preposterous farce.

VV couldn't not know who Lolita's father is. He simply tried not to think about it—the way we don't think about how we will sooner or later die. Actually, we all behave exactly as if we were immortal.

Perhaps that disgusting Sunday he and Gediminas intentionally got the better of Lolita, the offspring of an accursed family. But afterwards that accursed offspring turned into a miraculous flower, the center of secret hopes. It wasn't possible to think of her as her father's daughter. In VV's eyes, she was like some kind of orphan, a stray, his ward alone. They both needed to fence themselves off from the entire world—even from their own ancestors. Particularly from their ancestors.

The two of them had to stand all alone against the entire universe. Unfortunately it was, in any event, the Ass of the Universe they stood against.

That was exactly why VV rejected his father; that was exactly why he didn't want to see his grandfather. And after all, the senior Vytautas Vargalys was unique, perhaps the last descendant of the true Lithuanian gods. A heroic spy for Lithuania in Polish-occupied Vilnius. The secret coordinator for the forest brothers. A fearless rescuer of Jews from the Vilnius Ghetto. A man whom at least three governments should have shot no less than thirty times. The elder Vytautas Vargalys fought all his life and always lost. He was sufficiently intelligent and skeptical enough to grasp this.

I alone, as they say, accompanied him to the other world. He sobbed quietly and called for VV the whole time. He cursed me; the suspicion arose in his deteriorating brain that I was deliberately hiding him from his grandson. At times I would beg the Lithuanian god, bloated from his eternal snoozing, to not let the old man go on suffering, to finish him off quickly. At other times I was overcome with the heart-wrenching feeling that the last descendant of the true Lithuanian gods was

325

leaving this world in front of my eyes—left all to himself, forgotten by everyone, no longer needed, not even by his own grandson. At the time, his son, VV's father, was lying in a hospital in Druskininkai after his second heart attack. The old man kept wheezing:

"In my lifetime I had eleven passports of five countries under different names. Lithuanian, Latvian, Polish passports, Soviet passports and even a Swedish passport. Sometimes I'd forget my real name. Sometimes I'd forget my native language. I'd speak Latvian and Polish, German and Yiddish—anything but Lithuanian."

Colon cancer was on the verge of consuming him; they kicked him out of the hospital the last few weeks. The usual thing: so he wouldn't up and die on them and ruin the hospital's mortality statistics. It just so happened that the clinics were fighting to lower their mortality rating at the time.

"I've found a solution," mumbled the old man, "A solution for all Lithuanians. It's too late for me now, but I'll pass on the secret to Vytelis. He still can . . ."

It was sad and depressing. Here this all-powerful old man's entire life didn't even earn him a nurse at his deathbed! They kicked him out of the hospital so he wouldn't ruin the mortality rating!

The Soviet hospital is the most immortal in the world!

I kept thinking: and what do I have to do with this? Why me in particular? Somewhere I read this thought: one London money lender loved and suffered, stockpiled money and worried, in a word, lived his life, without even suspecting that the only purpose of his life, all of its meaning, was to catch the eye of an alcoholic playwright and to become the prototype for Shylock. More and more, I've come to believe the only purpose and meaning of my life is to be the commentator on VV's fate, to create an epitaph for him, and at the same time for Lithuania; to write my mlog.

"I've found a solution!" the old man wheezed. "Tear off your balls and don't give birth to any more Lithuanians! Tell Vytelis so he'll hurry! Don't let him wait until the end like me! He should hurry! Later it'll be too late!"

The old man, his covers pulled off, tugged at his masculinity like he really did want to rip it out. It was the second time in my life I had seen such a bulky sexual organ—the first one like that belonged to VV.

Things were even more fun at the old man's wake. The ghosts of Vilnius who gathered there awoke even my exhausted brain. You couldn't call those people anything else. Nearly hundred-year-old men and women. I never suspected people like that even existed. Some of them wore tuxedos. Greenish mold shone on their lapels. Spittle ran out of their mouths, and one old lady hiccupped nonstop and blew farts continuously. A lively old man most drew my attention. He was completely bald, and kept saying over and over that he's called Rafalas and is a count. He was the only one who didn't fall asleep during the night of the wake, but right before morning he peed on himself. With great dignity, he got up from the bench, leaned over and sniffed at the puddle, then sat down again somewhere else. Those ghosts were furiously intrigued by only one thing: would they bury Vargalys with his false teeth, or had they ripped them out? Choosing his moment, the bald Rafalas, with unexpected strength and agility, opened the corpse's mouth and pensively announced to the gathered crowd that the dentures were in place. The old folks spiritedly discussed this information for some time, and then quieted down again. A few hours later, he got interested again in whether Vargalys would be buried with or without his dentures. Rafalas inspected the corpse's mouth again. Everyone got lively again and discussed the news—in the exact same words they had used earlier. I thought I would go out of my mind. I was the only vaguely normal person in that company. None of that moldy crew went to the burial. I stood at the graveside all alone. I was soaked by an annoying, murky rain the entire time.

After that funeral, I wanted to punch VV in the nose. Since I'm like a dwarf in comparison to him, I had decided to smack him with some brick or a cudgel. I opened the door to his office panting with rage, and he raised his deep, intelligent, suffering eyes to me. I saw such despair in them that I immediately backed down. VV didn't live in our world; at that moment he was somewhere completely, utterly different.

"I've thought of it at last," he said suddenly. "The best thing to do would be to get castrated."

Some ancient nation (perhaps more than one) has already thought up a mythological God who, in disappointment with the world, fixed himself—so that his seed wouldn't prolong the degenerate human race.

To cut your throat means no more than to make an end of yourself. To destroy your seed means much more: to make an end of your entire family, of all your descendants. That was what the elder Vytautas Vargalys wanted to say, that it would have been better if neither his son nor his grandson had ever been born. That they shouldn't have been born, that in a certain sense they hadn't been born, they'd never lived. This thought inspired him with the desire to destroy the horrible future waiting for us all, that it would be better if it never came.

The defenders of Pilėnai, to a man, burned themselves alive, but they didn't become slaves for the invaders. *Homo lithuanicus*, smacking his lips in excitement, listens to the opera about Pilėnai, but out of all of Lithuania, only Kalanta burned himself to death. All the rest slave away quite valiantly.

At least the senior Vytautas Vargalys offered a decent solution. Without Lithuanians, the world wouldn't be either better or worse. Haven't any number of small ethnic groups disappeared without a trace? A sudden end would be quite a bit better than a slow death in the Ass of the Universe.

Why VV got the urge to castrate himself, I don't know. Despite the horrifying measurements of his sexual organ, VV was sterile. I know this for sure. I shamelessly questioned a plastered Kovarskis; he had tried to cure VV. Unfortunately, the Siberian permafrost irreparably locked up VV's seed; it stayed there, behind the barbed wire of the camp. No, his sexual prowess wasn't affected; he was unusually potent, but infertile.

Probably VV was particularly Lithuanian in this symbolic sense alone; the true apotheosis of *homo lithuanicus*: of gigantic proportions, enormous power, but absolutely infertile.

Perhaps because I knew this, I was struck speechless the first time I saw VV naked. His masculinity wasn't just gigantic. It was carefully tended, even, and smooth, without the slightest wrinkle or protruding vein. It was so flawless it looked fake.

It wasn't merely that he and Lolita had no intention of prolonging the human race; they were incapable of it. The two of them had been condemned beforehand to the divine suicide VV's grandfather suggested.

Poor Lolita was the victim of her origins, her position, and her passions. She was in a hurry to place herself upon the sacrificial altar. Perhaps she secretly wanted to be incinerated and at least rise up to the heavens in sacred smoke.

She didn't take into account that smoke can only go down in the Ass of the Universe.

When she sat on the floor in my room, she would look quite tiny, helpless, and defenseless; you could encircle her with one hand. I understood her rudeness—it was only a defense against the world.

Lolita, Lolita, Lolita! Where are you now? Is the other hell worse than the hell of our lives?


When I can think for at least a few minutes, I get tired right away. I've gotten unaccustomed to thinking. Today an investigator slunk into the library and was asking about everything under the sun. But probably least of all about Lolita and her relationship with VV. He was interested in weird things: V's habits, his predilections and buddies, even what bookshelves he would rummage through. What could that mean? I don't get it.

I'm going to that wretched coffee break. Our office's habits wouldn't change even if the prophecies of the Revelations started coming true.

"It's surely some kind of conspiracy," Elena declared as soon as I walked in. "They don't investigate things this thoroughly for no reason. It looks like there was an entire group at work here. Lola could have been sent here on purpose. You do know who her father is."

I sit directly across from her, like I always do. Even the places around the coffee table haven't changed. VV's and Lolita's chairs are empty, so Marija's left at the end of the table, seemingly cut off from the others.

"It's really awful about the meat," she replies pensively. "Yesterday there was nothing but boiled sausage for two-twenty in the store—and only one kind too. In the meat section just chicken and pig heads. It's just awful."

"They're not looking for clues just for the heck of it," Elena gives me a meaningful look. "I think they'll find them. These people are experienced."

It's funny how quickly those government flunkeys give themselves away.

"Pig heads—without the tongues. They cut the tongues out," Marija chimed in calmly.

That's how we converse. Slowly I sink ever deeper into the eddy of women's concerns. I'm the only man left. It must be that they simply forget themselves, or maybe they don't notice me. They used to take pains in front of VV, but they pay absolutely no attention to me. By now I've learned about the dreadful panty shortage. They used to bring them in as contraband from Poland, but now there's a shortage in Poland itself. Or maybe the customs agents got stricter. In a word, it's a huge problem. You have to patch the same ones over and over. The young man who claims he's my son adroitly uses this to his advantage. He brings panties by the sackful from his athletic excursions and divides them up among Vilnius's beauties—on condition that he'll take the old ones off and put the new ones on himself. That's his life. I don't understand how I fathered that huge imbecile. His eyes are expressionless and his muscles like a ship's tow line. When he comes by, he loafs about my room and curses the authorities—evidently, it's getting harder all the time to travel abroad, results alone aren't enough—the sporting masters need their palms greased.

But most important of all is that this belongs in my mlog too. Just like these gloomy rooms and the dust of books, just like our bathroom with the shit-covered toilet and the eternally broken water tank. If I were to leave this out, neither the deepest philosophy nor the most horrendous metaphysics would mean a thing.

"A friend of mine was in Paris." Beta interjects, "Well, you know, the one whose husband works at the Central Committee. She said all the girls were walking around with brown nail polish. Nails in any other color simply wouldn't be decent there."

They all sigh deeply and squint their eyes, giving homage to unattainable Paris, where everyone paints their nails brown. The ROF made a big mistake when it let people find out they could live differently somewhere else. Stalin was consistent in that regard: no one even suspected any other life was possible.

From my collection:

When the first Soviet people escaped for a bit out into the world, a relative quizzed a writer returned from America:

"Well, so how's the situation with food in America?"

The writer, somewhat surprised, answered that all was quite well.

"That's ridiculous!" the relative got angry, "Even we don't have anything to eat, so what's there to say about America."

Understandably, the writer and his relative were Russian. *Homo lithuanicus* always knew that it's possible to live differently. *Homo lithuanicus* experienced it himself, or at least heard from his parents, that abundance is possible, that not all that long ago a Lithuanian could not only dream of Paris, but go there too. Lithuania was independent for twenty years; this spoiled Lithuanians for the duration.

"And Moscow's full of Dior perfume and Lithuanian smoked sausage," Gražina remarked, stretching herself lazily. "They have that stuff for themselves. They took it from us."

"They do it on purpose," Marija agrees. "They're dying from envy that so far we've at least had enough to eat."

Elena frowns, but she's quiet. The ideological boundaries haven't been stepped over yet; she knows exactly when to take the women's rising revolt in hand.

The saddest thing is that if someone gave them good sausage, perfume and panties, they'd be entirely satisfied with life. Out of the famous formula "bread and circuses," only bread remains in the Ass of the Universe. In the best case, "bread and butter." It's the ROF's greatest success.

"But what can they do? They can't even manage to raise pigs for themselves!"

They! It's a miraculous term, *homo lithuanicus'* magic word. It's always them, not us at all. We've nothing to do with it. A genuine *homo sovieticus* is obliged to say: our revolution, our victory, our government, we did it. A genuine *homo lithuanicus* says: their revolution, their government, they did it. And we've nothing to do with it. By no means is this merely a lexical nuance; it's a key marker of an inner philosophy. *Homo lithuanicus* couldn't even explain who "they" are. They aren't us. We've nothing to do with it. The greatest downfall of the state doesn't worry him: they fell, but we've nothing to do with it. No victory cheers him: see how well things turned out for them. Unfortunately, we've got nothing to do with it. If some foreigner attacks him about the horrors of the Soviet state, *homo lithuanicus'* eyes bug out: excuse me, but what do I have to do with it? I'm a Lithuanian.

331

I have no idea if that's a good thing or not. That's simply the way it is.

"The coffee is awful," Marija announces. "It's gotten five times as expensive and they sell you manure."

Thank God, at least they're not talking about children today.

Children are the principal subject of my cosmic despair. The carefully regulated system of stupefaction sucks them dry by preschool. Our little children don't learn in preschool that they should love mama and papa. However, they find out right away that you have to love Lenin and the Soviet state. The kid can't hold a knife and fork yet, doesn't know how to read, but he already knows that Lenin was the best person in the world.

An absolutely authentic incident from my collection:

A teacher's aide was leading a group of preschoolers through the Antakalnis grove. Unexpectedly, a real, live rabbit ran right by them. The excited teacher's aide started prompting the children:

"So, who will tell me what ran by just now? So, who's the smartest? Who will tell me?"

The kids stood there gaping and said nothing. The teacher's aide got totally annoyed, she really so wanted to brag about her clever group of children when they got back.

"Come on now, remember, remember, what we talk about every day. So, what do we talk about all the time? We talked about it yesterday, and we read a book too. So, what ran by us? What do we talk about every day? Come on, what ran by?"

At that moment Aliukas, undoubtedly a future top student, shyly stepped forward, hemmed a bit, and answered:

"Was it Lenin?"

Incidentally, the Aliukases of this world are divine innocents only until the age of five. Later, they start comparing the lessons of kindergarten and the lessons of life—what they see every day on the street, in the yard, or in the store. The child slowly internalizes that all of life is a lie, so you must always lie. We are a country of liars, everyone lies and knows full well they're lying: they also know they're lied to, and those liars know their listeners know they're being lied to, and in their turn,

332

they lie too. And so on.

It seems I've thrown over my mlog and I'm starting a new dissertation about the education of children. I have to stop.

Elena summoned me; she's boss for the interim. I hope she won't start talking about meat, or else I'll start singing her a popular childish song:

> *One Russian, two Russians*
> *The trolleybus is full of Russians!*
> *There is no meat, there's nothing to eat,*
> *Just little red flags on the seat!*

God forbid, I really don't blame people for the fact that they've forgotten their souls. For a human to feel the hunger of the soul, he needs not just a well-fed body, but one maintained with tasteful food; he must be not just warmly, but nicely dressed as well. Only then can he reflect that it seems he needs some kind of nourishment for his soul too.

I understand everything. I don't blame those poor Lithuanians. Hell, after all, I'm exactly like them. I'm not blaming; I'm merely stating the facts.

Elena didn't talk about meat. She went on about newfangled bibliographic indexes, which from now on will replace the flawed ones VV had thought up. I had completely forgotten that our office was preparing a computerized card catalog. I mean, can you really be expected to remember what excuse they're using to pay you that beggarly salary?

I immediately replied that our card catalog ought to be like a layer cake. After all, the largest part of the collection is accessible only with special permission. And a significant part of it—only with special, special permission. So it's essential to invent special, layered indexes, which would immediately show who can read what. So the first thing you need to do is create special, indoctrinated computers, ones that would give out permission themselves. The problem is difficult. However, Soviet technology is, one way or another, the best in the world; no stumbling block is too difficult.

I was driven out of her office because of this brief monologue. And, by the way, I wasn't being in the least bit sarcastic. The Lenin Library's collection in Moscow is the largest in the world. It's a fact. Another fact: ninety percent of that collection isn't accessible to an ordinary citizen. Question: this being the case, what is a computer supposed to do? Hundreds of censors will have to sit there anyway, and judge the books—are they allowed, or are they part of the special collection? There's only one solution—to design an indoctrinated computer that would take the place of those censors too. That's not a joke. It's a general concept.

It's too bad Elena didn't let me finish my monologue.

For the thousandth time, listening to the divine Elena, I thought about whether *homo lithuanicus* really differs all that much from *homo sovieticus*: is it permissible to consider the former a separate anthropomorphous species, or is it merely a subspecies of the latter? Once more I decide it's permissible. *Homo lithuanicus* has characteristics that are absolutely atypical of the species *homo sovieticus*. *Homo lithuanicus* says "they," *homo sovieticus* says "we." *Homo lithuanicus* considers only Lithuania his country. To him the remaining parts of the USSR are as distant and as foreign as Mars. *Homo sovieticus* considers the entire USSR his home country. Just look at the Russians living in Vilnius or Tbilisi. They feel at home, in their own place; from their point of view, all these Lithuanians and Georgians aren't quite where they belong. *Homo sovieticus* doesn't sense any difference between Mogilyov, Ryazan, or Dnipropetrovs'k. (And by the way, there is none.) According to *homo lithuanicus'* understanding, Vilnius is as different from Saratov as the sky from the earth.

If a former *homo lithuanicus* quietly goes off to live in Moscow or Kiev—he's changed his skin. Then he says "we," and not "they."

In our office, only Elena says "we." Such converts are an intermediate product. *Homo sovieticus* talks in an Orwellian newspeak in which all the normal, age-old concepts are turned inside out and changed. The converts, like Elena, only speak newspeak from the rostrum. In other circumstances, they start talking in normal, human language despite themselves. They unconsciously drop their fake skin so the real one can breathe, for a while at least. They simply forget themselves.

This type isn't completely done for. True, you won't turn them back into humans anymore, but they're not yet genetically ruined. You can at least try to turn their children around.

Incidentally, on the subject of the converts' children. One rather highly-placed gentleman's wife told me, in horror, of an incident that embellished my collection:

Her son, a four-year-old philosopher, thoughtfully looked at Vilnius's identical buildings and unexpectedly asked:

"Mama, Lithuanians live in Lithuania, right?"

"Yes, my sweetheart."

"And the French in France?"

"Of course, sweetheart."

"And Americans in America?"

"Yes, of course, who else."

The philosopher looked around once more, listened to the passersby talking, sighed, and asked:

"Mama, then why are there so many Russians living in Lithuania? They've lost Russia, haven't they? They don't have anywhere else to live, right?"

His communist mother told me this in horror. Her opinion was that someone had maliciously taught this to her child.

She was a convert, so she couldn't grasp that there was simply still some good sense inside the child's head.

The first priority is to beat every scrap of good sense from people's heads as early as possible. In preschool, or in the first grades at the very latest. Comrade Molotov himself explained this to me. Yes, yes, the Iron Ass, Stalin's right hand. When I met him in Moscow, he was some eighty years old. I was running from one high office to another and fighting for my dissertation, while he had come by to pay his Party dues.

He paid his Party dues regularly, even though he had long ago been shouldered out of the Communist Party. But the Iron Ass will most certainly be returned to the ranks of honor! At least after he dies. If Comrade Molotov isn't returned to the ranks within the next five years, I'll go into shock.

I have no fear that he'll die too soon. I suspect that the Iron Ass will live to be at least a hundred and twenty.

Incidentally, the Iron Ass told me a sacred phrase:
"You Lithuanians never did understand anything!"

VV has his human ideal—the great ideologue Suslov. My eternal love is the Iron Ass.

On that occasion, he was suddenly overcome with sentiment for Lithuanians. When he found out that I was a Lithuanian, he took me home with him.

I must emphasize that in this respect the Iron Ass differs from the majority of Russians. He knew what Lithuania is, and didn't confuse Lithuanians with Latvians. The majority of Russians don't bother distinguishing Lithuanians from Latvians or Estonians. The name of their concocted generalization for all of them is *pribalt*, the people by the Baltic. In the minds of the majority of Russians, even Lithuanians themselves don't particularly distinguish who they are—Estonians or Latvians. The Russians always like to combine everything. Besides "pribalt," they've come up with other new races, for example, "caucasites."

The Iron Ass stated right away that inaccuracies of that sort irritate him. And then he added one more sacred phrase:

"You Lithuanians always got terribly in the way of the inevitable progress of history."

I'll explain for those who don't know what "the inevitable progress of history" is. That means the annexation of Lithuania and then the deportation of Lithuanians to Siberia—in short, freeing up the land for those who are more worthy of it. The Iron Ass didn't doubt in the least that this process was only temporarily halted.

I'll never understand why he took me to his home. Maybe the Iron Ass is assembling a collection too, one analogous to mine? He was extremely interested in pedagogy. I myself can bring home a shabby, grizzled bum, even though I'll have to disinfect all the furniture afterwards. It makes no difference to me, as long as the bum adds to my collection.

I didn't recognize him at first. Nasty suspicions arose when I saw a militiaman, who jumped up and saluted the master of the house, in the entrance lobby of the building on Granovsky Street. It slowly started dawning on me. When I took a better look, I could have bet it was Molotov. True, not for a lot of money.

The Iron Ass lived in a five- or maybe six- or seven-room apartment, entirely by himself. Apparently he was bored out of his skull. His lower lip sometimes sagged, but overall he was fairly energetic and reasoned perfectly logically. Lord knows, even now he would embellish the ROF. However, at that moment he no longer belonged to the ROF. The Iron Ass was a fallen idol.

He immediately grabbed the bull by the horns.

"Twenty-five years ago I used to know this Lithuanian who didn't understand anything, either," he stated hoarsely. "Your breed interests me a great deal. You are unique in your failure to understand the inevitable progress of history."

Never in my life—neither before, nor after—have I heard such perfect newspeak. There wasn't a single human word in its usual sense in his speech. This Molotov was the ideal new man—the type you don't even need to explain, just showing a good photograph is enough. No comment needed afterwards. I vividly pictured him saying, "There are no Red Army prisoners, there are only traitors." I could just see him with Ribbentrop chopping up the map of Europe: von Ribbentrop a bit agitated, breathing in quick gasps, and the Iron Ass with the cosmic indifference of a perfect automaton. He was terrible in his inhumanity. Everything human was foreign to him.

"He was called, uh . . . Krėva," he declared, never offering me a seat. "Do you know him?"

He had Krėvė-Mickevičius in mind.

"I finally let him into my office . . . yes, that was twenty-five years ago. Where is he now, that, uh, Krėva?"

"He emigrated to the U.S." I was startled to hear my voice sounding entirely natural.

The Iron Ass, dissatisfied, shook his head:

"He tried to escape the surge of the inevitable progress of history. A few individuals still can. For the time being."

It's a pity I can't recreate all the nuances of his newspeak lexicon. No matter how much I'd try, the Lithuanian language just isn't suited for it.

"I explained to that emissary of yours that the historical process is inevitable. That Lithuania can only exist as part of Russia. I showed him maps printed a year earlier, in which Lithuania was already a part of Russia. I explained that a great war would soon start, after which at least half of Europe would belong to us. That, uh . . . Krėva's historical task was to avoid bloodshed, if he wanted that breed of his to survive a while longer . . . A Bolshevik demands voluntary obedience first. Yes, almost always . . . We're humane. We got Lithuania back without spilling any blood . . ."

But he hadn't brought me home to listen to his memories. He wasn't in the least interested in the past. His gaze was turned towards the future. Moscow, the third Rome, was victoriously marching through the world: towards the Indian Ocean, towards the Dardanelles, through Africa. But I was much more shocked by the theory of the New Man, since it concerned children directly.

The Iron Ass was firmly convinced that children are their, that is, the iron asses', future. Listening to him, it suddenly occurred to me that all the principles of raising and educating children crawled out into the world from this room. I realized what boundless foolishness I had been full of until then.

I had quite sincerely supposed that my dissertation would open people's eyes, that everyone had merely been mistaken, and now they would willingly and quickly correct their unfortunate mistakes.

I really did think that way. Word of honor.

I thought this world needed intelligent people.

But the Iron Ass convincingly explained that you need to destroy even the most pathetic shoots of good sense, starting in infancy. He was programmed that way. That day I asked myself for the first time: who programmed these people? That is the only societal question a decent person must be concerned about: who programmed all of this? Who really rules the ROF?

Not even once did he say "the new man," certainly he didn't say "Soviet man," he simply constantly repeated "man."

The trouble is, he explained, man is born with a real muddle in his head. He called the intellect, or at least its rudiments, a "muddle." This muddle must be rigorously corrected. Children's preschools, schools, and universities are designed to do just that. The first steps in this direction should be taken while the child is still in nursery school. A child must absorb the correct ideology and the scale of values on the level of a reflex—like a trained puppy. The conditional reflex must become unconditional. To never pity a class enemy, to sincerely love the wise Party, to gladly execute the international responsibility of freeing nations—these must be neither thought out nor learned. They must lie at the level of a reflex; they should appear naturally and unavoidably, like saliva when a hungry person sees a cooked piece of meat.

Technology that allowed the dissemination of information irritated him to no end. He was preparing to entirely block the ether, leaving only a cable system that broadcast a single, solitary program.

He was similarly plagued by the problem of mathematics and computers. Abstract mathematics made him physically ill, because it was ideologically indifferent. But the most pressing problem was how to eliminate computers.

"Koba was entirely correct," he repeated, sighing, "to prohibit all of those cyberneticians. We've reached the point where they say a computer can verify the correctness of Marxism-Leninism. Of course, we won't allow it to do that."

I'm quoting him exactly. He did not say, "prohibit cybernetics," he said, "prohibit cyberneticians." That wasn't a casual mistake, but rather the expression of an inner concept. He was to speak again, and more than once, of the prohibition of people, entire nations, and even states.

"It was time to prohibit the Lithuanians a long time ago," he declared to me.

By no means did the Iron Ass think of himself as a tyrant, or as an advocate of a complete dumbing-down. He went by the Michurinian slogan: "We won't wait for blessings from nature, we'll modify it ourselves!" It's just that he was aiming to change humans, not a strain of apples. All of Judeo-Christian morality, love of one's neighbor, "Do unto others as you would have them do unto you," became obsolete a long time ago, he explained. It suited the old society, but hampered the new. That's why it's crucial to fundamentally change children while they were still in infancy. "Love," "brotherhood," "courage," must signify something entirely different than they had previously. In a friendly way, he suggested I take up an interest in precisely these things, that is, in the creation of newspeak and its implantation from infancy on. He vision was profound.

Newspeak isn't just some ordinary system of lies; it's a powerful weapon. All those Molotovs understood they wouldn't succeed in forbidding words. So they didn't forbid them; they did something much more clever—they stole or deformed the real meaning of words. They left the old words, but gave them their own meaning. A devilish invention: you can talk any way you want, but your words won't mean what they ought to anymore.

Clever Molotovs!

But I was particularly charmed by love for the wise Party on the level of a reflex.

From my collection:

A certain Marius Škėma graduated in history with honors. He was the Komsomol Secretary; he joined the Communist Party while he was still studying. When he finished his studies, regardless of his tender age, he was assigned the job of assistant to the director of the Revolution Museum. His work was thorough; the museum's collections and expositions constantly grew and improved. Marius Škėma was already approved for the directorship, but he suddenly disappeared. A letter was found in his apartment, in which Škėma vaguely explained that he had grasped the meaning of life and had left to carry out his great mission. It was also discovered that the museum women had seen him after work hours associating, in a singularly intimate way, with various images of Lenin.

Digging deeper, it slowly became clear that Marius Škėma had fallen in love with Lenin some time before. A union-wide search was quickly declared. His traces were found in Uljanovsk, Shushenskaya, and other Leninist places. Witnesses told of him explaining that he had to acquaint himself with every minor detail of the bearer of cosmic harmony. An absolute knowledge would eventually meld the seeker with the one sought; crudely speaking, Marius Škėma would turn into Lenin.

All that is known precisely is that Marius Škėma was captured and confined in a psychiatric hospital. Everything else I can only call a legend, even though all of this was sworn to by this old KGB agent named Mackus, a Narutis drunk, who never lied.

Mackus tried to convince us that Marius Škėma entered the Lenin Mausoleum along with the general public and tried to become completely one with the exhibit, considerably damaging the mummy in the process.

It's an incontestable fact that precisely at that time the Mausoleum was quite unexpectedly closed down for a long time.

Probably there's no need to relate what else the Iron Ass said. At the time it seemed horrifying to me; now it's simply boring.

Just one more interesting detail: he was completely convinced that only the Russian language suited the true teaching and upbringing.

"You Lithuanians, clinging to your flawed language, are perilously blocking progress," he said.

"We don't need Lithuanians, we need Lithuania. For the good of the Empire we must teach them only on the basis of the Russian language." This is what General Muravyov, the famous Hangman Muravyov, the most horrible character in school history textbooks, wrote in a report to the Tsar. Two hundred people, I believe, were hung at his command. Any single colonel in the NKVD, even the most inconsequential, destroyed the same number.

And I'm not talking about Colonel Banys.

Someone could get the idea that I really don't like Russians. That's ridiculous. There's quite a number of Russians living in Moscow and Leningrad whom I consider my friends. I believe they consider me a friend too. They proved to me that Russian culture is alive, just that it's not to be found in official art spheres. They honor that culture, they cherish it. Why should I dislike them? I envy them.

It's simply that there are Russians, and then there are Russians. I've already described the one, and as for the other . . . They dragged themselves into Lithuania after the war, frequently on foot, with bundles on their backs, hungry and rude, not even very well aware that this country is called Lithuania. Another category of this gang arrived in Party automobiles, still another—in tanks. These Russians don't honor or cherish anything; they just spit phlegm on the sidewalks and pretend not to understand Lithuanian. The bad part is, they're constantly showing their ass, while the others, the real ones, live far away. So, you get furious with the Russians, and then you get underground books from the others, the real ones, and fume as you read only in Russian, because Lithuanians don't have those kinds of books. Only Teodoras Žilys organized underground exhibits in his studio. But he burned up alive. Underground concerts, whatever their merits, were organized only by Gediminas Riauba. But Lolita drowned him. I've never held a single underground Lithuanian novel in my hand; I've never heard of any. Undoubtedly there's no shortage of graphomaniacs and other ignoramuses—I'm talking about a real novel.

The Lithuanian artist inevitably sells out and submits. He swears, moans, drinks vodka by the bucketful, or a three-liter jar at a minimum, but sure enough, he submits and sells out to the ROF.

This is a fundamental characteristic of *homo lithuanicus*.

I respect the Russians just because that characteristic isn't universal among them. But once more, I repeat: there are Russians, and then there are Russians. Worse yet, the first kind are constantly in your face, while the others are far away and busy with their own matters.

Maybe they're simply two different nations?

I've gone on way too much about myself. *Mea culpa*; however, without the Iron Ass my mlog would lose its skeleton. There simply must be something made of iron in it.

That's all, that's all, that's all. So, VV fell in love with Lolita. It looked ridiculous. There is no sight more hideous than mature people who are like teenagers in love. You want to vomit when you see them. Lord knows, it's sickening, seeing them holding each other's little hands and gazing into each other's eyes like calves.

Thank God, at least VV and Lolita didn't sigh, drivel, or hang around on park benches. On the surface, they behaved normally, naïvely thinking no one noticed their love.

As if you really needed to see it.

You'd notice the smell of that love from ten steps away. You'd handle that love when you shook VV's hand. You'd hear their marvelous words of love even though they were silent. The tastiest food would turn bitter in your mouth as soon as they sat down next to you. I suppose from envy.

The women in our office were terribly jealous of them. VV was showered with anonymous letters denouncing Lolita as a paid prostitute and an all-around syphilitic. I suppose every woman in our office secretly dreamed of sleeping with VV. However, that luck fell only to Stefanija.

Stefanija was VV's good fairy. Self-sacrificing women surrounded him all his life. Most men only dream of this, but VV had it without lifting a finger. Maybe he didn't even imagine it could be otherwise. Self-sacrificing women created the illusion of a better life for him—each as best they could. Irena, his former wife, managed to outfit a deserted island in the middle of glum Vilnius, where just the two of them lived. It seemed to me she herself didn't live at all; she would serve him up a piece of herself every day, without being in the least concerned about what would come later. VV swallowed her whole.

VV always was a cannibal. He was almost devoured by the Ass of the Universe himself—perhaps he was simply trying to recover his lost flesh. He devoured everyone, even me, sucking up my thoughts like a sponge.

But I could retreat at any moment, whereas Irena had long since become part of him, his organ, his third hand. The more submissively she crawled at his feet, the more VV scorned her and tortured her in refined ways.

Villain! Fiend! Pervert! I'd scream something stronger still, but an mlog is not the proper place for emotions. Only the facts are necessary.

Inside VV, two famous aristocrats were constantly at war: the Marquis de Sade and Baron von Sacher-Masoch. He was deathly afraid that Irena was secretly deceiving him. He was more jealous than Othello. But he would offer his wife to any man who came along. Whenever he went out of town, he would force some friend to look after Irena, and then he would plague her with his suspicions.

I find it unpleasant to go into this. He pushed and shoved Irena into the arms of a man who coveted her. This guy was called Justinas. VV hated him with all his heart, but that was exactly who he fixed Irena up with. I couldn't even say Irena was aware of what she was doing. Speaking picturesquely, VV himself undressed her, got her drunk, and shoved her into that Justinas's arms. The poor thing didn't even grasp what was going on; he forced Irena to make love to that guy practically in front of his eyes. Then he would call her a traitor, a pervert, his ruin, and the next day he again . . .

I don't understand these things and never will. But they don't stop existing on my account. The facts are what matter to me: in the end, after almost killing her, he drove Irena out of his house.

I visit her from time to time, even though it's more and more horrifying every time I go. She lives in a crumbling building on Gorky Street, right next to the Narutis. She slaves with a decrepit mother who doesn't get out of bed, washing and boiling her soiled sheets every day. Her whole world is stinking sheets and memories. And cognac. She buys herself a bottle of cognac every day and downs it all alone. Frequently she falls asleep right at the table. No one has the slightest idea about her real life. Irena is still beautiful. She looks like a suffering Madonna.

The worst of it is that she talks about VV as if she were talking about God; she absolutely doesn't blame him, doesn't even reproach him. Most of all she likes to tell stories about their nights of love, their entire days, even weeks, of love. Those stories are brimming with such divine poetry that even I listen to them as if I were mesmerized. I usually can't stand any talk of erotica. The fashion inspired by Daddy Freud of undressing in public is disgusting.

But I listen to Irena as if I were mesmerized. She goes on and on, always slower, always quieter, until finally she falls asleep right on the table. Her mother screeches harshly, chasing away some ghosts or another, and calls me the spawn of the devil.

That's the kind of scene left behind whenever the great Vytautas Vargalys goes by. But that fiend enthralls them somehow anyway!

I have no idea where Irena gets the money. The cognac alone comes to half again as much as her pay. Maybe VV's father sends it or brings it to her. In the Ass of the Universe, restaurant doormen make good money.

Stefanija couldn't be like Irena; she couldn't outfit VV with a deserted island. However, she did what she could too. She isolated VV from everyday worries.

If someone thinks that's not such a big deal, then they've never lived in the Ass of the Universe.

344

I can't imagine VV shoving in line for a bite of bread or washing out worn underwear. It was only thanks to Stefa's efforts that he was bathed, cleanly dressed, nicely outfitted, and tastefully fed, without even suspecting what supernatural efforts this required. She even spent her own money on his needs. Fact: VV would get maybe one hundred fifty per month. In the Ass of the Universe, wages are paid on the assumption that everyone procures another three times that much from the underground economy. Incidentally, a genuine *homo lithuanicus* isn't the least concerned about this. *Homo lithuanicus*, in the depths of his heart, has absolutely no faith in this government, so he doesn't expect anything from it. However, VV or Stefanija weren't even associated with the underground economy. Poor souls. Poor, poor souls. It's really tough for intellectuals in the Ass of the Universe—even economically. They have nothing to pinch from the state.

It may seem that I'm making a hubbub over nothing, that I'm whining about trifles. Unfortunately, the shortage of absolutely everything and the complete lack of order isn't just a physical phenomenon. It's a terrible hindrance to the soul. When you spend hour after hour hunting food and clothing and putting enormous efforts into creating a normal home, you get so tired that you can't do anything else. All of your thoughts die off like unfledged birds.

VV's thoughts were protected from this. VV wasn't a man of this world. And since he also had no other, he was a person without any world at all.

He merely attempted, in vain, to construct that world for himself.

Another thing I don't understand: Stefa accepted Lolita's appearance on the scene as if it were her fate. She went on serving VV as home economist and house maid—without getting any wages. In fact, it was quite the opposite; she was always supporting her master. You'll find that the families of declining Italian princes also operated under this kind of economy.

VV would bring Lolita home even when Stefanija would be sitting— or rather doing the laundry or scouring the rooms—in his apartment. Earlier, he at least slept with her occasionally, but when he fell in love with Lolita . . .

Lord knows, if I were a mystic, I'd believe VV has supernatural powers over women. I'm sorry for Stefa. I'm horribly sorry for Irena. On the other hand, they themselves are perfectly happy with their situation.

I often wonder: maybe a hunger to slave for someone really does lurk somewhere deep inside people? There's something Dostoyevskian in this desire, and at the same time something horrifying.

I swear: I, Martynas Poška, do not want to slave for anyone.

I believe it was Goethe who wrote that we must most beware the fancies of our youth. If they aren't fulfilled in youth, they crash down on you like a ton of bricks when you're already mature.

The great love that VV never experienced in the camps crashed down on him when he had already attained his second half-century. Once he took me to a remote bar and confessed his love for Lolita. He thought he was giving away a great secret, but the entire library was already buzzing about it. I listened to that lunatic, considering whether his story suited my collection. He explained his love for Lolita to me.

"She's the otherworldly gift of the sunset of my life," he gloomily disclosed. "It's like a fairy tale, or a poem. I fell in love with her in a dream, twenty-two years ago."

The bar was filthy and reeked of vomit. It was mostly alcoholic teachers and journalists who hung out there: there were two schools and three editorial offices close by. A great place for metaphysical confessions.

"She's like a sister to me, or maybe a daughter," VV complained. "I feel like a King Lear who's suddenly slept with his daughter."

VV is thoroughly poisoned by mythological associations. His erudite abbot, The Professor of the Gulag, stuffed his head full of legendary names and stories.

"I feel like King Lear," VV repeated grimly.

What could I say to King Lear? That he should down his cocktails with more restraint, because we'll be out of money in a minute? That he's no king, he's called Vytautas Vargalys, and he doesn't have any daughters? It's horrifying when a person merges with the sullied, stinking walls and becomes a nameless detail of the Ass of the Universe. But it's even more horrifying when an inhabitant of the Ass of the Universe drowns in cosmic visions.

Wouldn't you find it frightening at first, and then simply disgusting, if some worm wriggling through a puddle started discussing Heidegger with you?

In the meantime, VV, cowering in fear, without looking at me, continued unraveling the worst allusions:

"Lolita isn't her real name. She hid one letter. She should be called Lilita: Lilu, Lilitu, or Ardat Lili. She should be hairy and have wings. She shaved the hair off her body and tore off her wings, but only temporarily."

Suddenly I remembered how Lolita (or Lilita?) looked at the drowning Gediminas. I should have told VV about that look of hers, but I kept quiet. We're all no-account sneaks; not a single one of us is worth trusting. If I were to mention it, I'd first have to admit I was there and saw the whole thing.

"Every day I look for hair on her body," VV muttered. "Every day I look for scars between her shoulder blades, where the wings used to be . . . The Talmud advises men not to sleep alone in a house, because sooner or later Lilita will fly in to visit them."

It really is appropriate to give some thought to a woman whose husband burned alive, whose lover drowned, and whose latest eternal love raves Kabbalistic nonsense. But, as I've already said, I've grown unaccustomed to thinking a long time ago. I merely gave VV a nudge towards his Lithuanian heritage:

"Don't go rummaging through the Holy Scriptures," I said. "We Lithuanians should be afraid of Lithuanian succubi."

"I'm not afraid of her," VV said in an unexpectedly sober voice, "I'm not afraid, whatever she is. I'm afraid she'll fly away, that's why I check to see she's not hatching new wings."

She didn't fly off anywhere; she was slaughtered and disemboweled.

The investigator prowls around the library sniffing in every corner—it seems any minute he'll lift his leg and leave his doggy mark. Anything is possible—I'm not so naïve as to suppose a detective's psychology and physiology are analogous to a human's.

I really lucked out: I was summoned for questioning, so I saw VV's hideaway with my own eyes; I don't need to rely on legends and rumors.

The detective burst into my little room and took me with him. I was flustered at first, because he didn't explain anything. I supposed they knew everything. But in any case, he led me to the library collections. He deftly marched through labyrinths where even I would get lost. We probably walked several kilometers.

At first I had no idea where he had brought me. It resembled a night guard's corner. A broken-down couch, shamelessly supported by books from the shelves, a crooked desk, on it an electric teapot and two ashtrays full of reeking cigarette butts. Both corner walls were covered with drawings and portraits.

The detective asked hoarsely what I thought of all this. I answered quite sincerely that the rules for fire prevention had been maliciously broken.

"Cut the crap!" the detective bellowed crudely. "I didn't ask if you knew about this hangout. You didn't. No one's been here for a couple of weeks at least. If you'd known about it, you would have been poking around here long ago and left traces. So, what do you think?"

"So far, nothing."

"What are these?" the special collections director asked angrily—he was the second witness.

I studied the portraits. I recognized a still very young Kafka. Cupid, drawn by VV himself, was aiming at Franz's heart. Kafka was unshaven, like the drunks at the Narutis. Next to that smirked Camus's somewhat horsy face. In the engravings, I recognized de Sade and Nietzsche. Higher up hung Baudelaire and Roman Polanski. Only by racking my brains did I recognize, somewhat uncertainly, Jean Genet too.

"They're all writers, poets, one's a movie director," I spluttered. "I probably don't need to comment on the other wall."

On the other corner wall, each one larger than the other, paraded Plato, Marx, Lenin, for some reason Tolstoy with Picasso, and Chaplin. The company was crowned by the two great poker players who played for Europe, or maybe the entire world—the immortal Joseph and Adolph. Disdain and satisfaction lurked in their eyes as they looked at their cards. Lord knows I have no idea why VV didn't draw their cards. After all, he drew Plato with a handlebar mustache.

"He's carried a bunch of books from the collection over here," the special collections director announced sadly, squatting and looking them over. "He stole them, although I don't know how. Our security . . ."

"You'd be better off keeping quiet about it." I felt a certain glee that the detective spoke rudely with his colleague too. "I see that anyone who wants to can read your books. You'll make a list later."

He suddenly turned to me:

"Come on, give me a hand!"

Without a doubt, this was an acknowledgement of the worthiness of my intellect: he called on me, not my colleague, to lift up the couch. It would have been better if he'd recruited that flustered gray-eyes.

At first I thought my head was merely swimming, but then I recoiled in horror. Lord knows, a body chopped into pieces would have frightened me less.

Under the couch, millions of cockroaches crawled, twitched their antennas, and mated. All of the library's cockroaches, every last one, had assembled there. Black and brown, the size of a flea and the size of a matchbox, shining and matte, they clambered over one another, crawled in dozens of layers; they were actually leaping up and down and flying around. They were so numerous they could easily have devoured me, chewed me up a single molecule, a single atom, at a time.

And all of them suddenly rushed off, spread out, hid in the shelves and between the books, crawled into invisible cracks; it seemed they simply dissolved into thin air. After a few seconds not a single one remained—just that where the couch stood earlier there was a myriad of little black spots: the tiny shit-balls of millions upon millions of cockroaches.

I was shaking all over, while the detective started resembling a philosopher who had suddenly got hold of his *idée fixe*. He wasn't surprised; he didn't recoil, like I had. He just smiled wryly, and his eyes announced that this was just what he had expected.

In one of my collection's photographs, Lolita has an expression that looks as if cockroaches or ants were crawling all over her—over her entire body, over the most private and vulnerable spots. She stands there transfixed, because she knows there's no way to avoid the torture.

For some reason it's women like Lolita and men like VV who perish. In the meantime, everyone in our office and all my other acquaintances live on quite serenely; they're all completely content and satisfied. They don't fall in love with anyone. They aren't plagued by oppressive memories. They'll do their assistant professorships at the institutes, get bored in architectural offices, or paint the same colorful landscapes over and over.

Maybe if you really want to live, the only thing left is to perish?

I spend a lot of time with Lithuanian writers under the cover of the demands of my work. Supposedly, I consult with them, as is appropriate for devising a bibliographic index of *belles lettres*. Actually, I'm just scoping out new material for my collection. Lithuanian writers give me fodder for both the collection and my mlog. Incidentally, they're constantly asking me if I don't know of a good plot. There's only one I've come up with.

It's a story about this Dane, or Dutchman, living with a pretty little wife in a pretty little house in the suburbs, who's very concerned about a lot of things. Salaries are extremely worrisome to him: they aren't rising particularly fast. He's troubled about national problems too: Danish butter (or Dutch cheese) is facing constantly growing competition in the world market. He works whole-heartedly and thoroughly, and in his free time he draws plans for tennis courts in his yard. They have to be special, different from all the other courts in the world. In addition, this Dane (or maybe a Dutchman after all?) signs every imaginable peace manifesto and supports the War on Drug Addiction League. At last, he decides to build his unique courts, but suddenly he sees that an unfamiliar white object has shown up on the spot in the yard that he's allotted for it.

This Belgian (or Frenchman) gets very annoyed. He immediately calls the municipality, but no one there answers the phone. Completely furious, he calls the police, but all he hears on the phone is a strange sound, like mumbling, like someone chomping.

Then that Italian (or Dane) angrily huffs over to the intruder. Getting closer to the white object, his resolution fades, because the object is very large. In front of him protrudes a gigantic ass—roughly the size of a twenty-story building. It's very clean, and perches there totally satisfied, as if it had been born there.

A footpath is already trampled up to it, and a sign in large, calligraphic letters announces: "Kiss every day from 4 to 6 P.M." The Dutch

Belgian is absolutely clueless. He hasn't heard of the Ass of the Universe, or if he did hear about it, he thinks it's imaginary. He calls the War on Drug Addiction League, the Peace Defense Committee, calls his lawyer, even the Women's Club—but all he keeps hearing everywhere is the same strange noise: like incoherent mumbling, like some kind of chomping. All there is on the TV is an entirely analogous picture of an ass. This Danish Italian calls every possible number again, getting more and more nervous, until, in a moment of inspiration, he suddenly realizes what he's hearing all the time on the telephone.

It's the satisfied and content farting of that same sublime ass.

I have also created a story about the love of a prisoner. This prisoner was confined behind barbed wire. Behind what barbed wire, or whether he's guilty or innocent, is completely irrelevant. At intervals, very infrequently, he'd succeed in seeing a woman from afar. She was so far away that he couldn't make out her features, so he would invent them himself. He would draw these imaginary women. Sometimes they would resemble madonnas, sometimes street prostitutes, but that prisoner of mine no longer remembered what either madonnas or prostitutes looked like.

One day a miracle occurred. A young girl showed up right next to the barbed wire. She came again the next day, and the next. She was the daughter of the prison warden. The prisoner's life acquired meaning. He could look at that girl. He would steal glances at her or watch her openly—she never noticed him, anyway. But others noticed.

In stories about convicts, they love to portray how brotherly they all are, how they help one another out. That's very nice, but in actuality things are completely different. I know this—we're all convicts, and I've never encountered any solidarity. The other prisoners cruelly mocked the young lover, told dirty jokes about the girl, and crudely assessed her attractions and her shortcomings.

The girl was the daughter of the prison warden. She didn't consider the prisoners human; she didn't even consider them animals. Her favorite entertainment was to sic the guard dogs on careless prisoners. She didn't feel hatred for them; she simply thought that these people were considerably lower than dogs.

However, my young man didn't see this; he didn't want to see it. He loved her, and that was all. He was envious of the shaggy dogs she petted. He was envious even of the bucket she carried out every day. Maybe he would have gone completely out of his mind, but the girl disappeared after a month or so and never appeared again.

Later, the young man was unexpectedly set free, slowly recovered his strength, and began to live almost normally. It was just that he judged women oddly. Not a one could please him. It seemed there wasn't a single woman in the world who could attract him. But that wasn't true. There was one such woman in the world. And my young man (no longer a young man and no longer a prisoner) met her. He recognized her immediately, while she, understandably, didn't remember him at all.

Here my story breaks off, because there's no way I can think of an ending. I really can't write stories. All I can write is an mlog.

The Lithuanian writers immediately jump on me the moment I say that prisoners don't commiserate with or support one another. They quote somebody's pretty phrase: people aren't united by common joys and victories, only by common sufferings and misfortunes. I agree, this rule holds true for some people. But it doesn't in the least apply to the human herd. I immediately give an example from my collection.

This took place during the time the new Brezhnev Constitution was under consideration. We all know how these considerations go. The people driven into the hall snooze off or read books, while the apathetic orators explain how wonderful everything is and how many rights we all have. But out of the blue, a scandalous incident took place at the Engineering Institute. One assistant professor of philosophy decided to actually consider the constitution project. He stated out loud that the articles of the Constitution should conform to the principles of the Universal Declaration of Human Rights. Furthermore, he had the gall to mention that our great country had signed that declaration and was obliged to follow it. Obviously, the meeting was hurriedly called off, its minutes destroyed, and the assistant professor dealt with. All of that's perfectly natural. That's everyday stuff for the Ass of the Universe. But perhaps you think his colleagues secretly shook the professor's hand and unanimously, even if quietly, supported him? Maybe deep in their hearts they were proud of him? Maybe they at least sympathized with him? No, everyone got totally furious because the Institute was immediately beset, like wasps to honey, by all sorts of commissions, so everyone had to write a million reports and plans for the future, and on the whole to tremble for their hides. Everyone sincerely cursed the poor upstart who had caused so much trouble and angrily voted to do him in. That's what he had coming, everyone thought, you live peacefully, doing nothing, and here this guy shows up—he gets a hankering for a Declaration of Rights, the rat!

Obviously, his defense of the Declaration wasn't at all why the professor was fired. It was painstakingly proven that he didn't have the proper qualifications. He didn't understand dialectics and other subtleties of Marxism. He couldn't nurture the younger generation. And so on.

Incidentally, about the younger generation. The students didn't react to this incident at all. The slogan of today's students is: "It makes no difference to me!"

This story also interested me because the ex-professor, after a prolonged and pointless search for work, was offered a job in a library.

More and more, I am beginning to believe that some metaphysical secret—some secret that I haven't grasped yet—lies hidden in libraries.

VV and Lolita liked to walked through Old Town. To them, those few blocks substituted for all of Vilnius. I met them there more than once. "Met" isn't the right word. They would apparently be going down the street, but in essence, they wouldn't be there. You'd think they were walking down completely different streets, through a city they carried within, inside themselves.

They walked through Vilnius as if through a library.

You could put it this way. The houses and side streets of Old Town are yellowed manuscripts, full of wisdom and undeciphered mysteries. The new districts are identical, faceless political brochures or ROF leaders' speeches that differ only in their title, and they're as short-lived as the block construction buildings of Vilnius.

I could go on in this vein, but I'm much less concerned about the library than I am about the readers—VV and Lolita. They could wander the streets for days on end. A strange pair: a calm giant with graying temples and a long-legged girl humming something under her breath, perhaps "The Last Tango in Vilnius." They searched for small joys and sometimes found them: a hunched-over, lisping old woman selling the first violets; a bristling little kitten, mewing non-stop, its little pink mouth wide open; a flaming, fancifully formed autumn leaf—unique and different from all others.

Say what you will, but it's miraculous when two worn-out people who have been halfway to hell manage to find such small joys, the way children find fragments of colored glass in a stinking garbage dump.

Lolita's father, Colonel Banys, performed unbelievable experiments on her in her childhood. She was an only child, and her father wanted only a son, an heir to his ideas. He tried to raise a future apologist for terror, a secret police genius. He dreamed of a dynasty of Banys KGB men. He would take the delicate girl to interrogations; he forced her to love the smell of jail. He beat his oppressive philosophy into her head.

It's not hard to guess what vestiges this left in Lolita's brain.

However, it's impossible to guess what vestiges his grown daughter's behavior left in her dear father's brain. No one could make sense of Colonel Banys's brain.

As far as I know, the Lord God denied having created Colonel Banys; he announced he didn't know himself how that one got put together.

I'm depressed by the abundance of "less:" face-less, sense-less, soul-less . . . All that garbage, mold, decay, and paralysis in my head . . . But I can't influence anything . . . That's the way it is . . . and will be . . . for eternity . . . Horror overtakes me, thinking it really could be this way for all eternity . . . It's horrible . . . A sober, hard-working people like the Lithuanians, slowly turning into, or already turned into, lethargic worms of the Ass of the Universe . . . The worst of it is, we probably couldn't live without the Ass of the Universe anymore. We're all imprisoned for life, that's why we don't have the slightest idea of what we'd do if we were suddenly set free. That's just horrible: we really wouldn't know how to live if we suddenly got our freedom. We've already gotten used to being slaves and pushovers. We got used to it just like America's blacks. Just like the blacks of the past century, we are gotten out of bed in the morning, fed, and driven out to work. In the evening, we're fed again and allowed to sing some sad blues. And nothing needs to be decided, nothing needs to be fought for, nothing needs to be thought about. No one will let you die of starvation; they'll always feed you . . . And nothing really awful will happen—in the worst case, you'll get the whip . . . Well, what of it—a lot of people get it . . .

An existence like this grows into the blood, even worse—it grows into the genes. You can no longer live any other way and no longer want to. Released into freedom, you'd probably return to the old plantation yourself and ask to be taken back into slavery . . .

Jesus Christ—what impelled me to be born in the Ass of the Universe?

I'd really like to be different, but there's nothing I can do. I can only console myself with my mlog.

But no one's going to read it!

Even if I were to think up a way to prevent myself from turning into a fat worm of the Ass of the Universe—by what means could I warn other people, other nations, other countries? How could I save them from this terrible fate?

There's no way.

No way, no way, no way . . .


VV doesn't want to withdraw from my life. He sends grim messengers and intrudes into my daily routine more aggressively than ever. His not being here is far more obvious than his being here.

Today this ghost, Giedraitienė, slunk into the library. She stank of overly sour cabbage. But she didn't ask me for a three-ruble note; she wasn't even drunk.

"Vytie is completely innocent," she announced in a smoke-ruined bass, "I'll testify to it in any court. He killed me, not that girl. This is my fault. But it's my rabbits that are most to blame."

She slumped onto a creaking chair, raised one leg over the other and gracefully supported her chin with her fingers. In amazement, I realized this woman must have been a beauty once. In the calmest of voices, she told such a bunch of humdingers that I didn't know what to think.

Giedraitienė raised rabbits; she made a living from them because she didn't receive a pension and her only son didn't concern himself with her. She had names for all of her charges and would take them to graze in a meadow. The rabbits obeyed her like trained dogs. But it was their names that mattered most. One hysterical rabbit with black ears was called Hitler. A stumpy, mustachioed one was named Stalin. There would be a Beria, a Suslov, a Genghis Khan, and a Mengele. There would be—because the rabbits changed, but the names always stayed the same. VV thought them up. According to him, this was so he wouldn't regret knocking them off. Giedraitienė herself couldn't finish them off. She would call on VV's help. He would take some Mengele and do it in with a single blow of his hand. At that moment, Giedraitienė would close her eyes and think about the real Mengele.

"My profession's depressing," she explained in all seriousness. "Who's going to kill them for me now? Maybe you could? Or maybe you know someone who would want to buy two hundred sixteen rabbits?"

I felt an irresistible urge to get all two hundred and sixteen names out of her. It would be a macabre map of VV's hatreds. I invited that witch home. I suppose Molotov was driven to invite me home by exactly the same sentiments. She gladly agreed.

"He ordered the very ugliest, mangiest one to be named Plato," she said, standing up. "He'd let that one die on its own—no one would buy a fur like that, anyway . . ."

I listened to Giedraitienė's tale until nearly dawn. The names of the rabbits got all confused; there were too many of them. Robespierre or Freud didn't surprise me, but I was shocked by Mozart, Camus, and Beethoven. Beethoven was a large female with floppy ears who would tap the floor of its cage to the rhythm of the Fifth Symphony. Every week, VV would knock off some Kant, Picasso, or Confucius.

Note: Giedraitienė related the following words of VV's to me, stated as he knocked off yet another rabbit:

"Unfortunately, they'll all be born again. Killing makes no sense at all . . . Unless you'd murder someone in the firm belief that by dying a martyr's death, he'll be reborn into a better world, or a better age."

This thought is worth taking note of. Otherwise, Giedraitienė's confession turned everything upside down. I found out that VV would visit her shack every week. A man who didn't visit his own father took care of some half-witted drunk. By the way, I slowly started to suspect that she's no half-wit at all. She eagerly handled the things in my collection, inspected them with a shrewd glance, and read the newspaper clippings and letters.

The thought flashed through my mind that it was no accident at all that she had shown up, that she had been sent to spy out my collection and was merely distracting my attention with her stories.

Everyone in the Ass of the Universe who has even the slightest serious little thought suffers from paranoia. It's grown into our blood. You immediately start thinking they want to steal that thoughtlet from you, and do you in because of it. You imagine spies everywhere. When you talk on the telephone, you don't doubt for a minute that you're being listened to.

If you're even a little bit out of sorts, it even seems as if someone is secretly recording your thoughts. This type of paranoia is a fundamental characteristic of the Ass of the Universe.

I asked, straight out, why VV was so kind to her.

"One way or another, I am his aunt," she answered calmly. "Actually, I'm practically his mother. Magdelė never gave a thought to Vytukas."

I hiccupped no less, and went into the kitchen to fix some coffee so I could digest this news. The situation was totally Vargalian. Up until now, I hadn't even suspected he had an aunt.

"Yes, his mother," Giedraitienė muttered, pacing around the room. "To my little sister Magdelė, Vytas didn't really exist. She kept forgetting his name. Her only child was of no concern to her."

"So what did concern her?"

"She was a reader. All she did was read. The make-believe world of books was much more real to her than life. You know? A book can be charming, but you always understand it's just a little pile of paper. But in her head, everything was upside down. To her the world of books was the great reality, and life—an utterly boring book you could fling away whenever you wanted. When she was reading some novel, she'd even start dressing in period costume and speak that country's language. Sometimes I'd come by and I wouldn't be able to talk to her: she'd be stammering in English."

"He just gravitated towards me," Giedraitienė repeated, "sometimes he was closer to me than my own child. Robertas felt a morbid envy towards Vytie, but he'll have to help him now."

My mlog is crawling with colonels. Here another one's showed up—Colonel Giedraitis.

Suddenly I realized who it was, that horrible evening, who was grunting as he scrambled through the bushes, and then walked deliberately towards the black car. I was hanging out next to the Banys's garden cottage, and I got a good look at that graying man. It was Colonel Giedraitis. I know this now as clearly as if his name had been stamped on his forehead. He had a finger in that nightmare too.

They had prepared everything in advance. Don't tell me they planned Lolita's death in advance too?

Giedraitienė kept meandering and embroidering her ridiculous theory—supposedly, VV hadn't killed Lolita, but her, together with all of her rabbits. And then suddenly, as if it were something everyone knew, she blurted out:

"When I went to prison because of him . . ."

It seemed I'd been hit by lightning. I swallowed her shoddy story as if it were a writhing snake.

"My very existence stretched all his nerves to the limit," she confessed sadly, "I'm the living rebuke of his past."

I listened to her disjointed tale, seeing it all with unusual clarity: a calm stream, its bend sheltering a few houses out beyond town, and a hollow overgrown with bushes where VV would come straight from the forest, risking his life, apparently completely unable to leave his childhood memories behind. I saw Giedraitienė's hurriedly prepared packet of provisions: a piece of ham, three cucumbers, and two thick, fragrant pieces of bread. The flowery towel with which the naked VV dried his reddened body, not in the least self-conscious in front of his aunt. Her tale was so vivid that I believed it all.

But Giedraitienė's legends lacked elementary consistency. According to her, VV reigned over the neighboring forest brothers; he would give the leaders his grandfather's instructions. I believe I've already mentioned that the elder Vargalys secretly coordinated the forest brothers' actions. I can't conceive why VV would have needed to endanger the entire unit to save his life. I'm even more confused about why he would have denounced the go-between Giedraitienė, his provider and protector. One sentence of Giedraitienė's made me prick up my ears immediately. Robertas, after all, couldn't have done it, she muttered indistinctly, he wouldn't have betrayed his real mother. According to her, in a moment of weakness VV had given the entire unit away, and then disappeared for parts unknown. She was the only one who knew about his betrayal, so she was constantly gnawing at him—the living reproach of his conscience.

I'd say two facts destroy her hogwash. First, VV really was imprisoned; there are way too many witnesses. Second, his leader Bitinas's unit was in operation for at least several years after VV's arrest.

I was much more interested in the news that a couple, a brother and sister who once looked after VV's mother, were still living quite peacefully in the village of Užubaliai.

I'd never even dreamed there could be live witnesses. They could tell me about VV's childhood! They could give me the link my mlog most lacks.

My mlog, compared to life, is as orderly as the alphabet. Life is much less coherent. After listening to Giedraitienė's ravings, I was planning to end up at VV's mother's nurses by early morning. But I ended up there after something like a week, because Kovarskis suddenly came to visit me and from the doorway announced that VV had visited him just before his fateful outing to the gardens.

"He dissected my stiffs." Kovarskis announced, "He often liked to amuse himself that way. Maybe he was a secret necrophiliac."

I didn't believe a word he said; these fantasies are Kovarskis's secret predilection. He thinks there are too few genuine horrors and abominations in the world, so they need to be invented too. That's all very well for him. I suspect he doesn't know himself which parts of his stories are true and which parts are complete fiction.

"You mean to say VV trained himself in advance to cut people up?"

"No," he answered in a somber voice, "Vytas would only prepare brains. The rest of it didn't interest him. But the key thing is that yesterday I was questioned about it by this humanized phallus."

I immediately knew he had the detective in mind, the one who had prowled around the library too. Kovarskis always had a knack for describing people accurately. I'd love to include Kovarskis in my collection, but he's as slippery as a snake. Even when he's drunk he never talks about himself. You can't figure him out. What is he, a man of such talent, doing in that morgue?

"That guy got nothing but shit, anyway. I told him Vytas and I would guzzle grain alcohol, and that he was terrified of corpses."

I looked at his twinkling eyes and wondered—is he one of us, one of theirs, or no one's? I had to risk it: life isn't lived without risk.

"What, do you suppose, was VV looking for there?" I asked carefully. "In those brains."

"Cockroaches!" Kovarskis replied, without blinking an eye.

I had barely managed to include Giedraitienė's rabbits in my collection when other creatures started determinedly intruding on it too. I have cockroaches in mind.

The cockroaches in the den VV had set up between the library's bookshelves. Cockroaches in the brains of the dead. Cockroaches in all of my acquaintances' apartments—bold, menacing, invincible. The cockroaches of Vilnius are no longer an object of nature, rather a purely metaphysical one. It's impossible to overcome them. The best poisons from Holland and Germany affect them once and only once. They return after a few days and just get fat on the poison. They're secretly watching us when we empty our bowels in the toilet or make love to women. There's even cockroaches in birthing centers. They accompany us from the first moments of life. And accompany us to our very death-bed. Cockroaches breed even inside sealed refrigerators.

I visited VV's mother's former nurses anyway. They met me by the gate, as if they had been waiting there for a long time. Little brother seemed enormously suspicious: he demanded I show my documents. The two of them lived on a farm, and where the village of Užubaliai itself was tucked away, I never did find out. Apparently a minimalist artist had decorated the interior of the cottage: a table, chairs, and a shelf. Even the curtains were patternless. The owners looked like ascetics from the Middle Ages: thin, tight-lipped, untalkative.

Like a magician, Julius (that's how he introduced himself) pulled out a bottle, filled three shot glasses and snapped his fingers:

"We'll drink the first one on an empty stomach!" he said threateningly.

It was pure grain alcohol. Julius glanced at me more agreeably and poured seconds. Janė (that was his sister's name) somehow, who knows when, managed to quickly cut up some sausage. Outside the window a red sun was solemnly setting.

"You see, this guy was just here," Julius said after a silence, "who was pretending to collect material for an encyclopedia. But he gave off a familiar smell."

That was how I found out that the detective had already managed to make a visit.

"So, what are you collecting?" Julius inquired rudely.

Suddenly I decided I had to tell them about my collection and my mlog. They understood everything immediately.

"Oh, you want to understand the world, for whatever that's worth," Julius stated calmly.

We drank grain alcohol all night long, and the two of them kept on talking. They never went to church, so the confessions they had never made had been accumulating for years. They didn't spare themselves or defend themselves. They really did make confession: they tried to remember all their sins, not hide them.

After the war, the Vargalys house was left without owners. The two of them drank the fine wines that were left behind and paged through incomprehensible books, until the Russian soldiers arrived with some guy who pronounced them Vargalyses.

"So we're part Vargalys too," Julius smiled wryly.

"We sat out two months in the can for being Vargalyses."

"Why didn't you deny it?" I asked, somewhat drunk already.

"What's the difference? When they found out who we really are, they sent us to Siberia, anyway."

"Bullshit," Jané suddenly interrupted. "We both wanted to somehow atone for our sins against the Vargalyses."

That's how their great confession began. Jané and Julius were abandoned as children; they went forth into life from an orphanage. The mythology of orphanages is difficult for those of us with parents to understand. We can't comprehend the belief penetrating the orphan's soul that he is, at the very least, a prince kidnapped by fairies.

Orphanage mythology stated that Jané and Julius were left by an expensively dressed lady who swore to come back for them later. Actually, they don't even know if they really are brother and sister. All their lives they felt a secret attraction for each other, but they lived like

361

brother and sister. The Vargalyses took them in as servants. According to the orphanage mythology, they seemed like they could be Janė and Julius's parents. And "could be," to those throwaways meant "probably were." Slowly it began to mean, "without doubt they are." This was obvious nonsense for many reasons, but it didn't seem to matter to Janė and Julius.

They remembered the Vargalyses with sympathy and a strange, pathological love. Telling erotic stories was among Julius's duties; he had to tell them to VV's mother while giving her a daily massage. She utterly loved erotic stories, even though she herself, both of them confirmed, didn't sleep with her husband after VV was born. Janė had to suffer with VV's father's illnesses. He was a terrible hypochondriac; he surrounded himself with potions and pills.

"It was Vytie I was sorriest for," Janė explained. "They would really torture him."

The mother taught VV every day—up until he was grown. Two, three hours at a time. Who knows what she would teach him, but she didn't leave him a free minute. She was a maniac mother: she was afraid that if her son were separated from her for even a minute he would instantly be ruined.

"I'd feed him secretly," Janė burst out, "The lady was a vegetarian and a dieter, so she forced Vytie to starve too."

The two of them considered VV their younger brother. God's ways are mysterious: the two of them loved and protected VV, but began hating his parents more and more. They figured everything this way: the Vargalyses are trying to atone for their guilt; they don't pile them up with work, pay well, but won't acknowledge what mattered most: that they are their parents. This paranoid idea slowly took over Janė and Julius's entire being; they rose and went to bed with a single thought in their heads: how to take revenge on their traitorous parents.

Even now they couldn't agree as to which one had thought of killing the Vargalyses first.

Julius's pure alcohol slowly did its dirty work: it all seemed unreal to me, you'd think I'd been listening to some legends. I saw VV's mother proudly pacing the house's winding corridors. She wanted to do good for everyone, but didn't know how. I saw VV's father: pale, his hands trembling, but able to kill a bull with a single blow of his fist, if need be.

I saw the young VV too: frail, downtrodden, frightened of who knows what, pressing up against Janė, who protected her little brother. Suddenly I noticed Giedraitienė's absence; suddenly I remembered that her tale was completely different.

"Yeah, there was a cow like that around," Janė confirmed. "She was dying to charm everyone—even the barnyard animals. She'd mince around even in front of our dog. And her boy, they say, was a spy for the *stribai*."

"What aunt? What sister?" Julius eyes widened. "Why, she's a Pole! Her maiden name's Stefanovič!"

I no longer tried to make any sense of it or understand it; all I did was listen avidly. Janė and Julius related how VV's mother drowned herself. At that moment, the war was driving exhausted uniformed men through their yard. The first to appear were the Germans.

"Why are you retreating?" Vargalienė asked them all. "Why are you retreating when you have technology like that? What—do the Russians have better?"

"Technology's useless, ma'am," explained a polite little Silesian German. "My machine gun jams when it overheats, but they just keep coming and coming. This week I've mowed down some thousand Russians, but they just keep coming and coming, sticking out their bare chests. Technology has its limits, but the Russians are limitless. We don't have that many bullets, ma'am."

The next morning the Germans moved out, and Vargalienė announced out loud:

"We'll be overrun by locusts, giant locusts. A single one can bite off a person's head."

VV's father, forgetting his potions, was sipping champagne.

"But they've already been here," he kept saying. "They're not locusts. At best they're stinking, starving, dirty little people."

But Vargalienė didn't hear anything; she just kept repeating that it'd be better to kill yourself than to wait for the locusts to devour you.

Janė and Julius were still considering how to execute their metaphysical decision. However, VV's mother beat them to it; she drowned herself like some Ophelia. They pulled her out of the creek themselves; they were the ones who rolled her into the wagon. Vargalys's pockets were bulging with banknotes. There wasn't a single soul around. VV had disappeared somewhere; the two of them should have knocked off his father (their father), but they couldn't do it.

"She was lying on the hay with her head tilted to the side and looking at us with glassy eyes. I kept waiting for her to open her mouth and say: 'Locusts.' I forgot everything; all I could do was look at those glassy eyes. I still dream of them."

"Me too," Janė echoed.

VV's father rode off to the west with his wife's corpse, completely forgetting his son. The wagon creaked off after the setting sun and melted into oblivion. All that was left lying in the yard was a graceful, austere, thousand-pound sterling note.

Only now do I understand why VV hated his father so: he couldn't forgive him for forgetting him.

Most of all I regretted mentioning my mlog to them. Up until then, no one knew about it. I've been jumping up in my sleep with a nightmare for several days now. What the hell got into me?

By the way, don't you find locusts remarkably similar to cockroaches?

The locusts and cockroaches so affected me that I got interested in all sorts of abominations: Old Town garbage cans, backed-up sewer pipes, and the city's public toilets. The latter are interesting in a purely semantic sense. The writings on the walls of toilets are the last refuge for free speech in the Ass of the Universe. A person squatting down to make an effort manages to give birth to a crumb of truth together with his excrement. Apparently, the need for it is physiological.

Unfortunately, *homo lithuanicus* doesn't even keep a toilet log. Practically all of the writing in Vilnius's public toilets is in Russian. This isn't the result of etiquette or upbringing. *Homo lithuanicus* simply can't even poop the truth. He can't even write up toilet walls.

This is an essential characteristic of *homo lithuanicus*. Muscovites of all sorts still hope it's possible to say this or that, to change this or that, to wait for something. *Homo lithuanicus* knows *a priori* that it's absolutely impossible to say, expect, or hope for anything. That's why he doesn't waste his breath unnecessarily; he's supposedly saving his spiritual potential. It's just that no one knows what for.

What do I have in mind? Concrete results. The world knows of some dozen Russian writers. But they don't know of any Lithuanians, and they won't, because the Lithuanians don't waste their breath over anything; they're supposedly saving their spiritual strength.

*Homo lithuanicus*, unable to express himself freely, would rather carry his soul to the grave without it ever being put to use. That's how nations die.

By the way, about the extinction of nations. The Hungarians, Czechs, or Serbians one meets, with a single voice, claim that we should be proud of being Lithuanian. You've preserved your language with such a monster next door! You don't realize yourselves what a heroic deed you've accomplished! Even the Irish lost their language!

But that's meager consolation. The Irish remained Irish all the same, while language . . . Perhaps I'm horribly mistaken, but if a few Lithuanian Joyces would show up, or a Beckett and a half—let them write in Swahili for that matter. But let them at last write, paint, or play music.

But they don't write, don't paint, and don't play music.

There's something here I don't understand.

*Homo lithuanicus*, unfortunately, realized only too well that to lose is very easy and comfortable. Then you can blame everything in the world—just not yourself. Lord knows, it's really comfortable. And gracefully, elegantly sad. *Homo lithuanicus* tends to do nothing but feel sorry for himself and bemoan his melancholy end.

I was so affected by my trip to the Vargalyses' past that I even forgot VV's most recent exploits. I no longer dreamed of Lolita with her disheveled hair, or that wretched house in the garden. I took up an interest in the past.

I don't get along with my subconscious. It interferes with writing my mlog. My brain's probably full of cockroaches. Or maybe it's simply gotten overgrown with fat. It must be that Lithuania cannot give birth to an mlog genius.

Beset by these kinds of thoughts, I ran into Šapira, an old Jew and VV's former neighbor. VV called him Ahasuerus. That was irony, apparently. Quite the Eternal Jew—the embodiment of austere elegance and stable business. Šapira's shoes shine even in the worst slush, his suit never gets wrinkled, and his hair doesn't get disheveled. He looks half the age he really is. Šapira is a walking calculator, a walking clock, and a walking encyclopedia of the black market. VV used to play chess with him, even though he didn't otherwise care for chess.

"Such a clever head for playing, and he fritters his time away," Šapira used to say regretfully when he lost.

He would beat everyone else, so he would invite VV to a duel over and over again.

"Fool," he would say, losing yet again. "You should honor a gift from God. With that kind of talent, you could be a millionaire."

I don't think Šapira was really all that mercenary. He merely thought that if you had an aptitude for that kind of business, you should use it.

Šapira turned out to be virtually the only person in Vilnius who didn't in the least believe VV could cut a person into bits.

"If I were in the investigator's shoes, I'd check out all the Narutis thugs," he mused sadly. "Comrade Vargalys used to like hanging out there, but he turned into a normal person later. I'd think the dregs of Narutis hated him for that. It could have been their revenge."

Šapira is always right. I had no right to leave out an object of such significance as the Narutis. VV was always attracted by its characters. He felt like a pig in shit at the Narutis.

What pig, in what shit?

In the old days I used to go there myself, out of curiosity. I would drink some dreadful slop with this ex-security agent Mackus. After Beria was shot, Mackus was responsible for the destruction of NKVD documents. He burned everything he was supposed to, but he kept the files on several acquaintances for his own amusement. He showed me the record of VV's interrogation. That's the type that attracted VV to the Narutis.

The Narutis wasn't a bit changed. The same grotesque figures drinking the same grotesque slop by the tumblerful. I never felt comfortable there. I spat out the last gulp of wine straight into the tumbler and got up, but someone commandingly put a hand on my shoulder. Turning around, I should have gasped, but I just smiled wryly.

"Let's go for a walk," the drab detective said hollowly. "It's not at all far."

He didn't explain anything, didn't ask anything. To tell the truth, it was all obvious to both of us; we were too lazy to pretend. He took me to Teodoras Žilys's studio.

We turned into a gloomy side street; he went first. It occurred to me that this detective was ideally faceless. No one could paint his portrait in words. You could describe his walk, his gestures, you could even characterize his smell—but not his face, not his eyes. He had no face; he didn't even wear a mask. I don't think he was human at all.

He was a bleeding hemorrhoid of the Ass of the Universe.

It's difficult not to be astonished when a hemorrhoid starts pontificating.

"We're walking in the same footsteps," the detective's back said to me. "God has hitched us both to the same wagon."

The Old Town pigeons cowered at his words; cats in the gateways arched their backs in fear.

"What are you looking for? What are you looking for, my man?" the hemorrhoid's back continued. "Was he your friend? Buddy? Lover? What are we looking for in this world, pal? Why are we tracking down these cold leads?"

I followed in his footsteps, even though nothing was forcing me to act that way. I could have spat at the hemorrhoidal back and gone on my way. I could have flown off together with Vilnius's grimy pigeons. But I followed behind him. Some excited women were shoving by the shoe store: apparently, something had been delivered.

"Maybe we're looking for his diary? His notes? A tape recording? A sign?" The detective turned into a gloomy gateway without even glancing to see if I was following. With commanding movements, he marched up some creaking stairs. He spent an instant picking the lock.

"No man's land," he announced, finally turning around. "The studio doesn't really belong to the wife, but no one's agreed to move into a dead man's quarters. What are you staring at? Come on in. I'll use you like litmus paper. Like an indicator."

Teodoras's artist's quarters didn't look at all forsaken. Obviously, Lola and VV stopped in here. The bunk squeezed between the sculptures was unmade; if you wanted to, you could see the marks of a naked body on it. At the head of the bunk loomed Teodoras's famous Iron

Wolf. I winced when I saw its head had been taken off. The headless symbol of Vilnius. And we are all Vilnius's headless wolf cubs.

I stared in wonder at the nude drawings of Lola; all the walls were covered with them, from floor to ceiling. It was only Lola here; she reigned supreme. The studio was overflowing with her divine nudity.

"You've slept with her yourself?" the detective asked brusquely.

There's no way I can devote myself to my mlog. Now I'm hindered by a disgusting mortification I simply cannot forget.

Lola was visiting me at the time, like always, sitting with her fabulous legs stretched out. Things were particularly difficult for her: VV had fallen into one of his deep crises, and at those times he wouldn't spare even Lola. She looked like a mangled bird. I simply felt terribly sorry for her. I kneeled down next to her and stroked her head like a little sister's; all I wanted by it was to console her. She raised her eyes and fixed her penetrating, hypnotizing gaze on me.

"I understand," she said after a moment, "I understand everything."

Slowly, lazily, she stretched out her hand and ran it over my short hair. I never thought a person's hand could be so soft.

"Oh, you, lambkin, my little lambkin," she said in a strange, sharp voice. "Do you think I'm blind? You think I don't feel anything? You think I'm a hyena, tearing off pieces of live meat for my own amusement? Don't worry, I understand, I understand everything."

I, the fool, still didn't get what she was talking about. I'm not naïve or a complete idiot; I was simply lulled by her penetrating gaze.

"I understand that you're melting, swooning, and sighing with love, my dear lambkin. You've earned sainthood; you could walk into heaven alive. You knew your love wouldn't be requited. You didn't have the slightest hope, but you sacrificed yourself for me anyway, helped me, saved me. You'll be rewarded—here and now. And later, whenever, the moment you want it."

Speechless, I watched as she began a nymph's striptease. At first her bare toes began to stir, to wave, then the feet, shins, knees. The lightweight summer skirt appeared to slowly rise by itself. The buttons on her blouse slipped out of their holes themselves. She rocked her hips dreamily, caressed her thick hair and didn't shut her mouth for a minute:

"This is all I can give you, but believe me, it's no small matter. It's a great deal, Martis. I'll be your slave; I'll be as obedient as death. You'll be my ruler—for a while, a very short while, but you will be, really you will."

She finally shut her mouth and froze; she finally realized what my eyes, my entire pose, was screaming. But she wasn't flustered in the least, she just shrugged her shoulders and buttoned up her blouse.

"I wanted to do what was best," she uttered hollowly. She nimbly jumped up from the floor. "Don't see me out, I'll find my way."

She hurried off just in time—in another minute I would have slapped her and forcibly thrown her out. I was boiling all over, until I was overcome by a boundless mortification and disappointment. Disappointment with the entire human race.

She dared to think that I'm a sighing lover, of all things! She dared to imagine that I'm swooning and spiritually masturbating while I'm looking at her!

Blows like that happen to a person once in a lifetime.

What let her think that? Perhaps I did love her in my own way—like a younger sister. Perhaps I was a bit afraid of her; I didn't dare to drive her out when she got too tiresome.

However, I never gave her cause to humiliate me like that! I was accused of being a cat with its mouth vainly watering in front of some out-of-reach bacon.

I lost faith in the entire human race. People can't believe anymore that it's possible to help someone without expecting a concrete reward. People don't believe in any honorable feelings anymore. People are despicable.

After that evening, Lord knows I almost started despising her. I tried to find excuses for her, but an angry feeling kept winning out. Even if she considered me a swooning ninny, she could have rewarded me some other way. She could have offered at least a smidgeon of human warmth and closeness, she could have trusted me with some sacred secret, with anything but her defiled body, even if it was a nymph's body. I hated her.

Only her death settled everything at once. Death demands objectivity. I had put that undeserved wrong out of my mind until that faceless detective reminded me of it.

369

The detective spent a long time turning a roll of canvas, which he'd pulled out of the Iron Wolf, in his hands; he even sniffed at it. He started tracing over that canvas with a finger, as if he were reading a missive—line by line. I snuck a glance over his shoulder: it was a painting, a peculiar painting—countless tiny little faces in identical frames, very tidily arranged and painstakingly painted. All of them different, and at the same time unbelievably similar.

"The dispatch has been found," the detective muttered indistinctly.

I was totally confused. The detective rolled up the canvas and stuck it into an inner coat pocket. It seemed he only now remembered I was there.

"Let's go, pal," he said in his usual brusque voice. "Let's get out of here. And not a word about it to anyone."

We went down the creaking stairs and through the crooked little yard. In a corner by the gate, some grubby kids were playing store. The five-year-old saleswoman was arguing furiously with customers of the same age.

"I told you, they didn't bring it!" she yelled in a shrill voice. "I'm the only one here, and there's lots of you! You should try working in my place!"

The detective stopped and with his hand outstretched announced very loudly:

"My sense of smell is no worse than that dog's!"

Who knows how good that dog's sense of smell was, but his body was horrific. Extended along the ground, deformed, of an indescribable color. His ears dragged; it looked like he'd step on them any minute. But that dog's eyes were intelligent. They weren't the eyes of an ordinary doggish intelligence.

While I was staring at that degenerate, the detective disappeared. I saw his back off in the distance already. He paused in front of a store and apparently exchanged words with some hunchbacked dwarf hanging around the entrance. That was a remarkably strange detective.

Suddenly it occurred to me that I didn't have the slightest idea of where he had materialized from, or who he was. He didn't show anyone any identification. *Homo lithuanicus's* frightened respect for the authorities is so powerful that he's immediately speechless as soon as some brazen guy casts a commanding eye. In amazement, I came to the conclusion that I have no reason whatsoever to consider him a representative of the KGB or the public prosecutor.

Absolutely no reason. Who knows who he was.

Behind my back, the children continued to skillfully imitate a Soviet store's irritations and quarrels. If you want to get to know a country, then carefully observe what the children there play.

The children of the Ass of the Universe unfailingly play the Ass of the Universe.

The detective nonchalantly showed up a few days later at the library. He wasn't in the mood to so much as greet me.

Stefa's glommed on to me again. I've spent many lonely bachelor nights with her, so I can't just rudely push her away. You might ask— why did I lay my hands on her? You need to get by somehow. If a person can't stand all kinds of sexualizing, it doesn't mean that . . . Besides, it doesn't have any greater significance for my mlog.

So, Stefa glommed on to me. She mysteriously rolled her eyes and whispered in a muffled voice:

"What do you think, would my testimony save Vytas? I know every-thing. I saw everything. Even though she's dead, that slut wants to hurt him."

The quieter two women's fight over a man is on the surface, the meaner and crueler it is. I dampened Stefa's heat somewhat. I decided to invite her over to my place after work.

"Don't even ask, I can't!" Stefa shot back, and turned her insulted little fanny at me. "You're not at all concerned about Vytas!"

If she only knew how concerned I am about Vytas! He's all I'm concerned about. I wanted to straighten her out, but I restrained myself.

I always did want to straighten everyone out. The last gasp of an educator's talent hasn't left me yet. I'm dying to teach children and grownups. I want to teach cats and dogs. I'm a teaching maniac. If I lived in a normal country, I would found my own sect.

What would I teach?

I would lecture everyone on the history of *homo lithuanicus*; I'd explain that creature's composition and structure. I'd attempt to eluci-date why he doesn't hunger for freedom. After all, everyone, absolutely everyone, seeks freedom. A bird struggles to escape its cage. A dog tries to break its leash. Even amoebae try to drift freely. It's an instinctive desire. You have to have a brain, an intellect, to be able to destroy it. Only humans manage to do this. And *homo lithuanicus* manages best of all. That's why it's imperative to research this creature thoroughly. Perhaps he shows us all of mankind's future. Perhaps in understanding his structure, we'll realize what's unavoidably awaiting all the rest.

And so forth, and likewise.

Thank God I live in an abnormal country, where it's forbidden to found any organizations. My sect would dissolve after a month or so.

I'd bet no one would want to listen to me.


How is *homo lithuanicus* produced? Starting early in childhood—best of all, still in the cradle—is of prime importance. The core of this process is its essential three-pronged approach. The government teaches one thing and real life teaches something entirely different. And in addition, the parents, shutting the door, tell sad legends about some Lithuania, a nation, an honorable past, and similar oddities.

Opponents could maintain that such a situation is characteristic of all the nations of the Ass of the Universe. By no means. The Russian past can be praised out loud, without the door shut—and that's where the essential difference lies.

So, the junior *homo lithuanicus* grows up in triplicity. He's told about a nation, but the kid doesn't find one. He's told about socialism, but the kid can't see it anywhere. He's told to make a buck, but the authorities plant him in jail for that.

So, the above-mentioned creature gets completely confused and turns into a nothing.

Opponents will ironically observe that *homo sovieticus* is exactly the same. That is a totally unscientific assertion. *Homo sovieticus* is a creature that lives a double life, or more accurately, two lives. *Homo lithuanicus* doesn't live a single one. *Homo sovieticus* deciphered the structure of the Ass of the Universe and adapted to it. *Homo lithuanicus* didn't adapt to anything, which is why he's a nothing.

A real, true *homo sovieticus* isn't so terribly rare among the Lithuanians. But the much more common and more interesting case is that of *homo lithuanicus*.

*Homo lithuanicus* isn't entirely doomed. He just sleeping the sleep of hibernation, like a badger in winter. He secretly believes that one of these days the sun will shine again, the snow will melt and the flowers will bloom.

Poor, naïve *homo lithuanicus!*

Once again, I give grave warning: the entire world is slowly turning in the same direction. Everyone who throws out his books and stares at the television, or ruins his cousin over three thousand dollars in questionable earnings, is unconsciously laying the groundwork for that kind of existence. All it takes for the lethargy viruses to start madly multiplying is to doze off spiritually.

And then all that's necessary is for the Ass of the Universe to slowly slither into such a snoozing, virus-infected country.

I've lost the main thread of my mlog again. And there is no Ariadne to offer me hers. If Ariadne was named Lolita Banytė-Žilienė, then for a guide like that, no thanks. I never did understand what fundamental quality of hers she wanted to realize.

Let's say I haven't managed to realize my teaching talent.

Gediminas failed to embrace the entire world: neither mathematics, nor music, nor heaven knows what else.

VV failed to realize his love.

I frequently think about what it was VV really loved. Without question, he loved his past and all of his dead—the real ones and the ostensible ones. And the same goes for himself—the young VV brimming with strength and illusions, who is long gone and could never be again. But worst of all—he loved people. I emphasize—people. Not robots, not the little worms of the Ass of the Universe, but people, who are rarer and rarer in our ancient city.

I know quite a bit about his mature life, and I've learned a few things about his childhood, but the worst is that I know everything about his wretched end. Not the end of his life, just about VV's end.

Sometimes you'd give anything not to know what you know.

More and more often it occurs to me that one of the most important roots of VV's destiny was his infertility. He and Lolita desperately needed to adopt a child.

I'm probably talking nonsense. VV needed his own and only his own son, and he couldn't have one. When he was drunk, he kept threatening to go to Siberia to search for something he had left there. I knew very well what he had in mind.

It seems to me that all of VV's horrifying sexuality was a futile attempt to return what had been lost to the ages. You'd think he secretly believed that sooner or later quantity would turn into quality, according to the laws of dialectical materialism.

VV was a sexual Marxist.

VV would fall hopelessly in love every week, so Stefa had to constantly suffer the torments of hell. It was even funny to hear VV's sighs and see his misty eyes. But that youthful love would last no more than a week. To me it seems he was always waiting for Lolita; he would deceive himself for a while every time, thinking she had already come. I vaguely remember Nijolė and Aušra. And then there was Aurelija, Rolanda, and another Nijolė. But Vaiva was the one I took the most note of.

I didn't like her from the start. A giant Afro-style haystack of hair, coarse movements, and an insolent disposition. She radiated the attractiveness of a healthy young filly. She was screaming for a good stud.

Vaiva immediately became the leader of our community of women. Even Elena would let her take the lead a bit, to tell dirty jokes and pour cognac in the coffee. Vaiva went after VV shamelessly, sometimes almost obscenely. She offered herself publicly, I'd say triumphantly.

I don't know myself why this disgusting story sticks with me. I really don't want to remember it, but something keeps telling me it's significant.

I could certainly understand VV's male desire, but I really didn't grasp how a person that intelligent could make that filly his closest associate. She was in his office constantly and knew all of his plans. VV became nervous, rude, and I'd say stupid. This couldn't continue for long; it ended suddenly, and in an unanticipated manner.

I became a completely unintentional witness to that affair. I stayed in the library Saturday night, as I wanted to look over some books that weren't allowed out of the building. I had no idea that VV and Vaiva had stayed. For some reason I didn't reveal myself when I noticed them; I stuck in the background. Perhaps unnecessarily. It would have been better if I hadn't seen all that.

VV stood by some shelves and paged through a book, while Vaiva rubbed up against him like a giant cat. He didn't pay the slightest attention to her, but she didn't let up. She got on her knees and nonchalantly started undressing him: voluptuously and vulgarly, panting heavily. He just continued calmly paging through the book. Now it was too late to come up to them; my only option was to exit quietly, but, in astonishment, I continued watching them. I saw something I'd never seen before. The details really aren't necessary. I'll only say that when I returned home, I scrubbed my entire body some ten times under the shower, attempting to wash off an invisible slime.

And VV stood there as if it were no big deal, looking at a book!

By then it was too much for me. I wanted to run away, but I bumped into a bookshelf and several volumes fell off with a huge crash. I was so frightened I couldn't even manage to move. The crash seemed to awaken VV from a deep sleep. He looked around with amazement at what was going on. A look of disgust appeared on his face. He suddenly went nuts.

It was horrible to see how he worked her over. I thought he'd break her arms and legs, smash her skull, and knock out her teeth.

"Kanukas!" He screamed this strange word out loud. "Kanukas!"

I didn't even try to rescue her. I'm a coward and I know it. I had absolutely no desire to be crushed like a pear. For what? For Vaiva? For that filly? She got what she deserved.

I couldn't understand any of it: neither her earlier triumph over VV, nor VV's strange fading, nor that outburst of madness. Afterwards VV immediately recovered his good mood, agile wit, and sense of humor. You'd think he'd come out of some kind of fog. He didn't remember Vaiva at all.

What did he beat and kick between the shelves that horrible night in the library? Surely not a rather vulgar young woman with an Afro hairstyle, not a real human being. But what?

By the way, right after this incident, the infamous story of Sharon Tate and Roman Polanski broke. The satanic Manson, Sharon Tate's brutal murder, and so on.

For a few days afterwards VV walked around under a black cloud and moved his lips soundlessly. It seemed Roman Polanski was his brother, or maybe Tate his sister.

I took note of this, because VV grimly predicted that Polanski would shortly meet with a vile misfortune. And that's what happened: he was accused of raping a minor.

VV would frequently make predictions like that, and he always guessed correctly. He saw connections everywhere that were invisible to everyone else.

I saw that Polanski, in one of his own films, *The Tenant*. Lord knows, he somehow reminded me of a much smaller version of VV.

A hundred, a thousand times I've thought: God surely could have made VV smaller: his size, his passions, his edginess, his . . .

It seems to me that someone already undertook narrowing a person's soul. Was it Dostoevsky perhaps?

It's an extremely dangerous pursuit. Extremely. The ROF also undertakes this narrowing of souls. Apparently, cutting off even some evil or ugly human characteristic can't be done—it'd be better to cut off an arm or leg. Even without some appendages, a person's essence remains. But without a part of his brain, a person instantly turns into a worm of the Ass of the Universe.

I either have to admit that VV could have been the way he is and only the way he is, or not talk about him at all.

I agree: sometimes he was horrible. I agree: Lolita met a particularly hideous end. But apparently it couldn't be any other way. Otherwise, there would never have been a VV, either.

I ran into Giedraitienė again today. She was hanging around Lenin Square and constantly glancing at the KGB building, looming on the other side of the street.

"Hello there!" she wheezed. "I'm waiting for Robertėlis. He'll save Vytelis. I'm going to testify in court."

All of VV's female acquaintances have decided to testify at his trial, which most likely won't ever happen. However, this one didn't appear to be brimming with resolution; rather, she seemed confused. In the meantime, a sullen, gray-haired little guy who resembled an alcoholic carpenter darted out the side door of the KGB building. I had seen this guy before. Alas, I had seen him before.

Colonel Giedraitis got terribly frightened. It seemed he simply couldn't think of how to escape. Lord knows what a particularly elegant meeting between a mother and her son that was. The conversation didn't last long, maybe a minute. In the end, Colonel Giedraitis gave his mother a rather hard shove and instantly disappeared into the opening of the door. Giedraitienė, rubbing her injured side, smiled widely and muttered in a low voice:

"He'll listen to his mommy. Robertėlis is a good son. He was always an obedient child."

The detective stopped zooming around the library, but I run into him suspiciously often in the street. He's dressed differently every time. It's rather strange—a normal Vilnius male simply doesn't have that many different clothes.

A ridiculous idea came into my head: you'd think he was copying a character in Teodoras Žilys's painting—the one that was always dressed differently, staring out of a bunch of identical little frames.

Who knows if it's at all possible to help VV. Without Lolita he won't last a month. I can swear that there won't be any trial—he'll pine and fade away much earlier. It's a shame you can't write in our jails and leave the world your last opus.

Son of a bitch—that would be some opus!

Unfortunately, for the time being I have to make do with my mlog and my collection. Incidentally, the latter is rarely replenished anymore. Here's the latest record:

I went to the clinic to fix my teeth and listened to the conversation of two old coat check ladies. Both of them were Russian—that's why their chatter attracted me.

They discussed Brezhnev's health. They concurred that he had no more than a year or two to live. They discussed his possible heirs.

"Poor old man," one lamented. "And he'll be replaced with another old man."

"No, no," the other one disagreed. "This time it'll be a younger one."

"It won't, it won't," the first one glumly replied. "Now all those old men have to be in power for a while. Just think about it: they killed so many people, they were literally bathing in blood. So now they have to rule at least!"

What would a *homo lithuanicus* have to say on this topic? He wouldn't discuss it in the first place. It's absolutely the same to him who from the ROF will die or which leader will replace another.

There's only one area in which *homo lithuanicus* expresses his true feelings. That's in athletic contests.

From my collection:

An international basketball contest was held in Vilnius. There were several strong teams playing: U.S. students, the Spanish I believe, and some others besides. Plus a USSR team and—lord love a duck—a separate Lithuanian team. Someone from the central Sports Committee overshot himself terribly.

Truly beautiful things were going on inside the Hall of Sports. When the USSR team played, the crowd unanimously cheered for their opponents, whoever they might be. There was thunderous cheering when the Russians missed. Quite understandably, this didn't last long. Militiamen started guarding the entrances to the Hall of Sports. They dealt with it quite simply: they'd take the ticket away from anyone whose expression they didn't like. Anyone who tried to protest was taken straight to jail. I myself paid a ten-ruble fine. See, I tried grumbling that they didn't have the right.

The free spaces that opened up were filled by workers chosen for that purpose, Russians, of course. They supported the USSR team quite harmoniously.

Sincerity can still be found at sporting competitions. Less and less often.

Lord knows VV should have played basketball. That's the only chance for a Lithuanian.

They're fond of passionately telling us that a Harlem black's best chance is basketball or boxing. In this respect, all Lithuanians are black.

Lithuanians aren't allowed to occupy high posts in the hierarchy of the Ass of the Universe. They aren't allowed to rule themselves, much less others. Basketball is all that's left.

We're all basketball players, resignedly plotting mind-boggling plays, gracefully tossing balls into a dead-end, tied-up basketball hoop.

Lolita never loved VV. That's the kind of conclusion you invariably come to when you find yourself in a dentist's chair. It's impossible to explain to a civilized human being what a Soviet dentist's chair is like. It's impossible to explain what Soviet medicine is like.

It's not just our life, our wants, and our minds that the ROF seeks to control. They have to control our life and death too. The medicines ROF representatives get are absolutely off-limits to a normal person. You're left to quietly die of something that special medicines cure in two weeks.

From my collection:

The wife of a friend of mine had a raging temperature; death, as they say, was staring her in the face. By mistake, her frantic husband dialed the number of a special hospital. A doctor came over immediately, quickly looked the patient over and declared the situation critical. Only then did it become clear that the doctor had driven over through a mistake, and that my friend's wife didn't belong to the special hospital class. The doctor packed her already prepared syringe away and headed for the door. My friend begged her on his knees, even suddenly invoking the Hippocratic oath. The doctor, fittingly, looked at him like he was nuts, and calmly left.

Hippocrates with all of his oaths, and even more so all of his followers, are particularly dangerous dissidents. We must wage a fierce battle against them!

When they're putting in a filling for you that will fall out in two weeks, knowing perfectly well that it will fall out, there's nothing left to do but decide that Lolita didn't love VV.

The arguments: If she loved him, why did she drag her father into this? Why did she turn poor VV's head, why didn't she marry him? Why didn't she have a baby with just about anyone and then announce that it was VV's child? He would have been delighted. Why . . .

The whole thing bores me to death. I'm afraid. I don't know what of, but I'm terribly afraid. I am as alone as the finger of God in the Ass of the Universe. Even Stefa refused to comfort me—physically at least.

Lolita didn't love VV. She was egotistically striving for something. VV was striving to comprehend mankind, to defend it from the encroachments of the Ass of the Universe. And what of it? I'm striving for that too. And what of it? I'm not going to hand out proclamations on Broadway; I'm not going to publish my own newspaper. Even if I were to find the philosopher's stone, no one would find out about it, because I live in the Ass of the Universe.

It's a place where you cannot have any hope, because all hopes here are in vain. It's a place where you won't do anything, because it's impossible to do anything here. It's a place where it's dangerous to even think, because you could suddenly hit on something good. And that's the worst of all: you could know an important secret and you couldn't tell anyone about it. No news can escape into the world from the Ass of the Universe. We're sealed up inside. Better to not know anything. At least your conscience won't gnaw at you.

I don't know any VV, I've never heard of any Lolita. I haven't the slightest idea what the word "Colonel" means. Amen.


I've had it with that dog already. He's hanging around under the windows all the time. I could swear it's the same dog I saw by Teodoras's studio.

Suddenly I feel like writing my will. This means I must decide two things: what I will leave behind and whom I will leave it to. The first part of the answer is obvious: I'll leave my mlog and my collection.

But to whom?

To my son? He's not interested in it and never will be interested. He's generally not interested in anything. I'll confess to a terrible secret: my son isn't even a *homo lithuanicus*. He's long since been a typical *homo sovieticus*.

Of course, I could have left the results of my lifetime efforts to VV, but even that's no longer possible. I look out the window at my shitty neighborhood. The street is just the same as anywhere else. Everything's exactly the same as it is anywhere else. This isn't even Vilnius, who the hell knows what this is. At least the color of the buildings could be different in each neighborhood, or at least some minor detail. But oh, no! The Ass of the Universe doesn't need any differences, much less my legacy.

Anywhere else, absolutely anywhere else, I would find someone to bequeath my legacy to. Just not here. Just not in Vilnius. Just not in the Ass of the Universe. Damn it, and I'm an atheist to boot, so I can't expect to be judged and rewarded even after death, in the other world.

I'm not going to throw a stone at that horrible dog. He's just the one I'll going to leave my collection and my mlog to.

I threw him a piece of sausage, but he didn't even deign to sniff at it. I felt ashamed, no less. Lord knows that's not the kind of dog you should throw slop to. That's a completely different kind of dog.

That's my heir.

Son of a bitch, it should be possible to at least save the children. It takes my breath away to see what's being made out of them.

The ideology of the Ass of the Universe declares that no human can oppose the inevitable progress of history. If that's the way it really is, then Lord knows it's best not to bring children into the world at all. And even better not to be born yourself.

But what can you do, if you've already been born?

I'm going to go get drunk.

After two shots: it's still the same.

After four shots: it's absolutely the same.

After six shots: I remember I sat here once with VV. On a day of incredible miracles, when our store was visited by the great emissary of the ROF, Suslov.

Have you noticed how I never even mention any Lithuanian masters? They mean nothing. They're zeroes.

That's why I keep on talking about all sorts of Molotovs, Suslovs, and other similar Leodead Brezhnevs.

We don't even have our own masters!

It was at this very bar, the Erfurtas, that this disheveled little guy with a pistol under his jacket glommed on to us. He kept intruding; probably he'd noticed right away that we didn't give a shit. In turn, he let us know it meant nothing to him to fill the two of us full of lead.

"Just try to escape!" he emphasized, waving a crooked, drunken finger.

He badly wanted to make a deep impression on us.

"Yes, Suslov is as scared as a rabbit," he mused, commanding his tongue with difficulty. "Do you know why? He's visited you here twice and kept having to run for it. The first time, in Kaunas, there was a boxing championship, your guy beat ours up, but the judges of course declared ours the winner. Your guys got angry and sent the militia packing. The boss had to flee in a special airplane. He came calling a second time—that guy of yours poured gasoline on himself and burnt himself up. Another riot. Now he's sticking his neck out for the third time. He's shaking like an aspen leaf, but he's still sticking his neck out. Why?"

"Criminals always return to the scene of the crime," VV snarled, but the guy didn't understand him, he only understood Russian.

"Hey guys!" he roared, "I'm all right, believe me. I'm a sharpshooter and I love to hunt. I up and shot a forester. So, what came of it? Five years of hard labor, or you're welcome to come work for us. Now I'm a gorilla. And so be it! I'll eat caviar and drink champagne for breakfast. What other choice do I have?"

The gallant agent downed a glass of champagne in one gulp and instantly passed out. He was hit by an alcoholic stupor. VV suddenly got up and hurried down the stairs. I followed behind. I follow behind someone way too often. We got into the store without a hitch. Inside, Suslov really was shuffling around with his entourage. VV unexpectedly dived into the workroom and returned with a giant, maybe two-foot-long knife. I saw a murderous gleam in his eyes. I jumped in front of him without hesitating. You'll laugh, but I used to play rugby. I smacked him in the stomach with my head and pushed him back into the workroom. VV lost his breath momentarily, however, he could have recovered at any instant. There was a pile of pineapples standing next to us; I grabbed the biggest one and smacked him on the head. I've never hit anyone on the head with a pineapple before. I'd never even tasted them. VV was more astonished than stunned. I grabbed the knife away from him, threw it into the refrigerator, and blocked the door with my body.

"Wake up!" was all I managed to say.

"Maybe you're right," VV unexpectedly agreed. "If there's no dragon, there's nothing for the brave prince to fight. Let's go down to the river. Let's go down to the river."

We hurried past all the guards who were posted near the store without anyone stopping us. It was only then that I saw I was still holding the pineapple in my hands. Apparently, it had become our authorization.

The two of us quietly polished off the pineapple next to the Neris. We sat down on the river bank across from some construction site, the Exhibition Hall, I believe.

VV really loved the banks of the Neris. Although, hell, he didn't love it. The Neris drew him the way a loved one's grave does. He would talk about something to the dirty current of the Neris. Probably the Neris seemed alive to him.

After eight shots: I don't care about anything, everything is shit. Well, I'll have some hangover tomorrow!

I was quite right: the hangover is horrible. I no longer know whether today is Sunday, or if it's Monday already. I went over to see this alcoholic writer, got some money, and was sent out to buy some wine. I bought twelve bottles.

Elena will fire me. But no, the KGB won't let her. After all, I'm working at the place they chose for me.

I'm behaving like a pure-blooded *homo lithuanicus*. Alcohol is a great way to hide from everything.

Monday or Tuesday: "non stop."

Tuesday or Wednesday: I called Elena at the library and told her I had a dreadful cold. Elena, in the voice of an executioner, announced that even over the telephone I reeked of booze. I boldly asked her to join me; I said girls were in short supply. Apparently I hit the mark. You can never figure these communists out. She giggled and in a completely pleasant voice explained that I had better show up at work in the morning. Otherwise, it was curtains for me.

Just think—it was already curtains for me a long time ago.

I've emerged from those nightmares at last and can work at my mlog again. I perceive the world with unusual clarity. A frequent post-binge sensation irritates me intensely: the feeling that everyone's following you. Even the basement cats. It's a truly disgusting sensation. It seems like everyone's counting the remaining minutes of your life.

I shouldn't drink so much.

VV mentioned a dragon more than once. Maybe he really did feel that he was a prince, sent to save the princess. Was Lola really a princess?

But oh Lord, what a prince!

Apparently, a person can only take it up to a certain point. If you pass that, something disintegrates. Something irreplaceable.

VV would raise essential questions much too often. Let's take the most ordinary one: who really rules the ROF? Asking questions like that is deadly. But what an itch! No person in their right mind would believe that all sorts of Brezhnevs and Suslovs actually rule. So, who really does rule us? Who planned and created the Ass of the Universe? Who assembled the mechanism for crippling children?

VV asked questions like that all the time.

I'm secretly envious of him. We all envy people who do what we couldn't do or wouldn't dare to. I, for example, do nothing; I just rattle on.

Unfortunately, people can't choose their path in life. They have what they've been given—from heaven or from hell. By the way, I suspect it's nothing more than two different names for the same institution. So, I live a wonderful life. Like everyone else, I don't do anything at work, and for that, like everyone else, I receive beggarly alms. I dress like everyone else. I eat what everyone else eats. In addition, I get to feel spiritually superior to others. Those others certainly don't envy VV, write an mlog, or gather a collection.

Lordee, I'm such a brave man!

Someone has rummaged through my room. Everything has been left lying where it was, even the dust on the tables hasn't been touched, but someone has obviously rummaged through my things. By the way, it's long since time to get used to it. In Vilnius even dissertation manuscripts disappear without the slightest trace.

I wouldn't be the least surprised if some uninvited visitors didn't from time to time cut off a little piece of a person's arms or legs. Anything is possible in the Ass of the Universe. No one would be surprised by it, no one would object. They'd grumble for a week or two, then they'd get used to it and wouldn't pay attention to it anymore.

That's the psychology of the inhabitants of the Ass of the Universe.

If it were different, the Ass of the Universe itself couldn't have been constructed. The psychology had to be altered first. Alter the children. Create new conditional reflexes.

And so on.

Why have they gotten interested in me just now? I know the answer, but I'm afraid to say it even in my thoughts. I'm afraid to even think about it.

Every inhabitant of the Ass of the Universe is afraid to think. What's more, he imagines a nimble dwarf with piles of notebooks, cameras, and tape recorders is poking around in his brain.

For the third day, I haven't been able to add to my mlog. I haven't even touched it. The word "touched" sounds funny when you're talking about a purely metaphysical object, doesn't it?

However, the only means of staying alive in the Ass of the Universe is to devoutly believe that the fruits of your imagination are far more real than so-called reality.

It can't be otherwise. In the Ass of the Universe, everyone, by definition, is shit. So the only solution to avoid simply fertilizing the earth, is to turn into thinking shit. This is a byproduct of the Ass of the Universe, and its most advanced creation: thinking shit, or *homo lithuanicus*.

The abyss gazes at us, or perhaps we've long since been gazing at the world from out of the abyss ourselves.

Everyone keeps asking me about VV. But what can I say? "The man has killed the thing he loved, and so the man must die." Every Lithuanian, intentionally or not, has murdered an abundance of things he loved. He's murdered everything he loved.

Although for some reason, he hasn't killed himself. Apparently, he never loved himself.

If even I feel this way, how must VV have felt all his life?

How must he have felt visiting Lolita's father, the Colonel Banys we all love and revere?

After all, Lola's father wasn't some abstract monster to him. VV had literally been through Colonel Banys's hands.

I know this for a fact. That former KGB agent Mackus showed me the records of VV's interrogation.

It follows that Banys and VV were especially old acquaintances. The executioner and his victim.

Christ Almighty, what's going on in the Ass of the Universe!? Some things are impossible to comprehend. Impossible to bear. Impossible to even imagine.

VV had to socialize with Colonel Banys on a family footing!

Maybe, like that time in the Erfurtas store, he had a gigantic knife inside his jacket? Or maybe Colonel Banys was already sharpening his own knife?

One way or another, when two such opposing elements collide, the occurrence of a cosmic catastrophe is inevitable.

I never liked to wander through Vilnius, but now that's all I do. VV was a true poet of Vilnius, while to me this city always seems to be a soulless mechanism, a vengefully wheezing machine of inexplicable purpose. Even on our madly spinning planet, speedily rolling to its doom, cities of this kind are rare.

We don't have our own city. There are Moloch cities and tyrant cities. Museum cities and Tower of Babel cities. Snoozing cat cities and cities of the absurd. But ours is a nothing.

Like the Jews, we're eternal exiles, but we don't even have our own Israel. I'll add that we don't even have our own Jerusalem.

Dammit—why was I fated to be born in a crossroads trampled by whoever gets the urge? Why did I have to be born in the Ass of the Universe, through which every conceivable shit pours?

The *dramatis personae* of VV's life have encircled me. Every day I run into Kovarskis and Šapira. I have something to ask each of them, but the questions still need to be precisely formulated. I'm greeted pleasantly by Giedraitienė carrying rabbit furs, and once I even ran into Julius, the Vargalyses' former servant. We both sucked down a glass of vodka and parted without saying a word to one another. What's there to talk about? Everything's already been said. The circle narrows. If a gigantic fish were to come swimming up the avenue and swallow me, I wouldn't be at all surprised.

I'm someone's skinny little beer-drinking prey.

I'll add: every *homo lithuanicus* is inherently someone's prey.

I'm drawn to those horrible suburban gardens, the place of Lolita's murder. Inexorably attracted, as if I were a murderer unable to resist showing up at the scene of the crime.

I'm wracked and torn by the desire to tell everything. I can't stand it anymore. I'm horribly afraid. I have to put this down in my mlog as quickly as possible—for the first time in my life, I wonder if I might not make it.

I'm just looking for a rationalization. I'm magically drawn to those damn gardens, and that's all there is to it. I admit: by complete coincidence, I was there the day Lolita was murdered and I saw everything. I saw absolutely everything.

There! I've up and said it. What will happen now?

For the time being, nothing. I haven't been struck by lightning. My pulse didn't even speed up. That's it; I'm getting a taxi and going.

I've visited those gardens many times. Several writers have plots here.

387

One lets me live in his pseudo-folk villa during the summer. That's how I commune with nature. Ha, ha—that's a joke.

Today I'm nothing more than a pathetic little spy, the victim of my own dangerous whims, glancing about fearfully. Every *homo lithuanicus*, whatever he does, glances about fearfully: maybe I'm doing something wrong, maybe someone will get angry.

That other evening I was also going down this path towards my temporary abode. I didn't care if I ran into the owner or not—I knew where the bottles were stashed. The owner wasn't there; with a glass in my hand, I went out on the porch to smoke. The Banys's garden cottage was right in front of me. The sun was already setting; it shone straight in my eyes.

But today it's foggy and windy, the leaves blow along the little road as long as they don't get stuck in a puddle. I turn into the Banys's garden as if I knew exactly where I was going and why. I pause at the entrance. Next to me a gray bird, hanging upside down, serenely pecks at the wild grapes.

It's unbelievable, but the door to the house isn't sealed. Any curious passerby could look over the scene of the crime. And I, by the way, am an interested party.

Interested in what?

In any event, I cautiously step inside. Inside it smells of decay, of dirty, rotten leaves. Lolita's flaming blood has soaked into the old floorboards. The marks shine like my spilled school ink once did. This is where Lolita was defiled, chopped into bits.

Suddenly an insane notion besets me: to find even the tiniest little piece of her body and take it for myself. There must, there has to be more than that congealed blood left here.

My collection contains everything. All it's lacking is a little dried piece of Lolita's body.

The drone of an engine drew my attention on that other damned day. A black Volga reluctantly crawled up the small hill to the Banys cottage. The two of them got out quietly. I was doubly surprised: the cottage was completely empty all summer, and Lola never rode in her father's car. For good measure, I downed yet another glass. When I went out onto the veranda again, the Volga was no longer there, but I sensed that Lolita and VV had stayed in the cottage.

The first question: who brought them here? The father himself? His driver? If they came themselves, who drove the car away?

An elderly man sat by the cottage next door and smoked greedily. He meant nothing. He was meaningless. A gray-haired, glum little guy, with a beaten dog's eyes.

By no means do I think he was meaningless now, because now I know it was Colonel Giedraitis sitting there.

I'll have to arrange everything logically later. Divide all the triangles into rhombuses and pentagrams. The triangle: VV, Giedraitienė, and her son. What role did Colonel Giedraitis play in this story? After all, he and VV knew each other since childhood.

Childhood! . . .

I had a desperate itch to spy on VV and Lolita. I was somewhat inebriated; a passion for spying seized me. I talked myself out of it, I believe out loud even, but I knew I was going to sneak up to the cottage window and listen to what they were saying anyway. With the purest of intentions: just for my mlog. A person finds rationalizations for just about any amoral action. Only the Marquis de Sade was conceptually amoral—for the sake of amoralism itself.

That damned night I was downright driven by the devil. I was the devil's flunky.

To my astonishment, they were chatting very calmly and idly about Vilnius's history, Lolita's grandmother, the village enchantress, about breeds of dogs. Banalities or mystic poeticisms. Apparently, that was how they talked all the time. I stood there, my arms scratched by thorns, and swore a bit. I was horribly disappointed in them. It seemed to me that they were surely obliged to speak meaningfully, inhumanly, supernaturally. And there they sat making small talk. Then they leisurely started undressing. Without any heights of rapture, each one separately, very efficiently. How ordinary! VV introduced himself to Colonel Banys, and now rides in his car. Everything's perfectly ordinary. Banys's driver brought the two of them to the garden to make a bit of love in the arms of nature. How charming!

I went nuts. VV's horrible and lamentable story was taken away from me—no, no, not from me, from Lithuania, from the entire world. He was no more than an ordinary, one-dimensional little figure. And I was no more than an idiot.

My fury kept growing. I decided to march over and tell them what I thought of them. Thank God, I didn't burst in the door; I carefully glanced in through the window.

And it was then that I saw.

No ghosts have showed up yet. I crawl over the floor and look for even the tiniest little piece of Lolita's body. I saw it: there were a lot of them, a whole lot of them; they were practically broken down into molecules. Give me at least one molecule of Lolita's body!

At first glance, I saw everything at once; I grasped everything beyond a shadow of a doubt. VV stabbed her with a gigantic knife, just under the right breast, with the accuracy of a professional killer. He went down on his knees, holding up the falling Lolita. She was already dead when she collapsed on him. That was no outburst of insanity; he did everything with precision and a maniacal calm. The worst of it was that in the last moment of her life, Lolita did not fear him; she looked at VV with a lucid gaze and smiled. At first I thought they had agreed to commit suicide together; they had simply been delaying, and that was why they were making small talk. However, VV hadn't the slightest intention of killing himself. He looked around and turned his gaze straight at me. He instantly jumped up and ran out.

I knew he would kill me too, but I couldn't move. It wasn't that I was paralyzed by fear, but by some kind of all-consuming despair. Suddenly I understood that now nothing would be the same. Neither Lola, nor VV, nor me. However, VV jumped straight into the bushes and ran off like a wild beast, breaking the branches and tearing at the leaves.

My second thought was this: he killed the devil's seed; that is, not Lolita, but Colonel Banys's daughter. Maybe she had told him something? Maybe the father said something to both of them? That's probably ridiculous. It's too primitive. People aren't murdered on that account. However, at that moment, that was exactly what I thought.

And immediately I saw Colonel Banys himself.

*Just one molecule!*

*It was here, she was lying right here!*

She was lying on her back, very naturally, as if waiting around for Colonel Banys to solemnly step inside. Not the slightest little muscle on his face twitched. With difficulty, he kneeled down next to his daughter's body. He looked at her for a long time, as if choosing a favorite spot. Then he determinedly pulled the knife out of the wound.

Blood gushed out onto the floor.

I didn't see them, but I sensed quiet figures milling about. A pair stood in the bushes beyond the cottage; another figure a bit further, near the road. The black Volga's darkened headlights stared at me indifferently.

I didn't see the first cuts; apparently I must have been looking around at that moment. When I glanced into the cottage again, Lola was already headless. Her father was slowly, methodically slicing her into pieces, at intervals wiping his bloody hand on her belly. For some reason it occurred to me that this certainly wasn't the first time he had done this kind of work. For a while I watched as if I had been mesmerized, without any horror—it was much too similar to a nightmarish dream. But I could pinch myself as much as I wanted. I could close my eyes and open them again. Nothing helped: it was reality. For another moment yet I saw all the details. Then I felt sick. Thank God, I didn't scream or run off horrified through the bushes, I just threw up.

I'm pathetic; I'm the embodiment of *homo lithuanicus*. I didn't think of Lola or VV, I thought only of myself. I knew that if someone ran into me here it would be the end of me. I had seen too much. I was the only one to see Colonel Banys's deed; even all his assistants were some distance away. All I thought of was how to escape unseen. I tried to vomit as quietly as possible.

That I succeeded in.

I don't know how many times I've jumped out of bed at night, always seeing the same thing in front of my eyes: Colonel Banys, methodically butchering his dead daughter. That was all I saw, even though in my dreams I probably ought to have seen a more accurate, deeper truth: Colonel Banys butchering VV alive.

That's all I know for sure. If someone were to even suspect that I know this . . . It's awful just to think about it.

But I know it all the same.

They say even gods cannot change the past. So then who the hell needs gods like that? I demand that this be changed, erased from my memory! Can't I demand at least one thing in my life?

I haven't been able to shake off the feeling that I am Lolita, sprawled on the garden cottage's floor and being cut up into little pieces. That's the way I walk the streets of the city—being cut up, or already cut up. And slowly going out of my mind. The only reason I don't go entirely out of my mind is because my mind is cut up into little pieces too.

An awful thing happened today: I was getting ready to write the horrible history of the garden into my secret computer disk and ran into the insolent traces of an intruder. Someone had read my secret records, my entire mlog.

I won't explain it in detail; a non-specialist wouldn't understand anything anyway, but believe me—the record was encrypted four ways. No one could get into it without me. It seemed that way to me. I didn't appreciate people's ingenuity.

But no—I did appreciate it. After all, I had entered one last marker. If the record had, in spite of it all, been read (and that, it seemed, was impossible), I would know it immediately.

And I did know it immediately. They didn't appreciate my ingenuity, either.

So, that's how things stand. I was saved only because I hadn't had time to enter the horrible story of the garden. And the records in my brain, I trust, really are impossible to read.

Why am I convinced of this? If they could, they would have read it a long time ago, ergo, I would have long since been disposed of.

Devilishly logical.

Everything else is completely illogical.

Why, why, did VV murder Lolita? If it were a Shakespearean play, I'd believe everything—Will liked to throw corpses about. But this is life, after all! VV's, Lolita's, my life!

Yes, life has everything: absurdities, horrors, and afflictions. But I still can't believe that this inexplicable nightmare belongs to my life too.

I must get closer to VV's secret, to Lolita's secret. On stinking Vilnius's secret. I must understand them all, whatever it may cost me.

The most metaphysical object in the Universe is our office. Under no circumstances can it chance by so much as a hair's breadth. I burst straight into the coffee break with all my horrors and questions, and I was charmed.

"I know for sure that French perfumes are going to go up in price," Gražina immediately declared, yawning openly. "Good lord, they're already insanely expensive."

What does she need Dior perfume for? Explain this to me, for God's sake.

"True, true," Marija agreed at once. "We've decided to change our apartment. You know, the five of us are squeezed into two rooms. We saved up the money, found someone willing to sell . . . and the Executive Committee won't allow it."

"What Executive Committee!?" Gražina declared mercilessly. "It should be called the Exasperation Committee. They do everything just to make things harder."

"That's their purpose," Beta says enigmatically.

"The price of coffee is going up again . . . And cigarettes . . ."

"Yesterday I went to the studio, I look and . . ."

"Rimutis says to me: Mommy . . ."

And so forth, and so on. No one has been chopped into bits. No one is sitting in jail. Everything is the same as it always was, and you, Comrade Poška, are simply hallucinating.

Ever since that silly telephone conversation during my binge, Elena looks at me gently and benevolently. I answer with a polite smile, however, a holy terror grips me at the thought that she could demand something of me too.

"Martynas is in a lively mood today," she chirps, "I'm thinking he'll run out for a wee bit of cognac. I saw that Tallinn had these tiny little bottles. You could bring back a few . . ."

Only now do I see the homemade cookies and petit fours on the table. Apparently, it's someone's name day. Well, okay, a little cognac is a little cognac. Why just a few bottles—I'll stuff my pockets full.

Outside, the dog greets me immediately. He doesn't come closer; I'd say he follows me respectfully, like an uninvited entourage. Suddenly it occurs to me it would be worth my while to talk to him. Maybe he speaks English? If he follows me the whole way, I'll talk to him on the way back.

At the crosswalk, a roaring truck nearly runs me over. That's weird—trucks aren't allowed on the avenue. Some special truck. Every Soviet law has so many exceptions that no one person knows them all.

There was a line by the tiny little bottles. Apparently our office wasn't the only one that had gotten wind of them. I take five of them; I'll take the others home. Very handy: you open it up, suck down those four ounces, and there's none left over; the cognac's alcohol doesn't evaporate.

Vilnius has been engulfed in fall by now. The sidewalks are wet, the air damp. Glum figures creep by: they're known as Vilniutians.

The dog is waiting for me on the other side of the street; he knows I'm coming back. Unconsciously I start thinking up elegant phrases. I really must talk to him. I'll ask him about VV.

A gigantic truck roars right by the sidewalk, it's already turned around. Good Lord, he's hunting me down. I'll check out his plate number and report him to the traffic police.

Suddenly I spot Šapira on the other side of the street. I even get a pang in my chest. I must have secretly been hoping to run into him, because suddenly I realize what I have to ask him. I know now: it's just one little thing. Everything is unexpectedly falling into a harmonious scheme. If VV . . .

I quickly stuff the bottles into my pockets and jump into the street at an angle. Šapira could disappear at any minute, he's always in a hurry. I see his old face, his wise eyes. I know now what I'll ask, I almost know the answer too, I hear a horrible roar from the left, I turn and

# PART THREE
## TUTEIŠA

Miss Stefanija Monkevičiūtė. October 30, 197 . . .

The best thing would be to buy a heap of gauze and cut it up, like I did that time in Palanga: everyone was running to all the sundries stands, bitching and griping, while I, as pretty as you please, bought myself a roll of gauze, cut it up, and it was first-class; this always happens when you're at a resort or on the road, where there's neither the conditions nor friends, nor even a good place to get washed up, you go around stinking like a barrel of herring, it seems everyone's turning their nose away, although men probably don't smell it, only dogs, like this one: raising his crooked snout up, his doggy balls hanging, it's so embarrassing, you could just sink into the ground—you probably should go to the veterinary pharmacy, sometimes they have some sitting there.

When they picked him up all bloody, the street got blurry, I couldn't see the people anymore, his gray tweed jacket was all bloody, the guy with the mustache was emptying his pockets, pulling out one little bottle of cognac after the other, and everyone nodded their heads: see, he was drunk; but I knew for sure that he was stone-cold sober, I wanted to say something, but the mustachioed guy emptied the last pocket and everyone shut up, because at the very bottom of the pocket was a finger, a real, live human finger, I swear to God, just like in Vasilis's hut in the swamp: fingers of corpses, faded bundles of herbs and dried bats all hanging on strings; he went out for ten minutes and you find him run over, with a human finger in his pocket. I'm not afraid of death, I've seen lots of them, but I can't be calm like that young miss: a light blue miniskirt with patch pockets, a Dior handbag on her shoulder, looking down indifferently and chewing gum, she doesn't think it at all horrible, she's a genuine Vilniutian, but I'll never understand this city as long as I live, I'll live like I did in my village cottage in rotten, stinking Bezriečjė; you won't resurrect Martis, but I would like to so much, I never wanted to resurrect anyone that much, except maybe my cat Tomas, when Stadniukas crushed his skull, and I cried and rubbed dirt into my eye—later Vasilis washed it with a potion of herbs and cussed quietly, I kept saying: poison Stadniukas, poison him, but Vasilis answered gloomily: he's poisonous himself, poison wouldn't touch him; Stadniukas was the live embodiment of the Soviet government in our area, he did away with both people and cats. Martis was as independent as a cat, but as modest as a teenager, he always had to turn out the light beforehand, and he'd get terribly flustered if I squeezed that thing for him, but afterwards he wasn't a bad little guy, true, not large, but is size what matters; now he's lying there dead like an executed forest brother—how many of those I saw in my childhood; they would lay them in the village square: maybe someone who recognized them would gasp or start crying, then they could send them off to Siberia. That's why I don't cry or gasp now, I've seen too many of them, I've built up a reflex, like dogs do; that dog has gone completely nuts, he keeps getting underfoot with his snout raised—shoo, shoo, you monster, get lost, I'm not a bitch, I'm a member of the human race, even though Vargalys would sometimes say: you're not entirely of the human race. Lord only knows what he had in mind, no one could understand him.

No one could understand any of the Vargalyses; their and the Giedraitises' villas stood a bit outside of the village, by a bend in the creek;

they were genuine Lithuanians, but who knows what the rest of us were, tuteiša, tuteiša, the men repeated during the registration after the war when they were asked for their nationality, in other words, we're locals, but what could they say: to this day I don't know what part of me is Polish, what part Belarusian, or how much Lithuanian blood there is in me, now I think in Lithuanian, but maybe I thought some other way earlier. I threw a last glance at Martis, if they ask me to come identify the corpse, I won't go, because I always remember that early morning in the town square; father rattled off to get a spot at the market, and I said I wanted to go pee-pee, but that wasn't what was on my mind at all, I stayed in the square because there were four of them laid there, and not a living soul about. I was terribly interested in that growth between men's legs, I knew I'd never have one, I kept grabbing boys in that spot, but how are you going to feel up a grown man, and here they were, four of them no less; I knew they were sleeping and wouldn't wake up, I could take a look at them in peace, the morning was cool, their clothes and faces didn't concern me at all, I unbuttoned the one on the edge, felt around with a trembling little palm, but I didn't find anything, I spread the slit and saw there really wasn't anything there—just a gaping bloody clot. All four of them were like that; I ran away like crazy, screaming daddy, daddy, but I couldn't explain anything, I just kept repeating: they're lying, they're lying there, father stroked me and whispered: you can't go there, don't go near them, or else you'll be taken away.

I really need to go to the veterinary pharmacy, the trolleybus would be the best way to go, but I can't stand Vilnius's trolleybuses: in the old days they were attractive and mysterious; it seemed that climbing into them you were surrendering to that quietly growling creature, it opened up and swallowed you, you'd melt inside of it, melt . . . Now I find trolleybuses disgusting, I'm a genuine Vilniutian by now, I've already gotten spoiled, better take a taxi, even if I'd rather not spend the money, never mind Elena if it should take awhile; when Vargalys was here you could run around wherever you liked, he would do everything for everyone himself, but that one instituted a regime, we all sit there like sardines in a can. Beta tilts her little head with her bangs and straightens the lace trim at her breasts, the stuff they brought her from Czechoslovakia, well, I don't know if it's all that nice, it's kind of showoffy, although Martis likes lace underwear, he always says . . . liked,

liked, said, said—I can't get used to the idea that Martis is gone forever, funny crew-cut Martis—for sure he'd pick at Beta's lace now, he'd stick a finger between her breasts like it was an accident, but Martis is no more, nor his finger, just that other little finger in his pocket; Beta's pocket's lacy too, Lord, what a show-off, whatever you say, and she asks for five-fifty too—you could go out of your mind.

Marė sits there like the cat got her tongue, Lord, just like a wax doll, you'd think she'd flown off somewhere and left her body behind. Vargalys would often stand there like that. He could stop and fall asleep in the middle of the street: shake him as much as you want, you wouldn't wake him up. The whole family was weird; Vasilis liked to tell stories about them, as if those Vargalyses didn't live right next door, but off somewhere off in the wild blue yonder, back in the days when people still understood the language of birds; their house looked like a fairy tale castle where ghosts live, black blood flows down crooked corridors, and at dusk the obscene bird of night chatters. Many times I made up my mind to secretly look over the House of Horrors, but I never got up the nerve, I was afraid to meet Vargalienė on the creaking stairs with a knife in her hand, or Vargalys's naked father, putrefied like Lazarus. When I saw him again many years later, he was a bald fatty, he panted constantly, guzzled beer, and blathered nonsense, even I knew it was nonsense, while Vytas Vargalys frowned and fumed, his father whiningly begged for money; his pension wasn't enough, he spends it all sitting at the Neringa, tiresomely cursing the government, a government, which, by the way, didn't short-change him like it did other people, it gave him a pension for a few years of lecturing at the University; maybe someone changed places with him, the sorcerer Vargalys was left to live in his house and he deliberately sent a bald fatty, a foolish womanizer, out in his place; he even tried to seduce me—and just think, there was a time when he had god-like powers, mornings the village girls would secretly run around the bend in the creek, Vargalys's naked father would come there, stand on the shore looking at the current, and the girls would gasp and elbow each other in the side: look, look, you'll never see another one like that in your life, no matter how long you look, there isn't another like it, ones like that don't exist. It's horrible what age does to a person. Marė surely has some, she even buys flour in reserve, but how are you going to ask; there should be a special stockpile: whoever buys some puts it in the stockpile, and then everyone can use it, after all, everyone needs it; it really would be nice, but now wrack your brains and stink like a bucket of dishwater.

I can't stand any stench, instantly I remember the wash, scads of dirty underwear soaking in a wooden barrel whose sides leaked, mother's red, swollen hands, kneading the stinking, wet bundle: it would slurp and burble, steaming at the sides—and even the steam spread an overwhelming stench, like those who were lying in the town square, right next to the churchyard. It's no fluke that they say the Germans boiled soap out of corpses; maybe ours was from corpses too, even if it wasn't German—its stench would cover even the stink of sweat. I hated all the soap in the world, it was only later, in Vilnius, that I washed myself with my roommate's soap and I was amazed: my underarms were fragrant, my skin too, even my crotch spread a soft aroma—and again I thought Vilnius really is a city of miracles. But our swamp stank of a bloody past, of tears and rotting trees, people said that once the *stribai* surrounded and drove an entire platoon of forest brothers into the swamp, they got stuck and one by one drowned in the watery peat, while the *stribai* stood on the shore and watched the others disappearing into the black quagmire: only Vytas Vargalys escaped alive and brought out his leader, who was as bald as a rock, with horrible burning eyes, his gaze made birds freeze mid-flight and fall to the ground like stones—the swamp stank because of those forest brothers, it didn't want to take their bodies, at night it kept pushing one or the other up to the surface; lots of times in the mornings the shepherd boys would see one stretched out on the black water, and then sinking back again, condemned to journey that way for the ages: up, down, up, down, giving birth to the unforgettable smell of the mire. I can tell immediately if someone is from our area just by smelling them. Vargalys never smelled that way, that stench didn't stick to him, he was steeped in a completely different one, a musty basement smell—he'd say that's the way the prison camp smelled. He'd get furious if I forgot and started smelling his chest, his arms, his knees; he didn't want to be reminded of those other times, but every one of the cells in his body had soaked up that smell, it couldn't be washed away, rubbed away, or obliterated. I kept secretly smelling Vargalys anyway; that smell seemed to represent his past, which I knew nothing about, because he never told me anything, you'd think he had been born when he returned from the camp. It's drizzling outside the window, what a pain, I really won't get there on foot, it's weird even, how much I've started to love walking by myself, for no reason at all—before I'd run around with my pants on fire, looking for some tasty morsel or something for Vargalys, and then all of a sudden I had oodles of free time, right after that long-legged woman showed up. Lord, I'm talking like a fool, like legs had something to do with it; she bought him off with other things, with her youth first, then probably luxury. Rain or not, I need to get out of here—it's afternoon already, in a minute everyone will start zooming around the stores looking for meat, they'll leave me and Beta to mind the shop, see, we don't have husbands, so we don't go looking for meat, they sigh and say they envy us, but really they think we envy them; they think it's better to have any husband than not to have one at all, even if the husband is worn-out and useless, like Marė's, even if he drinks day and night, like Gražina's, even if he collects branched horns, like Elena's; no, if you're going to take one, then only a Martis or a Vargalys, those two were up in the clouds, but I couldn't fly, maybe I'm too heavy—Lord knows, I need to lose weight, it doesn't seem I eat all that much, but the rolls on my stomach keep getting bigger. Vargalys would bite them and quite seriously offered to sauté me—when was that, it's terrible to remember. As soon as I think of Vargalys, something stirs in my crotch, not a nice feeling, particularly today, I'll really start gushing blood, but as soon as I remember—it stirs: Vargalys was right to say that women think with that place. There's some kind of program on the desk, command lines, GOTO, RETURN, why on earth did I start up with those computers, why aren't I a knitter or a seamstress, I remember I sewed Gražkė a jumper, a loose one out of brown corduroy with big patch pockets and appliqués—it turned out rather nice, Gražkė was even surprised; she's often surprised, there's nothing but surprise on her face, as if she can't understand why she has to live in this world; I don't understand, either, but I don't show this to anyone, even Vargalys never understood me. I was sent to Vilnius to investigate this city, to investigate it using myself like some kind of guinea pig; it's been a long time since I've been to Bezriečjė, a long time since I saw Vasilis, he's gotten completely decrepit, he doesn't recognize me, he sent me to Vilnius, but now he'll never explain why; age does you in, although the old Vargalys was some hundred years old and his eyes still flashed, he did nothing but swear at the food, that it didn't taste good, at the girls, that they were ugly, and he called me a Polish spy, he kept suggesting that he and Vargalys gang rape me, and you could believe the old man could do it. Vargalys Senior, the king of the Jews: they say he stole some thousand Jews from the ghetto and hid them in the villages; mostly children—all the Jews of Vilnius would lift their hats to him, but later they left for Israel, while old Vargalys stayed here and gave lectures on the history of Vilnius; tons of people would cram in, but then they banned him from lecturing because he was always insulting the Poles, and after all, we have the brotherhood of nations. We're all such friends that it stinks to high heaven: the Russians hate the Lithuanians, the Lithuanians the Poles, and everyone despises the black Muslims at the market who sell pears, melons, and pomegranates out of season; the Russians hate the Jews who haven't left yet too, but, most of all, everyone to a man hates the Russians, but I myself don't know who to hate; I'm a mongrel, so one part of me should hate the others: the Polish part the Russian, and the Lithuanian the Polish, but I don't know how to divide it up so accurately, I don't even know what I am—a tuteiša, that's all, even though I think in Lithuanian. It's too bad Martis is gone, we'd be sitting in a bar somewhere now, sipping vermouth, and he would tell me about some new thing in his collection. The first time I saw it, I thought he speculated in clothing, there was so much stuff piled in his room; he was doing an inventory and his son sat in the corner and gave us dirty looks. His son hates Martis, the son is as straight as an arrow, he's a terrible Communist Youth leader, I always wanted to seduce that little hottie, corrupt him, so he wouldn't be so straight; he despises women, riches too; he just hungers for power. I can't stand it when teenagers preach, and that one was always teaching his father how to live, like from some textbook or a newspaper editorial, and Martis would listen with one ear, even though after his son left he would glumly call him the junior dictator; I've never seen a young man who was so ambitious for power, heaven only knows about those apples falling from the tree, no one could make sense of it—the father so intelligent, and the son a Communist Youth activist, a hypocrite and a good-for-nothing. Thank goodness I don't have any children, I'm horrified by my memory of that evening—when Vargalys begged me, on his knees, to keep his fetus. He insanely wanted a son, and I refused, I said, I'll abort it, and later I almost agreed, but suddenly I miscarried—God himself saved me; if kids really turn out so inside-out, like Martis's, then Vargalys's son would have to be some kind of slobbering sadist, like Stadniukas—he'd strangle cats and dogs, since they don't let you strangle people anymore—as it was, Martis's son was there to see, it's all as clear as day, Vargalys is under arrest, Martis, Gedka, Tedka are gone; maybe I really should go back to the village, even old age isn't bad there, no one pays attention to age there, in general there's neither age nor time there, I only sensed time when I ran away to Vilnius. It's just terrible to remember how amazed and flustered I was when I landed on this ant hill; everyone was moving, hurrying somewhere, they had a purpose, and I couldn't even talk to them, I stuttered a mixture of several languages, I wanted first of all to find a miraculous translator in Vilnius who would translate not just my speech, but all of me into this city's language; that wish came true, however strange it may be, all of the others came true too, just not at all like I had imagined, maybe that's the worst of it—if they didn't come true, you can at least hope they still will, the worst is if they do come true, but not in the right way. Tedis grabbed me in the middle of the street and thunderously declared he had to sculpt me; I didn't understand a thing, I didn't even know that there are people like that, who do nothing but make sculptures, but I believed it all immediately, because Vilnius is a city of miracles; I undressed for him without hesitation, while he smacked his lips, kneaded his clay or plasticine, smacked his lips again, carefully stroked my side or even my breasts, he would go off a bit and come closer again, but I wasn't in the least bit shy, I stood there stark naked and felt only pride; later Tedis said he wanted me like a stallion, but didn't dare to even touch me—I was so proud and pure, that's why even now art seems pure and unpolluted to me, although that's probably rubbish. Let it be rubbish, I myself am a slowly fattening bit of rubbish with rolls of fat on my stomach, a wrinkling face, and I'm running like a broken bloody faucet today too, but it's an honor to be even the rubbish of Vilnius, particularly if you're an alien from a stinking swamp, from the kingdom of frozen time; once a year I return to my home town and hurry back as fast as I can: my parents are gone, Vasilis doesn't recognize me, and my brothers and sisters are so foreign, they stink so bad of manure and moonshine, and they talk so strangely that I need a translator again, like I did before. To hell with it—if my underwear's soaked through, I'm done for; I don't have an extra pair. There's no help for it, purse over my shoulder and I'm off for the restroom, its growing stench is inviting me, one look at our restroom would be enough for men to lose their sexual drive for three months: toilets covered with poop and bloody balls of gauze on the floor, women pretend and preen their pretty feathers only in front of men, left on their own they get three times as disgusting, so that later they can convincingly blush at men's filthy talk, which, compared to their own secret filth, is no worse than baby talk. One, two, three, I change the tampon quickly, my last one, thank God, my underwear's clean, one, two, three, and out of here as fast as possible, back into the corridor; Lolka didn't use our restroom at all, she'd hold it in until lunch or run home, I respected her for that alone, she really was clean, not just for show. She was always a bright, long-legged little girl with an insolently protruding little fanny, maybe that's why she died, I remember her genuine naïveté when Tedka started to win her over and she was charmed by his sculptures and the daring of his unofficial shows, she fluttered her long eyelashes and was on cloud nine; I'm probably the most to blame for her getting mixed up in the business of men like that, she followed behind me; I rushed headlong into Vilnius like into an ocean of wonders, and she was still a child—it's not right for a sixteen-year-old girl to be in the company of avant-garde artists, or maybe it's exactly right, who knows. That time she asked me with maddening naïveté: Tedis wants me very much, what should I do; I felt like her older sister, Lord knows, I didn't say anything, my tongue was tied, but my hands of their own accord opened up my purse and handed her a packet of pills. You always act first and think about it only afterwards, men do exactly the same, it's just that afterwards they prove to themselves and everyone else that they've done everything correctly and sensibly, while we just torment ourselves—maybe they really do think more, but only afterwards, when everything's over and done with. If Martis could respond from the other side, he'd for sure prove, with impeccable logic, that it was particularly intelligent of him to get under that truck, that it couldn't be any other way: that's the way men are. Even in our village they'd sit next to a huge bottle of moonshine in the evenings and start jabbering, nothing that happened could disturb those rituals—neither flood, nor fire, nor someone dying. The library corridor is like a tunnel; it wasn't that long ago that Lolka and I would smoke here, hour after hour we'd chatter about everything or be quiet, it was here she admitted she was sleeping with Gedka Riauba and didn't know how to tell her husband about it—I even gasped, thinking of how much that sixteen-year-old innocent had changed in a few years; she looked at me coolly and repeated: I gave in to him by mistake, and now I can't escape, maybe they should fight it out or cast lots, it's too hard for me with both of them. Why is it too hard, I asked like a fool, and she answered: for some reason men want all of me, it's not just that they don't want to share me with others—they won't even leave me to myself, and I haven't yet met a man who was worth giving myself up to hook, line, and sinker; listen, Stef, maybe it's better to make love to yourself, to give up men entirely? I never considered men an unnecessary appendage of mine, it's more like I felt that I'm their appendage, I always got involved with the ones who needed me, I could have had ten of them at a time, I don't begrudge them, I'm generous, Lord knows, generous; I never bother about what use it'll be to me, what I'll get out of it, I've never held on to anyone if they wanted to leave, I never got insulted if they found someone else, I never thought that they used me or took away a part of my essence—a woman should be generous.

"Daydreaming?" Elena's voice startled me. "I've never seen such a sight: you're putting your fingers to your mouth like you're smoking, but without a cigarette. Want one?"

Huffing and puffing, she tears open a fresh pack, sticks a cigarette in my mouth, lights it; she's always that way, she loves to supposedly look after you like you were a little kid, apparently she thinks she's the Big Momma, even though she's nothing but an old brood-hen.

"There were visitors from the Department again today." She rolls her eyes in a hideous way and keeps panting, "they say Vargalys set up secret quarters deep within the library, that he was gathering information from books. This reeks of dreadful things, mark my words. Her father—you do know who Lola's father is . . ."

I don't hear her anymore: I've seen Lolka's father many times, he's a history professor or something, he always speaks very learnedly, but only of the past. Vargalys liked to say it's enough to toss him some concocted historical fact for him to disappear from this world for a couple of weeks, living in the deep past; he's old-fashioned and very pious, once—a long time ago—he burst into Tedka's studio and started begging Lolka on his knees to leave that den of iniquity, and she kicked him with her foot, Lord knows, she kicked her own father with her foot, that's the way she was. Elena rolls her eyes and croaks, she resembles a giant frog, a frog from our swamp, deceptively swollen, its throat puffing, luring you towards it, into the black muck of the swamp, I saw that frog once from as close up as I see Elena now; careful, Vasilis warned me then, that's no ordinary frog, that's Madam Vargalienė.

That time the frog plopped into the thick mush, like Elena now plops into the mush of the library's smells: plops and rows herself off with her fat paws, thank God, I won't have to listen to her chatter.

"What Vargalienė?" I shot back rudely, even though I had heard many times about both Madam Vargalienė and Mr. Vargalys's ghost, smoldering in gray ashes.

And how could I not have heard when my mother, the moment anyone mentioned my birthday, crossed herself three times: after all, I was born that very night in forty-four when Vargalienė met her horrible end.

Vasilis changed me, out of a half-wild village girl he molded the real Stefa, who, you'll find, no longer exists; that real Stefa melted into Lola, Martynas, Vargalys, scattered herself about the streets of Vilnius; it's like there's nothing left of her when she's alone, she must have others, I really need others, I have to find at least one person who can't survive without me. If the grand sourpuss Vilnius can get by perfectly well without me, it's best to go back to the village and grow cucumbers in a hothouse for the market; although it'd be better all around to kill myself than to go back to Bezrečjė—kill yourself with life itself. No, no, enough of hanging around here, better go outside, I can't stand the bookshelves, I can't stand the sticky repository dust, I even hate the books themselves: the best way to drive a person to hate chocolate would be to give him a job in a candy factory.

It's real fall by now, that day in the gardens a wonderful Indian summer lingered: it's drizzling, people are creeping down the avenue, stepping around the puddles, and wet, scruffy pigeons are perched in the square across from the library—and why are they perched there in the rain, what are they waiting for? I didn't even notice how I got into the shoe store, my feet took me there themselves; the brown ones are completely worn out already, I need to look around, even though you always overdo it, the shoes they've displayed in the store window aren't at all bad, you just about decide to buy, start matching colors, sew a skirt, dig a purse out from who knows where, but by the time those shoes make their way to the shelves, their color changes, it fades, you're left with a skirt and a purse that don't match anything, even at the shoe factory it's the same propaganda: if they promise something, then for sure it'll never happen, think that way and you'll never be mistaken, always think that way.

There's a huge line of people shoving at the housewares store—they're selling German kitchen tablecloths, with all kinds of fruit, and hams, and spices, and other colorful dainties. They're drawn so beautifully you even start salivating, but it turns out to be propaganda too—where would you see all of that if it wasn't drawn on that tablecloth; oh, what a show-off, she's fixed herself up in a light-checkered suit—pants, a long jacket nipped at the waist—it doesn't matter that it's rainy, she's probably dreamed of it for half a year, she's gonna wear it now no matter what, let it rain cats and dogs. I should drink some coffee, maybe eat something too, I haven't had a thing all day and it's eleven-thirty already; in the Žarija they're already serving vodka, those two boozers, of course, put away three shots apiece and are rushing back to their offices; if some do-gooder would tighten up on serving vodka, office work would come to a stop—none of the guys would get anything done, except for figuring out where to get a drop the day after, like in our village after the wheat or potato harvest. All the Lithuanian farmers would come to have a look at those horrors—the gulping of water, the trembling of hands, the exploding of heads—that horrible morning when it became obvious that the harvest celebration had gone on too long, that all of the hooch, every last bit of it, in the entire village, in all of the cottages, was drunk down to the last drop, that now there wouldn't be any hair of the dog. Even the Day of Judgment couldn't compare to that sight. Zombies with dried-up mouths and parched lips would hobble around, holding on to the fences around the houses, falling into the yards, vomiting, retching, drinking water, and vomiting again; children, women, old people; the women suffer more than men, but they don't let on—and in the entire village not a drop of vodka! On a day like that, for an itsy-bitsy bottle, anything would be given away, the most horrifying agreements signed, and unbelievable deals made. On that day the Lithuanians from Užubaliai would show up, curious but dignified; they'd paw over everything like some slave traders, everyone hated them, but they'd give anything away for an itsy-bitsy bottle of murky moonshine; the girls would even go offer themselves to the Lithuanian boys, who would take a long time ruminating and bargaining. All the Lithuanians ruminated and bargained. They planned their business and their future, but all our folks needed was vodka, those horrible mornings all they needed in the whole world was vodka: both the men, and the girls, and the children, and the old people: everyone just wanted vodka and hated those ruminating, bargaining Lithuanians' guts. Vasilis saved me from that horror, from that hate, from that universal hangover, from myself. He came at the beginning of one of those crazes, when the hooch was still pouring in rivers, when I got plastered for the first time in my life and staggered around the yard; he came, threw my helpless body over his shoulder and carried me out—no one was worried about it, no one missed me, the village drank for five more days.

Vasilis was the first one to tell me that there is this Vilnius, a city of miracles; now I'm walking around in it, breathing its air, eating its salads—there now! I sit down at the counter and gasp, because Liovka Kovarskis is sitting next to me; he always smiles sadly; like me, he doesn't know what nationality he is, he always says: when I meet a Jew, I want to be a Pole, when I talk to a Pole, I want to be a Lithuanian, when I drink with a Lithuanian, I want to turn into a Russian, but operating on a Russian, I get the urge to turn back into a Jew.

"Hiya, Stef," Liovka smiles sadly and pushes his coffee over to me, "I haven't touched it yet, I'm letting you have my place in line. I'm really a Pole today: you see how gallant I am."

He knits his god-like hands under his chin, he's sad, probably he's butchered someone on the operating table again; Levas has three surgical groups and a department next to the clinics, he just never had any luck, both his wives ran off; Laima said it was impossible to live with a person like that, all he needed were those scalpels, scissors, and needles, those disemboweled stomachs and chests. I'm sorry for Levas—he's so kind, sincere, and gentle, his sweaters and jackets are always in warm, soft shades; he likes to wear white slacks a lot.

"I've already heard about Martynas," Levas says glumly. "Aren't you afraid at the library? One butchered, another run over, the third they'll probably execute. It's cursed. I'd run from a place like that without a second thought."

I even spilled my coffee: good Lord, I hadn't even thought of that, maybe the angel of death is stalking me already; sometimes you think about suicide in all seriousness, but the thought that someone could do you in barely crosses your mind and you break out in a cold sweat.

"By the way, it's been all the same to Vargalys for quite some time," Levas says gloomily, "I can talk about it now. He came to us for tests: his cancer's in such a stage that . . . I almost understand why he murdered that girl. He didn't want to leave her to the world, he wanted to take her with him."

It's just my luck to spill coffee today; I can't tell anyone what I know, what I was doing in that damn garden—maybe I should tell Liovka? I look him in the eyes and he smiles sadly; he's wrong, he's mistaken, should I tell him, or not?

"I don't like that Vargalys, we've chatted over a drink several times, but when I'd run into him he wouldn't say hello. Stuck-up. That's the kind that butcher people."

Suddenly he gets up off the barstool and leaves, he's always that way, let him go torment himself over his dead patient and his two runaway wives; I meant to eat a salad, it seems I'm not cramping anymore, the narrow bar is packed, the starving ones are hanging over the backs of the ones who are eating, it looks like they're going to snatch a bite any minute, I can't stand it, to this very day I can't stand it, I instantly remember those famines, when everyone in our village would look that way at someone who was eating, eating was a rare thing, every stranger's bite would make us drool, it's awful to remember; some people boiled roots or bark, or went to Užubaliai to steal pig's slop, because the Lithuanians had everything, no famine affected them, they always had everything, like some kind of miracle workers, and they didn't live at all far away; the creek, then the Vargalys mansion, the hills, beyond them the fields and the Lithuanian farms—it'd be easy to see if it wasn't for those hills. Before the war, when I wasn't born yet, the border went along the creek: Bezrečję was in Poland, and Lithuania started with the Vargalyses— good Lord, what a joke; we were never Poles, tuteišy, tuteišy, the men repeated even then, after the First War, when the Entente's inspectors checked the administrative border. But why were the Lithuanians different, what does a creek or a hill or border police have to do with it? Why are they different, why am I, who have turned into a Lithuanian, or faked being one, different? Everyone envied those Lithuanians, and I envy that Lithuanian Stefa too; the one who lived when Vargalys, Martis, and Gediminas were here, and now she's probably dead.

Vasilis kept his promise, he cast me into Vilnius like a blind kitten into a pond, believing that I'd swim—it would have been better if I'd stayed in my village, drowned in the swamps, turned into the queen of the frogs; I no longer have the strength for my journey, I found my way, but it suddenly came to an end, because there's no Gediminases, Martynases, Teodorases, or even Vargalys; I was like a mother to all of them, a little mommy, I fussed over them as if they were babies, I hugged them all to my chest like the Great Mother, like the earth, like nature itself—tell me, does the earth feel any kind of pleasure? It's simply made for a seed to fall into, for a tree to grow out of and bear fruit; the earth is the earth. I'm the earth too, I think like the earth, I feel like the earth, I need them all, and at the same time I don't need a single one—they're the ones who need me, they won't go anywhere; they'll come to me, I'm the only one who can satisfy them, because I'm like the earth: they're my children and my lovers at the same time, because everything turns in a circle and returns to the beginning again—the dead will rise, there's nothing to be afraid of; I should finish this salad, today there's nothing but meat salads, they're expensive here.

"Staselė honey, get me a little salad! I don't need bread," I finally stopped that bustling barrel.

Will I find a new Teodoras, Gediminas, or Martynas, will I free Vargalys? Yes, I saw it; yes, I know; yes, I can tell the truth, but will it save Vargalys?

No one will want to believe me, even if they know I'm telling the truth. Or if they do believe me, I'll be afraid of retribution, most of all I'm afraid of Vargalys, probably I don't want to see him, I'm absolutely most of all afraid of Vargalys himself; I immediately remember his eyes, the horrible look he fixed on me that time in the library, between the bookshelves, and not just that time; many, many times, suddenly turning into something that was no longer human—a hideous spawn of the devil, capable not just of murdering you or injuring you, but of doing something unspeakably horrible, something you couldn't even describe; I was always afraid of him, he was as unfathomable as some diabolic riddle, he was the most horrible of my babies, even though I can't even imagine myself without him. The salad is disgusting, but what can you do, there's nothing to choose from, thank you Staselė dear, drop dead fatso; it's drizzling outside again, oh no, spare me, what a butt, and squeezed into disco style pants, and the color, the color, a Gothic gold, oh no, I'm gonna die, and the purse is round too, like a disk—it's completely insane, that's all. Even my butt would look better, Gediminas liked to pinch it like some redneck, even though he was from Kaunas; once we went off to visit his parents—a garden of paradise: his father was a famous tailor, his mother rented wedding dresses, she had some two hundred of them, a house like the Vargalys mansion, all the militia in Kaunas bought off, everyone who came just bowed, Mr. Riauba, Madam Riaubienė, only then did I realize where all of Gedka's Opels and Mercedes-Benzes came from—he never said anything about his parents, apparently he was ashamed: such a smart, spiritual guy, and here you have a veritable fortress of money; he would dress like God, his suits grayish or bluish, they'd fit him like they'd been molded, tight jeans to emphasize his slender waist, shirts invariably unbuttoned so the hair on his chest would stick out—it went really well with the gold chain on his neck—all youthful and headlong, more hip than his students, even though he was the professor; he was always torturing himself that he couldn't take in everything, the whole world, at once, he complained that the dragon got in his way, he was always going on about that dragon: Tedka even sculpted this piece of junk that reached to the ceiling, and he'd say it was Riauba's dragon, even though the sculpture was named The Deformer. On the left Lenin stretches out his hand, I should go into the record store, maybe they've put something out at the end of the month—although no, if I listen to something good, I immediately remember Gedka and cry. They say they've promised to name the mathematics lecture hall at the University after him, but I don't believe it—he died too young, they only honor old people here, the old folks in the government fear the young ones even when they're dead. They should put up a monument to him, they all need one—Tedka with his eternally ragged sweater, and Vargalys, and even

412

Martis; they'd sit deep in thought, and between them all—me, the little mommy, with four arms stroking their little heads, or maybe the other way around: they would all be walking in different directions, gazing off into the distance, and I would be kneeling, grabbing on to their knees, but they wouldn't pay any attention to me, they wouldn't even notice me: that would be the most accurate monument. I'm cramping again, Lord love a duck, I stick my nose into the pharmacy even though it's hopeless; of course, there's none there and couldn't be any there, that's the motto of our lives—if you need it, it surely won't be there, it's probably done on purpose, so you'd be looking for some item all the time and that's why you wouldn't look for anything else, be it love, or answers, or truth, or freedom. My stomach gurgles, I shouldn't have eaten that salad; stop at the light, all the trucks in Vilnius are murderous, now you can go, I won't go into the fabric store, on purpose I won't, oh Lordee, there's nowhere to hide, maybe I should pretend that . . . it's too late already, what can you do, I'll stop, even though it's really awful. Vargalys's father blinks his little bloodshot eyes a lot and strokes his bald pate, I haven't seen him in a long time, like it or not, I'll have to talk to him.

"Let's stop in here, Stefutė, come on," he waves his arm nervously at the Neringa. "Don't leave me by myself. I can't stand looking at those mugs anymore."

"Mugs"—that's Lord's Corner, a little collection of retirees and near-retirees, the last intellectuals of Vilnius's cafés; in a while even these will be gone, they'll smoke them out of here—who needs those geezers criticizing the government under their breath—although maybe they won't touch the old guys.

"Here, Stefutė, here, we'll sit with our backs to those mugs," Vargalys's father shuffles, stirs, runs to order champagne, smiles pathetically from a distance.

I won't listen to what he says, it's been a long time since he was a sorcerer, it's been a long time since he had anything to say and I know how to grouse myself; everyone's gulping coffee and eating crepes. Vilnius goes on as if nothing has happened; these people don't burn up, don't drown, don't fall off mountains and don't chop their lovers to bits—that's what's most important. I see the old man's writhing lips, his wrinkling forehead, his tired eyes, how old is he anyway, seventy

413

at least—wasn't it last year or so that we celebrated Vargalys's fiftieth? Vargalys's father will never find out we already met twenty years ago, that day when I finally got up my nerve to visit their decrepit villa, when I stepped inside barefoot, climbed the creaking stairs, opened doors, startling the spiders, rats, and bats, shaking all over, coming across the strangest things: a skull, an opened bottle of wine, the butchered skeleton of a goose. No one had been there for years and years; our folks feared that cursed house like fire, and the Lithuanians had been deported a long time before—Užubaliai had sunk into the earth. A heavy black dust had settled everywhere, it crunched between my toes; little tracks of rat footprints meandered here and there, from time to time some frightened rodent would squeak irritably and get in my way, but I wasn't afraid of anything anymore, I felt like the owner of the house, that was how Vasilis had taught me. I really did feel like the owner of all of that treasure—nothing had been looted, neither the clothes, nor the dishes, nor the books; now everything belonged to me, because I was the first to dare to step over the forbidden boundary, to go into the cursed house; I came across Vargalys's father on the second floor, in a big room whose walls were hung with pictures, weird pictures: they were covered by an undisturbed layer of gray dust, they were all equally mute and dead. I thought he was a ghost, because there weren't any footprints in the dust; he was unbelievably huge, already starting to lose his hair, the dried-up chair creaked beneath him when he waved his hand at me:

"Come closer, little girl. Tell me where my son is. He has disappeared, vanished, but he's alive, I feel it. Maybe you know? I'll give you everything: the pictures, the crystal, the silver, even the books. It will all be yours, just find my son."

Now he sits across from me and grimaces like a clown—what kind of world is this, where sorcerers turn into clowns, heroes into impotents, and geniuses burn up alive? I found his son for him—that's the weirdest thing—I really was the first to run into Vargalys, I carried out his father's wish, but where are all those paintings, silver, and books now? You'd think it had all sunk straight down into the earth like the village of Užubaliai; the champagne really is good, my heart doesn't even feel so heavy anymore, Lord, I understand drunks—you drink, and nothing bothers you, but I don't have time, I need to pull a fast one on Vargalys's father, otherwise he'll get it into his head to come with me; I'll pretend I'm going to the bathroom, the Neringa's curtains are heavy, he won't see: I ran away that time too, even though he kept repeating:

"Don't go, little girl: imagine you're my daughter. Don't you want to be my daughter? Imagine you're my daughter and you're looking for your brother. You must find your brother who's wandering somewhere in the wide world. Don't you want to find your brother?"

I ran away, I didn't want to learn the Vargalyses' horrible secret, it was whispered by the walls of the Vargalys house, murmured in the webbed wings of the bats, squeaked by the rats, woven into the cobwebs by the spiders, but the Vargalys legend overtook me, merged with me; that evening I turned into part of the Vargalys history myself, it penetrated into me and hasn't left me yet, it's always with me, like the Lord God.

What if I really was Vargalys's sister? After all, I slept with him and even carried his child; as soon as I think of it I want to be a man—like Vargalys's mother did, that witch with the mannish haircut who did men's work and practiced jujitsu every day with the giant Julius. She kept saying that Lithuanian men were completely sissified, all that was left was for her to take their place, to turn into a man, or else Lithuania would be doomed; most of all she liked to break in wild horses (where did she get them from?), they say she'd fly into our village on the back of some crazed mustang, driving the border policeman nuts, he was always meaning to arrest her for crossing the border illegally, but he was afraid to even get near her; everyone was scared of her, even our village boys. She would beat them, cruelly and unmercifully, with all of her jujitsu mastery. And the sorcerer Vargalys didn't pay the slightest attention to people, all he was concerned with was the spiritual and monetary system, they say it was thanks to him alone the litas was so stable; many times people saw him leading the dazed servant girl Janė, his connection with the other world, around the yard. The mother raised Vargalys like a girl, made fun of him and humiliated him, called him a little sissy, little girl, girly-girl, yet one more woman among Lithuania's womanish men, she would undress him and yank him by that thing, saying it was a fake, a worthless appendage, it would be best to rip it off and throw it away; she hated her son, hated him with a passion; after all, she wanted to be a man, and men can't give birth, the son would instantly remind her there's a womb inside her, which had already given birth and could give birth again; probably that's why such a giant body had such a pathetic, helpless, tiny little thing, I've never seen anything like it; it shrank from the mocking and humiliation in his childhood, that's why Vargalys tried, all his life, to prove to himself and everyone else that he was a real man, a man of all men. I've never met such a rude, pompous, snarling person whose insides were so vulnerable and frail, no man ever stroked my hands and cheeks that way, no man ever kissed my feet that way, but only when we were alone—in front of others he would instantly turn coarse, cruel, and unmerciful. He didn't want to come to terms with aging; he wanted to always stay young and powerful, although he never was powerful, that drooping little thing of his got smaller every day, it kept shrinking—phooey, what am I going on about, he was the only one I never compared to anyone in that respect; he was a Vargalys, that says everything. I want to howl, maybe it wouldn't be so bad to start howling right here, next to the Central Committee building, or better yet, inside—but they won't let me in; a militiaman with a pistol glances at the passersby suspiciously, even though he's never had to shoot and never will: everyone's calm, quiet, and obedient, and dressed alike: I've gone down nearly the whole boulevard and I've met maybe three ladies with smarts, so what if it's silly, but it's smarts all the same; on the face of it, everyone seems to dress differently, but so alike that you can blink as much as you want but you can't even tell yourself apart; you try and try and all the same you look as alike as peas in a pod; here, take this one: a shabby, nothing coat, a rumpled, nothing hat; oh Lordee, it's Šapira, it's not right to talk about Šapira that way, he's special, you can't figure him out, you'd think he was trying to look different every day, as if he were an actor on the stage, one day suited up like a gentleman, the next dressed in rags like some bum, he wanders the streets of Vilnius, looks, listens, and knows everything; they say he's secretly writing a book, the great history of Vilnius: a genuine eccentric, sometimes I get the urge to make fun of him, but you just look at him and you see he's smarter than you are, he surely knows what he's doing, even though no one knows what that is.

"At one time I used to play cards with Vytautas's grandfather," says Šapira approaching, "he'd always beat me. He was smarter than any

Jew, that's what strange. Strange, because he lived foolishly. I kept suggesting we trade, let him be a Jew, and I'll be a Lithuanian."

We go past Gražina's haberdashery, I planned to take a look at the gloves, well, Optica doesn't concern me, for the time being I get by without glasses—oh, I didn't stop at the pharmacy on Totorių Street, but what of it: if they had them, women with bags would be running around, all the ministries would be rushing to lay in a supply.

"Vytautas was a smart guy too," Šapira mumbles, "A poor guy, a smart guy, a martyr. His mother tormented him, that girl tormented him, his own thoughts tormented him. He should have been giving sermons on the mount, but instead he hid from everyone. He brought Vilnius to a stop, but he still didn't discover anything. He thought he could achieve victory just by being on the defensive. Do you know he hung himself in solitary? Or maybe someone hung him?"

I grab Šapira by the sleeve, but all I do is catch at the air, the old man's gone, it's always like he's dreamt up a bunch of stuff and he always reports some misfortune; don't tell me it's true, don't tell me I won't need to decide, don't tell me my knowledge, my testimony, is worthless now. Once more I see Vargalys slowly standing up, straightening out, and looking down with a wooden expression, looking at the mutilated body just as he had looked once before—on that horrible night when I was born.

He found his dismembered mother on our hill: he knelt by the mutilated body in the exact same way, then in the exact same way he stood up and straightened out, in the exact same way he glanced downwards with a wooden expression—I didn't see it the first time, but I saw the second. On that day in forty-four when the Russians came back his mother went completely crazy, she rushed to go to battle; none of you men have balls, she would scream, none of you have balls, I'm the only one who's a real man, then she started saying she was Lithuania itself and she was standing to battle immediately; in the evening she secretly escaped from the family's care and stood to that battle, all alone against the entire Russian army; apparently she really felt she was Lithuania itself. Vasilis saw that battle of hers, as always, he stood there aloof and watched: she met the first Russian soldiers and attacked them like a she-wolf; they were provisioners, they didn't even carry automatics, and their hands were full, they were dragging soap, as much as they could carry; they

417

had come across a warehouse the Germans had abandoned and were whistling happily because they'd finally gotten some soap, they thought they'd finally wash up like human beings, all they were dreaming about was a sauna, and suddenly they met a she-wolf. There were maybe six of them, but Vargalys's mother scattered them in all directions, kicked them, trampled them, tore their faces with her nails, she even forgot her jujitsu mastery, but the Russians slowly came to their senses—stunned, humiliated, with bloody, harrowed faces; a few more emerged from the forest, and that was it for Vargalys's mother: the soldiers chopped her up with shovels, they didn't even have any other weapons, they didn't just kill her, but chopped her to bits; blinded by an inhuman anger, they chopped at her brutally and for a long time. Vasilis said that pieces of her body were strewn everywhere, and they kept chopping until they tired. Only then did they come to their senses: they got horrified themselves, or maybe they only just then realized they were mutilating a woman; they ran off, some even crossing themselves, scattering pieces of soap. All of that happened on our nameless hill. Sometimes it seems to me that all of my childhood happened on that bare hill. Gediminas Hill looms over Vilnius, but nothing's happened on it for a long time now, the exhausted castle pokes out like some worthless addition to the city; inside the knights' armor, Lithuanian swords, and silver ornaments are sleeping, they're sleeping and will sleep through the ages, and we're dozing right alongside; a slight mist covers the castle, like an aged coquette's veil; I was inside only once, with Gedka and Vargalys, this alcoholic artist worked there as the museum's night watchman, we partied all night long in the middle of all that armor, those cannons and swords, but the spirit of the old Grand Dukes didn't wake up, anyway: it couldn't even manage to get insulted; enough about the castle, on the other side of the street is the corner of miracles, a bit of paradise, the kingdom of dreams, on the other side of the street is—the dollar store. I simply can't believe a world like that even exists, that's the way I'd feel when Martis would listen to that radio from the other side: I'd hear people's voices, they would utter completely understandable words, but as soon as I'd try to imagine them sitting in some room, to imagine that there are streets outside their window, that trees grow there too, and cars zoom around—it would never work. They're like Martians to me. Apparently they exist, but they don't, they're imaginary, like this Martian store, Ali

Baba's cave: you say, Open Sesame, and like hell it'll open; they just yell—a foreign passport and dollars! Only Martians come here; once I lived in the swamp, from there even Vilnius looked like a Mars of some sort, but now I'm a bit Martian myself, when I go back home, that's just how everyone looks at me. But after all, I could have been like them, if not for Vasilis, the great phantom Vasilis, my teacher and creator. He lit a spark in me that I didn't have when I was born, turned me into a human and a woman, opened up a world for me that I didn't even suspect existed; all I knew was our village life, it seemed there couldn't be any other. You know, it really is comfortable not to know anything: when you don't know anything, you don't want anything either, the wheel of life turns evenly and smoothly, nothing changes, nothing worries you; it really is awful to find out you can live some other way, that knowledge is devastating, but Vasilis managed to patiently nurse my spirit, so I went out into the world prepared to oppose it fearlessly.

Vasilis loved and respected all forms of life, be it ants or wolves. Once I saw a louse crawling through the hair on his chest, I wanted to smash it, but he didn't let me: it's God's creation too, he said, it's needed too, it's needed under God's canopy, honor every living thing, this louse matters just as much as a star, or Gediminas Castle, and you don't, after all, put out stars or wreck Gediminas Castle; lice, tigers, goats, and cats live among people too—and it's forbidden to destroy a single one, all of them are equally important, a louse could still turn into a tiger, or a cat into a flea, what matters most is to want something, to want something very, very, badly. Then he kept telling me about Vilnius, that city would appear in my dreams as a land of miracles, where people, tigers, cats, fleas, and elephants live together, all of them get along, socialize, turn into one another, and there's music playing everywhere, the towers stretch to the sky, plants of paradise you've never seen before sway in the breeze; I wonder who this babe is—she's sewed herself a poncho out of Scottish plaid and walks around that way—a mouse, a cow, or maybe a magpie? I found the real Vilnius to be different, completely different, but no less amazing; it seems to me that Vilnius enters my body like a man, my eternal man, who will give me sons; God almighty, I should have had children, I desperately needed to have children, a lot of children—they could have had so many fathers. I keep remembering Gediminas, his scholarly language, that music of his that made my teeth hurt; I probably loved him, but I loved Tedis too, and Martis; Lord knows, one heart is not enough for me, I should have been born with a couple of them; I didn't love Vargalys, he's not a creature of this earth, I was afraid of him, but at the same time I respected him, maybe respect and fear are inseparable things. His child, a son of course, fell out of me himself, committed suicide before he was born, I'm afraid to even think of what he would have been like, what marks of the Vargalyses he'd carry, that accursed family, who, according to Vasilis, was perhaps destined to save Lithuania: maybe it was because of his family's importance that Vargalys wanted children so badly, after all, he left his wife because she was infertile. I know Irena quite well, occasionally we call each other, go out somewhere to sit; I don't visit her at home, she lives too luxuriously, her new husband is a black marketeer—a Volvo, carved furniture, and a Japanese television—the realization of the Soviet man's dreams. I don't know what it was that tied me to Vargalys—huge and miserable, unhappy and terrible; no, I didn't love him, not even in the beginning, and certainly not later, when that business with Lolita started, so that's why I suddenly feel so free now. If Šapira's right . . .

But I can't be free, I must devote myself to something every day, every hour, every minute—to men, to Vilnius, to the air or the stars, that's my nature, that's my essence, that's the way Vasilis taught me; Lord may he gain the kingdom of heaven, or maybe he's long since there by now—I don't remember when I last visited Bezrečjė.

But the village is stalking me, it even gives me the shudders. Madam Giedriatienė, Vargalys's eternal escort, his good or evil spirit, his grand-father's like-minded friend, is slowly approaching with a dignified air; it looks like St. John's Church is sliding down the hill right at me. Madam Giedraitienė is very close; she raises her serious, piercing eyes at me and says in an impatient voice:

"We're going to my place, Stefanija. I've something serious to talk about."

"He hung himself," suddenly bursts out of me, "he hung himself in the solitary cell."

"I'm just coming from there," Giedraitienė shoots back, as cool as a cucumber. "He's as healthy as he could be. Healthier than ever."

She turns and walks into the gateway next to the Narutis, climbs the creaking stairs, unlocks the door, she's already taking off her coat and stepping into her slippers, she's dignified and noble, dresses conservatively, now she's wearing sleeves with crinoline, her hair's tied back with a shiny barrette, she drinks endless cups of coffee and chain-smokes Marlboros, her son Robertas is a diplomat who works in West Berlin.

"What's this you've thought up, you silly thing," Madame Giedraitis mutters angrily, "You should put a sock in it."

"Šapira said so."

"And you listen to a Jew's rubbish. Some black marketeer hung himself. And he heard about it and decided it's Vargalys. No Vargalys ever killed himself."

The Giedraitises were never either witches or werewolves. Giedraitis Junior, they say, joined up with the *stribai*, his mother even disinherited him and went to Siberia to find out where Vargalys was confined; she made peace with her son only after fifty-three, when people started coming home, and Robertas, after sufficient breast-beating, went off to study at the International Relations Institute.

"I've mustered all my acquaintances and connections," says Madame Giedraitis, pouring coffee out of a thermos. "He can be saved. It all needs to be thoroughly investigated. Vytautas couldn't have done it."

He's alive, he's alive—what should I do with my knowledge, what should I do with that wretched sight: Vargalys slowly stands up, straightens himself out and looks down with a wooden expression, looks at the hideously dismembered body; it'd be better to see something else. If you could look right through the walls, you'd see Tedka's studio, it's right nearby: gloomy, piled up with sculptures, the walls covered with my portraits: me naked and me dressed; me with black hair, blonde hair, and even bald; me, sorrowful and saintly. Lolka was terribly jealous of those portraits, but Tedis was immovable—I continued to be his painting muse, even though Lolka shoved me out in real life. Lolka, Lolka, monster Lola, disgusting Lolita, she always had to push you aside, step past you, then ruin and humiliate you; she always had to take whatever it was that belonged to you alone—not because she really needed it, but just so she could humiliate you. It wasn't enough that things were good for her, she needed it to be bad for others too; no, she wasn't like that at first, she turned that way slowly, it seemed she siphoned up the worst she found in everyone—from both Tedis and Gediminas, even from Vargalys. The old lady's head shakes a bit, but her speech is clear and articulate:

"They even took his medical file, looking for mental deviations. I didn't think there would be anything to it—after all, Vytautas was so tough. It turns out he was constantly looking for diseases—I would never have imagined it. He got checked out at the clinics and at the oncologists, looking for cancer. They didn't find any. He even had himself checked for . . . well, I can tell you . . . he had his semen checked, to see if he wasn't infertile. Everything was hunky-dory. In short, his medical file is as fat as a Lithuanian novel, but there was only one answer: Vytautas is as healthy as a horse. Mentally as well."

Well then, Kovarskis was full of it too; all you need to do is mention Vargalys and it starts raining legends—that he hung himself, that he was ill with cancer, that he was impotent—apparently you can't say anything definite about him.

"Do you understand what's at stake here?" I suddenly ask. "He chopped Lola to bits. That's a fact. If they don't send him to prison, they'll shut him up in an insane asylum. Forever."

"Not forever, Stefanija, not forever." To my surprise, Madam Giedraitienė visibly rallies. "There's treatment, be it real or fictitious, and most of all—time for everything to at least quiet down a bit."

"Well, what of it?"

"You don't know what it means to have powerful connections," Madam Giedraitienė says proudly. "Connections mean everything. They elevate and ruin. They turn black into white, and white bloody. If they don't kill Vytautas, we'll get him off."

I almost start believing her, even though I'm immediately horrified: if Vargalys shows up again in this world, if he touches me again, I'll probably go out of my mind, I'll remember what I saw and did in that damned garden that damned day; Madam Giedraitienė shuts up, smokes maybe her tenth Marlboro, maybe; I feel stupid, even though it's so understandable to a woman: forgive me, perhaps ma'am . . . you know how these things are . . . I know, it's awkward . . . Madam Giedraitienė's best quality is that she's never surprised at anything, doesn't condemn anyone, and doesn't gossip about anyone. After a minute she comes back with a nearly empty package of sanitary napkins, proudly hands it to me; it's still something, even if it's only enough for today.

422

"It's been lying there for awhile already," says Madam Giedraitienė. "I can't just throw it out. I was ready to use them, and it turned out I didn't need to anymore. A horrible feeling. I had to hide it from the old guy. Vytautas's grandfather was potent up until the very end."

I run to the bathroom, make it just in time: everything's soaked through, the first day is always awful; I look down and I'm amazed; that stinking, bleeding cavity is what all men are after, and if that wasn't enough, everything that's alive comes out of it, although no one came out of mine and maybe won't now: cover it up, hide it, squeeze it shut, and suffocate everyone hiding in there. Now it seems to me they're all holed up in there: Tedis splattered with clay, and Gedka whistling jazz, and even Martis with the woman's pinky finger in his pocket. But they've died, they're gone, I'm all alone—oh Jesus, just don't think about it, think about anything—just not about that; oh, Vargalys's grandfather was potent right up until he died—well, she's full of it, he was a hundred maybe when he died; I remember his funeral perfectly well, just about all of the ancient Jews of Vilnius came, you heard ten times more Yiddish around than Lithuanian. The Jews came to honor their rescuer, one even tried to give a speech: he compared him to Wallenberg, that's some Swede who saved Jews too, and Vargalys kept fuming that the deceased's last wishes hadn't been carried out, the others pleaded with him every which way—who could carry it out? The old guy told him to set a silver bucket full of excrement next to his casket and to hang a sign reading, "Death to the Poles."

It's time to move on, you could describe all of our lives that way: time to move on; Madam Giedraitienė politely escorts me to the door, I go down the stairs, at last escape into the air. Didžiosios Street finishes rising here, well, how can you not love Vilnius, it's so big and sad, and comfortable at the same time: even Didžiosios Street is a only few yards wide, the houses on either side stretch out their hands to each other and quietly sigh. I go past Tedis's studio, try not to think about him, but my eyes turn to the left on their own, look over the clothing store too, and the leather repair shop, and the famous beer kiosk, the Mecca of Old Town's drunks, until at last I see the buildings of Bokšto Street; the street dives down so suddenly it seems the houses are half buried under the earth—the strange houses of Bokšto Street, which bring back gloomy memories. The time Stadniukas appeared on our hill with two

truckloads of soldiers; Lord knows, all the most important things happened on that hill; Stadniukas walked about puffed up like a rooster,
choosing which village to start with, he called it collectivization, the
soldiers smoked cigarettes and yawned, they knew they wouldn't need
to shoot, they were NKVD and didn't mind anything. Stadniukas went
down the hill to our side, there was no need to summon people, everyone was milling around at the foot of the hill anyway; sign up for the
collective farm, Stadniukas yelled without any introduction, or else—
but he didn't need any or else, our village was obedient, Stadniukas was
disappointed, he wanted to beat, to cut, to burn, but no one resisted;
but he got his wish in the Lithuanian village, his eyes shone no less than
they did when he wanted to rape me, he was delighted because the
Lithuanians glared at him from under their lowered eyes and had no
intention of signing up for that collective, Stadniukas finally got to do
some beating, he particularly liked to kick children, and in about two
hours all the people were gathered into a row. Covered trucks appeared
out of nowhere and roared off towards the railroad station at dusk. That
morning in the village the cows still lowed, geese cackled, children
screamed, but after that night Užubaliai was left voiceless; the open
doors to the cottages yawned like eyes that had been poked out, the
smell of people still drifted from inside, coals still glowed in the fireplaces, but the village was gone, only Stadniukas was left: he was the
first to go around the cottages, he collected the valuables and roared
away in his black car; it was only afterwards, following the government's
example, that our folks fell upon the cottages in Užubaliai too; they
carried off everything: bedding, clothing, furniture—after all, the others hadn't had time to pack anything up, they had to leave almost everything behind. I was only five years old, everything seemed like a fairy
tale—there was a village, and then the village was gone—I crept around
in those empty cottages too, but I didn't take anything, really, I didn't
take anything, even though I badly wanted those wonderful rag dolls,
there was one in every cottage; I could only dream of things like that, I
wanted them badly, but I didn't take them, and everyone was dragging
clocks, wagon wheels, even benches and chairs over the hill, until the
village idiot Piotrusis joyously hobbled over the hill, screaming horribly: "The houses knelt down, the houses knelt down." At first no one
understood, then no one believed him; it was only on the third or fourth

day that the men of the village gathered to talk it over: Užubaliai village was steadily sinking into the ground. At first just the doors seemed to get lower, and it was still possible to doubt that the village was sinking, but slowly the windows ended up even with the ground, then they sank even further, were half hidden, disappeared completely: our folks didn't just stop looting, they were afraid to even go near those sinking houses, only the kids, ignoring their parents, climbed around on the straw roofs that ended up entirely underfoot, hooted down into the chimneys, and teased the astonished stork—you could reach its nest just by jumping up; I wandered around there too, with a terrible heartache I watched all the rag dolls disappearing beneath the ground, they vanished like that, together with whole houses; for a while a stork's nest, built on a wheel, stuck above the grass, then it sank into the ground too. There was just a bare space left where the village once was, people erased it from their memories, and the village was erased from the surface of the earth. That vision stands before my eyes when I look at the houses of Bokšto Street now; they're slowly sinking downwards and no one's worried about it, the men standing next to them calmly drink beer, it means nothing to them that all of Vilnius could sink beneath the ground any minute, nothing will remain but a bare space—the castle and the very tallest buildings will sink too; for a while the television tower will continue to stick out, like a sign that there was a city here once. A puffy face turns towards me from the beer stand and stares at me: he resembles Stadniukas, the way he was then, already relieved of his duties, hanging around the village, ordering the chickens and the goats around, killing the dogs and cats. When he looked me over, I got terribly scared; I complained to Vasilis, he nodded his head sympathetically and gave me a dagger, a strange, exotic weapon with a three-sided blade on which was written SACRUM—just pull it out, you only need to pull it out, he taught me, and turn the blade in the light, all the Stadniukases in the world will avoid you forever; I made it just in time, maybe a day or two later Stadniukas caught me, cornered me by the double trunk of an old willow, and grinning vengefully, grabbed me by the breasts; I didn't scream, I didn't resist, that unnerved him a bit, but just for a little while, he immediately saw fear and hate in my eyes—that which he needed most—he didn't hurry; quite the opposite, he enjoyed it, that introduction of horror was what mattered most to him; he slowly pulled down my skirt, even more slowly bared one breast like on some Amazon, but I didn't think about the horror awaiting me, or about any rapes, there was just one thing on my mind: what would be if everything would happen and then I'd give birth to a child, Stadniukas's child, whom I would have to strangle before its first cry, a child of hell, who would have to be drowned, buried underground, burned up. Stadniukas slowly moved his hands towards my crotch, giggling foolishly, sucking on his teeth, while I secretly pressed the handle of the dagger and repeated to myself: now, when his fingers reach the mole on my thigh; now, when he touches the triangle of hair; now, when he lasciviously squeezes that hair: now it will be enough. But I resolved to do it only when he started unbuttoning his fly; his hands were busy for an instant, and I stabbed him—I didn't turn the blade of the dagger in the light, I didn't intimidate him, I didn't warn him; I stabbed at him at once without picking a spot—if I had hit the right spot, Stadniukas would never have strangled cats again. I remember Gedka half tried to take me by force the first time and was struck speechless when he saw the dagger, the three-sided blade with SACRUM written on the side, in my hand. I pulled it out automatically, not thinking of anything or planning to do anything; that instant it was simply an extension of my hand, to me it was like a bee's stinger, an inseparable part of my body, and Gedka was so stunned he wasn't able to do anything more that evening. The Stadniukas-like mug finally turns away, thank God, all I need is to attack someone, better calm down, look around. Well, now, I'll go in the consignment store to gawk at the leather coats, even though I'll never buy one like that: what can you buy with our pathetic little salaries, just let an Englishman or American try to get by in Vilnius, he'd walk around ragged, hungry, and finally go out of his mind, while we manage just fine; one thousand two hundred, thank you very much, and this one's eight-fifty, that's more like it, but all the same. Lolka always ran around decked out in leather and pretended to be my friend; she kept offering to give me something to wear like I was some kind of beggar, she always pretended we were friends, even when she started beating Vargalys away from me—oh, what didn't she try, she about crawled out of her skin, the outfits she changed: Vargalys cost her at least several thousand, if not more. She changed her feathers, but Vargalys didn't pay the slightest attention to her, that's the way he was: a person could be running around under his nose for ten years, and Vargalys, meeting him on the street, wouldn't recognize him; darts at the chest, pleats gathered on top, tiny lapels— let's see, an even thousand, an entire half-year of your pathetic salary, Stefanija, plus some; don't eat, don't drink, don't breathe for half a year, and you'll be dressed like Lolka; those eyes, those wretched eyes of hers, I can't forget them, like that time I went over to Gedka's and found her there for the first time: I unlock the door, smell a strange scent and I'm furious already, and Lolka crawls out into the corridor stark naked, totally shameless, not feeling guilty, just smiles a bit, calmly lights a cigarette and puts on a robe, my robe, staring at me all the time with shameless, fierce eyes, as if that's the way it had to be, as if that's the way it always was, as if it couldn't be any other way: Gedka didn't look me in the eye for some two weeks, and she goggled her pretty eyeballs at me as coolly as can be, invited me to lunch and, as if nothing was the matter, chattered on about her great new dress. No, dear friends, I'm outta here, the prices here are horrendous; Martis put it well: we don't get wages, we get unemployment compensation, for that compensation all we can do is not work, which is what we do. Martis's crushed body stands before my eyes again, the gloomy guy turns the woman's little finger over in his hands and I know whose finger it is, Martis is gone, the finger's owner is gone too; Martis was the only one she didn't steal from me, the honorable Martynas; I remember I was at Gedka's, I don't know how it happened, I never made love with two at the same time again, but that time it turned out that way; they pulled long black stockings on me, Gedka ran around the rooms, yelling that I'm the Circe of Vilnius, that I've turned them into beasts, and suddenly Martis came by, he came to borrow some books or something, I was so out of it I barely knew what was going on anymore, I stumbled into the living room with those black stockings on and only then did I come to my senses: Martis was adorably flustered, he tried not to look at me, and when he couldn't control himself and glanced at me sideways, I saw so much suffering in his eyes that Lord knows I came to completely. He was embarrassed, even I got embarrassed, he couldn't understand that I am like the earth and I belong to everyone, it was the only time I was ever sorry I'm not a prude and monogamous; poor straight arrow Martis wanted to create the great museum of Lithuania, year after year he collected exhibits, and then they took everything away from him, destroyed his museum; Martis searched for justice for a long time, he even went all the way to Moscow, there he was accused of being a nationalist and nearly arrested, probably he was a nationalist—as long as he was listening no one could say anything at all bad about Lithuanians, Martis would immediately start arguing about it, even fight about it; listening to him, you'd think Lithuanians don't have any shortcomings or flaws at all—then he started collecting a museum in his house, he didn't care about anything, losing his job, or his wife leaving him, I even envy him, I always envy people who believe in something. Poor Martis, Martis the little corpse, children were his other mania, he would sit in the courtyard and chat with the kiddies, and then he'd write down their wisdom in a notebook—don't tell me we really are destined to lose—loving children the way he did, the son disappointed his father terribly by turning into a careerist. Horrors, I only just now realized it so clearly: not a single one of them had children, only Martis—and the one he had was like that. My God, there's nothing left of them anymore, not even their seed is left, there's no seed of theirs left even inside me, the earth mother; I feel myself slowly stiffening in horror, I'm probably turning into a rock, I'm no longer living; it takes my breath away, thinking there's no sign left of them all, not a trace—how is that, what's to blame for it? The cupola of the Orthodox church gleams with brand-new gold paint, there's so many Russian Orthodox churches in Vilnius, four at least, and how many of those Russians were there here earlier, there were a hundred times more Jews and only one synagogue, although it's all the same to me, I don't know my nationality, I don't even know my faith, I don't know what I am—probably the profligate earth; after all, the earth belongs to everyone, it doesn't have a nationality, doesn't profess any religion or professes them all at the same time; I'm like the earth, I can shelter and comfort anyone—that dejected little hook-nosed Jew too, who's standing there deep in thought with his hands in his pockets, he's probably thinking of his little Jewess—I can comfort everyone, although maybe not today; I'm a human, after all, not the earth—the earth doesn't bleed and doesn't go looking for gauze to plug up its little hole. I'm not the earth anymore, I don't have anyone to comfort, that's what's the most horrifying—so why did Vasilis send me to Vilnius, what was I supposed to find here or do here, why did I have to desert my village and become an exile, an exile's fate is always hard; in a new place he feels foreign, unnecessary, and I was terribly envious too, I brought that envy with me from Bezrečjė like a dreadful disease, I envied the Lithuanians their streets, their houses, ideas, manners, language, looks, clothes, love, food. Why, why, I kept asking myself, how can they be that way, who gave them the right, why are they that way, so I'm forced to envy them, and yet they're still unhappy about something, they constantly bitch and moan about the government; my God, if I were like that and had that much of everything, I'd pray to that government; they should try to live in our village, they should try to live somewhere in the middle of Russia, I'd count them as something then; it's terrible to remember, I so wished them ill, a hundred times I did—to Tedis, and Gediminas, particularly Gediminas; he was so great and so out of reach with those mathematical articles of his, his concert piano, and the letters Sartre wrote him; he was a giant, and I was an ant, but Vasilis, seeing me off, said: that dagger is miraculous, it's meant for you too, if you feel the dragon of evil rising up inside you, remember the dagger. I remembered it too, when I felt that wretched envy I would stab myself in the left thigh, even now there's a bunch of little scars on it—I wasn't fooling, stabbing my left thigh, really: you envy Lolka her outfits, take this! Take this! You envy Gražkė her trip to Paris—take this! And this! You envy Gedka his ability to feel at home everywhere—take this! Take that! I spilled a lot of blood before I overcame my envy, before I became what I am: the humble earth that knows its eternal purpose. I fell in love with Gediminas first; he liked to be consoled like a fragile little missy, but he was a real man when he had to face some serious business, work or war. But I fell in love with him just because of his fragility and shyness; I'd comfort him with tears in my eyes, he'd be clinging to the piano, banging its black lacquered surface with his fist in despair. All his life he wanted to learn how to play in some special way, all his life he tried to create special mathematics; he'd work at night, and in the mornings he'd rip up the written pages, nothing was enough for him, being the youngest professor in Lithuania meant nothing to him, he was seeking something beyond reach, that's why he was unhappy: Gedka was a demigod, but he thought he was a failure, that was the most beautiful thing about him. He really loved this ruined square across from City Hall, true, the monument to Kapsukas didn't perch here yet then; Gedka would sit here, smoke, and think up his fantastic stories about everything under the sun; he was always longing for something, some other life, as if a mysterious city stood somewhere, his real city: Gedka's family would live there, his children, his real friends and companions, and there was no way he could get there, he felt he had lost all of that forever. Once he even let it slip that he longed for death, the kingdom of death as the house of his birth, perhaps he sensed what was already waiting for him in that canyon in Tian Shan? Tedis really did sense it, a week before he died in that fire he suddenly turned pale and glum, sculpted nothing but wolves; his studio was stuffed to the gills with all kinds of wolves, there almost wasn't room left for anything else, just my portraits hanging on the walls: me with dark hair and blonde hair, me without breasts or without a head; sometimes I think that Lolka set fire to him, wretched Lolka, stepping over corpses until she became a corpse herself, tyrannizing the best men in Vilnius—I hate her full lips, her shameless gaze, her long, too thin legs. Going through that many men, she hated them all, feared them too; that was why she didn't give herself to anyone— she'd take them all herself, she said, even making love she always tried to stay on top; she didn't give anything to anyone, she just took, plundered, pillaged. I am the earth, and she was a leech, but I was friends with her all the same—and who can say why?

Here's St. Casimir's Church. Casimir, I believe, was Lithuania's guardian saint—as Martis liked to say, saints like that should be relieved of their duties forthwith: some guardian saint, he guarded only too well, maybe it was true, as Martis claimed, that some holy ones secretly joined the Communist Party—but what do you want from poor Casimir, how could he protect all of Lithuania if he couldn't defend even his own church? Like one Hungarian visitor of Martis's said, I've seen churches turned into a lot of things, but no one's thought of putting a museum of atheism in a church before; Vargalys told a good story too: they set up a little wine bottling operation in this old Vilnius church courtyard; they'd bring barrels of wine from the south and bottle it in that church—I wonder what that Hungarian would have said, although what could he have seen in his lifetime, except maybe the famous Budapest revolution, but he would have been little then; I was even younger when the forest brothers raged through our area, I remember them vaguely, when they drove them into the swamp and drowned them I was maybe five, but I remember people's talk well: the forest brothers, they said, can't be caught or surrounded because they weren't hiding in ordinary bunkers, but rather in the sunken village of Užubaliai, everyone has his own cottage there; we children listened to that talk and then doggedly searched for the burrow to the mysterious underground kingdom. I remember Vargalys's grandfather too, the great leader of the resistance; he would arrive at the deserted Vargalys villa wearing a long coat that reached to the ground, suck on a bent pipe and be completely nonchalant, our folks would say: the buzzard's flown in, expect corpses; and then we really would hear about some daring exploit of the forest brothers; once they even took over a town and held it for four days, calmly fending off the NKVD attacks until the army with tanks and artillery was called in, then the forest brothers deftly retreated, not losing a single one of theirs—I just can't understand why they didn't lock old Vargalys up, apparently because our folks could betray just about anyone, but they were afraid to even pronounce Vargalys's name: Vytas Vargalys was nuts too, he walked through the villages and fields without disguising himself, he'd bathe at the same time every day in the creek, and when he was warned by some good-hearted old man, he'd shoot back angrily: what should I be afraid of, why should I hide, I'm in my own country, in my own home, they're the ones who should be afraid and hide themselves. That's the way a Lithuanian should be, Vasilis lectured me, it's just a shame there's so few of them, but as long as there's at least one the world isn't doomed. Maybe there aren't any left now, although no, there's at least one—Martis told me, he knew about things like that—there really is one, I don't remember his name, once they tried him for who knows what, for some literature, he declared he wasn't going to say anything, he didn't recognize a court of that sort, refused defense, and then calmly dozed off: while he was sleeping they salted him with ten years or so in the camps. Maybe there still are genuine Lithuanians left; now look, I've passed up a pharmacy, when you're wandering through Vilnius you get completely forgetful, Vilnius stirs up dreams and summons ghosts, it puts you under a spell, carries you off to distant times, to other worlds, but the pharmacy with the swan in the window expects me, and I expect at least one roll of gauze that isn't here and couldn't be here; the line aroused a naïve hope, but everyone's buying one thing or another, there's not so much as a whiff of gauze, the typical battle for healthcare continues: I want this—we don't have it; I want that—it's not to be found in all of Vilnius; I want this other—go to the twenty-eighth pharmacy at the far end of Antaka-lnis. In the hospitals doctors with degrees sharpen dull needles with files, the patients have to hunt down bandages and gauze themselves, there aren't any in the hospital, not to mention sheets or other bedding, slippers, robes, hot water in the radiators—that, in sum, is what's called protecting the public health. There's a crowd by Polena, I wonder what they've put out—of course, French eyeliner, there's a terrible shortage: that was the only kind Lolka used, although you'd never suspect she wore makeup at all, she really did have subtlety, a peculiar elegance. I don't know if she would have won Vargalys without my help, but any-one else really wouldn't have been hard: Vargalys is Vargalys, there are all kinds of people, blacks and Jews, Latinos and Asians, French and Swedes, a zillion of all kinds of variations, and among them all one more—Vargalys, an otherwise undefinable subspecies of human, maybe not even human, maybe there's really only two different kinds: human and Vargalys. If you close your eyes and think hard, you can imagine anybody, but not Vargalys; you pretty much have an idea of everyone's inclinations and activities, but what Vargalys was doing on this earth no one knew, not even me, even though I was constantly alongside him. We wandered the library collections together; I brought him books and wrote summaries—so what of it: one time he'd write page after page about tiger hunts, another time about a cave city in Iraq, and then, let's say, something about Camus's last days, or a species of wild pigeon: no system, no meaning, and no results. So I never did experience what the whole of Vargalys is, I only got to know a lot of his separate parts. He was as inscrutable as Vilnius itself, I've never been able to understand this city either, it mocks my efforts: every day it's different, intangible, unnameable; even now Vargalys is holed up inside me, he won't leave me alone, whatever I think about, in essence I think about him, what-ever I may say, I say it to him, and what matters most—I almost believe he hears me. I don't feel wronged on account of his horrible behavior, his complete lack of consideration for me, I understand him: I became a part of his own self, a part of his body, a part of his soul; after all, you have the right to behave with yourself however you see fit, anyone can hurt or harm himself, pay no attention to himself; I was the one who wanted to completely devote myself to him, no one forced me to, unless it was my own nature, or Vasilis's great teachings, or my endless loneliness. If there really is a lonely person in the world, it's me—I'm a stranger in this city, in this world; no matter how much I put on, I'm still stuck in the swamps of my childhood, I still hear the croaking of the frog queen, I still long for Vasilis's slow and careful caresses. I'm still a tuteiša, nothing more. On the days of your period you're always drowning in depression, and why is a person so dependent on their body, on that wretched flesh; no wonder Vargalys hated his body so, he really was a strange person, but irredeemably authentic: no deception, no pretense, no desire to look better than he really was; Vargalys reeked of authenticity, it's hard for people like that, but you can't not love them: you're charmed by their daring—it is so hard, after all, to be yourself, to not put on a show, to not pretty yourself up, to not try to sell yourself as best you can. It always seemed to me that he's the incarnation of Vasilis, he's the wizard of Vilnius, in exactly the same way that Vasilis was the wizard of our swamps; I was always afraid I'd call him Vasilis, Vargalys wouldn't have forgiven me for that. I remember an episode, one of his short-term romances with this Vaiva, our intern, she showed up in our office, very pretty and unbelievably proud: Vargalys was instantly taken with her; maybe she was worth it, Vaiva really did have something proud or even queenly about her, but as a woman she didn't pay the slightest attention to him—Vargalys was old enough to be her father; however, he immediately discovered Vaiva's soft spot— she liked to feel intelligent and smart—he'd do her work for her, but so cleverly, it would turn out she'd thought it all up herself, and even offered some good ideas to the others. He went at her from all directions at once, he divided himself up into a legion of Vargalyses, each one more elegant and magnanimous than the last; Vaiva melted right before your eyes, and to him it was like some contest or something, he entranced her like a wizard, the poor girl really was under a spell, she didn't get it at all, but all of a sudden Vargalys slapped her in the face and threw her out of the library; I saw it happen: he was triumphantly squeezing the poor thing right between the library bookshelves, and she accidentally called him by someone else's name; she said, "don't Rimutas," or "not here, Romutis." Vargalys went nuts, the same way he did once when he found me looking at the pages he'd marked in a book—he smacked her in the face, gave her a black eye, and the next day threw her out without giving her credit for her internship; Elena was crowing: now he'll get it, a commission will come, but absolutely nothing happened; Vaiva disappeared into thin air, and not a peep. To call Vargalys by someone else's name wasn't just a horrible insult, but a bad omen too; to me it seems that without his name Vargalys wouldn't have been anything at all, his power hid in his family and his name, he was a Vargalys of those Vargalys sorcerers, his grandfather and a host of ancestors stood behind him, he was encased in legends and the respect of the neighborhood, he couldn't be a Rimutis or Romutis, he couldn't even be a Vytelis—he was Vargalys, that said it all. Mad Vargalys, glued together out of ridiculously opposing parts, parts that couldn't have anything in common, the way his grandfather had nothing in common with his father or his father with his mother; the street is rising uphill, it seems I'm climbing the hill next to Bezrečjė, all the important things happened there, apparently something will happen today too. The bonfire of the Great Fire burned on that hill, set by Vargalys's father, who smelled the Russian tanks advancing on Lithuania's cities and towns from afar; he decided to meet the tanks the new government was bringing with a huge fire, he burned his entire archive, and he had a ton of paper, papers on Lithuanian finance, Lithuanian politics, and Lithuanian history; Julius kept dragging out more bundles, and Vargalys's father turned into a sorcerer, the eternal ruler of the flame; he probably burned up all of Lithuania, or its spirit; since he didn't dare to burn himself up, at least he sacrificed his papers, where all of his essence hid, to the flames; once he'd destroyed them, he couldn't be a sorcerer anymore. Vargalienė ran around the bonfire and danced an insane dance of victory, only it wasn't obvious who had won what here, because there were no winners, only losers; today on the hill there's neither a fire, nor Stadniukas with soldiers, this isn't the right hill; on the other side of the street are the gates to the market, a remnant of the old city, it's still possible to buy a thing or two there, even though the market went downhill a long time ago: no one bargains anymore, a lot of the sellers are too lazy to even hawk their wares, they just write the price on a bit of paper like they were in a store. In the pavilions the Uzbeks make an uproar with their melons, at least they've retained the spirit of an eastern market, they bawl, praise their wares, grab passersby by the sleeve;

Lolka and I liked to stroll through the market, even though we never bought anything, it was just that Lolka always had to swipe something; she had enjoyed stealing at the market since she was a kid, maybe she was a thief by nature, she was always grabbing others' things: others' apples, others' victories, others' men. All the same you'll have to admit your great shame, Stefanija, no matter how much you don't want to, you'll have to remember your terrible mistake and humiliation: true, Lolka is gone, but you're still here, and there's nowhere to hide from yourself—admit it, Stefanija. When Lolka starting weaving her net of long legs, sexy breasts, and bewitching glances around Vargalys, I shuddered; as always, she was shockingly brazen, she even had the nerve to ask me about his favorite things, what his weaknesses were, the willful, insane look in her eyes would paralyze me; you're defenseless in front of a person like that because you instantly realize no weapon hurts them, you cower in front of them like a monkey in front of a boa constrictor and surrender, an iron-bound villainy like that intimidates and crushes you—my little sister slowly turned into a monster, and I helped her myself. I still think of her as my little sister, even though she's long since been a monster, her toothy maw aimed at Vargalys; thank God, Vargalys paid no attention to her shameless attacks, Vargalys didn't pay attention to anything, he didn't need to answer to anyone—people like that are rare, people like that can't exist at all, only a Vargalys could be like that: all of Lolka's shameless attacks shattered on his indifference, sent her into complete despair, Lolka fumed to the point of insanity, her toothy maw snapped, catching nothing but air. I felt a wicked pleasure, I felt I was taking revenge for everything bad she had done to me, even for what she had only yet to do, I hated her, the way only sisters can hate each other: I'd imagine what I'd say to her when she'd try to get my sympathy, I picked out mocking, murderous words with pleasure, but when the fated hour struck I was speechless again. Lolka didn't ask for sympathy and she didn't complain, she topped even herself: with the smile of a vestal virgin she demanded I help her nab Vargalys, my help was her last resort, she didn't see any other alternative. She thought I should organize a little orgy, with Vargalys and the two of us, I was to lure Vargalys into a snare, shove Lolka into bed with him myself; when I heard this I felt I was a corpse, a dead thing, I should have killed her, bitten through her throat, poked out her brazen eyes. She chattered on as if it were nothing: you know that Vargalys doesn't take you seriously. I should have killed her on the spot. But I just mumbled like a fool and promised to think about it. The worst of it is that I really did start thinking. Even now, remembering this, I feel like that carcass swaying on a hook, yes, it's fall already, lamb has shown up at the market: Vargalys liked lamb roast, he'd marinate a nice leg for a whole week in red wine with seventeen herbs, that evening we gorged on just such a roast, but all of that was later, at first I just started thinking; a person's worst ability, his true ruin, is thinking, particularly if it's a woman who takes it up. I knew, I saw that Vargalys didn't pay attention to her, but I was completely overwhelmed by a weird premonition that Lolka would inevitably nab him—the more openly Vargalys ignored her, the more that conviction flourished. I should have tossed sulphuric acid in her face, poked out her brazen eyes, but a frightened voice whispered, don't you dare touch her, let everything go on behind my back, better I agree, like it wasn't for real, like it was a joke, so I could control everything, so that at least in some weird way I'd stay in charge; I couldn't do it, I simply couldn't, I couldn't even think about it, so I did it without thinking: we devoured that roast, got drunk, and when I went out I left Lolka with Vargalys, in the depths of my heart refusing to believe he'd take her, but it was as if I were pushing him into it myself; I couldn't even imagine it, but I agonizingly foresaw that would be just the way it turned out; dreaming he'd smack her in the face like he had that Vaiva, that he would spit in her face, mock her in public, but knowing full well that I was giving in. I gave in, I was and still am a tuteiša, what could I do up against Lola the Lithuanian, the owner of Vilnius, she had the upper hand, she kicked me back into the quagmire, into Bezrečjė's stench, and I gave in practically without a fuss, because I never did become a true Vilniutian, I've always been a tuteiša, a wretched, miserable exile. I wrote my own sentence, no one forced me; I condemned myself to long years of imprisonment because I couldn't leave Vargalys. I really am like that lamb carcass, there's just that much sense in me and just that much strength. I continued to be friends with Lolka too. I wore her leather coat, and I have it still. I continued to buy clothes and food for Vargalys, to clean his apartment, that's why I came to Vilnius from my swamps, that was the meaning of my life; I don't want to leave the market, even though the veterinary pharmacy is across the street,

I'm fascinated by those carcasses, they're saying something to me, it's just that I don't understand their language yet, but some day I will, because today blood is running out of me like it does out of them, and today both they and I are crucified, because God has forsaken us.

I was supposed to find a strange country here, one called Lithuania; it really is here, but is this how it's supposed to be: at least a quarter of the city's inhabitants are Russians brought here from who knows where, and the Poles of Vilnius—the poor Poles—graduate from the Russian schools and don't speak Lithuanian; break the spell on Vilnius, Vasilis, boil up a potion of bats, crows' feathers, and wolf-berry, break Vilnius's spell, Vasilis, if you still can, if it's at all possible anyone still can. I was to find the spirit of the ages here, it actually does linger here, but will it last much longer: Gediminas, the dour brainiac of Vilnius who went by the name of a Grand Duke, lies somewhere on the glaciers of Tian Shan, Vargalys, the other one with the name of a Grand Duke, is neither dead nor alive, even plain old Martynas lay down in front of a roaring truck—the soul of Vilnius is fading by the day, you aren't needed here, Stefanija. Don't think that way, don't; you're needed, Vasilis will break the spell on Vilnius yet, he'll pull the pink, violet, rose-colored mists of our swamps out from under his arm and he'll show everyone; he'll dig the sunken village of Užubaliai out of the ground too; he'll summon the forest brothers, slowly drowning in the muck of the swamp but rising again to the surface every night, out of oblivion, and if he doesn't do it, if he is no more, it's destined that you, Stefanija, do it: you really are needed. The ladies are buying onions, there aren't any in the stores again; it's time to get out of this market, the veterinary pharmacy will close for lunch any minute, I go across the street and there's a long-bodied little dog with short little legs traipsing around by the pharmacy, some kind of perverted dachshund, exactly the same as the one I saw by the Tallinn, it can't be the same one, it couldn't have scurried this far—that's just the way it is in Vilnius: the people here are all alike, and the dogs too, and the buildings in the new districts, even Old Town's vain efforts to remind you of the real Vilnius don't help. Shoo, shoo, you clumsy thing, you're all I need, don't tell me menstruation really does smell like a bitch; the door creaks stupidly, there's a bit of a line: salve for fleas, fish oil, and this one doesn't know what he wants at all. Lolka feared her fate, but she feared old age most, even a mature age, she foolishly tried to stay young forever; when she had a bit to drink she complained that she was slowly losing her body, I didn't know what she was talking about, but she kept repeating it to me, it turned into her mania. Earlier, her favorite pursuit had been abusing Vargalys: what a wimp he is, how old, how hopelessly in love. Lolka tormented him, she'd make him tell her about the camp, drag him to discotheques, threatening to one day force him to shave his head bald for the fun of it—Vargalys, the great Vargalys, would complain to me, or maybe not to me, but rather to himself: he'd sit down in the room and talk out loud; the really horrible part was that he didn't say a single bad word about Lolita, he'd only complain about himself, about how old and wimpy he is, and undeserving of Lolita's love—I'd be overwhelmed with horror: it was Lolka who wasn't worthy of licking his boots, and this was how she'd brought him down: Lord knows, if she'd demanded it, he would have shaved himself bald. I'd console him like a little child, stroke him and hug him, and he'd lie there naked, feeble, with that childish, helpless little thing of his, but he really wasn't either old or wimpy, he was worth the love of all the women in the world, it was just that slut Lolka who destroyed him. And suddenly she started complaining that she was losing her body: she kept showing me her fingers, which were supposedly distorted, bent at the joints, she'd get completely undressed to prove to me that supposedly there were fat lumps of flesh gathering on her hips, her thighs, under her breasts, Lord knows, I didn't see anything, I got really tired of her, although that mania had its good points: Lolka stopped torturing Vargalys, became more attentive and more loving, she even told me secretly that she was afraid to get undressed in front of him, for a moment I even had hope that maybe she'd leave him alone. Lolka lived just for the myth of her perfect body; suddenly that body started going downhill, or maybe, for all the good it did, she got scared that sooner or later it'd start going downhill and that would be it; she lost her crutch, she started acting like a fool, lost the meaning of her life: everyone's that way, they hang on to a house, or a car, or a job, or some other trifle, and if it vanishes unexpectedly they don't see any sense in living . . . I've off and philosophized, it's not just the clerk giving me dirty looks, it's the line behind my back too: why doesn't that dolt ask for something; and the dolt, that is to say me, just stammers: if maybe, by chance, even just one package; they have it, they have it, I stuff the roll of gauze into my purse, I don't even take the change, I slip out to the street, take a deep breath of air—oh, how happy I am, I want to sing or turn somersaults, all the people are so good-looking and smart. I got some gauze, I got some gauze—do you hear, I got some gauze to plug up my stinking, dripping little hole! It's time to go back to work, I smile like some kind of a fool, even my cramps have stopped: look here, how nicely that girl has tied on a scarf, I could learn from her, I follow her with my eyes, my glance falls on a tall young man's figure, he turns and I recognize Žilvinas, Martis's son—how old is he now? Seventeen? Eighteen? All decked out and slicked down by his mama, brown corduroy pants, a jacket with at least six appliquéd pockets, gracefully tied with a belt, the ends hanging loose, the expression on his face proud and a bit insolent, a real Communist Youth leader, an exemplary youth; apparently I wasn't destined to be happy for long, my heart stirs with a sad, sad longing: Martynas is gone, Teodoras and Gediminas are gone too, Vargalys is neither dead nor alive; Vilnius is emptying, the real people, the real Lithuanians are dying, and who will replace them, who will come in their place, what will their children do, their one and only child, Martis's son? Žilvinas saw me, he's walking towards me, another two young men follow after him, they don't look like Communist Youth leaders at all, more like gangsters in the making.

"Aunt Stefanija, what a pleasure!" Žilvinas greets me somewhat mockingly, his buddies nod their heads with unusual solemnity. "I didn't think we'd see each other until dad's funeral."

A velvet voice, large, deep eyes, a manly, handsome face; he reminds me of a young Alain Delon—really a handsome boy. It suddenly strikes me that I've always loved him, he's the only one I can open up to, reveal all of my loneliness to, show myself the way I am—weak, miserable, gushing blood—and ask for comfort, he's the only one who can understand me, surely he'll understand; his eyes are kind and wise.

"How are you doing, Aunt Stefanija? We haven't seen each other in a long time." He doesn't change his tone, and his buddies are standing next to him without moving, not even blinking, unpleasant characters, worn-out leather jackets, patched jeans, frayed sweaters: they're like twins.

"At my age not much changes. And how are you doing? You're still working on your professional Communist Youth career?"

"Sure," he answers calmly. "I've been elected to the City Committee. Maybe you'll stop in for a minute? We'll honor dad's memory."

Suddenly I get sad, so sad—here he is, the only offspring, the offspring of them all, he's the only one I can tell everything to and be comforted by, the future is in his hands, he's inherited Vilnius now. I go with him like I'm under a spell, the twin gangsters in the making hold me by the arms, I go up the stairs, held commandingly. It's a bit intimidating, but I know Žilvinas, after all, he knows me, I have the dagger, and Žilvinas is a Communist Youth leader, everything's okay, we're just going to stop by some apartment, the boys apparently have some wine or something, they'll probably ask me to put in a ruble or two—that kind is always penniless, well, Žilvinėlis, I really didn't expect it.

"You see, it's right nearby, Aunt Stefanija," says Žilvinas; his velvet voice is calming, all of my fears disperse, I smile to myself: how intimidated we are, we immediately imagine robbers, or hooligans at least; when someone asks for a cigarette in the street we instantly smash him on the head, and then it turns out the poor thing really did just want a smoke.

"We won't be long, Aunt Stefanija," Žilvinas goes on, locking the door, "We're speedy guys. We've got all kinds of business. You'll have time to get back to the library too. The lunch break is almost over, isn't it?"

He smiles pleasantly, Žilvinėlis really is suited to be a leader, he'll look fantastically handsome on whatever podium, a dashing boy. His friends are taking off their jackets, I throw off my coat too, step into the room, and suddenly I want to scream. A huge, messy couch wallops you with the oppressive smell of soured sperm; caked syringes and empty ampules roll around on a dirty table, there are little bottles with a whitish fluid and a bowl of dried poppy heads standing there; hanging on the walls—what children they still are!—there are pictures of Stalin, Hitler, Castro, all of them stuck with kids' toy arrows: one dangles right out of Stalin's eye. I've never seen a room like this before.

"Wow, what a little liar you are," I say quite calmly—it's strange even to me. "A Communist Youth leader! When did you have the time to change so much?"

"I'm a little liar?" It seems to me he's sincerely astonished. "Why?"

"Well, the Communist Youth committee, you're building a career . . ."

"That's true," his eyes are so calm, self-confident, and oppressive, that I instantly believe in him. "I'm a member of the City Committee, and this . . . it's nothing, just a little relaxation."

"They're from the Committee too?" I unsuccessfully try to joke, even though I don't feel at all like laughing; he really wouldn't have brought me here if not . . . if not for what?

"Of course not. Let me introduce you, Aunt Stefanija, so you'll know who you're dealing with. Raimondas, otherwise known as Roza, he doesn't know himself why. Viktoras, otherwise—the Dolby Master. He's an awesome talent, the first in Vilnius to set up a Dolby system—it suppresses the noise of magnetic tape, maybe you've heard of it? They're both unemployed at the moment—but no conflicts with the justice system, no criminal cases. I warned them—your first conviction, even if it's probation—and I don't say hello anymore."

"And what are you planning to do now?" I ask, like an idiot. Žilvin-ėlis just shrugs his shoulders.

Suddenly I want to scream, but it's hopeless, the old masonry walls of Vilnius won't let any sound through, everyone's at work, no one will be home; it was so long ago, I see Stadniukas's eyes before me again, but I don't feel the fury and determination I did then, I just feel awful and really depressed: here they are, here they are, my children, our future; the eyes before me aren't Stadniukas's, they're completely different, bleary, with enlarged pupils; the faces are quite young, but two are already puffy, and the third, the very worst of all, is smooth and handsome, like in a painting: the most important thing is to not be afraid, or actually, not to let them see that you're horribly afraid, to say something or ask something, or scream, or scold them, or . . .

"Boys, have you gone completely nuts?" There you go, my voice squeaks like a mouse whose tail's been stepped on; it trembles and breaks off. "Žilvinas, I could almost be your mama."

"Yeah, it ain't worth picking up old women," one of them agrees with me, Dolby it seems. "She's probably worn out."

"What do you know, my child," Žilvinas says to him in a dreamy voice; they're talking over my head, not paying attention to me at all, I'm just a thing. "What are you talking about!? An old woman? She's a

441

woman in the prime of life. A specialist. An expert! She'll get into it; you'll see, she'll knock us out! We'll have to hide from her yet, you'll see!"

I can no longer get a word out: I'm just opening and shutting my mouth; Žilvinėlis's clear eyes are already undressing me, I feel faint, but when they start undressing me with their hands I suddenly get my strength back: it seems I'm struggling, it seems I'm biting, where's my dagger—you don't even need to stab, it's enough to turn its blade in the light; the blow is sudden, short, brutal—jujitsu? Karate? Kung fu? It's even better this way: the fear subsides, I feel faint and my head spins a bit, God knows, it's almost pleasant.

"It's okay for Dad, but for the son, you say no way? That's not nice, Aunt Stefanija, it's simply not right."

"It's no fun with an old woman," one of them muses to himself. "Once, when I was maybe sixteen, this widow glommed on to me. Phew! I tell you for real—phew!"

"Listen, Roza," Žilvinas calmly lectures, "so, you go catch yourself some local bimbo, fuck her—and what of it? She's a little fool, she's powerless. And this is a mature woman, old enough to be your mother, and you . . . Don't you get what the thrill is? Use your brains! Think about it!"

He shuts up, because suddenly I get my voice back:

"Boys, come to your senses . . . Boys . . . Boys . . . I can't . . . I have my period . . . Really, really . . . It's my period, I can't . . . I bought gauze, see, gauze—there, in my purse . . ."

Žilvinas' face twists up unpleasantly, probably it's a smile; even Stadniukas didn't know how to toss off grimaces like that.

"Aunt Stefanija, what do you take us for!?" he snarls, his voice not at all velvety anymore. "What kind of childish excuse is that, what kind of lie? You know we'll check."

He snaps his fingers, I try to resist, but that's naïve and in vain, the gangsters in training know how to hold on, and it's Žilvinas who checks, who else; he really does look, I've never experienced a feeling like that before, it's indescribable, after that all that's left is to die, while Žilvinas calmly raises his finger to the light, he even sniffs at it—what's going on here, maybe it's a dream—I stand there a mess, my skirt turned up, my underwear pulled down and there's nothing, nothing, I can do against this impossible villainy: this is a dream, this kind of helplessness is possible only in a dream.

"It's true," Žilvinas says with a strange gaiety. "And here I was thinking: why is that dog sticking to her? Aunt Stefanija isn't lying. The tampon's bloody too, and it stinks to high heaven."

"The old lady won't suck. Probably doesn't even know how," says Roza disappointedly, he's called Roza, I'll remember that nickname all my life. "It's useless."

"So what, if she doesn't suck. We'll get one on anyway—what's the difference. Don't tell me you're going to go out looking again?" This one was quiet up until now; don't tell me they're going to, after all, it hurts me, it hurts, boys, it hurts me, you can't during my period, the first day, I'll die; have pity on me, boys.

"Come on, it's not that bad," Žilvinas firmly contradicts me. "But it's a subtle thing—the blood could get infected, then she'll die. Are we some kind of murderers?"

I start laughing out loud, hysterically, everything is mixed up inside me: death, menstruation, gang rapes and the massacres after the war, the churches of Vilnius and wads of gauze, the fog of the swamp, Lolka's little finger in Martis's pocket. I laugh uproariously, they pull back, talk among themselves, paying no attention to me, and I laugh: screw me, yes, I was the earth and I belonged to everyone, but I won't belong to you, screw me, shit on me, try and force me—I'll bite you, I'll taste fresh blood; too bad I have my period: I'd surrender my whole body to you, torture you, put you to sleep, and then I'd trample your wretched balls, I'd take revenge for Martis, and Gedka, and Tedis, and Vargalys, and for myself. For myself.

Probably they'll just scare me and throw me out, I need to remember the apartment number, maybe something can be done to them, but what—I no longer have anyone to advise or help me: I look closely at Žilvinas's face, Žilvinas was the king of the snakes, this one's a snake too, his face is calm and pretty again, elegant men like that always give women their seat on the trolleybus, his buddies would scare you to death in a dark alley, and you'd run to him looking for help, I've long since stopped laughing because his gaze stops my heart—what have they thought up now, what else can you think up?

"I don't know . . ." Roza breaks off doubtfully.

But Dolby even licks his lips, that one's really insane, he could do anything; for the moment I don't believe my ears; this is unreal, this doesn't happen, it's really not me they grab, force face down onto the couch stinking of sour sperm; it isn't me whose clothes they're taking off, my body's totally limp, but I still resist, I can't scream anymore, I've probably torn my vocal cords, I resist again, my shoulder really hurts, they must have sprained the joint, but now it makes no difference, now it makes no difference at all, I'm not here or I won't be soon—what's the difference.

"Hand me the cream," Žilvinas mutters, "And hold her."

They lift me, put me down on all fours, my body's completely limp, all of my muscles are slack, I'm as calm as a corpse, my thoughts are numb, how nice it is that they hit me on the neck, uh-oh, I'm gonna let loose in a minute, says Dolby, I see him when I turn my head, he's sitting on a chair; Žilvinėlis presses up to me, aims at me, I feel his thighs against my thighs, his pubic hair on my fanny and—oh, it almost doesn't hurt, how hopelessly calmly I'm thinking, or maybe I'm not thinking at all anymore, I just try to move my shoulder where it won't hurt so badly anymore, I just hear my farting, smell the double stench—from both fore and aft; it's not true, it can't be true, I'll die, this is a nightmarish dream, it almost doesn't hurt, it's just revoltingly unpleasant, no, this isn't happening for real, I'm not here, I'm not, I'm not, my rear hurts, but does that matter—I'm already dead, I'm being done in by the dragon, then I'll turn into a dragon myself too.

"Well, guys, cool!" says the dragon in Žilvinas's velvet voice.

"Oh yeah, sure," Roza doubts, "you're all shitty."

"What do you know," mutters Dolby, he's taking off his pants; opening my eyes, I see his hairy thighs right here, I quickly close my eyes again.

This isn't true, this isn't even a dream, it doesn't exist at all, my butt stings even worse, it doesn't just sting anymore—it seriously burns— it's the flame of a bonfire, it'll burn out my guts and I'll die—that would be best.

"Blood!" Dolby announces, charmed. "Like a hymen, huh?"

"Bloody shit," Roza corrects him angrily. "I'm not interested. Let her get dressed."

"So we managed it, and you're clean as a whistle?" Žilvinas's velvety voice suddenly turns into sandpaper.

"I held her," Roza says calmly. "I'm a co-author. I don't want to, and that's that. You stick yourselves into that bloody shit. I'd rather hit the needle instead."

"Let's hit a needle!" Dolby agrees; that one's insane, he can do whatever he wants. "Maybe she needs a hit too, so she can't go and complain?"

"It's a waste of a dose," Žilvinėlis is completely velvet again. "How's she going to complain? Everything's been thought out—figure it out yourself. Where? How? Besides, Aunt Stefanija has to go to work. She's in a hurry. She stopped by for a bit, we sat and chatted—that's all. Why should Aunt Stefanija complain—nothing happened, everything's just hunky dory."

I clamber off the reeking couch, the bloody tampon falls to the ground from between my legs, all of it's true, it happened, my rear burns like fire; I stagger to the bathroom, they didn't tear my clothes, even all the buttons are in place; I am a machine, I work according to a program, that's why I don't need to think, what matters most is that I don't need to think, yes, Dolby is washing up in the bathtub, he playfully splashes me with water, pinches my right breast, I have to wait until he leaves, I'm a machine, he gets out of the bathtub, I get in, Dolby stares at me, and I'm already washing up, I am a machine washing itself, he smacks his lips, licks them, sighs, and goes out, where's my purse, a dagger with a three-sided blade impatiently waits for me there; SACRUM is written on it, but that has no meaning, because by now I know what I am going to do.

I'll wash up carefully, get dressed slowly, comb my hair, I'll even put on makeup, then I'll quietly slink into the room, they'll be drawing the whitish fluid into a syringe, like a cat I'll sneak up to Žilvinėlis—he'll be sitting with his back to me—I'll aim carefully, and stab. The blow is short, sudden; the dagger instantly flies to the ground, Roza picks it up, turns it in his hands.

"I respect character," says Žilvinas, rubbing the wounded finger on his right hand. Jujitsu? Karate? Kung Fu? "I suspect we'll be seeing each other again, Aunt Stefanija. I like you. When I get promoted, I'll hire you as my secretary—by then secretaries will need to know how to use a computer."

"Wow, what a knife," Roza is charmed. "I'll take it, okay?"

"No way," Žilvinas lectures. "First of all, when a guy has a knife in his pocket, he really starts itching to put it into action. And second— this is a subtle thing. It's antique. Return it to Aunt Stefanija. What are we, some kind of thieves? Robbers?"

Roza very unwillingly obeys; I stuff the knife into my purse, pull on my coat, rush out sobbing hysterically. The apartment number is eleven—and what of it, I no longer have anyone to help me or advise me, I don't want them anymore; I don't want anything anymore—not even Vargalys, let them all get lost, let Vargalys himself get lost, let all of Vilnius get lost, I won't be here anymore. I go down the stairs, go out into the street and turn upwards, up the hill: I could jump in front of a car, but Martis already did that, besides, it might just injure me, not finish me off; no one will advise me how to act, no one will advise me what to do with my secret—to tell someone or to tell no one what it was I saw and did that damned evening in that damned garden?

I saw everything: I can testify in an earthly court, even in a heavenly one, that Vargalys didn't kill Lolita. When he ran back from the garden, she was already dead. Would testimony like that save Vargalys? But what does he need to be saved from? From a death sentence, from an insane asylum? Is it worth it? All of us would be better off in an insane asylum, all of us would be better off dead. And no one can save Vargalys from Vargalys.

I'm not worried about any Vargalyses, I don't know anything and I don't want to know anything, I didn't see anything, I can't testify to anything. Of course, only if I testify—I can't be the accused. I'm no longer here, that's my ghost climbing the steep stairs, going who knows where—without a reason why, without meaning; I was in that damned garden on that wretched eighth of October, I saw everything with my own eyes. For some reason I was certain they would show up in that garden, certain that they would come to the neglected little wooden house; I wandered around the empty footpaths, stared at the little houses, some of them were like little fairy tale castles, others reminded you more of a giant doghouse. By then it had been a long time since I'd had anything to do or anything to worry about, while I was schlepping around that damned garden I thought about whether it was worth getting a dog: a scotch terrier or a cocker spaniel; better a cocker spaniel, even though they're expensive. I believe I cried, or maybe not; in the end I snuck up to the cottage where they had been sitting for almost a half-hour already; holding my breath I settled in by the window and looked inside; I wanted to pull back at once, but I didn't even close my eyes: the two of them were naked, caressing each other; I immediately remembered our village, the kids, who, like Indians, used to crawl around by the woods following twosomes, sometimes for hours on end—until they got what they were trying so hard for. On rare occasions they'd take me along too; I'd spy patiently, breathing hard and swallowing my spit, but the most important part would just get started and I'd close my eyes and cover my ears: that wretched October eighth, for the first time in my life, I didn't turn away, I greedily watched them, without feeling upset, or ashamed, or angry; Lolita's body was slim and elegant, grasping and greedy, but slowly I realized that nothing was working out for them, nothing at all, something was blocking them, neither poses nor imaginative caresses helped, absolutely nothing worked for them, apparently I had showed up there so I could see it with my own eyes, I needed to see it, that's why I watched—for the first time in my life. Vargalys kept getting redder, Lolka got more and more furious, but all their efforts were in vain, I gnawed on my fist and waited, I even drew blood, but still nothing worked for them, absolutely nothing, the more they tried, the more horribly they failed; I don't know whether I was glad, probably not, what was there to be glad about if Lolka suddenly kicked, that's right, kicked Vargalys away, jumped up raving, her hair tousled, breathless out of fury or lust. Vargalys looked at her like a beaten dog; the sun was setting by now, painting that wretched scene the color of blood.

"You're impotent! A damned impotent!" Lolita shrieked. "You've got no balls! I'll tell everyone! Tomorrow. Immediately. I'll hang out posters. An impotent and a madman! I've read your writings. I've secretly read your blatherings. I'll publish them too. Why are you reaching out your hands? Don't touch me!"

I couldn't intrude, I couldn't suddenly show up and calm her down: she screamed again and again, screamed horrible words—she was stretched out, standing in a rapacious pose, she worked Vargalys over, her fingers really were twisted like a beast's claws, disgusting globs of flesh as slimy as a jellyfish really did quiver between her thighs, under her breasts, on her hips—that was how her evil erupted, it barged and busted out of her; Vargalys stood up too, and Lolita kept screaming, I

447

didn't pay attention to the words anymore: Vargalys turned pale, his entire body turned white, practically transparent, then he roared like a beast and jumped out, ran off through the bushes stark naked, between the trees, leaving shreds of skin on the sharp branches. My feet calmly lead me towards the station; I'll get into a trolleybus and ride to the library, my rear hurts, it's burning all over, it won't let me forget the whole thing really did happen, I'll have to continue to live, the worst of it is that I'll have to continue to live: Lolka stood there like a post, like a perverted monkey-man statue, she didn't see anything around her, didn't hear anything, didn't sense me; she collapsed gradually, it seemed she slowly, comfortably, laid herself down, trying not to hurt herself; meanwhile, Vargalys was running around the garden naked. He returned much later, when she had already started to stiffen: he didn't have anything to do with it, I could testify to this, even at the heavenly judgment; when Lolka collapsed, my heart didn't race, I smoked a ciga- rette and carefully fastened my purse for good measure, so it wouldn't fall out. I nearly ran right into Vargalys, he returned from the side where I had been standing, but he didn't see me, he didn't see anything, he didn't smell the smoke from my cigarette, he was completely out of his mind, he collected himself only when he saw Lolita lying already dead on the floor; he probably doesn't remember anything, it wouldn't be hard to convince him he killed Lolka, Vargalys would believe it whole- heartedly, especially since from that moment on he acted consciously, he knew all too well what he was doing: I was condemned to see it, I had to watch everything to the end, apparently that's the way it was written in the great Book of Life; he wasn't at all sadistic about dis- membering Lolka's body, not at all; not at all, he did his ghastly work carefully and attentively, looking for something; he didn't disfigure that body just any old way, he was looking for something, something he was certain was there; you'd think he was digging in the ground trying to come across something, but not a treasure—I understood that from his expression—surely not a treasure: more like a terrible bomb that could blow up all of Vilnius, maybe even the whole world—I don't know if he found it, but he stood up slowly, looking down at the dismembered body with a wooden expression, the way he had looked once before, thirty-five years ago, on the hill next to our village, next to Bezrečję. Only then did I retreat from the window; I went to the bus stop, just like I'm going down the station platform to the fifth track now; I don't know anything, I can't testify to anything, because I'm no longer here, all that remains is a burning rear and a fresh memory of the coming generation; I don't know any Vargalys, I know now who I am and what I'm doing, I'm going home, here's track five, my train, it's waiting obligingly, the clock shows there's two minutes left before it departs: I'm going home, I'm a village girl from the swamps, without a nationality and without an education, I never lived in Vilnius, I don't have a single acquaintance here, I'm as alone as alone can be, a silly, bestial, genuine tuteiša from the swamps—I'm calm, I'm all right, Vasilis said more than once that people like that have it easiest. The train moves, I sit down on the left side, so I won't need to see Vilnius disappearing in the distance, that dying city I'll never visit again; empty cars slowly move by, gloomy figures; suddenly I'm afraid Vasilis might not recognize me, very afraid, but in time I remember that I have a sign, a password he will surely remember, even lying in a coffin; I pull it out of my purse, it accomplished one great deed; I carefully stroke the three-sided blade, there are still traces of hated blood on it, three dried rust-colored spots, and that's all—how ordinary it all is. I put it back in its place—what a fancy purse, and my clothes are strange, like some city lady's, but it's nothing, at home I'll change in the blink of an eye; beyond the window the last houses of the city have already gone by, I cast a farewell glance at my past, which probably never was; for some reason it seems as if someone should see me off, wave a handkerchief, but there's nothing behind me; only by turning all the way around—at the very last moment—does it occur to me that a long-bodied, perverted dog, hopelessly lagging behind, is scurrying after the train, but it's just a thought—there's really nothing there, in the entire world there hasn't been anything real for a long time; only the three rust-colored spots on the three-sided blade of the dagger, they've held fast on that blade for the entire three weeks.

# PART FOUR
## VOX CANINA

Trees have become particularly significant—each one is like a different person. Some stand there naked, only their bark smells; others still spread the scent of profuse foliage. The scent is always different: some trees are bland and a bit dry, others are as juicy as the aroma of just-opened buds. But perhaps the multifarious trees are the most significant: a part of them are luxuriantly crowned, a part dried and weakened, yet another part is as red as blood. They're multifaceted. They've crumbled inside; they live like people who have lost their harmony. Like the real people of Vilnius.

I find it difficult to look at the crowns of trees. They're too high up.

We look at trees entirely differently than we once did. Before they were just plants that could provide shade or bestow fruit. We didn't sense that just about any tree could be one of us. We didn't sense that every one of us is at least somewhat a tree. Now we sense it; we look at them as one of our own. Nothing happened; it's just that people became a bit more wooden, or the trees became a bit more human. And in any event . . .

And in any event—there's nothing to be seen in the empty autumn road. And the road itself leads nowhere. Don't drag yourself down it; it doesn't lead to the secret, to the unknown, not even to ruin. It doesn't lead anywhere at all, because every road in Vilnius always leads nowhere.

I can no longer brush my hand over my face. I no longer want to look in a mirror. Vilnius was a city of churches, but now no one prays in them. Vilnius was a city of lindens, but now the lindens have been ravaged by acid rain. Even I cannot bathe in the insatiable waters of the Neris. The really awful thing is that I can't play the piano. Sometimes I hear jazz pouring out of some window. I want to weep. But I can't even cry anymore.

Who am I? I'm called Gediminas Riauba; I was born in 1930 . . . That's funny; it's funny and meaningless. I'm not called Gediminas Riauba. I wasn't born. It's more like I died.

We don't remember our death. That's natural—after all, we don't remember our birth, either. The beginning and the end are always covered in fog; that's why every ending can turn into a new beginning.

I don't mourn. And I don't torment myself. And I'm not glad. All emotions are either similar or completely the same. The truth of it is, we don't feel emotions—they are, after all, based on the effect of glands. The effect of human glands—and we're no longer human. We feel only memories of emotions or remember the feelings of emotions. These remarks are no more than a pathetic tautology, but I don't know how to express it better. The language of humans isn't suited to our non-world, to our timeless non-life.

The little bushes by the railroad bed are scraggly, their leaves are miserable, but they're still alive. Their smell is the smell of the abused. A person would smell the same way if he were secretly splashed with gasoline, fuel oil, and other chemicals. Through all of those odors, a smell of shock, injury, and misery emerges. Perhaps those bushes were once happy and carefree. The people of Vilnius were never carefree and happy, at least I've never seen any like that. They're depressed and upset—most of the time because of trivial concerns. I was exactly the same: I can assess this objectively because I'm dead. To me it's no longer worth lying. We don't lie at all, because the truth is always simpler than lies, however complicated it may be. See, the truth already exists, while a lie needs to be invented and constructed without contradictions. So we never resort to lies. The state of the dead has its advantages; it's just really different. When we're alive, we don't at all worry about what we'll do when we're dead. That is a huge mistake. The world is extremely deficient in schools about life after death. The paradises of Christians, Muslims, or the other religions that are popular on earth are very funny and absolutely pointless. We are acutely aware of this here.

While I was still in the world I read about a rat paradise. The scientists constructed it as follows: as much food, drink, and sex as you want. At first, the rats were happy, then they got lethargic—they even stopped reproducing—and in the end they got completely unnerved. The most athletic ones attempted to break out of paradise, but it was surrounded by high tension wires. So the ones who wanted to escape would die. The other rats saw and smelled the corpses, and quickly realized that the white, shiny wires carried death. But they went on trying to escape, even at the price of their lives. The hedonistic rats, those who hadn't tried to escape, didn't merely stop breeding, they stopped moving too, and then eating: they calmly and quietly died out. The rat paradise was left vacant. It's strange that people haven't been able to think up a paradise in the least bit more sensible than the one even the rats scorned. The best they've thought up is to renounce it entirely. To strive to turn into nothing, like the Hindus. Or to believe that there's nothing after death, like the atheists. The latter really suffer here; they feel insulted. They've finally died, and now they're forced to continue existing. Most of the time, the atheists rush to get back to earth in the form of a fly or a cockroach. Those are the rules here. You can return to earth, but you won't have a consciousness. You can keep your consciousness, but you won't turn into a human. Those are the rules here. You can choose the form yourself, but only once. For myself I chose the one that suits Vilnius best.

For the time being it doesn't get terribly cold, so I feel all right. True, the drunks and the kids throw glass shards everywhere, so I have to be careful. If I cut up my paws, no angels will lick my wounds. When you choose a form, you get both its advantages and its disadvantages. Those are the rules here. There are quite a few rules here.

There are rules everywhere, because nothing can exist without any rules at all.

I frequently ask myself—just what were the rules of Vilnius? I can think freely, I am a thinking dog of Vilnius, and that's what I'll be as long as a car doesn't run me over or a dogcatcher doesn't finish me off. It's quite tolerable; it's just that the general symphony of smells greatly hinders your concentration. Even strangers' thoughts smell, all of them differently. And then there's that Stefanija. True, a stench that strong smothers all smells, but it wears on the nerves. It's like the blinding blue flash from a soldering gun, or the roar of an airplane taking off. And at the same time like a sophisticated porno movie shown to a sixteen-year-old who is bursting with unreleased sperm. We find physiology particularly oppressive. I can't even masturbate. Nor can I chase after bitches—after all, I have consciousness. The hardest part is food. I'm most certainly not a metaphysical dog. I'm an entirely real Vilnius dog with a human's intelligence and memory. I could even help someone, save them from misfortune or encourage them to do a good deed, but only with doggish behavior. It's too bad Vilniutians don't pay proper attention to dogs. It's a rare person who goes searching among the dogs for one like me. That's probably sensible. You could spend your entire life searching, become well-known as a madman, and find absolutely nothing. Better to search for treasure. There are considerably more treasures than there are those like me.

Maybe I should have turned into the Iron Wolf.

But it's too late, I'm a dog; even my thoughts are slowly getting doggy. I'm always afraid I'll lose my chain of thought. It's tough for me, I admit it. We don't know how to lie to ourselves, either. Lying is worthless to us, because any lie at all is temporary by its own nature. A lie hides the truth, but only for a while. Lying is a mute admission of death's inevitability, practically its anticipation. And here we don't have anything to anticipate; you won't die even if you turn into a tree. The majority of Vilnius's trees are reincarnated Hindus. No theory of Vilnius is possible without accounting for this sad fact.

But I'm hardly concerned with Hindus who have turned into trees: I'm much more attracted by live Vilniutians. Yesterday, or a month ago, or sometime, I met Vytautas Vargalys next to the fence of Lukiškių Prison. He didn't recognize me—and I had so hoped for that. Vytautas Vargalys is the only one who could have recognized me. He never considered dogs to be just dogs, or birds just birds. He didn't even consider himself to be just Vytautas Vargalys. That's why he was a walking corpse—every excessive knowledge kills by degrees. He didn't recognize me—well, what of it? One of our biggest advantages is that everything's absolutely same to us. We don't immediately escape from the eternal wheel of fate: at times we feel fear, hate, or ignorance—without them the soul couldn't exist, and we do have a soul, even though we're surprised at that ourselves.

Human language hampers me. In our world there is no "at first" or "later," and language can't get along without words like that. Unfortunately, a language corresponding to what I know would be comprehensible only to me. I suppose this is the way the gods feel: they talk non-stop, but no one understands their language. At the very most single words, or individual sentences. But even complete sentences seems unlikely.

It's difficult to get used to a new body. I keep wanting to stroke my mustache. Or knit my fingers together. It's rather odd to sense my old body, which I'll never have again. I'm like a soldier; I still feel my amputated legs and arms.

It's difficult to get used to the new Vilnius too. It's totally different than the city I remember. I no longer see the rooflines, I no longer see the crowns of the lindens—dogs don't look upward, only into the distance. I don't see faces well: around me there are just knees and more knees, girl's legs, and sometimes dogs happen by too. Children have become strangely close; their faces are the only ones I can get a good look at. But I immediately distinguish every person's scent; Šapira went by here not so long ago, and here, a bit earlier, maybe even yesterday, stood one of my former students: I recognize his smell, I just don't remember his name. The scent of Vytautas Vargalys drifts from the basement of the KGB Building, and an impossibly reeking pool of vomit, which never dries out, gathers under the little bench by the statue of Žemaitė. The streets of smells sprawl in an entirely different way than human pathways. The Vilnius of smells is mysterious and poorly researched. When I was a human, it never occurred to me that scent is the only sense that can reveal the past directly. The smells of ancient events and ancient sufferings don't fade. They slowly settle on the grass, the sidewalks, the walls; they penetrate into the city's body and remain for the ages—like an everyday, ordinary landscape, the landscape of smells. I am perhaps the only inhabitant of that landscape. Other dogs smell it, but they don't understand it. People would understand it, but they don't smell it. No one going by the KGB turns their head like I do, no one pulls the mournful and angry scent of Vytautas Vargalys into their nostrils. He would frequently smell of anger, agitation, and fear. His father is fat and sweats heavily. People sweat to cover up the smell of their emotions. Sweat smells only of physiology; it smothers the perfume of the soul. Love doesn't smell of roses or the blue of the heavens at all. Love smells of sleepless nights, death, and insanity. When I run down Vasaros Street, it smells as if nothing but Romeos and Juliets, Tristans and Isoldas, Orpheuses and Eurydices were pining away on the hill of madmen. Smells reveal unexpected connections of things and phenomena, confirming those I only suspected before. Smells are an important language of the world, and Vilnius is a city of smells. If people's sense of smell were like that of dogs', the world would change radically. Many secret thoughts would immediately become plain, as people's emotions, and most often their thoughts too, have a distinct smell. You can learn to conceal yourself, to never give yourself away by expression, voice, or movements, but you can't change your smell. People can't smell like dogs do, otherwise the world would fall apart. The world is the way it is only because the greater part of people's thoughts and intentions are unknown and unpredictable to other people. But we, the dogs, can smell all of that. Even the most ordinary mutt smells what his master wants before he even wishes for it himself. The semiotics of scent could be the most profound knowledge in the world.

My thoughts keep getting more dog-like.

I am the secret God of Vilnius, but at the same time, I'm the most ordinary of dogs: I reek of dog; I can eat offal; I urinate with my leg raised. It's harder for me to understand people than it once was, even though I know more about them all the time. More and more all the time. The essence of Vilnius is deceit. If you understand the deceit of Vilnius's prisoners, you'll understand the Vilniutians themselves.

Life in Vilnius is a giant poker game, played by madmen. Everyone hides his cards, raises and raises the bet, grimaces and makes faces, hoping to deceive the others, but no one ever finds out what his cards really are. It's a madmen's poker game, there is no logic or sense in it:

here they pass with four aces and raise to the skies without any face cards. Here everyone plays jeopardy, but no one wins the jackpot. Our life is an endless game of Vilnius Poker: its cards are shuffled and dealt by a scornfully grimacing death.

I no longer play: I fell out of the game. Many have fallen out, but Vytautas Vargalys, Ahasuerus Šapira, Levas Kovarskis, and Stefanija Monkevič still sit at the table . . . As long as the game continues, I don't have the right to reveal the cards in play. And it continues; it will end only when the last one rises from the table. A pointless and meaningless game played by madmen: the last one left at the table won't by any means win the jackpot. The jackpot will come to nothing, the cards themselves will come to nothing: everyone knows this, but they keep heaping more and more into the jackpot, even though a pile of corpses, sleepless nights, hysterical tears, suicides, and murderers are piled up there already. I suppose Lolita Banytė-Žilienė was a suicide. She smelled like a suicide.

I don't understand why all of this worries me so much, what I still want to find out about that wretched Vilnius Poker and its players. What are they to me, what meaning do they have anymore? It's pointless for us to be interested in the fate of the world: it doesn't concern us anymore. It's unproductive to study the world because there's nowhere to put any new information about it to use. Rummaging around in people's actions and thoughts is like playing chess with yourself.

But the dragon of Vilnius won't give me any peace. Vytautas Vargalys searched for him, Teodoras Žilys molded him out of clay, and Lolita Banytė-Žilienė caressed him and made love to him. Ergo, he really does exist.

If he didn't exist, I wouldn't need anything in the gloom-wrapped city of Vilnius. I can remember the past without idling around the crooked little streets of Old Town.

I listen to old man Vilnius wheezing heavily as he breathes. Cities fall ill too—their illnesses are similar to human illnesses: they suffer from both hypertension and cancer. Cities die in horrible pain as well. But what's even worse is when cities rot alive. When people peck around in stinking putrefaction, thinking that's what life is. In my human life, people often asked me why I didn't defect to some other country. I don't know the reason myself. I had to die before I finally realized why. I was agonizingly interested—and even now I'm interested—in the people of Vilnius. People like that aren't found anywhere else. Where else would I have found Vytautas Vargalys, who had traveled through the hell of the prison camps and then through the horrifying hell of the abyss? And who had, in the end, created his own private hell, which even I can't fathom? Where else would I have met Lolita Banytė-Žilienė, a bird of paradise with a poisonous beak and the claws of a dragon? Or Martynas Poška, the crazy collector and guardian of Vilnius's rot? In what other country would I have been able to play crushing, meaningless Vilnius Poker?

It's a shame I don't know how I died. One of the crazy players of Vilnius Poker who's arrived on our side could tell me that, but even that won't happen. We don't recognize one another here and we don't have names. That's natural: all names apply only in a single lifetime. They change all the time: they mean nothing. I was the mathematician Riauba, now I'm a dog—so what should I call myself? You're all sorts of things, but you are always you, and your name—every one of your names—means nothing. It only marks one of your many lives. Those are the rules here.

Hindus frequently turn into the trees of Vilnius. Others travel to Vilnius as mice, pigeons, or cockroaches. Vilnius is crawling and teeming with aliens. They want to fathom the secret. We all want to fathom the secret, each his own. But why is there such a profusion of aliens struggling to get into Vilnius in particular?

It's only Vilnius Poker, or its hands, that could answer, but what its cards are is an unknown. Who will answer, who will explain? Maybe Lolita Banytė-Žilienė, whose father was a KGB colonel, or a history professor, or . . . Or what? The strange logic of humans demands an explicit answer. As if it were possible to find out! For some reason, people yearn to resolve and explain everything, even that which I didn't find out—what it is Vilnius Poker is hiding. Lolita's father was neither a KGB colonel, nor a history professor, nor . . . Then what was he? Either one or the other, or nothing—poker is poker, one can only make conjectures in this case. It's easier for us thinking dogs: Lolita's father always smells like Lolita's father, and nothing else is important. People's strange logic doesn't apply to us. In general, no logic applies in Vilnius. You won't find unarguable answers or absolute truths in it. Vilnius is a city of infinite possibilities. Vilniutians sit at the table and get cards you won't make any poker hands out of. But you have to play anyway. If you fold—you'll transmigrate into the company of the Bangladeshis. It's only when you fold that everything becomes obvious. A Bangladeshi is a Bangladeshi. Sometimes I visit them in the giant city garbage dump beyond Fabijoniškės. They sleep in piles of rags, cardboard boxes, or the heating pipes; they dig around in the decay of the dump. They're the only ones who understand me. They don't feed me reeking pieces of meat, like others do. They talk to me. One elderly man, who cut off his frostbitten toes last winter with a jackknife, frequently explains his theory to me, and I almost agree with him.

"Vilnius is a city under a spell, my dear dog," he likes to explain. "We both know this is true. Vilnius was the ethnic capital of Lithuania, then it belonged to Polonized Lithuania, then Russia, then Poland, and now it belongs to Russifying Lithuania. Where else is there a capital of a country that has belonged to one, another, and a third, a capital that wasn't a part of Lithuania even when Lithuania was independent? Can you imagine Paris belonging to Spain? No, Vilnius could only be compared perhaps to the Armenians' Ararat, which isn't in Armenia. It's a miraculous mountain too; it was no accident that Noah disembarked there. But Vilnius is ten times as miraculous. To a thinking person it reveals ten times, twenty times as many secrets. That's why I sit here, in a garbage dump, my dear colleague."

I thought the same way myself once. I don't know why I never found myself in the city garbage dump. I had to die to visit it. You make all of your most important discoveries after death. When you're alive, you can't find the time for them. You need to earn your bread, satisfy your ambition and your ego, drive out fear, and pour out hate. And if you live in Vilnius, you have to play that wretched Vilnius Poker too.

The Bangladeshis dig around in the Fabijoniškės garbage dump like shabby ravens. Real ravens often fly in too. I'm convinced that there are scores of new arrivals among them. From here, almost all of Vilnius is visible—as if it were a giant continuation of the garbage dump. Vilnius is an inside-out city. Other cities give birth to their garbage dumps, while this dump secretly gives birth to Vilnius itself. The view of Vilnius looks like a dream to me: people walk slowly, automobiles drive by slowly, there are no sounds—you have to concentrate hard to hear a vague hum. It was that Vilnius in particular that Vytautas

461

Vargalys worshipped: he predicted the city would stop altogether at some point. In my dreams it doesn't stop at all; that lethargic world suddenly explodes, really explodes—all of the people crack and split like over-ripe pears, and jellyfish-like gelatin, revolting slime, and warty tentacles that drip poison start gushing out of the cracks, striving to snatch up and entangle everything around them.

At least I'm trying to get inside my old friends' heads now, to untangle their deceptive labyrinth of scents. At its center, like a Minotaur, sits the worn-out, sickly dragon of Vilnius. He feeds on people's dreams, desires, and scents. On scents above all else.

Vytautas Vargalys arrived on this earth permeated with the smell of misfortune. He was never an infant; he was never a five-year-old bambino. At birth, he was already a nearly six-foot-five young man with gigantic, bottomless eyes. Everything about him was gigantic—his desires and his thoughts, his arms and legs, all of it. In some other place, he would have become a sports star, a great philosopher, or the president of a country. Even now the scents of all those possibilities lurk within him, and scent is never deceptive. But he tied his life to Vilnius. And Vilnius does not give birth to triumphs—this city gives birth only to a boundless, oppressive dreariness, or a fiery hell. I know I'm trying to explain too much, but I want to understand, in death at least, how people manage to live the life of Vilnius, why they've surrendered to the dragon, what axis their world revolves around.

Unfortunately, the people of Vilnius don't smell of self-love. If they possessed it, they wouldn't allow themselves to be treated that way. The ignorance of Vilnius doesn't smell of any hope; it's a hopeless ignorance. The axis of Vilnius's world is hate, fear, and a blind, black ignorance. No wheel of the world can turn on such an axis. Vilnius is a wheel of the world that has ground to a halt.

Vytautas Vargalys sensed this. He discerned many things that are known only to us, the dead. He was always a bit dead. But Lolita Banytė-Žilienė was even too much alive. You wouldn't even suspect they would become so close. They were people from entirely different worlds. In the great dream of Vilnius, it seemed they couldn't possibly dream together. Vytautas Vargalys was an aging giant, consistently destroying his own world. And Lolita Banytė-Žilienė was a beauty gushing with youth, for whom one world was too small.

It's only here that we finally realize that the world is the way we imagine it to be. Only here do we find out that attempts to change the world are ridiculous. All possible worlds are hiding in the boring—you'd say immutable—flow of life; you just need to come across them. Lolita Banytė-Žilienė truly made a great deal of progress in this quest if she managed to find Vytautas Vargalys.

I watched their acts of love many times. We don't think that spying on people or reading their diaries is taboo. That moral standard applies only in human life, where you can use others' secrets for evil. There's no benefit in it for us. If the secret is impressive or horrible—that's great for us. If it's banal or sentimental—we feel like we've wasted our time. For example, Martynas Poška's life was brimming with secrets, secrets that were as tiny as gnats. I know quite a bit about him. We know a lot in general. But by no means everything. Suffering and ignorance are universal commonalities. The gods people invent, gods who know absolutely everything, couldn't exist. They would suffocate in cosmic tedium. They'd simply kill themselves. If gods couldn't commit suicide, what kind of gods would they be—what would remain of their omnipotence?

There was a time when I loved Lolita very much. Even from here, it was a bit sad to watch her giving herself to someone else. We don't feel envy, but love is a feeling everyone can understand. I loved her, so I wanted her to be happy. But no one can be happy once they've taken up with Vytautas Vargalys. I could have told her this, but I didn't feel I had the right. What would happen if all the aliens started teaching people? The world would fall apart in the blink of an eye—people wouldn't want to play that wretched poker game anymore, they'd just wait for someone to tell them what cards their opponents were holding.

We don't pay much attention to all the others' secrets, to all our knowledge. We're already dead. It's all the same to us now.

Gediminas Riauba would have saved Lolita. But I'm not Gediminas Riauba. I'm already dead. It's all the same to me now.

Sometimes I just can't manage to remember Lolita's face; then I crawl into Teodoras Žilys's studio through a broken window. The children of Old Town stare, amazed, when they see a dog clambering over the rooftops. Lying down comfortably, my tongue hanging out, I stare for a long time at two of her portraits, hung in an old-fashioned vaulted corner of the room. Dust constantly settles on them; I keep licking it off. In her portraits Lolita Banytė-Žilienė is more real than in life. It seems she's going to step out of the canvas any minute and pet me. I hate being petted. Particularly when children pet me.

Even now I haven't completely fathomed Vytautas Vargalys. The first time I saw him with a dog's eyes, the first time I smelled him, I immediately sensed that he was carrying an important secret. I even imagined he wasn't playing poker with the others, but rather with the Lord God himself. The paradox is that God doesn't exist anyway. Even we don't experience him directly. So who was Vytautas Vargalys playing against? Who is he playing against now, hidden away in the basement whose windows towards the avenue are covered in glass block, smoking cigarette after cigarette? They let him smoke; they even provide him with Winstons. I suppose it's so the smell of smoke will get in the way of me smelling other, more meaningful smells: "a cover of smoke" is a concept that applies to us thinking dogs too.

He always carried a great hatred and an even larger fear inside. He was as smart as any devil, but he was never wise. He didn't know how to stop, or even so much as pause. That ability is essential for a wise man. The wise man doesn't rush about: he waits patiently until it all comes to him. As far as I remember, Vytautas Vargalys is always running, striving, chasing after that wretched dragon of Vilnius. Or talking about the prison camp. Here we regard all camps, massacres, and tortures much more phlegmatically than on Earth. It's not the exterior that's important, nor the barbed wire, nor the guards with bloodthirsty dogs. Nor crematoriums or monthly plans of annihilation. What matters most is the camp that unfurls within. What's worse is when people spend their entire lives confined inside a gigantic camp without seeing any barbed wire, without smelling the smoke from the crematorium. When they don't even realize that they are imprisoned. That's the biggest victory of the prison camp system. It's practically impossible to fight against a system like that. That's the very worst of it. We ponder this a great deal. We consider whether people need freedom at all. We look at today's North Koreans or Vietnamese, who are grateful to their government for allowing them to sleep a bit, eat a bit, and work a great deal. They die almost happy. There's still a lot of things here that just aren't clear to us. Maybe it's best for a person to be a slave? Maybe striving for freedom is no more than the invention of individual deviants?

Only Vilnius can answer questions like that. Vytautas Vargalys could explain a great deal. In the prison camp, everything was obvious to him; the confusion started only when he escaped it. Confusion always arises when you have choice. I was able to choose my new form, so for that reason I tormented myself over it for a long time. A person doesn't get to choose anything; he must be born a human. He is born in a concrete place and at a concrete time. This doesn't depend on him. Perhaps that's just the way a person's entire life should be? No choice, no substitutions, no freedom? You get those wretched poker cards, and your goal from then on is to prove to everyone that your cards are completely different. Not necessarily that they're better. Merely that they're different. Those are the rules of poker. Why is this necessary, if death is the only prize?

I keep comparing Vytautas Vargalys to the weakened, tormented vegetation of Vilnius. I search for universals in his life. Vytautas Vargalys grew exactly the same way the trees or grasses of Vilnius grow. Or maybe the foliage of Vilnius took over the principles of his growth. First, an unhealthily lively and luxuriant youth, a voluptuous branching. Then a prison camp of gas exhaust and power plant coal dust. All of Vilnius's trees start out longing to escape to an invigorating freedom. But slowly a gloomy resignation is born: the trees stand there submissively, and their branches are continually clipped and clipped. I know what's awaiting them, but there's nothing I can do about it. The biggest mistake our beginners make is to presume it's possible to fix a lot from the other side. I'm no longer a beginner. By now I know we're destined only to assess, but not to change. We can record and know, but we cannot condemn. I don't condemn Vytautas Vargalys, whatever he may have done. One way or another, here we know that death is not annihilation at all, rather just a change of form. So, it's all quite natural. Lolita was born only to die young.

Today there are an unusual number of people on the streets. Today Vilnius is unusually dead. A real, true necropolis; a profusion of the dead creep around the narrow little streets. What else is there left for corpses to do?

Perhaps some other thinking dog once looked at me in exactly the same way. Looked at me and considered me a dead man. Why, for what? I wasn't a corpse. I was just quiet, because it's impossible to speak out loud in Vilnius—otherwise you won't last. Sometimes it seems to me that I'm only allowed to wander freely through the city because I'm always quiet. Probably the power of the dragon of Vilnius reaches our world on the other side too.

Wandering the dismal little streets, I sink into oblivion more and more often. More and more often Vilnius recedes, disappears into the mists. Earthly matters worry all of us less and less, even though I do my utmost not to forget it. But I have to inhale through my nose for a long, long, time before I sense the city's smells again. The sad shoes of a sad person slowly approach from the left, pause, and go around me. I smell everything again. The sad person smells of hysterical goodness. From the nearest window drifts the smell of many days of drinking. It's a bit sad that we dogs can't get drunk. My pelt is damp from the fog. I nervously shake myself from my ears to the tip of my tail. In the sluggish mists sway all the Vargalyses, Poškas, and Banytės. They don't scream, struggle, or call for me. More and more often I reflect: are they really all that significant and important? Is their fate really worth my attention? Everything intertwines in the cramped dream of Vilnius; then it seems I wake up and once more feel the bitterness of a truly doggish life, but it hampers me less and less. Sometimes I'm more sorry for the trees of Vilnius than for the humans of Vilnius. And I should be sorry for them both, at least equally.

Probably solving even a single problem is too much, not just for a person's life, but for a thinking dog's life too. We can't even recognize other aliens. I've tried many times to associate with the more dubious of Vilnius's dogs. I've tried giving them signs, but without success. Perhaps they were ordinary dogs. Or maybe they didn't want to start up with me. You can't make sense of anything in this world, much less in the other. My non-life crumbled into pieces. There are many pieces of meaningless, aimless trots through Vilnius. Between them, like wandering rocks, float mysterious and doubtlessly particularly meaningful episodes. Sometimes it seems to me that they are different every time, that they change, like dreams seen many times.

Here's Vytautas Vargalys, walking slowly towards the Narutis and disappearing in an entranceway. Before vanishing, he smelled of pure hate and revenge—that biting smell still burns my nostrils. And just now I saw, right here in the gateway, Vytautas Vargalys's father; the two of them passed each other as if they didn't know each other, even though they almost crashed into one another. Vytautas Vargalys's father smelled of pure hate and of revenge as well. Vytautas's father—an economist or a physicist, a retiree or a ghost, or the doorman of a Druskininkai restaurant—who is he really? To me that's not what's important, there isn't any "really" for us; he really did smell like Vytautas Vargalys's father, that's enough for me. I sit in the gateway and shiver—and not just from the dampness and the cold. I find it horrifying that a son might kill his father, or a father his son. But I haven't yet managed to gather my senses when I see the third player. I see, and I can't believe my eyes, because I mostly rely on my nose now. Irena Giedraitienė slowly creeps towards the Narutis. I recognize her smell; I can't be mistaken. She smells of herself, but she doesn't at all look like Madam Giedraitienė. She has a completely different appearance. It's as if she changed into a stranger's skin. No human would recognize her, but you can't fool us thinking dogs: she forgot to change her scent, or maybe she couldn't. What does Madam Giedraitienė, who is seemingly now no longer Madam Giedraitienė, intend to do here? She smells of indolence and erotism—could they all be gathering here to make love? Giedraitienė/ not Giedraitienė pauses next to me, rummages around in her purse, and throws me a cold sausage. Then she determinedly sets off behind the Vargalyses. I pant with my tongue hanging out; suddenly breaking out in a sweat, I sniff at the stairs they all climbed, but the scent of their feet isn't there. It's unfathomable, everything loses its meaning; if only I could return to the so-called heavens, but from there, I'd hurry back to Vilnius again.

It's autumn in Vilnius now. Almost all of the trees have dropped their leaves and an annoying rain often falls. All scents weaken in the fall: because of the dampness in the air, because of the vegetation's apathy, because of the sad drowsiness of animals and people. Sluggish people smell differently than lively ones. Sleeping people smell different still. They smell of dreams. The intoxicating scents of dreams are not for me. Only house dogs enjoy them. All I can do is smell the dream of some traveler dozing in the railroad station. But even that's out of bounds. Some drunken militiaman might shoot me. I hide from the rain in the gateway and try to remember everything. To gather the floating islands of the more important episodes into a whole.

What was Vytautas Vargalys always hiding, and what is he continuing to hide?

I clearly remember his fear and its numerous forms. I saw it when I was still alive and smelled it as a dog; even thinking back on it, I can actually feel it, literally grasp it.

Fear is always growing in Vilnius; even the autumn dampness doesn't cover its scent. I was always afraid myself. I'm afraid even now, as a dog: it's terrifying that someone might kill me or injure me. In other world cities dogs aren't so fearful. And what was I afraid of as a human? Fear in Vilnius is multifaceted. You fear the future most of all, because it doesn't exist.

I never liked mathematics, but I was a topologist because that was the safest and most convenient thing to be. That's the reason I always returned to wretched, despicable Vilnius. I was afraid that if I stayed abroad, I'd suddenly realize that I could have, that I should have, been something else entirely, but it was already too late. I was afraid to look about and see my true possibilities, the ones I'd lost. That's why I kept coming back to Vilnius, where the only thing I could be was a mathematician. But in Vilnius an even more intense fear would overtake me: I feared irretrievably losing yet another of my possible futures. But I was afraid to leave Vilnius, because I would instantly come across a profusion of my own long-lost futures, droves of lost possibilities, abroad.

The other essential Vilniutian attribute is hatred. First of all, you hate yourself, because you are afraid. The worst of it is that love doesn't compensate for that kind of hatred. You can't love yourself, because there's nothing to love yourself for. I couldn't love myself for the fact that I was a professor and others weren't. On the contrary—I hated myself, because I made a living by hanging onto a decent mathematician's position, even though it contradicted my nature. By nature, being a terrorist suited muited me much better. By nature, Vytautas Vargalys was suited to become a prophet, to found and defend some new religion. But all he became was secretive.

I'm restless. I worry that I won't find the den of Vilnius's dragon. I hate the dragon of Vilnius. Hate of myself instantly turns into hate of Vilnius's dragon, because he is the most to blame for everything.

Over there a numbed Vytautas Vargalys waits patiently next to the Russian Orthodox Church on Basanavičiaus Street, glancing about fearfully. His eyes are like a madman's; a horrible fear wafts from him. Now he sees something I can't perceive. His hands shake; even his protruding lower lip shakes like an old man's. He cringes and suddenly takes off—I don't know why, I don't know where, I don't know what for. He's no longer a man; he's the embodiment of fear. The dragon, the dragon alone, is to blame for this.

Over there Martynas Poška sits shut up in his apartment and pages through brittle sheets of paper. He tries to invent a humane world in an inhuman city. However—oh horror!—he tries to create it on sheets of paper alone. The living don't concern him; he's not trying to change anything. He didn't even change his own son—the one that's a knuckleheaded athlete, or Communist Youth leader, or a drug-addicted rapist, but that's not what worries Martynas Poška. With a sarcastic smile, he assembles a paper world. He's sorely deceiving himself. He convinces himself that his collection is immeasurably important, even though he knows it has no meaning.

Over there Lolita Banytė-Žilienė dresses to show off in town. This ritual can take an hour or two. She starts with her toes and finishes with the ends of her hair. For a long, long, time, she massages one little muscle in her thigh, driving the fat from it, even though there isn't any there. She minces in front of the mirror naked, and then covers herself with layer after layer. The heavens could split, or the earth open up, and she would fuss over herself all the same, swaying her thighs, flourishing her chest, carefully choosing that day's ideal mask. I perfectly understand Vytautas Vargalys's spontaneous desire to rip off all her clothes, all of her covers, to tear even her divine body to bits—just from the desire to find something inside her.

And now here they all three come together. Vytautas Vargalys, as straight as a stone pillar; Lolita Banytė-Žilienė, shining with an oppressive beauty; and an unsmiling, crew-cut Martynas Poška. A little game of Vilnius Poker begins. It actually hurts to smell it. Only as a dog do you realize deceit isn't people's flaw. It's their means of existence. It's impossible to condemn them for it. What madman would scorn people because they eat or breathe? And deceit is even more vital to them than air. I know. After all, I was a human myself. I would sit down at the piano just so I could, for a brief moment, avoid pretense and openly play my despair, my spiritual impotence, and my hatred of myself; so that I could, for at least for a few minutes, be a terrorist who blows it all up.

So a little game of Vilnius Poker begins. The trio begins torturing one another. Martynas Poška lets ironic witticisms fly, even though he's not at all happy or funny. Actually, he only envies Vytautas Vargalys his height, his looks, and even his intelligence. He reeks of envy. Most of all, he envies him Lolita Banytė-Žilienė. And it's not just the scent of French perfume wafting from her—the smell of death wafts from her. She is as cold as Death. It isn't blood flowing in her veins, but dilute nitrogen. She always wants to win. That's why she pretends to be a victim who needs comforting and protection. A proud, practically unapproachable victim. That's the kind that attracts men most. She irresistibly attracts Vytautas Vargalys, so he pretends he's in love. But he smells only of fear. He doesn't love anyone, because he's horribly afraid of love itself. In love, he loses his vigilance, and Vytautas Vargalys is always tense and watchful.

That's the way three particularly close people play.

It's hard to understand people, even for us. They are born for a single, tiny second, in order to die after it rushes past. But even so, they do their utmost to make it as senseless as possible. They lie, pretend, deceive, get an instant of profit, and rejoice over trifles. They all ignore any responsibility to eternity. They don't feel any responsibility. A human life is a competition of ingenious idiocies. Everyone desperately tries to exceed the others with the boundlessness of their stupidity. I was by no means a laggard in this contest myself. Sometimes a terrible nostalgia comes over me; I get the urge to get mixed up in a group of people and take up endless little stupidities again. Only a human being manages to act as if he were immortal. We thinking dogs cannot do this. We know too much about the world. That's why we sometimes get an irresistible urge to turn into a human. You just need to decide, and return to the world as some insect, fly, or a tree, and then patiently wait, turning in the endless circle of change: sooner or later, you'll turn back into a human. But once you've turned into one, you'll no longer have the experience you gained in the afterlife. Those are the rules here.

Maybe that's what I should do? I'm already tired of searching for the truth. No one knows it.

Believers say that God knows it. Even if I believed in God I wouldn't take that for granted. The creator of the universe, the most powerful being in it, couldn't be interested in a poker game dealt by piddling little people, or in some truth of theirs. He wouldn't have either the time or the desire for it. He'd be worried about entirely different things: the collision of galaxies or the birth of stars. I'm certainly not anyone's creator, nor am I particularly powerful, but individual people concern me less and less, even my former friends. Then why should God himself be concerned about them?

So, who knows the real truth?

I suppose no one does. It's dangerous to positively assert anything about a human. A human is significantly larger than any proposition. Maybe it would be more appropriate to speak of them only in negatives? Lolita Banytė-Žilienė's father was not a shoemaker. She was not bald, she wasn't lame, she was never a boy. You could go on this way indefinitely. But there won't be any real answers anyway, because only Nobody knows.

Perhaps the dragon of Vilnius is that Nobody? Or maybe that Nobody is the very air of Vilnius, the gloomy noise of the streets, the misleading labyrinth of the city's smells?

Lolita Banytė-Žilienė concerns me less and less: the firm-breasted, big-boobed, or chestless KGB colonel's, or history professor's, or not a shoemaker's daughter, murdered, or a suicide, or maybe dead from a heart attack. She is all sorts of things, but it concerns me less all the time. The same with Vytautas Vargalys and his grandfather, who died or didn't die, who was buried by Martynas, or Stefanija, or Vytautas Vargalys himself; and his father, the aviation inventor, or artist, or economist, a helpless invalid, or super-sexed athlete, or mystical sorcerer, who had emigrated, or disappeared without a trace, or got a government pension. It no longer matters to me if Vytautas Vargalys wanted children, or didn't want them, or was impotent; had a wife, or never had one, if she is now the wife of a successful businessman or a lonely alcoholic; if he knew Lolita's father or not, or if he knew him, then which one—the KGB agent, or the historian, or not a shoemaker. That which I have seen or known doesn't necessarily mean anything. Nothing means anything, because only the nameless Nobody knows the complete truth. And if you want to get to that Nobody, you need to at least know what Vilnius is.

A hell, in which only those who light the fires under the cauldrons have it good? A desert, where only lizards and snakes live, and everything else is no more than tiny grains of sand? A city of the dragon, in which all of the princesses are already devoured? I don't know what Vilnius is.

Maybe Vilnius knows what I am? Maybe I'm a ghost of the Gediminas Riauba who once lived. Or maybe a creature whose name hasn't been thought up yet. I crawl out of the gateway, splash through the puddles, smell the scents of Vilnius that have been weakened by the damp, and keep doubting everything more and more. Yes, I feel my paws, my restless tail, my ears flopping as I run. They keep flopping over to the sides—then I hear better. Then they lie down next to my head again—immediately I hear worse. I can look at the mirror in some store window and I'll really see a dog. A monstrous, mutty creature with intelligent eyes. I'm not imaging it: passersby who see me say "dog" about me too. You'd think I really was a dog. But I doubt that more and more. I take food from the half-witted little old men of Old Town, and I'm doubtful. Completely starved, I heroically squeeze my way into filthy little cafeterias and whine pathetically. They always feed me: even the meanest cook, seeing my eyes, suddenly quiets down and throws me an entirely human morsel. They don't act that way with real dogs. Real dogs aren't shown such respect.

I can't save anyone; I can't do anything at all. I don't resemble some supernatural being with miraculous powers in the least. I'm just as miraculous as any other dog. Would life in Vilnius change in the slightest if all the city's dogs were intelligent? Not at all. If you want to move the jammed wheel of Vilnius's existence, a much more terrific effort would be required.

Lord knows, it would have been best to be reborn as a dragon. Only a more powerful dragon could triumph over the dragon of Vilnius. I should have returned to Vilnius with miraculous powers and proclaimed my laws. But I never wanted to rule. I have no desire for everyone to obey me. And I don't now, either.

All I am is a degenerate dog—always soaked through and frozen, always hungry and tired. Apparently I wasn't destined to become powerful in any life. Apparently, it's clearly written in the book of fate that I will always be cold, always suffer, and never find the answers. Who knows whether it's worth dying just to find that out. Apparently no true Vilniutian will find happiness, even after death.

By the way, I don't particularly torment myself over this. I said I would want to save everyone just to say it. I'm probably lying. I rarely want to find out anything anymore. I'm becoming more and more indifferent. Here, where we are, indifference isn't considered a flaw. It's a natural state after death. Those are the rules here. I have felt neither sadness, nor guilt, nor happiness for a long time. My thinking has been nothing but indifferent for a long time. True, here we sense a strange nostalgia. We secretly long for foolish emotions, senseless pain, and even the silliest human errors. Perhaps it's the errors we long for most. Here, unfortunately, we don't make errors: we don't behave either well or badly. We know all too well that it's absolutely the same no matter how we behave. Whatever happens is absolutely the same. All variations of fate are equal, we realize this; naïve human hope has been taken away from us. That's why we long for the foolish—but ever so dear—human naïveté, for the belief that it's possible to change at least a thing or two. We long for tears of helplessness or outbursts of anger. Only we understand how agonizingly beautiful it is to lose irrevocably. Only we know that human despair is really a giant ball of unrealized hopes and possibilities.

In my human life I had a purpose: to run as far as possible from here, as far as possible from the soullessness of Vilnius, from that moribund city's despair. It would seem that in dying, you really could end up as far away as it's possible to get, but it's the reverse: you dig deeper into the decay of Vilnius. I could choose freely, and that's why I chose Vilnius anyway, why I picked the dragon that holds everyone in his jaws, or maybe has already swallowed them. Around me, inside of me—Vilnius is everywhere; perhaps the entire world is Vilnius.

Although Vilnius itself really isn't the entire world—those empty streets of the night, those corpse-like neon lights, the pale riddle of dusk. I go so far as to terrify myself—maybe the city really is extinct, maybe no one lives here anymore. Maybe even the riddle is no more; it remains only in my memories, in a strange cryptogram of old scenes.

Over there, Vytautas Vargalys climbs up a ladder, lifts the trapdoor, and finally ends up on a flat roof in Lazdynai. He carefully settles in behind the elevator tower. He smells of exhaustion and senseless determination. He carefully glances down at the square by the shopping center. Militiamen are already gathering there; gloomy figures in markedly civilian clothes stand guard in all of the passages between the buildings. Vytautas Vargalys slowly takes a long case from his shoulder, unbuttons it, and lays it down next to himself. His hands don't shake; he breathes perhaps just a little harder than usual. He doesn't smell of fear—only of fulfillment after an endless wait. The figures in the square next to Lazdynai's weather vane suddenly begin to move. Apparently, the dragon is approaching. Vytautas Vargalys carefully screws on the stock, and then adjusts the telescopic sight; even a fraction of a millimeter is important. He raises the rifle to his shoulder, aims, closes his eyes, and aims again. He carefully lays down the rifle, pulls a small leather sack out of his pocket, and smiles wryly. He unties the knot, sticks a finger inside and rolls out a bullet. The casing's copper is appreciably darkened, while the bullet is entirely black. This bullet has waited thirty years. It smells of despair, old blood, and sacrificial smoke. Vytautas Vargalys, with a crooked nail, scrapes the bullet; silver sparkles under the blackness. The bullet is silver, as is appropriate. Only one like that can slay a dragon. It has waited thirty years; Vytautas Vargalys has waited just as long. The silver of the bullet blackened, while Vytautas Vargalys's black hair coated itself in silver. But the hour has arrived nevertheless. Life gives every person at least one lone chance. A patient man will surely live to see it.

The square is in his power; even a scrawny basement cat couldn't run through it unseen. Today is Vytautas Vargalys's day; he instantaneously turns thirty years younger. Now he isn't fifty, but nineteen. He has gotten Bitinas's clear instructions, a sacred mission from the nation. The silver bullet will fly straight at the target: the dragon must be destroyed. He carefully sets the bullet in place and checks the safety. The automobile cavalcade is visible by now, guiding and accompanying the beige Volga, their sirens blaring. The dragon unwinds, flashing its brilliant blue eyes and howling. No, he's no longer nineteen; when he was nineteen the dragon hid day and night, it didn't howl and didn't flash its lantern eyes. It even slept inside a tank. Now it only fences itself off with a wall: the square opposite the shopping center is completely empty. Vytautas Vargalys continues to wait until the great visitor climbs out of the car; only when he recognizes him does he raise the rifle to his shoulder. Now he doesn't smell of anything, he smells of absolutely nothing at all. The old man's hunched figure is easily seen through the scope. He's as scrawny as a basement cat: his long coat flutters around him as if it were hung on a pole. Vytautas Vargalys doesn't hurry; he chooses a spot under the temple, by the ear. He knows he won't miss, that he'd hit him even with his eyes closed. He gently presses the trigger. The sound of the shot is unexpectedly harsh; it rebounds very loudly. For a few seconds there's nothing to be seen, but then he sees the hunched-over figure, as healthy as can be, step into the store. Vytautas Vargalys's face is twisted, and his smell just doesn't take shape. That's the way an injured beast smells, a drowning person; that's the way a recurrent nightmare smells. Vytautas Vargalys doesn't howl, doesn't tear out his hair, doesn't sob. He looks over the rifle's safety, torn out by the explosion, touches his scorched cheek, and again smiles wryly. The smile of a hired killer doesn't suit him at all.

When did I see this scene? Did I see it at all? I remember my paws burned as they stuck to the hot bitumen of the roof. There wasn't so much as a hint of a breeze. And it occurred to me that I could, for all it's worth, change the course of events. I could have jumped up and knocked the rifle out of his hands. But I couldn't explain anything to him.

It slowly gets lighter. I've sat in the gateway the entire night long. We dogs think very slowly.

I'm drawn to run to the village, to Stefanija Monkevič. I'm drawn to Lolita Banytė-Žilienė's grave. I'm drawn to the barred basement window, behind which Vytautas Vargalys sits and smokes. If I were three dogs, I'd run everywhere at once.

But even alone, I sense, I smell the essence with all of my doggy being. I almost understand what the dragon is doing with my Vilnius.

The people of Vilnius can't avoid lying, because Vilnius itself lies.

Probably all the cities in the world lie sometimes. They want to appear prettier, smarter, or more lovable. That's a nearly innocent lie. Vilnius lies all the time—consistently and maliciously. Vilnius wants to deceive; perhaps that's the only purpose of its existence. It lies with people, because people are the city's words. But it lies with its streets too, and with its houses, and even with its past.

Today I don't believe nighttime Vilnius, either. It wants to pretend it's the same as always. It's a clever pretender. If St. Anne's Church were to suddenly disappear, or Gediminas Square were to turn into a swamp, everyone would notice it. Vilnius lies in a much more subtle way; its deceptions are always covered in mist. Only a thinking dog can fathom them.

First of all, Vilnius dissembles with its smells.

The city's smells form in layers: with effort, you can smell out even the very oldest, ones that dispersed once upon a time, in the depths of the ages. Ancient smells don't air out; it would seem the stench of gasoline ought to cover everything—but no, you sniff and sniff, carefully smell it out, and finally you sense that an Old Town crossroads smells of ancient blood and ripened hatred, Jewish love and Polish honor. The new building crammed in place of an old mansion spreads an abundance of smells, but they don't conquer the scentscapes of old wine, aurochs roasts and ruinous gold. In the world of scent, the ancient mansions are more genuine than that new building. In the scentscape of Vilnius, the twentieth and the fifteenth century exist side by side. The flow of time doesn't apply to the smells of Vilnius.

I'm so accustomed to that city of smells that I keep forgetting people can't smell. Although I suspect some can; they just don't reveal themselves to anyone.

And then I suddenly found out that the city changes its smell. Early in the morning I dashed down to the square next to Symphony Hall; at least a couple of streets run together into a single spot there, like creeks. The smell of river mud and a gloomy craving for freedom always hung around there. That smell was just as familiar to me as the way the square looked. I sensed the new smell from a distance. It was strange and artificial. I couldn't be mistaken—a dog's nose doesn't lie. The square smelled neither of river deposits, nor of a craving for freedom— merely of narcissus and a silly cheerfulness.

It was unbelievable. The scentscape of Vilnius, the most immutable, eternal part of the city, had suddenly unraveled. It was a bad omen.

After that morning, I scrambled to examine my map of smells. To my horror I realized it was all constantly changing. The scentscape of Vilnius turned out to be unstable. The smells of the city were playing an incomprehensible game. One morning, the fundamental, centuries-old smells of streets, houses, and rivers would suddenly change. A hundred times I had smelled that right here, in this intersection, there was once a leather workshop, and later, perhaps a century later, someone had murdered all the women and children nearby; one morning I would suddenly discover that none of it had happened. There was no leather workshop; there was no slaughter of women. Suddenly the intersection would smell only of an expensive banquet and Dominican hymns. True, the real scent would return sooner or later, but not always. Sometimes it would be shoved out by yet another, completely unexpected smell. It seemed the city was furiously changing its own self, hiding its true past, its own essence.

As a former jazzman, it instinctively occurred to me that Vilnius was secretly swinging. That it simply improvises a bit—so it wouldn't be so boring. There is the basic smell theme, the familiar map of the city's smells. But that's only the theme; it can be varied and expanded, returning over and over again to the beginning. That's exactly what ancient Vilnius took up. I smelled those threatening changes and naïvely judged them to be a game, musicianship without any hidden purpose.

I can't be angry with myself for that. I was merely a novice. I still didn't know anything about Vilnius Poker.

I had to run around as a dog for five years before I realized that Vilnius lies intentionally. Little by little, it accustoms its inhabitants to not feel or notice the deceptions. A little at a time, it takes up playing tricks on not just the sense of smell, but other senses as well. The pavement on the cross street above Pilies Street is at one time polished slippery, at another time coarsely rough, and later it turns slippery again. At first, you think you're only imagining it; later, you don't even notice it.

Unfortunately, people don't notice even drastic changes, and Vilnius lies a little bit at a time, very carefully. Some old house will just get a foot or two smaller; a week later by the same amount again; then more and more. Its color slowly changes too. Regardless, a few years later the house is completely different. And Vilniutians don't even notice this. These changing people are accustomed to a changing city. If you left Vilnius for a long time, on your return you'll no longer find some cross street: it simply won't be there anymore. The inhabitants of Vilnius, with perfect equanimity, will say it never was. And they won't even think they're lying. Only people like that can live in a lying city.

This morning is lying too. Street cleaners in orange jackets sweep the bare asphalt with brooms. Maybe they see fallen leaves there? The streets are still empty; the lights don't dispel the dimness in the least. It's the dimness swallowing their light.

"Oh, look, what a doggy," says a fat woman to her stripling assistant, who is mysteriously gathering leaves one at a time. "A hungry doggy. A stray."

The urchin raises his mysterious eyes to me, and picks up a whiff of a warm winter hat. He's thinking it wouldn't be at all bad to skin my hide.

Skinners like that didn't proliferate in Vilnius before. Besides, I wouldn't make a warm hat—I freeze quite a bit in this hide myself.

Sometimes I think I'm lying myself: I pretend to be a dog, although I am by no means an ordinary dog.

Vilnius slowly awakens from its doze, a howling police car flies by: some Vilniutian met the morning no longer in this world. I'm dejected, I'm unbelievably depressed, although, thinking logically, this can't be. We thinking dogs don't have feelings. Maybe we don't have them, but I remember them anyway. I dream them, and dreamt feelings are even more intense than real ones.

Although I'm not convinced even of that. A human inevitably believes in something. I haven't believed in anything for a long time now.

There's nothing real in Vilnius anymore. Its houses can change, switch places, disappear, and then show up again. Its people apparently can be several places at once, act several different ways at the same time, and invent not just their future, but their past too. It's always because they have neither a real past, nor a real future. It's always because the city itself lies shamelessly, so it has taught its inhabitants to lie too.

It's always because I am a homeless thinking dog, because I don't know what I really am, because I was Gediminas Riauba, and now I'm nothing.

I'm a dog in any case, a hungry puppy—without rights, without friends, without a future. I never did get used to living without the fear of death. I'm not immortal, but I know, after all, that I won't die; in the worst case, I'll change my form.

There's nothing genuine in Vilnius anymore. Who can say if those two huddled figures are genuine, or if they're only Vilnius's morning trick? One figure is a woman, the other a man; the two of them creep along the wall as if they were looking for something in the dark.

I know the woman's scent. She's drastically changed her appearance again, but she won't fool me. I can smell her very well; it's a regenerated Irena Giedraitienė: a quite young, slender witch in the semidarkness of a Vilnius morning. What is she doing this early in the morning, in an empty street dominated by sleepy street sweepers? I run up closer; she gazes at me intently, looks into my eyes, and smiles.

"A spy?" asks the hunched-over man in a hoarse voice.

"No, it's just a little dog," she answers melodiously. "It's just a little lost dog, it doesn't know itself what it's looking for."

She chats on and on, smiling and smiling. It bodes ill when witches smile, but that's not what disturbs me most. Irena Giedraitienė smells me: she greedily pulls my scent into her nostrils and sways her head, as if she were trying to remember something.

"Let's knock him off, and be done with it," says the tall man angrily. He smells like a holy man who has murdered his own God, and also of a profound intelligence and an unspeakable sin, and of old age too, a profound old age; he's maybe a hundred years old.

"Stop it, Bitinas," Giedraitienė calms him. "After all, this isn't the dog of hell. That one's supposed to have three heads, isn't it?"

Bitinas angrily waves his hand; the two of them slowly slink off along the wall, carefully sniffing at the air. The two of them sniff at everything, as if they were large, hunched-over dogs.

This isn't the first time I've seen people sniffing like that. Incidentally, those sniffers don't resemble humans at all. Lord knows what they resemble. Their heavy, blocky heads are grown right into their shoulders, their fingers are crooked, their joints swollen, their gaze is strange and insane. Lord knows what they resemble.

In any case, they really don't resemble today's Giedraitienė and her Bitinas. Those two are slender, with long necks and straight fingers. But they can smell too!

Only now do I suddenly realize that all the sniffers must inevitably fathom Vilnius's lying.

"You know, he smells of a human," she says suddenly.

"If an owner slowly begins to smell like his dog, why can't a dog smell of his master?" Bitinas thoughtfully answers, his head, as bald as the back of your heel, tilts to the side.

"Maybe, maybe," she continues. "But why is he following us?"

I'm no longer following now; I quickly turn into Rūdninkų, while they prowl on down Vokiečių Street. Evil ghosts have beset morning Vilnius: Giedraitienė and her Bitinas have ruinous intentions. If I were a human, I'd be completely unnerved; I'd probably break into a sweat, I'd be short of breath out of impatience and fear. Everything would worry me enormously. But now practically nothing bothers me. We thinking dogs don't even break out in sweat. I nonchalantly sniff at trees my fellows have peed on and trot off, I don't know myself where. I just feel horribly depressed. I want to be a human again.

I so want to turn into a human again.

I want to fear again, and to thrive in a horrible unknown, to doubt and to hope, again and again. I want Irena Giedraitienė's changes to shock me and Vytautas Vargalys's tragedy to move me to tears; I want to know again that I will die, and to desperately try not think of it. I want to be a human again: flawed, lost, and weak.

It's a really weird nostalgia that's tormenting me. I don't long for my country, not even my past: I pine for a human form. It's too difficult and pointless to be a thinking dog. Too difficult and too pointless. I finally felt a tiny little twinge of feeling inside me. It's like some little wavering flame in my non-existent doggy soul.

I need to become even more human. I would give up all of my life after death just so I could laugh and cry.

Lord knows, I'd gladly exchange my life after death for one more human one.

My doggy brain works furiously. Irena Giedraitienė and Bitinas distend through it like a black knot of thoughts. I'm beginning to fathom Vilnius's fateful system, all of Vilnius's insane jazz. Giedraitienė wandering around here is no accident. When a person is connected to every episode, to all of your acquaintances—apparently by chance, apparently for no reason—that person himself is the cause as well as the essence. Irena Giedraitienė was creeping around everywhere, all the time; her scent almost never faded from my nostrils. Could she have been the secret manager of Vilnius Poker, could she have dealt marked cards to the players?

There's street sweepers toiling next to the Cvirka monument too. Good Lord, an inhabitant of some other planet, seeing Vilnius for the first time this morning, would suppose it's a city of street sweepers, that all Vilniutians dress only in orange jackets. A bit further, on the boulevard, the first trolleybuses are already rumbling. Vilnius is brazenly awakening.

And I keep running at a steady trot, as if I had a clear purpose. But what could my purpose be? Life after death doesn't offer any purpose. You thank the nonexistent God that at least you have the right to visit your own Vilnius.

Of course, everyone's Vilnius is completely different.

My Vilnius is Vilnius. In this respect, I have precedence over many of the dead.

And now I'm running at a trot, not knowing where, not knowing why. Although no—I'm rushing to see Vytautas Vargalys. I'm rushing to warn him, and most important of all—to ask him. He'll answer me: via scent, sound, or something else besides. Now I'll understand him, whatever he may do. I've suddenly begun feeling the secret jazz rhythm of this city of sweepers. It pulses in my veins; some piece that would allow me to put it all together is still missing, but thank God, I know the key to the cipher. It's called Vytautas Vargalys. Only now do I realize his importance. Every act of his, every word, was significant. In my human life, he was my pal, my drinking buddy, and later even my friend, but I never understood him completely. For that I had to die and spend several years in a dog's hide. Only this morning did I begin to grasp that Vytautas Vargalys isn't just a human—like I was, and maybe will be again sometime. All of his family's memory and understanding lurk within him. The Vargalyses somehow managed to connect their human lives with their after-death ones. What one Vargalys experienced after death, all of the Vargalyses—if even only the tiniest bit—felt in their own lives. It's been that way for generation after generation.

We desperately need to make contact, to talk a bit. It's not true that a dog is so helpless. I can write with my paw in the damp sand by the sea. I could even type on a typewriter, if someone would outfit it with a special keyboard. Thank God I didn't turn into a fly or something. I'm a dog, I can answer questions by barking—at least "yes" and "no." I can . . .

I can do anything, if I just want to. And I've wanted to for a long time now.

I've even gotten a bit out of breath running, but the destination is close by. Here's Pamėklių Hill, here's the most disgusting building in Vilnius, and here I am—breathless, irritable, but happy.

I almost had a sensation of human feelings. All the more since the wind is blowing at my back, so I don't smell anything. Here's Lukiškių Square. Here's the record store; despite the early hour there's a crowd of teenagers milling around next to it: for several days now rumors have been going around the city that they're going to deliver a Paul McCartney record. And on a bench next to the toilet, as pretty as you please, sit Irena Giedraitienė and Bitinas.

I don't understand how they could have gotten here before me, but that's not what matters most. Their faces are serene and blissful; it seems they're looking at me: scornfully, and a bit proudly, as if they had carried out a secret mission by beating me to the punch. I don't want to believe it, but now the wind is blowing at me from the KGB Building, so with appalling clarity I smell everything clearly.

From out of the basement, from out of Vytautas Vargalys's cell, spreads one and only one strong scent. I know it very well; it's always identical, even though it's colored differently every time. But those weak hues are merely a deception, mere smoke in the eyes, because the scent is always the same. Spreading or entwined, but at the same time unique and completely ordinary. As ordinary as death.

There's no other way it could be, because that is the smell of death.

Just now, there in the basement, Vytautas Vargalys died.

The square, the building behind my back, Vilnius in its entirety has turned into an ineffective theater set. The wind tossed the solitary leaves on the trees; the badly made-up street sweepers played the part of street sweepers. The musical teenagers played excited music-obsessed fans. The trolleybus intentionally rumbled and sped, playing a trolleybus. Every last thing here was acting—even the trees. Only Irena Giedraitienė and Bitinas continued to be unrelentingly real. As real as fate. As real as destiny itself. Their thin, doggishly quivering nostrils greedily caught at the scent they had dreamed of. Their thin faces, seemingly sculpted out of wood, shone with bliss and an evil joy. Staring at me brazenly, they got up from the little bench and waved their arms strangely. Then they awkwardly swayed their hips and took a few small steps in opposite directions. Only then did I realize they were dancing.

An unimaginably fat, mustachioed man leisurely waddled out the door to the KGB building, grasping a bluish-white lump in his hands. Squatting with difficulty, he put the lump down on the sidewalk and stroked it tenderly. Another trolleybus clanged by. Irena Giedraitienė and her companion danced slowly and ostentatiously. Straightening up, the fatty stared at them, and then earnestly clapped his plump hands. His mustache-covered mouth grinned; his palms were so plump that the clapping couldn't be heard at all. He was completely toothless. He glanced at his watch, stroked the bluish-white lump again, and yawned. The lump unexpectedly shook itself and spread out its wings. It turned into a pigeon right in front of my eyes. And the pair of doggish sniffers kept dancing, even attracting the attention of the musical devotees.

I didn't care about them anymore, all I saw was the bluish-white pigeon; the mustachioed fatty finally left it alone and returned to his office. I carefully ran across the boulevard and stopped in front of that oppressive bird.

It was a filthy, shabby city pigeon. Like all pigeons, it squinted at me with its deranged little eyes. But it didn't try to fly away. It merely hobbled to the side, swaying badly. Its left foot was shorter, or maybe injured. Probably it couldn't fly at all. Without a doubt it couldn't; it didn't have the right to rise up into the air; it was eternally tied to the ground. A disgusting, soiled pigeon of Vilnius, with plastered-down feathers and the eyes of a dangerous maniac.

Scent once more betrayed all and explained all.

A threatening and tangled scent, which had forced its way through the stench of congealed feathers and soiled three-toed pigeon, through the hopeless whiff of the sniffing couple's dance, through Vilnius's armor and deceit—it was faint, but plainly sensed, and inarguably the scent of Vytautas Vargalys: murderous and mocking, like the idiotic squinting of the pigeon's eyes.

The mangy, insane pigeon of Vilnius's morning smelled of Vytautas Vargalys, because it was Vytautas Vargalys.

If they'd let me choose a nightmare, I'd agree to any of them, if only I wouldn't have to see this sight. Vytautas Vargalys in the shape of a revolting, frightening, crazy-eyed pigeon of Vilnius. Vytautas Vargalys, who knows what even I don't know, what no one else knows. Vytautas Vargalys, who despised pigeons with a deathly hatred. That Vytautas

Vargalys was standing in front of me now and glaring maliciously with its fierce little eyes. I'll never talk to him now; I'll never see him. I won't even smell him—a few days will go by and his scent will fade, all that will be left will be the stench of a soiled, scruffy, lame Vilnius pigeon.

The malicious hand of the demiurge of Vilnius turned him into the one creature in the world that was the most disgusting to Vytautas Vargalys.

Apparently, those must be the rules.

Every decent dog would, sooner or later, start finding those rules oppressive.

Vilnius doesn't stop playing a cheap comedy. Like any decent dog, I despise that old comedian. The doggishly-sniffing couple growl and wag their tails, even though they don't have them. The city calmly awakes, yawns and stretches nonchalantly, because nothing matters to this city. It has no soul; in place of its heart hides a putrid, lethargic dragon.

I'm left completely on my own. The last person who tied me to this city has turned into a pigeon. He didn't want to give the secret of Vilnius Poker away to me.

I don't realize myself that I've sat down in the middle of the avenue and started howling. On my left looms the KGB Building, on the right the Lenin monument. And I howl like the Iron Wolf. Only just now do I realize: I am the Iron Wolf. The prophet of the New Vilnius. I sit in the very center of the city, my snout raised to the skies, and announce the news to the entire world. And the glory of Vilnius flies round the farthest lands; every place on earth resonates with my howl.

Rejoicing, the morning trolleybus comes tearing along directly at me, but I don't budge, I just howl louder still. The trolleybus even screeches in its jubilation and flies towards me. The sullen guy at the wheel, with puffy bags under his eyes, has brightened up; he even leaned forward—he was one of those drivers who invariably speed up when they have a chance to crush a cat or a dog.

I calmly think that not a single person had the strength to do this. Neither Martynas, nor Teodoras, nor even Vytautas Vargalys. None of them committed suicide. I think calmly that perhaps I'll manage to carry out the most human of acts, an act that is impossible for any ordinary dog, in exactly this way.

Maybe this is exactly the way I'll manage to break all the rules.

Earthly life didn't satisfy me, but the afterlife is even less satisfying. There has to be, there must be something more.

It'd be better, even if it takes a hundred other transmigrations, to be born a human again. With all those foolish hopes and weaknesses. Most importantly of all—with foolish hopes. It'd be better . . .

Thank God, the trolleybus doesn't let me think for long.

First, my howl is gone, then my body, but then for a long, long time my last thought, the most important insight into Vilnius Poker, remains. This thought broke out of my howling brain as a black luminary, as an explanation and an answer, even though I don't know what it means, and now I'll never find out:

DOGS DON'T DISTINGUISH DREAMS FROM REALITY.

*Vilnius*
*1979-1987*

Ričardas Gavelis was a prose writer, playwright, and publicist. He published his first book—a collection of short stories entitled *The Celebration That Has Not Begun*—in 1976 and went on to write six novels, three collections of stories, and several plays before passing away in 2002. His other novels include *Seven Ways to Commit Suicide*, *The Last Generation of People on Earth*, and *The Life of Sun-Tzu in the Sacred City of Vilnius*. This is his first novel to be published in English.

Elizabeth Novickas graduated from the University of Illinois-Chicago with an M.A. in Lithuanian Language and Literature. She has worked previously as a bookbinder, newspaper designer, cartographer, and computer system administrator. *Vilnius Poker* is her first full-length literary translation.

Open Letter—the University of Rochester's nonprofit, literary translation press—is one of only a handful of publishing houses dedicated to increasing access to world literature for English readers. Publishing twelve titles in translation each year, Open Letter searches for works that are extraordinary and influential, works that will become the classics of tomorrow.

Making world literature available in English is crucial to opening our cultural borders, and its availability plays a vital role in maintaining a healthy and vibrant book culture. Open Letter strives to cultivate an audience for these works by helping readers discover imaginative, stunning works of fiction and by creating a constellation of international writing that is engaging, stimulating, and enduring.

Current and forthcoming titles from Open Letter include works from Argentina, Austria, Brazil, France, Iceland, Norway, Spain, and numerous other countries.

www.openletterbooks.org